Caroline Harvey ... Trollope, the highl... selling contempora... *... Show, A Village Affair, A Passionate Man, The Rector's Wife, The Men and the Girls, A Spanish Lover, The Best of Friends, Next of Kin, Other People's Children* and *Marrying the Mistress* are all published by Black Swan. *Other People's Children* has recently been shown on BBC television as a major drama serial. She has also written a study of women in the British Empire, *Britannia's Daughters*. As Caroline Harvey she has written several historical novels including *Legacy of Love, A Second Legacy, Parson Harding's Daughter, The Steps of the Sun, Leaves from the Valley, The Brass Dolphin, City of Gems* and *The Taverners' Place*, which are all published by Corgi Books.

Joanna Trollope was born in Gloucestershire, where she still lives. She was appointed OBE in the 1996 Queen's Birthday Honours List for services to literature

THE TAVERNERS' PLACE

Caroline Harvey

CORGI BOOKS

THE TAVERNERS' PLACE
A CORGI BOOK: 9780552168847

Originally published in Great Britain by
Century Hutchinson Ltd

PRINTING HISTORY
Century Hutchinson edition published 1986

Corgi edition published 2000

9 10

Set in 10/12pt Plantin by
Phoenix Typesetting, Ilkley, West Yorkshire.

Corgi Books are published by Transworld Publishers,
61–63 Uxbridge Road, London W5 5SA,
a division of The Random House Group Ltd,
in Australia by Random House Australia (Pty) Ltd
20 Alfred Street, Milsons Point, Sydney, New South Wales 2061, Australia,
in New Zealand by Random House New Zealand Ltd,
18 Poland Road, Glenfield, Auckland 10, New Zealand
and in South Africa by Random House (Pty) Ltd,
Endulini, 5a Jubilee Road, Parktown 2193, South Africa

The Random House Group Limited supports The Forest Stewardship
Council® (FSC®), the leading international forest-certification organisation.
Our books carrying the FSC label are printed on FSC®-certified paper.
FSC is the only forest-certification scheme supported by the leading
environmental organisations, including Greenpeace. Our
paper procurement policy can be found at
www.randomhouse.co.uk/environment

Printed and bound in Great Britain by Clays Ltd, St Ives PLC

THE TAVERNERS' PLACE

Chapter One

November 1870

Scufflings from the aucuba japonica under his dressing room window showed Tom Taverner that Meggy Bradstock was trying to attract his attention. The leaves shook intermittently, there was a glimpse of a muddy black boot and the corner of a plaid shawl and, audible even through the closed window, an exasperated exclamation. He stood looking down and grinning. Meggy's round face emerged briefly, like a coin thrown into a pond, then vanished, to be succeeded by a plump arm in a rolled up sleeve, which flung a pebble upwards. It missed the window.

Tom leaned his arms upon the windowsill and waited. Again Meggy's face swam through the spotted leaves to cast an indignant glance at the point on the wall her stone had struck, then sank beneath the surface. Again her arm sprang up and threw a pebble. Again the pebble bounced off the house wall and dropped softly into the lavender bushes underneath. Tom opened the window.

'It helps to look where you are aiming, you know.'

All movement among the yellow leaves ceased at once.

'Meggy. It's me. Tom.'

An eye and a bright cheek became visible.

'You shouldn't have come, you know, Meggy. You shouldn't be here. Not at the house.'

Meggy twisted her face so that her mouth was in the open air.

'I 'ad to come. I 'ad to wish you 'appy birthday.'

'But you did. In the coppice last night. I told you not to come up to the house. You know that.'

'Yesterday wasn't the day,' she said stubbornly. 'Today's your birthday.'

'Meggy—'

'It's ever so early. There's never no-one round this side this early. I often comes. Sees you dressin', through the blind.'

The idea was at once exasperating and exciting. She was, as he had known now for six months, as loyal as a dog and as stubborn as a mule and those two qualities were often quite impossible to distinguish.

'Meggy, you absolutely must go now. And don't come back today. Do you hear me?'

'Can' I stay a minute more?'

'Not a second.'

'You can' make me go. You've only your nightshirt on—' She subsided into a stifled giggle.

'If you don't go now, I shan't meet you tomorrow. Nor the next day. Nor the day after that.'

Silence.

'I only came to wish you 'appy birthday,' she said in a small voice, 'seein' as it was your comin' of age. Seein' as 'ow you'm master 'ere now.'

'You've done that. And I'm very grateful. Now *go home*.'

He withdrew his head and shut the window. For

a minute or so there was no movement among the japonica leaves, then an irregular quiver began, travelling towards the wall where a hydrangea bloomed in summer, and where there was a door into the park beyond.

It was his mother's idea to celebrate his birthday with a shoot. He liked shooting, adored it even, but what he liked about it was roaming the woods with Bradstock, while the pheasants rose loudly whirring from the bracken, or crouching by the flight pond in winter twilights waiting for the mallard to come heavily in. What he did not like was organization and butts and the whole estate workforce pressed into beating and the cream of the county shots mowing his birds down with relentless skill. Most of all, he did not like the game cart in the dusk, its ridge-tent-shaped frame solid with feathered bodies, the odd woodcock, a bird of whom he was particularly fond, swinging ignominiously at the back, apart from the pheasants. Pheasants were imported and painted foreigners; woodcock – as softly, neatly dappled as the leaf mould in which they nested – were as English as old ale.

His mother was the sort of woman you sidestepped if you saw her in time advancing head on at you. She had borne down upon Tom announcing a birthday which would begin with a late breakfast for all the guns, proceed to a shoot (with a luncheon in the house for the ladies) and end, after a suitable interval for shutting one's eyes in the smoking room and changing, in a dinner and a ball. She also intended to summon a photographer from Bath who would record each stage of the day as well as the indoor and outdoor staffs grouped in turn on the steps below the south terrace.

The results would fill a morocco album to be left in the drawing room in a prominent place. Faced with this avalanche of entertaining, Tom seized upon the notion of a shoot as the least of the evils and clung to it enthusiastically, until the main body of the onslaught had roared down the mountain past him, and exhausted itself on the indifference below. The morocco album he vetoed at once and with horror.

'People will think it very strange,' Charlotte had said accusingly, 'very strange indeed. The heir to Buscombe comes of age and only a few hours' celebration – and only for the men at that.'

'We'll make it a day to remember. I'll get Bradstock to put down twice as many birds and we'll be hotter on poachers than ever before—'

'I feel you are failing me,' said Charlotte, who could never accommodate both her own intense desire to have her own way, and everyone else's equal right to theirs. When force of personality failed, as now, she was given to bringing up reinforcements of moral pressure and personal hurt.

'I am not *failing* anyone, Mother, but I should fail my guests horribly were I to invite them to an occasion at which I do not in the least want to see them. We dine together all year long and I am miserable dancing. Anyway,' he added with a flash of petulance, 'it is *my* birthday.'

'It is not only your mother you are failing,' Charlotte insisted, 'but your father also.'

Sir Thomas Taverner, born at Buscombe in 1820, eldest of three brothers, had died in the Crimea at the age of thirty-five. It had been no mean death of typhoid, but rather a glorious episode in which he had been shot down as he stood waist deep in the icy waters of the River Alma, urging his men to perform that most courage-taxing of military operations – wading across a river under enemy fire while holding their rifles above their heads to keep the powder dry. His body was buried then and there, on the southern slopes above the river, where Russian sightseers from Sebastopol had stood shortly before to picnic and watch the battle. His widow put up a plaque of polished stone quarried from the estate, in Buscombe church, which enumerated his qualities as a man, a husband, a father, a soldier and an employer.

Tom was six when his father died, his sister Catherine seven, and his sister Elizabeth eight. Of his father he could remember little, and certainly not enough to know his opinion on the proper behaviour of an heir upon coming of age. Sir Thomas had left a bluff, fair portrait of himself, whips, guns and rods, a blotter which bore the blurred backwards image of the last letter he had written from Buscombe, and a row of riding boots bent to the idiosyncrasies of his feet. These last still stood in the gun room and were respectfully dusted each week. Tom's sister Catherine, who was sharp and clever, said she personally doubted Mother cared to remember what Father had been like with any accuracy and, to cover that up, invented him, anew, by turns paragon and disciplinarian as occasion demanded.

Whatever he had been like, Tom felt his father's presence powerfully about him as the great birthday drew nearer. It was not so much a sense of the individual man as of family continuity, of Sir Thomas finally handing to the young Sir Tom the house and the park, the fields and woods, the farms and cottages with all the souls who lived in them and worked the land. He had always previously felt, standing in the home park and gazing to the east where a swell of land hid the Bath road, or urging his cob on inspection tours of newly ploughed fields or newly planted woodland, that all this was on loan to him only for the moment, and that it knew quite well the real owner was surveying it from some heavenly vantage point. But of late that respectful feeling of being the estate's tenant had dwindled, and somewhat to his embarrassment, Tom had found he wanted to embrace the trees and crush handfuls of earth in his fists and lay his cheek against the stone of barns and walls. There was cool reason for this sudden and passionate sense of ownership, for although he would still turn for guidance to the trustees, his two uncles, he was about to be literally and legally his own master.

That realization too brought dimensions he had not previously considered. He could ride exultantly through the woods letting an outstretched hand slip from tree to tree with a muttered incantation of 'Mine, mine, mine!', but that very possessiveness brought with it a strong sense of responsible guardianship. A broken fence, a sour and neglected pasture, choked woodland aroused an emotional anger in him; he could not bear the pain of the neglect, he felt a personal wound. The house itself looked to him like some vast and trusting beast, its honest and sturdy Jacobean bones still there under its elegant Georgian shell, with the absurd Gothic tower his father had added in 1845 to celebrate his marriage to Charlotte Cooper. It was to him personally that Buscombe Priory turned its sash windowed face, to mend its roof, rip the ivy from its walls, repoint the great ashlar quoins that defined its corners, save its soul. Late at night he would tour it with a lamp, profoundly excited by the drama and unaware of the melodrama of his own feelings.

Just at this moment, he knew he did not want his rooms full of people. He did not want people scuffing his floors, crushing his carpets, squashing the drawing room chairs – touching girlish chairs in the striped slip covers that his mother had clothed them in, as her grandmother had learned to do from Thomas Chippendale himself, in Yorkshire in the 1770s. He did not want them eating and drinking at his table and spilling things and filling the air with the debasing atmosphere of revelry. He would ideally have liked to spend the morning with Bradstock, some of the afternoon with Meggy in the granary loft – that rendezvous was becoming chilly in November but he was damned if he could think where else to go – the remainder of the daylight in the gun room fiddling about with oil and pads, and whistling, and then family dinner which would include partridge and oysters rolled in bacon as well as a really good argument with his sister Catherine.

Obligation undoubtedly had to march hand in hand with inclination. His uncle John, the soldier, and his uncle Robert, the Member of Parliament, were extremely hot on reminding him of his duty, and when he had burst out to his cousin Harry, three years his junior, that he felt dutiful to nothing but his inheritance, Harry, who wished to be a soldier like his father, had said simply, 'I think you ought to do what people expect.'

'But why? It is my house and my land and my birthday.'

'If I were in your place,' Harry said reasonably, 'I should do what everyone expects of me just this once, to keep them quiet, and thereafter I should do what I wanted. Within reason.'

What was expected of him seemed immense; the dining room laid for the most lavish of ladies' luncheons, the drawing room filled with new books and new magazines to amuse the ladies when they had eaten, pyramids of flowers and fruit in all corners. Charlotte had evidently compressed the energy and lavishness of the three parties she had wished to give into the one she had been allowed to give.

'It is Mamma's last chance, you see,' his sister Elizabeth said, meeting him and Catherine in the dining room doorway where they were surveying the banquet-like arrangements. 'You must make allowances.'

'But so should she,' Catherine replied, 'and realize that this is not the end of her reign so much as the beginning of Tom's.'

'Oh, I don't mind—'

'Then you had better start practising minding. Or Mother will mind for you, every time.'

'But she didn't over this,' he protested. 'I've ruled out the dinner and the ball.'

'Then I suppose,' Catherine said, waving an arm at the white and silver blaze of the table, 'that this is her small revenge.'

Robert Taverner, Member for North Somerset and founder-owner of one of the largest warehouse systems on the Bristol docks, could never suppress a smile driving up to Buscombe. It was the amused and faintly patronizing smile of a man who has not, being a second son, inherited his family house and who needs to reassure himself that he is in truth better off without it. It was a pleasant house, of course, one couldn't deny it that, and a good sized, well situated house, but Thomas had really made a laughing stock of it with his tower, like putting a pink ribbon round the neck of a gun dog. Without the tower, the house had possessed a homely dignity; homely because however severely elegant the façade of 1770, whose plans John Wood the Younger was said to have cast an approving eye over, the proportions and ceiling heights within were uncompromisingly Jacobean.

The first baronet had bought his title from James I for eleven hundred pounds. Before that he had just been a member of the solid country gentry whose support James so coveted, living in a house which was basically a medieval hall house and which he had filled with little rooms for more modern living until the interior resembled a dovecote, with the great old crown posts bursting through walls here and there with all the disproportionate size and primitive energy of trees brought indoors. Once he was Sir Thomas Taverner, he began to regret his ancient associations with medieval alehouses, and to remember with growing enthusiasm his equally ancient Catholic connections which were, after all, only to be encouraged under the Stuart king. With the substantial income drawn from fat Somerset farmlands – he was worth at least two thousand pounds a year, as much as a minor peer – he set about building a house fit for a baronet in the gentle green country where the last spur of the Cotswold hills dips to the south towards Bath. Bath itself was no place then, a sordid, hilly little town, but Bristol was within reach and so was a road to London, and the quarries of the surrounding hills could provide him with wonderful stone, easy to work, enduring, and as deep a gold as the best honey. In addition, there was a good site available, near water, untouched since Henry VIII had turned the monks out of their humble settlement at Buscombe, stripped the lead from the roof, removed the few vessels and books from the chapel and library, and set fire to the remainder.

There was no question of the new house being a courtyard house; that would have smacked too much of the Middle Ages for the new baronet's peace of mind. No, it should be a compact house, a single E-shaped block, facing north of course for health, with the wings stretching forward for the private chambers, and the southernmost oblong for hall and gallery and great chamber. Guests approached great iron gates set in a wall of pierced stonework that stretched between the wings, enclosing in the space thus formed behind it a motif garden divided into balanced halves, each centring upon a mulberry tree, planted as a particular compliment to the monarch. Around each tree spread a neat pattern of beds, edged in box and separated from each other by paths of golden gravel from the locality and blue and white stone imported from the quarries of the Exmoor hills. The north facing walls of the wings and central block were Dutch gabled, the stone mullioned windows were latticed, the ceilings were richly plastered and the walls lined with new pale yellow oak. Mindful of both his new status and his Catholic ancestry, the first Sir Thomas named the house Buscombe Priory.

And so it remained for half a century, the rooms renamed as fashions came and went, stoutly Royalist during the Civil War, largely untouched by the Commonwealth, on account of its seclusion and the absence of its owner in France, the family rooms buffeted by the winter winds rushing down from the Cotswold escarpment, the mulberry trees – which rapidly became the house's guardians in the family's eyes – shrouded from the worst blasts in shaggy wrappings of sacking. The third baronet went to Paris with Charles II and returned to Buscombe at the Restoration with Baroque ambitions. He extended the main block of the house across part of the formal garden to give himself a hall with a great parlour behind it, sliced off the Dutch gables, hipped the roof and replaced the lattice casements with rectangular sashes. Beyond the southern side of the house he laid out a balustraded terrace, and a long oblong lily pond in which the Priory's face was brokenly reflected among the lily pads. He was on the point of stripping out all the panelling inside, putting pilasters up the front and urns on the roofline when he decided he detested country life, so he contented himself with changing the name from Buscombe Priory to Buscombe Park, and went back to London and his sovereign and some fun.

Bath, only ten miles to the south, began to grow and become fashionable. Warily the Taverners watched it evolve from a scruffy jumble to a place where first royalty then the beau monde flocked to gossip and gamble and dance, and to wade, clad in yellow canvas smocks, through the filthy waters of the ancient baths in search of health. After fifty years, they could remain spectators no longer. Darting in and out of the city as the parades and squares and crescents went up, the fifth baronet – who had slipped quietly out of the Roman Catholic church in obedience to his natural protestant instincts and his desire for Government office – resolved that Buscombe Park must be a worthy neighbour to such elegance. Plans were drawn up by an architect from Bristol, who alleged that they had been admired by the creator of the Royal Crescent and, within two years, Buscombe was unrecognizable.

To begin with, it was turned back to front and the drive now broke from the Bath road two miles further south – sweeping up to the old south front of the house, the original Jacobean central block. This face was now sheathed in smooth new ashlar blocks, a pediment and columns rose around the new front door with a curving flight of steps to the gravel below, the whole reflected most gratifyingly in the third baronet's lily pond. Inside a severe symmetry attempted to organize the old Jacobean muddle to create a ring of rooms around the central hall, and although nothing could be done about seventeenth-century ceiling heights – the bedrooms would only have been fit for pygmies if the ground floor ceilings had been raised – the oak panelling could be painted white, the old oak doors replaced with twin leaves beneath carved pediments, and the hall, flagged in diamonds of local stone and black Cornish marble, was quite large enough to take eight pillars, painted by a craftsman from Bath who swirled the paint skilfully about with a feather so that it resembled marble. Kitchens, stables and outhouses formed a courtyard on the eastern side, a lake was dug to the southwest and a walk made around it with strategically placed statues to give points of interest. The fifth baronet pronounced himself very pleased.

They had all remained very pleased, Robert reflected as his gig turned the corner and revealed to him the handsome yellow house with a sharp autumn sun full upon its face, until his ass of a brother Thomas. Thomas was always impulsive, always obsessed by the current enthusiasm, and unfortunately just wealthy enough to satisfy most of them. As luck would have it, the enthusiasm, which dominated the years just before his marriage in 1845 was a passion for the Gothic. The seeds of this passion had been sown ten years before when his maternal uncle, something of an aesthete, had given him a slim green cloth-bound book for his fifteenth birthday, bearing the title *Gothic Furniture in the Style of the Fifteenth Century*, and the initials, stamped in gold, of Augustus Welby Pugin. The following year he bought for himself *Ancient Timber Houses* and the argumentative *Contrasts* by the same author. Between lecturing his insensitive family upon the essential truthfulness of medieval architecture as opposed to the imported shams of all subsequent styles, he set off on tours of Pugin's masterpieces, even going as far as Stockton-on-Tees and Manchester to see the master's churches.

This thoroughness of enthusiasm was, Robert considered, the chief quality in his brother responsible for his death. There had been no need for him personally to stand so visibly in the Alma exhorting his men; that sort of function was the very thing sergeants existed for. It was no false and showy heroism in Thomas to be sure, but rather the vigorous, wholehearted application of his entire being to the scheme or idea or person which had for the moment caught his fancy. Robert's sister-in-law, Charlotte, had once confessed that her courtship by Thomas had been the most relentless and exhausting six months of her life, six months crowned by his announcing that he wished to celebrate their union by building a Gothic chapel in which they would be married, the first ceremony in a long line of dynastic celebrations stretching into the twentieth century and beyond. Charlotte, whose natural self-assertiveness had by no means been diminished by having Thomas Taverner as a lover for half a year, refused point blank. She hated Gothic, the house was very well as it was, and to be married in a family chapel smacked to her of popery.

Robert could recall the ensuing row even now. It lasted quite as long as the courtship and was every bit as energetic. He was a young man of twenty-one himself, and had been most admiring of the way his future sister-in-law stuck to her guns, inducing in her future husband a violent desire to triumph over her and an equally fervent determination to marry, at all costs, this strong-minded girl. The conclusion was of course a compromise, since Charlotte was as bent upon marriage as Thomas. The Gothic element was to remain – Charlotte's concession – but the chapel was to be muted into a slender tower – Thomas's accommodation. It rose beside the library on the west wall of the house, pinnacled and lightly buttressed, crowned with a green copper finial and pierced by long windows with trefoil tops. Inside it was a single tall hexagonal chamber, galleried in the upper half, lined with bookcases between the windows and furnished with extremely uncomfortable carved and painted chairs in the Gothic manner. Its purpose was never quite defined as it was too cold to work or read in for any length of time except in July and August on account of having so much glass and no fireplace (a chimney would have ruined the appearance of the exterior), and so it gradually became the place where members of the family took each other for solemn talks or for quarrels. The ceiling height gave an impressive resonance to angry voices and one could pace furiously and endlessly in a circle around the room while haranguing one's victim penned somewhere in the middle in an unwelcoming pointed chair.

The first quarrel had been, most appropriately, between Thomas and Charlotte over the renaming of the house. As the last flowering of his Gothic fervour, Thomas wished to revert to the old name of Priory, and Charlotte eventually agreed, defeated not by his arguments, but by the overpowering sickness and faintness of her first pregnancy. In honest appreciation of her submission, Thomas presented her, when his first daughter was born, with a suite of garnets and pearls, and enough writing paper to last a lifetime, heavily embossed with 'Buscombe Priory, Somersetshire', in Gothic script. Charlotte never wrote upon a single sheet.

There was no doubt, Robert thought, that some of Thomas's good-hearted, insensitive energy had been handed on to his son. There he was now, that nephew of his, deep in talk with the keeper on the steps below the terrace, while all manner of guests milled about on the gravel waiting for a lead. Of course, Bradstock had been a sort of substitute father to the boy – Charlotte had on her writing table a photograph of a solemn eight-year-old Tom beside Bradstock in gaiters and bowler hat, spaniel beside him, gun broken over his forearm – but that was no reason for letting natural enthusiasms overcome manners. Bradstock was a good fellow and, in the long run, probably better company than most of those men unnecessarily shouting at their dogs on the gravel, but he was a keeper not a guest.

'Uncle Robert!'

'I must congratulate you, my boy.'

'Thank you, sir.'

Robert looked round.

'Thwarted your mother in the matter of a ball, I hear.'

Tom coloured faintly.

'I am afraid she is rather disappointed—'

'She'll get over it. She had a ball apiece for the girls. When they beat the Long Coppice, Tom, I don't want the sixth stand. Two or eight please. Six you get all the wind and no birds. Don't forget.'

'I won't, sir. How's Aunt Mary? And Charles?'

Robert stepped down from the gig, whistled to his liver-spotted springer and motioned the gig away.

'Your aunt kept me awake half the night wanting to decide on the baby's name. She wants Victoria, I've no objection, but it didn't stop her arguing. Charles isn't so good, poor little chap. They think it might be asthma. Hard on a lad of five – makes him a namby pamby, cooped up all day with the women. Ah! Creighton! How does Chancery Lane? And Forrester—'

Freddie Forrester had been asked to please his sister Elizabeth, Arthur Creighton because, although he was a Catholic, he was an excellent lawyer and Charlotte was adept at extracting information she needed out of him for nothing. This she preferred to do rather than consult Edward Martineau, the family lawyer, who was not in the least afraid to be firm with her, and to whom the family owed its financial calm during the years of Tom's minority. Arthur Creighton cherished a small but bright hope of supplanting him, and an even smaller expectation that his daughter, Rosamund, might prove the key to the door. She and her mother were now in the house with Lady Taverner, and he was standing out here on the drive conscious that the other guns seemed infinitely more anxious to speak to Martineau than to himself.

Uncle John Taverner was in South Africa, where he had gone after being sent with the British armed expedition to Ethiopia in 1868, to assist with the consolidation of the Cape Colony, and his representative at the birthday was his son Harry, Tom's eighteen-year-old cousin, whose sheer goodness of heart made him

22

open to exploitation by his mother. Aunt Rachel behaved most of the time like a war widow, wore black – or lilac on particularly skittish days – and had perfected an act of pretty, broken courage. She was inside the house now, telling anyone who would listen that dearest Harry's coming of age would be but a melancholy thing by comparison with this splendid day, with his father absent overseas, so sadly missed, so badly needed.

'Rachel,' Charlotte said with decision after the third repetition had caught her quick ear, 'Harry will not come of age for three years, by which time John will be home. And even if he is not, he is only absent and not dead. When Tom was Harry's age, his father had been dead twelve years.'

Mrs Creighton and her daughter exchanged glances; Lady Walgrave caught their eyes and nodded conspiratorially, passing the intelligence silently but firmly to the Hon. Mrs Bough who was always disposed to pity poor Rachel Taverner. Catherine, from childhood a warm supporter of her cousin Harry, gave her mother a nod of approval, but Elizabeth, frustrated by the drawing room being the far side of the house from the drive, was too taken up with fretting that she could not watch Freddie Forrester moving elegantly among his fellow guns to care who said what to whom. Mrs Bough, in order to deflect herself from her own compassion and to fill a small pause, said, 'There are new people at Marsham Court.'

'Jews,' said Lady Walgrave.

Young Mrs Martineau, second wife of the family lawyer from Bath, and currently wholly preoccupied with the necessity of providing him with children, said mistily, 'They have an enchanting baby called Rose.'

'Jews,' said Lady Walgrave.

'Rose has blue eyes and flaxen curls and a complexion like her name.'

'Jews,' said Lady Walgrave, with dangerous emphasis.

There was an instantaneous rustle and flutter in the room, and the company was somehow smoothly divided into a group admiring the growth of the new tulip tree from the north window, and a smaller group from the west window regretting the appearance of two molehills on the croquet lawn. Mrs Martineau found herself next to Catherine Taverner.

'Is du Cros a Jewish name?'

Catherine smiled out at the molehills.

'No more than Walgrave, I think.'

Out in the long meadow below the beech wood, they drew lots for their stands. Tom found himself at three, between Edward Martineau, by a long way the best shot of them all, and Freddie Forrester, by an equally long way the best dressed. Above them in the hanger, a quarter of a mile away, Bradstock's well-drilled line of beaters whacked and whistled their way through the low undergrowth in an advancing crescendo. Tom imagined the pheasants scuttling under the bracken, as determined not to take off as the beaters were to dislodge them. There were hundreds up there; he and Bradstock had seen to that.

'Do you ever,' Edward Martineau said casually across the few yards that divided them, squinting up into the bright air, 'think of following your uncle?'

Tom said, 'No hope, really. He has a son, you see.'

'But a sick son.'

'He's only five. He may pick up as he gets older.

Uncle Robert is quite set upon Charles being Member after him.'

'Parliament is changing, you know,' Edward Martineau said. 'Ever since the Reform Bill. Your uncle was set right against it. He told me we had over two million voters in the country now on account of it, and he looked as if he was tasting lemons. But that Bill is only a beginning. What is more is that the counties are fast losing their power and Parliament is taking over. If you want to do right by Somersetshire, you will have to do it from London. We mightn't like that, I know, but that is the way things are going. It doesn't seem to me that resolutely turning one's face is going to help anyone much, and it certainly won't halt progress.'

The first roused pheasant flew low and heavily straight out at Freddie Forrester. He aimed, fired and missed, and the bird sailed calmly over his head down to the coppice below.

'Too young,' Edward Martineau said. 'Give them another month and they'll learn to fly higher.'

'Unfortunately my birthday couldn't wait another month.'

Edward grinned. 'This is quite something to inherit, eh?'

Eyes upon his beeches above him, gold and copper against a sharp blue sky, conscious of his own cold, wet grass under his boots, Tom said gently, 'Oh yes, sir. Yes, it is – something indeed.'

A sudden chattering whirr and over two dozen birds exploded in the air above them, with an almost simultaneous crash of shotgun fire. When it was over, and Tom was conscious that Bradstock, who was loading for him, was most restrainedly not commenting either way upon the fact that only one of the birds brought down was his, Edward Martineau strolled over towards him and said casually, 'But if it isn't Parliament, what is it to be?'

Tom tried not to look at the feathered pyramid mounting round Edward's stand as his two dogs sped importantly to and fro.

'I don't think I quite follow—'

'You are twenty-one. You have a good – well, reasonable – education, you have inherited an excellent little estate; you have a farm manager to oversee the tenant farmers, a keeper to see to the game, three men to weed in the woods and fell timber. What are *you* going to do?'

Tom said, blushing and foolish, 'I've always been busy—'

'My dear boy, so could I be in your place. There's enough occupation on these two thousand acres to keep a gentleman contented every day of the year. But, though I cannot say this to your mother, this is 1870 not 1770. We are no longer in a landed age. Look at your uncle Robert. Certainly he used such family money as was his to start his company, but he is a rich man by his own energy and enterprise.'

'Do you mean,' Tom said, feeling the day was suddenly dimmer, 'do you mean that my money will not last?'

Edward Martineau looked at him with sympathy.

'It will last, my dear fellow, it will last at least for you. All I want you to realize is that both you and the estate would benefit from some extra effort from you, not just in financial terms, but in the progressive ideas you might bring to it. Progressive ideas do not, I fear, grow on the trees at Buscombe. You must go farther afield. And you must think of Buscombe *after* you. After all, what you have been given today is the fruits of other

Taverners' labours. I sound a deal more solemn that I wish to on such a day, but I am simply taking the chance of a word alone with you. Shall we join the others?'

'What should I do?' Tom said. 'Shall I come and see you? Should we talk again?'

'Willingly, when you have thought some more.'

'I am grateful,' Tom said suddenly, 'I really am – if in a rather worried way—'

Edward laughed.

'Put it out of your mind for the rest of the day.'

As they approached the other guns, they passed the line of beaters being marshalled into a farm cart before going off to the Long Coppice. The last beater was a foot shorter than the others, and dressed in a drab green garment almost to his feet and a huge cap that enveloped his head in a tweed parcel. As Edward and Tom passed him, he turned his head quickly towards them and with a grin of pure triumph revealed himself to be Meggy Bradstock.

CHAPTER TWO

May 1871

Freddie Forrester had been, with a slightly sinking heart, conscious of the inevitability of Elizabeth Taverner for a year. He had always known his own fundamental enjoyment of domesticity would catch up with him in the end – as would the results of living beyond his slender means – but he was afraid to abandon the mildly socialite image of himself that his looks and manners had enabled him to adopt. He knew quite well that he had never uttered a witty saying in his life – he had confessed this once to Catherine Taverner when he thought she might be an ally in saving him. She had replied that he must content himself thus and told him of the poet Wordsworth who had admitted to one witticism only, the repetition of which reduced the company to regretting bitterly it had ever asked him – but Forrester had a friendly polish and an ability to laugh just the right amount which made him appear more amusing than he was. The Prince of Wales seemed to like him very much and this of course raised his stock without any further effort on his part, particularly as he was prudent enough never to boast of it.

He knew that, at forty-one, with five hundred a year and the expectation of only a few thousand on his mother's death, he was not a catch. Elizabeth was, though not quite as delicious a one as she had been five years before at eighteen when her particular kind of highly coloured golden beauty was enhanced by being so new and young. By thirty she would be a handsome, solid, settled woman in appearance, and that, coupled with the mixture of determination and sentimentality in her character, gave Freddie little stabs of unease. But then, so did the prospect of his own future life which showed no prospect of advancing, since he was unfitted for any occupation but that of being a pleasant guest. He did not doubt that, as a married man, he would make an equally pleasant host, and that entertaining on the scale he enjoyed would be possible with a wife such as Elizabeth Taverner, whose own income from her mother, drawn from the Coopers' Nottinghamshire coalfields, so wonderfully exceeded his own. Fidgeting between his fears and his inclinations, afraid both of losing his freedom and of acquiring a dreary middle-aged loneliness, blown hither and thither by all kinds of moderately held conclusions, he eventually and not entirely intentionally, laid the whole problem in Elizabeth's eager lap.

She was in the small south sitting room, perhaps the most charming room in the house, its high, wide windows draped in long falls of white muslin and yellow velvet, its Regency furniture arranged in welcoming groups around a table in the window and a low one before the fire. The carpet was Turkey, but pale coloured, the walls washed a dim duck egg blue; there was a proliferation of cushions and little padded stools, of books and photographs and plants in pots, and in the window a canary sang, in a brass wire cage like a pagoda. Elizabeth, in blue and claret striped silk, was sitting in the window, painting assiduously on a piece of velvet, and the spring sun was falling brightly and becomingly on her yellow hair, plaited ornately on the back of her head. Freddie had in fact driven over to see Tom. He had told himself that and in order to make it true, had also told his man so. He wanted to ask Tom about the chances of a little mayfly fishing in a month or so, but had unluckily chosen the day of the Bath Assizes to come and make this request, and there was only Elizabeth, all alone, at home, since her mother and sister had accompanied her brother into the city.

When he had been announced, and welcomed, and placed in a chair on the other side of the small table, Elizabeth could look at him with all the delight she felt. To her he was dashing, handsome, sophisticated, amusing and, she fancied, much sought after by other women. He also seemed a little afraid of her which she found entrancing. She leaned forward to add a highlight to a violet leaf in her picture and said, 'We have hardly seen you since Tom's birthday, you know. I suppose you can't resist London and we are all so dull down here in the winter by comparison. Is that not so?'

'By no means,' he said gallantly, thinking how much he liked the spectacle of her painting but how equally much he regretted her choice of purple velvet as a canvas. 'It happens every year, by a kind of accident. I intend to remain down here and improve myself no end by reading and so forth and then the invitations begin to come, and I go to one or two things in town, and before I know where I am, I have done yet another season.'

Elizabeth thought the picture of him as a solitary reader touching, being ignorant that the real reason for his winter intentions was to economize by living in the country. She looked up to give him a smile of studied tenderness. He explained a little stumblingly about the mayfly. She replied very smoothly that she was sure Tom would be delighted to see him on the river. He then rose and walked about the room admiring things, while she admired the cut of his high-buttoned pepper and salt tweed suit and felt pleasantly in control of impending excitement. He then came across the room holding a scarlet lacquer box he had picked up from a side table and stood very close to her and said, apropos of nothing he had said previously,

'Oh, Elizabeth!'

His voice was full of appeal. She laid down her brush and looked up at him. He seemed very agitated and was gazing at her with a kind of desperation. She rose, gently removed the scarlet box from his grasp, replaced it with her own hands and calmly replied,

'Freddie.'

He said, 'I dare not, I cannot – I beg you – help me—'

In her mind's eye she saw the falling stricken faces of all the other women who so surely loved him. It was the high noon in all her life as she said to him, to help him,

'Do you love me, Freddie?'

He nodded vigorously, mute, his eyes fixed and pleading. She leaned forward and laid her mouth for an instant on his and then turned her cheek to put it against the shoulder of his coat while she said, 'And I love you.' They stood like that for a long moment while Freddie's heart hammered beneath his expensive linen and his brain whirled with a thousand reflections. He tried to speak again, but could only bleat a little, so he put his

31

arm around her firm blue silk shoulders and waited to see what she would do next. What she did was to raise a radiant face to him and say softly,

'I have dreamed of this for so long. I have never wanted to marry anyone but you.'

Somehow, suddenly, it was over. He had swum through the waterfall and was on the far bank, dripping wet but alive, with a view before him that had a great deal in its favour. He was seized with gratitude towards her and led her to the fireplace, where a small coal fire burned as a token to the changeable April weather. They sat down together on a yellow velvet sofa, clasping hands, and began to talk, very sentimentally, of their future life together.

Catherine said sharply, 'You are a fool, Elizabeth.'

Elizabeth, buoyed up by her own delight, lounging in a chair in her sister's bedroom, said idly, 'Why so?'

'Because he is so dull and so stupid. He is certainly kind and undoubtedly handsome, but he has rich tastes and no money and hardly an idea in his head. He will bore you to tears in months.'

'Mamma does not think so.'

'He is being very charming to Mamma just now.'

'Tom does not think so.'

'Tom knows you wish to be married and that Freddie will not knock you about. But Tom has not given marriage a thought. He has never considered the companionship it ought to bring, the delight in one another's conversation, because he is still a half-baked boy. But I have thought of those things and I tell you that you are a fool.'

'Why must you try and spoil things for me?' Elizabeth said, pouting a little.

Catherine came across and lowered her sharp, fair face close to her sister's.

'Because you are my sister,' she said crossly, 'and I love you.'

Besides her sister Elizabeth, Catherine Taverner loved her brother, her mother and particularly her cousin Harry. She was four when he was born, a benign and amenable baby who grew into an obliging and cheerful child with, from his earliest years, a strong human sympathy. Taverners all came fair, but some, like Tom and Elizabeth, came square and fresh complexioned, and some, like Catherine and Harry, came narrower, paler, and bony, with long hands, thick hair and a smile of extreme sweetness. When he was in a room with her, however many other people were also present, she could feel his natural understanding of her flowing down an invisible pipeline between them, and it was one of the few elements in her life that gave her true comfort.

Much of the time, as Charlotte constantly pointed out, Catherine was restless and dissatisfied. She was given to reading books that only increased her inquietude, and had written out, and pinned up above her dressing table, a quotation from Charlotte Yonge's *The Clever Woman of the Family*, a speech made by the heroine, Rachel, on her twenty-fifth birthday:

'Here am I, able and willing, only to task myself to the uttermost, yet tethered down to the merest mockery of usefulness by conventionalities. I am a young lady, forsooth! – I must not be out late; I must not choose my acquaintance; I must be a mere helpless, useless being.'

Above her bed, Catherine had pinned another stern warning, this time from Florence Nightingale:

33

'The family uses people not for what they are, nor for what they are intended to be, but for what it wants them for . . . This system dooms some minds to incurable infancy, others to silent misery.'

On her writing table, lay a menacing remark from Charlotte Brontë's *Shirley*, its corners weighted by four horn buttons snipped from her father's old shooting coat.

'Men, I believe, fancy women's minds something like those of children. Now that is a mistake.'

The last sentence Catherine had underlined in red ink. Other injunctions of a like kind curled on walls or in the corners of picture frames like yellowing moths, but Catherine would not take them down lest she might seem to be slackening in her quest for fulfilment. That quest she pursued almost wholly in her bedroom, a large and characterful room that faced north and west above the drawing room with a single small window looking east straight into one of the ancient mulberry trees. One had to be careful to keep that window closed in late summer, or gorged and drunken wasps, sated with fruit, dragged themselves across the windowsill to lie on the carpet below, waiting for passing bare feet.

Catherine's bed, of curly brass with a half canopy of convolvulus patterned chintz, faced the west windows. Her writing table stood at one of those windows, and her dressing table, immaculately ordered with its swinging toilet glass, stood by the north one. There were chintz-covered low chairs by the fireplace in the south wall, and bookcases ran right round the room to chair rail height containing what Tom had once teasingly called A Young Lady's Library of Discontent. The walls were crowded with pictures, the top of the wardrobe piled with boxes and along the flat surface of the bookcases marched the dolls and wooden horses of Catherine's childhood. It was an extremely full room and yet a very disciplined one. In it Catherine painted garden plans, wrote fierce little social satires, practised the flute, read and paced and chafed.

'What troubles me,' she said once to Tom, 'is that I cannot *think* what will become of me.'

'Shan't you marry?'

'I don't really feel any inclination to, you see. I don't have Eliza's desire to organize a house, nor do I particularly like mothering people, otherwise I should no doubt have run away to nurse before now. And I don't have to marry for money because I can support myself.'

'In that case, you may please yourself!'

'That is precisely the trouble,' Catherine said, turning a grave gaze upon him. 'I cannot seem to discover what *does* please me.'

Now Elizabeth said to her, 'I think you are cross because you are envious that I know how my life will be and you do not.'

'Heaven forbid! I would rather have my uncertainty any day than the deadly certainty I see for you.'

'I wish you could try to be just a little pleased—'

'Dearest Eliza, I am pleased that you have what you want, and I will make every effort to become fond of your Freddie. But I cannot help seeing what I see and I must, for the love I bear you, tell you of it.'

Elizabeth rose and stretched and wandered to the north window.

'There are buds on the tulip tree!'

'Oh good,' Catherine said absently.

'I shall ask Lilian Traill to stay. She knows Freddie in London. She will be happy for me.'

'Does that mean Mr Traill too?'

'I shall simply ask Lilian. He can spare her for a week or so and I must have somebody to talk to. She can come shopping with me in Bath. She is a very good listener.'

'Why,' Catherine interrupted wildly, 'do you all marry this way? What are you all thinking of? There is Freddie, eighteen years your senior with nothing in common with you whatsoever. There is George Traill, at least thirty years older than Lilian, with no appreciation at all of her gentleness and compliance. Are you all *mad*?'

Elizabeth moved to the door and said stiffly,

'There is nothing to be gained from talking to you when you think this way. Your prejudices are piled so high you cannot see over them.'

'And you,' said Catherine rudely, 'have your eyes so deliberately closed that you cannot see *at all*.'

May that year was a very pretty month. The hedges were pink and white with hawthorn, cowslips dappled the banks and in the soft, cool evenings, the brown trout rose handsomely in the little chalk stream that ran out of the Long Coppice and away through the level meadows to the south. Tom rose early, breakfasted quickly with his mother and was in the stableyard before nine. He had established a routine of inspection of the estate on a weekly basis, partly because his strong instincts led him over and over and over his own ground, but partly also to avoid thinking too much about Edward Martineau's admonition that he must come to terms with the fact that the landed gentleman was rapidly becoming a thing of the past.

Unlike his sister Catherine, upon whom he doted, he knew exactly what pleased him. Buscombe did, house and land, and after a day out on the estate, he came to the dinner table buoyant and satisfied, and when he closed his eyes in bed later, saw his own trees and slopes and walls printed in a marvellous frieze behind his eyelids. He could not conceive of anything he could do in life that would interest him as much as his growing knowledge of which crop was best planted where, of what weather to hope for when, of how woodland should be cared for. He spent whole afternoons learning the laborious rhythmic craft of building a dry stone wall, or splitting and weaving the stems in hedges to thicken them, and days behind a plough or in the lambing pens. He could not bring himself to drive into Bath and talk to Edward Martineau who would, for the best and most farsighted reasons, gently try to put a stop to this life he so loved. He would assure Tom that economically it was short-sighted to live on rents and farming profits – all very well for 1771, but not well at all for a century later – and that those profits must be put into some scheme that would, in the future, support Buscombe. It was too late to train Tom for a profession – Charlotte had, with old-fashioned ideas and a powerful obstinacy, seen to that – but he had a perfectly sound intelligence and a strong sense of duty. Those two Edward intended to play upon, and Tom knew it.

The thing seemed to be, Tom thought, to counter Edward's suggestion – whatever it might turn out to be – with another, preferably before he even made it. His confidant was Bradstock whose comfortable, philosophical presence reassured Tom of the fundamental immutability of all the things he held most dear.

'Course,' Bradstock said, 'wages never bin so 'igh as now.'

They were standing at the yard gate of the home farm, and watching men at work on four new good brick labourers' cottages, finished now but for stout slate roofs.

'Twelve shillings a week,' Tom said, 'and a brood of children apiece—'

'It were five shillin' but twenty year ago, and just as many babbies. I never seen anything like the last twenty year for farming and, to speak fair, I thought the enclosure would be the end of the land. I did.'

'Progressive farming, Bradstock.'

Bradstock pulled a face.

'Can't abide machines.'

'We wouldn't be so productive without them. The two best decades for farming this century.'

'The forties was 'ungry.'

'The seventies won't be!'

'Dun't look like it. Twelve shillin' a week—'

'I ought to buy more land,' Tom said suddenly, 'that's what I should do! Capitalize on the farming boom, take on more men, produce more—'

'Steady,' said Bradstock, adding after a pause, 'sir.'

'Perhaps I should take over the farm management myself, too.'

Bradstock sucked his teeth.

'Saving on Howitt's wages, I could take on three more men without putting up the wage bill!'

'Howitt knows what he's about.'

'I could learn!'

'Takes time.'

'I'm a quick learner. Remember teaching me to fish?

And shoot? You said I was even quicker than your own lads.'

'Farmin's different. There's—' Bradstock paused, searched the sky for words to express his objection, and said finally, 'There's all the money to do with farmin'.'

Tom grinned.

'I did go to school, you know.'

''Tisn't the same, sir,' Bradstock maintained. 'So much depends upon it. Deal of people, sir.'

'But that would be such an incentive for me! I should relish that kind of responsibility. Buscombe and all the people here could only benefit!'

There was a pause and then Bradstock said, 'I'd best be getting back to the river, sir. Temptin' time of day this, when they start risin', for those as 'as no business there.'

'Of course,' Tom said, hardly hearing him, 'of course.'

He was in a fever of elation for days. The scheme seemed to answer every problem, and would provide solutions to Edward's anxiety as to how he should shape his life, as well as solve the more practical problem of how Buscombe's livelihood would be assured. To raise capital, he would sell out part of the investment in his uncle Robert's business left to him by his father and with full pockets he would approach his new neighbour du Cros and make him an offer for the five hundred acres of pasture and arable land that joined his own. He would thereby have increased Buscombe's farming and production capacity by twenty-five per cent. Du Cros was known to be a businessman who had bought the Marsham estate for the house and garden rather than the land. Tom, in his impetuous desire to be plunged into this new scheme, could hardly refrain from riding over at once, and making an offer for the land before another sunset.

The Gothic tower, however, served the family as a warning against reckless hurry as well as a refuge for rows. In the short blue spring nights, Tom wrestled with his own eagerness and battled to force himself to work out this plan so that he might present it to Edward, having previously considered and allowed for every possible objection beforehand. If he were to take on more men, he would be at least two cottages short; if he persuaded Edward that upwards of five thousand pounds must be invested, he must be able to show how quickly, by present prices on the world market, Buscombe would again be paying its way; he must bone up most earnestly on agricultural economy and probably, though he felt a great pang at this, he must stop talking to Bradstock, who for all his comforting unchangeableness, was unprogressive to a degree.

Another thought then thudded down upon that last – Meggy. A man of his ambitions, a man aiming to show the landed classes of his own country that, if they seized the new mechanical advances and harnessed them to the traditional richness of English farming, their day was far from done, such a man could not continue any longer a liaison with a gamekeeper's daughter. He was fond of her, to be sure, and grateful to her for allowing him a year of freedom and exploration of her solid little body. He knew that body inch by inch, its different textures and colours, its interesting responses and secrets and he knew too that it was very much more absorbing than Meggy's mind could ever be. He had liked her monosyllables and her long silences to begin with; they were peaceful and left him free to make all the fascinating discoveries that, in the early days, had driven him almost daily to the granary loft. But lately he had to admit, Meggy had seemed duller than before, her dumb compliance almost irritating, also her puzzlement that what used to stir him up in an instant now only had him rumpling her hair absently while his attention wandered.

He was abruptly furious with himself. How could he have let it maunder on so long? How could he have let it even begin? What was he thinking of, to choose in the first place the daughter of a man who trusted him and to whom he owed so much of the pleasure and security of his growing up? He was flooded with hot shame and rage with himself, almost to the point of rushing, middle of the night or not, to the Bradstocks' cottage, and relieving himself of all his unbearable feelings by confessing everything. But that course of behaviour would be utter luxury for himself and absolute torment for Bradstock – the burden would simply slip from the young man to the older. He must consider a gentler scheme, a subtler plan; he must not hope to clear his own conscience; and he must try not to inflict too much pain . . .

'What'm you sayin'?' Meggy asked him.

They were sitting on a south facing bank on the edge of the Long Coppice not far from the spot a year ago where the gleam of Meggy's white thighs, as she relieved herself among the bushes, had first caught Tom's eye as he went down to the river in the May dusk. Meggy looked much the same as she had then with her bright cheeked round face framed in rough brown hair, her plump white arms ending in small reddened hands (the result of hours in the cold water sinks of the dairies and a source of strong early attraction for Tom) and her body bundled up in shapeless dark stuffs that made her resemble, when on the move, a scuttling hedgehog.

'I'm trying to tell you about my plans for Buscombe. For the farm.'

Meggy sighed.

'I only got an 'our.'

'You must try to listen, Meggy, because it concerns you.'

'I don't know nothin' 'bout farmin'.'

'You don't have to. You just have to try to see that with all my changing plans – plans that will make this place and all the people who work for it safe for the future – I have to change too.'

Meggy surveyed him silently as if she expected to see his yellow hair turn black and his long legs shrink to bandy stumps like those of old Veale the coachman.

'I have to change my ways. I have to behave differently. I can't do all the old things I used to do, even things I liked to do.'

'If you *liked* 'em—' Meggy said reasonably.

'Liking isn't the important thing. If I don't change my kind of life, I can't change things here, and then we will all suffer. I've got to learn how to manage the farm.'

'You'm a gentleman,' Meggy objected.

'But a gentleman has to bow to change. If I resist the changes in our society, I will simply get left behind and all Buscombe with me.'

Meggy shook her head uncomprehendingly. Tom took up the nearest little red paw and said earnestly,

'If I don't improve things, change things, to enable the estate to make more money, there might not in the future be enough money to pay your father and Veale and Mr Howitt and the maids and the farm men and – and you.'

The first small flicker of suspicion came into Meggy's blue-grey eyes.

'Why'm you tellin' me?'

'Because you must be part of the change.'

Meggy took her hand away and folded it in her other one. She sat for a long time staring before her, stoutly shod little feet thrust out below her skirt, the wind blowing fuzzy wisps of her hair gently about her head. Then she said,

'You'm tired of me.'

To his horror, his eyes suddenly filled with tears.

'Not tired, Meggy. I'm so fond of you. I'll never forget you—'

'You'm of age now. You'm man and master. You'll be needin' a wife soon and a son to grow up be'ind you. You'll be lookin' for a lady to be your wife.'

She scrambled to her feet and began to cry. He got up too and put his arm around her, trying to mop her face with his free hand and to say comforting things, but she was crying too hard to hear him. Her tears ran down her round cheeks and splashed onto his mopping hand, while she simply stood and wept helplessly, her own hands hanging limply, her mouth open. Then she stopped, suddenly and completely, as if a tap had been turned off.

'Tom?'

'Meggy—'

She gave a huge sniff.

'You do summat for me?'

He was about to say 'Anything', in his rush of

gratitude at her lack of reproach but remembered his new self-imposed role and said instead, 'If it is in my power, of course I will.'

'Come to the granary with me, then.'

'No, Meggy—'

'Last time—'

She took his hand and began to tug.

'Tom. Just the last time. Then I'll never bother you no more, I promise. Just one last time to remember you by.'

'I shouldn't—'

'You shouldn' all this year, then!'

She came close and turned her little tear-pinkened nose up to him.

'C'mon. I only got 'alf an 'our. Just this last time.'

The granary was set apart from the other farm build-ings, raised up on a dozen stone staddles like giant mushrooms, out of the way of the rats, and usefully – for those who did not wish to be seen approaching – set about on two sides by hawthorn trees. There was a door in the wall which gave onto a stone staircase leading to the loft which had its own high door for loading wagons. At the far end of the loft, someone had partitioned off a section for an apple store now unused, and this had been a secure bolt-hole all winter, screened by the sacks of grain and bales of hay stacked against it and down the length of the building. Tom and Meggy had made a narrow tunnel which they carefully blocked with bales each time they left. Now, in the spring, with winter feeding over and the grain mostly gone to be milled, the apple store was more vulnerable. Their security lay in the fact that, until the harvest and the replenishing of supplies, nobody would need to come to the granary again. Cider scented and thickly strewn with hay, its single tiny window furred with cobwebs and dotted with fly corpses, the apple store was the place where part of Tom, at least, had come to manhood.

Gratitude and obligation overwhelmed him as he sank beside Meggy into the tickling haystalks. She was just the same, biddable and heavily limp, helpfully opening bits of her clothing, saying nothing, not even sniffing reproachfully. She guided him into her, watched him steadily while he rode her, and held him when he had spent himself, patting the back of his neck and head. He lay panting for some time, then raised himself to say,

'Oh Meggy, I do thank you!'

Then he struggled to all fours, up onto his feet, and turned, as he always did out of some instinctive point-less courtesy to do up his trousers with his back to her, to find Bradstock regarding them both from the doorway with an expression of the deepest sadness.

Lilian Traill arrived to a house silently bursting with some great secret. Lady Taverner was very grim, Catherine very sharp, and the big fair brother with the ready smile, most unnaturally silent. They ate the first luncheon together – a chicken fricassee and early peas – with great conversational difficulty, and then Lady Taverner went to lie down, Catherine to her room and Tom to ride, leaving at last Lilian alone with a glowingly satisfied Elizabeth.

Lilian hoped Elizabeth would enlighten her, but Elizabeth only wanted to talk of Freddie. Lilian thought Freddie had as much amusement value as a tailor's dummy and did not want to talk of him all. They fretted irritably around each other for a quarter of an hour or so until Elizabeth, for want of anything other to say, asked after George Traill, whereupon Lilian burst into sudden tears and said that everything was too awful and she simply could not think what she was going to do.

Even Elizabeth was fascinated out of her complacency over Freddie. Lilian looked lovely even when she was crying, and she was not so much crying now as howling, rocking herself about and saying over and over again that she had never dreamed that marriage could be as horrible as this.

'What kind of horrible?' Elizabeth asked. 'Are you lonely?'

'Oh!' cried Lilian furiously, 'I should love to be lonely! He disgusts me—'

She stopped to blow her nose, vigorously. A tendril or two of soft russet hair escaped from the rest on account of her vehemence and curled against her collar.

'Disgusts you . . .'

'Elizabeth, Elizabeth, I must tell somebody. I must, it is so shameful. When we married two years ago, I was twenty-two and he was fifty. Within three months I discovered he had kept a mistress for ten years, in a flat, would you believe it, off the Bayswater Road, that he was having a liaison with – well, with a peer's wife and – oh, Elizabeth, this is the worst, this is terrible – his friends nickname him Two Shilling Traill because he'll pay anyone, he doesn't mind, off the streets, *anyone*, and then,' her voice rose in a scream, 'he comes home to *me!*'

Elizabeth was transfixed.

'You see, all my money went to him,' Lilian went on. 'My guardians liked him so much and thought he would be a father to me as well as a husband. While he was courting me he was quite different, *quite*, I mean, I always wished he were not quite so old and I should have loved him to have had soft, thick young man's hair, but I could not believe the sort of brute he turned out to be!' She got up and began to pace very vigorously about the sitting room. 'You cannot believe what a relief it is to be here! Of course, he didn't mind a bit if I came because it gives him his horrible freedom. All he wants of me is my money and a ba—' Lilian looked as if she might be sick and pressed both hands to her mouth. 'What *am* I going to do?'

There was no reply to be made. Elizabeth got up and made soothing, silly remarks to comfort her distracted friend, and gave her little fluttering pats.

'I am sorry,' Lilian said after a while. 'What a frightful outburst. Unforgivable of me, particularly when you want to talk about Freddie. Let's talk about Freddie now.'

Elizabeth found that, just now, she did not seem to want to talk about him as much as she had done ten minutes before. The golden word 'Marriage' had abruptly developed a dull tarnish in her mind. In any case, Lilian's revelation had left her excited and jumpy; she could not settle to the usually comfortable prospect of where they might live and how many travelling dresses she should order for their wedding journey. So, rather without meaning to, she said to Lilian,

'I'm afraid we have terrible news here, too. It absolutely mustn't go beyond you – you really must not tell a soul – but Tom has been caught having a – a – well, with the keeper's daughter, by the keeper if you please, and we really do not know what to do with ourselves.'

'Oh!' Lilian breathed, eyes wide.

'The keeper came to Mamma. She said he was quite

wonderful, very calm, just full of sadness that Tom should behave that way, and full of shame that his daughter should. She has been sent off with a sister to lodgings in Lyme Regis – Mamma is paying for them – in case there is a baby, and if there is not, she will be sent straight into service. Bradstock – that's the keeper – offered to leave Buscombe, but Mamma wouldn't hear of it and said he was not to blame and the estate could not do without him. Of course, he and Tom can't meet just now and Tom is in agony about it all. Mamma feels let down, Catherine thinks Tom the biggest booby in all the world, Tom cannot hold his head up – so you see what a cheerful house you are come to!'

Lilian said sadly, 'Do you think all men are the same? I mean like this? Wanting this – this thing all the time?'

'I hope not,' Elizabeth said with a sudden shiver.

'What will happen to the baby, if there is one?'

'I think it will be adopted.'

'Perhaps the girl loved Tom, really loved him.'

Elizabeth shook her head. A girl of Meggy Bradstock's class did not know about proper love.

'I expect she was flattered.'

'Poor her,' Lilian said. 'Poor her, all the same. And poor Tom.'

At dinner that night, Tom thought he saw gleams of sympathy in Lilian's grey eyes across the table. If they were there, they only made him feel worse. He would not have believed it possible to feel so tormented, but every time the pain in his mind tried to find a smooth, cool place to lay its burning anguish, he could hear Bradstock's voice saying quietly to him, 'I don't want to hear nothin' from you, lad. And I don't want to say nothin'. You'll be sayin' all the things I might say to

48

yourself in the next few weeks, and that'll be 'ard enough for you to bear. Just get out of my sight and stay out, lad, stay right out just now.'

Mrs Bradstock, expecting a seventh baby when little Fred, the sixth, wasn't crawling yet, had gone into hysterics. Meggy had simply gone dumb as a post. Tom could face nobody for several weeks. It was all made a great deal worse because his mother and Bradstock were being so bloody *marvellous* about it all; it was far easier to bear the tongue lashing from his sister Catherine.

He was glad Lilian had come. He hardly knew her but she was gay and amusing and very pretty. Catherine said she was quite clever too, but moved among people who despised cleverness, so she pretended not to be. He watched her for a while, spearing the first strawberries on a cloudy glass plate patterned with vine tendrils, and when she looked up, she caught his eye and gave him a clear level cool glance that was peculiarly comforting. Then she turned to Lady Taverner, who liked her and thought her a good friend for Elizabeth, and said, 'Have you ever thought of building a conservatory? They are all the rage, you know. And I think I know just the place for one here, at Buscombe—'

CHAPTER THREE

August 1871

'I don't like any of your schemes,' Robert Taverner said to his nephew, 'except the conservatory.'

Tom, red from August heat and equally red from being thwarted, jabbed at the turf with his boot toe. They were standing about Arthur Creighton's green and plushy lawn while his daughter, her dark and greedy face alight with animation, held an archery party. It was a charming spectacle: Elizabeth Taverner (to be Mrs Freddie Forrester in a week) and Rosamund Creighton in white, Catherine in blue, Aunt Mary Taverner in green and in wild Irish high spirits, Alicia Martineau in cream lace, Lady Taverner and Mrs Creighton in unfortunately similar striped silk, the men in pale flannels, all grouped gracefully about against a backdrop of rhododendrons and azaleas that were the talk of the neighbourhood in May.

'You should not be selling any part of your share in the company, Tom. We are expanding across another five acres and with free trade, business can only get better and better. I can't stop you selling even if I think it the height of folly, but I do beg you, if you do sell – and there's no shortage of people ready to buy I can tell you, in fact I'm thinking of turning the whole thing into a limited liability company – if you do sell, do *not*, whatever you do, buy land. Houses, furniture, shares, anything you like, but not land. Don't touch land.'

Tom began again, too angrily, on his defence of the present agricultural boom.

'I know, I know,' Robert said, cutting him off, 'but it isn't going to continue. I'll stake my last shirt on it. The Americans are farming with machinery we haven't dreamed of yet, those miles and miles of the Middle West are going to flood the world with cheap grain in a few years, and then you'll be able to buy English land for boot buttons. Five thousand pounds' worth of farm-land this year won't be worth your croquet lawn in three years' time. You might as well bury the money in the muck now and have done with it.'

Tom had the sensation of trying to break down a brick wall with his bare hands. Disappointment and fury made him careless.

'I wish you would listen. I wish you would at least try to see that my position will be different because I shall learn how to run the land as a business. I intend to be as progressive as you think you are and when I've succeeded I'll do everything in my power to help younger men with my kind of ambition and enterprise, rather than break their heads because they don't see everything my way.'

'We will speak of this again,' Robert said sharply, 'when you are cooler.'

'Now then, Robert,' Mary Taverner said, catching his sleeve as he strode past her a moment later, 'what have you been saying to the boy?'

'I talk sense to him. He spouts moonshine back.'

Robert Taverner had found Mary Costelloe while

hunting in County Kildare when he was forty-one. She was physically brave, extremely argumentative and could do almost anything she liked with him. In six years of marriage she had given him a son whose physical frailty neither of them could understand and a small composed daughter whom they understood at once, and had poured a great deal of vibrant energy into her husband's life and interests. He called her a baggage and adored her recklessness on the hunting field.

'He believes his moonshine,' Mary said, looking across the lawn at Tom's morose figure drooping against a young willow on the edge of the lawn.

'He wants to throw money to the wind. He wants to sell out the only good investment he has, besides the estate, and buy half du Cros's land. He says I'm breaking his head because I don't agree with him.'

'Maybe you are. You've the tact of a charging bull, Robert Taverner. Why can't you get at the boy more gently?'

'He'd think I agreed with him.'

'Not if you were clever and quiet about it. Will you look at that girl? She never misses.'

Rosamund Creighton was exquisitely aware of her own skill and grace. She was not pretty, but her dark face with its quick, darting glance, her secret smile, her air of self-assurance more than compensated. She wore white because she liked the drama of it with her black hair, just as she liked watching the white arrows fly against the dark leaves of the rhododendrons and land, quivering, in the white targets set up on the grass beneath the blue-green branches of the cedar trees. She liked, too, the little currents of excitement fizzing through the calm hot afternoon – Tom Taverner's angry red face, his uncle's set pale one, Lady

Taverner's fidgeting, because although the Creightons were useful to her they were, she always remembered uncomfortably once on their property, also Catholics. Rosamund thought Lady Taverner a stupid woman who attempted to cover up her stupidity by being over-bearing. Her daughter Elizabeth would be much the same in time – but not Catherine Taverner. She was another matter altogether, a creature of quite enough discernment to give Rosamund some pause. It was a small but real consolation that she was such a poor shot. Rosamund had heard Harry Taverner say to her,

'I like watching you, you know, however you do it and even I know you are not doing it very well.'

'Oh!' Catherine said, laughing, 'I would find you a comfort even upon the gallows!'

Rosamund was shooting beautifully. Arrow after arrow flew down the lawn in a shallow measured arc and plunged into the heart of the target. Arthur Creighton watched her with a fatuous pride for which she would punish him later. Her mother was as usual talking too much, inevitably, of her elder sister Florence who had married a minor Italian duke and lived in a little castle in Tuscany. She said to Elizabeth at her side,

'I believe I must go and tease your brother into a good humour.'

Elizabeth, more than reconciled to the idea of marriage now that Lilian's disturbing presence had gone, and unable to see anything except through a kind of rosy prenuptial filter, said,

'Oh, I wish you would. I dread him behaving like a bear next week. He has to give me away, you see.'

'Are they going to make good brothers-in-law?'

'My dear,' Elizabeth said, fitting her arrow and raising the bow, 'nobody could fail to get on with Freddie.'

The arrow rose too high, described a graceful rising and falling curve and buried its head in the outer edge of the target.

'Too high,' Rosamund said unnecessarily and crossed the lawn to Tom.

He was not conscious of her until her white skirts were almost swishing over his boots.

'Would you rather be playing croquet?'

He said, stammering a little, 'I'm afraid not. I'm rather bad company today. I must apologize.'

She stood and looked at him with her intense, darting glance, without speaking. He felt yet more hot blood rising in his heated skin and said with a kind of desperation,

'I'm no kind of guest, I know, but sometimes things are just intolerable—'

'What is your quarrel with your uncle?'

Tom said stiffly, 'I cannot speak of it.'

'But you must. You cannot come to my party and make the atmosphere so awkward by quarrelling and then refuse to disclose what was so important that it could not wait until another occasion.'

She sounded consolingly like Catherine, which melted him.

'It is the age old struggle between the young man and the older man, father and son I suppose, and Uncle Robert has been some kind of substitute father since I don't have one of my own. I am come of age, as you know, and he wishes to treat me still as the boy who must be guided in all things. Not only do I not wish to be guided, I am very certain that many of my fresh ideas are better than his!'

'And what are these fresh ideas?'

'I should bore you—'

'Not at all. If I thought I might be bored, I should not ask you.'

He told her. As he spoke she saw in her mind's eye the lands about Buscombe swelling, glowing green and gold, bursting barns and granaries, a great workforce lined up for a harvest home, and the house at the centre of it all, windows blazing with light, ringing with voices and music. When he stopped she laid two cool fingers on his hand – this was most agitating – and said,

'Of course you are right.' Then she turned from him and surveyed the lawn and her guests and the too-new, too-yellow, too-Italianate house her father had built and said, 'I want to hear more, but I cannot just now. What will you do next?'

'I must steel myself and go to talk to Edward Martineau.'

'I should like to know what he says. Will you come here, and tell me?'

'Oh,' he said with intensity, 'I should like that above all things. It will give me heart for the meeting.'

She turned and gave him a swift nod over her shoulder.

'Good,' she said.

'I don't much like Miss Creighton,' Harry Taverner said to his cousin Catherine. He had brought her a dish of blackcurrant leaf water ice and was sitting beside her on a stone bench while she ate it.

'Oh? Why not? You like everybody.'

'She is too dark and secret.'

'She has the reputation of being most devout. As a child, her mamma says she had visions.'

'Visions of blood, I shouldn't wonder.'

Catherine smiled and put a spoonful of ice into her mouth to hide it.

'Did you hear about the conservatory?'

'Yes. Yes, I did. I am so delighted.'

'Oh, Harry, so am I! I sometimes worry that it is a measure of the narrowness of my life that I can be transported at the suggestion of having a mere glass room added to the house. But it will be beneath my bedroom window, and I think constantly of looking down into that green world under its glass dome and knowing that I can keep summer there all year long. I've made such lists of plants I can't describe to you. I am being quite absurd. I lay awake at night last week worrying about how to keep alive a gardenia – gardenias are notoriously delicate and difficult, you know – a gardenia, I do not even possess yet. So you see!'

Harry very much wanted to put his arms around her and had to content himself with saying,

'I love to see you so excited.'

'I shall do heaps of it myself, you see. Turnbull and the boy have more than enough to do anyway, outside, and I shall so love it to be my kingdom.'

'May I help you,' Harry asked diffidently, 'before I go?'

'Go?' she said.

'I lost the battle. I'm going straight into the army.'

Catherine's eyes filled with sudden scalding tears.

'But you wanted to go to Oxford!'

Harry shrugged.

'Harry!'

'You cannot argue with a man by letter from South Africa.'

'But Aunt Rachel wants you to go to Oxford!'

'Not enough to keep on fighting for me.'

Catherine said fiercely, 'But it's absurd! It would only postpone entering the army by three years.'

'In my father's view it would postpone promotion disastrously and what I would learn at Oxford would unfit me wholly for military life.'

'That says nothing at all for military life, then,' Catherine declared. 'Are you sure you want to be a soldier at all?'

'Oh yes,' Harry said. 'Quite sure of that.'

'Even if it means losing Oxford?'

'Even if it means that. Nothing would stop my reading.'

'But why are you so bent upon the army?'

He reddened.

'You know why.'

'Because of England and the Empire and freeing people from oppression?'

He nodded.

She said, 'Oh Harry, I am so sorry. About Oxford, I mean.'

'Yes. So am I. But I think we should now talk about your conservatory.'

'I should watch that girl,' Mary Taverner said to her sister-in-law. Charlotte followed her glance to Rosamund Creighton seated in the shade with Elizabeth and Alicia Martineau.

'My dear?'

'Ambitious, she is. And not slow to see' – Mary waved an arm at her surroundings – 'that all this is what money rather than breeding can buy.'

'Don't add to my worries,' Charlotte said. 'You be

thankful your babies are scarcely old enough to talk. Mine are more trouble to me now than you can conceive of.'

'You mean they will no longer do as you say?'

'They do it,' Charlotte said a little grimly, 'but it takes much longer.'

'There's trouble brewing between Robert and Tom. Of course, I will do what I can—'

'There is no obstinacy in the world,' Charlotte said vehemently, 'to compare with the pigheadedness of the Taverners.'

'Except,' Mary said, knowing she could get away with it, but not really caring even if she could not, 'for your own.'

Edward Martineau's offices were on the south side of the Circus in Bath, which gave the partners gloomy grandeur at the front of the building, and the clerks a sunny warren of converted servants' rooms at the back. Edward's own room was on the first floor, with long windows behind a balcony and an air of old fashioned austerity that also clung about the occupant. The paintings were a few eighteenth-century views of Bath, the furniture of the same age – apart from a large golden mahogany desk – and pushed back against the walls, leaving great unwelcoming spaces of carpet for Tom to cross, without a friendly chair back or table top for support on the journey.

'I'm glad to see you,' Edward said, putting a severe wooden armchair three inches forward for Tom. 'I began to think you were not going to come.'

Tom muttered inaudibly.

'You see,' Edward said, 'I spoke to you in November and it is now September. Ten months.'

'I – I had to have time to consider things. Think things through.'

Edward regarded him for a moment and then said in a kinder tone,

'I hope your mother was as much pleased with your sister's wedding as she had every right to be.'

Tom said quickly, 'It seemed to be a great success.'

He had personally found it very peculiar. Only a night or two before it took place, it had suddenly struck him, in the middle of a conversation with Freddie, that this future brother-in-law of his, at twice his own age, was never going to alter materially from what he was now. And that Elizabeth was going to have to love, trust, confide and find delight in this dull emptily smiling fellow for at least the next twenty-five or thirty years until his death released her into widowhood. The prospect was appalling; the marriage must be prevented. Tom tried to speak to Elizabeth in the first impulsive flush of his discovery but found his attempts greeted with an imperviousness, a calm confidence and seeming knowledge and ready acceptance of everything he was trying to say, that caused his words to die on his lips. She *wanted* Freddie, appeared to love him with excitement as well as warmth. Tom went to see Catherine.

'I know,' she said to him. 'I have thought that from the moment she began to encourage him. But you might as well try to push Stonehenge over with one hand.'

'I'll go to Mother.'

'What for? Do you think that, just now, she would be in the least inclined to listen to you?'

'But, Catherine, what happens if Elizabeth regrets it bitterly, later?'

'She will have a house and a social life and a status to

59

sustain her and we shall have to console her for private losses as best we may.'

As a result of all this, the wedding day had felt most disquieting, rather like a drawing room charade that the actors were suddenly insisting upon making into real life. Everybody came from miles around, and a huge smart contingent from London included Lilian Trail with a cold-eyed, cigar-smoking husband in tow. The entire ground floor of the house was opened up for the wedding breakfast as it had been designed to do a hundred years before, and the crowd swirled and swished in an animated river through it, and out through the garden doors of the hall to admire the pattern of little white pegs stuck into the grass beyond the drawing room to indicate where the conservatory would soon rise in towered glass splendour. Two of the Prince of Wales's equerries were present, three members of the House of Lords, a substantial number of baronets, two archdeacons and a bishop. The air was thick with the studied drawl of those affecting the highest *ton* and the scent of late Gloire de Dijon roses massed on tables and in corners. Both bride and groom had looked extremely beautiful and wore smiles of the greatest satisfaction. Halfway through the festivity, it struck Tom that he was actually giving precisely the kind of party he had refused to give for his own birthday, and that oddly enough, his pride of owner-ship was augmented rather than diminished by knowing that a hundred and eighty people were guests beneath his roof. This discovery made him feel extremely benign which was in itself a difficult emotion to reconcile with the distaste he now felt about the marriage.

Edward Martineau now said, watching Tom's face,

'It was what Elizabeth wanted, you know. Freddie Forrester will not go down in history books, but he is kind enough, and a gentleman.'

Tom nodded.

'Sit down,' Edward said gently.

Tom sat.

'I haven't any inclination to shout at you or carpet you, you know. I am just afraid that some things are not quite clear to you, and that you are bent upon making decisions that are based upon some misconceptions, even some ignorance. I know how seriously you take your responsibility to Buscombe and I know, I think, where your inclinations lie, and my purpose – if you like, my aim – is to try and harness the one to the other.'

Tom gripped the arms of his chair.

'My uncle Robert—'

'I know,' Edward said swiftly, 'I know. You are men of a wholly different temper. He spent fifteen years building up with astounding enterprise and industry a business which began with an old rope walk on the Bristol docks and now covers acres of the most modern warehousing system. Naturally, for him, that is the first and best way for money to be made. But he is shrewd and he is well informed. You must not forget that his parliamentary experience makes him far more than just a west country businessman. His predictions for the future are important to listen to.'

'He is wholly anti-agriculture.'

'I think not. He simply sees the writing on the wall. He is not an advocate of free trade, I know, and feels we should impose tariffs on imported goods to protect our own markets. This is a measure of the dispassion of his view since free trade after all keeps his warehouses full and expanding. One might expect that the businessman in him shouted down the politician, but this is not so. He would not warn you about dangers from American farming as a mere whim. Can you not see how illogical that would be?'

Tom got up and began to walk quickly about the room.

'I am not disagreeing about America. I'm sure the Middle West will soon be producing enough grain to feed all the world if they are as sophisticated in their methods as my uncle claims, and we will have cheaper bread than in all our history. But I am not going to farm in the old traditional way that competes with huge American grain farmers. I am going to run such a mixed farm that whatever is not doing well at any one time is balanced by something else that is. And I can't do that without a lot more land because I need space for the variety. I can't buy land out of income, I must spend capital, and such capital as I have outside that represented by the estate itself is in Taverner's Warehouses. I don't need to sell out completely, though I should like to, but I do need at least another five hundred acres, and I need to build more cottages, not to mention machinery.'

When he stopped, Edward went to a side table and poured two glasses of Madeira. Handing one to Tom, he said thoughtfully, 'Have you spoken to Howitt?'

'Howitt is stuck fast in the farming of the forties.'

'It is your uncle's opinion that he is a most able farm manager.'

'He is obsessed with sheep and corn.'

'Perhaps your land is best suited to sheep and corn.'

'He will not think of a dairy herd or pigs or orchards or vegetable crops.'

'Perhaps he has good reasons.'

'His reasons are his own ignorance of anything but sheep and corn.'

Edward let a little pause fall and then said,

'And what of your own ignorance, Tom, even of sheep and corn?'

Tom put his glass down upon Edward's desk with such emphasis that Madeira splashed out onto the golden wood. He rubbed at it impatiently with a forefinger until Edward leaned across and blotted the pool with a handkerchief.

'I can learn!' Tom said in almost a shout. 'I *am* learning. I've lived at Buscombe all my life, I'm not exactly a stranger to the land, I'm prepared to work at farming with every ounce as much energy as Uncle Robert put into his warehouses! And I'll wager you anything you like that when he bought that rope yard he wasn't made to run the gauntlet as I am being—'

'There was perhaps some seventy pounds involved, rather than one of the best small estates in the west country.'

Tom took a deep and careful breath and said,

'If I do not do what I want to do, what would you and Uncle Robert have me do?'

'He would like you to join him in the company.'

'Warehousing?' Tom said in horror. 'I would rather die.'

'Only for a few years. Only to help it through the next stage of expansion while your uncle is committed in London, and to put yourself on your own financial feet the while. If it becomes a limited liability company as he proposes, it will grow very fast indeed with the injection of new capital. It is a very handsome offer.'

63

'I could not countenance it.'

'It is a better, safer route to help Buscombe than the one you propose.'

'It is an intolerable route.'

'I think,' Edward said, rising from his chair, 'that we cannot take this conversation further today.'

Tom strode to the door, laid his hand upon the knob, withdrew it, paused, turned and came back to the desk.

'I do not mean to be intemperate, Mr Martineau. I do not want to quarrel with either you or my uncle. But you can perhaps sympathize with my feeling that my strong desire to make my way my own way is being thwarted almost entirely because it is not a way tried and tested by a Taverner before. My uncle knew nothing about warehousing twenty years ago just as I, by my own frank admission, know little of farming. But as he learned, may I not learn? Can you convince me that your reluctance is really more than prejudice against my inexperience? Can you not rather help me to do what it is in my heart and my every fibre to do?'

Slowly, Edward came round from behind his desk and put an arm about Tom's shoulders.

'Oh, my dear boy, perhaps. My responsibilities are as great as yours and I have been carrying them a lot longer, so maybe my back is wearier than yours. Will you sit down once more?'

In the stableyard at Buscombe, to Tom's inner discomfiture still, Bradstock was waiting.

'May I have a word with you, sir?'

A groom led horse and gig clattering over the cobbles, leaving them in the blue early autumn dusk lit by the dim yellow blooms of the stableyard lamps. Bradstock held his hat in his hands and turned his square and honest face towards Tom's.

'You should know, sir, that Meg's gone as housemaid to a house down Bridgwater way.'

'Why, Bradstock—'

'I thought to tell you, sir, to put your mind at rest.'

Tom swallowed.

'Bradstock—'

'I'll be saying good night then, sir.'

Tom went straight to his sister Catherine. She was seated at her worktable with the design for the conservatory pinned to a drawing board before her and was moving around it, like draughtsmen, little painted cutouts of ferns and shrubs and climbing plants.

'Look,' she said, 'plumbago in a great mass because of the heavenly blue, but it has no scent, so if I intermingle it with jasmine which does have a scent – but that will not work because they do not flower together—'

'Edward Martineau has promised to talk to Uncle Robert.'

Catherine wore small gold rimmed spectacles for close work. She took these off now and laid them carefully across a Black Hamburg vine.

'My dear Tom—'

'I won him over! I explained to him that change and progress only happen because risks are taken, and that disasters often befall us because we cling to what is fatally outmoded. And the upshot was that he will speak to Uncle Robert and set about seeing to my realizing some capital from Taverner's Warehouses!'

Catherine rose and put her arms about her brother's neck.

'I know not the first thing about farming but I know you, and I have great faith in that at least. I am so very, very glad for you.'

She took his hand and led him over to the low chairs before the fire.

'What will happen next?'

'I shall explain the scheme to Howitt and if he cannot adapt to me, he must find another place. I shall write to Mr du Cros and make my offer. I shall send for books and pamphlets. I shall plan a journey of the farms of the Midlands and East Anglia. Catherine, I shall *begin*!'

She looked at him.

'Will there be great changes here?'

'Only that I will be so busy that you will hardly see me.'

Her mouth twitched a little.

'That will disappoint others besides myself.'

'Oh?'

'Miss Creighton. Miss Rosamund Creighton called this afternoon, gorgeous in dark green with cream ruffles, and stayed a full hour, talking chiefly of you. You are blushing, Tom.'

'She is clever,' he said a little defiantly. 'She is interesting to talk to.'

'She is not quite reliable.'

'She is the only woman besides you who is sufficiently interested to listen to my plans.'

'I think I would not be too ready to believe her interest lay solely in your plans. I know she is Catholic which makes for difficulties but she is also very determined indeed. Tom, you are blushing quite tremendously. You must be very resolute, you know, as, since the Meggy business, Mother is fully determined

66

you should marry young, like Sir Thomas More, to keep you out of further trouble.'

Tom said, grasping at the relief line she had unwittingly thrown him, 'I met Bradstock just now. Meggy has gone into service, so she is not – there is no—' and then a silence fell between them until Catherine put out a hand to take his and said,

'Tom, may I tell you something? I am so truly happy that you know what you are going to do, and my understanding of your happiness is all the greater because I at last know, as well, what I am going to do.'

Tom took her hand in his and looked towards the paper conservatory which bloomed and fruited on her writing table.

'My dear Catherine, I am so glad and I only wish I had thought of it before, years ago—'

'Oh no. Not that. Not even that, lovely though it will be. No, this is something quite different, though you will recognize it the moment I tell you as the inevitable and natural and right thing that it is—' She paused, slid her hand out from between his, and said smilingly, 'In two years, when he comes of age, I am going to become Harry's wife.'

Tom said, 'But you cannot. He is your cousin. He is younger than you—' and then, furiously, '*Catherine*.'

She rose and went to lean against the chimneypiece.

'Neither of those things are of the least consequence. He is right for me, as I am for him. There is no hurry, we have all the time in the world and nothing to prove. We can wait.'

'But he is about to go into the army!'

'Don't shout, Tom. I know he is. I said there was no hurry. He will probably be posted abroad, and in two years I shall join him.'

'Officers may not marry until they are twenty-five. And then only with permission!'

'Then we will wait until he is twenty-five. I can go to India or wherever to be near him sooner. I will travel with a sketch book, I will collect plants, I will get out of this stifling cocoon and live the kind of life I am meant to live. I have the money to be independent, after all.'

'Mother and I control that until you are thirty or marry. You know that. Oh my God, Catherine, there will be such a row—' He got up and put a pleading hand on her arm. 'Must you be so – so *revolutionary*?'

'I call it honest,' she said.

'Do you have to speak of it openly?'

'Of course I do!'

'There isn't a hope, of going to India or of marrying Harry. I can tell you that before you begin. I think you are just in one of your discontents, and you think this crackbrained scheme is the answer. Harry is too young to know his own mind, and he feels thwarted about Oxford. Travel about India picking flowers! Oh my dearest, my *silly* sister, please, please see sense!'

'You would not talk so if I were a man!'

'This idiotic proposition would not have come from a man.'

'Please go away,' Catherine said. She bent her forehead down onto the hands that gripped the chimneypiece ledge and repeated in a low voice, 'Just go away. I hoped you would understand but you are as blinded by prejudice to my vision as Uncle Robert is to yours. So go away.'

As he closed the door behind him, Tom heard her catch her breath and say, with great passion, 'Oh Harry!' to the flames in the fire.

CHAPTER FOUR

February 1872

The curtains of Charlotte's bedroom – chosen to resemble as nearly as possible the reputation of the Queen's chintz curtains in her bedroom at Osborne House – were drawn against an afternoon of steady, slashing sleet. The south view, of which she was so fond, over terrace, lily pond, drive and tree-scattered slopes was today no more than a roaring steel grey blur, best excluded behind a consoling wall of pink and green flowers blooming on a pearly ground. Only one lamp was lit, which stood in the centre of the tartan-rug-covered table at the foot of her bed, throwing a soft yellow pool of light which did not quite reach her in her chair before the fire. A savage headache gripped her skull in an iron cap, but she regarded lying down as a craven way to fight it and would, if words had not writhed and leaped about the page, have been reading or working just to show the headache how little material difference it made to her life, and therefore how hollow its victory.

For the moment, however, she had to admit defeat and lay back rigid with resistance, her head as painful within as without. There did not seem to her, that grim afternoon, to be a single corner of her life she could turn to where sunlight fell warm on a breeze-blown meadow. The headache was indeed a physical manifestation of her disappointment, her anger and – almost worst of all – her impotence. Her life seemed to her like a beautiful landscape painting to which some delinquent force that wished her mindless evil had taken a knife and slashed the canvas across and across until only little snippets of calm sky, little patches and fragments of trees and lakes and parkland remained to remind her, so poignantly, of what once had been.

She could not face the possibility that her energetic – but, she earnestly believed, benevolent – rule was somehow coming to an end. It was like walking through a familiar wood and finding that every tree you touched dissolved into mist at your fingers' ends – indeed, the only tree in her wood which seemed to retain any solidity was her brother-in-law, Robert, of whom she was fond because she had known him nearly thirty years, but had always regarded as cold and intransigent. Although he was as opposed to almost all the proposed upheavals and sure disasters as she was, he somehow still did not manage to make himself seem her ally, but seemed rather to criticize some weakness in her for letting matters reach the pitch they now had. But what could she have done beyond what she had done? She had been the faithful trustee of Buscombe and a loving and upright mother to her children, instilling duty and honour. She had managed well for the Taverners. How came it now that she seemed to have failed?

Her hands plucked and fidgeted at the rug on her knees, strong capable hands heavy with old fashioned Regency family diamonds. Even Elizabeth was not satisfactory just now – straightforward, womanly

Elizabeth was writing often, far too often for a girl married but six months, to suggest long visits home in the spring.

'I can hardly refuse her,' she said to Catherine on one of the rare days she could bring herself to speak to her younger daughter, 'but it is quite wrong that she should come so soon, and even worse that she should wish to come alone.'

Catherine, thinner than ever, and knowing the impossibility of explaining Elizabeth's state of mind to her mother, made some anodyne reply. Her own letters from her sister lay with a few forbidden ones from Harry under books in the shelves in her room, letters almost impossible to answer.

'I am so puzzled,' Elizabeth wrote, 'and I am afraid I am, in some way that I am ignorant of, to blame. Here we are in Mount Street, in a house I was so happy to come to, and we see nobody. I mean it, Catherine, *nobody*. Freddie does not wish to. All the people who were, I do believe, such a delight to him, are now quite distasteful to him. I cannot understand it and he cannot explain it. He does not want to dine out, he does not wish people to dine here. He does not want to go to the theatre or to the opera, he only wishes to spend each evening after dinner by the fire with me and discuss our remove – our *permanent* remove – to the country with which he is now obsessed. I think he would discuss drawing room hangings and the perfect qualities for a parlourmaid all night were I agreeable. But I am *not* agreeable. I have never been so bored. If it were not for Lilian and her friends with whom I can spend the luncheon hour and the afternoons while Freddie goes to his club, I think I should go mad.'

'I thought of many troubles for her,' Catherine said

71

to Tom, 'but I did not think of that. Freddie is not just dull, he is irredeemably domesticated. That is why he was so afraid of marrying because he knew that this is what would happen. And yet because it was so strong and unacknowledged a part of him, he could not resist it. Poor Elizabeth! All those dreams of sitting down to dinner never less than twenty-four—'

To her mother, Elizabeth wrote of little ailments, headaches, lassitudes, loss of appetite. Charlotte wrote brisk replies.

'It is no more than the natural consequence of the change from country to city air, and from being able to please yourself to being bound to please another. It is also very common for young women to suppose themselves unwell before they bear their first child.'

When pleas for sympathy over health failed, Elizabeth wrote sentimentally of Buscombe.

'Oh how I miss the dear place! I had no idea of how strong my attachment was, how much it was a part of me.'

It was her duty, Charlotte reminded her, to think that way of Mount Street. Had not she, Charlotte, felt just such a pang at leaving her childhood home and adapting to Buscombe as a bride? But Elizabeth would not give up. If it were not her health or her childhood home, it was her family she was missing. London did not suit her, the season was not what she had supposed it would be; she would be down in March, she wrote over and over again, to see the first dear Somerset primroses, and she would bring Lilian who was not well either and needed country air.

Charlotte did not want either of them. It was quite wrong; their place was in London by their husbands' sides, the quality of those husbands being almost immaterial. Given half a chance, she would have sent Catherine to London instead, but she was afraid of what Catherine might do if she took her eye off her. There was no predicting that Catherine might not simply board a ship and follow Harry scandalously to India; that was why she had temporarily cut off Catherine's allowance, to prevent any possible madness. Catherine's response was silence and invisibility, hours and hours spent shut in her room, meals sent up on trays, a correct but unspeaking presence in the carriage to church on Sundays.

'What I cannot comprehend,' Catherine said furiously during that awful row they had all had in the tower room about her announced intention of marrying Harry, 'is that your refusal is for ever. We are not proposing to marry until he is of age. Will you not even agree that you will reconsider this when that day comes?'

They were all present, upright in the Gothic chairs, Robert and Mary, Rachel crying softly like steady drizzle, Charlotte, Tom, Catherine on her feet facing them, trembling with misery and anger. Harry was not there; he had tried to be but his uncle Robert, in obedience to barked telegraphs from South Africa, had acted swiftly. Harry, as a second lieutenant of the Queen's Own Dragoon Guards, was dazedly on his way to Calcutta almost before he could blink.

'A lancer, you see,' he wrote to Catherine. 'I should so much have preferred a local infantry regiment, but Father would not hear of the South Gloucestershires. At least these 9th Lancers of mine were the ones who gave such a good breakfast to the women and children they released from the siege of Lucknow. Oh Catherine, Catherine!'

Tom had thought Catherine mad; her older relations thought her wicked. Harry was her cousin, had no money and was four years her junior. It would be folly for her and lunacy for him. He did not know his own mind, she had played irresponsibly upon the susceptibilities of a romantic boy, in any case by the time he was twenty-one he would have tired of her. Stubborn and cornered, Catherine lashed back.

'You do not know him, you do not know me and you misjudge us both. You only wish us to behave in a way which suits your own purposes, not our inclinations. We have ambitions for each other, can you not see that? Can you not see what kind of a wife I might be to him in India, what happiness and interest *I* might find in such a life, how happy I might make him because I am *not* designed by temperament for drawing rooms and house parties? He has such honourable purposes and he can fulfil them so much better with support, my support. If you deny us, can you begin to conceive of what emptiness and futility you are condemning us to?'

Then she fled, locking herself in her room in a storm of angry weeping.

'She'd make a grand wife to an Indian Army officer,' her aunt Mary said, 'she's right in that. But it should not be her cousin Harry.'

Through a handkerchief Rachel Taverner attempted to say that dearest John most unfairly seemed to assume that it was on account of some fond maternal laxity on her part that Harry was in such trouble. Robert had patted her shaking shoulder absently and remarked that the whole thing would soon blow over – it was a common sort of young people's nonsense.

'Not to be expected of Catherine,' Charlotte said, 'not Catherine.'

She had stayed in the tower room when they had all gone and paced round and round it until Tom came to retrieve her in the dusk and said,

'Uncle Robert is right for once. It will blow over. You will see.'

For five months it had blown nowhere. Forbidden to write to Harry, forced to ask for every penny even for the most mundane article, Catherine was as rebelliously unreconciled to her fate as at the beginning. Neither she nor Charlotte, even though they might speak of objective matters, would take one step towards each other on the one essential subject. Pride and anger forbade Charlotte to acknowledge that she knew letters still passed to and fro; defiance forbade Catherine to trouble to conceal them with any care.

'If I cannot marry Harry, I shall marry nobody,' she announced to Tom.

Tom shrugged.

'Then an old maid you will surely be.'

Charlotte could not bear to think of it, and would not accept it. Catherine must bend, crack, even fall ill, given enough time. It was a war of nerves, Charlotte against Catherine, a series of campaigns fought in silence, ruining meals, making social life at best awkward and at worst impossible. When the truce came, neither side needed to budge an inch; they were united in an instant and completely, in their horror at what Tom was proposing.

He had straddled himself in front of the drawing room fire, hooked his coat tails over his arm and announced blandly,

'I've asked old Arthur Creighton for Rosamund.'

He did not add that only the day before he had asked Rosamund for herself. He had called on the pretext of returning a book – there were months of such pretexts behind him now – and found her as usual alone, scribbling fiercely in a book she shut up the moment he came in, holding it provocatively behind her back and staring up at him with her challenging dark eyes. He made as if to snatch it – it was surely her journal – failed, and found that she was instead pressed against him, her face flung up to his. So he kissed her. When he lifted his head she said, 'Again,' so he kissed her once more and this time she was fierce and greedy and pushed her tongue deep into his mouth, dropping the book and winding her arms tightly about his neck. He was wild with excitement. When she pulled free at last, and whisked behind a chair to laugh at him, he said, panting and unsteady,

'Will you marry me?'

'I am a Catholic.'

'Your father isn't a Catholic!'

'You are not marrying my father.'

He fell on his knees.

'Rosamund, I beg you, please—'

She came to stand over him, her hands on her hips, eyes glinting. He flung his arms about her waist, butting his head into the rustling depths of her skirts and petticoats.

'Why do you want to marry me?'

'Because I love you. Because I can talk to you. Because I am lonely.'

'You have your mother and your sister. They will not want you to marry me.'

'It is my wanting that matters. I want you.' He looked up. 'Do you love me?'

She swayed a little in his arms.

'I think so—'

'Should you not like to be Lady Taverner?'

'Oh yes,' she regarded him keenly, 'but you are so young.'

'I am older than you—'

'Only in years. Stand up.'

She reached up and took his face in her hands and guided his mouth down to hers again with its hungry flickering tongue. He moaned a little, seizing her, until she pushed his head away and said,

'Well? When will you ask my father?'

Arthur Creighton was all complaisance. His daughter could hardly do better. He was himself a Protestant, married to a Catholic, the daughter of a convert, a schoolmaster who was, like Arthur, pleased to see his child marry well materially, if incompatibly spiritually. Arthur seized Tom's hand cordially. He and his wife had never fallen out over Church matters – he was sure Rosamund and Tom would not either.

'There is my mother—' Tom said.

Arthur had thought of that. Lady Taverner was indebted to him for a good deal of advice she had no scruple in extracting from him under the umbrella of friendship. He had given her advice she preferred to that of Edward Martineau, and he had given it free. Some little speculative investments in northern industries, small shareholdings in foundries and machine-tool factories, had paid handsomely – on his advice. If she was difficult, he might gently remind her of past favours indicating that he would be disinclined to suggest anything further. She loved to make money; it fuelled her obstinate independence and her love of power.

'Perhaps when you have first spoken to your mother, I should do so?'

'If you would,' Tom said gratefully.

'He is calling tomorrow,' he said now nonchalantly. 'He and Mrs Creighton are very pleased.'

Without a word, Catherine crossed the room to sit by her mother on the sofa.

'I forbid you,' Charlotte said.

Tom said, easily, 'You cannot.'

'I must! She is in every way unsuitable. She is a Catholic!'

'She is not unsuitable. I want her for my wife. She is clever, she will support me. She loves this house. Her being a Catholic is of no consequence at all.'

Charlotte rose, shaking.

'You must listen to me!'

Tom moved towards the door.

'I will listen when I wish to hear what you have to say. In the meantime you will not, cannot, change my mind. Perhaps you would both now prepare yourselves for giving Rosamund a deserving welcome.'

Charlotte could not eat that night nor sleep, even though Catherine sat up with her and sponged her forehead with eau de cologne and listened to all the frustrated, furious things she had to say, over and over. The next morning Arthur Creighton came, seeming suddenly egregious and disagreeable, and she was too fatigued and distraught to feel herself in any way in charge of the interview, only able to concentrate on the necessity of getting rid of him. When he left, smiling and attempting some disgusting familiarity of farewell, a headache dropped upon her like a violent blow and drove her to her room. She had remained there ever since, having commanded Brixton to draw the curtains and light the lamp, and wrestled with the pain in her head and her despair.

Beneath her, in the library, just to add to her

wretchedness, she imagined she could now hear Arnold du Cros discussing the sale of his land to Tom. When he had gone, the room would smell of whatever disgusting oil he used on his hair, patchouli or musk, and she would be unable to resist – as she always, inevitably, was unable to resist – asking Tom every detail of what had passed, then objecting to it, and finally bewailing his folly in buying more land at all at such a time. She had told Tom quite bluntly that he should gratefully accept his uncle's offer and work in Bristol for three years. Tom had seen straight through this, and said so.

'First, you want the running of Buscombe back in your own hands and you prefer your own way of doing things to mine. Secondly, you want me out of Rosamund's way in the hopes that I shall cease to want to marry her. In both cases, I am ahead of you. Buscombe is my life and Rosamund shortly will be also.'

It was as disagreeable to listen to as many of the things Catherine had said when baulked of marrying Harry. Quite incapable of self-analysis herself, Charlotte disliked intensely having the job done for her, and felt herself most injured, all the more so because the consolation she might have gained from confiding in Elizabeth was also – by Elizabeth's fault this time – denied to her. She was, she felt, much injured by being without a husband's proper support, particularly as his brothers appeared to make no allowances for the solitary struggles of her widowhood. One brother-in-law managed to make her feel the whole unhappy situation was on account of her own failure to manage her children properly, the other wrote irrelevant and out-of-date letters from South Africa saying the girls needed a firm governess and Tom needed a spell of soldiering. Her sisters-in-law, though secretly she felt much interested in all goings on at Buscombe, an interest she could not believe wholly altruistic, were too much absorbed in their own lives to have much time to spare for hers. Round and round her tired and angry mind went, like a mouse on a wheel, until Brixton, looking in with a tray of Earl Grey tea and a cold compress, damp-ened with Hungary water, found that she had fallen into a profound and scowling slumber punctuated by regular, indignant snores.

Charlie Taverner was told by his mamma, with the excess of vivacity she used for imparting special excite-ments, that he was to be an attendant at the wedding of his cousin Thomas. He was not much interested in the information, or rather was much more interested in the arch he was carefully building out of blocks made of different polished woods. It was imperative that he finish the arch before his sister Victoria was released from her afternoon rest in her crib and allowed to crawl, as she always incomprehensibly was, slap through the middle of whatever he had made. He was supposed to rest too, but had discovered recently that if he said he could not breathe when he was told to lie down and didn't want to, he was allowed to get up and build the bridges and towers and tunnels that were his heart's delight, quietly on the nursery floor.

This new and interesting turn of events had come about as the result of a visit by Doctor du Cros. Doctor du Cros had driven down from London in an admirable gig, and had been very likeable for five minutes admiring a railway station Charlie had made, and then tremen-dously boring for at least an hour listening to Charlie's chest and peering into his eyes and ears. He then talked for an equally long time to Mamma and to Nurse, in which he said much that was incomprehensible but also, emphatically and most valuably for Charlie, that when a paroxysm threatened or arrived, Charlie was the best judge of his position while it lasted. If he wanted to sit for hours by an open window, even on a winter night, he must be allowed to, and he must never be kept lying down against his will. He further won Charlie's approval by declaring that the hated practice of Nurse's holding Charlie's hands in basins of very hot water while he struggled for breath, was useless, and left instead instructions that nitre paper should be burned in the room, and tincture of lobelia – in a most desirable tiny sapphire blue bottle – should be held under his nose. Neither smelt very nice, but neither hurt. Doctor du Cros had then bent over Victoria, who ignored him with the self-possession she had perfected in fifteen months of life, had said how much of an age she was with his niece Rose whom he was about to visit at Marsham Court, and had departed in a whirlwind of Mamma's most voluble Irishness. Since the doctor's visit Charlie had eluded his afternoon rest, built bridges at three in the morning and found that a display of distress or temper brought invariable adult capitulation. Neither, however, had the smallest effect on his sister Victoria, so he gave up trying them on her.

'Blue velvet breeches,' his mother said persuasively, 'and a jacket with brass buttons, a blue velvet jacket. And only you, not Victoria.'

'She can't walk,' Charlie pointed out.

'You're to be the special one, all the same.'

'I don't think my train will fit through here. I wish I had a small train – as well as my big train.'

Mary Taverner took a grip on her patience. She disliked her hours in the nursery, hours she might have spent doing more energetic things, and it was only Doctor du Cros's insistence that all emotional disturbance must be avoided, even the danger of Charlie's feeling that his illness was in some way distasteful to his parents, that drove her dutifully upstairs twice a day. She sat down encouragingly on the floor in an inflated balloon of green skirts.

'You are to have a new Aunt Rosamund. She will wear a beautiful cream dress like a princess with a thing like a little crown in her hair, of diamonds and pearls, that I wore when I married Papa, and Great-aunt Charlotte wore at her wedding. After the wedding there will be a party and there will be ices and you may stay for a while because you are the special attendant who is going to carry Aunt Rosamund's lovely flowers.'

'If I had a little train,' Charlie said, 'I could push it through here. And then I could make a big arch for my big train, and I could push them both through and they could crash. I don't want to carry flowers.'

'I see,' Mary said. 'You don't want to be the special page. You don't want lovely blue velvet clothes. You don't want to come to the party with ices where there are only grown-ups and you are the only lucky, privileged child. Would you rather Victoria was that lucky, special child instead?'

Charlie sighed tiredly, added the final arch-shaped mahogany block to his building and said again, '*She* can't walk.'

The night before the wedding Catherine could not sleep, as she had known she would not be able to. It was equally impossible to fix her attention on any alternative to sleep, so she roamed restlessly from window to window, peering out at the pale April night, clutching

82

the last letter from Harry in her hand, with an apprehension sharp as toothache for Tom in her feelings.

'Don't give in,' Harry implored her from Cape Town on his way east. 'If you can simply stay silent on the matter, but show no acquiescence, we will win through. I have had dreadful sessions with my father here, who is as anxious to move me on to India as if I had bubonic plague, but don't worry, I'm as solid as granite I find. I don't think I'm cut out to be a cavalry officer. There are too many silly asses among them—'

The great misery that lay waiting always at the edges of Catherine's mind began to lap in towards the centre. 'Don't give in,' Harry wrote, free Harry on his troopship going east, purposeful Harry with a decided life ahead of him. He missed her, he wrote, but his tone was often too buoyant for her comfort, his sympathetic appetite for new people and places too keen, his relish of things too manifest. What could she do about herself just at the moment, penned in and penniless? She felt herself to be two people inside one skin, the first incisive, ambitious, adventurous, the person who pinned up stirring admonitions from achieving women around the walls and chafed against her confinement; the second a frailer creature, a person given too easily to self-doubt and to despair, a person who needed to be led by the hand across the boggy parts of life. Harry could do that, young as he was, Harry had offered her the chance, in India with him, of becoming in reality the strong person she so longed to be. Harry could help her in her frailty but he had gone and left her. Now he had gone, she felt prey to all the old black fears – she could not manage to be happy and fulfilled on her own.

From outside her door came a stealthy creaking. She opened it an inch and saw Tom, lamp in hand, descending the staircase towards the pillared hall. She was about to call out but stopped herself, instead simply slipping out after him. At the foot of the stairs he put the lamp on the floor and began a strange and stately progress around the hall, running his hands over architraves and door panels, touching pictures and chests and chairs, even putting his arms around the pillars and laying his cheek against their painted marbled smoothness. In the dim ochre glow of the lamp, his face looked very young and craggy with exhaustion, his shoulders sagged a little, he moved heavily. He took the lamp up and went into the library, then the drawing room, releasing from each room a threateningly sweet blast of the scent of the forced lilies Rosamund had insisted upon, then the dining room and sitting room, repeating his poignant and loving ritual of touching and caressing the objects in each one. Crouched on the staircase in the near dark Catherine watched him in pity, since the thought came to her, unwelcome and unbidden, that Tom was instinctively making some kind of farewell.

For Rosamund, the wedding day was all triumph. She felt queenly, for the very simple reason that she was. Everyone had done what she wanted, without too much trouble – and a little trouble was titillating anyway – she was marrying a man who was, most excitingly, a little afraid of her, and was to make him, his house, and their life, both impressive and glittering. She had outdone her sister Florence whose little Duce, however ancient of lineage, was just faintly comic opera and more than faintly short of cash, and whose castle, at first all romance and the source of constant emotional transports, had proved too hot or too cold, damp, dirty, hideously uncomfortable and staffed by deeply suspicious servants. Rosamund had sent a glowing description of Buscombe to Tuscany, and a watercolour painted by her new sister, Catherine. Florence replied staunchly that she loved to think of her little Rosamund in her very own castello. Rosamund sent a sketch of her wedding dress, cream because Florence's had been cream, frilled and flounced, studded with bows and pearl buttons, the back caught up in bouffant swags by cascading brown velvet and cream satin ribbons. She was to wear Taverner pearls in her ears, Taverner diamonds and pearls in her hair to anchor a waterfall of cream Brussels lace, a Taverner necklace Tom had had redesigned for her at her own request, and a pair of matching bracelets. Florence, who had not been allowed to wear the Duce's family jewels because his mother was so angry at his marrying an Englishwoman, replied that she thought the effect very pretty, if a little showy perhaps?

Rosamund wanted to be showy. Her Catholicism meant that she could not be married, as she would have liked, in Bath Abbey, with a crowd gawping in the square outside, bells ringing across the whole city, and a resplendent bishop to marry them. Instead the new church at North Cheyney must suffice.

'I shall not go,' Charlotte declared.

'You must, Mamma. Not for Rosamund perhaps, but for Tom.'

'Tom does not care. All he cares for is defying me.'

'That is foolish talk,' Catherine said patiently. 'We all care. We may not want this marriage but we must give it all the help we can.'

'She is a Jezebel,' said Charlotte.

Rosamund wore a gleaming smile throughout the day; her eyes were alive and at their most darting. She flickered them often towards Tom, handsome in a grey frock coat and a waistcoat of grey satin, his face set with a slight aggression, a little flushed, head very high, shoulders very squared. The church was full, Buscombe after it even fuller, so much champagne, such heat, such overpowering vases of forced lilies, such noise and laughter. On the staircase Tom found Charlie, pale in his blue velvet, peering through the bannisters.

'I have something for you, old fellow.'

'A present?'

'Yes. Come with me.'

Charlie put a faintly damp and sticky hand into Tom's. They climbed the staircase, and turned away from the racket along the corridor that led to Tom's dressing room, above the dining room, facing north towards the park.

'Do you like this house, old fellow?'

Charlie shook his head.

'No.'

'Why not?'

'I like my house.'

'I hope you like this—'

Tom reached on top of his compactum and brought down a parcel wrapped in blue paper.

'It is a thank-you from Aunt Rosamund and me. For holding her flowers. I don't think you much wanted to.'

Charlie coloured.

'I – I didn't mind—'

'Open the parcel.'

Charlie sat on the floor, slid the paper off with great precision, and opened the box. It contained coloured stone bricks like exact architectural samples, pillars and architraves and pediments and chimney pots.

'And I think you need one of these.'

Tom bent down and put beside Charlie on the carpet a small tin train.

'Do you like them?'

Charlie nodded furiously. 'They are the best in the world. In the whole world.'

'Now you can build exactly the house you like. I have to go back to my guests. You stay here and play. I'll tell Nurse where to find you.'

Charlie looked up.

'I nearly prayed for a little train.'

'Your Mamma told me you wanted one.'

'I don't want anything any more.'

'I'm glad about that.'

'I quite liked,' Charlie said with a huge effort, 'holding those flowers.' Then he turned away and began to pick bricks out of the box, lining them up carefully across the carpet.

CHAPTER FIVE

October 1875

Rosamund's eventual pregnancy, Elizabeth declared confidingly to her women friends, was the best thing that had happened to Buscombe since Tom came of age. With luck, the baby would be a boy, and his arrival would unite all the warring factions and stop these terrible quarrels which were such a regrettable part of life at Buscombe now. The women friends were, on the whole, rather sorry to hear this because an invitation to Buscombe in the last three years since Elizabeth had virtually resumed residence there, had meant a week or two of considerable fascination. Family quarrels were excellent spectator sport for the uninvolved, after all, and there was always the delicious indecision of whose side to take.

Old Lady Taverner, admittedly difficult and head-strong as she was, deserved considerable sympathy. Rosamund had returned from her wedding tour to a very expensive progress through France and Italy, where she insisted upon purchasing an enormous number of busts and statues, whose authenticity Tom greatly doubted, and which were set about the house. The cool quality of restraint, almost of Georgian order, that Charlotte had brought into the very air her children breathed, vanished beneath the onslaught of Rosamund's desire to be fashionable. The blond and black diamonds of the hall floor were covered with a Turkey carpet, and the hall itself became Rosamund's notion of baronial, furnished with clumps of heavy red velvet chairs grouped around gate-legged tables thick with books and magazines, and each one bearing a parlour palm in a brass pot embossed with quasi Indian deities. The eighteenth-century silver sconces were ripped out, and the lighting came from a series of new and massive brass chandeliers. Around the pillars, statuary fought to see through a jungle of rubber plants and in the centre of the room a white marble swan balanced on the edge of a white marble font and gazed gloomily down into the maidenhair fern with which it was tremblingly filled.

The drawing room got away no less lightly. Such eighteenth-century chairs as were allowed to stay were glaringly re-gilded and re-upholstered in sapphire blue velvet. A fleet of tables moved in, a regiment of whatnots and jardinières stood about on new and brilliant Indian rugs, and the grey stippled walls were exchanged for startling new ones of dark yellow damask. The old and faded rose moiré curtains gave way to heavily draped swags of blue and gold, and across tables and pianos and sofas crept a tide of fringes, embroidered cloths and shawls, framed photographs and china objects, glass paperweights, fans, tropical shells and small bronze statues of Mercury and Ceres poised on pink marble plinths.

Rosamund was relentless, unheeding, impervious even to Charlotte's angry declarations that she was turning the house into a middle-class villa.

89

'It is the fashion,' Rosamund said.

'It is unutterably middle class,' Charlotte retorted.

Rosamund did not care. The old rosewood dining table was banished to the attics and replaced with a massively thighed monster in red mahogany. The dining room should be masculine, Rosamund declared, as masculine as the drawing room was feminine. The sitting room next—

'No,' said Catherine.

'It is absurdly dowdy. I have no boudoir. I cannot be comfortable in such a shabby room.'

'No,' said Catherine.

Elizabeth stood behind her. Rosamund left them to cool a little and turned away to fill the library with antlered heads, busts of men whose music she never listened to and whose books she never read, and vast oriental pots big enough to hold a child. The tower room, its Gothic tracery newly gilded and picked out in plum red, its original chairs exiled to the stable lofts and replaced with Jacobean imitations, all bobbled stretchers and fringed cut velvet seats held in place by huge domed brass nails, became a smoking room.

'I do not,' Tom said more gently than he felt, 'want a smoking room.'

Rosamund rolled her eyes.

'There isn't a good house in the land without a smoking room. At house parties, Saturday to Monday house parties, where do you propose the men shall go after dinner?'

'I do not propose to have house parties.'

'Oh?' she said and then gave the little whiplash laugh she had acquired with her new commanding status. 'Well I do.'

Briefly, Elizabeth became her ally, bored, frustrated,

useful Elizabeth with her list of London friends and her disappointing husband. Freddie, with the mulishness of the obtuse, had simply gone back to his old life, in a subdued form, and society, always adaptable as long as its fun is not threatened, was perfectly happy to accept him back, virtually a bachelor still. He had more money now, as well, which he spent not lavishly, but certainly steadily. Elizabeth, not witty nor stylish enough to be a plaything for the beau monde in her own right found that her strongest card was Buscombe. People – idle women particularly – liked an invitation to Buscombe, especially now that Rosamund, the new chatelaine, charged the air of the house with such electricity, and gave such excellent parties. She persuaded German pianists and Italian tenors to come down from London and gave her guests magnificent food at the new table. It was now adorned with vast candelabra held up by lavishly bosomed caryatids with imitation emerald eyes, around a silver epergne as big as a fountain, spilling ferns and fruit and sugared almonds.

'It is vulgar!' Charlotte insisted. 'Even the way you eat now is offensive. The joint should be placed before your husband and carved by him, not brought ready cut and handed to guests as in a common inn.'

'It is the new way,' Rosamund said serenely. 'It is called dining *à la Russe*.'

She ordered venison and poussins and ortolans, she had champagne always on ice, and when Catherine's conservatory could not supply what she had a whim for, she summoned gardenias and camellias, and out-of-season roses and lilies, from London. Elizabeth's new friends were her eager first audience.

'Dearest,' Tom said, leaning in their bedroom doorway and watching her brush her crackling black hair, 'I fear we simply cannot afford all this. I cannot afford the time to play host and the farm is declining.'

'Get a manager, then.'

'I dismissed the manager precisely to do his work myself. I do not want a manager, but I cannot manage the farm if the house is so full that I am committed to being a host all day, and, when I am not being a host, to pacifying my mother whose life here is wholly disrupted.'

'It is my life here now,' Rosamund said, brushing on relentlessly. 'It is my house. She has her rooms and in them she may live as she always has.'

'You make her a prisoner.'

'It is her own doing. She is queer and abrupt with our guests which makes having her in the drawing room awkward.'

'Rosamund,' Tom said warningly, 'this house has been my mother's home for thirty years and the life she lived in it was a peaceable, old fashioned country one. It is not just to expect her to know suddenly and by instinct how to deal with society people, urban society people. I insist you respect her right, at least in part, to live here as she always has, and as suits her.'

Rosamund said nothing but stopped brushing her hair.

'You are making us all look fools,' Tom said, a little sullenly, 'all this fashionableness, this extravagance. We are becoming a laughing stock, we are losing our dignity. And we are losing money—'

She spun round.

'And whose fault is that?'

'Yours!' he shouted, suddenly out of control. 'You spend and spend and spend! We do not have the kind of money to spend like this, hundreds on hothouse flowers and French food nobody eats more than a mouthful of! Thousands on new furniture while all the old pieces, the pieces that belong to this house and are part of this house, lie in the attics. I cannot support such spending, particularly if I can never get away from the demands of guests to spend time on the farm—'

'Then hire a manager,' she said quite calm and still at her new dressing table flounced like a crinoline in lavender silk. 'Do what, as a gentleman, you should do. Go in for politics.'

'There is no money in politics!'

'There is status in politics. There is power. You tell me there is money in farming. You go on and on and on telling me there is money in farming. You always have. Then hire a manager to manage the farm and make your money for you, while you go into politics. It is *you* who are the laughing stock, the hayseed baronet left over from some ridiculous Georgian comedy—'

He lunged at her then, as she had calculated he would, and the quarrel ended fiercely in bed. It had been that way since that tumultuous wedding journey, where Rosamund's violent and contrasting appetites, sometimes so passionately pious, sometimes so savagely physical, had left him feeling like the loser in a prize fight. Her personal fastidiousness, her insistence upon the best of everything – even though she might easily refuse it, having commanded it, when it came – her energy and greedy sexuality, her capriciousness and terrifyingly quick temper made dealing with her a matter of tiptoeing across eggshells. She fulfilled none of the notions of womankind he had been brought up with, not even that most obligingly basic one of providing him with an heir, despite night after night

93

of the battling coupling she relished so, rushing after-wards from her bed to fall gabbling and gasping at the Spanish prie-dieu – hideous to Tom in its un-English blatancy of ebony and ivory – which stood in pride of place, its constant and flickering candles watching with prurient eyes every act, every human moment. He could not imagine her pregnant, she was too like some glittering insect, too unreliable, too contradictory to do anything so substantial. But for all that, suddenly, she was.

Catherine wrote to tell Harry. It was not a love letter; she had not written a love letter for two years. It was a sisterly letter. Harry had forsaken his cavalrymen for the 28th Battalion of Foot, the South Gloucestershires, the regiment he had always longed to be part of, and wrote warmly of his life.

'It is a policeman's duty, to be sure, much of the time, but out here in Malta, it is more in fact, and we are the administrators of justice as well as the keepers of the peace. Sometimes I am tempted to leave soldiering for administration proper, but I could not, I think, bear to leave the men. I suppose they are in a way my family. When you come—'

He always wrote that: 'When you come—'. At first she assumed he meant it but now she assumed he did not, but that his habit of natural kindness made him still say it. Charlotte and Tom had reinstated her allowance well over a year ago, and she had never bought her passage to anywhere. Less and less did she suppose she ever would.

'We get on so well, we English and the Indians,' Harry wrote, 'because we both come from societies built upon a hierarchy of class. Speaking of hierarchy, I rejoice to know Buscombe is to have an heir, although

I cannot quite envisage the dangerous Miss Creighton (I cannot think of her by any other name) as a softly doting mamma.'

For Tom, the news fell like summer rain on a thirsty landscape. It was the first strongly natural, right event of the last three years, the first time he could feel – he who so yearned to feel – that he was succeeding in doing deservedly by Buscombe. He had inherited it from a Thomas Taverner and he would now be able to pass it on to another. There was no doubt but that the baby would be a son, a son who could take the house and the land forward into the new century. Briefly, the contemplation of the future took Tom's mind off the inescapable and growing anxieties of the present, anxieties all the more miserable to bear because they were of his own making.

He was not a man to cry over spilled milk, but neither was he resourceful about what to do with it, once spilled. It was most assuredly not his fault that five years of poor seasons had diminished his harvests, but it was nobody's fault but his own that he had determinedly expanded his farm at the very moment – a moment he had confidently acknowledged and then equally confidently dismissed – when the American prairies were becoming grain lands such as the world had never seen before. Defiantly he might insist – and rightly insist – that the English remained better farmers scientifically, but that made no difference to the sheer volume, cheap sheer volume, of American produce steaming remorselessly across the Atlantic to a nation whose belief in free trade was as unshakeable as its belief in God. Other nations in Europe, mindful of their peasantries whose presence gave their societies stability, protected their farmers, small and large, by the imposition of tariffs upon imported goods. To England, such a notion was literally unthinkable – after all was not her wealth and imperial power built upon free world commerce?

Already, two labourers had come to Tom and announced they were going up to Birmingham to find work. They made no apology for this. The farm was losing money, their wages had fallen – only sixpence, but it was a fall – and they did not care to stay and watch them fall any lower. Tom found himself almost spiritually anguished by their departure.

'It appals me,' he said to Catherine, snipping eternally away in her green jungle, 'to think of them in some filthy tenement in a city when they might be here, in clean air, in a decent cottage. It cannot be right to live in a town when you might live in the country, it cannot be right for an Englishman. We are a nation of countrymen, it is the countryside that has shaped us. That is our *rhythm*. Do you not see?'

'I am not,' Catherine pointed out, 'even arguing with you.'

'There will be others. Quite honestly, I cannot conceive of how to stop them. I cannot pay them more. Even the pigs are not paying their way because imported pork is coming in and, inevitably, it is cheaper.' He caught sight of his face in the glass between the lapageria leaves. 'I look forty, Catherine. I look forty-five and I am twenty-six.'

'Should you perhaps,' she said carefully, 'sink your pride and go and talk to Uncle Robert? Or even Mr Martineau?'

'Martineau couldn't help. In the end he was persuaded by me into the notion of expansion. And I cannot, Catherine, I *cannot* go to Uncle Robert—'

She said nothing. She thought of the places on the estate where fences were not mended any more, of the great granary almost empty, of the new dairy herd that seemed seldom to be anything but trouble.

'Perhaps Rosamund is right—'

'Rosamund?' Catherine said, abruptly and furiously. '*Rosamund?* Do you know that she has ordered a new piano this very day and has summoned Mr Linklater from Bath to see about the decoration of the top rooms for the nursery?'

Tom gestured unhappily.

'She thinks I should get in a manager and turn to politics.'

'And how is that going to pay for pianos and nursery wings?'

'A manager might make a better job of farming. If I can't farm – oh, Catherine – if I can't farm, perhaps I should try to do something in public life to defend agriculture. Before we lose it entirely. I do believe in that so passionately, you see. I do believe that as a nation our very selves have been shaped by our contact with the countryside and that we are in peril to try and make ourselves as urban as we seem to be doing.'

'Human values,' Catherine said musingly, 'spiritual things—'

'Yes. *Yes.* We can become as industrial as we wish, but no industry, not one, can give people what agriculture gives them. We will suffer if we lose touch with the land, our souls will shrink—'

Catherine stopped snipping and looked at him, admiringly.

'How eloquent you are!'

He said miserably, 'I care so. I care so and look what my caring has brought this place to—'

'That is not entirely your fault.'

'Oh yes,' he said calmly, 'yes it is. Every decision here, every decision in my life in the last four years, has been made by me. And all I can hope for now is that I have the strength to pull it all out of the mire it is stuck fast in.'

'You admit so much. Can't you just admit one more thing and acknowledge that you need help? Cannot you go to Uncle Robert?'

He shook his head.

'No. Not that. I must find some other plan.'

'What other plan? Surely not Rosamund's?'

He sighed.

'Even that,' he said.

In the week before the baby was born, while the sounds of carpenters putting the finishing touches to the nurseries pattered from the top windows, open to let in the new soft spring air, Robert Taverner could restrain himself no longer.

'I must see the boy,' he said to Mary, bursting in on her as she sat writing home to County Kildare in her flamboyant black hand. 'Will you listen to this? I've a letter from Martineau this morning saying he has heard two more men have gone to Bristol from Buscombe this week, and a third threatens to follow them. And that there is an advertisement in the *Gazette* for a farm manager for the place. I must go at once. I must know of whatever he plans to do, or the estate will be ruined.'

She twisted in her chair.

'Perhaps getting a manager is a good sign! Perhaps he will come to you after all.'

'Pigs might fly!' Robert said.

'And what is it you'll say to him?'

'He must take advice on any manager he hires. He

must work out a plan for the next five years – he must set himself goals, financial goals. He must think again, very hard, about his own earning capacity for the estate.'

Mary grimaced.

'I'll wish you luck, then.'

With indifferent grace, Tom led his uncle to the tower room, and seated him in the southwestern window which looked down, along a wide grass path, between newly planted rhododendrons, to the far-off glitter of the lake.

'A heavy shrub, those,' Robert said, 'not really suited to this house. Why have you planted them so close to the walls?'

'We have, I believe,' Tom said a little tensely, 'great models in Panshanger and Alderley and Waddesdon Manor.'

'Rothschilds!'

Tom inclined his head and waited.

'Well, my boy? Why must I come to you? Why have you not come to me?'

Tom said truthfully, 'Because I knew what you would say, and I did not wish to hear it.'

There was a fleeting but softened gleam in his uncle's eye.

'So we understand each other this far. What do you now propose?'

'Politics.'

'My dear boy!'

'I have to. Somebody has to point out to England how shortsighted she is on agricultural policy. There are no plans for the future. This can't be the only farming estate in real trouble. Look at all our cornlands, vanishing under grass! How will that be in ten or twenty years? What will have become of American farming, of world trade then?'

Robert sucked his teeth.

'You will be whistling in the wind. I don't say you aren't right, but nobody will listen. Government won't see it is important, I can promise you that. They have bigger fish to fry, social fish like education, administrative service, even Parliamentary reform itself. And we are going to have trouble with Southern Africa before the twentieth century comes in, mark my words. Any breath of war and it will blow Government wits clean out of the window. We haven't brandished a sword since Sebastopol.'

He got up and walked to the window, standing there hands in pockets, staring out at the glossy dark shrubs below him.

'I'm going to try and speak softly to you, my boy. Your aunt Mary advised it years ago, and she was probably right. She usually is. You can't afford to trust to your own instincts a second time. The estate can't take it. I'll admit I've ridden round it a bit recently and I don't need to tell you what I saw. You can't let it get worse, and you can't spend another penny, not one more of those gloomy things planted out there, until you have halted the slide. I came with a lecture all prepared, about cutting back, but I am going to dispense with that. Instead I'll tell you my plan. Forget politics. Take advice on hiring a farm manager, but cut the farm down by at least half, only growing what you can use or sell. Turn the rest of the estate over to game. Make this the best sporting estate in the southwest and rent it out to the moneybags of the Midlands. Du Cros would be your first taker and he doesn't have a friend who isn't a banker or an industrialist.'

'Hire it?' Tom said in horror. 'Hire Buscombe out to strangers for shooting?'

His uncle turned.

'What do you care about most, then? Buscombe or yourself?'

Tom's voice was angry.

'Buscombe, of course. But I cannot have paying strangers on my land! It turns Rosamund and myself into – into *innkeepers*!'

Robert said, 'I repeat my question.'

'No!' Tom shouted.

'You're a young fool. This place is not yours to squander, it is yours in trust. For that child your wife is carrying.'

'She would not countenance your scheme!'

Robert shrugged.

'That is your affair, my boy. I'd advise you not to let her caprice weigh too heavily with you and I would add that the offer I made to you four years ago still stands. Five years working for me in Bristol, five years of renting out the shooting here, and you will be back where you should be. Maybe better. And I'll tell you something. Don't daydream that you can take my seat in Parliament after me. It isn't for you. My seat in Parliament is for Charlie and none but he shall have it.'

Tom opened his mouth and with stupendous self-control, closed it again. Charlie, who had become something of a pet of Catherine's in the last year or two, had spent the day with his cousin at Buscombe only the week before. A sweet faced, frail ten-year-old with an unexpectedly steely resolve and quirkiness beneath, his passionate absorptions were as much with building and with things of the past as they had been when he was a tiny child. Catherine had bought for him the romantic account of the archaeologist Schliemann's discovery of what he claimed to be the treasure of Priam at Mycenae. Sitting, round eyed, beneath the starry showers of jasmine in the conservatory, Charlie had listened to the story of Schliemann, accompanied only by his young Greek wife, coming upon the ancient chest among the excavations and hastily dismissing all the workmen so that only he and she might share this stupendous moment. Out of the chest he drew bracelets and diadems, rings and goblets and daggers, and loaded them piece by piece into the girl's outspread scarlet shawl. Then they had crept back to the hut they were using during the digging season, and in secrecy and wild exaltation, Schliemann had hung the jewellery upon his trembling wife and told her she was wearing the gold of Helen. Charlie was enthralled. Tom had come in and seen him, rapt and still, listening, listening. Even at ten, it did not seem that a mind so fervently caught up in an archaeological legend of such consequence, could easily turn itself to the nuts and bolts of Parliamentary administration. But all he said was,

'He is only a child—'

'He'll grow. And I have fifteen years' service left in me. I am only fifty-three. He knows it is what I want of him. And you know what I want of you.'

Robert crossed to the central table and leant heavily upon it, making the castor oil plant in the middle clatter its stiff and shiny leaves.

'If you want to pass on something worth inheriting, my boy, you must listen harder to others than it has been your habit to do up to now. You have to bite the bullet.'

* * *

The birth of the heir was quick and straightforward, and Rosamund fought it every second of the way. Elizabeth and her friend Lilian Traill – an increasingly frequent visitor to Buscombe – listened from easy chairs in Elizabeth's bedroom, filled with a mixed consciousness of what they themselves were missing and, simultaneously, had been spared. Catherine sat with her mother. Tom paced around the hollow square of the landing in a state of terrible agitation. When he was at last summoned – it had been no more than five hours – to his wife and son, and tumbled to Rosamund's side in a fever of loving gratitude, she turned a blazing white face to him to say, 'Never again!' and then snapped her head away in the opposite direction. By contrast, his son was bright red, seemed extremely self-possessed, and when handed to his father he curled drowsily over his shoulder as limply as a little sandbag. In tears, Tom went to tell the others. The sight of him in Elizabeth's pretty room, so large and ruddy and so plainly not in charge of himself for the most honest and human of reasons, had a profound effect upon Lilian Traill. She put a hand out to him, murmuring a conventional pleasure, and then, to her astonishment, found that she had put her arms about his neck and was crying heartily and attempting to speak through the crying, to tell him that she did understand his feeling that this hour-old child might be a talisman for the future. Elizabeth was much surprised.

'My dear Lilian—'

'Forgive me,' Lilian said incoherently into Tom's waistcoat, 'forgive me, but I am so delighted – so thankful – I do understand – everything is going to be all right and he is a boy, a healthy boy – forgive me, but I think I know something of what you wish – oh, I am absurd—'

and she disengaged herself clumsily and burst into fresh tears.

Tom was deeply touched. She had quite forgotten her poise, her society manners and was badly in need of a handkerchief more substantial than the morsel of lace she was howling into. He proffered his, not trusting himself to speak, just gently touching her arm. She nodded violently, took the handkerchief and gave him a wild and grateful glance before subsiding into her chair once more. Elizabeth, most visibly in control, motioned Tom to leave.

He recounted the episode, with some awe, to his mother.

'Overwrought,' Charlotte said, unable to think of anyone but her new grandson.

Catherine shook her head, but said nothing. She put her hand briefly into her brother's and squeezed. He looked down at her.

'Here beginneth?' he said.

Tommy showed at once that he meant not only to be an agreeable baby, but a thorough Taverner as well. A thick pale down soon covered his head, his eyes were as clear a blue as his father's and he seemed amenable to everything but late meals. His mother did not care for him. His needs and instincts offended her, his conception and arrival became entangled in some dark corner of her mind with a savage violation, and she found his company pointless. She earned the outward disapproval, but inward delight, of his grandmother by leaving all nursery decisions to her and to the aunts. This was achieved by means of a row Charlotte had no trouble at all in engineering, since Rosamund, her nerves flayed raw, had no control over her temper at present. Charlotte made a practice of carrying the baby, attended by a solemn train of nursery servants, to visit his mother every morning at precisely the moment that Rosamund liked to say her morning office. It was each day, Charlotte felt, an opportune moment to deliver a little homily to Rosamund, not a syllable of which would be wasted on the nursery maids, whose presence would restrain Rosamund's powers of retaliation. What Charlotte omitted to take into account was Rosamund's complete carelessness of servant opinion. On the fifth morning, after a sanctimonious little sermon on Rosamund's duties as mother of the heir to Buscombe Priory, Rosamund leaped up, flung her hairbrush, which she happened to be holding, among the bottles and jars clustered on her dressing table and screamed.

'This is my house and my baby and Tom is my husband and you are – you – you are *obsolete*!'

Charlotte's grip tightened vice-like about the baby. He began to cry.

'You are not yourself, my dear,' Charlotte said, head high, thrillingly conscious of the nursery maids.

'I have never been more myself,' Rosamund cried. 'I have never been able to see more clearly! You are *using* me, you Taverners, you are using me for your own dynastic ends!'

A nursery maid surreptitiously tried to ease Tommy from his grandmother's arms. She clung to him. The little maid, genuinely anxious for the baby, pulled harder, and Charlotte suddenly let go of both him and her temper in a single moment. She advanced upon Rosamund.

'You little *Miss*,' Charlotte said, 'you little plotting middle-class meddler, with your canting ways and deceiving wiles that you practise on my poor boy. Use you! Indeed, I wish we could, but you are no use to us. You are *privileged* to be here, do you hear me? Privileged to bear our name, to live in this house, to bear a child for it—'

'Get out!' Rosamund screamed. 'Get out, get out!' She ran to her dressing table and began to scrabble among the clutter for her hairbrush. 'Tyrant!' she shrieked at Charlotte. 'Wicked old woman! You have made a fool of your son but you shan't make one of me!' She found her hairbrush and began to wave it wildly about. 'Get out! Get out! Get out!'

The little group of servants shifted uneasily towards the door. Charlotte took a step backwards. 'You have not heard the last of this—'

'Nor have you!' Rosamund said. 'You just wait! Nor have you!'

One by one the maids were slipping out and Tommy's mewings could be heard fading along the landing. Before she closed the door after her, Charlotte said, 'Never have I seen such a disgraceful exhibition.'

Rosamund flung her hairbrush. It hit the door.

'Of course you haven't because you are too busy making one of yourself!'

After that, Rosamund refused point blank to see the baby. She even banished, in an hysterical outburst, his father from her bed, and shut herself up for hours on end in her darkened room. Through the closed door, her muttered, rapid prayers could be heard.

'It is enough,' Catherine said contemptuously, 'to give the Catholic Church a bad name.'

Rosamund would not see her parents. They called frequently, bewildered and anxious, their pleasure in the child quite destroyed by her behaviour. She came out onto the landing once, dressed entirely in black and glittering with Taverner jewellery, and announced to her parents, gazing apprehensively up at her from the hall, that they had persuaded her into this marriage and its consequence, and were as much to blame for her wretchedness as anybody else. Her voice was both loud and clear, and not a servant in the central part of the house could avoid hearing every word. Tom leaped up the stairs and forcibly pulled her back into her bedroom. She was in tears.

'It is a punishment,' she cried to him. 'The pain is a punishment!'

He tried to hold her but she fought free.

'Dearest Rosamund, the pain is over! The child is here, and blooming! And you need never' – his heart sank but he persevered, 'you need never bear another child—'

'Not just that pain! All the pain! The blighted hopes! The longings! I am trapped, I am punished. What will become of me?'

He could not understand her; he could not comfort. He did not know what she had wanted and failed to get, and she would not explain. She insisted he was to blame and refused to tell him why. He left her sobbing and took his confusion to the nursery. It was full of women. His son was quite swamped in skirts. His entry was greeted with indifference or little exclamations of irritated surprise. Even Catherine gave him a small push back towards the door and said lightly,

'Dear Tom, you really must go. You take up too much room and there is nothing for you to do.'

He went down to the library in a most solitary frame of mind, to the disordered pile of farm accounts that had lain there, unattended, for days. A soft April rain was pattering at the window. As if answering its summons he went to the south window and looked across the terrace and the drive, down the long green sweep to the lake where the trees were showing their pale new growth. A triangle of mallards flew in, calling, from the west, dark against the light spring clouds, making for the little creek where duck had nested every year he could remember, reedy and secluded. A crippling fatigue afflicted him suddenly, the fearful tiredness of one who, halfway swimming across a lake, doubts and hardly cares if he will make it to the other side. He closed his eyes and leant his forehead on the glass, and then, with an enormous effort, dragged them open again. He crossed the room back to his desk, almost stumbling, and crashing into a chair, pulled towards him one of the sheets of headed writing paper that his father had, with such high delight, given to his mother on Elizabeth's birth.

'Dear du Cros,' he wrote, 'I am told that you, and friends of yours, are looking for some shooting for the coming season. As you know, this estate provides excellent sport, and I find I have more shooting available than I need. You are, of course, familiar with the precise acreage I mean which adjoins your own—'

There was a tentative knock on the door. He said, 'Come in,' without looking up.

'Would you prefer not to be disturbed?' Lilian Traill said from the doorway.

He was much surprised.

'Mrs Traill – Lilian – no, not at all, I am delighted – please come in. A chair – take this chair—'

She said, 'I have not come for anything at all specific. In a way, I do not know why I have come except – except that my own life is such a confusion and all too often a disappointment, that it makes my eyes very keen to see others who – who – oh dear, I am being absurd again—'

'Please sit.'

She did, bowing her graceful russet head.

'I may have made a terrible mistake in coming. I do not think I am at all a good judge of character. Some people hate to be pitied while others feel it to be a balm, and honestly I do not know which category you would fall into. But you see, I have watched you covertly for weeks, ever since little Tommy's birth, and I have thought that less and less have you anywhere to turn, and more and more are you excluded from all the lives in the house, and suddenly, seeing you in the nursery just now, I was filled with an impulse to tell you that I had seen – and been so sorry. I – I really do not know what good I thought such a revelation could be. That is the trouble with obeying impulses, do you not think?'

He said, gratefully, 'You are quite extraordinary.'

'Oh no,' she said earnestly, 'only a goose.'

He laughed. It was a vast relief. There did not seem to have been much to laugh about for some time.

'My sister Catherine,' he said in gentle teasing, seating himself close to her, 'says you are a very clever woman who must hide your intelligence to suit the company you keep.'

Lilian blushed deeply.

'Is it not ridiculous?' she cried. 'To spend so much of one's life simply drifting with the tide, ending up in a whole series of creeks and bays that do not suit one at all?'

'We cannot always help it.'

'I could help more than I succeed in doing. I have the decisive powers of a jellyfish!'

'You also have a most sweet understanding.'

She murmured something inaudible. He said, on impulse,

'I have to go round the woods tomorrow. Would it amuse you to come?'

She shook her head.

'It would, but I should not. In any case, I must with the greatest reluctance tear myself away and return to London. I have been here far too long.'

'That is not possible. Assure me you will soon return.'

She looked at him, and nodded, and then said with a little laugh,

'I run a grave risk of sounding exaggeratedly pathetic, but really, I have nowhere else to go.'

From the bedroom above came the imperious banging of a stick upon the floor – Charlotte summoning Brixton. Lilian gave Tom a conspiratorial smile.

'I think your trouble might be, you know, that you are entirely hedged about with extremely strong-minded women.'

He said, more lightly than he felt, 'Then do you not consider me to be in grave need of rescue?'

CHAPTER SIX

August 1878

In the summer of 1878, Meggy Bradstock returned to the neighbourhood of Buscombe, as parlourmaid at Marsham Court to Mr and Mrs Arnold du Cros. Her father had been much against the move, but her mother, desperate for the near support of a grown-up child and a dangerously nervous woman in any case, wore down his opposition with a mixture of pleading and nerve storms.

Meggy bore no resentment about the past, only feeling a satisfying pity for her old lover's sorry state in the last eight years. She had progressed steadily from lower dairymaid to a respectable indoor position, while he had married a shrew by all accounts, and mishandled the estate to a shocking degree. Her father said it was kept going only by the severest economies – the labour force was down to a handful – and by letting all the shooting, every acre but the Long Coppice where Sir Thomas still roamed nostalgically with his gun, to the kind of new rich man Bradstock declared the old baronet would not have given the time of day to. The only good aspect of the degrading business was that Bradstock was the one really fully stretched employee, to the extent that he now had two under keepers. For all that, his cottage roof badly needed repair, the agricultural parts of the estate were almost all down to grass, cropped by a small unproductive flock of sheep, and the neglect of every corner that would not be seen by the rented guns cried louder with every passing week.

Meggy was interested to see it all, particularly from the ultra comfortable viewpoint of Marsham Court with its fleets of footmen and prodigious ceremonies. The eventual goal in Meggy's life was a housekeeper's place and the du Cros household – not born to money but too intelligent to misuse it or to underrate the things it could buy, like good servants – was an admirable beginning to her climb upward. She worked with unflinching diligence, just visibly enough to suit her purpose, and on her scarce afternoons off – whose allotted hours she never exceeded by so much as a minute – she would take circuitous routes to her father's cottage, in order to make mental lists of signs of Buscombe's decline, and also in the hopes of seeing members of the family driving out.

Sometimes there were rich rewards, like the day she saw in the sheltered meadow by the old granary, a stout fair little boy in a pannier strapped to a pony of similar proportions being led about by Miss Elizabeth and Miss Catherine. On another day, in sudden summer rain, the family carriage dashed by her, almost hurling her into the ditch, but giving her a compensating glimpse of a staring dark woman in black, leaning forward as if urging the vehicle to go even faster. Tom she only saw once, a solitary figure on a cob cantering along the edge of the high beech hanger. Her father said he had grown quite stout and although there had been a year or two when his spirits seemed almost broken, he had rallied a bit recently and taken more of an interest in things. There had been a rift between him and his uncle; they hardly spoke now, though the boy came to see his cousins, an odd bookish boy whom Bradstock said would never make a sportsman.

After a judicious interval, Meggy took herself upon a visit to old friends in the dairy and the kitchens. The outside of the house, she observed, needed repainting, and the stableyard would have broken old Veale's heart – a single blade of grass in his day and he'd be bellowing at the stable lads, 'What do you suppose this place is? A bloody *meadow*?' Now there were green tufts everywhere between the ridged bluish bricks that floored the yard, two downpipes to the rainwater butts were broken, and she could only hear a single tuneless whistle emerging from the harness room where there used to be a whole chorus. She shook her head with a regret reinforced with complacency.

They had a deal to tell her in the kitchen. When the new mistress had come, the whole house had been turned upside down, papered and painted, new-furnished and carpeted. The attics were piled high with all the old tables and chairs; it was rumoured she had wanted to sell them but the master had put his foot down. Then she had lost interest overnight, when the boy was born. No more guests, no more parties, you could break your heart dusting and polishing and she'd never notice, she who had been such a stickler for detail that a single fingermark on the piano threw her into a passion. She spent hours in her room, brooding, or drove out to Bath, to Bristol, even to London, just on a whim, never saying when she would be back. If it wasn't for his aunts, the little boy wouldn't know any mothering. Of course, the house was quieter now –

Meggy should have heard it a couple of years back! Quarrels? There wasn't an hour without them. You couldn't help hearing every word, even if most of them made no sense. It was hardly to be wondered at that Sir Thomas should drink a bit—

'The bottle?' Meggy said sharply.

Not so much now, but for a time he'd be hours in the dining room after dinner alone, and it would always be Miss Catherine who came and helped him upstairs. She was grown shockingly thin, as thin as Miss Elizabeth – one should say Mrs Forrester but it didn't seem right when she never left Buscombe now and Mr Forrester never came to visit her – had grown plump. Her old ladyship had thought of nothing but the boy at first, but of late, with her young ladyship so queer, she'd taken over some of the reins of the house again and one couldn't say other but that it came as something of a relief. At least you knew where you were. But it wasn't what it was, wasn't really a happy house. The boy was a little cherub, of course, but the atmosphere was sort of nervy, you never quite knew what would happen next and how could any household so uncertain be happy?

On her way out, slipping around the stableyard walls to the gates into the park, Meggy saw Tom riding in. He did not see her, but she had a long opportunity to gaze at him. He looked heavier, certainly, but healthy, almost blithe, and as he went by, she noticed to her surprise, almost to her annoyance, that he was humming.

Having left his horse, Tom took the path through the shrubbery in which Meggy had hidden on his birthday almost eight years ago, and came out onto the lawn between the dining and drawing room wings where the two old mulberries stood crookedly and patiently confined in their collars of the white painted seats. It was a cool place for the summer, though hazardous with wasps, making Catherine and Elizabeth urgent with little cries about the dangers for Tommy. The nurserymaid detested afternoons out there, most of which were spent crawling on her hands and knees in pursuit of somnolent enemies, when the huge garden was full of shady places without wasps where Tommy could tumble about in safety. There seemed to be some family tradition about the mulberry trees, however, and they clung to these afternoons beneath them with a senseless and sentimental obstinacy.

Catherine was there now, with Lilian Traill, the former drawing a glistening beetle skewered to the top of her drawing board, the latter doing nothing beside her. Tom had passed his son and his sister Elizabeth, a stable lad and the nurserymaid, making a solemn progress down to the lake on the fat pony. Tommy had on a huge white linen sun bonnet framing his scarlet face and was shouting peremptory and unintelligible commands at his attendants. His aunt remarked fondly to his father that he was quite the little soldier. His father, in the greatest flush of contentment he could remember, equally fondly agreed.

The enormous happiness of the whole summer was quite awe-inspiring. The agonizing over the estate, the frustration of his political ambitions, his own inability to commit to a prudent course of action, such as working for a brief while for his uncle, his incomprehensible and unhappy marriage all seemed for the first time to be manageable. The compromise solution for the estate might not be socially perfect, but it enabled him to live, if he was careful, like a country gentleman, and to farm a little, and shoot a little and eat trout that had risen to his own mayfly. Politics, it seemed suddenly, could wait.

He wasn't thirty yet. Uncle Robert would mellow as Charlie's manifest uninterest grew unavoidable, and by that time agriculture would have picked up again, and the estate could turn out these profitable industrialists and businessmen who were, for the moment, such a lifeline. As for his marriage, it came to him that poor old Rosamund might benefit from a winter abroad, seeing her sister, visiting new places, being distracted from whatever nightmare it was she clung to so madly and would – or could – not explain.

And the reason for this absurd happiness, this almost unnatural optimism, was sitting there beneath the mulberry tree with his sister Catherine. After the comfortable exchange – almost, he sometimes thought, a mutual recognition – in the library after Tommy's birth, Lilian had gone quickly back to London and not reappeared at Buscombe until the autumn. When she had come back she had been very pale and disturbed, and needed rest and quiet, and Catherine and Elizabeth had spent hours shut up with her. Tom had badgered and pestered to know the trouble and it was Catherine who had relented at last and told him, with ill concealed revulsion, of Lilian's ordeals. She had, it appeared, some years before, finally confronted her husband, revealed what she knew of his public strayings and declared that she would remain with him, for the look of things – 'And of course, the money,' Catherine said in disgust. 'He owns all her money. She is destitute if she leaves him' – as long as they led, henceforward, entirely separate lives.

'To her astonishment, he was dismayed to find that his habits were well known, and began to attempt promises of reform. She spurned him and it seems they lived on her terms in separate rooms in the same house until last month when Lilian discovered a further horror.'

She stopped.

'I don't find the next part easy to say.'

Tom waited. Catherine took a deep breath and said with a kind of expressionless rapidity,

'It seems that there are laws passed now to remove from the streets any woman – any common woman – who – who is diseased because of – because of what she does. For money. It is called the Contagious Diseases Act. It is,' Catherine's mouth twisted, 'for the protection of men. The sick women are put into special hospitals called Lock Hospitals, until they are cured, and the expenses of these wards are paid for by public subscription. By innocently admitting to the house the well-intentioned governor of such a hospital, Lilian discovered that a large annual sum, no doubt drawn from her own fortune, was being paid by George Traill to fund a Lock ward. This, while he still wandered almost nightly in Covent Garden and St James and the Haymarket—'

Tom shouted, 'It is loathsome.'

'It is true.'

'It is evil, it is the worst of hypocrisy!'

'That is what she most courageously told him. There was a terrible quarrel and I fear he struck her repeatedly. It was after they had dined and he had consumed almost an entire decanter of claret alone.'

'She must leave him! She must never go back.'

'She does not have a single penny of her own. Do you know that the law of this land not only makes all a wife's property her husband's, but allows him, if he so chooses, to make her a prisoner in her own house? We are a nation of barbarians!'

'She must leave him! I will support her!'

'Oh,' Catherine cried in scorn, 'what a romantic fool you are! How do you suppose that would look? What do you imagine Rosamund would say to such a plan?'

Lilian, it appeared, had in any case worked out her future. She had retired to Buscombe to recover, George had departed upon a tour of Switzerland and the Italian lakes, accompanied by a friend who if not exactly upright, was at least not hopelessly debauched. After Christmas they would meet again and attempt to resume the life that fed and clothed Lilian yet gave George Traill his unappetizing freedom. Nothing Tom could say, with his particular open hearted boldness, could shift her. Back to London she went in the raw January of 1877, to find that her husband had preceded her. She found him in bed, racked with pneumonia and a blazing fever. Three days later he died in a state of great fear and self-pity, the cynicism of his life no prop at all to him in the end. And Lilian Traill found herself free, the mistress of a good house in Charles Street and a respectable portion of the money she had brought to the marriage almost a decade before. It was, as she wrote to Elizabeth Taverner, an encouraging way, in the circumstances, to begin one's fourth decade.

She spent a year abroad. From time to time Tom thought of her with affection and a faint nostalgic hunger for that brief and sympathetic encounter in the library at Buscombe. In the spring of 1878 she appeared once more, blooming and responsive. Strangely and touchingly, Rosamund seemed as pleased to see her as anybody, begging her not to leave them and whispering her grievances and fears to her for hours with a kind of beady eyed intensity. Lilian was very patient.

'She talks very madly,' she said to Elizabeth, 'but I do not believe she can help it. There is a spring broken somewhere inside her which makes all the old machinery just limp along, and she fights the broken rhythm all the time. The only thing that sustains her is to believe that her state of mind is somebody else's fault.'

'Tom was speaking of a change of air, a winter abroad. I do believe' – dropping her voice confidentially although they were quite alone in the sitting room – 'that this is quite common, after a confinement, with a highly strung—'

There had been a most uneventful three weeks, driving to Bath, or to see Mary Taverner, entertaining Mrs du Cros who brought with her a fairy-like child of ten with a cloud of pale curls, dreamy and biddable, who liked nothing better than to be allowed to dawdle about alone in Catherine's conservatory.

'You must find us so dull,' Elizabeth said to Lilian, meaning that she did herself.

'Not at all,' Lilian replied without perfect truthfulness.

Such dullness as there was, however, was short-lived. One afternoon, excused from the ritual pony excursion with a headache, Lilian took Ruskin's newest volume of lectures in his capacity as Slade Professor of Art at Oxford, a straw hat and four cushions out to a seat beneath one of the mulberry trees. For half an hour she dozed and read and listened to the fat, contented sounds of the summer afternoon, and then Tom Taverner appeared, very agitatedly, from the direction of the rose garden, and with disconcertingly few pre-liminaries, told her that he loved her.

'Oh!' she cried. 'Please do not confuse sympathy and friendly understanding with love!'

'And do not you confuse,' he retorted, 'what is socially convenient but false with what is socially *inconvenient* but true.'

She regarded him with admiration.

'I have surprised you,' he said, 'of course I have. I have had since that day in the library over two years ago to become used to the knowledge that I loved you. You have had too much recovering to do to think of it.'

'I think,' she said, 'I think you are perhaps in love with the idea of me. You are so very romantic. If I had not had this hideous experience, if I had not been so close to so much pitch, I doubt I would seem so attractive to you.'

'Why do you wish to explain me away?'

'For self-preservation. I am determined never to take anything on hope or trust again, only to move forward where I can see clearly.'

Tom bowed his head and thought for a moment.

'Lilian, I am so much in earnest. I would not wish you to have the faintest misconception – illusion, anything. I do indeed want to protect you. What man would not, could help himself? But I love you because I know you, and because you know me. You are such a relief to me because I do not believe you expect the impossible, only the human. You have had the bitterest disappointments, yet you are still hopeful. My poor sister Catherine cannot hope as you can. I need this strength in you.'

'Suppose,' Lilian said, looking away from him to the cream and pink profusion of the rose garden across the grass, 'suppose I am not – as I fear I am not – really strong, and that what you see as optimism is in truth only the sheer relief of being free once more? Suppose what I feel for you – and I do indeed feel something for you – is not love, but affectionate pity?'

'In the first case,' he said, smiling, 'I do not believe you. In the second, I will make up the deficiency.'

She burst out laughing.

'I am very doubtful! But' – she turned to him almost eagerly, 'I should like an adventure and—' She was about to add that her freedom often left her feeling most solitary and with a yearning to be of particular significance to somebody, but decided upon impulse not to say that yet. Instead she said, 'Oh, what an abuse of hospitality!' but she noticed that she said it in a tone of high delight.

Two nights later, he came to her room. It was imprudent and ridiculously easy. His dressing room, and her allotted room looking north to the rose garden, were separated by a short L-shaped corridor, a single helpfully silent passage door, and no other members of the family along the route. It was a visit of enormous pleasure to both of them, the first of many. Lilian, having never provided George Traill with an heir, had not been in the freewheeling state of many of the women of her set who, duty done, could please themselves as to lovers. For a woman of her social sophistication, she was physically inexperienced, sufficiently so to be openly and flatteringly delighted with Tom's body, the quality of his skin and the thickness of his hair. For Tom, making love to Lilian was the end of a very long and wearisome journey, a haven from which – and he had no doubts about this whatsoever – he could set out on extraordinary forays to achieve the impossible. If anything as purely wonderful, as absolutely trusting as this could happen, he thought, then no future problem would dare to proclaim itself as being of any consequence at all.

They were elaborately circumspect by day. Tom turned to the harvest – such as it was – with a vigour he had not shown in three years; Lilian, declaring herself a drone in the hive, threw herself into being the most useful of guests, assisting Catherine among her green fronds, planning itineraries among her friends in Europe for Rosamund with Elizabeth – her conscience was not quite easy over this so she chose not to listen to it too scrupulously – patiently bearing both Lady Taverner's and Rosamund's complaints of each other and the upbringing of the boy. Apart from impersonal and pleasant exchanges at meals, she scarcely spoke to Tom.

'I must not be in the same room with you,' he said, 'because if I am, I must look at you.'

They avoided any occupation in the day that might bring them together. The deprivation, with the secret nights between, was almost pleasurable. Whatever direction Tom would ride off in, Lilian chose the opposite for walks with the sisters, or even occasionally alone, on errands for Lady Taverner if she could, to revel in her satisfaction and happiness. One afternoon, having volunteered to take veal broth and two flannel shawls to Mrs Bradstock – confined again and with her usual frenzied inability to cope – she waited until Tom had set safely off to see the last of the hayfield baled, before tying on her straw hat and picking up the basket.

She did not care for charitable errands. The helpless disorder of the Bradstock cottage offended her as much as it did Bradstock himself, who often had to see to it personally that he had the daily stiff white collar and well brushed bowler without which he would not have stirred outside. She gave the rabble of children a token caress, endeavoured to admire the baby, left the broth and shawls and Lady Taverner's instructions about both, and escaped thankfully into the cottage yard, where Bradstock's dog muttered drowsily from his kennel, and a few hens scratched without much hope in the dust.

With renewed energy, and her white parasol up against the sun, Lilian struck out across the park towards the smudge of Long Coppice which would give her a quarter of an hour's shade on the journey back to the house. A horseman, coming up the shallow slope from the south towards the lake, revealed himself to be Tom unable to resist meeting after seeing her unmistakable white figure crossing the empty landscape above him.

'Oh my dear! My dear – you must ride on—'

'Five minutes,' Tom said firmly.

He dismounted, and hitched the cob to a tree at the edge of the coppice.

'Somebody might see!'

He waved an arm, laughing at the huge empty bowl of land around them, blank and bland in the sunshine.

'Let them! The whole lot of them! In any case, what is wrong with a man telling the woman he is going to marry that he loves her in the daylight for once?'

She was outraged and delighted.

'Marry? Marry? Tom, you are ridiculous, you cannot marry, you *are* married!'

'I shall obtain a divorce. I decided upon it an hour ago in the hayfield. It is the most obvious, the most natural thing to do. I am going to marry you.'

'You can't! It's impossible, shocking! We should have to live abroad—'

'Nonsense. We should live here.'

'It is never done—'

'We shall do it!'

He reached out for her but she held him off, saying,

'Tom Taverner, you go too fast. Trying to reason with you is like shouting at a hurricane to be still. You cannot throw such an idea at me and expect me not to reel a little. I will not, I absolutely will not, discuss it any more just now.'

He kissed her nose.

'I adore it when you are firm with me. If you will not talk to me, will you kiss me instead?'

'No,' she said.

'We'll see about that!'

Meggy Bradstock, taking her personal and illicit path through Long Coppice on her way to visit her mother – Mrs du Cros had given special permission for a few extra hours' absence on account of the new baby and Mrs Bradstock's urgent distress – could hear voices long before she could see their owners. Her reaction was not to consider her own safety and wait until they had passed on, but simply to move steadily forwards but with redoubled stealth. Twenty yards from the edge of the coppice she halted behind a hazel clump and observed Sir Thomas Taverner and a lady who was most certainly not the staring lady in black, in each other's arms. Her sudden and miserable anger almost stunned her. It was only right, was only the natural and proper way of things that Tom should have abandoned her to marry a lady as befitted him, in order to bring into the world the heir who would inherit Buscombe and to sustain his due position in society. That Meggy had never questioned, any more than she had resented – for she had never seen it in that light – being used for some energetic and youthful sexual experimenting. But this spectacle before her was breaking all those rules, destroying the whole edifice of right and wrong, of the interdependence and usefulness of society's various levels to each other. Peering through the hazel twigs at Lilian's graceful white back in the circle of Tom's tweed clad arm, Meggy knew herself to be a used thing, an abused thing, a discarded and valueless thing. She hated what she saw and she could not look away. She wrapped her arms about her solid little body and rocked and swayed in silent pain.

At last Lilian drew away, laughing and insisting that Tom must go on, re-tying her hat ribbons with elaborate decision, and holding the basket before her as a kind of shield. He mounted the cob with the greatest reluctance, trying to stoop and catch Lilian from the saddle, but she evaded him and ran laughing into the trees, passing so close to Meggy that the wind of her going blew gleefully into Meggy's face. Meggy stared after her with hatred until her flitting white form had quite vanished, and then, making sure that Tom was still cantering away with his back to her, set off in a turmoil of resentment and resolution to the teeming cottage across the park.

Lilian lay across her bed and held her temples.

'Stop it, Tom. I cannot bear this. I cannot bear a scene.'

'You must listen to me! I am in deadly earnest!'

They were speaking in furious whispers. The curtains were closed, but the window was open to the hot August night, and across the dark space of garden and the mulberry trees was Catherine's window, closed it is true, but the night was still. Lilian swung herself up.

'You mistake yourself. It is not serious. It is melodramatic. You are trying to persuade yourself that a fantasy is possible, that we could overturn everything society holds dear and re-write the rules without a breath of objection.'

'Do you not love me?' Tom demanded. 'Do you not want to be my wife?'

Lilian sighed impatiently.

'Yes, I love you. Yes, I would like to be your wife. But the one does not automatically follow the other. You not only have a wife but a sick wife who needs care. And the scandal and the difficulties would be simply frightful.'

'Are you telling me that you do not love me enough to face them?'

'I don't know. I have never loved anyone as much as I love you, but I cannot, for a moment, countenance the future you are proposing for us so I – I suppose I cannot have a very great capacity for love. Not enough for your scheme in any case.' She paused and then said pleadingly, 'Please try to use a little imagination in what you are asking of me!'

He began to say he was asking nothing but her love and trust, but the sentence seemed to have the hollow tones of mock heroism, so he stopped himself and said as gently as he could,

'Please do not put an end to everything. Not after such a summer.'

She began to pleat and release a fold of her grey silk wrapper.

'It is, I suppose, a characteristic of all human relationships that they must either develop or die. You can never keep them still, even at the most perfect moment. So silly of me – such a goose – to think – hope that I could just always have this summer!'

'I cannot bear it if you go.'

'Tom—'

He waited.

'Tom, I must go away and think. I must go and see the other side of my life and live in my house a little. I am a bit wrapped away from things here—'

'Then you are not denying me all hope?'

She thought for a bit and then said uncertainly, 'I suppose not.'

He got up from the side of her bed and moved to the door. He said with his back to her,

'Will you go soon?'

'In the morning.'

'How will you explain that to my mother and sisters? Will it not seem very extraordinary?'

'I expect so. It is extraordinary but I do not think you are in a position to point it out. You are proposing a scheme to me, after all, which is not so much extraordinary as preposterous.'

He opened the door. She observed, even though his back was turned to her, that he was extremely angry, and this observation made her long to be transported at once, out of these horrid complications, back to Charles Street.

'Good night,' he said and opened the door.

'Tom – Tom – I am so sorry.'

He looked at her hard for a moment, and then he said crisply, 'The milk is spilled,' and went out and closed the door behind him.

She did not see him the next morning, nor his mother, nor Rosamund confined with a migraine as she so often was. To Catherine and Elizabeth she made a brief and clumsy explanation of suddenly, foolishly, wishing to see her house, to be in London, a caprice really, she knew, but a strong one—

'London?' Elizabeth said. 'In August? But, my

dear Lilian, you were to stay another month.'

Catherine, whose sharp observation had not been idle the last weeks, who had remarked to herself the change in her brother, the almost languorous bloom of Lilian, said simply,

'Do not fuss her, Elizabeth. She is her own mistress. Would you like me to order the carriage for the station?'

Lilian, sensing herself detected, stammered her gratitude. Catherine said no more, beyond briefly, while helping her to pack, 'I will tell Tom you are gone. He has not looked so well for years.' She could not reply. Later, her trunk and boxes strapped behind her, the carriage bore her away towards Bath. As she was taken rapidly down the drive, she was too bent upon fighting back impending confusion and misery to notice that she passed a dumpy little woman travelling with great determination and audacity towards the front door of the house. It was Meggy Bradstock and in her pocket she carried a laboriously written letter for Rosamund.

A franker woman than Meggy would have sought advice from her friends in the kitchen as to how to get her letter to Lady Taverner and probably confided the contents of it, too. But Meggy had learned cunning in her steadily ambitious life, and she was well aware that the best way to cause the sensation she desired was to play upon the animosity between the two Ladies Taverner. Old Lady Taverner she dared not approach directly, on account of the past, but she knew it was essential that her information reach Charlotte's ears as well as Rosamund's. She said her good mornings in the kitchen, and then she went to her father's customary stool at the dresser end to wait, and watch the morning hubbub around her. Punctually at eleven, Brixton came in to make, with her own hands, the green tea Charlotte drank at this hour. Meggy slipped from her stool and went to stand beside her.

'May I 'ave a word, Mrs Brixton?'

Brixton was a loyal and sensible woman who had refused to take part in the below stairs furore over Tom and Meggy. She put a spoonful of tea into a Coalport pot.

'What is it then, Meggy?'

Meggy pushed her face close to Brixton.

'I know something their Ladyships ought to know. It's really important. I've come special. I ought to tell her Ladyship – Lady Thomas that is – but I don't like to ask. And I ought to tell her old Ladyship but I dursn't.' She pulled the letter from her pocket. 'Would you give this to her Ladyship, Mrs Brixton, and ask her to be so good as to give it to Lady Thomas?'

Brixton looked suspicious.

'Is it gossip?'

'They ought to know—'

'What sort of gossip?'

'It's about the nurse they've got for the little fellow. I know about her. It's for the baby's sake. I want to help, you see.'

Brixton took the letter reluctantly. She peered at the writing.

'Did you write this?'

'Yes,' Meggy said proudly.

Brixton grunted.

'I wouldn't conceal my name,' Meggy said, 'I'm an honest woman.'

'I'll see what her Ladyship says,' Brixton said. She put the pot onto a tray beside a cup and saucer and a single piece of shortbread on a plate. 'You needn't wait. If there's anything needs doing, it'll be done.'

Meggy grinned.

'I'm ever so grateful—'

Brixton explained the matter doubtfully to Charlotte.

'I hope I did right, bringing it to you. But as it is for the baby—'

'Perfectly right,' Charlotte said. 'Bring me my paper-knife. I always knew there was no real harm in Meggy Bradstock.'

'She's done well for herself,' Bradstock said, 'I'll say that for her.' She watched Charlotte slit the paper wrapping of the letter. 'I hope it isn't bad news, my Lady.'

After a moment, Charlotte looked up. Her face was absolutely frozen. She rose.

'I must go to Lady Thomas at once.'

'But my Lady—'

'Open the door,' Charlotte commanded. Holding the letter before her, she swept around the galleried landing and flung open Rosamund's door without knocking. Rosamund, crouched on the window seat and glaring with loathing on the summer's day outside, sprang up in amazement. Charlotte opened her arms.

'My poor child—'

She surged across the room and enveloped the astounded Rosamund in her tremendous embrace. Then she thrust Meggy's letter at her daughter-in-law.

'Read this, my dear child, read this, and then let me comfort you.'

It was, Catherine thought later, when she could bear to think of it at all, as if all the Old Testament manifestations of divine wrath, whirlwinds and tempests and pillars of fire, had descended simultaneously upon Buscombe. Self-control, it seemed, was a quality neither Tom nor Rosamund had ever heard of, along with restraint, decorum or propriety. When Charlotte, appalled by the virulence and sheer volume of the quarrels rolling like thunderstorms through the rooms, demanded that her son remember his position and his manners, Tom roared back at her, quite beyond control, that losing his temper was the only luxury left to him and that he meant to indulge it.

Paradoxically, the revelation of his liaison with Lilian, though it opened floodgates of jealous fury, also served to slip back into place the cog in Rosamund's brain that had caused her mental rhythm to miss a beat in its circuit ever since Tommy's birth. Savage, even vicious, she was, but she was highly articulate and though blazing eyed, her eyes were dry.

'Weak!' she screamed at him. 'Soft, feeble! Hardly a man, only a puppet! Flattered and fawned upon, fit for no woman of principle! Disgusting beyond words—'

Charlotte attempted to suggest that a man might divert himself without impairing his devotion to his wife. She was met with scalding, withering scorn. Elizabeth could profess nothing but dismay mingled with a much explained – if anyone would listen – sense of her personal betrayal by Lilian.

'It is hardly to be thought of! I cannot understand it, truly I cannot. She has been like a daughter of this house, a sister to me. She seemed so grateful for our kindness, so docile, so unconscious of any thoughts of such a kind. Truly, I do not know what to make of it except that I must admit to being deeply, oh very deeply, hurt—'

Catherine found that whenever she was alone, she could not help herself crying. She cried for Lilian's falseness and her vulnerability, for Tom's lost happiness, for her own lost hopes. She cried for Rosamund's bitterness, the poor baby's unpromising future, her mother's bewildered, angry sorrow and for her beloved birthplace which, it seemed, the gods were determined to frown upon. There seemed no way out, no future that would not be hopelessly scarred by things that could not be changed, things that had happened which no amount of wishing could make unhappen. The best thing to wish for – such a dreary thing to wish for! – seemed to be a degree of resignation. As a kind of purge, she wrote the whole saga down in a letter to Harry, but on paper it was sordid and bizarre, reflecting well upon nobody and unreal besides, so she tore it up. When Rosamund announced her plans, Catherine was ashamed to feel a sweet flood of relief.

She would, she said, go to Italy. She would go to her sister in Tuscany, to a pious Catholic environment where she would endeavour to heal herself, to put behind her the horrors of her time at Buscombe.

'The boy?' Charlotte demanded, bracing herself for a battle she would die to win. 'The boy?'

Rosamund flung out her hands.

'He must stay. I cannot take him. You have all made sure he hardly knows me. He is all Taverner,' she said in disgust.

Tom said, shaking so with such a mixture of emotion he hardly knew what he wished the answer to be, 'And will you return?'

Rosamund kept him waiting, while she looked around the room, the drawing room, at the colours she had clothed it in, and objects and furniture she had filled it with, the spirit of her age she had sent in to chase away the spirit of its own age. Then she said, almost with a smile,

'You must wait and see. I simply cannot tell.'

'*Will* not tell,' Charlotte said later to Brixton, while

her hair was being brushed. Brixton clucked a little; there was, after all, nothing to be said that everyone in the house, above and below stairs, had not said already a thousand times. It was a matter for rejoicing, in Brixton's view, that this turbulent spirit which had made their lives such a misery the last six years was finally packing her bags and taking herself off. Perhaps there was a chance now that the household could stop behaving like a madhouse and return to what it was supposed to be, the country household of a titled English gentleman, with all that was proper to such an establishment. And the poor mite in the nursery could be allowed to grow up in the manner nature intended for a child.

She looked at her mistress's reflection in the mirror. Still handsome, but haggard handsome now. Brixton had been looking watchfully at that face for over a quarter of a century, and there wasn't a new line she would miss.

'I'm an old hag,' Charlotte said to her. 'Look at me!'

Brixton gave her shoulder a little pat.

'Give yourself a year, ma'am. A year of decent living and you won't know yourself.'

Charlotte snorted.

'Decent living!'

'That will begin,' Brixton said, turning the bed down with practised little tweaks and tucks, 'when her highness takes herself off.'

Rosamund left Buscombe in the second week of September, taking every single possession she could possibly claim as her own – Tom, on the last evening, sarcastically offered her the marble swan and its font – and her maid. When the carriage had rolled out of sight, and the grinding of its wheels had faded on the still morning air, a stricken dumbness fell upon the watchers on the terrace. There was nothing to be said that suited both their feelings and their various senses of what was proper. In silence, they filed into the house and dispersed into various and separate rooms. Only Charlotte had the energy and purpose to make straight for the rooms her daughter-in-law had just quitted, leaving the air in them still charged with the force of her going.

Climbing the steps to the front door in the Circus in Bath, Tom realized that it was the first time he had done so in six years. Nothing there had changed, the same plum coloured stair carpet, the same dim little views on the walls of Bath from every surrounding hill, the same papery, dusty smell overlaid with polish. Only he was not the same, climbing those stairs, being ushered into Edward Martineau's unchanged office, walking across that blank unhelpful space to where Edward stood – a little greyer, a little leaner – hand outstretched.

'My dear boy, I am so profoundly sorry.'

Tom inclined his head.

'I suppose I am reaping where I have sowed—'

Edward gave the hand he held in his a little shake.

'Now, now. Bitterness is a poison. Never confuse ill desserts with ill luck.'

'I cannot avoid the consequences of my own determined decisions over the last six years.'

'Ah. But you must use what you see as the foundation for the future. I am trying to avoid repeating the cliché of "profit from experience", I hope you notice. Sit you down. There now' – putting a drawing of a tiny man in a huge moustache, apparently carrying a giant comb beneath his arm, into Tom's hand, 'that is my boy

134

Frank's notion of Isambard Kingdom Brunel. As you see, he is carrying the Great Western Railway under one arm. He was Frank's hero last week. This week it is Alexander Graham Bell. Does the idea of the telephone appeal to you?'

'Not as much at the moment as joining the redcoats to fight the Zulus or going out to Panama to help Mr de Lesseps dig his canal.'

He put little Frank's drawing down on the desk. Edward watched him a moment and then said as gently as he could, 'I cannot help you with a divorce, you know. You are unfortunate but I fear there are others as helpless and as unfortunate. In any case misfortune is not enough. The most I can offer you is a judicial separation at the moment – which gives you no freedom you cannot exercise in any case – with the possibility of a dissolution of the marriage if, over the years, your wife persistently refuses to return home.'

Tom raised his head.

'I do thank you. But divorce is not the reason that I have come.'

'Ah. Then perhaps I may be of use to you after all.'

Tom rose and leant on the desk, holding his face out towards Edward Martineau as a kind of added emphasis.

'I have come to you because my wife has taken every last gem of the family jewellery to Italy with her. The aquamarines and pearls were my wedding gift to her, so was a pair of diamond clasps from my mother. But the rest, suites of the stuff, pieces that have been in the family further back than anyone can remember, was not hers to take. It was my mother who discovered the loss after Rosamund had gone, and found all the jewellery cases in their accustomed place, but empty. But she did not make this discovery until yesterday when Rosamund had been gone three days and was halfway across France.'

Edward Martineau had closed his eyes as if retreating behind his lids. When he opened them again, he said with elaborate calm,

'Can you be perfectly certain that it was your wife who removed the jewels from their cases?'

'Perfectly. The Taverner jewellery was the one aspect of marriage to me that Rosamund rejoiced in. It was kept in a safe whose opening process is known only to her, to my mother and to myself, and she was in and out of it constantly. In any case, such an act rings true. It is her last word, her revenge.'

Edward shook his head and sighed.

'It is not something I have ever been faced with before. Preventing something leaving the country, yes. But retrieving something that has passed beyond the powers of English law, now that is quite another problem. I should have to begin by ascertaining beyond all doubt that your wife has the jewels in her possession.' He looked up at Tom. 'Are you maintaining your wife?'

'Naturally. I shall make her a quarterly allowance.'

'Perhaps that could be used as some kind of lever. My dear boy, what an ugly business.'

'Yes,' Tom said.

'We must, I fear, involve the police. You must make a statement.'

Tom nodded.

'You look all in—'

'I keep dragging myself over horizons only to discover there is another, more mountainous still, ahead of me.'

'I wonder,' Edward said watching him, 'what history will make of this age of ours. No doubt the glorious progressiveness of the majority will quite obscure the pain and difficulties of those who sought to preserve the best from the old, the traditional, order of things. Unfortunately one cannot choose to own the cast of character and the beliefs that are best designed to profit from the particular age in which one lives. I'm a child of the Regency in spirit if not in years, and I venture to think that you might be another. My dear Tom, forgive me. This is hardly businesslike. Will you allow me to summon my clerk that we may take down all the particulars? The precise missing items for instance, and as much as you can tell me of their disappearance—'

Tom said suddenly, 'I want you to know that this is no vendetta of mine. I could not sleep last night and in my wanderings I realized that I did not want the jewellery back for myself. Indeed, in all my sorrow and confusion at what has become of Rosamund and myself, I think I should be quite glad for her to have it, I should feel it was a small thing to give her in place of what I once hoped to give her. But it is of course not mine to let go in this way. There are pieces of my mother's, pieces that are to become my sisters'. The jewellery is in my care, like everything else I have, and therefore I am not free to choose what I would do about it. But I should like you at least to know that a legal chase across Europe is not what I would do if I had a chance.'

He rose and went to the window. The Circus was empty except for an immense old woman, bundled in shawls, being pushed in the direction of the Royal Crescent in an invalid chair by another woman, half her size and clad in thin and rusty black. For a moment he speculated, in wonder, as to whether the little woman had actually managed to propel her mountainous charge up the steep slope of Gay Street to the Circus in the first place.

'Will you –' he said, not turning towards Edward, 'will you summon your clerk?'

CHAPTER SEVEN

September 1882

'I cannot beat about the bush,' Edward Martineau said. 'I have to confess that I have come home empty handed.'

Five pairs of Taverner eyes regarded him unwaveringly – Tom, Charlotte, Elizabeth and Catherine, against whose shoulder six-year-old Tommy leaned.

'You must understand,' Edward continued, gripping the Gothic chair back before him, 'that I found I was powerless.' He paused. He was terribly tired, longing only to get home, to be soothed by Alicia who believed the Taverners to be quite merciless in what they expected. It had been a dreadful journey in any case, August dust and heat and a deep knowledge that the whole business was a wild goose chase, even before he began. 'I must explain—'

'Yes,' Tom said.

In the last week of July, Edward had crossed the Channel and taken a train down the length of France to Marseilles. In Marseilles he had caught a steamer to Leghorn and from Leghorn had been driven to Pisa where he spent the first night for a week in a stable bed, a bed he shared with enough fleas to leave him enraged with itching by morning. Unrefreshed and jaundiced in outlook, he hired a carriage to carry him up the hills to Lucca where he took a hotel room and then made himself known to Signor Forcole, lawyer to Paolo Buonvisi, Duke of Montemagno and brother-in-law to Rosamund Taverner.

The beauty of Lucca that August morning was quite lost on him. The richly green surrounding hills, the broad tree lined walks along the old city walls, the glitter of the River Serchio, the celebrated pleasantness of the Lucchese themselves only managed to be irritating. Edward had spent three years writing elaborately patient letters to both Rosamund and to Signor Forcole arguing that as the jewellery was not, in law, Rosamund's to take, it must be returned to the lawful owner, her husband. Indeed, under English law, even those pieces he had given her remained his, but he was generously intending that she should keep those as long as the bulk of the pieces, some four thousand pounds' worth, were handed back. Rosamund had ignored all the letters; Signor Forcole had replied that the jewels were perfectly safe in the possession of a wife who was merely recovering from great distresses, and who had by no means set her face against the possibility of returning to her husband. He hinted also that Italian law on property did not see the matter in the same light as English law, and pointed out, with dangerous courtesy, that it looked very much as if the law in England concerning the property of a married woman was about to be materially changed – to her benefit. It was that last letter that had caused Tom to despatch Edward Martineau to Italy almost without giving him time to pack.

Signor Forcole's offices were in a charming saffron washed building in the Piazza San Martino with an

140

arched Renaissance balcony on the first floor and an inner courtyard tiled in marble diamonds where a fountain played into the mouths of four upended stone dolphins. In a huge cool room looking down onto this pretty sight, Signor Forcole, small and grave with a short white beard and immaculate linen, settled Edward into a high carved chair padded in crimson cut velvet, gave him cold white wine in an ancient gilded Venetian glass and a plate of tiny macaroons, and composed himself to listen.

When Edward had finished, he refilled the Venetian goblet and explained in careful, charmingly accented English, about the Buonvisi, whom he had the honour to represent, just as Edward represented the Taverners. Historically, Lucca was a city state of tremendous prosperity, notably for merchants in the early sixteenth century and for bankers, such as the Buonvisi, in the latter years of the same century. Lucca had minted its own money and from the mulberry trees that grew so plentifully in the lush countryside outside its walls, developed a silk trade whose products were prized all over Europe. The Buonvisi family had been bankers extraordinaire with agents all over France, in Germany and Portugal, even as far flung as Constantinople. Until the end of the eighteenth century the family had been of immeasurable consequence, building many of the beautiful villas around Lucca, but regrettably dying out since then except for one minor line, and being subsequently forced to live in comparative seclusion and simplicity. What Signor Martineau must not forget, however, was the undying significance of their lineage and of the house which extended to all those who joined it, even foreigners. The Lucchese were something of an exception to every rule; their little state had preserved

141

its independence until only thirty-five years before, the only Tuscan state to do so.

Edward replied, somewhat but not entirely soothed by the wine and the surroundings, that he did not question one word of what Signor Forcole had so interestingly said, but that none of it seemed to have any relevance to his mission to Lucca.

'There is no suggestion of any imputation upon the reputation of the Buonvisi, Signor, but you must acknowledge that they are sheltering my client's wife who has taken beneath their roof property which was not hers to take. Any involvement arises simply from that fact.'

Signor Forcole put the tips of his fingers together.

'It is indeed true that Lady Taverner lives at the Villa Buonvisi. It is the magnanimity of the Duke that permits this. But in no way can he be held responsible for her actions if those actions contravene English domestic law.'

'Can he not bring pressure to bear upon her, as both brother-in-law and guardian in effect, to do what is honourable, let alone what is legal?'

'There is,' Signor Forcole said very, very quietly, 'a little complication—'

Six months after her arrival in Italy, Rosamund announced that she wished to go to Rome. Her purpose, she said, was purely religious. Judging from the excessive piety of her behaviour, and the hours she spent alone in the Buonvisi chapel, nobody had any reason to doubt her. Her sister would have accompanied her, but was in the seventh month of a trying pregnancy and it was judged best she did not attempt to travel. Rosamund was away from Lucca for a month, returning exhilarated and fervent from her trip, which had consisted of visits to convents it seemed, conversations with pious old Roman duchesses and hours upon her knees in all the major churches of the capital. Nothing was thought or made of it. Two months later, a second son was born to the Duchessa whose frailty absorbed the whole household to the exclusion of all else. When letters came from Bath on the subject of the jewellery, Rosamund forwarded them unanswered to Signor Forcole, requesting that her reply should be what it had always been, namely that the jewels were safe and that she had by no means decided never to return.

'Then comes the little complication. Last summer came a festival at the Villa Buonvisi, to celebrate the fifth birthday of the eldest boy, and the visible strengthening of his brother. All the noble houses of Lucca were invited. During the preparations, the Duchessa asked Lady Taverner if she would at last wear some of the celebrated jewellery on such a magnificent occasion. Lady Taverner replied that she was unable to do so as she had sold every last gem. Permit me to refill your glass.'

'No,' Edward said, 'I thank you, but no. *Sold*—'

'To a most distinguished and reputable jeweller in Rome who believed Lady Taverner to be an English noblewoman distressed for money abroad. It is not uncommon. The jewellery has since been resold all over Europe, every piece bought with the utmost propriety and in the best of good faith.'

Edward pulled out his handkerchief and covered his eyes.

'I must make the position quite clear to you,' Signor Forcole said gently. 'Under Italian law, a purchaser of items who buys in good faith and in a proper manner

143

acquires a good title to those objects he buys notwith-standing any defect there might be in the seller's title or in the title of previous sellers. In this case even the seller, the Cedri Brothers of the Via Condotti, had no defect having bought themselves in good faith and a proper manner. It seems some defect may indeed lie with Lady Taverner as seller to the Cedri Brothers but as all transactions happened here in Italy, Italian domestic law must apply, making such a defect irrelevant to the subsequent sales.'

Edward's initial dismay was being rapidly overtaken by anger at finding himself so outmanoeuvred, and so ill prepared. Vaguely in the recesses of his mind he could recall some general rule of international law which said that property must be governed by the law of the land from which it came, but he could remember little and that little only dimly.

'I regret it, Signor.'

'I would be obliged,' Edward said, restraining his rage with difficulty, 'if you would arrange for me to see Lady Taverner and, if possible, the Duke.'

'I must regret again. It is not possible. It is essential, for all the reasons I told you of, that the Buonvisi family are kept from even a breath of ill repute.'

'Then I shall go to the villa myself.'

'I fear you will find it empty. The family are removed to a summer house only three days ago.' He opened a drawer in his desk and took out an envelope. 'I have here a letter from Lady Taverner to her husband. I have no idea of the contents. My instructions are simply to give it into your hands.'

Edward took himself off with as little ceremony as he was allowed to get away with, and walked rapidly past the church of San Giovanni, ignoring its celebrated west front, to the Piazza del Giglio. He sat down at a café table in the shade of a plane tree and ordered coffee. It came, thick and black and bitter in a heavy white cup. Edward regarded it with distaste. He drummed with his fingers on the table top, gazed irritatedly about him at the pretty, sunny square, glared at the little neoclassical theatre opposite, scowled at passers-by, and finally got up, his coffee untasted, and strode off in search of a carriage.

An ancient fiacre eventually consented to drive him to the Villa Buonvisi. It was an entrancing drive up into the luxuriant hills above the plain of Lucca, among myrtles and lemon groves, winding up a white dust road along whose verges cypresses marched in plumy pairs. Fretting in the fiacre's dusty and airless interior, Edward saw none of it. He felt responsible for the catastrophe – he was responsible in large measure – and he felt too that the combination of Rosamund's personality, the dreadful lapse of time since the jewels had gone and the rules of Italian civil law had brought him up short against an impenetrable wall. He hated Tuscany for her grasshopper-ticking hills, her beauty, her charm and her thyme scented high summer air. He hated Signor Forcole for his dapper courtesy and clear headedness. He hated the sheer amiability of every Italian he had dealt with since he landed at Leghorn, and when the fiacre stopped at the most marvellous rusting gates of baroque ironwork, he hated the Buonvisi more than any other of their countrymen.

He indicated to the driver that he now preferred to walk. A drive ran up from the gates between pillars crowned with urns and cypress trees, a weedy and neglected drive in which he could see, in his present mood, no romance. It ended in a prospect so lovely he almost despaired, a crumbling terracotta washed baroque house, peeling shutters linked against the sun, whose long frescoed portico looked down a cascade of balustraded steps to a pool and a ruined garden and, five miles below, within its ancient walls, the little city of Lucca. Winters here, he thought crossly, imagining long driving cold rains seeping into the soft rust walls, blotting out the view, reducing the hanging vegetation to slimy strands, winters here must be terrible.

A small, square man in black emerged from the portico and asked if he could help. Edward offered him a card and said that he wished to speak to the Duke and to Lady Taverner. The man bowed and replied that il Duce and the family were in the mountains. Where? Edward demanded. The man bowed again and said that it was not possible to say. When would they be back? Again, it was not possible to say.

'You will be good enough to present this to the Duke,' Edward said, insisting upon his card being taken.

'Of course,' the man said. With great politeness, he indicated Edward's path back to the gate. There was nothing to do but to go, past a choked Bacchus' head whose fountain had dried up, past a broken nymph clothed only in pink climbing geraniums, past a fat putti face down in the gravel, tumbled from his plinth, to the gates and the fiacre and the drive down to Lucca and the telegraph office.

For a week he struggled on. Two more interviews with Signor Forcole brought no more than copies of the impeccable receipts from the Cedri Brothers of the pieces they had sold, more white wine, more implacable regrets. Telegraphs to his clerk in Bath brought the bloomy news that in the only relevant important legal precedent – Cammell v. Sewell, 1858 – judicial opinion had eventually decided that the law of the land in which goods were disposed of must take precedence over the law of the land in which the original owner was domiciled. *Lex situs*, it seemed, must prevail; if goods are disposed of in a manner binding according to the law of the country where they actually are, however they got there, that disposition is binding everywhere. There seemed no way out of facing the fact that Taverner jewels now gleamed perfectly properly around two Italian, three French, a Dutch and a German neck, to cite but a few. Worse than that, Edward had to go home and say so.

The saying so, standing there tense in the tower room, took very little time. When he had finished, he bowed his head and looked at his white knuckles tense on the chair back and waited for the fury. Charlotte and Elizabeth began simultaneously on a volley of outrage, demands that more enquiries should be made, refusal to believe that the matter could be taken no further, insistence that Rosamund should at least hand back the money she had received from the sale of the jewellery. Tom said nothing. Catherine put her arm around her nephew, silently offering him her watch and watch chain as a distraction. Edward handed Tom Rosamund's letter.

'She informs me,' Tom said levelly, a moment later, 'that she will use the proceeds of the jewellery, which she always regarded as her own, to support her for the future. She does not wish to draw upon the allowance I make her. She wishes to be free of all connection with the Taverners. She declines to enter into any further correspondence on this or any other matter.'

Tommy raised his head from the watch and looked gravely at his aunt. Catherine, who alone of her family,

147

felt it wrong that Rosamund's son should be brought up to regard his mother wholly as a villainess, looked gravely back. In the new clamour made by his mother and his elder sister, Tom rose slowly to his feet and said with great emphasis that he had now had enough of the whole affair, ten years in all of the most unbelievably wearying and destructive wrangling, and that he wished to hear no more about it ever, from anyone.

'You are not serious!' Charlotte exclaimed, almost leaping from her chair. 'You cannot mean that you will let the matter rest here, that you will not try to see justice done!'

'I do mean it,' Tom said, moving inexorably towards the door. 'It is but a drop in the ocean of our troubles. We will drown finally if we expend one more penny in what seems to me a hopeless pursuit. In any case,' he paused in the doorway and looked back at them all, 'I simply do not care. Not any more. I do not give a damn, I find, not a *damn*.'

If Tommy seemed an uncomplicated child, it was to his aunt Catherine he largely owed his open and sunny disposition. He depended upon her for his lessons, for honest replies to questions, for stimulus and for the satisfaction of most curiosities. He turned to his nurse for daily routine, to his father and old Bradstock for information on the absorbing outside world, to young Fred Bradstock for interesting disclosures on the natural appetites, to his aunt Elizabeth for peppermint lozenges, and to his spaniel for comfort. He tried not to turn to his grandmother for anything. His mother – whose portrait had been removed by his grandmother and discreetly replaced by his aunt Catherine – he thought of as dead. There seemed to be no other explanation of her.

When he left the tower room that September afternoon, one hand in Catherine's, the other tightly around her little watch in his breeches' pocket, Rosamund's deadness did not feel as complete as usual. The letter his father had read out had been written by his mother. His mother lived in Italy, he had been told that. If they had said Heaven or Peking it would have made no difference to his opinion of her complete and final absence from his life. Italy was utterly unrelated to Buscombe and she was stuck there; that he could see and accept. But this letter unsettled the finality of Italy. Letters came from person to person, by some ordinary human agency, very much alive and everyday. Letters did not come from people who were buried in the earth like Mrs Bradstock had been, when she died and all the servants said poor soul, but what a mercy and what a relief for Bradstock, looks ten years younger already. He gave Catherine's hand a tug.

'Where is Italy?'

'Southern Europe. If you cross the Channel, and drive all the way down France, you will come to Italy. It sticks out into the Mediterranean Sea like a long boot.'

'Can you go there?'

'Oh yes. Plenty of people do. That is where Mr Martineau has just been.'

'And he did come back!'

'Most certainly.'

Tommy thought for a moment, and then said calmly, 'Why does my mother not come back?'

'Because she would rather live in Italy.'

This seemed perfectly logical. Tommy had, after all, no need of her. There was not a gap in his life that he was aware of that a mother might fill – indeed, he was not at all sure what a mother did. His cousin Victoria, who was twelve and whose bravery filled him with a desperate awe, had a mother who behaved much like Aunt Catherine, except that she was crosser, which did not say much for mothers.

He followed Catherine into the conservatory. It was roofed with the blue trumpets of morning glories and gave off the scented warm and earthy steams that made it so particular a place, even in the winter.

'Can I go to Italy when I am grown up?'

'Of course you can.'

'Why does my mother like Italy?'

'Because she is not very well and Italy is warmer than Buscombe and because she can live with her sister.'

'Is it warm like in here?'

'Drier. Dry and warm.'

'Oh look,' said Tommy, 'an awful slug. A black one.'

'Put it on a trowel and take it outside. But not near the delphiniums or it will eat them.'

Returning, Tommy said, 'When can I go to Italy?'

Catherine put down her scissors and looked at him.

'When you are fifteen.'

'Will you come with me?'

'Yes,' Catherine said.

Charlotte summoned a family conference. It was inevitable she should do so, and equally inevitable that such a gathering could decide nothing. Ignoring the charms of the drawing room with its new glass doors thrown open into the depths of the conservatory, the family moved, impelled by traditional instinct, towards the tower room. The drawing room must be reserved for more lighthearted things.

Aunt Rachel, in pale grey silk and violet ribbons, was

escorted by Uncle John, briefly home from the exhil-
arations of defying the Zulus and prepared to bring
precisely the same straightforward prejudices and bluff
energies to family affairs that he applied to foreign ones.
Robert and Mary entered with the air of people who had
seen all this kind of thing coming, warned against it, had
their advice ignored and were now realizing the tired
harvest of being right to no effect. They had brought
Charles and Victoria with them, ostensibly for a family
occasion however grim, but in reality, in Robert's mind,
to impress upon Charlie the awful consequences of a
lack of responsibility towards people and property.
Charlie, distressingly, showed a marked indifference
towards both. Both cousins were then excluded from
the tower room by their great-aunt and sent to amuse
their cousin Tommy in the conservatory. Elizabeth, still
grieving volubly over the loss of the jewels she had
particularly looked forward to inheriting, took up her
seat next to Catherine, who was thinking longingly of
the children in the conservatory, and hoping that
Victoria was not inciting Tommy to attempt feats
beyond his agility or courage. Charlotte was in her
element; Tom almost entirely silent.

September sun fell in broad yellow bars through the
lancet windows onto the circle of chairs, the central
table and its rattling castor oil plant, the ring of heads
and hands, tweed clad shoulders and spreading silk
skirts. This is my family, Catherine thought, and I know
exactly what each one of them is thinking and is going
to say and how inconclusive it will all be. My uncle John,
not being in the direct line of inheritance, will tell everybody what should have been done now that it is too
late to do anything, and on the drive home, will empha-
size to his wife what a sorry mess Tom has got the estate

and the family into, which is of course partly Tom's own fault and partly my mother's. Aunt Mary will say what else could you ever expect from a family as pig-headed as the Taverners, and Aunt Rachel will, with a sly look at me masked in false sentiment, say how glad she is that Harry is in the army, now a captain, and safe from the distress of witnessing yet a further family humiliation. Elizabeth will say how especially hurt she is not to be able to wear the particularly fine set of pearls and aquamarines to which she had looked forward since she was a child, and my mother will volubly and repeatedly blame Rosamund for everything and demand that we all rush out to Italy in a body and make a tremendous fuss. I will say nothing and poor Tom will say as little as he can get away with, and at the end Uncle Robert will get up and remark that in the absence of Edward Martineau, they lack final confirmation of the legal position, so can decide nothing, which makes the whole gathering as pointless as he told Aunt Mary over breakfast this morning that it would be. She stood up.

'What are you doing, Catherine?' Charlotte asked.

'I am going to see to the children.'

'Nurse is with the children. Please sit down. There is much to discuss.'

'No,' said Catherine, 'there is nothing for me to discuss. I have no opinion on the matter except that, like Tom, I should like to hear no more of it. I have nothing to contribute to any discussion.'

Charlotte said furiously, 'Sit down!'

Catherine looked at her brother.

'Please let her go,' he said tiredly. 'For two pins I would go with her.'

Aunt Rachel remarked to Elizabeth in an audible aside that Catherine had not been herself, not quite in control of herself, you understand, since the regrettable business over her poor cousin. Elizabeth looked blankly back and said that as Catherine, plainly, if incomprehensibly, did not care about jewellery that was her rightful inheritance, she did not see why she should stay.

'May I go?'

Charlotte nodded with unnecessary vehemence.

In the conservatory, Tommy and Victoria were floating beetles in a watering can. Nurse was nowhere to be seen and Charlie, folded up awkwardly into a monumentally uncomfortable wrought-iron armchair, was absorbedly reading.

'Where's Nurse?'

Victoria looked up. She was a neatly made child with a determined expression and her mother's glossy dark hair. In order to facilitate movement, she had deftly tucked up her skirts and petticoats revealing, to Tommy's interested admiration, very pretty legs encased in grey and white striped stockings.

'Out there.'

She was supposed to call Catherine, Aunt Catherine, but never did. It was a compliment on Victoria's part.

Under a mulberry tree, Nurse was composedly mending. It was a waste of her skill and enthusiasm with a needle that Tommy's clothes did not have torn frills and tucks and ruffles constantly needing her attention.

Catherine said, 'What is Charlie reading?'

'I don't know. Some book about old stones as usual. Black beetles are very good swimmers, you know.'

Catherine went over and sat down by Charlie. He unfolded himself slowly and stood up.

'Please don't stand up, Charlie.'

He sat down again. 'Have they finished?'

'No. I came out before they started. There suddenly

seemed no point in staying. What are you reading?'

'The usual thing,' he said, grinning and holding out the Schliemann she had bought for him years before.

'When do you go back to school?'

'Tomorrow. It's my last half. Then six months in Europe, then Oxford.'

'Charlie!'

'I'm seventeen, you know.'

'I don't feel that I was seventeen very long ago. Or poor Tom. Even less time ago.' She looked round the conservatory and up at the yellow walls of the house, at her own bedroom window, through the frond-obscured glass roof. 'He had such ambitions – such high hopes – he so loves this place.' She let her gaze fall on Tommy, kneeling on the tiled floor and poking, giggling at the water's surface with a stick. 'It will all be his, of course. I am rather glad that for the moment he does not know what that means.'

'Poor little chap.'

'Poor?'

'It doesn't seem to me,' Charlie said, 'that inheriting something like this is much of a pleasure. Ever since I can remember Buscombe has been talked of as a problem, as some great burden that you are not allowed to put down, yet haven't the strength to carry. I mean, when Father dies and The Hall becomes mine, it is simply a big house I inherit, it isn't a sacred trust. I can sell it. I probably will, it's most undistinguished. But this—'

Catherine looked at him with affection.

'What a good thing you are for the family, Charlie. A most refreshing change. Too many Taverners have lived here for too many hundreds of years and have built up a sense of duty that is sometimes positively stifling.

Even I have it in some measure. If I hadn't, I would be a captain's wife by now and I would have seen Malta, Hong Kong, Singapore and Ireland—'

Charlie did not hear her. He was thinking of the idea that had just come to him, unbidden, of sometime in the future selling The Hall. The freedom this abruptly suggested was tremendously exciting. He looked at the little boy on the floor.

'Poor Tommy.'

'You don't know,' Catherine said, looking too. 'He might be just what the house needs. He might turn out able to manage everything. His start in life is unorthodox enough, goodness knows.'

Charlie stood up and stretched and was instantly doubled up by coughing. Well trained, Catherine took no notice. When he had finished, he said breathlessly,

'You see, what I should hate so violently would be knowing I was so many people's little white hope.'

'In your case,' said his sister from the floor with great clarity, 'there is absolutely no chance of *that*.'

CHAPTER EIGHT

November 1888

To celebrate his daughter Rose's twentieth birthday, Arnold du Cros took her and a few of her chosen friends to the new Gilbert and Sullivan opera, *The Yeoman of the Guard*. Rose enjoyed it unashamedly but was conscious that one of the party, Charlie Taverner, was fidgeting. In the interval, Charlie told his host – with unnecessary emphasis, Rose thought – that almost simultaneously, St Petersburg was hearing Tchaikovsky's new symphony, his fifth, and that he wished himself in Russia with them. Arnold du Cros replied smoothly that it was a wish he rather shared.

'Have I offended your old man?' Charlie said to Rose.

'Yes,' Rose said, 'but it does not signify because he is more than a match for you.'

Charlie loved Rose. He always had, from the far off days when she came to his sister Victoria's nursery and he had had to defend her sweet blond vagueness from Victoria's frequently awful purposefulness.

'I only came tonight to see you. I can't bear all this trumpery, jokey, amateurish stuff. I wish the Tower of London would collapse in revenge on Mr Gilbert's facetious head.'

'But as my father's guest, it is hardly manners to say so.'

'Oh Rose,' Charlie said.

Where had she come from, changeling child of these two massive dark parents? Their house was wonderful of course, the most intelligently furnished house Charlie knew, full of enterprisingly chosen pieces – Arnold du Cros was a great patron of new craftsmen – but usually populated by pretty awful people. Charlie was slightly afraid of du Cros, he seemed so much more in charge of things than most men Charlie knew, and of course was enviably in possession of his daughter's heart and admiration.

'He has wonderful *judgement*, you see,' Rose said once. 'I think he often understands people better than they do themselves, and therefore can decide what course of action they should take. He is truly wise.'

In the second act, Charlie could not sit next to Rose. On one side of him was Mrs du Cros, whom he liked although he was never able to think of anything to say to her, and on the other a modern young woman dressed in the disconcerting loose and flowing lines dictated by the Aesthetic Movement who informed him, irrelevantly, as the curtain rose once more upon the Tower of London and little Phoebe, that the only shop in London with any kind of progressive taste was Liberty of Regent Street.

'Progressive?' Charlie said. 'Imported lattice screens and ginger jars *progressive*?'

'My dear man,' said the young woman, rattling her amber beads, 'you clearly do not understand the true meaning of aestheticism.'

Charlie said, too loudly, 'Rubbish.' Mrs du Cros begged him to be quiet.

'I am so sorry—'

'Try to remember,' Mrs du Cros said, knowing precisely how to appeal to him to behave, 'that this is Rose's party.'

He tried. He thought about Rose and how incomprehensible it was that she should *enjoy* these folderols; he thought about what the Liberty young woman had said to him and how much he should like to test her intelligence and to explain to her that Whistler and Oscar Wilde and tasselled oriental silk cushions from Regent Street were only part of a cult, as opposed to a true movement, which used aestheticism as a label to make itself seem more interesting; he thought how much he disliked the lavish plush and gold interior of the Savoy Theatre and how equally much he would like to lecture the entire audience upon the merits of the most modern architecture – which brought him to the thing he thought about most these days: his quarrel with his father.

It was a difference whose very birth Charlie still found bewildering. All his conscious life – and he was very, very sure about this – he had been consumingly, tirelessly, visibly interested in buildings and their history. He knew perfectly well that he had never, throughout the cosy days in the schoolroom and bleak days at Winchester, been more than casually interested in anything else at all. He loved reading, he loved the acquisition of knowledge but nothing fired him with quite the same single minded absorption and appetite as architecture. He not only was perfectly certain of this, but was equally certain that this one overriding enthusiasm had been plain for all to see since he built his first unsteady tower of bricks on the nursery floor over twenty years before.

It now appeared that his father had been so equally fervently besotted by his own ambition for Charlie, that he had succeeded in ignoring completely Charlie's own desires for himself. It was incomprehensible to Charlie that Robert should have been able to disregard entirely his son's utter indifference to public affairs and political life purely because it was the reverse of what he wanted to believe. It seemed that Robert was planning a campaign, to begin on Charlie's twenty-fourth birthday in a few months' time, to ease himself out of his seat in Parliament, replacing himself with a son who mirrored his own beliefs and had the energy of youth to push them forward. The campaign was on the verge of collapse because the son refused point blank to have anything to do with it.

'I should be miserable and miserably unsuccessful,' Charlie said. 'As much as you would be if commanded to be a dancing master to young ladies. I want to be an architect. It is all I have ever wanted to be. There is nothing else I want to be except that I should quite like to be an archaeologist as well.'

'Do you not care,' Robert shouted, 'what happens to this country?'

'Of course I care, sir. I care very much indeed. But I have not the aptitude, nor the gift with other men, to be able to contribute anything worthwhile. No country can possibly benefit from being run by men who have no talent or enthusiasm for doing so.'

Charlie did not even look much like a Taverner. He had his mother's Irish colouring – softened slightly by an injection of Taverner fairness – and he was tall, and lean and stooped a little. Asthma still attacked him, periodically, but he would never have it spoken of.

'If I let them,' he said to his sister Victoria, 'then they

do it all the time and it entirely conditions how they think of me.'

Victoria, who had never doubted but that, in parent–child relationships the child must have the upper hand, entirely agreed. She was sympathetic to his cause, though considered architecture a peculiar and pointless way of life when one might be changing the course of history, and so were his Taverner cousins over at Buscombe. He had ridden over a great deal recently to talk to them, and both Tom – for whom he had a particular devotion – and Catherine were as clear as he was himself that his bent had been unmistakably marked out since he was a tiny child.

Buscombe was not an especially happy house to go to, but it still had the undeniable attraction of a house which felt lived-in. It was a mess to look at, Charlie considered, sprouting random towers and conservatories and stable blocks, and he knew it was precariously maintained by renting out most of the suitable land for shooting, and by the income that his aunt and her daughters drew from the coalfields outside Nottingham. He knew that each year his cousin Tom sold a few more shares or acres to meet the inevitable gap between income and expenditure, and he came to know, by degrees, that the seat in Parliament he would do anything rather than occupy was silently coveted by Tom. It seemed to Charlie the perfect solution, satisfying everyone's ambitions and keeping the thing in the family which was what his father wanted. But – no, Tom said.

'No? But I thought that was the one thing upon which you had set your heart!'

'I have. But your father has not. We had rather strangled discussions about it over – oh, twelve years ago or so – and he has always been adamant that the next member for North Somerset is you.'

'And if I do not want to be?'

'He wants you to be too much for himself to be able to acknowledge that.'

'Well,' Charlie said, 'he will have to think again. Short of trussing me up and carrying me bodily to Westminster, he simply is not going to get me there. And don't tell me he would not rather have you, if he can't have me, than a stranger, a non-Taverner.'

'Can you afford to defy him?'

Charlie shrugged.

'I've four hundred a year of my own from my mother, so even if he were to cut off what he gives me, I shouldn't exactly starve. But I don't think he would do that. He is not a vengeful man, just rather unimaginative. He cannot visualize being anybody other than himself.'

'And can you?'

Charlie grinned.

'Not very well. I am his son after all. But I think I do it fractionally better than he does.'

Tom said, 'So what will you do now?'

'I'm going to London. Charles Voysey has agreed to take me on as a pupil.'

'*Voysey?*'

'Yes.'

'But, my dear Charlie, he is quite extraordinary, unorthodox, no respect at all for the traditional styles—'

'Precisely,' said Charlie.

And now here he was, Charlie Taverner, living in rooms at the top of a house in Swan Walk and spending his days on the downpipes and slate specifications for a projected country house near Malvern called Castle

Morton. His head, so long filled with the symmetry and splendours of antiquity, now swam with Voysey's highly individual view, a world away from the Gothic of his contemporaries, a view of long low roughcast houses, with little leaded mullioned windows, steep gabled roofs, buttresses, small rooms filled with furniture designed by Voysey, fabrics designed by Voysey, wallpaper, accessories, even stained glass designed by Voysey. *That*, Charlie wanted to explain to the pseudo-aesthetic young woman in amber beads, was progressive – and English to boot. Progressiveness necessarily means rebelling against the established order of things which, at this juncture in his life, suited Charlie fine.

In Swan Walk he had a large bare room looking at the river, and a small bare room looking at a wall, and in the mornings Mrs Marsh, who dwelt darkly in the basement and had been in service in her youth, brought him shaving water and breakfast. In the evenings, if he wanted it, she brought him chops and made unenthusiastic enquiries about his laundry, but mostly, he did not want it. Charlie had discovered Chelsea.

If it wasn't for Rose, that was where he and his fellow pupils would be now, masquerading as friends of Burne-Jones, tipsily composing appalling prose poems in execrable imitation of William Morris's *Dream of John Ball*, carefully artlessly draped in blowing scarves and full skirted coats. Charlie loved it, even if he couldn't believe in it. The freshness of vision, after rural Somerset and a way of life fundamentally unchanged for two centuries, was intoxicating as was the passionate concern for the visual and the craftsmanship of things. So was the freedom. His sister Victoria envied the freedom so badly, she wrote, she nearly burst with it.

'I have decided that I shall have to leave home, just

as you have done. I am eighteen after all. But the question is how. What do you think of journalism? I have read several articles in the *Pall Mall Gazette* by someone called Flora Shaw who seems to be the magazine's correspondent in Egypt. Well, if she can, I can. I am going to write to her. Have you any other suggestions?'

Charlie invited her to Swan Walk but she was not allowed to come.

'Such a pity,' he wrote, 'I was even going to make my bed. Or ask Mrs Marsh. Don't despair – it may not feel like it, but you have plenty of time.'

So curious that Victoria and Rose, only two years apart in age and from similarly prosperous and sheltered backgrounds, should be so absolutely different – different in what they wanted as well as in how they lived. You couldn't *live* with Victoria – she would drive one insane with her determination, her voluble persistence, but living with Rose was all Charlie felt he needed to make life so absolutely perfect – well, that, and, if he was honest, his father's rage to subside – that he would have nothing else left to wish for.

The final chords crashed and boomed, the curtains rose and fell interminably upon the enormous cast. Charlie made a stupendous effort to be decidedly and conventionally grateful.

'When will we see you in Somerset?' Arnold du Cros asked.

Charlie grinned.

'When Voysey is commissioned to build a house there.'

'I like his work. My only objection is that the interiors are too small for a man my size.'

Charlie said, 'I'm sorry I've been a bore this evening, sir.'

'To prove I've forgiven you, come back to Lowndes Square for supper. It's a surprise for Rose. She thinks the evening ends here.'

Out of gratitude and enjoyment, Charlie drank too much and talked too much. He was seated next to Rose and that was as inebriating as the champagne, particularly as she was so happy herself that she could not stop laughing. The dining room at Lowndes Square had been newly panelled in wood and mirror glass in a stylized pattern of lily pads. Charlie toasted it. He toasted his hostess, his host and Rose. He even toasted Gilbert and Sullivan.

There was a moment, as dessert came, when the conversation flowed away from his end of the table, leaving him and Rose suddenly together and quite private.

'Shall I peel you a peach?'

'I couldn't eat another thing—'

'Well, something smaller. A grape?'

'I can't *bear* grapes peeled—'

'Rose.'

'Yes.'

'Are you listening to me?'

'Yes.'

'Rose, will you marry me?'

'Um,' she said.

'Rose. Will you?'

'Ask me again,' she said, 'when you're sober.'

'I am getting nowhere,' Robert Taverner said, glaring at January out of his business room window, 'am I?'

Mary, in the swivel chair at his desk, took a deep breath and held it.

'I'm sixty-six. I have a business that bores me now but which flourishes whether I trouble myself with it or not.

I have a seat in Parliament I no longer want now that every last turnip-headed labourer has the vote, and local government is going to take over all the administration that was Westminster's. I have a son designing middle-class cottages, living in a garret, who fantasizes Arnold du Cros will let him have his only child. I have a daughter who wants the vote too and tries to run away unless I hobble the horses and padlock her bedroom door. I have a nephew who has made, in under twenty years, such a mess of the family estate that he is virtually living off his mother and his sisters. I have you. Of that whole catalogue, only the last item gives me any pleasure at all. I am very angry, very tired and very disappointed.'

He had not finished. Mary, who knew it, played idly with the little brass canister of lead shot which held the pens upright on his desk.

'Politically,' Robert said, 'I am an old Whig gentleman. For years I believed I was not, that I was in fact a new Liberal, but my reaction to recent events has shown me my true colours.'

When he got worked up like this, over Charlie, or the Franchise Bills, or the surrender to the Boers, or that appalling debacle in Khartoum, he always ended up blaming Gladstone. He couldn't forgive Gladstone for not remaining admirable, nor could he bear, being a believer in self-control, Gladstone's soul-baring style of government.

'We have made such a muddle of Ireland!' he cried to Mary. 'We will never understand the Irish mind!'

She regarded him.

'That's for sure,' she said.

What was also for sure was that he found he wanted now to go back to the old way of running things. How

165

could the country be governed if every barely literate labourer was allowed his say?

'We can't go back,' he said and his voice was thick with misery. 'And we are going forward the wrong way. Salisbury is the wrong man. I haven't got the energy any more to see that a new way of doing things is a good way of doing things, but I'm experienced enough to know that you cannot halt progress just because you don't like the look of it.'

The climax, Mary saw, was coming. She took her hands off the desk and folded them in her lap.

'You see, Charles has precisely the right cast of mind for these changes. He is not afraid to go forward. He is not held back by any sense of tradition. He brings an entirely fresh mind to problems at a time when the most fundamental changes in parliamentary thinking, in government generally, are happening. And yet he is my son. He is a Taverner. He is my natural successor. And this is the moment, with the new single member constituencies, for the change to take place most easily. You must talk to him, Mary. You must make him see the sheer logic of it all. He couldn't resist that.'

Mary rose from the desk and joined her husband by the window. The view was the discouraging one of a large, dull, well-stocked garden deep in its mid-winter sleep, too early yet for even the most intrepid snowdrop.

'Robert.'

He grunted.

'You'll have to face the fact that nothing on this earth will get Charlie even to consider Parliament. It's no good ranting at him or at me. He has never shown the slightest interest and I don't believe he ever will. The pity of it is that Victoria would make a splendid parliamentarian, and there she is a girl, so quite out of the question. But you'll be driving yourself insane going on at Charlie and you'll be driving me there with you. I'm telling you.'

He turned angrily towards her.

'Have you not heard one word I've said? The logic of my argument?'

'Every one,' she said calmly. 'And most of them several times before. Don't talk to me of logic, Robert Taverner, or I'll walk out on you this minute. Would you think it logical to be forced to be an architect, a calling for which you'd neither taste nor talent, when your whole soul cried out for Parliament? You'd fight tooth and nail. And that's no more than Charlie is doing in reverse. How do you know what your father would have said to your going into business when hardly a man? I'll bet you he would have said no son of his was going to ruin the family name by touching trade and that you were too young to know your own mind in any case. Your luck was that he wasn't there to say either of those things, so you were free. That is all Charlie is trying to be! Don't mistake me, I've no opinion at all of the houses he works on, but he is as entitled to his own life as you were to yours.'

Robert left the window and stamped around the room for a while, impeded in his progress by book-laden tables, atlas cases, mahogany filing cabinets, and a series of captain's chairs on huge groaning swivels in which he liked to spin and think. The walls bore a kind of chronicle of his life in photographs, framed in black, and a large water stain, memory of a moment of temper eight years before, when Mr Gladstone had swept unexpectedly back to power, and Mary, understandably feeling that her husband would be delighted, had put a huge vase of sweet williams on his desk. Robert, who had been scenting something he did not like at all in Gladstone's handling of Ireland, flung vase and flowers at the wall. Servants had picked up the mess but Mary had spiritedly refused to have the wallpaper, a damask rose print in two shades of deep green, replaced. The stain spread to resemble a map of the Iberian peninsula and Robert grew quite used to it. He stood in front of it now and traced the inlet on the coast that might be the mouth of the River Tagus, and said over his shoulder,

'What do you suggest I do, then?'

Mary let a tiny moment pass before she said,

'Offer the chance to Tom. He'd have to win it for himself of course—'

'*Tom!*'

'Yes.'

'Are you mad? He is all passion, no reason. He cannot think straight to save his life. Do you remember Parnell, keeping the house up for thirty-six hours while he ranted on? That would be Tom!'

Mary rustled back to the desk.

'I don't think so, Robert. Not now. Ten years ago, maybe. But he's sadder and wiser, poor Tom. And he'll be forty in nine months.' She paused, and then she said, 'It might be just the thing for the estate too.'

'How?'

'If Tom got as involved in campaigning for a seat as it is in his nature to do, he would have to hire a farm manager again as you have been wishing him to these last ten years.'

Robert shook his head.

'There'll never be money in land again. Commerce and industry are taking all the profits that used to go into the land, and that won't change for generations.'

'All right,' Mary said, 'Buscombe will never provide

the income it did for your brother, but at least it won't be a dwindling shabby place that's a shame and a disgrace to us all. It might find its self-respect again.'

'Come on, Mary. Out of my chair. I've work to do.'

'Robert—'

'Yes, yes. Don't fuss me. I have a hundred things to do before I leave for London, and by the late train too by the look of things.'

She rose and went to the door in silence, but as she closed it behind her, he shouted, 'I'll think about it! Don't nag me! I'll think about it!'

Soon after the Easter recess, in the same week that Arnold du Cros told his daughter Rose she might marry Charles Taverner if she really and earnestly still wanted to do so in two years' time, Robert Taverner applied for the Chiltern Hundreds. To the thirty-seven thousand inhabitants of the county constituency of North Somerset, most of whose menfolk had only had the vote for four years, the matter was intensely interesting since it would give them, at a by-election, only the second chance to flex their enfranchised muscles. The candidates were equally interesting. The Liberal candidate, in surprising succession to his uncle, was Sir Thomas Taverner of Buscombe Priory; the Conservative, Mr Arthur Creighton of Codrington. Sir Thomas was known to have land; Mr Creighton to have money. Miss Rosamund Creighton had become Lady Taverner sixteen years ago, but had disappeared to Italy soon after a hailstorm of scandal and acrimony. Mr Creighton, it was believed, was unable subsequently to regard the Taverners as anything other than the root cause of a mental breakdown that had deprived him of his daughter for ever. This personal animosity added a nice extra edge to political differences.

It seemed to be a pretty equally weighted contest. Creighton had the money – electioneering expenses couldn't come to much less than a thousand in a constituency this size – but Taverner had the name and all the old landed associations that weighed still so heavily in county politics. The present prime minister, Lord Salisbury, was a Tory but it was the last prime minister, Gladstone, a Liberal, who had brought the vote to the farms and small industries of the constituencies. The constituency was traditionally Conservative – as was the case in almost all the English counties – but the Reform Acts had injected a heady sniff of change into the air that blew across North Somerset. It was too an unexpected excitement to have the seat contested; nobody could remember when the Member – once Whig, now Liberal – had ever had any opposition to his election. The constituency sat back expectantly.

The one thing it did not expect, and was much astonished at, was the fervour with which Tom Taverner campaigned. Posters appeared in every village from Bath to Shepton Mallet, from Clevedon in the west to Frome in the east; you could read the name 'Taverner' on barn and cottage walls, on gable ends and gateposts in Kingston Seymour and Chapel Allerton, in Priddy and Binegar and Norton St Philip, in Whitchurch and Mells, in Rode and Rudge, in Holcombe and Butcombe and Compton Dando – anywhere where a huddle of houses meant at least one vote. Pamphlets appeared on doorsteps, under doorsills, handed out in the streets of towns, left under milk churns. Tom himself spoke at meetings so frequently that it seemed he must hardly sleep. He spoke on agriculture largely, and on the need to have disease in stock animals controlled but he also spoke – it was the Liberal directive to do so – on Home Rule for Ireland and on the growing industrial unemployment that was clearly to be blamed upon the Conservatives.

He was extraordinarily happy. Furnished with money from his mother and sisters – some Cooper family shares had been sold to raise it – and fuelled with a sense of purpose and an outlet for his enormous energies, he was a man renewed. Visits to London assured him of the warm support of headquarters for his particular cast of personality. He took to wearing a copy of the grey frockcoat suit that was such a hallmark of Gladstone, with an imitative flower in the buttonhole, and found it all too easy to speak with the emotional and gesturing energy, the tremendous moral emphasis, of the Liberal leader. They were speeches seen by the opposition as no threat, those speeches about land and Englishness and a way of life and birthright, during which the speaker was so visibly moved he had frequent recourse to the huge yellow handkerchiefs his sister had given him as a small political joke. His speeches were not thorough and well-informed and plentifully supported by figures as Arthur Creighton's were, but they were better theatrical value. In Frome, one market day, the auctioning of beef cattle was suspended while the crowd listened to a speech on England's traditional agricultural values worthy of the death bed of John of Gaunt.

The only occasion upon which his path inadvertently crossed that of his father-in-law, Arthur Creighton chose not to acknowledge him. Tom's own exuberance and warmth would have driven him to shake Creighton's hand but he was forced to acknowledge that such a gesture might only lead to a large and visible public embarrassment. Creighton, it was rumoured, had only taken up politics to escape from a house now morbidly centred upon his sick wife, prostrated by the fates of her daughters, forbidden to see her grandson only a few miles away, and in any case, the kind of woman without a single resource in adversity. She was so far from being any kind of support to her husband in his new ambition that, having quite altered the tenor of their life together for the last ten years by the unvarying dreary persistence of her broken health, she chose the day after the by-election to die unspectacularly in her sleep. It was not a good day for Arthur in any case, since he woke with his defeat heavy in his head, like a hangover. Looking down at her still silly and discontented little dead face, he could not but reflect that if she had only died the day before the election, she might have at least gained him some sympathy votes.

Tom's jubilation was like a great sunrise. Never had he paid over seven hundred pounds as joyfully as he handed the money to the returning officer in Bath to defray the polling charges. He was too exhilarated to care whether or not he was being charged for services never performed. He paid for a brass band and bunting, for a most feudal distribution of beer and beef and bullseyes. He went home to a late dinner at Buscombe, the newest and most exultant of the four hundred and sixty-five members of the English Parliament, ordered champagne to be brought up, and announced to the table, swollen for this evening by local party officials, that they would all yet be proud of him. Tommy, asleep with the utter absorption of one who has spent a whole day cheering himself hoarse, was woken and brought bemusedly down to share in the celebrations, which he could later chiefly remember for the acute self-consciousness of being the only person in a nightshirt and dressing gown at too old an age for such apparel to be proper, let alone endearing. He was offered sugared almonds off the table by all the lady guests who could think of no other immediate way to make themselves charming to him, and to whom he had to reply, individually and laboriously, that he really did not like them very much. Edward Martineau, whose own son was only two years Tommy's senior, watched him with affection and thought what a solitary fellow he looked, as solitary as his own father had looked at much the same age. Perhaps at last Tom had found some kind of road he could travel.

After a while Catherine took Tommy away and put him back to bed, despite his protestations that he would go up alone. As he climbed in he asked if his father and grandfather would go on being enemies, now that the election was over.

Catherine thought of Arthur Creighton eating the solitary chop of widowerhood and defeat in that tremendous crimson dining room he had furnished so proudly twenty years before.

'Not enemies—'

'Well, they both wanted the same thing and Father won it. And they won't speak because of my mother. So, enemies.'

'Opponents.'

'Well, will they still be those, then?'

'I expect so.'

'I'm not going into Parliament. I'm going to be a soldier. I shall enlist in the Gloucestershire Regiment, in the first battalion, the 28th, because it is the oldest.'

'Not cavalry?' Catherine said, thinking of the young Harry with a brief and sudden longing.

'No. I want to be a real soldier.'

173

Catherine turned the lamp out.

'Sleep well. At least we will all wake tomorrow knowing something lovely has happened.'

'I'll tell you what isn't lovely,' Tommy said from the darkness, 'and that is sugared almonds. Sugared almonds are awful. They taste like scented soap and old corks.' He began to giggle. 'Scented soap and old corks—'

Catherine closed the door on him and went down the stairs and as she went she could hear Tommy giggling above her and below laughter and voices rose from the dining room in waves of triumph. She would not say that here was a new beginning at last, she told herself, she would only prudently say, as befitted a disappointed spinster of forty, that she very much hoped it was . . .

CHAPTER NINE

1891

'You promised me,' Tommy said.

'Yes.'

'I won't make any fuss. I don't want to stay on in Italy or have a grand reunion. I just want to see her, even for a few minutes. Then I won't ask any more.'

'Then we shall go,' Catherine said.

There would of course be hurdles. Charlotte, having successfully pretended her daughter-in-law was dead for twelve years, would object violently. The journey must not only be planned, but planned in secrecy since if Rosamund or the Buonvisi knew they were coming, they would no doubt remove themselves again to some obscure hilly stronghold, and all that toiling across Europe would be wasted. The money from the sale of the jewels – it was incredible, but Elizabeth was still regularly lamenting their loss – had never been pursued, chiefly because Tom had maintained his refusal to have anything more to do with the matter. But Rosamund would not know that; if she were to hear that Catherine and Tommy were coming, she would assume that the money was what they were after.

'It will have to be in the school holidays—'

'April,' Catherine said.

'Will you ask my father?'

'I won't *ask* anybody. But your father must be told, and you must do that.'

Tommy squirmed.

'If you don't,' Catherine said, 'I won't. And then we cannot go.'

When Tom returned from London exhilarated from the first week of a new parliamentary term, Tommy met him in the hall and holding the marble swan's neck in one hand for confidence said, immediately,

'I hope it won't upset you, sir, but I am going to Italy with Aunt Catherine to see my mother.'

Tom, still swathed in greatcoat and scarves, looked at the trunk and hampers lying strapped up inside the hall door.

'I thought you were going back to school.'

'I am, sir. We are going to Italy next holidays. Just for a short time. I just want to see—'

He stopped. Tom nodded.

'Was this your idea or your aunt's?'

'Mine. She said she would come with me.'

'You are,' Tom said, 'most fortunate in your aunt. I am going into the library. Will you ask her to come and see me? And find someone to bring me some whisky.'

Catherine brought the whisky herself. She put it down on the huge desk covered in battered red leather at which innumerable Taverners had wrestled with estate accounts and went to kiss her brother.

'My dear,' he said affectionately, 'you are going quite grey!'

'I am forty-three. Have you summoned me to scold me about Tommy's scheme?'

Tom looked immediately absent.

'Oh. Oh, that. No. Do take him. I am – I am sure he should. But I can't—'

'No. Of course not. Do you want water in this?'

'Please,' Tom said. 'Catherine, I saw Lilian Traill this week.'

Catherine waited.

'She is to marry Arthur Creighton.'

'Oh –' Catherine said on a long note, shutting her eyes, 'oh, Tom—'

'Ironic, eh? More than ironic, I'd say, damnable really. There was I, all these years, dancing discreet attendance, writing only when she said I might, never pestering her, asking nothing except that she did not utter the final no, and there she is, out of the blue blushingly telling me she is to marry my father-in-law, as if she hadn't given me cause for hope but days before, as if she did not know what I would feel at the news, as if there was any reason in the wide world for her to marry a man old enough to be her father without wit or charm or anything very much but money. Do you know, I believe she honestly expected me to *congratulate* her?'

Catherine put her arms round her brother's neck.

'She was flaunting her freedom at me,' poor Tom said. 'The freedom I don't have. Of all men in England to choose! Sixty-five and Rosamund's father, *Rosamund's*! I told her she was heartless and unprincipled. I think I said she had no moral sensibilities. I certainly thought it. I do think it. She is outrageous. I don't know whether to be furious or heartbroken. It's like some shopgirl's novel – former mistress weds lover's father-in-law in spite. *Can* it be spite?'

Catherine took her arms away.

'Boredom, more likely.'

'But why? She has not complained of it. Her life

177

always seems full in a female sort of way, that hasn't changed.'

'No, but she has had over twelve years of it. Perhaps she would like to be the mistress of a house again without the commitment of loving the master. Perhaps she wants a new role as a pampered younger wife. Perhaps – oh, I don't know, Tom. I've never known with Lilian.'

He said, 'If we weren't up to our ears in Home Rule for Ireland just now, I think this would fell me. I had dinner with Balfour last night, fascinating, such a grasp of Ireland, best Chief Secretary we have ever had. I shouldn't wonder—'

Catherine put a hand on his arm. 'I think you ought to change. Mother hates late dinner on Fridays enough as it is, and she is not pleased about the Italian scheme.'

'No.'

'Tom. Do you not feel anything at all about the prospect of Tommy seeing Rosamund?'

'My dear Catherine, can you not see that I am most earnestly and deliberately trying not to feel anything? Morally, I believe he should go. Instinctively, I wish he would not. But I will defend his going to Mother and I will buy you both your tickets. Now, what news here this week?'

'Your cousin Charles and his bride are back from their wedding tour, and have declined The Hall because they prefer to live in London. Robert and Mary are rather dashed because they had quite braced themselves for a move – Robert has found a site at Bathampton he likes – and now don't know how to feel about not moving. The estimate for the roof of the east wing is two hundred and thirty pounds – yes, I know, but all the beams are rotten – two ewes have lambed early and the lambs died, Elizabeth has finished the last hassock

178

for the family pew and Tommy has finally succeeded in teaching me how to play bezique.'

Tom finished his whisky.

'I have not got two hundred and thirty pounds.'

'Then we will continue to put buckets around the maids' beds in wet weather.'

Tom said, suddenly morose, 'Things don't change, do they?'

'No,' Catherine said, 'they do not. All that has changed is that you are in London now and do not feel the decay so poignantly. Look at those curtains! And those are quite new, comparatively—'

'Tommy has to be schooled. And we all have to be fed and clothed. I try to live modestly in London—'

'I think you need dinner. I would be much obliged if you would arrange for Tommy's tickets and mine. But I will pay for them. It will be best like that. Tom—'

'Yes?'

'Try not to grieve about Lilian. I don't truthfully think she ever had the capacity to make you lastingly happy.'

'All right!' Tom shouted, abruptly, exasperated by coming home, by the leaking roof and the dead lambs, by the resurrection of Rosamund, the faithlessness of Lilian and above all by his sister's good sense. 'I'm not a fool, you know, not a complete fool!'

On their way to Dover, Catherine and Tommy spent the night in London. They took the early afternoon train to London and then a hansom cab which clopped them all the way from Bayswater to Westminster to visit Tom in the House of Commons. He met them punctually in the Norman porch of the Victoria Tower, wearing a confident and altogether more impressive air than was customary at Buscombe. He and Tommy shook hands.

'I bid you both welcome to the Palace of Westminster.'

They inclined their heads. Tom then led the way past Westminster Hall through St Stephen's Hall, and into the Central Lobby, where he conducted Tommy to the Tudor rose which formed the central motif of the tiled floor's extraordinary pattern and said sonorously, 'You are now, my boy, standing at the very centre of the British Empire.'

Tommy, unable to respond to this overwhelming thought, merely nodded. Catherine said, 'Not geographically?'

Tom glanced at her. 'Don't be so literal.'

Tommy looked confused.

'Tommy', said his father, drawing the boy's arm through his, 'knows exactly what I meant.'

Catherine followed them out onto the Terrace. Both were, she could see from their gait, filled with an enormous pride. Every so often a passing man would say 'Good afternoon, Sir Thomas', and once or twice Tom presented his sister and his son and the pride in him swelled his voice like an organ. On the Terrace, he released Tommy's arm to gesture expansively and eloquently at the building and the river, indicating, with a poignancy he was hardly conscious of, all that greatness and his awed elation that he should somehow be part of it, and a useful part at that.

Consciousness of his father's glory shone on Tommy's countenance like reflected sunlight. He looked up at the crocketed turrets along the skyline, and east to the clock tower and the bridge, and across the great river, and he turned to his father and said gruffly, 'Splendid, sir.'

'Yes,' Tom said. He put a hand out. 'I wish you

all you wish yourself, for your journey to Italy.'

Tommy looked up, his glance suddenly clouded. 'Am I wrong to go, sir?'

'No,' Tom said, glowing, generous. 'No, my dear boy, you are entirely right.'

Catherine and Tommy were to spend the night with Rose and Charlie, who had bought a tall house at the top of a sloping square in Holland Park. Tommy was much impressed by it, with the bare polished floors, the spare elegant furniture and most of all with the lamp-shades which were like pale-coloured inverted water lilies and which shed a soft and pearly light. The drawing room was on the first floor, opening onto a balcony, with a fireplace tiled in iridescent green and peculiar simple furniture made of thin black lacquered wood. The walls were white, there were almost no pictures but plates were hung up instead, and there were extraordinary lattice screens and blowing strips of lily-patterned gauze instead of curtains.

'My dear,' Catherine said laughing to Rose, 'how very advanced.'

There were several bathrooms in the house too, tiled brilliantly in white, and at the very top was Charlie's studio with the drawings of his first commissioned house pinned to huge angled boards beneath a skylight. It had a high roof through which flat topped dormers thrust, a wide arched porch and deep eaves. Tommy could not get used to it, so far was it from Buscombe or the ornate massiveness of The Hall, and kept going back to the drawing board. It was a house he could imagine living in; he could visualize cats on the window-sills, riding boots kicked off in the porch, people opening those little leaded windows and shouting things down to the garden. It suggested to Tommy a very attractive and cosy way of life. He sighed; his grand-mother would say it was middle class.

Dinner was far less formal than at home. There was only one parlourmaid and Charlie opened the wine himself and, talking away, filled Tommy's glass as a matter of course. After dinner, Charlie took him out into the garden and lit a cigar, and they stood in the cool damp air and looked at the London night sky, reddish brown and indigo, streaked with cloud.

'When you get to Pisa,' Charlie said, 'of course you'll go to the Field of Miracles, and look at the Tower. But look at the Cathedral more closely. It is built entirely of marble and has wonderful bronze doors. It was begun about the time William the Conqueror landed here. I envy you going to look at Tuscany.'

'I am not really going to look at buildings—'

'No,' Charlie said coolly, 'but you won't be able to help it.'

Tommy slept that night in Charlie's dressing room.

'I do hope you do not mind,' Rose cried, 'but we have not yet got anywhere else to put you!'

There was a photograph of her on the chest of drawers among the brushes and boxes and also, touch-ingly, one of Tom, in riding clothes, standing under the arch that led into the stableyard at Buscombe. Tommy looked at it for a long time before he climbed into bed. Someone had put a stone bottle at the foot, full of hot water. Tommy grinned to himself; at home he was only allowed such a thing in January.

His cousin Victoria came to breakfast, to wish them Godspeed. She wore a grey flannel coat and skirt with puffed shoulders and a tiny waist, over a tall collared striped blouse, and no jewellery. She looked as neat and pretty and self-possessed as she always had. She told

Tommy she now lived in Charlie's old rooms in Swan Walk, with a girlfriend called Maud Bryce, ate a great deal of toasted cheese because it was so easy and they were both endeavouring to become journalists. Victoria had had an article accepted by the *Fortnightly Review* for four guineas, and was being much encouraged by Miss Flora Shaw, now colonial editor of *The Times*, and by a new circle of friends who believed in the inevitability of the vote for women.

'What was your article about?' Charlie said, grinning and offering muffins.

'Education for girls. The need to extend it to fit women for work in the professions. A great deal is being done, but it is not enough. There are still far too many women in teaching and philanthropy because those are the only two spheres society is yet comfortable to let them occupy.'

Catherine thought of those admonishing little scraps of paper that had fluttered about her own bedroom at Victoria's age, and the earnestness with which she had meant to obey their exhortations. She looked across the table at Victoria's composure, her effortless sense of enterprise. Victoria's parents had made almost as much outraged fuss at her proposal for life as the family had made at Catherine's, twenty years before, but Victoria had simply gone steadily ahead and physically removed herself – sustained, if Catherine was honest, by a very much smaller private income than Catherine had had herself.

'I do admire you,' Catherine said.

To everyone's surprise Victoria blushed.

'Good Lord,' Charlie said, 'I didn't know you could!'

After breakfast, Victoria took Tommy up to Charlie's studio.

'Do you like this?' she said, bending over the drawing boards.

'I can't quite get used to it. But yes.'

'I don't much. But I think it is a kind of architecture that will be very influential. Because it is classless, and rightly. You could copy that kind of house along a thousand suburban streets. Tommy—'

'Yes?'

'Why are you going to Italy?'

Tommy sat on Charlie's high stool and hooked his toes under a stretcher. It was always entirely comfortable to talk to Victoria.

'I want to see what she is like. I don't want her to be a mother to me, there's no need and anyway it is too late for that. But she *is* my mother, and if I don't see her I shall keep on imagining her and I will probably imagine her all wrong.'

'Does anyone at Buscombe ever speak to you of her?'

'No. Well, Aunt Catherine sometimes. If I ask.'

'Where would you be without Catherine?'

'Can't imagine,' Tommy said gratefully, rubbing his thick fair hair into a crest.

'Has your father said anything about your going?'

'No. We don't seem to talk very much just now. He is very wrapped up in Westminster, you see. I think he really likes it.'

'He took me out to tea,' Victoria said unexpectedly. 'He was very kind. Charlie has always thought the world of him. Look.'

She went to a tall built-in cupboard under the eaves and took out a battered wooden box which she brought over to Tommy. Inside were bricks like exact little pieces of real architecture, pediments and steps and balustrades, all ranged with precise neatness. In the middle, for some reason, was a dented tin train wrapped in a handkerchief.

'Your father gave those to Charlie on his wedding day, when Charlie was a page. I was never allowed to lay a finger on them. If I did Charlie flew into a rage and then he started wheezing and I would be spanked with a hairbrush. I expect he feels just as possessively about them now.'

'Why the train?'

'Because Charlie loved them. He had two clockwork trains, I don't know where the other one is, and he would build long tunnels and then wind up the trains and set one off at each end. Your father gave him that too.'

She put the box back in the cupboard and closed the door.

'Italy might be very disappointing, you know. I don't think it will be, but you must be prepared for it, in case it is. Just remember that whatever you find there won't change anything here.'

She bent forward and gave him a quick kiss.

'We'd better go down. Catherine said you were catching the ten fifteen from Victoria. Boat trains! What luck!'

The journey remained in Tommy's mind long after some of the rather disconcerting subsequent events had faded in their confusion. Before that journey, Tommy had been to Bath, school and London and in summer, with Aunt Catherine and increasingly without Nurse, to Lulworth Cove and Studland Bay in Dorset, for sea air. He had spent two separate weeks in Norfolk with a schoolfriend, wildfowling across the empty Broads. That was the extent of his travelling, and this new journey bore no resemblance to any journey he had ever taken before.

It began with the French train, so high and hissing, with its tremendously upright seats covered in a kind of dark patterned harsh plush that could not possibly have been English. The porters smelled of an entirely alien tobacco and some other interesting things he could not define, and dinner, eaten with all ceremony in the dining car like a real, rocking little dining room, was composed of absolutely recognizable things which tasted completely different. Why should slices of meat, and potatoes and beans, apparently just boiled as they were at home, taste like different substances altogether? Catherine said the beans had been cooked with bacon, the potatoes in some kind of stock like a thin soup, and the meat roasted with garlic. She gave Tommy two glasses of red wine and he noticed that two women in the dining car, women who looked neither revolutionary nor unprincipled, were smoking cigarettes.

He said, 'Oh, it's grand, Aunt Catherine, it is absolutely grand!' and she laughed and said, 'Isn't it exciting?' and poured more wine into their glasses.

'Ought we to be more solemn?'

'Not tonight.'

He slept with great thoroughness and woke delightedly to the sway and rhythm of the train, and to a brightly lit landscape outside the window, yellow earth, dark green hills, rust roofed villages, huge pale cows in the fields. There was a basket of rolls for breakfast, buttery, sweetish rolls that collapsed in one's fingers, and black bitter coffee in huge cups. Catherine had smudges under her eyes.

'I can't sleep being shaken about. Too old. I expect you slept like a puppy.'

'I don't want to get off this train!'

At Marseilles, there was an Italian boat waiting to take them to Leghorn. They had a tiny cabin on the upper deck, very clean but smelling wonderfully of abroad all the same, and the sailors were barefoot with rolled up blue trousers and long straight blue jerseys with the shipping line's name embroidered across the chest in scarlet. They shouted to each other, so did the men on the quayside among the bundles and boxes and crates, and so did the gulls wheeling overhead, screaming to each other in French. When the steamer started up and chugged her way among the ships and boats in the harbour, Tommy could not tear himself away from the open deck despite the dense black coal smoke pouring from the funnel, and came down to the cabin at last with glowing eyes and hair full of smuts.

'I think,' Catherine said, 'that I should tell you what I plan. When we get there.'

Tommy nodded. At the moment the purpose of his journey was absolutely obliterated by the exhilaration of the actual process.

'There is a good hotel in Lucca, the Universo, where I have taken rooms. I think we should settle for a day, walk about Lucca, but not as Taverners. It may seem a little melodramatic, but I shall use my mother's name. Then, on the second or third day, depending upon how we feel, we will take a carriage up to the Villa Buonvisi in the late afternoon which is a time when people are invariably at home. From then on, we will simply have to see.'

'What happens if we are turned away?'

'I will make myself as difficult as possible to turn away. This is the most adventurous thing I have ever done in my life and I mean to make the most of it. In any case, I do not think any mother could resist a glimpse of her own son.'

If France was wonderful, Italy was better. Tommy was in a state of rapture. In Leghorn they stayed in the old quarter of Nuova Venezia, in a tall pink hotel on a waterway, and ate ices in the Piazza Grande and found a marble statue of Ferdinando I, which much intrigued Tommy because of the four great bronze blackamoors in chains groaning under the weight of the pedestal. He ate clams and pasta, learned the Italian for 'Please' and 'Thank you' and 'Delicious', and, in a certain confusion of feeling, watched a chanting Holy Week procession move through the streets towards the Cathedral, carrying aloft in a kind of gilded glass box the image of the Madonna delle Brazie, patron saint of Tuscany. Perhaps, in Lucca, his mother was following just such another procession, black robed, black veiled, holding a candle. He knew nothing about the Catholic Church except that it was somehow unpatriotic, and certainly morally inferior to Protestantism. There was a boy at school who wanted to be a missionary in Africa, like David Livingstone, a missionary explorer, but of course he couldn't because he had to go into the family bank. Missionaries were Protestant, Tommy was pretty sure of that, because they had a special energy in this age of Victoria, a special divine gift that they were called upon by God to hand over to the heathens. Nobody had ever mentioned Catholics being admitted to this charmed evangelizing circle, so perhaps they were not. Certainly they behaved differently, and their churches smelled extraordinary. If his mother was one, how apart did that make her?

In Pisa, they had rooms in an hotel on the Lungarno Pacinotti and Catherine tried to insist that Tommy should have the one that looked out onto the slow flowing Arno, a marvellous view down two curves of the river. Tommy refused and won.

'You say this is a special journey for me. Well, it is for you, too, and you are giving it to me. Anyway in the daytime I can come in and share your view, and in the night I sleep so absolutely that I might as well be in a wardrobe for all I notice.'

The room was floored in russet tiles across which the spring sun fell in a syrup coloured oblong through the open windows. Catherine pulled a chair up to the windowsill and leaned her arms on the warm wood and looked across at the little church of Santa Cristina where the guide book said St Catherine of Siena had received her stigmata. It was a day without wind and the green shuttered yellow houses on the opposite shore looked down into their own perfect reflections, upside down in the water. She felt, for the first time in years it seemed, absolutely, tranquilly happy, partly because it was so lovely here and partly because she was doing the kind of thing that it suited her to do, going on an adventure with a purpose. Then a maid came in with a pile of rough linen towels and told Catherine smilingly that the view was 'il bello di Pisa', followed by Tommy saying that they must go out, at once, because there was so much to see.

They stayed a day longer in Pisa than they had intended for that very reason. Roaming through the old northern quarter, marvelling at the four wondrous pale buildings rising from their green lawns on the Field of Miracles, trying *mallegato*, the strange Pisan salami dotted with raisins and pine kernels, sitting on the Lungarni while Tommy ate sweetened cheese pastries and Catherine drank coffee and glasses of moscato.

There were eels from the Arno on the menus, and wild pig, and on the streets you could buy dried black truffles from the hills of Umbria in twists of brown paper.

'We mustn't stay,' Catherine said, 'we must go on.'

A looping railway line ran north from Pisa to Lucca, through the low green hills. The sun went in. They sat in their carriage and stared out at a landscape which looked abruptly deadened and said very little. Catherine offered Tommy the mint sugar sticks she had bought at the station, but he shook his head. When they reached Lucca, they climbed out in silence and Catherine, now well practised, commanded a fiacre to take them inside the city walls, beneath the Porto San Pietro – the portcullis pleased Tommy by the sheer size of its teeth – and up into the square where Edward Martineau had sat in such a fury of frustration nine years before with his untasted cup of coffee. There were the plane trees, there was the little neoclassical theatre and there opposite was the old hotel, where Augustus Hare had once stayed, the Universo. Catherine turned to Tommy as the fiacre stopped and a boy ran out for their bags.

'It is always easier to travel than to get there, but we would be great fools if we stopped enjoying ourselves now. Whatever happens next.'

Tommy nodded.

The day remained grey and still and cool. They looked at the Cathedral and its treasury, they wandered through the Piazza Napoleone and up the Via Fillungo because Catherine felt she might like to buy something, a little terracotta pot, a bit of ivory, a string of beads, but when it came to any actual purchase she knew it to be only a distraction; her heart was not in it. For dinner, she made an especial effort and put on the best dress she had brought with her of sage green silk, its low neck filled in with a high tight frilled collar of spotted muslin. She attempted to tease Tommy into trying the lasagne with hare that the hotel insisted was its speciality, but to no avail. He pushed risotto round his plate instead, seemed disinclined for the puddings he had so far been ecstatic about, and then excused himself before she had even ordered coffee, and went to bed.

In the morning, for the first time, he had shadows under his eyes.

'We are going today,' Catherine said firmly. It seemed unfeeling to have slept so well herself, but at least one of them must be in command of themselves and whatever lay ahead. A carriage was ordered, Tommy's appearance inspected and passed, and under a high thin grey sky behind which the sun swam like an imprisoned coin, they began the climb into the hills.

It was a lovely landscape. Against a backdrop of wooded slopes, tilled fields ran between ochre buildings roofed in ribbed tiles the colour of soft copper, and as they climbed higher, the fields grew fewer and there were no more farms, and herbs and bushes, showing pale bright tufts of new growth, straggled onto the road between the cypress trees. Birds were singing – perhaps, thought Catherine, relations of those thrushes whose poor little roasted bodies on twigs she had been pressed to buy in the street the day before – and in the grasses, southern insects ticked spasmodically, waiting for the sun. It came out, apologetically, as the carriage stopped before the gates of the Villa Buonvisi. They were open.

'Drive on,' Catherine said.

The drive was green with weeds and strewn with winter debris at the edges. Someone emerged from the bushes by the gate and shouted after them, but

Catherine simply said, 'Drive on' again, and looked out of the window.

'Oh, my dear – do look—'

The drive had swung them out onto the side of the hill, into a gravel circle for turning, with a fountain in the middle choked with leaves and brambles, and below them the land fell away to the view that had maddened Edward Martineau so by its sheer loveliness.

'I don't feel,' Tommy said, torn between tears and sickness and a great many other things he could not immediately identify, 'that this is really happening.'

Catherine put her hand in his and held it hard.

'Look at the house!'

It was set at an angle, the face towards them crowned with urns in which dried up weeds waved like ancient hair. The walls were faded, patched, bleached pale russet, the barrel windows pedimented, the archway leading into some central courtyard flanked by gates as marvellous as those at the end of the drive and great bay trees planted in fluted stone tubs five feet across. To the right of the main façade, a long portico ran away from them along the villa's south face, over whose balustrade it looked, unbelievably, as if the tops of trees planted thirty feet below were spilling.

Dogs appeared suddenly from the courtyard, angular thin-skinned dogs with great square heads, barking furiously, and followed at a distance by a man in some kind of livery, a faded green coat with crested buttons worn with what were plainly his own breeches. He stopped in the gateway and called to ask them what they wanted. The Duke, Catherine said. The Duce was in Florence. The Duchess, then. The man came nearer.

'Your names, then, Signora.'

Catherine hesitated. To lie might gain them entry

more easily but put them all, once in, on a very poor footing; to tell the truth risked not being admitted at all. She took a card out and wrote on it:

'Miss Catherine Taverner. Master Thomas Taverner. Only a few moments, please. We have come particularly but without design.'

The man took the card and vanished down the portico. They waited apprehensively, Tommy scuffing the moss-choked gravel, Catherine looking steadily at the view and seeing nothing. When the man came back, he stood at the end of the portico and shouted to them.

'The Duchessa will see you!'

At the far end of the portico incongruous beneath a frescoed ceiling where nymphs and satyrs frolicked among vines, stood a small stout woman dressed in a braided frock of dark red wool. Her hair was taken up into a bun high at the back of her head except for a neat row of curls along her brow, and she wore gold and pearl crosses in her ears and a huge one on a velvet ribbon on her ample bosom. She stood waiting for them with her hands clasped, and when they at last reached her – the portico seemed half a mile long to Tommy – she said,

'I am the Duchess of Montemagno. I was of course Florence Creighton—' and then she stopped and gave a little scream and put her arms round Tommy, covering his cheeks with kisses. It was disconcertingly Italian.

'It is so good of you to see us,' Catherine said.

'Oh my dear Miss Taverner,' Florence Buonvisi said, mopping her face, 'I cannot tell you – really, such a shock – but oh, a good thing, I think, and so fortunate that the dear Duce should have business in Florence! Will you come in?'

She led them through double doors into a room

193

floored in green and white marble whose pilasters, niches, pediments and statues revealed themselves, to Tommy's delight, to be ingeniously painted onto the wall. Huddled on a rug by the empty fireplace was a nervous group of upright armchairs, a basket of needlework and one of tiny – and to Tommy's mind, revolting – dogs with starting eyes, ears like wings and deafening little voices. To this island in the sea of marble, the duchess steered them.

'I am so surprised – shocked even. It never crossed my mind I should see Thomas, though of course I have always thought of him so much, being of an age with my own boys—'

'I was afraid,' Catherine said, 'that if I wrote and warned you that we were coming, you might refuse to see us. It was not the most courteous way to arrive, springing ourselves upon you, but I am bound to confess I thought it would be more successful.'

The duchess spread her hands.

'Things have been so difficult – you see, my father even no longer comes here. I never saw my mother before she died – I had not seen her in years. The Buonvisi are so proud, you see, and when Paolo wished to marry me – he found me, you know, gazing at the Bridge of Sighs in Venice, I had gone with my parents for an Italian tour, what could be more romantic? – when he wished to marry me, the old Duchessa was so angry because I was not of an old Tuscan family. She was angry until she died, and now her sisters are angry in her place. It is so difficult—'

She was, Catherine thought with a sudden small affection, exactly like her mother. She remembered Mrs Creighton at garden parties twenty years before, prattling and chattering, so good hearted and so absurd.

The duchess looked about her and gave a little shrug. The marvellous *trompe l'oeil* walls were blotted with damp and there was not a stick of furniture beyond the chairs in which they sat and a lifesize statue of a classical man in a toga who regarded them impassively from a corner.

'It is not easy—' the duchess said.

'Are your boys here?'

'Oh no! They have gone to Florence with their father.' She looked at Tommy. 'I wish they were here! You are cousins and you are as unalike to look at as you could be! You're so fair and they are as dark as I am, and like their father.' She turned the great cross on her bosom over and held it out to show the miniature on the back. 'That is their father.'

Catherine and Tommy looked respectfully at a small dark face that might have been an indifferent portrait of Napoleon.

'Of course, he is not a *tall* man— My dears, refreshment?'

She jumped up, grasped a small bronze bell that was sitting alone in the empty marble hearth, and rang it furiously. After a long interval, the same man in his battered livery coat appeared and was despatched for wine and cake and fruit syrup for Tommy.

'We make our own panforte, you know. I am most particular. It must be white cane sugar, and only fresh orange and lemon peel, and our own almonds. Cinnamon is such a price!'

'This is the most beautiful place,' Catherine said.

The duchess looked vaguely out through the open door to the blue and green lines of distance, the dark spears of the cypresses.

'It is not easy—'

A table was brought in, and on separate and laborious journeys across the echoing floor, a tablecloth, three glasses, plates, a carafe of water, a decanter of wine – 'The local vinsanto, our dessert wine, my dear, quite excellent!' – a jug of red syrup, a dish of almonds, a silver plate of panforte nestling in a paper frill.

'There!' the duchess said, bristling and moving things about. 'We shall have a little party!' She cut a huge wedge of pastry and put it in front of Tommy. 'I have not seen anyone English for so long. I hardly ever speak it. I really see so few people—'

Tommy put a piece of panforte in his mouth. Catherine was looking at him. He chewed, swallowed and took a mouthful of the red syrup which tasted oddly of the smell of geraniums. He did not know how to address an Italian duchess, so he simply said,

'I have really come to see my mother, you see.'

The duchess put down her wineglass.

'Oh my dear. How stupid – but perhaps you don't understand – Oh, how difficult!'

Tommy waited. Catherine said, 'Where is Rosamund? What has happened?' at almost the same time that the duchess said, 'Your mother is a nun. Near Sestola, halfway to Bologna. I only see her once a year upon her name day – it is a closed order, you see. She entered it – it is a convent dedicated to Our Lady, Our Lady of the Mountains because the Appennines are so close, you see – eight years ago, a year after Mr Martineau came. Oh, I remember his coming! Oh my dear' – to Tommy, 'and to think I should forget that you did not know—'

To his horror, huge ungovernable tears rose in Tommy's eyes and slid heavily down his cheeks.

Catherine sprang from her chair to kneel and put her arms around him.

'I think it is a Franciscan order in origin,' the duchess was saying, 'but of course the Poor Clares usually live and work in the community and at Monte Cimone they are quite closed although they do take in the sick, most skilled in nursing I'm told, particularly in diseases of the stomach. Presumably they grow the herbs—'

'*Please*,' Catherine said furiously. She reached out for her wineglass and held it to Tommy's mouth. 'Have just a little, dearest boy. It is very pleasant and sweet. There now—'

Tommy gulped.

'I'm s-sorry—'

'Don't you dare be sorry. It is just a horrible shock.'

'You see—'

'Yes.'

'You see, if she went into a convent she knew she would never be able to see me. She knew that when she went there. But she still went.'

The duchess came to kneel too, and irritatingly patted the bits of Tommy she could reach.

'I shouldn't say this, I suppose, it isn't loyal and it is the sort of thing children are not supposed to know, but you are hardly a child, are you, Tommy – Ros – your mother, I think your mother went into the convent because she was so – so ill. She went in to be healed.'

'Ill?' Tommy said, straightening himself and glaring at her. 'What was the matter with her?'

The duchess put a fluttering and tentative hand to her brow and gestured clumsily.

'In her mind, my dear.'

'Are you saying that my mother was mad?'

197

'No,' said the duchess with a decisiveness she had not shown before, 'not mad. Simply, unhappy. Thrown off her balance, so that she could take pleasure in nothing. She cried for a year when she first came to us. She kept saying she did not want to live—'

Catherine shot her a warning glance.

'I could think of nothing to make her happy. It was so difficult. Nothing here is ever easy, but that was more difficult than anything, living with someone who does not want to live. It was Paolo who thought of Monte Cimone. Such an aristocratic house, he has a cousin there and an aunt before her. Rosamund is so calm now, quite serene—'

'Then why doesn't she come home?' Tommy demanded.

The duchess scrambled to her feet.

'We never talk of the past. I am not at all sure she remembers it. I am not sure either that she knows I am her sister. She is called Sister Annunziata and does not answer to Rosamund any more. My dear, I think she has forgotten everything but Monte Cimone.'

Tommy got up and went out into the portico. A hazy, quivering sun cast a pearly grey glimmer on the extraordinary garden below him. He leaned his arms on the balustrades. Those *were* thirty-foot trees down there, growing in ruined beds with broken stone rims, and staircases swept down to them with heads and urns at every corner. Down and down the staircases went, swinging between fountain and terrace in a kind of dancing movement, to a huge pavement some hundred feet below, laid out like a giant marble chessboard beneath a wall set with niches and basins that divided the garden from the valley. Neglect lay like a spell upon it all. The statues had broken noses, creeping weeds filled the fountain basins, exhausted dry geraniums fell from urns with missing handles, rusty spires of sorrel rose from the marble pavement. His mother, Tommy reflected, had last looked at it all when he was eight – no, seven – before she had gone away and simply shut the door on the past. He sighed, shuddering. It was absolutely incomprehensible to him and, as it was plain – the only thing that was plain – that she would never see him and would not know him if she did, there was no point in even trying to understand it.

As Victoria had said, nothing in his ordinary life, his English life, had changed. Buscombe was still there – he thought of it with a sudden clutch of love, sitting blond and confident in its English fields – so was dear Aunt Catherine and his father and the cousins. He had come on a quest and had been given an answer, even if it wasn't the answer he had been seeking. Already, he could not remember what he had thought he was going to find.

'Tommy?'

He turned round.

'Shall we go back to Lucca?'

He smiled uncertainly.

'Pisa. Can we go straight to Pisa—'

'Of course. Back to the Nettuno.'

The duchess came out after Catherine and said, 'Will you send my love to my father? And tell him I am very well and the boys so tall and handsome. They are at school in Florence now, they had a tutor here but Paolo insists that now they must go to school. Tell my father that I am very contented here, will you, it is such a beautiful place, and give my warm regards to your mother and to Elizabeth, oh! I have the happiest memories of Buscombe! Wait—' She darted inside and came

199

back with the remains of the panforte wrapped in its paper frill. She thrust it at Tommy. 'There now – for the journey. I know how you boys are, always hungry—'

A mile from the villa gates, Tommy threw the pastry into the thyme bushes beside the road.

'I couldn't eat it—'

'No,' Catherine said.

They slept two nights at Pisa and went back to see the Baptistery and the Tower. It was calming. Catherine decided she would not talk unless Tommy manifestly wanted to. She had herself a new fact to digest, something the duchess had told her while Tommy was out in the portico; that the money – almost five thousand pounds in sterling – which Rosamund received from the Taverner jewellery had been given by Rosamund's wish to the nuns at Monte Cimone. She had intended it to support her and support her it should. It would certainly, finally – and this came as a relief to Catherine – never be retrievable. The chapter was at last closed, however unsatisfactorily. In Leghorn as luck would have it, a steamer was sailing for France that night, and in Marseilles there was no more than half a day's wait for a train north. By Marseilles Tommy was talking again, by Dover he was almost himself.

'Must we say?' he said, in the train to London. 'Must we tell them?'

'Yes. But very simply and no fuss—'

Catherine telegraphed from London and the familiar carriage was in the yard at Bath station.

'Oh,' Tommy said in joy at the sight of it. 'Oh, look!'

It was an exquisite light, clear day, cream and pink may in the hedges, cowslips and bluebells in the grass, lambs on every sunny slope. Tommy was humming.

They turned the familiar corner of the drive and there was Buscombe, square, honey coloured, welcoming . . .

The carriage wheels on the drive were suddenly muffled. Catherine looked out. Straw – straw thick on the gravel. And the curtains were pulled across, every window blind, the knocker wrapped up in something black. She flung open the carriage door, not waiting for Fred Bradstock running from the stableyard to open it for her, and hurried up the steps. Charlotte . . .

'What is it?' Tommy said to Fred. 'What's happened?'

And Fred, who had been told he must say nothing, but who had known Tommy since he was a baby, blurted out, 'It's your father—'

It was a massive haemorrhaging they said, nothing could have saved him. No-one could have survived a kick like that, not right at the base of the skull. Such a reliable horse that had always been, and Sir Thomas only bending down with Bradstock to see to some inflammation around the frog on the near fore hoof. Must have touched something tender, to make him lash out unexpectedly like that. It was a terrible loss. Only forty-two. And all going so well with him in Parliament, everyone said.

Tommy did not want to see anybody. He did not much want to see his father's rigid waxy body either but somehow there was no evading that. He did not cry, nor did anybody else, although it was perfectly clear that they had been, even Fred Bradstock. Bradstock himself was inconsolable. Tommy went up to his room on the top floor and looked sternly out of his window towards the lake. He told himself that he was now virtually an orphan and certainly a baronet. Neither fact meant a thing. He wrote on a piece of paper, 'Please send for

Victoria' and pushed it under his door for the next person who came up to find. Then he put a chairback under the door handle, rolled himself in the top blanket on his bed, lay down and fell at once into a profound and dreamless sleep.

CHAPTER TEN

1893

Tommy left school without any marked regrets, the summer after his seventeenth birthday. By his own choice he was to spend that summer and autumn at home – his grandmother wanted to take him to Nottinghamshire on a little tour of showing him off, his aunt Elizabeth thought he would meet the right sort of people if he buried the family hatchet and went to Scotland at the Creightons' invitation, and his aunt Catherine told him he should go to Greece – and in the new year, go to Sandhurst for the first of two terms training as an officer. Upon passing out, he would sail to join the Gloucestershire Regiment as an ensign.

The choice to stay at home in the summer was, he knew well, sentimental; the decision to go into the army, absolutely was not. Buscombe, though his legally in just under four years' time, was not his in essence at the moment. He hoped that when he was older and more authoritative – surely the army would teach him that? – he would be able to detach, kindly but extremely firmly, the hands that grasped Buscombe so decidedly just now. The drawback to going off soldiering was that it gave the most recent pair of hands, the large, smooth ones of Arnold du Cros, the chance to clasp Buscombe even closer. But then, if he stayed, a raw, largely ignored schoolboy having to ask advice at every turn – advice that Arnold du Cros was unvaryingly able to give – he knew he should go mad with frustration and resentment. It was best to go away for a while and return with some authority.

He had come to this decision quite alone. He had thought of asking his cousin Charlie, at present designing tea rooms for some huge company in the Strand, a commission which gave him the chance to design everything from the exterior to the teaspoons, but had shied away from the problem of not being able to sound other than antagonistic about Charlie's father-in-law. Edward Martineau would treat him as a boy, Uncle Robert . . .

At his father's funeral, Arnold du Cros had taken him aside and with a small but eloquent gesture at the band of black clad Taverner women, had said,

'If you need an ally, dear boy, against the governing body—'

Tommy said stiffly, 'I have Uncle Robert.'

'Of course.'

They both knew he had not. Robert Taverner, believing himself frustrated of everything upon which he had set his heart, in addition to everything that was no more than his due, had all but turned his back upon his family. He was seventy-three and had, in retaliation for his concession over the matter of his son, his nephew and Parliament, devoted himself since to inflexibility. Not even his beloved Mary could shift him if his mind was made up – which it increasingly was, over mountingly idiotic things like the precise colour of toast at breakfast or the meticulous regularity with which he expected to hear from his busy children – and the strain was telling upon her open temper.

The Hall was shut up and Robert and Mary were living most inconveniently in the Royal York Hotel in Bath while a large yellow villa, not designed by Charlie, rose on the site at Bathampton Robert had purchased three years before. It was to have a loggia from which to appreciate the spectacular views, and to it Robert went every day, as punctually as if he were bound by office hours, to harry the workmen. He never went to Bristol and seldom to London. He drew still a most substantial income from Taverner Warehouses, but the controlling interest now belonged to the new managing director. He was the obvious choice – Rose had suggested her father to Charlie who, wishing to please Rose and not being in the least interested in the business beyond the income it gave him, suggested Arnold to Robert.

'Capital,' was all Robert said.

The year after Tom's death, there had been a General Election, which returned Mr Gladstone as Prime Minister for his fourth term, and Arnold du Cros as Member for North Somerset for his first. He was elected by a far greater majority than his predecessor. Tommy was furious about the whole thing and Arnold knew it, but Arnold was not in the least afraid of Tommy's sulks.

'You are, my dear fellow,' he said gently to Tommy, 'in cricketing parlance, a very straight bat.'

It was perfectly true and strangely infuriating to be told so. He played energetic rugby and, he hoped, thoughtful cricket; he rode to hounds and had made himself, by sheer effort, into a passable oarsman. He sang lustily in chapel, punched bullies, read Kipling avidly and his hero – like half the boys in his house – was

Cecil John Rhodes, Premier of Cape Colony at thirty-seven, who was going to turn all Africa pink and glorious for the Empire. Tommy believed in the Empire without thinking. It was as immutable as God, as natural and right and inevitable as his inheritance of Buscombe, as benevolent and judicious as only an English institution could be.

He was aware that Arnold du Cros did not so much not believe in the Empire, as believe it could not last. He shook his head at Africa.

'We should not be carried away by our possession of India. Even that will turn sour on us one day, remember the Mutiny. How else can it be when we educate our possessions to understand about administration, about government? Naturally, in the end they will want to govern themselves. Africa is a far more complicated and diverse problem, even than India. Such different tribes, countries, make it up, all at war with each other, all intractable. It will drain our coffers and our young men if we become drawn in—'

Tommy could not help listening to Arnold du Cros – he was, in any case, the only man who talked to Tommy in this way – but he did not want to believe him. He preferred to believe in the glory of the newspaper reports that described the warlike Matabele rising up, howling against the British South Africa company, and being coolly crushed by Dr Storm Jameson. He did not want to hear such an episode compared ironically by Arnold du Cros to a rugby game between two schools.

'He is a dear, good boy,' Arnold said to Catherine, whom he admired, 'but he has little imagination.'

'He is so much a Taverner. Taverners do not have imagination in abundance.'

'What does he feel about inheriting this?'

Catherine sighed.

'I simply do not know. He has become very private since his father died. I expect he just assumes it will always be here, going on, when he comes back covered with glory from the North West Frontier or wherever. Like me, he has never known anywhere else. He will make a good soldier.'

'Not too good, I hope.'

'Why do you say that?'

'I am thinking of your uncle John.'

Catherine said after a tiny pause, 'But you have not met my cousin Harry.'

He looked at her. She was extremely thin and her hair, the colour of faded straw, was pulled back too tightly from her clever, humorous face. She invariably wore grey and if she was in the conservatory as now, a huge blue apron over it which gave her the air of a stern little nurse.

'May I have a gardenia? I know no-one who can grow them as you do.'

With the straightforwardness for which he so liked her, she put a perfect flower unselfconsciously in his buttonhole.

'You are no coquette, Miss Catherine.'

'No,' she said.

'I should like to meet your cousin Harry.'

'There is every reason to suppose that you will. He might even be Tommy's commanding officer and will come down this summer. He has been in the East or Mediterranean or Ireland for twenty years.'

'You have not seen him for twenty years?'

'No.'

'Then it will be a considerable meeting.'

'No,' Catherine said, 'it will not. I am going to look

at the fjords of Norway and I shall not be back until late September. I sail on the *Blackness Castle* next week with four new sketchbooks – and a special white straw hat lined with grey flannel to wear while using them. You see, it is all arranged.'

'Bravo.'

She smiled at him, but all she said was, 'I think Mother is hoping to see you.'

Charlotte, over seventy and extremely robust, was very happy. She had grieved for Tom very properly, and grieved still over the disappointments of his life, but she was at the helm in a way she had not been for almost a quarter of a century. Managing though she was, she had moments of extraordinary sensitivity and in one of these had decided that she would alter none of the changes Rosamund had brought to the house. It was perhaps some inarticulate tribute to Rosamund's genuine disarray of temperament, even some acknowledgement of how difficult a mother-in-law she herself had been. She opened up the attics, and once a week sent up a reluctant maid to polish at least one piece of the old furniture, but she did not bring down a single item to disturb the rooms as Rosamund had left them.

She was unashamedly delighted with Arnold du Cros.

'You are like Queen Victoria with Benjamin Disraeli,' Catherine said to her.

She bridled but she smiled. Taverner Warehouses in his hands, now a limited liability company, was doing handsomely by its shareholders. The roof of the east wing was mended, the rotten windows on the north side would be replaced this summer and Elizabeth had begun to ask her friends once more, a sure sign that the house was recovering. Arnold had dealt entirely with the aftermath of Tom's death and increasingly with her own affairs, those horrible depths and grim little cottage rows in Nottinghamshire that had really kept Buscombe going these last twenty years. She had not needed to see Edward Martineau in months.

Charlotte liked Arnold's presence too. His large masculinity and tremendously good clothes flattered and soothed her. To live the life he did, he must have enormous energy, but it was a quiet purring energy, quite unlike poor dear Tom's bounding vigour, that of some field dog puppy. He could tease her and he could manage her and to her amazement she found she objected to neither. When he came in to her from Catherine, she said,

'Now I am not in a hand kissing mood, Arnold, so don't try any gallant tricks with me.'

'Ah. So I am out of favour for some reason.'

'Not at all. But we must be practical.'

'I am very glad to hear it.'

He sat down in his usual chair opposite to her in the window where poor Freddie Forrester – now a foolish and faded old beau on the edge of dubiously smart sets, whom no-one at Buscombe spoke of any longer – had proposed to Elizabeth. She handed him a sheaf of papers.

'These are my plans. In answer to yours.'

Two weeks before, Arnold had outlined a scheme for Buscombe for the next five years. He proposed that all the land except for five hundred acres should be sold, preferably as a single block to someone who would wish to build a house on it and make his own estate. Arnold would then invest the proceeds for capital growth, using the income for a modest but steady scheme of repairs.

He suggested that they should return to the farming mix of twenty-five years before, sheep and wheat, since there was a local demand for the former in the woollen mills of the Golden Valley that ran through the steep hills around Stroud, and wheat of high quality was finding an appreciative market after years of cheap imported grain. Charlotte had said she would think about it. Looking down her proposals set out in her delightful idiosyncratic old-fashioned hand, Arnold saw that she had simply put every suggestion of his into her own words.

'So,' she said challengingly, 'now, what do you think of that?'

He was not going to pander to her any more than he was going to humour Tommy's surliness.

'I am going to say, my dear Lady Taverner, that I am not in the least taken in, and that I am delighted to have your agreement.'

She was not remotely abashed.

'Then we may go straight ahead. I have an estate map here and I suggest we mark out the portion we should sell.'

'One thing first—'

'Yes?'

'Lady Taverner, you should tell your grandson. Or rather, you should suggest and explain it to him.'

'Tommy?' Charlotte said indignantly. 'Don't be absurd.'

'He is not a child. He is only a few years away from possessing Buscombe. How can he be expected to manage the estate well if he is excluded from such plans?'

Charlotte was really quite cross.

'Of course I shall not tell him. He is quite unfit to understand, only a schoolboy.'

'My dear Lady Taverner,' Arnold said quietly, 'you sound precisely as I imagine our dear old Queen sounds when it is suggested to her that she informs the Prince of Wales of some urgent matter of state.'

Charlotte rose.

'I will explain all these things to my grandson when he comes of age, when it is relevant. If I were to explain to him now he would feel he must object to show his independence of mind and we should have difficulties that I do not want. He will be extremely grateful in the future that such a scheme ensured him a comfortable livelihood.'

'I am afraid,' Arnold said patiently, rising also, 'that he will not thank you at all for excluding him. And I will have sympathy with his resentment.'

'Mr du Cros, kindly have the courtesy to allow me to know my own grandson. He is too undeveloped either to comprehend what you wish to explain to him or as yet to value this house and estate sufficiently to be interested.'

Arnold waited a moment and then said,

'Perhaps you would be good enough to show me your suggestions for sale on the estate map.'

Three days later after a long sitting in the House, he went, as had become his custom, to his daughter Rose's house in Holland Park.

'Between them, my darling daughter, between Lady Taverner and the Home Rule Bill, I shall be ground to a powder like corn between mill stones. At least today in the House Mr O'Connor was quiet and nobody actually struck anybody else as they did two weeks ago, but I believe Lady Taverner would have struck me on Monday if I had pursued my point.'

'What point?'

'That Tommy should be included on any major decision about the estate.'

'And she won't?'

'She won't!'

'I am so glad she is not my mother-in-law.'

'So am I!'

'More brandy?'

'Please. I was half minded to tell the boy myself, but of course he mistrusts me, believes me to have some sinister purpose in advising his grandmother. And I should have alienated Lady Taverner.'

Rose said, 'I'm sure your purpose isn't sinister—'

'It isn't even a purpose. It is a manner of accident, of a connection which arose when you wished to marry Charles. I want to talk to Charles. I should like to commission some furniture from that outrageous Scot, Mackintosh—'

'You should get Charlie to do it of course,' Rose said, pricking herself and sucking her finger.

'I was, my darling dolt, just saying that I would talk to Charlie before I did anything.'

'Not about chairs. About Tommy. Get Charlie to tell Tommy.'

'Clever girl.'

'Tommy trusts Charlie. What is the plan, anyway?'

'To sell enough land to invest for modest repairs. Very simple.'

'What a good thing. The house looks a disgrace just now. I am so glad I don't have to inherit it. I don't want to live anywhere but here. Papa, it is time you went home to Lowndes Square. What was Mamma doing tonight?'

Arnold stretched.

'Breakfast was spent testing the rival claims of Mr

Wilde or Mr Pinero, but I think Mrs Tanqueray was going to win.' He got up. 'You are right, however, and I must go. The theatres will just be finishing.'

In the hall, handing him his hat and stick, Rose said, 'Why do you bother with the Taverners?'

'Because, my dear, they are everything I am not. They are what your grandmother was, and she is why you look as you do and not like me or your mother, your little fair English grandmother, who married a Jewish banker in Geneva on an impulse I believe she much regretted. He was a kind man, my father, but only lastingly in love with money. It must have been a great disappointment to my little mother that I should have turned out looking as I do.' He made a face at himself in the hall looking glass.

'I love the way you look.'

'Don't flatter me, Rose. It always makes me suspicious.'

'Is that why you were sent to school here?'

'Is—'

'Because your mother missed England and was unhappy in Geneva?'

'I think so. She left me three hundred pounds, a memory of her great fretfulness and an abiding romantic fascination with the old landed classes of England. My father left me everything else.'

'More usefully, probably,' Rose said, laughing.

He kissed her.

'My good wishes to my son-in-law. My dear, my dear, what a family! Tell him about Tommy. I feel for the boy.'

'No,' Charlie said, 'I am not going to interfere.'

'But it is for poor Tommy!'

'Tommy is not poor in the least. He won't care

whether he is included or excluded as long as old Buscombe keeps ticking on until he has finished killing Hottentots or whatever, and wants it.'

'You are very heartless,' Rose said, 'and I don't think you are right, either. I think Tommy feels that everybody but him has got a finger in a pie that really belongs to him. My father thinks that too.'

Charlie finished brushing his thick brown hair with Rose's brushes, and climbed into bed beside her. He patted the mound of her belly.

'Look at you.'

'I wish it would happen. I'm tired of looking like this.'

'Why doesn't your father tell Tommy himself?'

'He says Tommy does not trust him and it would make Aunt Charlotte furious.'

'Oh,' Charlie said, '*that*.'

'They have so much to do with one another now.'

Charlie said with meaningful emphasis, 'I know.'

'Don't be unpleasant.'

'I am not unpleasant. But your father is an extremely clever man. I am merely observant.'

'And I,' said Rose, 'am extremely uncomfortable. Nowhere is comfortable.'

'Would you like me to sleep in the dressing room?'

'I should hate it.'

'So should I.'

He folded his arms behind his head and contemplated the ceiling.

'We are so lucky not to have anything to do with it. We don't even have obligations to The Hall any more. Absolutely our own masters, thank God. I've been asked to design a really important house in the Lake District. Someone wanted Voysey but he is too busy and so he suggested me.'

'Charlie!'

'Come up to Windermere with me and we'll look at the site together.'

'Oh! I'd love to but I daren't—'

'After the baby, then.'

'Boy or girl?'

He squinted at her belly.

'Tonight – boy.'

'Boy it is then,' she said contentedly, turning on her side. He blew out the lamp.

'It sounds a wonderful site,' he said in the dark, feeling for her hand, 'on a kind of broad south-facing ledge above the lake. Why don't you design the garden?'

'Because I can't even put bread and butter on a plate without it looking a mess.'

'The new gardens are a mess.'

Rose began to giggle. Then she stopped and said, 'Poor Tommy—'

'Shush about Tommy. It is not our problem. Think about the baby.'

'Very well.'

'And sun-filled holiday houses by English lakes. And people saying to you, "Are you the wife of *Charles* Taverner?"'

'Are you going to be famous?'

'Yes,' said Charlie, 'now go to sleep.'

'Very well,' Rose said again, and did.

Rose's baby took fourteen hours to arrive and caused her mother great pain and fright. Nobody, not even her own sensible mother, had told Rose how much it would hurt, nor how much she would feel, in the face of knowing that the baby must be born, that it never would be. When it was at last over, Charlie did not seem to understand that it was necessary to tell him, describe to him, what agony it had been. He was delighted with their daughter, delighted with Rose, and all agog to have her back to himself so that he might take her to the Lake District.

The baby was named Anna. She had her mother's colouring and she cried pitifully and ceaselessly. Rose seemed to take for ever to feel better and could not stop wanting to cry. Tommy came up to London to see her on a particularly weepy day, and it was a profoundly unsuccessful visit as she was unable to be cheerful and he was in a rage about Buscombe.

'Do you know what they have done, your father and my grandmother? They have sliced off a whole half circle of land – almost everything that you cannot actually see from the house – and put it up for auction. And the first thing I knew of it was a newspaper advertisement. Nobody told me. They sell half my inheritance and nobody tells me. *Nobody*.'

'My father wanted to. He tried to persuade Aunt Charlotte—'

'Oh?' Tommy said disbelievingly.

Rose remembered Charlie's refusal to intervene and felt tears rising.

'Tommy – I – I – am sure they all meant well—'

'Bosh,' Tommy said.

He left soon afterwards and carried his sore and angry feelings back to Buscombe.

'Well,' his aunt Elizabeth said, 'and did you see the baby?'

Tommy stopped.

'No,' he said. 'No, I didn't. I forgot.'

'And Cousin Rose?'

'She seemed a bit upset—'

'Perhaps because you did not ask to see the baby. Tommy, you are to go in to your grandmother.'

He knocked on the door of the morning room – which Elizabeth, in deference to the modish influence of friends, had rechristened the sitting room. Charlotte was sitting in a sea of maps and papers.

'Ah, Tommy.'

'Yes, Grandmother.'

She took off her spectacles.

'Major Taverner will be here from Friday to Monday of this week. Your cousin Harry. Your responsibility will be to see that he is properly mounted. The cob, perhaps. Will you see about it with Fred Bradstock?'

'Yes, Grandmother.'

Charlotte waited.

'Grandmother, may I see the maps?'

'There is,' Charlotte said, 'no necessity for that at all.'

Tommy's face was scarlet with fury and distress.

'Nobody will tell me anything. I do not know anything that is going on. I am treated entirely as if I were a little child. If it wasn't for Fred I shouldn't know anything, it was Fred who told me that it was the Creightons who want to buy the land, but I know the Creightons are family enemies though nobody will tell me why – even though Mr Creighton is my grandfather. I never see him, I haven't seen him since I was tiny! I should not have stayed here this summer, I should have gone with Nat Grant to Norfolk, he asked me to go. It's awful here. I don't feel it's mine and I don't feel I belong. I'm just a childish nuisance and they would all be so much better off if I wasn't here.' He stopped. 'I – I'm awfully sorry, sir. I shouldn't have—'

'I asked you, you know,' Harry said.

'I'm jolly glad you came,' Tommy exclaimed.

'So am I.'

He looked around him at the tilted basin of land below Long Coppice through which they were riding. So familiar it almost hurt—

'I haven't seen this for twenty-one years. I had been away for four years when you were born.'

'I want to get away too.'

'I know.'

Tommy said truthfully, 'I am a little nervous, sir, about the army—'

Harry turned to look at him.

'Only because it is unfamiliar. That will last a week. Then I think it is one of the easiest of lives. Much easier than here. You are very like your father to look at.'

Tommy privately thought this lean brown and sympathetic cousin very like Aunt Catherine in looks, but knew it would be impertinent to say so.

'We were all brought up together, your father, your aunts and myself. I was here as much as I was at home. I thought about this house so much – Tommy, in time, you know, all your troubles will smooth themselves out. You must simply wait patiently to be a little older.'

'While people my family will not speak to or even mention, live in half our estate?'

'I shall ride over to see Mrs Creighton,' Harry said.

'Oh, sir—'

'It may come to nothing. But it is worth a try.'

Lilian apologized at once for her predecessor's fussy taste. She waved a hand about the drawing room.

'Terrible! Terrible! The whole house – Oh, but it is extraordinary to see you! I have not set eyes on you for – oh! – over twenty years! Such a happy thing you should come home!' She looked veiled. 'And how do you find Catherine?'

'She is sketching in Norway. I came to see the boy because he joins my regiment next year. Mrs Creighton—'

'Oh!' she said, putting a hand on his arm, 'Lilian. Lilian, please—'

She had grown plump and soft, her prettiness had a petulant edge after two years of Arnold Creighton's ponderous devotion. She said to herself, often, in the mirror now, 'Being spoiled doesn't suit me'; but she had thought that was what she wanted, to abandon herself to cosseting care, not to have to think or decide any more. She did not like the way she was behaving with Harry Taverner. She was like any faded beauty making a fool of herself with an attractive man. It seemed to happen too often these days, a kind of discontented silliness would rise in her breast and make her crave a man's attention and sympathy.

'Lilian. I must confess I have not come to renew old acquaintance, great pleasure though that is. The truth is, I have walked into a bit of a tangle at Buscombe with that poor boy beleaguered in the midst of it and you might help me.'

'Buscombe?' Lilian said on a high note.

'I really want to know why you wish to buy the land?'

'I hate this house,' Lilian said, tears of self-pity starting to her eyes. 'It is a hideous house. You must see that. I can't live with all her things, her terrible taste. I want my own house—'

'You do not,' said Harry with the level calm he used to reprimand his men, 'have to choose the one site in all England upon which to build your house which would cause immense distress to a family you have wronged.'

Lilian tossed her head, gave a little laughing yelp.

'You dear old-fashioned thing—'

'It is some kind of spite. There can be no other reason.'

'Not spite. Disappointment.'

'You will make others suffer for your own disappointment?'

Lilian said piteously, 'I am not happy!'

'And so you will punish everyone else for that?'

'You are very hard,' she murmured.

'I am quite angry,' he said. 'And my heart is wrung for that boy. He does not even know why he may not see his own grandfather.'

'I suppose Catherine told you. I suppose she wrote to you—'

'Only this spring, when she knew I was coming from Ireland to see the boy. It was a brief and factual letter so that I should not be in the dark.'

Lilian went over to the window. She was wonderfully dressed, striped silk, ropes of pearls, a froth of lace around her throat.

'I do want that land. I was so happy at Buscombe, it was the only house I ever really loved. I could build a house there I could love. I would not be in anyone's way. The wounds will heal, you know, when Lady Taverner dies, and it will all be forgotten—'

'I must beg you not to.'

'I could outbid anybody now. And the Taverners need the money.'

'Perhaps not so much that they will tolerate you as a neighbour.'

She spun round.

'*Tolerate!* As if all the fault were mine!'

'I did not say or even imply that. Is your husband in favour of this plan?'

Lilian wrestled with herself a moment and then said, 'Not entirely.'

Harry thought of kind, industrious Arthur Creighton, so proud twenty years before of having built up a law business from nothing – a law firm that dealt with companies not individuals, which brought him money but no social cachet, a lack he would never understand. He thought of Creighton's new house, his daughter the Duchessa, his clever, ambitious second daughter. He was probably now just as proud of Lilian, and as bewildered by his inability to make her satisfied as he was by his firm's inability to attract gentleman clients.

'He likes this house—' Lilian said with faint distaste.

'Of course. He built it.'

'But he would build me another. If it would make me happy.'

How spoilt I sound, she thought, why can't I manage this interview, where has my sense of humour gone?

'Is anyone else,' Harry said, 'interested in the land?'

'I believe the Martineaus—' She came very close to Harry and looked up at him intently. 'I am not being perverse, I do not want to give anybody much pain. But, you see, the only way I can be happy myself – and why should I not be? – is to live in the one part of England where I really have known happiness.' She wanted to say that she felt she had had a very sad life, as she did so often to Arthur – with results that irritated her more and more – but felt it would only earn Harry's contempt. The impulse was followed by a second one to confess that she believed she had really loved his

221

cousin Tom, but that thought, too, seemed doomed. She shook her head, and backed away.

'I must leave you,' Harry said.

'When do you return to London?'

'On Monday. We are posted to Malta.'

She said recklessly, 'Will you come back for the auction?'

'No.'

'Oh!' she cried. 'Oh, don't think badly of me!'

He put his hand upon the door knob and twisted it with a jerk.

'I shall endeavour,' he said in exasperation, 'not to think of you at all.'

On 21 September 1893, five hundred acres of the Buscombe estate went under the hammer of Millings and Thompson, auctioneers, in a large dim back room of the Francis Hotel in Bath. By lunchtime, Edward Martineau, his wife Alicia and his nineteen-year-old son Frank, had emerged a little dazedly into the thick sunshine of Queen's Square as the new owners. On 24 September, newly returned from Norway, Catherine Taverner drove into Bath to see about the mounting and framing of the best of her sketches and, calling in at The Circus offices to congratulate Edward Martineau and to tell him of the sheer relief that pervaded Buscombe, learned that almost a third of the money that had enabled Edward to be top bidder, had been lent to him by Harry Taverner, in the strictest confidence. Even the indulgence of Arthur Creighton, it appeared, had its limits. It was despite this relief, a difficult autumn – Tommy sulking, Charlotte commanding – and she longed to pack her bags and boxes and be off again. It was for Tommy only she stayed. On 9 January

1894, his hair newly cut – it would be cut again within a week – his bags packed and strapped up with unaccustomed precision, Tommy Taverner left home for the Royal Military Academy, Sandhurst. It happened to be the same day that Rose Taverner, sick and damp skinned on the white tiled floor of her shining bathroom, realized that she was pregnant again. It was a realization that filled her with nothing but despair.

CHAPTER ELEVEN

1894

When Tommy passed out of Sandhurst at the end of 1894 and was gazetted an ensign of the 1st Battalion, the Gloucestershire Regiment, Fred Bradstock left Buscombe to enlist beside him. There was nothing to keep him at Buscombe any longer, not since his father had died, the previous spring. While Fred went into several weeks of gruelling training at Horfield Barracks in Bristol, Tommy took his Sandhurst uniform to Hawkes, the regimental tailor, had it altered to regimental pattern and adorned with the celebrated sphinx buttons. His red serge coat was trimmed with a white collar and cuffs for ordinary parades, he acquired a white helmet with the distinctive back badge – a lavishly bosomed sphinx reposing in a laurel wreath – a patrol cap, a fatigue cap, three belts – white, brown and spectacular gold – two sashes, a sword, a revolver and a tin trunk to pack all this glory in.

He went round to Swan Walk to show himself off.

'Perfectly beautiful,' Victoria said, 'even if I think you quite mad.'

'I'm going to Malta.'

'Oh!' cried Maud Bryce. 'You will melt in your scarlet splendour!'

'No more than anybody else. Have you seen the back badge? We are the only regiment to have one in the British Army.'

Victoria peered.

'Why Egypt?'

Tommy's eyes glowed. He stood straighter.

'Twenty-first of March 1801. Historic order given at Alexandria by Lieutenant Colonel Chambers in the face of a French cavalry charge to the rear of the 28th. "Rear Rank 28th! Right About Face!" The rear rank wheeled about, backs to their comrades, and fired a musket volley of remarkable steadiness into the French cavalry. So successful were they, that after that single volley, they turned about again and resumed firing into the enemy in front.'

He stopped. There was a small silence. The young women exchanged tiny glances.

'What about Buscombe? Aren't you going down to show yourself off there?'

Tommy drooped a little.

'I don't think so—'

'I quite understand your feelings,' Victoria said briskly, 'but I think you might regret it later.'

Tommy grew red.

'I cannot talk to Grandmother just now. And Aunt Catherine has gone to hunt butterflies in Palm Springs.'

'Should you like to see the house before you go?' Maud Bryce asked.

'No.'

'I think,' Victoria said, 'that you are sulking.'

'I am not.'

'Tommy. Take off all your fancy dress and let us go to the Army and Navy stores together. I want to see what fascinating things a soldier needs.'

'For an article?' Tommy said suspiciously.

'Perhaps. What does it matter? I can hardly make politics out of camp beds.'

'My dear,' Maud Bryce said admiringly, 'you could make politics out of anything.'

In the Stores, Tommy and Victoria bought a chest of drawers which packed into two cases and ingeniously became a cupboard, and a chair neatly folded into another case, which in its own turn became a table. There was a camp bath which held a washstand and a tidily assembled bundle of black iron rods and angles rolled into khaki canvas which would make up into a bed.

'Just think,' Victoria said, 'of Fred Bradstock setting this up for you all over the world. It even makes me feel almost sentimental.'

It made Tommy feel violently so, particularly with Victoria beside him, so infuriatingly independent of his constantly offered arm, so self-possessed, so self-contained.

'Will you come and see me off?'

'Where from?'

'Southampton.'

She considered.

'Yes. Yes, I will. I can work on the train each way.'

HMS *Himalaya* provided him with a horrible cabin on the pandemonium deck, right on the waterline, and he had to share it with two other ensigns going out to Malta, neither of whom did he much like the look of. Standing at the rail looking down at Victoria's neat grey figure, he had a sudden tremendous longing for her, for

Buscombe, for Catherine, for his dead – and even when alive, remote – father. He swallowed hard. Victoria would scold him for self-pity, and she would be right. His right hand moved to a tunic button and he held it for comfort. At nineteen it was absurd to feel like this; it was *right* that a man should get away . . .

The journey was as horrible as the cabin and his companions uncongenial as he had feared. But once past Gibraltar, the grey northern winter turned into a clear southern one and his spirits rose irresistibly, rose and rose until, steaming into the astounding prospect of Valetta harbour, the soaring walls like massive yellow cliffs in the sharp sun, he found he wanted to sing.

> *Floriana Barracks*
> *4 February, 1895*

My dear Victoria,
    What a lark! I have bought a pony and am learning to play polo. I have to learn fast and faultlessly – so as not to disappoint Fred, whose ambitions for me are sky high. He certainly turns the pony out for me better than anyone else's. And there is a regimental yacht I find, so I shall learn to sail, and I'm being pushed into the officers' boat for the regatta. Cousin Harry is a brick. He must be the best liked man in the regiment, and we are much envied having him as second in command of our battalion. We are allowed an hour and a half to dine at the Club in the Strada Reale and we all go there to a man, because you are allowed to remove your sword. Tuesdays, we may have ladies to tea—

'Thank goodness,' Victoria said. 'Perhaps it will stop him making calf's eyes.'

'You always maintained it was good for him to practise early romantic yearnings on a cousin!'

227

'I know. But recently I began to feel it was not so good for the cousin. A boy's enthusiasm is very manageable, but an almost-man's are something quite different. You cannot talk to a man who supposes himself in love with you because he is only listening to hear you say one kind of thing. He is not considering your character properly at all. Being in love makes people very untrustworthy.'

'And how,' said Maud Bryce tartly, 'would *you* know?'

Victoria said coolly, 'From the keenest observation, my dear,' and went away to work.

Floriana Barracks
2 March, 1895

My dear Victoria,

I am sure you have heard from the man himself how happy Tommy is. I try not to see too much of him in order to make him stand on his own feet, but the dear affectionate fellow is often difficult to avoid! Instructed by Fred, he will make a capital polo player – a credit to the regiment in that respect however cheerfully wild in others. I always forget, between each new batch of ensigns, what puppies they are.

My dear, I write to beg a favour from you. I had hoped to get leave this month to come home and see my mother, who has taken my father's death so hard, but we are ordered to Alexandria for two years, and there will be no chance. I am a little anxious on account of her last letters and feel an alarming situation is brewing which must, if possible, be prevented. She has declared her intention of letting Thickwood House – it became mine on my father's death – and moving to Buscombe with Aunt Charlotte, Catherine and Elizabeth. The place struck me two years ago as a tinder box already and she would, I fear, provide an admirable match since Aunt Charlotte and she have made such a mutual career of despising one another. Frankly, it only

228

needs your own father to leave your mother a widow who
also feels her loneliness might be assuaged by moving to
Buscombe to complete a truly terrifying prospect. A prospect
which is – and this is why I fear it – this dear open boy's
inheritance.

  I write to you because I can write bluntly. I know this task
should be Charlie's, but I also know he abhors family affairs
and might, therefore, well not have his heart in the matter.
Will you go down to Somerset and, if humanly possible,
deflect your aunt Rachel from her collision course? If you
succeed, you will feel such scorching waves of gratitude from
Egypt as will singe your hair. Even if you do not, will you
write and tell me what occurs? Mustapha Pasha Barracks,
Alexandria – and very unpleasant they are too, I am told.

  Write to me too of your opinion of colonial matters. I am
most uneasy myself and think we should be going to South
Africa not Egypt. A war in South Africa would be really so
very serious, and so bitter, that if I were in top command, I
should send us all down there now to do a policeman's job
and thus prevent a soldier's one ever being necessary.

  With my earnest thanks, your most affectionate cousin,
                                                Harry

Victoria went straight to Buscombe. There was little
point in starting with Aunt Rachel, wholly absorbed
in her elaborate grief for a man she had hardly seen in
thirty years, and Victoria had no time to waste. In any
case, there was a measure in which she and her aunt
Charlotte understood each other very well.

Buscombe looked modestly improved. The garden
was less shaggy and there was new paint on the
south-facing window frames, but the interior had
the slightly thin-blooded air of a house that lacks,
for the moment, an energetic masculine presence.

Charlotte and Elizabeth used the morning room almost exclusively, even dining there comfortably by the fire in winter, so that the drawing room and library, the dining room and the tower room smelled neglected. Even the conservatory had changed character on account of Catherine's constant absences, tended now by Albert Bradstock, Fred's younger brother, whose mania for tidiness – inherited from his father – had given the place a slightly municipal air.

'Oh!' Catherine had cried on her last return home. 'All I need in here now is a bandstand—'

The morning room, Victoria thought, could have done with a little of Albert's disciplining hand. It wasn't so much the yellow velvet curtains, faded unevenly to the colour of old straw, or the dim walls where darker squares showed the previous homes of various pictures, but the crowded feminine clutter of the room, workbaskets, piles of papers, pyramids of cushions and books, jars of paintbrushes, music stands, plants in pots, photographs and, on the now battered yellow velvet sofa where Elizabeth and Freddie Forrester had rejoiced so sentimentally over their engagement, a small square pug puppy who was bouncing and barking.

'Your cousin Elizabeth's,' Charlotte said. 'I have never cared for dogs.' She came forward and offered a downy old cheek to Victoria. 'Sit down, my dear. Be quiet, Pug.'

The puppy jumped from the sofa in order to show off on the floor.

'He is rather engaging.'

Charlotte said severely, 'He imagines he is.'

'Aunt Charlotte, I believe you rather like him.'

The puppy became all alert for the answer.

'At least he knows who is mistress with me. Victoria,

I hardly open a paper or a periodical these days without seeing your name, and now you seem preoccupied with this nonsense of women's rights to vote.'

'You sound like the Queen, Aunt Charlotte. She calls it this "mad, wicked folly of women's rights".'

'There has never been any problem in a strong minded woman achieving precisely what she wanted and the vote will make no difference.'

Victoria sighed.

'Of course it will. Among a hundred other differences it will force society to see women as a sex with the same rights to educational and professional chances as men—'

'And where has that ever got a woman?'

'Precisely, Aunt Charlotte. All down the centuries, nowhere at all.'

Pug yapped sharply.

'Aunt Charlotte, I do believe you have a feminist dog.'

'Did you come down to Somerset to enlist me in the campaign for women's suffrage?'

'Of course not. I came because of an impending problem with Aunt Rachel.'

It was Charlotte's turn to become alert.

'Rachel?'

'I had a letter from Harry, from Malta. The regiment is about to go to Egypt, so he can do nothing himself, but Aunt Rachel has informed him that she wishes to let Thickwood House and move here—'

'Here?'

'Yes, Aunt Charlotte. She is lonely after Uncle John's death—'

'Fiddlesticks! They could not abide one another. They lived together long enough to achieve Harry and were then, by mutual agreement, together as seldom as possible. There is no question of Rachel's leaving Thickwood and even less question of her ever living here.'

'So what is to be done?'

'I shall ask her to come here and tell her plainly that she must forget any such scheme completely.'

'You would not go to Thickwood? Or permit me to go?'

'Certainly not. Coming here will give Rachel something to do. She has never had enough to do. Idleness is the curse of silly women.' She waved a hand at the piles of papers that lay on every surface, weighted with lumps of quartz and crouching bronze animals. 'I am never idle. I have the house and the estate to run which of course I must do single-handed since Elizabeth has no grasp of such things and Catherine has succumbed to some kind of travel fever and is never here. Of course I can always rely on Arnold and now Frank.'

Pug tiptoed across to Charlotte and stared fixedly up at her with brandy ball eyes.

'He knows Frank's name. He is very fond of Frank. Frank Martineau, Edward's son, and the dearest boy. Almost another grandson to me. I believe he is going to be a better lawyer than the rest of them put together. There is his picture.'

On the chimneypiece among a crowd of china shepherds and spotted dogs, clocks and candlesticks and photograph frames, a thin faced, dark young man in a stiff collar and black silk cravat looked seriously back at Victoria.

'He looks very intelligent.'

'Highly intelligent. He can understand things that mean nothing at all to our poor, dear Tommy. He is wise enough to listen to the voice of experience, you see.'

'And their house—'

'The foundations of Combe Place,' Charlotte said in the satisfied tones of a successful fairy godmother, 'are to commence being dug in the first week of April.'

Swan Walk
3 April, 1895

My dear Harry,

There is nothing to fear. Aunt Charlotte was appalled at the notion and the scheme is scotched. There were, of course, interesting elements in her reaction that neither of us could have imagined, but the truth is that Aunt Charlotte is building up a little Empire down at Buscombe and is outraged at the thought of a possible fellow Empress, even a dowager one. Elizabeth is lady in waiting, Arnold du Cros both Prime Minister and Lord Chancellor and there is a promising new courtier in young Frank Martineau. In fact, I shall keep an eye on him because however honourable he may be, Aunt Charlotte must not be allowed to think of him as heir to the throne. Court jester is an endearing pug puppy with a great sense of humour and an equally great understanding of his Empress.

I am afraid Aunt Rachel was much upset and felt herself unwanted. I invited her to London for a while – we have now expanded across the whole top floor here and are living in quite a domestic manner so there was a room made ready for her – but I don't think our way of life or our friends quite suited her, and she went home to Thickwood within a week. Charlie took her to see a house he is building for a banker, out at Putney, and she showed great spirit and said she would not put a gardener in such a house.

Aunt Charlotte's scheme to occupy your mother was to

attempt to make her President of the Somerset Women's Institute, so in defiance she is devoting herself to making a friend of Lilian Creighton who must be a case of real loneliness, ostracized as she is. What a hotbed! Give thanks for the crude simplicity of your licentious soldiery—

Egypt, Tommy decided, was pretty good fun, though not so much good fun as Malta. He was given command of a small detachment which was a little sobering in itself, and lived for the most part in a tent pitched in an old mule yard, so was powerfully bothered by flies. There was, however, excellent shooting – duck and quail and snipe – to relieve the monotony, as well as Alexandria, only three miles distant, and the military camaraderie which he had found, ever since putting foot on Maltese soil, so entirely to his taste.

Letters from home reassured him he was missing nothing. The Buscombe chimney stacks were being repointed, new lead was ordered for the roof valleys, experiments in winter wheat were most successful, Catherine had fallen from a mule in the Atlas Mountains and broken her left arm, the walls of Combe Place were now up almost to the eaves, his uncle Robert had had a bad winter and could not seem to rouse himself. He was no better the following winter, a winter enlivened for Tommy by the fact that Catherine, nursing her arm, stayed at home to organize her diaries and her sketches and so had time to write to him.

Buscombe Priory
20 February, 1896

Dearest Tommy,
I have such fidgets sitting here that I even envy you your flyblown tent. I am cheering myself by planning a scheme for

the Nile in the late autumn, which would of course include Alexandria and you. Please do not get involved in all the bother brewing down in the Sudan before I get to you. It is really a great nuisance as I should so much like to look at Khartoum.

I am sketching now in sepia ink and a wash of Chinese white, and am very pleased with it as a medium for buildings. I am slightly aghast at the sheer bulk of material I have collected in only five years but at least the organizing of it keeps me out of the conservatory and from quarrelling with Albert, who is as highly strung as his poor mother was, and very possessive. He is good, however, and nurturing anything I bring home and is longing for a banana tree. This longing seems to me an excellent excuse for the West Indies but I must save that until next year.

Nothing really progresses here save Combe Place which will be ready for the Martineaus in June. Frank is here a great deal, and most patient with Grandmother. He asks wistfully after you at every visit feeling, I think, that the life of a solicitor in Bath does not compare favourably with that of a soldier in Egypt. He is clever and thoughtful – I feel they will make excellent neighbours. We are sorely in need of company.

Your uncle Robert is no better. I went to Bathampton last week and found a cross and apathetic old man rolled in rugs. Aunt Mary said sadly that sometimes she longed for him to lose his temper with all the old gusto, but all he does is complain ceaselessly in a thin high voice he has invented for the purpose.

Now write and tell me details of your life; what you eat, how you spend your days, what you have seen of Egypt! I wonder what news from South Africa filters up to you? England was both spellbound and horrified by the Jameson Raid which I fear might only be the beginning of serious *trouble between us and the Republics. Needless to say, the one member of the family to profit from it is Victoria, whose help has been asked for by the great Flora Shaw, Colonial Editor of* The Times, *and friend of Rhodes, in preparing a reply to a Parliamentary inquiry on the matter. What do you young men think of this new breed of young womanhood, I wonder?*

Your most affectionate aunt,
Catherine.

Two days before Christmas 1896, Robert Taverner died in his sleep at the age of seventy-three. It was Rose who insisted that they should at once abandon all preparations for the London Christmas they so much enjoyed and go down to Bathampton.

'Your mother—'

'My mother is the most practical woman on earth. She will not expect us until Boxing Day.'

'If I was her, I should be extremely hurt. And with the children about she cannot be so sad. Of course we must go. Victoria thinks so too.'

Charlie put his arms about her.

'Dearest Rose—'

At Bathampton, Mary Taverner had indeed been practical. The house was decently sombre and shrouded, but she herself was quite composed and had even put a small Christmas tree in the room where the little girls were to sleep and on each pillow a gingerbread star wrapped in gold paper. Robert had died without pain, it appeared, after only half an hour of difficulty with his breathing, leaving the house and its contents to her, The Hall to Charlie, and his shares in Taverner Warehouses to all of them. Victoria was also to have his books, and his granddaughters the two cornelian fobs from his watch chain which they were to wear on ribbons round their necks for his funeral. On Christmas Day, while Charlie carved the turkey and two-year-old Kate beat irrepressibly upon the table with her spoon, Mary announced that she was going back to Ireland.

'Mother!'

'Oh! Have you really thought about it – hush, Katie – so far from us all – should you not wait a little?'

'No,' Mary said, 'I have thought about it for two years, ever since Robert began to decline. I knew he would die before me because his love of life was quite gone. And I'm telling you this. I've no taste to stay about here as just another of the old Taverner widows and I've no great liking for this house either. It was put up in the wrong spirit, bless the man.'

Victoria looked at her mother with affection and admiration.

'Bravo, Mother!'

'And I'm missing Ireland. I always have been, but I've felt it more keenly these last years, me getting older and him quieter. I've two sisters to go home to and more money that I know what to do with so we can do up the old place handsomely.'

Kate beat a triumphant tattoo on her tumbler. Nurse was not there to say don't and her mother did not know how to.

'We'll be wicked old Irish ladies together, my sisters and me. You can come over each summer and see.'

'What will you do?' Anna asked, wide eyed.

'Breed wolfhounds, I shouldn't wonder, Irish wolfhounds and Connemara ponies. And wear our boots in the drawing room and drink whiskey like the menfolk do—'

'Wolves—' Anna breathed.

Charlie came round the table to give his mother a kiss.

'I do believe you are bent upon being a legend in your lifetime, Mother.'

'No more than you are, my boy!'

'Do you know,' Rose said later, when Mary and the children had gone to bed, and the three of them remained in the drawing room, 'she has such a light in her eye! It's a new life beginning for her, I do believe, after years and years of helping your father to live his—'

'She was born half a century too early,' Victoria said. 'What the suffragists couldn't do with a spirit like hers!'

Charlie was laughing.

'Whiskey and boots on the sofa! She will too. And she won't give tuppence when I sell The Hall.'

'Sell The Hall!'

'Sell The Hall?'

'Of course,' Charlie said coolly, 'why not? Do either of you want it?'

'No – but—'

'Charlie, so soon—'

'Why keep it?'

'A sort of decency—'

'Rubbish. Nobody really liked it but Father, and he liked it because he had built it. Architecturally, the late fifties were a disastrous time for building. It's far too ornate and unmanageable to run. In any case, you haven't heard what I shall do with the proceeds.'

They waited.

'I shall buy Swan Walk. The whole house. Victoria shall continue to live on the top floor and the rest will house my new practice. My new and independent practice.' He put one arm round his wife and one round his sister and whirled them around him until they shrieked. 'Do you realize? Do you realize that now I have enough money to set up entirely and absolutely on my own?'

Fort William Barracks
Calcutta.
4 July, 1897

Dear Victoria,

You will never guess, but I am sharing an officer's bungalow with its own compound here, a luxury that almost makes up for the disgusting disappointment of missing Omdurman. Can you believe such a thing, being transferred just before an engagement like that? This place is pretty good though, a huge star-shaped fort on the Hoogli River, and there are race meetings, and dances at Government House, so I am being, as you would tease me, very jolly. We are the only British regiment in Calcutta, so much in demand. Rather a lark!

I've had a rather solemn letter from Grandmother on the subject of Buscombe. So odd – as a schoolboy I could not wait until it was mine, almost counting months and weeks, and now that it is, I'd much rather be here. Harry suggested I should apply for leave and come home for a little family ceremony, but I'm not too keen, especially as I'm now to be sent to the School of Signalling at Subathu in the Simla Hills which gives me at least a chance of becoming Brigade Signalling Officer. Buscombe won't change, it hasn't changed all my lifetime. It can wait.

We have mounted paperchases every Sunday – have to take old screws out on them because the ground is like iron and would wreck the legs of anything decent. Fred is worth his weight in gold and the envy of everyone. We had our own little toast to Buscombe, just the two of us, on board coming here on my birthday.

239

*What do you need a vote for, may I ask? You are quite
enough trouble without one. (Only joking.)*

Write soon.

Yours, and you know the rest,
Tommy.

In 1898, Lord Curzon was appointed Viceroy to India
and it was Lieutenant Thomas Taverner – only a month
promoted – who, as Brigade Signalling Officer, organized the twenty-one gun salute that acclaimed his arrival
in Calcutta. That same year, Miss Flora Shaw, Colonial
Editor of *The Times*, acquitted herself splendidly before
a Parliamentary inquiry into her part – if any – in the
Jameson Raid, and, in recognition of the research done
to help her in her answers by Victoria Taverner,
commissioned her to travel to South Africa on behalf of
the newspaper and report on the political situation there
as she saw it. She travelled on the *Scot*, the ship which
had the previous year taken Sir Alfred Milner, High
Commissioner for South Africa and Governor of Cape
Colony, to Cape Town, the only woman journalist on
board, arriving with a full notebook and an already clear
grasp of the muddle that years of drift and compromise
had got England into, in Southern Africa.

'I am afraid you are quite right,' she wrote to her
cousin, Major Harry Taverner in Calcutta, 'and we
have got ourselves into an awful fix. First we repudiate
all right of interference in President Kruger's state of the
Transvaal, and now we try to force upon him all kinds
of reforms – such as giving a vote to foreigners – in his
own internal affairs. I think our eagerness to interfere is
the mask for sheer greed for all that gold. We cannot
bear to think the Boers shall have it all. However
patriotic I am – and I am, as well as being something of

an imperialist too – I think our behaviour is immoral as well as unwise. Sir Alfred Milner is coming back to London to talk to Mr Chamberlain, but I shall make every effort to interview him before he does.

'I have been up to Johannesburg and seen the mining camps and I am horrified. Johannesburg is all new money, raw manners and vulgar luxury, not a breath of civilized values anywhere but at least I did not frighten them, as I do the good citizens of Cape Town, by being that alarming phenomenon, the New Woman!

'Have you news from Home? Catherine went to a lecture given by Mary Kingsley, the traveller and anthropologist, and is now absolutely bent upon going to West Africa herself. Charlie is a coming man – someone named Edward Hudson has started a magazine called *Country Life*; it is all the rage and Edward Hudson thinks Charlie's houses wonderful. My mother sounds in her element to be home in Ireland again – she declares her newest ambition is to be the first lady master in County Kildare – and there is no doubt but that the Empress of Buscombe is having the time of her life.

'Could it be, miraculously, that for a brief moment we are all happy and satisfied?'

Allahabad, Tommy thought, kicking his heels through interminable dusty hot days, was a hell of a hole. If it wasn't for mounted paperchases and a spot of polo, he did not know what he should have done. Fred could have told him that life in the lines was a hundred times as unbearably boring and uncomfortable as that in the officers' compounds, but Fred was not a complainer, any more that he was – a quality he shared with Tommy – fretting for home. Home was where the regiment was.

'Durban!' someone shouted.

They were playing aimless bridge in the mess under a punkah that only stirred the stale hot old air about and kept the dust nicely airborne without bringing a single cool breath.

'Durban?'

'Yes! Yes, look!'

An order was slapped down on the table and they craned to see. War looked imminent in South Africa, the English towns in Natal particularly vulnerable; the 28th were to entrain for Calcutta forthwith, embark at once and proceed to Durban.

'Five years in the Army, sir,' Tommy said to his cousin on the cantonment station in Allahabad that night, 'I have had five years in the army, if you count a year at Sandhurst, and I have hardly seen a shot fired in anger.'

Harry grunted.

'I am afraid that the Boers are very angry indeed—'

On 25 September 1899, the officers of the 28th battalion lined up at the rail of the SS *India* to be photographed, moustachioed, eyes screwed up against the glare, sun-helmets in hand, before the ship, hooting mournfully, swung away from the banks of the Hoogli and began her journey across the Indian Ocean.

Chapter Twelve

1899

President Kruger beat the 28th to it, by a single day. They landed in Durban on 13 October to find that war had been declared on Great Britain twenty-four hours before. The regiment disembarked, entrained at once in three trains of open trucks and clattered northwest to reach Ladysmith in the middle of the night. The remainder of the night was spent bivouacking on a piece of scrubby waste ground outside the station while trains banged about in the shunting yard next door, and in the morning four vast mule carts, drawn by ten beasts apiece, arrived to take baggage and equipment into Ladysmith. Behind them, the men marched into the garrison, dry mouthed, gritty eyed and smeary with smuts. Tommy, at the head of his detachment, was humming.

If you had a competition, someone suggested, as to which was the worst hole, Aldershot would only win by a very short head. Both places shared the grim red regularity of a railway town, Aldershot or Ladysmith, Ladysmith's romantic origins as the crossroads of great cattle driving tracks of the past being now quite obliterated by hideous parallel lines of tin roofs and an uncompromising architectural style of harsh ugliness. Life there might have been redeemed by being able to dwell on the green ridge that lay on the northeast of the railway or even on the hills that ringed the town, and where, it was feared, the Boers might set up their guns, but those were luxuries not offered to the men of the 28th, put into lines of dusty bell tents on the dusty plain with no view but the latrine trenches in one direction and the back of the railway sheds in the other.

To Miss Victoria Taverner
Mount Nelson Hotel
Cape Town
South Africa

Ladysmith
26 October, 1899

My dear Victoria,

So – we have had our first engagement and a fine blunder it was. The only person whose spirits seem unquenched in any way is Tommy who appears raring for another go. We were sent out of the garrison to a place about eight miles away, called Riet Fontein, to try and stop Free State Boers joining up with Transvaal Boers. I am afraid we failed. We also lost half the mules in a stampede I simply cannot account for, and, far more seriously, our commanding officer, Colonel Wilford, who broke cover where the action was hottest and deprived us of himself, a whole company and a Maxim gun.

The only cheerful note in the day was my feeling a sudden warm trickle running down my leg and, looking down to see if I had been hit, finding a bullet had only pierced my water bottle and it was army regulation tea and not Taverner blood that was filling my boot. And something rather decent – we went back the next day to pick up our dead and wounded, and found that although the Boers had taken all British boots, they had also removed towels from the haversacks of every dead fellow and covered their faces with them.

We struggled back to camp through a thunderstorm I have never seen the like of – only the lightning (pink and blue and green out here and hundreds of feet high) reflecting in puddles showed us the way. I don't like the look of things. The Boers are digging in all round us on the hills. It looks like a siege for sure, to me.

What news? You say you are recalled now that war has been declared. When do you sail?

Ever your fond cousin,
Harry

Buscombe Priory
Somerset
16 October, 1899

My dear Tommy –

It is now almost five years since you left home, and two since you became a man. I expect your thoughts turn often homeward to Buscombe and that such thoughts are a great comfort to you. It is with pride I heard that you had been made a lieutenant, and that you are proving such a credit to your regiment.

I believe I am safe to say that fortune smiles just now upon the family. We are so fortunate in our new neighbours at Combe Park which has turned out a handsome house, thought not of course with the presence of this. I am glad to be able to tell you how well all things prosper here. We are to repair the stableyard in the spring and I have engaged a new boy to help in the garden since the two remaining Bradstock boys have gone to seek employment in Bristol. That would never have happened had their father still been alive. We are trying Herefords on the top pastures too, to see how they thrive, and mean to turn our hands to cheesemaking.

I have not been too well this summer but Catherine gave up her notion of coming to South Africa as a nurse, to look after me. It is for the best and I am fast improving.

God keep you, my dear boy,

> Your affectionate grandmother
> Charlotte Taverner.

> Ladysmith, Natal,
> 2 November, 1899

My dear Victoria –

I cannot write any more letters to you, for we are now besieged. The railway line to the south has been cut and at 2.30 p.m. our telegraph line went dead. How long we are in for it, nobody can tell, but I do not like this being cut off, so I shall continue to write to you, a kind of journal, as if I could still post the envelopes.

I expect you all know more of what happened to Cousin Harry than we do, stuck here. Sir George White, who commands the garrison here, tried to dislodge the Boers from the hills to the north. It wasn't much of a plan in the first place, but it was made much worse by sending about two thirds of our battalion out with the Royal Irish Fusiliers and ridiculously small guns, in the middle of the night to capture a Boer held hill and block their retreat. Cousin Harry took C company out last of all in the blackest night you ever saw. The pack mules carrying the gun stampeded I heard, it was all the most awful confusion.

Two of our fellows came back dead beat to camp the next day. The whole thing had been a fiasco. The attack, at a place called Nicholson's Nek, had failed and there was an order to retreat and the men just broke ranks and wandered off. A sickening sight, they said. One of them saw Harry chuck his sword away rather than be taken prisoner with it and then he was marched off down towards Elandslaagte

Station with some other officers. I suppose he has been taken to Pretoria. I should think he is as disgusted at the bungling as we all are. Eleven dead for nothing and all because of the strategy of a half wit.

It is odd not to have Cousin Harry here. He has been within a mile of me for five years—

30 November, 1899

This isn't much fun. We had eight days of full rations after the siege began, now we are down to three quarters rations. They are making bread out of Kaffir meal which is pretty disagreeable. We are on watch constantly, and the Boers have begun to shell us with their Long Toms, day and night. They can't do much steady damage but it stops us playing cricket and polo and the noise is damnable. And now it's raining and we are a sea of mud and boredom.

Christmas Day, 1899

Long Tom dropped a shell in today which turned out to be a Christmas pudding wrapped in a Union Jack! We could have done with one each – half rations for two weeks now, two pounds for a dozen eggs if you can get them, no flour, no rice and sugar is like gold dust. The bread is always mouldy, and now all the troop horses have been slaughtered, we are on to mule meat. Too awful for words.

A couple of men were brought to me yesterday who had been caught stealing starch from the laundry. I couldn't even be angry with them. They confessed they had stolen it to eat simply because it was clean, as every other mouthful we get is putrid or filthy or covered with mould. We are catching rainwater in the tarpaulins over our shelters, and it tastes of rusty nails. The Boers have tried to flood Intombi Relief Hospital where a lot of our chaps are lying with dysentery, and to poison the stream.

I was asked up to Convent Ridge for dinner with the staff last week. Six courses, silver candlesticks and polished boots while we regimental officers pig it in the trenches in boots we haven't taken off for a week, trying to pretend burnt mealies taste like coffee. Makes me sicker than old Buller making such a stew of things on the Tugela. There's a lot of bitterness about the staff officers; I'm not the only one—

10 January, 1900

When I come home I shall want to sleep in clothes I have worn for a week, somewhere out in the park, and I shall require someone to water me well every so often and someone else to fire my shotgun close by my head now and then. I shall want to be given boiled grass that you assure me is spinach – this was issued to the men today, we are now on quarter rations – and mule bone broth, they call it Chevril, how's that for the year's worst joke? and I shall only require to shave every few months.

28 January, 1900

I weigh seven stone twelve pounds; I started the siege at eleven stone three pounds. We all look like scarecrows, uniforms hanging like bags on sticks. An order came round yesterday instructing us to keep the civilians in the town cheerful. I haven't the energy to keep a laughing hyena cheerful for half a minute just now.

I've had word that Harry is in Pretoria, a prisoner in the Model School on a diet of bully beef and boredom. Even writing the word bully beef makes my mouth water. I don't know where the fun and glory has gone but it certainly isn't in Ladysmith any more. We have sent out skirmishing parties to raid Boer guns, but I couldn't say they do much more than provide a diversion. Apparently old White is sitting up there on Convent Ridge with his head in his hands and can't decide a single move to save his life.

I've an awful headache the last few days, probably the sun, and I can't seem to sleep despite having the energy of a sick kitten when I'm awake. I seem to be thinking about Buscombe a great deal – odd when I haven't given the dear old place more than a passing thought in four years. I wonder if there's snow. Keep thinking I can hear the pheasants rising out of Long Coppice and that long cry of the foxes on winter nights. The days are so hot here you could fry an egg on your boot toe. If you had an egg.

6 February, 1900

They have put me into the 24th Field Hospital. Mild typhoid, I'm told, but I don't see much is the matter except the headache and a bit of fever and the odd nosebleed. Fred has made himself into my orderly and a shocking old woman he is too. I'm living on watered milk and sago but can't raise much of an enthusiasm for it. Do you remember beetle swimming races in the watering cans in the conservatory? The sun is like a ball of fire through the tent wall but I was lucky not to be sent out to the camp at Intombi where all typhoid cases are supposed to go – horror stories from there would make your hair curl. Fred found me a bottle of Armagnac and said all the cavalry horses were being slaughtered for food – the cavalry are up in arms because they feel themselves now reduced to the level of the infantry. Buller's very close, shouldn't be long now to relieving us. Are the snowdrops up yet? Write—

Railway Cuttings Camp
Ladysmith
2 March, 1900
Your Ladyship, I write in great sorrow to tell you that when Gen. Buller relieved this place two days ago he was too late

to save the life of your grandson. I am taking the liberty of writing to tell you he died an officer and gentleman on 27 February worn out in the third week of illness and with a fever and internal bleeding we could not stop. I have lost the best master and gallant officer in this regiment but must try to take comfort knowing he died for the British Empire and was talking of Buscombe before the fever took him. I have no heart left for the army now he is gone and will apply to be discharged as soon as this war will allow me and come home to Buscombe to take up my duties as before if that so pleases your Ladyship.

Your obedient servant,
Fred Bradstock.

Buscombe Priory
8 May, 1900

My dear Victoria,
I fear I have not the heart just now to come to London. I expect you are right and I should avail myself of a diversion but I simply cannot bring myself, rouse myself, yet, to do any more than drag through the days. It haunts me that I went to the West Indies rather than Egypt and so missed a chance of seeing him there in early '97, and then gave in to Mother over this nursing business in South Africa. Even to have been on the same continent, I feel, would have been a comfort. Ever since he became a soldier I told myself that he must be allowed complete freedom to live his own life until he chose to come home of his own free will but now I feel myself to have been neglectful and selfish and am as racked with remorse as I am with grief. I have written to Monte Cimone to tell his mother, but really I do not know why I did.

If you could spare time to come here, you would do so much good. Mother is not just prostrated over Tommy but also over the fact that the house must now go to Charlie, who, much as we all love him, does not like it or want it. You tell me his practice is flourishing. Perhaps he will decide to refuse Buscombe? Edward Martineau says he is quite entitled to, it does not go automatically with the baronetcy. It then becomes Harry's, I suppose, and I am sure he does not want it either. How much hung upon that one dear young life!

Freddie has sent word from London that he is not well at all and would like Elizabeth to go up and nurse him. She has refused, properly I think. The only things I can even begin to look forward to are the possibility of your visit, and to Fred Bradstock's coming home when he may give me a first-hand account of my darling. With fondest love,

Catherine.

Lowndes Square
21 June, 1900

Dear Lady Taverner,
After a long conversation with him yesterday, it is my earnest belief that your nephew Charles will, in the fullness of time, come to appreciate the desirability of his inheriting Buscombe. Having no axe to grind but my regard for the family and my fondness for your late grandson, I believe my son-in-law will listen to me and come to see the amount he might gain as well as give in assuming his proper place at the head of the family. I see no difficulty in his combining such duties with his architectural practice – there is plenty of room in an energetic man's life for several and diverse preoccupations. Will you be so good as to leave the matter with me?

Yours sincerely,
Arnold du Cros.

CHAPTER THIRTEEN

1903

It was no use for Rose to pretend that she felt anything but the sharpest apprehension as the carriage drove up to Buscombe. The drive was already choked with the great vans that had preceded them, and which were now disgorging their dear London furniture onto the gravel. It looked as miserable and out of place as she felt. Where could it possibly go, in those solid and traditional rooms, muffled and smothered in carpets and curtains, littered with unnecessary bits and pieces? A longing pang for the polished floors and calm empty white walls of Holland Park shot through her so keenly she felt tears rise. This would not do. There was Anna and Kate to think of, now gazing soberly out of the window at their new home, themselves both on the verge of bottomless doubt. It was her fault they were doubtful, Charlie was quite right to point out how they caught a mood from her, but oh the prospect was so hopelessly depressing, that great beast of a house she had never liked, inhabited immovably by Lady Taverner and the aunts, and the memories of doomed and disappointed men—

'It is a very nice day,' Anna said staunchly.

She was ten, as fair and as amenable as Rose had been

at her age. She wore a drop-waisted sailor frock, sashed low with black silk, and a sailor hat with black ribbons, and black slippers with bows of moiré ribbon on the toes. Kate, a year younger and a shade darker, wore blue and white striped cotton and carried in her clenched fist the small ivory pig that was her most successful talisman. For every visit to the dentist, her father gave her a tiny lead or china or ivory animal as an inducement to behave with proper stoicism. The pig had acquired a special aura since that particular visit had happened not to hurt at all.

The pig was only necessary because Rose's unmistakable dismay at leaving London and fear at the prospect of Buscombe had persuaded Kate that something unpleasant must be ahead. For herself, leaving Holland Park was sad, certainly, but since all the people and the possessions who mattered to her were coming too, the adventure of a change seemed to be dealing most effectively with the sadness. Anna clung to the old house as her mother did, certain too that no other place could make them all as happy. Kate was sorry about this but could hear in her own voice an edge of briskness when she and Anna talked about it, the same briskness she could hear in her father's voice.

'My dearest Rose,' Charlie said the night before they left, 'can there *please* be an end of this? You know my feelings, you know I do not want to leave here, you know we never planned to live in the country, you know how much I enjoyed our freedom from my family. But you also know that it never crossed my mind that I should inherit Buscombe. The fact that I have must change things. Harry and I are the only men left in this benighted family and he is in India. I no longer have a choice about my life any more. Perhaps I was lucky to have the luxury of a choice for thirty-eight years and I should not forget that. But please understand this: I do not want to live at Buscombe, and I have to. Because you and Anna and Kate are my wife and children you must come with me. It was a choice made *for* us, not *by* us. If you go on and on lamenting, you will make yourself and all of us miserable. Why should we not' – leaning forward and giving her shoulders a little shake – 'make something of our life at Buscombe?'

Rose said all the usual things. That she did not much like the country, that she did not at all like Buscombe, that she was afraid of Lady Taverner, that the house would not be theirs at all.

'Then *make* it so,' Charlie said.

How could you, she thought now, stepping out onto the gravel into a small congregation of their ladder-back dining chairs, make anything of a house that had had four hundred years to make something very decidedly of itself already? It stood on its weed-sprinkled terrace and looked down at her, huge and solid and shabby, sooty smudges under its windows and defining every ledge and crevice, the tower absurd beneath its pointed hat of green copper.

The children got out after her, and stood waiting for a cue for their reaction.

'You see how big it is!' she said. 'And how much space there is. I think there is a lake down there—'

'A lake? With a boat?'

'Which will be our room?'

Rose looked up at the dormer windows in the roof.

'Probably up there—'

Kate said, 'Did Tommy sleep there?'

Tommy had become a sad and sacred little myth of their last nursery days. Their nurse, deeply sentimental

254

by nature and deprived of going out as a proper nurse to South Africa by a slight hump back, had made a grisly little shrine on the day nursery mantelpiece, with a photograph and a candle and a vase for flowers. There was a black tasselled ribbon draped across one corner of the photograph, taken of Tommy in uniform at Sandhurst. He had been born at Buscombe, they knew that, and now he was dead and so was his father and his mother, Charlie had told them, was a nun in Italy.

Anna said, 'I do not think I want to sleep in Tommy's room.'

'No,' Rose said hastily, 'you shall choose. Perhaps the new governess will sleep in Tommy's room.'

In the now faded blue and yellow of Rosamund's drawing room, untouched since her refurbishing of it, down to the last little cloisonné object of indefinable purpose, Charlotte waited for Rose. Beside her, Elizabeth sat embroidering a stout satin stitch lily on a stole for the induction of the new rector at Buscombe Church – a bachelor of fifty, most promising – and beyond her, in the conservatory, Catherine was pruning dead flowers off the Himalayan jasmine. Catherine was brown-skinned; she was newly returned from Morocco.

Charlotte was humming with good intentions. Rose was a dear, Charlie was at last showing a most proper sense of responsibility, and it would be delightful to have children in the house again. Charlie would of course have to spend Monday to Friday of each week at his practice in London, but he assured her he had ample time left to devote to Buscombe. Charlotte was over eighty and had never felt better. The household looked after her most carefully – it had no option to do otherwise – and enabled her to conserve her splendid energies for managing things. Elizabeth did the housekeeping – it was no use counting on Catherine for that, with her boxes corded and labelled for somewhere outlandish almost permanently in the hall these days – and Fred Bradstock combined being keeper with overseeing the few remaining outside staff. Charlotte interviewed Fred, Arnold and Cook (she liked to reassure herself daily of Elizabeth's competence), kept a journal and the account books and required the newspaper to be read to her after luncheon and the novels of Charlotte M. Yonge to be read at night. She intended to vary this in future by playing patience and canasta and bezique with her little great-nieces. On their behalf she had already interviewed Cook and explained about the wholesome simplicity necessary for children's food, an explanation which accounted for the dreaded trays of unadorned mutton chops and tapioca pudding cooling beneath its slimy skin, that were to ruin lunch time on the top floor for the next three years.

Rose, Charlotte decided disapprovingly, was looking very fashionable. It was perhaps only to be expected, fresh from London. Her tiny waist, her hugely flounced shoulders and bodice, all that braid and lace ruffling—

'My dear,' she said. 'Welcome to Buscombe.'

Anna and Kate lurked at their mother's skirts.

'Come, children—'

They advanced doubtfully between the armchairs.

'This,' Aunt Charlotte said, in the voice of one issuing a directive, 'is a very, *very* happy house for children.'

It was undoubtedly an interesting house for children, a kind of historic junk shop of endless possibility. That first summer, they spent whole days in attics and barns and stables, emerging breathless and cobwebbed with their arms full of curious implements and objects. On wet days they arranged these in an empty attic room they adopted as a museum, and on dry ones they spent anxious but irresistible hours with Fred in the orchard, learning to ride. Fred had recently married a girl from Romney Marsh who cried and cried for the dykes and the sea and told them, between sobs, her family's smuggling stories of which they were privately extremely sceptical. Fred said it was the fate of men in his family to marry nervy women. Was their mother, they wondered, nervy? Certainly they did not hear her laugh as much as they used to, but then, the sheer size of Buscombe meant that you couldn't hear everything, and perhaps she was laughing where they could not hear her.

The new governess was a pale thin girl called Ellen Napier, with an interestingly hot temper and a really wonderful talent for painting wild flowers and bees and birds. She refused, however, to paint the sweet dead mole they brought her which they thought unenterprising. Lessons were not to begin again until September and Ellen's job meanwhile was to help Rose settle them into the part of the house – the morning room and first floor of the east wing – that was to be theirs. Charlotte decided she very much liked the sound of Ellen's voice, so Ellen was deputed to read the newspapers and Miss Yonge.

She lived with the children under the sloping ceilings of the top floor, the bleakness of the rooms – this was all part of the simplicity for children campaign pioneered by the chops and tapioca – redeemed by southerly views across the dark blotch of the rhododendrons to the lake, and a good sight of whoever was coming up the drive, almost from the moment they left the Bath road. On Fridays, they watched for Charlie from this vantage point, and so did Ellen Napier who found a household of women – she had five brothers – a rather overpowering environment. Charlie's weekly arrival entirely changed the atmosphere at Buscombe.

So did the visits of Arnold du Cros, more frequent now that he had a daughter and granddaughters at the house. Those visits, Charlie knew well but did not acknowledge, were responsible for his weekly freedom in London to be an architect. It would have broken Charlie's heart to have to give that up now, particularly as a new romantic craving for country houses and the life they offered was making his practice absorbingly successful. The house in the Lake District had been featured in an article in *Country Life* and had brought Charlie more commissions than he could handle from country-loving businessmen, who not only wanted his kind of house but liked to have it designed by a baronet. That Charlie forgot he was Sir Charles Taverner most of the time only added to his cachet.

Arnold, paying punctual visits to Buscombe either end of his regular Friday and Monday visits to Marsham Court, was equally aware of Charlie's dependence and equally conscious it was best unacknowledged. His quiet pleasure at being increasingly indispensable to the family, his seat in Parliament, his purchase of two container ships that now plied between Bristol and the Continent (Taverner Warehouses now owned two expanding warehouse systems at Ostend and Calais) gave him the deeply satisfying sense that his ambitions of all kinds were being richly fulfilled. Buscombe was hardly restored to its former glory and there was only the barest sufficiency of staff to maintain it, but Arnold's patience, tact and diplomacy were all boundless. To rush anything, to appear to mastermind anything, would destroy at once the delicate and dignified structure of traditional life at such a house as Buscombe, which was so infinitely attractive and precious to Arnold. With Charlotte he had been sensationally successful: she believed all the steady small successes of the last ten years had been the result of her own adroit management of things. Charlie was too intelligent to treat in the same way and entirely without a need for domestic power, but he too was gradually succumbing, largely because it suited him so well to do so.

The only cloud on this sunlit horizon was Rose. It was not much of a cloud, and Arnold was sure it would disperse, but it was an indisputable little cloud all the same. That her apprehensions at the change had been terrible he both knew and understood; but it was less easy to understand her almost frightened inability to adapt herself to Buscombe and its demanding, but by no means impossible, inhabitants.

'But you are a man!' Rose cried when he pointed this out to her. 'Aunt Charlotte likes men—'

'My dear, she likes you—'

'Yes, yes,' Rose said fretfully, 'I know. But we need to occupy the same space in the house, if you see what I mean. I can't run the house because she and Elizabeth do that – it is Elizabeth's only occupation apart from fervent organ practice to impress Mr Aubrey on Sundays – so I can't be what I used to be. Ellen is a dear, but she is employed with the children, so I cannot interfere with that either. Catherine said of course I must treat the conservatory as my own before she went off to Egypt, but she said it with such a longing possessive look that I am terrified I might damage something. And I miss Charlie, Papa.'

Arnold suggested to Charlie that they might buy a

small house in London so that Rose could be with him during the week. Charlie said he would think about it. What he thought was that he would not like Charlotte to be in ultimate charge of his daughters, that he was working so happily and hard that he would scarcely have time to be at home if he had a London one again, and that the impersonal, practical life at his club suited him admirably.

'Then I must think of something else,' Arnold said.

Rose's own temporary solution was to try to re-create Holland Park at Buscombe. Though she did not dare to remove the carpets in their rooms, she persuaded Charlie to have the walls stripped of the papers that Rosamund had put up – papers of bosomy blossom and ribbons – and painted them cream with apple green woodwork instead, the heavy swagged curtains bundled up into the attics – where they made, Anna and Kate discovered, excellent nests for reading or giggling in – and the red mahogany furniture carried off to the stable lofts. In its place she put the delicate geometric modern pieces she and Charlie had so enthusiastically collected, so successful in the tall airy rooms of an eighteenth-century London house, so pitifully wrong in the uncompromisingly Jacobean proportions of the first floor rooms at Buscombe. The finished rooms felt neither interestingly new nor comfortably familiar.

'They look,' Rose said in despair to Ellen, 'like some beloved person who has been disfigured by an awful illness, don't they?'

Ellen was full of a fierce sympathy. Ellen's view of the world had changed very much since she came to Buscombe. She had to come because there was no other way to live in a family as proudly impoverished as hers, so she took the Taverners' roof and their annual hundred pounds and the charge of Anna and Kate with the imperious determination she took anything unavoidable. Motherless, she had grown up accepting the authority of the six men at home – her father was a minor civil servant who had wished to be an academic – and was used to undiluted masculine company. The subtle shifts and struggles for power among the women at Buscombe, their mutual dependence and antagonisms and rivalries, at first appalled her, then intrigued her and finally called out the predilection for taking sides that was so much a part of her. Charlotte roused her wary admiration and dislike, she despised Elizabeth, knew little yet of Catherine, found Anna dull, liked Kate and gave her whole intense heart to Rose.

Rose was the first person who had, in all her life, turned to her. All those men in the narrow, shabby house in Wilmot Street had needed her to see to their laundry and make marmalade and chivvy the series of kitchen girls – increasingly resentful kitchen girls because they wanted to be waitresses in the new teashops in the West End – but they had not needed her to confide in, even to talk to much. When Rose, so pretty, a little dishevelled in one of Catherine's huge blue aprons over a dress of soft white lawn spotted in grey, had burst into tears at the failure of her homemaking scheme, Ellen, out of pure instinct, put her arms around her and was, to her delight and amazement, not pushed away. Rose let herself be comforted, let herself be cheered. With growing elation, Ellen found she could do both, not just this first time, but the next, when Charlotte reminded Rose with elaborate kindness, whose house Buscombe had been for years, and the next, when Charlie said he must return to London on a Sunday night one week, because his schedule for Monday was so heavy.

'What do you think', Rose asked Ellen diffidently, 'I should do about the morning room? It is our drawing room after all—'

'Leave it,' Ellen said.

'Leave it! But it hasn't been touched for fifty years!'

'But it's lovely. So faded and pretty.'

'It's falling to pieces.'

'It doesn't matter. It is the nicest room in the house.'

'That is what Kate says.'

'Kate is right.'

'Oh! Oh – I don't know—'

'Don't think about it,' Ellen said. 'Come outside and I will show you what Fred showed me yesterday, a double camellia newly out, the colour of thick cream. You never saw anything so lovely.'

It was Ellen who started the custom of calling her Lady Rose. She blushed, but she liked it. It was romantic, pretty, and set her apart. Within a month all the servants were doing it too. Only Charlie teased her.

'Ah! The lady of a medieval ballad.'

'Don't be horrid. Anyway, you used to write medieval ballads.'

'In my foolish youth.'

'I liked your foolish youth.'

'Lady Rose! I should have a yacht or a racehorse named after you. I think Miss Napier is in the grip of a violent infatuation.'

Rose wanted to say that she wished Charlie still was, but simply said,

'The children are learning a great deal.'

'Very jingoistic history, from what Kate tells me.'

'You look tired. You work too hard.'

'Nonsense,' Charlie said. 'I couldn't work too hard, I love it, you know that.'

'Yes,' Rose said sadly.

'I always meant to be successful. Don't you remember asking me?'

'Oh!' Rose burst out. 'I am very proud of you, you know that. But there is no point in being proud of you here with no-one to see, no friends to talk to!'

Charlie knelt and put his arms round her.

'Oh, my dear—'

Rose burst into tears.

'I don't want to be unhappy, I don't want to be like this! But I did love our life before and now I feel so lost—'

'I will talk to your father again. He suggested buying a little house in London and your spending the week there. But you see, I am just so tied up, so busy, I should hardly be at home.'

'The children here—?' Rose said, hearing the reluctance in his voice.

They looked at each other.

'I know.'

'And this house *is* yours! It belongs to you!'

'Yes.' He kissed her.

Rose, cheered as she always was by sympathy, blew her nose and said resolutely, 'Perhaps we must just be patient. In a few years—'

Charlie kissed her again, more buoyantly.

'How good you are. Of course. Patience. Come, we must go down to dinner.'

On his arm down the staircase, Rose's brief recovery of spirits died away. How she regretted her hopeless compliance, her desire to please Charlie, to be easy! Why had she not at once said yes to a house in London and made him agree, there and then, so that she would now have something to look forward to, her friends again, the theatre, concerts, galleries. Oh she was such a fool! Anna and Kate would be quite safe with Ellen, so sensible and decided, they would never miss her. She glanced at Charlie. He looked back at her with affection and gratitude.

'Rose, you are so right. Patience is what we must have.' He grinned. 'And, as usual, you will have to have it with me, bless you.' He put his hand on the drawing room door knob. 'Ready?'

She nodded. Her chance was gone.

'Charles!' Charlotte said and waved the newspaper. 'Here you are in print again, I see. Rose, dear, you must be so proud of him. Now, come and sit by me and tell me what the children have been about today. And Charles, come and tell me about London. Oh! I almost forgot. Elizabeth! Elizabeth, tell them your news!'

And Elizabeth, composed and complacent Elizabeth, burst into sudden tears and cried, 'Oh! Oh, I am a widow!' and it was only Rose who thought to rise and cross the room to comfort her.

CHAPTER FOURTEEN

· 1904

On a thunderous July night, in their bedroom looking west into one of the ancient mulberry trees, Charlie had the worst asthmatic attack he had suffered since his marriage. He terrified Rose, and was for a time so frantic for breath, that he terrified himself. He was forbidden to go to London as usual on Monday morning. Two nights later, it happened again, and three nights after that, although neither of the two subsequent paroxysms were as severe.

Meredith, the family's medical practitioner, and Mr Carew, the specialist summoned from Bath, were of the same unpalatable opinion that these new attacks, always occurring at night while Charlie was resting, were symptoms of cardiac asthma, and indicated how gravely Charlie's heart had been weakened by the asthma of his childhood. Hardly had Charlie and Rose begun to digest this information, than Charlie developed a cold which within a few days manifested itself, with an agonizing dry cough and raw chest and throat, as bronchitis. Glaring at Mr Carew with eyes blazing with fever, he learned that he had chronic bronchitis which had arisen secondarily to his asthmatic and cardiac condition, and that in England bronchitis was one of the commonest causes of death. The cure, he was told, was to avoid all habits and ways of life that had given rise to the first asthmatic attacks. Since Charlie neither smoked nor lived in an unwholesome climate, the culprit was clearly overwork. If he wished to live, Charlie must change his professional habits.

Anna decided, somewhat understandably, that she would not go near her furious and wheezing father just now. Even Kate simply sidled in and looked sorrowfully at him for a bit and sidled out again. They were left very much to their own devices; Rose was looking after Charlie and Ellen was looking after Rose. Fred taught Anna and Kate to fish – Kate was too much of a fidget to be much good – and he told them about the Boer War and the tough little Basuto ponies the Boers rode that he had so coveted, and of how Tommy died. This last was particularly fascinating and a great revelation.

'Didn't he die of a bloody wound?' Kate asked.

'No, miss. He died of the typhoid.'

'But I thought all soldiers died of a bloody wound. That *that* was how they died—'

'Not 'im,' said Fred and then he said the most romantic thing he always concluded his reminiscences of Tommy with, and which they loved – it seemed so noble – 'I'll never 'ave another friend in all the wide world like 'im.'

'It makes,' Kate said afterwards, 'poor Fred seem so dreadfully, beautifully lonely.'

It was, Kate realized much, much later, for all the miserable anxiety about their father, also the last summer of childhood for either of them, the last summer of that carefree absorption in simple and messy occupations without the responsibility of worrying about other people's lives. Barefoot mostly, and in special pinafores of strong blue cotton with pockets to hold snail shells and pebbles and apples and pieces of string, which Ellen had made them, they dammed tributaries of the stream, scrambled about the beech hanger and in the disused apple store at the back of the old granary made a secret house furnished with objects smuggled out of attics and lofts. It had a very pretty washed Chinese carpet on the bare boards and two little low chairs covered in faded duck egg blue damask, beds of piled straw covered in old curtains, the now empty bird cage like a pagoda, a musical box, a sewing table with a bag below of pleated silk, a silver candlestick which could hardly be of any value since it was almost black, a globe, an ivory abacus, and a rosewood swinging toilet glass for Anna. When it was finished, they played in it for one day and then they left it.

'The only thing that's nice when it's over,' Kate said, 'is horrible German grammar.'

Ellen found them on the night nursery floor one evening comparing whose feet were the browner.

'Kate's are,' Anna said, 'because they are dirtier than mine.'

'They are *very* dirty,' Kate said proudly.

Ellen sat down and said, 'Your father is at last getting better. Really better. Meredith said that tomorrow he may leave his bedroom and sit outside for an hour.'

'Only sit?'

'He is hardly strong enough to stand. He has been *gravely* ill. Really seriously so.'

'Perhaps,' Anna said, 'he won't go to London any more.'

'No. I – I don't think he will—'

'He won't like that,' Kate said. 'He won't like not

working. He'll get awfully steamed up if he can't work.'

Ellen sounded worn out.

'The doctors think that if he works again, he will have another attack because he is unable to work moderately. And another attack might—'

Her own feelings were such a tangle. If Charlie stayed at Buscombe, she would hardly see Rose any more, and yet Rose was so happy to have him, even ill, not a tear in weeks . . .

'Kill him?'

'Yes.'

'Then he mustn't work,' Kate said, scrambling up. 'He must think of something else to do. I'm so *hungry*. I could eat a whole loaf by myself.'

A long cane chair was put on the grass beneath one of the mulberry trees and there Charlie lay, shadowy pale, bone thin and dangerously irritable. Mr Aubrey, sleek as an otter, had come over from the Rectory that morning, spent a delightful ten minutes being flattered by Elizabeth, and had then mounted the stairs to inform Charlie of the wonderful gift of *Life*, of simply being *Alive*. Charlie stared at him stonily and refused to speak. As the living was now in Charlie's gift, Mr Aubrey deemed it wise not to repeat his assurances of life's daily little glories – the love of a good woman! the primrose! the laughter of children! – and withdrew. As the door closed, Charlie threw a volume of Carlyle after him and felt disconcertingly close to tears.

It was almost unbearable, literally, to be in the grip of an enemy one had no weapons to fight. If he were to continue to pretend, as he always had so far, that he simply had no physical frailty, then it seemed the enemy would just rise up and lop him off altogether. If he allowed his students to run his practice he would be agonized that his standards were not maintained and that the work he had already done would acquire an inevitable tarnish; if he closed down the practice he would be saying goodbye to the great single achievement of his life at the very moment it was about to put him into the class of Voysey himself, or Ballie Scott. If he went to London in a sort of overseeing capacity once a week he knew he would go mad with frustration and would also lose all the clients who naturally wanted houses by Sir Charles himself, down to the last kitchen stool. As it was, he hardly dared to think of the problems that must have arisen in the six weeks he had lain here in breathless pain . . .

Kate came trailing across the lawn from the rose garden and fished a crumpled letter on thin crackling paper out of her pinafore pocket. She crouched beside him.

'I'm sorry it got so squashed. I think it is from Aunt Catherine for you. I was supposed to give it to you long ago, I mean long ago today, but then Fred said some stags were fighting beyond the beech hanger and it's pretty early for them to start, so I went—'

'It's from Athens. I thought she had gone to Constantinople.'

'Perhaps she went to Athens after.'

Charlie put the letter down on his rug swaddled knees.

'Shall I open it for you?'

'Later.'

'Shall I go away?'

'No.'

Kate was peaceful because she was not as exhaustingly sorry for him as Rose or Anna or Elizabeth. He knew she thought he should get up and get on with it now and if he had not felt as limp as a rag, he would have agreed with her.

'Did you see the stags?'

'No. I really wanted to find a bit of antler. But,' she coloured a little, 'I did see Mr Martineau.'

'*Young* Mr Martineau?'

Kate nodded.

'Did he speak to you?'

'Oh yes. He always does. Why didn't you design their house?'

'They couldn't afford me.'

Kate looked pleased.

'Serve them right then, that Combe Place is such a dull house.'

'Loyal child.'

She looked at him.

'You won't always feel so awful, you know.'

Charlie scowled.

'Do you know what I think?'

'What do you think?'

'I think,' said Kate, 'that when you are better, you ought to do something about *this* house.'

'This house? Here?'

Kate waved a hand at it.

'It's such a mess. I mean, Anna and I like it messy because it is more interesting for us, but we do think people coming here must laugh a bit, every room different and such a jumble and full of such funny things. We'd like the swan in our bathroom, please, to brush our teeth into. We put an old bonnet on him yesterday but Ellen made us take it off because of Aunt Charlotte.'

'The swan is a classic piece.'

270

'I thought classic meant Greek.'

'Not *classical*. Classic, meaning having intense historical associations.'

'What is it intensely associated with?'

'The extreme of fashionable taste thirty years ago and your mad cousin Rosamund.'

'Mad like Ophelia?'

'More mad, like Mrs Rochester.'

'I say,' Kate said, 'you're smiling.'

'I'm not,' Charlie said crossly.

'Well, stretching your mouth, then.'

'Don't argue.'

'You like arguing. Anyway, it's a sign you're getting better.'

'What is?'

'Arguing. And smiling.'

'I think you have grown very impertinent.'

'Ah,' Kate said, getting up and shaking the clattering contents of her pinafore pocket, 'I am a modern child, you see. Born a Victorian, brought up an Edwardian. Ellen said so. Shall I tell Mother that you are going to redesign Buscombe?'

'No.'

'Why not?'

'Because I haven't thought about it.'

'But will you think?'

'Go away. You exhaust me.'

She blew him a kiss and trailed away again across the grass, past the dining room wing and into the great dark solid mass of shrubs – he hated them, pure suburbia – until she reached the door in the wall that led into the park. On the still afternoon air, Charlie heard the faint slam of it swinging shut behind her. He picked up Catherine's letter.

Athens
31 August, 1904

My dear Charlie –

I have had the most extraordinary summer, chugging about the Cyclades in a series of funny little boats, and only yesterday did I go to the Poste Restante here, and find my mother's letter telling me about you, which had been forwarded from Constantinople. In my experience it is unlike the Turks to be either so competent or so obedient to one's instructions.

I cannot tell you how sorry I am. Having only discovered freedom very late in life, I now know what it would cost me to lose it again, which is, I suppose, poor Charlie, what you are facing. I can hardly bear it for you, but I do take comfort from my knowledge of the resilience of your character and your courage. I know you will come through and I am convinced that nothing you have done so far will be wasted. Nothing ever is – God and Nature are both very economical.

I discovered when I was in Constantinople that I did not after all feel like Turkey this summer. I was not in the right mood. So I found the captain of a little Greek ship carrying oil and dried fish – how I wished it had been wine and lemons! – and persuaded him to take me to Athens. We went straight down the Aegean, only stopping at Lemnos and Skiros and I was treated with great delicacy by the four hands on board whom I rewarded with photographs of themselves. A wild success.

In Athens I discovered it was not Turkey that had been wrong for my mood, but cities, so I found a boat that went to Paros and another to Naxos and a third to Rhodes and a fourth to Karpathos and a fifth – the worst – to Crete. There

I stayed for a month and not a day passed on that strange fierce island that I did not think of you.

Why? Charlie, on Crete – or Candia, the old name – Arthur Evans is doing of the ancient civilization of that island what Schliemann did at Troy. He is re-creating history, he is rebuilding the palace of a people he calls the Minoans, a palace built perhaps two thousand years before Christ. It is, literally, a breathtaking project, staircases and store-rooms, courtyards and throne rooms rising out of a steep rocky hillside, just as they looked nearly four thousand years ago. The hillside is called Kefala, the palace is Knossos. Would it not, dear Charlie, be a good place for you to convalesce? A dry warm climate for your poor exhausted lungs and an exciting project for your equally weary mind?

I will be home in October. I have decided to spend September walking in the Peloponnese, in the south, around the Gulf of Messinia. And I must see Sparta. I am as brown and leathery as an old shoe. Elizabeth will be horrified—

'It was Kate's idea, to be truthful,' Charlie said to his father-in-law.

They were sitting in the library, pale September sun in slabs on the faded carpet and through the open window, the faint sound of Rose on the terrace explaining something to Fred. Fred ran Ellen close second in his passion for Rose.

'You see, it's the heaviness of the rhododendrons I hate so. I want birches and azaleas, light airy things. Would birches like this earth, do you think?'

'What do you plan?' Arnold asked.

'Are you sitting firmly?'

'Certainly.'

'Number one. Pull down the tower.'

Arnold burst into a shout of laughter.

'My dear boy!'

'There is every reason, aesthetic and practical, to do so. It is a wasted room, it does not work as a room, there is no purpose it can fulfil. It is in itself ugly and ridiculous, impossible to heat, no pleasure to anyone. It has no possible sympathy with the exterior of the house which is largely Georgian or the interior which is a great mixture but still, I find, Jacobean or even baroque, in character. It is a perfectly frightful excrescence in short, and the sooner it is demolished, the better.'

Arnold said, smiling, 'And your aunt Charlotte?'

'We have to have a collision one day, about something. It is as inevitable as night and day. I am not afraid of her, you know.'

From the terrace, Rose said,

'Is there somewhere we could make a medieval garden, do you think, Fred? Lilies and grey leaved plants—'

Arnold said softly, 'I have no right, no wish to interfere, but if you are to commit yourself to living here, should you not be thinking of a son?'

Charlie looked down.

'Rose – after Kate—'

'My dear boy! Ten years ago—'

'She seems happier just recently. Since I decided to close the practice and just accept a couple of private commissions a year. This new interest in the garden, for instance. So perhaps—'

'Talk to her.'

'I shall be forty next year.'

'A wonderful age to start a new life.'

'Steady,' Charlie said. 'You aren't talking to Aunt Charlotte, you know. Every time someone congratulates me on my renunciation of the practice I still want

to break their necks. Never could take sympathy. Odd, but Kate is the only one who seems to understand that.'
He got up. 'Are you seeing Aunt Charlotte, or are you leaving straight away?'

'The latter. I have to go up to London. Now that you are so much better I really only need to see her as a courtesy. Is she well?'

'Terrifyingly.'

Arnold rose.

'I shall go and have a word with Rose before I leave. Give my love to the children.'

Since Charlie had brought his family to Buscombe Charlotte had – with a great deal of self-congratulation – lived a large proportion of her life in her own rooms. Her bed had been moved into what was once only her dressing room, and her bedroom, still draped in Queen Victoria's convolvulus chintz, the tables still covered in tartan rugs in imitation of photographs of the interior of Balmoral, had become a sitting room. In it she and Pug – who had adopted her as mistress in recognition of a character as strong and as quirky as his own – lived in a companionable clutter, keeping an eye out of the south window for all callers, and another out of the west windows for any preventable alteration going on in the gardens. Thus Charlotte knew Arnold had been, and had not troubled to see her, and that Rose and Fred were pacing about an area of grass below the croquet lawn in what looked suspiciously like a planning manner.

'Well?' she said sharply to Charlie's knock.

He was unperturbed.

'Well what?'

'What is going on? Arnold du Cros has clearly lost his manners and Rose is going to dig up the croquet lawn.'

'Arnold had no particular reason for calling, Aunt Charlotte, and did not wish to disturb you. I heard Rose say something about lilies to Fred, so I imagine they are deciding where to plant them.'

'Not on the croquet lawn.'

'I am sure not. It would be an idiotic place to plant anything.'

Charlotte grunted. Pug trotted over to Charlie and squared up to him.

'And you are an idiotic dog.'

Pug tried to toss back an insouciant ear, and failed.

'Rose is looking well, Charlie.'

'She is. It's wonderful.'

'People are always well at Buscombe. Charles, it is time Rose gave you a son.'

Charlie hesitated and then said, instantly regretting it, 'Her father has just said the same thing to me.'

'Ah!'

'Aunt Charlotte, you must say nothing to Rose. It is a matter on which she is desperately sensitive. The birth of the girls—'

'Childbirth,' Charlotte said, 'is not supposed to be a picnic. I should know. We none of us enjoy it but it is our duty and our privilege.'

'Not, perhaps, any more—' Charlie said faintly.

'Nonsense. You have the family and the house to think of. Rose cannot just think of herself. I will speak to her.'

'No, I beg you—'

'It will be better, coming from me.'

'Aunt Charlotte, please, it will be disastrous. And wrong.'

'*Wrong?*' said Charlotte furiously.

'Yes, wrong. It is for me to do, if anyone does.'

'I disagree—'

'Aunt Charlotte,' Charlie said upon an impulse of desperation, 'Aunt Charlotte, there is something I must tell you. It has been in my mind for some weeks and it would not be right not to tell you of my plans. You know, I think, that now I am more at leisure I mean to devote myself to the general updating of Buscombe? Well, the first thing I mean to do, and I cannot beat about the bush—'

'Yes?'

There was a frozen moment in which Charlotte and Pug glared at Charlie and then he took a reckless breath and said,

'I am going to pull down the tower.'

'Over my dead body.'

'There is no point to it.'

'It is part of this house.'

'It is cold, ugly and useless.'

'It was put up on the occasion of my marriage.'

'The house is mine.'

'I have lived here for almost sixty years.'

Pug seized a mouthful of Charlie's trouser leg. Charlie twitched himself free.

'What is the point of keeping it?'

'It has become part of this house,' Charlotte said. 'It is a landmark. I will not have things changed.'

'So you do not want the stone cleaned or the windows replaced or bathrooms put in or dead trees cut down in the park and replaced with young ones?'

'That is not change,' Charlotte said stonily.

'It was a change to put the tower up. A change for the worse. Now I propose a change for the better, to pull it down again.'

'No.'

'You have not been in it in months.'

'I need,' Charlotte said, 'to know it is there. It is my marriage tower.'

'You cannot even see it from this room.'

Charlotte went to the farthest right hand corner of the west window embrasure and pressed her cheek flat to the glass.

'I can.'

'Not unless you do that.'

'I am doing that.'

Charlie sighed exasperatedly.

'Aunt Charlotte, I shall leave you to think about it.'

'There is nothing to think about. Send Elizabeth.'

'As you wish.'

As he shut the door behind him, Pug burst into a volley of barking and Charlotte shouted with surprising strength,

'Over my dead body, I tell you! Over my dead body!'

It was stupid to broach the subject of a baby to Rose that night. Charlie knew it and could not seem to help himself. She was sitting at her dressing table fiddling about with all those pots and brushes, and he was roaming about behind her in his dressing gown before going off to his dressing room – that seemed to have become an unhappy habit since he was ill – and he let it all spill out, clumsily, and not properly thought out and of course she was in torrents of tears before he had even finished.

'You cannot mean it! You cannot make me again! You know how awful it was, you know how afraid I was, and how depressed I get afterwards, not wanting to hold the baby or look at it even. You can't want to frighten me like that again!'

'Dearest Rose, the last thing on earth I want to do is to frighten you. I know it was painful with the girls, and I remember how sad you were afterwards, but you are ten years older now. So am I. Everything will probably be quite different—'

She sprang up, hair flying.

'Will it? Will it? Oh yes, very different, because my body is older so will be far less flexible even than it was, because I will get tireder and sadder, because having just managed to get a little pleasure out of life here, I am pushed back into a straitjacket. You don't understand a *thing*, Charlie Taverner, you don't understand one single thing. You have no imagination at all and if you had you wouldn't use it. How can you suggest such a thing to me?'

Charlie tried to put his arms about her, but she backed violently into the window curtains and stood there trembling in her whirl of pale hair.

'Rose. Rose, *please*. I am not trying to harm you. I am trying to suggest that we give this place an heir. I am about to make it ours, really ours, with all my new plans, and when it is ours, we shall want it to belong to our son. Can you not see that?'

'And if I have another girl? Will you want baby after baby after baby like Henry VIII until you get your son?'

'No,' Charlie said, flopping tiredly onto the edge of Rose's bed, 'don't be so silly. Of course not. But I would like us to try and see if we can achieve a son.'

'*We!*'

Charlie tried a small joke.

'I don't believe you can do it without me.'

Rose glared.

'It is so easy for you! Everything is easy for you

because you don't put your heart absolutely into any-thing for long, except your houses—'

Charlie shouted, suddenly furious, 'I have given up my houses!'

He began to cough, doubled up. Rose was instantly all contrition, flying from the room for his inhaler, kneeling by him while he gasped and blew.

'Oh Charlie, I am so sorry, I never meant this—'

'I know—'

'It's just that I simply cannot face—'

'I know, I know, don't talk about it—'

She helped him to the window and threw it wide.

'There. There, is that better?'

He leaned against the frame, his eyes closed, dragging up breaths.

'You ought to go somewhere warm. Like Catherine suggested. You ought to rest somewhere warm.'

He shook his head.

'Not yet—'

She put her head on his heaving shoulder.

'I love you, Charlie.'

'Yes,' he said, 'yes.' He looked over towards her bed. 'May I stay tonight? As you see I can hardly—'

She nodded vigorously.

'I must tell Ellen.'

'What the hell has Ellen got to do with it?'

'She often reads me to sleep. Tennyson and Swinburne.'

'Naturally,' Charlie said.

'It's kind of her,' Rose said, a little nettled.

Charlie moved slowly away from the window and towards the bed.

'Go and tell her not to, tonight. Tennyson and Swinburne would choke me.'

Later, lying side by side in the dark, Charlie said,

'I told Aunt Charlotte today that I was going to pull the tower down. She blew up like a volcano. That was why she refused to come down to dinner.'

'Charlie! Will you go ahead?'

'Of course.'

'Charlie – could – could you not wait until she – she is dead? It was put up for her wedding after all.'

'She is going to live for twenty years. She is attached to it for the most insubstantial of reasons and never goes into it now. I think I will make some kind of loggia on its foundations. There is nowhere to sit on the sunny sides of the house at the moment.'

'I think you will hurt her.'

'Only because she is determined to be hurt.'

Rose said, 'Good night, Charlie. Sleep well,' and he put out his hand for hers and found that she had turned on her side away from him and composed herself for separate sleep.

Rose and Charlie were very careful with each other for several weeks, behaving with a grave and delicate courtesy, the wary politeness of people dealing with fretful invalids. Charlie slept in Rose's room for three nights, but the fourth night he was wakeful and restless and took himself off so as not to wake her, and the next night, he met Ellen in the passage carrying a book. It was in truth Ellen's decision, not Rose's. Rose was almost as afraid of alienating herself from Charlie as she was of becoming pregnant and bearing another child, but seemed to her own dismay, powerless, helpless. The certainty that she could not endure childbirth again burned her up, made her reckless, exaggerated – she knew it did, could see it did and could not stop herself.

Ellen was soothing, a kind of neutral alternative to either a baby or Charlie. She lay at night listening to the *Morte d'Arthur* and tried to think only of that, of the ruined chapel and the glimmering lake and Sir Bedevere grasping Excalibur in an anguish of desire, unable to hurl it into the water towards that silent, beckoning arm.

'Mother is mooning again,' Kate said.

'What?'

'Look.'

They were on the top floor, in their schoolroom, kneeling on chairs at the window with their German untranslated on the table behind them. Down below, in a long soft grey cloak that fluttered in the little wind, Rose was drifting down to the lake, head bent.

'Do she and Father quarrel?'

'No!' said Anna, shocked.

'It doesn't matter, quarrelling with someone you love. You love them just the same afterwards.'

'I don't. Quarrelling makes me not like people so much.'

'Well, you are always quarrelling with me.'

Anna climbed off the chair and went reluctantly back to 'der Sommerbesuch des Kaisers in Bad Homburg'.

'I don't count you. You are my sister.'

'Oo! A carriage! It's Grandpapa. Shall we go down?'

'We mustn't.'

'He is far more important than the Kaiser's summer holiday.'

'Let's do this German first, quickly and then go down—'

The parlourmaid told Arnold that Lady Rose was down by the lake.

'Has she been gone long?'

'No, sir. Not above ten minutes.'

It was a soft October day, high thin cloud, pale sun, gentle air. The trees to the south of the house were beginning, very slightly, to turn and the borders below the terrace were full of cream and bronze chrysanthemums, as big as mops. Arnold found Rose standing under a willow at the edge of the lake and staring emptily across it to the little obelisk the fifth baronet had put up as a focal point.

'My dear?'

'Papa!'

She gave him a smooth cheek.

'Your mother sends best love and a basket of mushrooms. Her charitable works have mounted now so as hardly to allow her a minute to eat or sleep. How are you?'

Rose said nervously, 'Very well.'

'Shall we walk a little?'

She put a hand in his arm.

'How lovely this will be in a month's time, when the trees have truly turned.'

'Oh yes.'

'And how is Charlie?'

'Oh – very well. Determined to pull down the tower. I am sure he should wait.'

'She will get over it, you know. She is the most resilient woman I ever encountered. And this house is now yours, you know, this house and lake and park, this piece of England, this piece of English history. You must make it yours, put your stamp upon it, enrich it as other generations have done before you to make it what it is. Charlie understands that, I think. Rose—'

She stopped walking and looked at him.

'Yes?'

'My dear, a house, an estate like this is a very precious inheritance. It has, because of its age, its traditions, and all the lives that have been lived in it, something indefinable and priceless that no money on earth can buy. One can feed off such houses, a diet more truly nourishing than any other, but in return one has a duty, a duty to give as well as to take. You must think about that, my dearest girl. This house is yours now and your responsibility now. But in the future you will not be here to take that responsibility, so you must ensure to the best of your ability that the house will be loved and cared for you—'

Rose said, 'No, Papa! No – no, not that! Not that! Not you too!'

And she wrenched her arm from his and turned and began to run with surprising speed away from him along the lake's edge, away from him and back towards the house.

CHAPTER FIFTEEN

1906

In the spring of 1906, Charlie left Buscombe for Greece. To the outside observer there was every reason why he should go, after a winter spent gasping and wheezing with bronchitis, wild eyed with frustration as much as with fever. He was the subject of the first question on the lips of every caller.

'So good of you to ask,' Elizabeth would say piously, 'but I am afraid I cannot give you much of a cheerful reply. Of course his heart was so weakened by childhood asthma—' He became something of a romantic local legend, a man of immense talent driven to become almost a recluse by his physical frailty. Kate thought this very bad for him.

'What he needs is something to *do*. If he is busy he won't wheeze.'

'Aunt Charlotte won't let him.'

Kate said in a fierce whisper, 'Aunt Charlotte is an old monster.'

Anna looked prim.

'There are far too many women here,' Kate said sadly. 'I think we are all driving him mad.'

He spent his days – and had done so for well over a

year – in the tower room hunched over plans on drawing boards he had set up in the windows that looked north to the croquet lawn. They were not plans for the private commissions he had intended to do – it had proved impracticable to accept work he could give no reliable date for completing – but for imaginary houses, and for Buscombe. Some of these latter plans were for meticulous restoration; for example, putting the hall back almost a hundred and fifty years to its graceful columned simplicity, empty of furniture, the walls pale and stippled, the floor stripped to reveal its polished chequerboard of stone. Of other plans, ideas for demolition or reconstruction or remodelling, he presently had little hope. He had met in Charlotte such an abiding, intractable antagonism, such a powerhouse of relentless energy in opposition, such a *relish* for domination, as had left him almost stunned. His first instinct had been to lock horns and fight back, certain that his own coolness of judgement and undeniable logic would, step by step, undermine her. Not a bit of it. She thrived upon their confrontations, seemed almost to swell visibly in stature as they fought.

'You have quite lost sight of what you are arguing for!' Charlie shouted in despair one day. 'You are simply arguing for the sake of arguing!'

It was the reddest rag he could have brandished at her. The last shred of any flexibility vanished. He tried to call her bluff and actually ordered a demolition team from Bath to set about the tower; Charlotte countermanded them personally. Short of an undignified family scene before an audience of interested labourers, there was nothing Charlie could do but concede her victory. She had no delicacy in it either and triumphed over him at meals, even in front of the children.

'She has no consideration for his feelings!' Kate cried indignantly to Ellen at night, brushing her hair out of its daytime pigtailed crinkles.

'She is old,' Ellen said. 'She has been here since she was less than twice the age you are now.'

Anna said, 'I think Mother is right. He should wait—'

'But he can't do nothing, waiting! And he is too ill to do what he wants to do. Ellen, Ellen, don't you think it is very hard for him?'

Ellen put down the hairbrush.

'I think,' she said with the straightforwardness that made her so reliable a companion, 'that life in this house is hard for every single person in it.'

'Do you think,' Kate said later to Anna, lying in the dark, 'that that is why Aunt Catherine is always going away?'

'What is why?'

'She goes away because life at Buscombe is hard? It *is* hard. It is so complicated, because nobody seems able to do what they want to do without there being a fuss.'

There was a new fuss because Rose had made a friend of Lilian Creighton. It was not deliberate. It was the result of a genuinely chance meeting in a milliner's shop in Gay Street, and a mutual admiration for a tilted summer straw, the brim lined beneath with rosebuds and ruffles of thick lace. Rose was wearing a most becoming dress of flowing cut with a little high cropped jacket and a jabot, and Lilian said, 'Oh, but the hat would be perfect for you!' and Rose put it on and they turned to the looking glass together to judge the results, and were both much pleased by their two faces, framed side by side. Rose paid for the hat, highly delighted, and the milliner called her 'Lady Taverner' copiously, and Lilian, encouraged by Rose's charm and the sudden intimacy of the moment, said,

'I am Lilian Creighton.'

Rose put her hand to her mouth, but she was laughing.

'Will you have tea with me? Shall we go to the Royal York?'

Rose looked at her watch. Ellen was taking the children to see the Roman Baths; they were not due to meet up for three quarters of an hour.

'Yes,' she said.

'Am I even spoken of?' Lilian said later, putting a slice of lemon into Rose's cup.

'At Buscombe?'

'Yes.'

'Oh no.'

'Not even obliquely?'

'I am afraid not.'

They both giggled.

'What a waste of a bad reputation. Are you happy there?'

'No,' Rose said truthfully.

'I loved it. But then, I did not have a sick husband to worry me. Are you lonely?'

'Oh yes—'

'So am I.'

'I miss London.'

'So do I.'

'Do you often come in to Bath?'

'Far too often. I am woefully extravagant, I shop all the time. I used to read but now I fidget too much to read. Will you call on me?'

'Oh!' Rose breathed, eyes wide. 'Think of the storm—'

Lilian shrugged.

'Or think of yourself.'

'Oh, the time! I must go – I am meeting the children. Charlie dared them a shilling each to taste the water but I think only Kate will have won it.'

'Please come and see me,' Lilian said. 'What harm can it possibly do? Please come.'

Rose went. It was delightful. She went again, and on her return Elizabeth asked the coachman where he had taken Lady Rose, and then she went to Rose's room and was very reproachful.

'She betrayed me as a friend, you know. I quite trusted her, and I helped her when she had troubles, and then of course I found she did not give tuppence for my friendship. It was very hurtful. I am not sure I am in the least recovered from the hurt. Mother will be hurt too. You should not have gone, you know.'

'Must you tell Aunt Charlotte?'

'Oh, indeed I must.'

'Don't go again,' Charlie begged Rose after the inevitable explosion, 'not when you see the consequences.'

'Why should I not have a friend?'

'Not *that* friend.'

'But *I* have no quarrel with her! And she is charming. We have so much in common.'

Charlie said tiredly, 'Then you must fight your own battles when you return from her house.'

But Rose would not fight. If there was an unpleasantness looming, she stayed in her room. She stayed there a great deal and Ellen would take up little meals on trays, so that Charlie was too often faced with dinner alone with Charlotte and Elizabeth, from which he would totter exhausted with the effort of keeping conversation neutral. Elizabeth, he decided, had become a monument of repetitive dullness, a woman content to live within visibly shrinking horizons. Charlotte was impossible, admirable and more exhausting than every other human being he knew put together.

As for Rose, she was simply bewildering. She had withdrawn from him, but where she had gone, he could not follow, and she did not seem to want him to. She still nursed him when he was ill, but absently, and he began to prefer Ellen with her straight answers, her tremendous commitment to whatever task it was she had in hand, from making his bed to teaching his daughters geography to adoring Rose. Rose drifted, elusive, managing to avoid even the lightest touch without actually seeming to repel him. When she spoke to him, or answered his questions, she hardly seemed to see him and answered him from far away. Arnold counselled patience.

'We have alarmed her. We must wait for her to come to terms with what we have suggested in her own time.'

Charlie waited. While he waited he chafed and coughed, tried to draw, fought with Charlotte, succumbed to bouts of fever. In the late winter of 1906, leaning on his drawing board staring out at the cold dead garden and the leaden sky, he became suddenly devoured by a flame of resentment. Why should he endure all this? Why should he be buffeted like a human tennis ball between tyranny and mystery? What on earth was he doing, idling, wasting, in a household rife with domestic politics of an intensity incredible to a civilized man? Life at Buscombe was a padded cell; he saw himself hurling himself at soft yet unyielding walls, screaming unheard for help.

'I shall suffocate,' he told himself. 'Quite soon they will decide I am breathing too much air – a decision they will arrive at quite arbitrarily – and cut off the supply.'

Kate came in, as was her habit, with a cup of tea for him and an arrowroot biscuit. He looked at it gloomily.

'Why may I not have a ginger nut?'

'Not so invalidish. Ginger makes you overheated. Are you all right?'

'No,' Charlie said.

She flung her arms around his lean middle.

'Why don't you go away to get better? Aunt Catherine suggested it ages and ages ago and you said you would and you never did. I should miss you terribly but it would be worth it. Go and see that palace. The one you have kept all the clippings of. The bull palace.'

'The bull palace—'

'It is hot there, isn't it? So good for your poor chest. If you went there you would get well again and I need you to be well because I think Anna and I ought to go to a proper school in Bath and I am going to need some help in *that* campaign. Aren't I?'

Charlie sailed for Athens in late April. In his luggage he had copies of all the excavation reports from Knossos which had been published annually by the British School of Athens, a copy of a catalogue from a Cretan exhibition at Burlington House three years before, and the text of a talk Sir Arthur Evans had given at Bath College in January 1905 which Charlie had been too ill to attend. He also had Homer. He had read no Greek since school and turned back to it with a trepidation that turned rapidly to excitement and wonder.

Out in the dark blue sea there lies a land called Crete, a rich and lovely land washed by the waves on every side, densely peopled and bearing ninety cities . . . One of the ninety cities is a great town called Knossos and there, for nine years, King Minos ruled and enjoyed the friendship of almighty Zeus.

Minos, priest-king of Knossos, ruled over a seafaring empire and delivered it from piracy, his deeds chronicled by Thucydides, his enlightened lawgiving acclaimed by Aristotle. It was his daughter Ariadne who saved Theseus, son of Aegeus, King of Athens, from his fate as part of the grisly appeasing annual tribute exacted by the Minotaur, the bull-man monster who dwelt beneath King Minos' palace in a labyrinth designed by Daedalus. Ariadne gave Theseus her clew, a ball of thread, which he unwound as he pursued the Minotaur to its inmost lair and slew it and then, winding up the thread once more, came up out of the labyrinth into the sunlight and the rejoicing. Ariadne loved him, and he carried her away with him from Crete but abandoned her on the isle of Naxos where Dionysius, son of Zeus, grandson of the King of Tyre, found her lamenting and took her as his wife. Devouringly, Charlie read on, legend and history, poetry and prosaic fact, bulls and priest-kings, monstrous matings and superhuman valour, love and cruelty and triumph and grief, and Crete riding the seas out there ahead of him like a stony dragon humped in the waves.

In Athens, he found that the British School was well accustomed to enthusiastic amateurs, even to the extent of sparing hours to lecture Charlie on the Acropolis. What Charlie would find on Crete was remarkable, he was told, since six seasons of digging had revealed an enormous palace, tiers of courts and staircases, magazines and rooms down a hillside, and with it a whole civilization of magnetic sophistication and force. He was taken round the museum and gazed absorbedly at vases and spouted jars, amphora and cups, objects made from pottery and crystal, faience and gypsum and stone, the objects of ritual and ceremonial and domestic life of a people three thousand years old. He was spellbound. There was controversy of course. Sir Arthur Evans proposed to reconstruct the parts of the palace that had decayed, but whose original form was still clear (he had indeed already covered the Throne Room with a pitched roof), partly as a scholarly exercise, partly because the gypsum of which so much of the palace was built melted like sugar in rain – and the archaeological world was sharply divided over such a proposal. At night, over tough Greek lamb and thin resinous Greek wine, they argued the case across Charlie until he felt himself caught up entirely in a world of extraordinary self-sufficiency and interest, a world where domestic issues were only of any consequence if they belonged to a civilization dead for more than a thousand years.

He was in love with it all long before he got to Crete. He took the night steamer from Piraeus, equipped with a newly bought pith helmet recommended for the high sun of the digging season, and came into Herakleion in a clear May dawn, with the mountains violet blue against a transparent sky. The Venetians had left their lion on the harbour walls, and a fort and a magnificent arsenal. Among these imperial remains, the Cretans moved with the confidence of a people hardly to be changed by any occupying force. Charlie had an address at which to find lodgings, letters from Athens to Sir Arthur Evans himself and to Christian Doll, his architect, a bag of comfortable clothes – the rest he had left in Athens – and a second one of books and papers.

His landlady proved not only used to Englishmen, but to Englishmen with an obsession for buried history. She gave him two rooms on the first floor of her house, looking out into a small courtyard with a pump, a few bright, muttering bantams and a lemon tree. The rooms were furnished with several large and useful tables, extremely upright chairs, a narrow iron bed with a horsehair mattress which thrust black spines through the sheets, and bright blue and scarlet rugs on floors of grey marble. It was cool and quiet. Charlie unpacked and spread his papers lovingly across the tables, weighting them with books. His landlady brought him a glass of water and a slice of flaking golden pastry soaked in thin honey smelling of flowers. He sniffed it. He went to his window and sniffed the air. He walked round lightly, touching objects, chair rails, the rough cotton of the curtains, the engraved glass globe of the oil lamp. He lay on his bed and sat on his chairs and inspected his thin face in a greenish mirror hung on a nail driven into the white wall. Tomorrow he would write home and tell Rose where he was – tomorrow, or the next day perhaps. But today he would be free. He would eat his honeyed pastry and drink his celebrated Cretan water and then he would go out into the streets of Herakleion and walk and walk, wherever he wanted to, for as long as he pleased, and nobody would know who he was or where he lived. He raised his glass of water and said, 'To both Catherines!' to the silent room.

He arrived at Knossos first on a Saturday, thinking to find the site empty, for a solitary prowl around its extraordinary discoveries. Instead he found, in the midday sun, a long line of wonderfully dressed men and women lining up before a little table under an olive tree, where a small moustachioed man in a white suit and a pith helmet and a tall moustachioed man in a straw hat were doling out handfuls of coins. The men, the workmen, wore marvellous voluminous draped trousers tucked into coloured riding boots, zouave jackets, brilliant sashed belts and headcloths wound into small turbans. The women, who spent their days washing sherds and pieces of pottery in great tubs of water, were shawled and scarved against the sun. They were all chattering and laughing, holding out dusty brown hands for piastres – forty-five for an average week, maybe fifty for excellence or a small find.

'May I help?'

Charlie turned. A short and smiling elderly Greek in a fawn suit, a straw hat in his hand, was holding out his free hand in a gesture of welcome.

'You are English?'

'Yes. Yes, I am. I have just come from Athens. I have letters from the British School—'

'Ah! So you are an archaeologist.'

'No. An architect.' He looked about him. 'But I am a very interested architect.'

'I am Doctor Mesara. Old friend of Sir Arthur. Like you I am not an archaeologist, but a very interested doctor from Chania. You know Chania?'

'I only landed on Wednesday—'

'Of course. Come, you must meet Sir Arthur. We have had a wonderful week – two giant pithoi, one patterned in medallions, almost complete. A good start to the season, heh? Come, he has almost finished—'

Sir Arthur Evans was not at all as Charlie had supposed a scholar archaeologist to be. His white suit, his handsome small face, the spotted silk handkerchief in his breast pocket all gave him an air at once dandified and formidable. He stood and held out a hand.

'You come at the end of our little weekly ritual, Sir Charles. When my house is finished I will of course summon them all up there – how many, Duncan? Two hundred and eighty? Two hundred and eight-three

295

'– good grief. That must mean close on a hundred pounds this week.'

'It does—'

'Sir Charles, my invaluable assistant, Duncan Mackenzie. Sir Charles, let me show you the beginnings of my villa.'

Charlie bowed.

'I had rather hoped—'

'The palace? Oh, but naturally. When you have lunched with us and we have told you a little? I am expecting the Director of the German Archaeological Institute at Athens – Professor Dörpfeld, Schliemann's chosen successor at Troy – who is, shall we say, a rather oppressive guest. So I am charmed to see you. An architect, did you say?'

Across the road which had brought Charlie down from Herakleion lay the foundations of a substantial villa, set among sloping olive groves and vineyards.

'Excavating will be immeasurably easier with a dig house on the site. You will be interested to meet Christian Doll since he is, like yourself, an architect by training. With whom did you train?'

Luncheon was spread out on uneven tables in the shade, dishes of pilaf with yoghurt and kebabs on piles of rice.

'Do you have a comfortable house in town? You should not have to pay more than twelve pounds for the season. Christian! One moment – Sir Charles, my architect, Christian Doll, my photographer, Georges Marayiannis. Please seat yourselves. Ah! A carriage – my distinguished guest. Will you excuse me one moment?'

If Athens had been wonderful, this was better, this scholarly yet romantic luncheon of extraordinarily knowledgeable men governed by the disciplining formality of Evans himself. Sun fell filtered through the leaves over their heads, dishes and plates and crumbled bread were removed and replaced with apricot-fleshed melons, the talk was of frescoes and rhytons and megara, of the mysterious stone tablets that had been dug up, covered with a strange and secret linear script. After luncheon, while Evans and Dörpfeld went their scholarly way, Mesara attached himself to Charlie.

'You see, to Sir Arthur this place is not just an archaeological site, it is a palace still full of the people who built it, and lived in it. He told me that one night last season he had an attack of fever and decided, for cooler air, to sleep on the observation tower that has been put up in the Central Court. He was restless and left his bed to look down the well of the great staircase and was sure that he could see, passing up and down, the great ladies of Minos' court, in their tightly waisted gowns, and the priests in their robes, and the sinewy elegant young men of the frescoes with their long curls flowing onto their shoulders. That is why he is an archaeologist apart. He has flair, as well as scholarship. Come, I will show you the palace.'

It was an afternoon of wonder and exhilaration, scrambling among the rooms and recesses, exploring the magazines where the great pithoi, the storage jars, had held the grain and oil and wine of that other world, treading corridors and courtyards, peering into baths and tanks, gazing in awe at the little gypsum throne which had stood in the throne room against its frescoed wall for almost three thousand years.

'If Sir Arthur were with us,' Mesara said, 'he would suggest to you that this is the throne of Ariadne. That she trod those stairs, leant upon this windowsill, passed through that portico. Mr Mackenzie is, shall we say, more scientific. But the workmen will do anything for him, Christian and Muslim alike.' He laid a light hand upon Charlie's arm. 'It is my luxury to come here in the digging season, each Saturday. I drive along the coast from Chania on a Friday afternoon and evening with my daughter Eleni – her mother insists she comes, to ensure that I return – and we drive home again on Sunday. It would give us so much pleasure if you would dine with us tonight. I have a small house in Herakleion which I think will interest you. My family descended from the Venetian occupation and the house dates from that time—'

Charlie, drunk, dazed with his day, accepted with gratitude.

'Then you will share my carriage back to Herakleion?'

'You are so good—'

'My dear Sir Charles, it is a privilege and a delight to see a man lose his head and heart to King Minos just as hopelessly as I have done myself.'

Dr Mesara's house was in a narrow lane of the old quarter behind the harbour, and had a pilastered Venetian front and a stucco covering of peach-washed plaster. Charlie, in the only stiff collared shirt he could find and the fine blond dust of the afternoon still immovably in the seams of his boots, was shown into a cool dark room with long windows open into a little court-yard where a stone dolphin threw a jet of water into a basin like a shell. Mesara was feeding sunflower seeds to a caged canary hanging on a bracket from the court-yard wall – 'An ineradicable Cretan habit, caging birds, my dear Sir Charles, always very shocking to the English, I know' – and a young woman in a dress of some soft blue stuff was bending over white geraniums

298

growing, apparently, in just such a pithus as Charlie had been shown so reverently that afternoon.

'Is that the same age of jar—?'

'No, no. That is a mere infant of some thousand years, dug up near Phaestos on the south coast. The island abounds in them. In the villages they are sometimes used as chimney pots. Sir Charles, may I present to you my daughter Eleni?'

Eleni Mesara was perhaps twenty, perhaps a little more. She was a fraction taller than her father with very thick smooth dark hair coiled high at the back of her head and despite a serious cast of feature, hazel eyes that were simply brimming with life. She held out a supple little hand and said she hoped Charlie would forgive dinner entirely in the Greek manner.

'You see, the cook we have in Herakleion has come from Constantinople, and it is enough for him to learn that he must not flavour everything with rosewater, without learning European ways as well.'

Her English was correct and only lightly accented. She made a little grimace.

'We are almost the Middle East here, you see. Middle Eastern people have a very, very sweet mouth.'

'Tooth,' said her father.

She laughed.

'Only one?'

'I shall relish a Greek dinner,' Charlie said.

'Allow me five minutes. I must see that all is ready.'

'It is the way of our society,' Mesara said when she had gone, gazing up at the darting arrows of swallow flight against the twilit sky, 'that we really do not use our clever women. I have two sons, one a doctor in Athens, the younger a lawyer here in Crete, but neither is as clever as Eleni. And what is she to do? Domestically, she

299

is extraordinary, in fact, she has enabled her mother to devote herself almost entirely to the little charity schools in the mountain villages that are her passion. But she could – indeed does – run my two houses with one hand! She is my secretary, she runs my practice, she arranges all my archaeological notes and drawings. As you see, Sir Charles, I am a very fond old father—'

'With reason,' Charlie said, gallantly.

'And have you daughters?'

'Two. One is also, as you have described, too clever to be a woman. But I have a sister with a career, a sister who has most doggedly become a journalist.'

'You must tell Eleni!'

'What must you tell Eleni?'

They both turned. She was standing in the doorway with an embroidered white apron over her blue gown.

'Sir Charles has a sister who is a journalist, my dear.'

Eleni's eyes shone.

'Then I am proud of her!'

'So am I,' Charlie said. 'She is formidable.'

'Come and eat.'

A table was laid in a long and narrow room that had once been a little colonnade, now glassed in, on another wall of the courtyard. Apart from the table, lit by a dozen wax candles in a magnificent branching bronze candelabra – 'Seventeenth-century Venetian, a little family piece' – and strewn with trails of young ivy and pale clumps of almond blossom, the room contained only fragments of ancient masonry, stone masks and capitals and plinths dotted about at random on the tiled floor.

It was well after midnight when a cloaked servant carrying a lantern – would the magic of this day never end? – escorted Charlie home to his lodgings. He left behind the candlelit table, cluttered now with books and prints and pieces of pottery – 'Run your finger there, Sir Charles, where the potter of King Minos ran his own finger to make that soft groove' – as well as with dishes and glasses. Eleni had brought them Turkish coffee in tiny cups, and Greek brandy in more astonishing goblets, and had then softly gone out and left them talking.

At the door of his lodging, Charlie offered his escort two piastres which were gravely refused. In his room there was no light except the dull glow of the moon reflected on the white wall opposite, patterned now with the sharp leaved shadow of the lemon tree. Charlie dragged a chair to the window and leaned his folded arms upon the sill and his chin upon his arms. He closed his eyes and a vision of the palace rose in his mind, the pillared tiers, the roofs crowned with bulls' horns along their edges in a spiked battlement of menace, all spilling down the hillside, earth red columns, flat grey roofs, gardens, fountains, ritual, dark blood and darker cypresses. The frescoes swam behind his lids, frescoes of blue and rust and black, of dolphins and flowers, priest-kings walking through fields of lilies, supple slender cup-bearers tossing their black manes of oiled curls, moving between saffron painted pillars on their missions of ceremony and threat. His forehead dropped upon his folded arms. He could hear running water piped in stone channels, a bull's roar, smell blood on stone pavements, feel throbbing about him that ancient life stalked by violence, by dark pulses, earth and wine, dark wine running into dark earth, the throb and beat of drum and heart, his own heart beating again, strong and buoyant, heart and head in tune again at last, at last . . .

*   *   *

Young Frank Martineau had tactfully withdrawn from Buscombe upon Charlie and Rose's arrival. He was still, in his father's place, the family lawyer but all necessary business could be dealt with through Arnold du Cros, a state of affairs which dispensed with Charlotte's interference and Charlie's indifference. Charlie's attitude to money was that it must not be allowed to become a nuisance, either by being too plentiful or by being too scarce, it must at all times be kept in its proper place of invisible usefulness. Accordingly, Frank went to Buscombe as a formality on quarter days, was given Madeira and a bossy little speech by Charlotte (often spiced with reproach for visiting so seldom – 'What can you mean, that your coming might interfere with Sir Charles and Lady Rose's life? Absurd! Whose house is this, I should like to know?') put his head round the tower room or library doors to say, 'Any problems, Sir Charles?' and then returned to his office. When the letter came from Italy, it was in early June and therefore not a quarter day, but he felt he must break his self-imposed rule and call on Lady Rose. He consulted his father.

'Heigh ho, more fat in the fire—'

'But I must tell her.'

'Of course you must. What a strange twist to that interminable saga!'

'It was your saga, Father. Should you like to go yourself?'

'I should detest to go.'

Rose was in the rose garden, appropriately, when he called, dead heading the bushes. She wore a huge straw hat, one of Catherine's blue aprons and special gloves, and the basket at her feet was a tumbled mass of cream and pink and yellow petals. Frank Martineau was

302

not the first to wonder what on earth had possessed Charlie, wandering off to Crete and leaving this vision unattended for even a single day.

She turned upon him her faint and abstracted smile.

'My dear Frank—'

He bowed.

'Such a surprise – what can you want with me? Come, shall we sit down here? Oh – I do so hope it is not anything I should not like—'

'I must truthfully say that it is a very peculiar matter, but I do not think you will dislike it.'

Rose seated herself on a stone bench held up by lions and patted the place beside her.

'Come and sit here. Peculiar? Oh, there is Kate. I hope you do not mind her hero worship. Look – she is watching from the shrubbery—'

Frank said, 'I am very flattered. I like her enormously.'

'She is much too clever for me. So is my father, and my husband.' She turned to him, laughing. 'And so are you! What a situation.'

He blushed.

'Lady Rose—'

She closed her eyes.

'Surprise me.'

'I must beg a favour first.'

'Oh! Oh, of course—'

'Lady Rose, your cousin – your husband's cousin – Rosamund, died a fortnight ago at Monte Cimone, the nunnery in Italy where she had withdrawn. I gather her father does not yet know because all communication between him and the Buonvisi family ceased almost a decade ago. Would you, since you are a visitor there, undertake to tell him?'

Rose said musingly, 'Rosamund dead – so strange,

because you see she has almost been dead for so long already – Yes, yes. Of course I will tell Arthur Creighton. Poor man, such blighted hopes, such cruel disappointments. Rosamund dead—'

'Of a haemorrhage in the brain—'

'Oh – oh, too horrible. Frank, how extraordinary.' She looked towards the north front of the house, the mulberry trees, Catherine's conservatory. 'To think she lived here!'

'Very powerfully, my father says.'

'Thank you for coming to tell me. I will of course tell her father but I am afraid you must tell Lady Taverner yourself.'

'I know. Lady Rose—'

'Yes?'

'There is something else. You remember the jewels?' Rose's face lit up.

'Indeed I do. Such an unbelievable scandal.'

'I don't know if you knew, but my father went to Italy in '78 to try and retrieve them or the money that had been received from their sale?'

Rose clasped her hands together.

'I know! And found Rosamund shut up in a nunnery and all the money with her!'

Frank said, 'She has left all the money to you.'

Rose started.

'To me?'

'Yes, Lady Rose. To you. The lawyers acting for her in Lucca have written to instruct me that the convent of Monte Cimone only had use of the money for Rosamund's needs while she lived there. She made a will after she entered the convent leaving the proceeds from the jewellery to the wife of the next baronet to inherit Buscombe. I imagine she supposed it would be her daughter-in-law.'

Rose got up, scattering the contents of her basket and began to walk rapidly about on the grass in front of Frank.

'I cannot believe it—'

'Five thousand pounds. Is that not believable?'

'It is miraculous!'

Frank thought of Arnold du Cros's wealth and Charlie's extreme financial comfort and was unable to suppress a wry smile.

'Oh, but this is something quite apart!' Rose cried, seeing the smile. 'This is my money! Do you not see? I do not have to ask anyone for it, or thank them afterwards! No-one has earned it either, so it has no moral responsibilities—'

'I must warn you,' Frank said soberly, 'that it will be Lady Taverner's view that the money belongs rightfully to the family. There will be some justification for her argument too—'

'In law?' Rose demanded.

Frank made an equivocal gesture with his hand.

'I don't think so. But a case could be made since the jewels were Taverner property and were taken out of England without their consent in the first place. On the other hand, the will is dated 1883, a year after the Married Women's Property Act which gives, as I am sure you know, all kinds of freedoms and protections that women such as yourself and Rosamund lacked so keenly before. There is no doubt but that under Italian law, the money was hers to leave, and under English law, is yours to inherit.'

Rose sat down once more.

'I could not bear another confrontation. I have no heart for them. But oh, if the money is mine—'

'I think,' Frank said carefully, 'that you will need some help in the matter. Sir Charles's support, for instance. Could you contact him?'

'Yes,' Rose said, doubtfully.

Frank looked at her.

'I will write.'

She did not wish to explain to Frank how remote Charlie seemed to be making himself, how his letters were all of Knossos, of Crete, bare sometimes even of questions as to how she was or what Anna or Kate were doing. Surely he would come for this, though, particularly if it were to support her against Charlotte? Tears of a sudden self-pity filled her eyes, self-pity not just for that happy lost London life but for all that she must endure here at Buscombe instead, her loneliness, her fears, Charlotte's bullying, and now Charlie's distance. She put her chin up.

'I will write to him.'

She rose. Frank got up too and stood looking at her.

'Lady Rose, you do know that you have my professional support. Should you need it—'

'Thank you. Thank you so much – Oh, do look—'

With elaborate nonchalance, Kate was dawdling across the lawn, affecting not to see them but waiting to be noticed.

'Kate!'

Kate leaped, like an exaggerated grasshopper. Rose was laughing.

'Go on, Frank. Go and say something to her. Oh my dear! Think of it! Five thousand pounds—'

CHAPTER SIXTEEN

1908

'It is astounding,' Arnold du Cros said to his wife, 'that so little should mean so much. Rose is quite changed.'

He was nettled by it, irked that this small private fortune should undermine part of his own power, break some of the silken but strong strands with which he bound the Taverners to him. Rose had not come to him when the news of her legacy broke, nor yet waited for Charlie's reluctant return from Crete but had confronted Charlotte alone; confronted her and won. Rose had gone to Frank Martineau for help, not to him, her own father. Charlotte had said she would never speak to Rose again and Rose had replied that she had got used, since coming to Buscombe, to a great many awkward things, and she would doubtless also get used to not being spoken to. Then she had gone to London, asking no-one, telling no-one but Ellen and the children, whom she swept away with her. She took a little house in Camden Square for the autumn of 1906, and there Charlie found her when he came home at last and deposited in her narrow hall crates and crates of stones and jars and broken vases.

'Oh!' Rose cried. 'An entire ruin in boxes in my hall!'

But she was laughing.

'*Listen*—' Charlie said, trying to catch her, dying to explain, 'I've so much to tell you of—'

He was laden with treasures, many of them incomprehensibly desirable lumps and blocks of masonry on which little scratchings meandered aimlessly.

'It is a script.'

Dutifully they peered.

'It isn't deciphered yet. But one day—'

'What will you do with them all?' Anna said, fifteen year old Anna longing to put her hair up.

'They are going to Buscombe of course. I am going to remodel the hall and make it a tribute to Knossos—'

'Like a museum?'

'Yes. It will be wonderful.'

'It will be very unfriendly.'

'I think you do not understand—'

At Christmas, the little house was given up and the four of them, with Ellen and the precious stones in their great crates, went down to Buscombe. They sang carols in the train. Rose had a new hat like a deep soft helmet made of cream felt with a huge cascading plume of cream feathers, and Charlie a new cashmere overcoat, pale fawn, that made his brown face browner. Kate was surprised to realize, as the train beat down through Reading and Swindon and out into the green country beyond, that she felt she was coming *home* to Buscombe.

'Are you afraid?' she said boldly to Rose.

'Of Aunt Charlotte?'

Kate nodded.

'Not any more.'

Ellen said quietly, 'One should always have something to fear, however small. It is healthier that way.'

'Healthier?'

'It balances one's personality.'

'Oh wise Miss Napier,' Charlie said.

Buscombe was very quiet. It turned a grave, restrained face upon them as they drove, still humming, up the drive. Brixton came to the door instead of a parlourmaid. Her ladyship was not well.

'Not well?' Charlie demanded. 'In what way not well?'

Brixton looked about her and then said with elaborate caution that it was one of her ladyship's forgetful days. Miss Elizabeth would explain.

Elizabeth and, to their universal delight, Catherine were in the drawing room. Catherine had been in Norway, learning, to the girls' awe, how to ski – 'Only across country, you know, but I do long to go faster' – and had brought home a crib carved of spruce wood that she had set on a little table by the fire in a ring of candles. It was she who had ordered Fred to bring in a Christmas tree, and she who had decorated it with ornaments she had pretended she had bought but which had in truth come with a card for Anna and Kate from Lilian Creighton.

Elizabeth offered a friendly cheek to Charlie and a cool one to Rose. To her mind, Rose still owed her the pearls and aquamarines that were to have been her share of the Taverner jewellery.

'You look so well!' Catherine cried to Charlie.

'Not a croak in months—'

'Aunt Charlotte?' Rose said courageously to Elizabeth.

'Not so well. Not well today at all. She cannot remember things sometimes, cannot recognize things—'

Charlotte had woken that morning and demanded roses. They had told her it was but two days before

Christmas and roses were not to be had. She said, 'Christmas?' indignantly, as if she had never heard of such a thing, and then she had shouted at Elizabeth to leave the room – 'I do not permit strangers in my room!' – and ordered breakfast the moment she had sent Brixton out with her untouched breakfast tray.

'She was well yesterday,' Elizabeth said, and her voice trembled. Rose put an arm about her but she shook herself free. 'You should not have done what you did,' Elizabeth said accusingly to Rose. 'She has not been herself since you defied her.'

Rose drooped. Charlie took her hand.

'Who put that fairy on the tree?'

'I did!' Catherine said. 'Is she not perfection?'

'For a fairy—'

'She is simpering,' Kate said.

'Fairies always simper.'

'So does Anna.'

'I do not!'

'You are going red,' Kate said unkindly.

Charlie said, 'Beastly children. Go upstairs. My dear Elizabeth, would you explain to us a little more?'

Charlotte's memory, Elizabeth explained haltingly, came and went, some days clear, others cloudy and doubtful. She was angry so often, interspersed with terrible sadnesses, like the day of her eighty-fifth birthday when she wept like a child into her slice of the astounding cake Arnold du Cros had sent down from London, and only wanted Brixton by her. On the bad days, she summoned the dead – her son and grandson, sometimes even her husband – insistently, imperiously, growing ever angrier at their failure to come. She grew frantic if she could not see Pug every second, and on bad days wept like a waterfall while the patient Brixton took him down to the garden for most necessary out-ings. Elizabeth thought the sight of the children would benefit her, but Anna refused to go.

'Don't make her!' Kate begged Charlie.

'Will you go?'

'Very quickly—'

Charlotte's room was stifling, the air thick and sweet and stale. Pug barked at her. Charlotte plucked at her shawl and peered at her.

'Kate?'

'Yes, Aunt Charlotte.'

'Why are you here? Why are you not in the school-room?'

'It is Christmas Eve, Aunt Charlotte. Anna and I don't have any lessons.'

'Nonsense.'

Kate said nothing.

'Where is Pug?'

'There, Aunt Charlotte. By your feet.'

'Send Brixton,' Charlotte said fretfully. 'Go back to your lessons. I have had no tea. Brixton forgot my tea.'

'It is eleven o'clock in the morning,' Kate said.

Charlotte's face puckered.

'I want my tea. Send Brixton—'

'It was awful,' Kate said later to Anna, 'I thought she might be going to cry.'

'It gives the house a funny feeling, Aunt Charlotte being like this. It doesn't feel *normal*.'

'I don't think life here is ever normal,' Kate said, 'but I agree this makes it more abnormal than usual.'

She waited until after Christmas – a strange subdued Christmas redeemed for her and Anna by Catherine – before she announced her plan. It was a plan that had been in her mind for almost a year, a plan borne of her unexpressed – even to herself – realization that life at Buscombe was making herself and Anna odd, separate, different from others of their own kind. They loved Ellen, but they should not rely solely upon her for all they knew, for all their attitudes.

'Anna and I should go to school.'

'School!' Rose cried, horrified.

'Yes, Mother. We should. We are becoming little freaks and we have no friends but each other.'

'Oh,' Rose said dismissively, 'friends—'

'You have friends, Mother. Every day in London this autumn you saw friends. Why should you do that if it did not give you pleasure and make you happier? And if friends mean pleasure and happiness to you, then they will mean the same for Anna and for me.'

'Perhaps a rather trivial reason—'

'There are others. We need to be taught by other minds than Ellen's. We need to be made to read things and learn things that are not natural to us, to broaden our minds—'

'I must talk to your father,' Rose said quickly.

'I have already.'

'Oh? What a little schemer. And what did he say?'

'He agrees.'

'I do not want them to go to school!' Rose wailed to Charlie.

He was in the tower room, bent over the long trestles with which it was now filled, and which bore his sherds and notes and drawings.

'Why not?'

'Because I want to return to London for the spring and I do not want them left here with – with—'

'These mad old women?'

'Yes.'

'Then why can they not go to London with you and go to school in London?'

Rose fidgeted.

'If they go to school – *anywhere* – I am tied. I must stay there. If Ellen teaches them, we can move when we choose.'

'When *you* choose. Have you been infected by Catherine? Do you want to travel?'

'I – I don't know. I don't want to stay here.'

'But the girls do. At least Kate does. And to go to school in Bath.'

Rose said petulantly, 'You should not listen to her, you take too much notice of her opinion.'

Charlie moved two pieces of dull apricot coloured pottery together and tried their edges, side by side.

'Only when it is a good opinion which, I am bound to say, it often is. I think she is right and that they should go to school. Go to London, if you want to.' He stood up and looked critically at the sherds. 'The girls will be quite safe. I am staying here.'

Rose said, on the edge of tears, 'You do not want to come to London with me?'

Charlie took his eyes reluctantly off the pottery and looked at her.

'I want to be with you, but I do not want to come to London. I want to arrange my collection here, and annotate it and file my drawings and read and learn. I may go back to Crete this summer. I may not. I should love you to come but I fear it would bore you very much as it is very hot and very dusty and the conversation is all of old stones. You have your independence now, Rose, as you constantly tell me, and you must be satisfied with that and not whine at other people's desire for theirs.'

313

Rose went to the south windows and looked down to the lake.

'So you propose I should go to London, and the girls should go to school in Bath and that you should remain here and sort your stones?'

'Roughly speaking, yes.'

'But – but – but it is so *irregular*!'

'Then what do you propose, if irregularity seems so unthinkable?'

'That we go on just as we are.'

'In other words,' Charlie said, suddenly angry, 'we do exactly what suits you, irrespective of our own desires or needs. It seems to me that a heady little dose of financial independence has made you exceedingly selfish.'

Rose burst into tears.

'Don't cry,' Charlie said, not at all contrite, 'just *think*. You want people and theatres and dinner parties and social talk. You *like* society. Nothing wrong with that. I do not. Nothing wrong with that either. Kate wants a broad, objective education for herself and Anna. Highly commendable. She wants to live here which may seem odd to you, but is not a reprehensible desire. I want to live here for the moment too, because the place is, after all, mine, and because it is an ideal place for my present purpose. Some compromise can be found and I have suggested one. All you suggest is that everyone but you gives up what *they* want to suit what *you* want.'

'I gave up so much for you, to come here—'

'Yes. And I know what it cost you. But I think you will admit you have been rewarded for your sacrifice, even if not in the form you thought a reward would take.'

'You are so *hard*.'

Charlie turned away.

'On the contrary, my dear Rose. But I am well, now. I have found something that suits me. So have you—' He stopped, on the verge of saying that if the choice was between their chosen ways of life and each other's company, and the ways of life were to win, so be it, and said instead, 'Please do not let us quarrel. And please let us try to help Kate with her most worthy ambition.'

In the third week of January, in pleated serge frocks of dark green, white blouses and regulation brown boots and fawn lisle stockings, Anna and Kate entered the fourth and fifth forms of Laurelbank School in Lansdowne, Bath. The same week, Rose took a house in Chelsea Square, taking with her – after a good deal of public reluctance – a parlourmaid whom Brixton had attempted valiantly to make into a lady's maid at three weeks' notice. Ellen, miserable to be parted from Rose, but with characteristic fair-mindedness, conscious that she was first and foremost responsible for the girls, remained behind at Buscombe. It was a dismal prospect, with Charlie oblivious of anything but his own projects, Kate and Anna only home to do their homework and go to bed, Catherine poised for flight and Elizabeth balancing precariously upon the seesaw of Charlotte's health.

Rose endured poor Palmer for a month, then she despatched her back to Buscombe, insisting she could do such menial tasks as the girls required as well as Ellen, and summoned Ellen.

'You may go,' Charlie said.

'I am in a dilemma—'

'I know. I can see it. But don't worry. Palmer can see to the girls' practical wants and I will see to the subtler ones.'

Once she had Ellen, Rose began to return from Friday to Monday of each week.

'So funny,' Kate said to Anna over the schoolroom table one evening, 'but do you remember waiting for Father to come home on Fridays? A sort of weekly excitement. And now it is Mother—'

Anna had bloomed. She had friends, went to their houses, to dancing classes, was envied for her cascade of waist-length hair, had discovered she could sing, *really* sing, well enough to be given solos at school concerts. Often she and Kate stayed in Bath at night, at the houses of friends, and trooped to school in the morning in a gaggle along the broad and curving pavements. Kate preferred to go home to Buscombe, to see her father, to give distracted Aunt Elizabeth a rest from those pointless readings from Charlotte Yonge, ignored if read, demanded if forgotten.

'You are a busybody,' her father said affectionately.

'How unfair,' she said, not minding at all, 'when I thought I was being really useful.'

'Is school a success?'

'Yes.'

'No regrets?'

'Only that Ellen turns out to have a far more interesting mind than the combined minds of Miss Peabody, Miss Mayhew and Miss Pratt.'

'Kate?'

'Yes.'

He put his arm round her and kissed her forehead.

'Nothing really. Just – Kate.'

It was, Ellen knew, junketing up and down to London all that year, into the next even, a way of life that could be no more than a stopgap. It was so because it led nowhere. It was like setting out on a journey that has no destination so that the travelling itself eventually becomes pointless, without savour. She wished she could say something to Rose but Rose was so happy, so pretty, so proud of her life, that Ellen could not bring herself to point out how unseeing she was.

There was no point in even asking her if she did not miss the girls. She would have opened her eyes wide and said, 'But I do see them! Every Friday to Monday!' and so she did, alighting at Buscombe like some fairy godmother, sustaining an improbable air of holiday for three days and then flitting back to London again. At least, Ellen thought, surveying her lovingly while she brushed her hair, there was no need to worry about other men. In her circle of women friends and that provided by her father and his parliamentary colleagues she seemed entirely contented, satisfied even.

'She should be at home, at Buscombe more,' Arnold said to Ellen one day, out of the blue.

'I expect she will be. In time.'

'You think she will tire of this way of life?'

Ellen nodded.

'I only hope you are right—'

Charlie did not go back to Crete in the summer. Instead he took Rose and Anna and Kate to the South of France – his own idea, his own plan – to bathe in the warm sea and to sleep in the first hotel bedrooms the girls had ever seen. When they returned, the hall at Buscombe was transformed, cleared of all furniture and carpets, the stone floor gleaming, the walls and pillars newly painted. In the spaces between the pillars, plinths and pedestals bore the best urns and vases, and all round the walls behind the pillars, newly built display cabinets of glass and wood held all the other treasures

Charlie had brought home from Crete. On the floor, here and there, lay the odd capital or lump of stone or broken column. The general effect was grim and lifeless and Charlie was entirely entranced with it. He had ordered classical friezes – great panels of plasterwork – which were to be put around the tops of the walls below the cornice, and specially designed bronze lamps like torches which would be hung from brackets on all the pillars.

Rose tried to imagine the thoughts of guests arriving in this gloomy shrine to antiquity, parking their bags irreverently on the nearest stone crag, calling hopefully for their hosts and getting instead a herd of sacred bulls or a procession of mincing boys bearing ceremonial cups and saffron flowers. She turned to Charlie. His face was alight with satisfaction and pleasure and he was moving from case to case with little grunts of approval.

'Some people from the Ashmolean Museum in Oxford came and arranged it all. On my instructions of course. They say it is a very fine collection—'

'Oh good—' Rose said faintly.

She went back to London in September and the girls to school. Anna was Helena in an all girls' production of *A Midsummer Night's Dream* – carefully doctored of the coarser comedy – and Kate was made a prefect, the youngest in the school. She wore an enamel and gilt badge like a laurel wreath with 'Prefect' and the school motto, *Et Nova Et Vetera*, in the centre, pinned on the bosom of her serge tunic. She was almost fourteen.

Charlotte was almost eighty-seven and Elizabeth not far off sixty. They lived now a strange and introverted life, a life coloured and shaped by the variable but ever thickening cloudiness of Charlotte's mind. Catherine had tried to help, to share in this particularly wearisome form of nursing but Elizabeth shook her off. She had found a vocation at last, a need, a space in someone's life she could most unquestionably occupy. Charlotte absorbed her days and wore her out with a kaleidoscope of fretful confusions and tempers, of pathetic bewilderments and deep depressions to which Elizabeth became a slave, priding herself almost on being the only one – not excluding Brixton – who could most surely read the signs of an impending mood, and deal with it when it came.

Charlotte's robust Regency appetite had dwindled to petulant pecking at bits and pieces. She slept at unsocial hours and was awake, and prey to miseries, at night. She called incessantly for Pug and banged her stick upon the floor for Brixton when Brixton was already attending to her. She grew afraid of the daylight and wanted the curtains drawn across, the fire lit, even on summer days, and then complained that she was being suffocated, could not see, while her strong old heart beat relentlessly, unkindly, on.

Because of her, invisible though she was, Anna and Kate did not bring friends home to Buscombe. More and more they stayed school nights in Bath. Kate joined the school debating society and persuaded her aunt Victoria – this was an enormous coup – down to speak and lead a debate on women's suffrage. Victoria was regulation neat and spoke with crisp decisiveness, causing much admiration in the aspiring bosoms of female ambition that listened to her. After the debate, Victoria drove to Buscombe for the night, dined with Charlie, took in the situation with Charlotte and Elizabeth, went back to London the following day and straight to Chelsea Square.

'You must go home,' she said to her sister-in-law.

Rose was lying in a low chair before the fire polishing her nails.

'It is the bleakest situation. Charlotte is clearly senile, Charlie obsessed with ancient rocks, Elizabeth wholly given up to nursing, Catherine abroad. It is as welcoming as a morgue. What about your girls?'

'But I see them every week—'

'Rose, it is not enough. That house ought to be a *home*, not just a building in which a collection of people lead entirely separate lives. Anyway,' with a disparaging look around the little drawing room which Rose had enthusiastically made so pretty, 'what on earth is there to keep you here?'

Rose said truthfully, 'Not as much as I thought there was.'

'Well, go home and make something of it. You can do what you like now, with poor Charlotte beyond noticing whether it is Christmas or high summer. And what about my poor brother? Eating a solitary dinner in that great room every week night with a book propped on the decanter—'

'I – I will think about it.'

'Take your friends there with you, for Heaven's sake. Like Elizabeth used to. Goodness, she has grown an old sofa of a thing, so odd with Catherine as lean as a rail. That house needs people, it always has. It won't affect Charlotte one way or the other if you fill it, but it will transform the house and the girls' lives there. I must go. I'm addressing a meeting in Kilburn, and I've left my notes at home.' She got up and stood looking down at Rose. 'I wonder what use the vote would be to you?'

Rose smiled up at her.

'None at all, I should think. I should probably vote exactly as Charlie or my father advised me to.'

'But your daughters won't. Kate anyway—'

'Kate, no. Victoria, dear Victoria. Thank you for coming. And I will think about what you have said. Really I will.'

At Christmas, she announced at Buscombe that she had given up the Chelsea house entirely. In January she ordered – to Kate's dismay – new curtains of apple green patterned linen for the morning room and tried out new colours for the walls on the panels behind the door. In February she went to visit Laurelbank and charmed the headmistress, the staff and the girls, and in March she had two spring house parties and discovered that the museum hall gave Buscombe, in the public eye, distinct social cachet. Charlie was, in a small way, suddenly lionized in his own house, regarded with admiration, sought out for instruction – he was good at that – on ancient civilizations. The second house party was such a particular success that Rose, quite exalted to find that both she and Buscombe had such singular and unlooked for social potential, allowed Charlie into her bed, the first occasion in almost four years. Eight weeks later, vomiting and sweating in a June dawn ten days before her fortieth birthday, she knew she was paying the most dread price for an impulse of delight and excitement.

It seemed an interminable pregnancy. She grew thin around her swelling belly, felt violently sick, worried about the sudden limpness of her hair, the puffiness of her feet. Mary came over from County Kildare, coarsened and enlivened by a life in the open air and full of all the cheerful enthusiasm that Rose could not feel one atom of, try as she might. Only once, to Ellen, did

321

Rose actually say in an agonized whisper, 'I can't face it,' but her apprehension was writ large on her forehead and in the dark smudges under her eyes and her reluctant smiles.

She spent most days on a sofa in the morning room window. The new curtains were up, brashly fresh and the wrong colour anyway for the dim and faded blue walls which had never had their new paint. She could not bear the scent of flowers suddenly, nor coffee or the smell of vegetables. She could not think what to do with the pointless days, could not read, could hardly bear to embroider, dreaded meals yet felt worse if she did not eat them, and looked forward with a kind of hunger to the girls' return from school, to Lilian's visits. That at least was a triumph – a concession gained from this horrible situation.

Lilian loved coming, even if Elizabeth was elaborately cold with her.

'So wicked of me. But I almost find it funny—'

She read to Rose and told her bits of gossip and tried to interest her in the serious redecoration of the room.

'Now, you have to start by admitting that those curtains are a mistake. Put them somewhere else. This room needs velvet.'

'So stuffy—'

'Not in the right colour.'

'I can't seem to mind—'

'Rose, will you pull yourself together? You have a delighted husband, a delighted father and two delighted daughters, not to mention a host of friends who are equally pleased. You are beginning to see what a dear house this is and what a satisfying life you might have in it. You are only *pregnant*, my dearest girl, not dying, and in three months it will be over and you will be wondering what on earth you made such a carry on about.'

'Am I making a carry on?'

'Yes,' Lilian said firmly. 'You are.' She gave Rose's cheek a little pat. 'I am very grateful to you, you know. Having you as a friend, being able to get back to Buscombe and the Taverners because of you, has rescued me from the most awful pit. I would not say I was reconciled to my own awful, vulgar house, but I can at least now bear – and this is more important – poor Arthur watching me every evening with the expression of a dog craving a biscuit.'

Rose began to giggle.

Little Robert Taverner was born after a protracted and painful labour on a spring afternoon in 1909. An obstetrician recommended by Lilian came out from Bath and caused Rose untold agony by trying to manipulate the baby, which had become crookedly wedged after fruitless hours of trying to be born, and Rose had fainted, only to be roused again by her own pain. Eventually forceps had to be used, and Rose was badly torn and screamed and screamed on a high sharp animal note that no-one in the house could escape hearing.

Battered and exhausted, the two dark bruises made by the forceps startling either side of his forehead, but breathing and shrieking valiantly, little Robert was bundled up in flannel layers and put in a basket by the fire. Everybody turned to his shuddering sobbing mother who was insisting she could not look at him, would not look at him. She was slippery with blood and sweat and crying, incoherent with recent pain and present exhaustion, her pale hair plastered to her wet skin. Kate and Anna, allowed in for no more than a minute, looked sorrowfully at her, with a kind of guilty delight at the furious yelling parcel of their new brother, and tiptoed out again. Rose would not look at them, nor at Charlie, but lay on her face in her damp pillows, her fists clenched at her side.

'It will pass,' the obstetrician said, 'when she has rested.'

It grew worse. She refused to suckle Rob, and a wet nurse had to be brought in, a stout friendly girl from Marsham Court, daughter of Meggy Bradstock, now Meggy Tilling since she had married the coachman. Rose did not want to see her or have her spoken of. Lilian, haunted by her memories of Rosamund's savage reaction to Tommy's birth over thirty years before, was almost beside herself with anxiety. Rose sank deeper and deeper, withdrew from them, farther and farther, into a profound and lonely unhappiness. Sometimes she would turn eyes huge with reproach upon Charlie and sigh from the very depths of her being, but mostly she lay and gazed blankly at nothing, or wept and wept, enormous silent tears that coursed down her cheeks unchecked, almost unheeded.

'Why does she not get better?' Kate demanded of Ellen. 'Rob is here and healthy and adorable. Why is she like this?'

'I cannot really explain, but it is something to do with the balance of substances and mechanisms that all come into play with childbearing. Perhaps there is a little *im*balance. But she will get better. I promise you that. It will take time, but she will get better.'

But Charlie discovered, quite suddenly, that he could not wait for that. His compassion, his delight in his son, even his love for Rose were not enough to bear those enormous accusing eyes swinging upon him like lamps, luminous with unspoken charges of cruelty. The cocoon was closing round him again, the sweet suffocating female world where he would eternally make mistakes because he could not, for the life of him, fathom the seemingly arbitrary rules by which it was governed. Even for Kate he could not stay. Surely Kate would understand? He would not be gone long, he would not confront anyone, he would simply go, best that way, quietly, at once . . .

'We have a letter from Father,' Kate said to her sister. 'Look. It was on the breakfast table in the schoolroom. He has gone back to Crete. It says it is best – best? Oh Anna—' She burst into sudden tears. 'Anna, what is happening to us? What are we going to do?'

CHAPTER SEVENTEEN

1909

Charlie stood in the garden of the Villa Ariadne. It had been finished in the same year that he had lunched by its foundations and infant walls, and now sat substantially in a garden planted with young date palms, as yet no more than three feet high, and with hibiscus and honeysuckle and jasmine and brilliant scarlet splashes of the pomegranate flower. To Charlie's left, where he stood on the cobbled drive that ran up from the road to Herakleion, a little statue of Dionysius had been set in a sort of shrine, with a stone basin below, and a flat topped wall bounding it.

There Charlie sat down, suddenly weary, dropping his bag at his feet. He had sent a message out to Knossos to say that he had returned to Crete, and an invitation had come at once, an invitation that was more like a command, to stay at the Villa. He accepted eagerly. He did not want to be alone; he yearned to be part of that absolutely absorbed male community who ate, drank and slept archaeology, their emotions rendered clean by their intellectual commitment. He wanted to find a refuge in that stout Edwardian villa as much as he longed for the adventure and fascination of the great city palace that lay across the road, revealing every year yet more and more of its luxurious, aesthetic and savage history. He wanted his sense of self back, as he had almost, three years ago, in this extraordinary place, managed to achieve. The sun fell hot and full on his tired shoulders like massaging hands, and for the moment he could not move but sat and stared about him, all at once bewitched and at peace.

The villa was single storey, built solidly of buff stone, eccentrically cut like some kind of crazy paving, the cement standing out of the stonework as if it were piped icing, dark green shutters linked against the insistent sun. The windows were classical beneath heavy pediments and an impressive flight of steps led up to the front door where a heavy leafed palm in an ancient pot stood guardian. One leaf of the door was open and a woman in black carrying a bucket came out down the steps, hurled the water from her bucket over the low stone wall edging of the nearest flower bed and came to tell Charlie, with the matter of factness of a person used to an arbitrary and constant stream of unexpected guests, that Sir Evans was in the swimming bath.

'Swimming bath?'

She pointed across the face of the house to the north east corner of the garden. Charlie could see a wall smothered in the huge purple blue trumpets of morning glory.

'Over there? Behind the wall?'

The woman nodded, stooped to grasp Charlie's bag in her free hand and set off back to the house with it. Charlie stood up. It was disconcerting to think of Sir Arthur in a swimming bath, however undoubtedly stately such a swimming bath, in his possession, would be. Perhaps he swam still wearing, for authority and dignity, his silk scarf swathed pith helmet. The vision this conjured up seemed to Charlie somehow impertinent. He crossed the garden and found a twin leaved door in the flowery wall which he opened apprehensively after a hesitant knock. Inside, to his relief, there was indeed a splendid swimming bath, equipped with vast rearing brass taps, but it was unoccupied. On a corner seat set in the surrounding wall, Sir Arthur Evans was preoccupied with a notebook.

'My dear Sir Charles, this is an extraordinary pleasure! You are come at such a significant moment. I am just about to undertake yet further work on the Grand Staircase itself, and then I shall embark upon a study of all the frescoes. I trust that you were well assisted by my colleagues at the Ashmolean in the arrangement of your collection? Good. Good. I resigned as Keeper last year, as doubtless you know? Such regrets, but inevitable as a decision with the pressure of work here. Are you well?'

Charlie sat down on the flat topped wall that edged the bath.

'Very glad to be back here, sir.'

'And I trust this time you can stay long enough to see some real progress? It is to be a vast architectural project, the restoration of the staircase. We cannot be too appreciative of all professional help since the great gypsum slabs we found very early on, on the eastern border of the Central Court, now reveal themselves as the steps and landing blocks of the fourth and fifth flights of the staircase. It is our intention to restore them to their original position. I have no doubt but that Mr Doll is quite equal to the occasion, but I have no doubt either but that the presence of a fellow architect can only be of assistance in the massive yet delicate task.'

'Will there need to be much new stonework?'

'Two pillars at least, it seems, at present, to elevate the landing blocks to their original lofty situation. Perhaps more.' He paused and with a humorous yet penetrating glance added, 'Is it an impertinence to ask what has kept you away these last two seasons?'

'Affairs at home, sir.'

'The same affairs, I imagine, that put such an untimely end to a most promising career?'

Charlie looked down into the water of the pool, its surface patterned with the hand shaped shadows of the fig leaves that overhung it.

'In part. But my health and my inheritance were largely responsible.'

'In my experience,' Sir Arthur said, closing his notebook over one forefinger to show that this interview would not take final precedence over his meditations, 'it is necessary to reach a point of eminence where one is indeed master both domestically and professionally, a point, shall we say, where no-one dares do other than obey.'

He gave Charlie a twinkling smile.

'I am afraid, sir, that I had not reached such a point when disaster struck. I was still, it seemed – it *seems* – at the mercy of human responsibilities.'

'Not here—'

'No, sir. Not here.'

Sir Arthur stood up and held out a small well-kept hand.

'Then may I bid you warmly welcome as my guest and co-worker. You will find Maria in the house who will attend to your needs, and I shall look forward to your company at dinner. Both Mr Mackenzie and Mr Doll are on the site.'

* * *

Charlie was shown to a cool monastic cell in the semi-basement where Sir Arthur had put all bedrooms to be out of the summer heat. Its schoolboy austerity pleased him, narrow iron bed, small deal table and rush seated chair, row of black hooks on the wall, white china bowl and jug for washing on a stand with an enamel pail beneath. Someone had left a tray of sherds in the corner and, on the wall above the bed, a curling drawing of double-headed axes, pencil on yellowing paper. The floor was of red tiles, polished to a high gloss. He sat on the edge of the bed and felt its satisfactory hardness, put a hand under the tough woven cotton cover to touch the familiar coarse sheets. The only soft element in the room was a single trail of plumbago which had wound its pale blue flowerhead between the half closed shutters and hung there swaying in the shaft of afternoon sun.

Upstairs, the villa was a country house, furnished with Turkey carpets and heavy curtains, the walls smothered in prints and pictures, shelves and tables stacked with books. Luncheon, Maria told him, was served in the long dining room, dinner on the elevated terrace at the back of the villa where jasmine was making brave beginnings at a canopy supported on black iron bars. Punctuality at both meals was rigorous. The food, Charlie found to his surprise – he had been expecting some fittingly ascetic frugality – was not rigorous at all. Sir Arthur imported all his wine, including champagne and most of his groceries, crate after crate of food arriving from Herakleion to the undying wonder of his Cretan staff. It was of course an indulgence that matched his silk scarves and handkerchiefs, his swimming bath in the classical style, his lordly formality.

'There is no need,' he said at dinner the first night,

catching Charlie's delighted surprise at his plate, 'to live meagrely merely because one wishes only to talk of numismatics.'

He was phenomenally rich. Those exhausting magnificent hours on the site in the pressing afternoon sun revealed to Charlie that there were hundreds of workmen whom Evans personally paid weekly. The site was his, this treasure stuffed hillside had actually been bought by him from the Greek government in 1900; he, an Englishman, was a Cretan landowner. After a few weeks, even that did not seem extraordinary. The power of the palace itself, where fact gave validity to legend and legend gave life to fact, the hidden, comfortable, scholarly world of the villa, the olive and vine clad slopes opposite and the great mountains to the west, the heavy sun and the nights where the moon was a soft warm silver gilt, quite another planet from the cold ice blue moon that hung in an English sky – all combined to give Charlie the sensation that he was being both healed and fed.

The villa was never empty. A procession of scholars and architects moved through the basement bedrooms, argued at meals, spent long hours straw hatted in the sun, making notes and drawings, roamed through the olive groves in the dusk to expound and explain to one another. Every Saturday morning, with a punctuality only matched by Sir Arthur's own, Dr Mesara appeared at Knossos, smiling beneath his straw hat, ever ready with his soft opinions and his deft and gentle hands.

'It must be admitted,' Sir Arthur would say, 'that his eyesight is not as keen as mine, but that his touch is remarkably delicate.'

Dr Mesara would laugh.

331

'Sherds and bodies, my dear Sir Arthur, equally as fragile and as meaningful—'

Understanding both the scholarly and romantic nature of the work, and the Cretan workmen, he was of invaluable assistance, and to Charlie, a source of extraordinary knowledge. The weekdays Charlie spent largely with Christian Doll, working out the massive, yet delicate, structural scheme by which the ancient landing blocks of the staircase Ariadne once trod could be hoisted up once more into their original position. On Saturdays, Charlie abandoned the staircase to accompany Doll around the site while he examined new finds and pondered over old problems and talked to the workmen.

'I have been coming here for almost a decade now,' Dr Mesara said to him once, 'and although nothing will ever equal those first two seasons when we seemed to find a miracle each week, I still cannot stay away. My interest may not be so passionate, but it is every bit as intense. I have come to feel protective too, about these ancient peoples as well as about their palace and their city. Archaeology is, I find, a humbling science, particularly in an age like ours where we see ourselves as such progressives, such achievers. It gives us back – how shall I put it? – it gives us back our sense of proportion.'

He did not invite Charlie to dinner again in his house in Herakleion – Eleni, it seemed, had to stay behind in Chania and nurse her mother and therefore the house was only fitted for the most meagre of wants – but as the relentless summer drew on through August, he began to suggest that Charlie should accompany him home to Chania one Sunday evening, and remain there some weeks to explore the western part of the island. Charlie hesitated. Digging was almost at an end under the fierce sun, Sir Arthur was preparing to go home to Youlbury, his Boars Hill house outside Oxford, the scholars and architects were beginning to trickle away to write up their summer conclusions for learned journals and lecture tours. Charlie knew that he should, in response to all those despondent letters from Buscombe which he had answered with a brisk purposefulness no doubt interpreted as sheer indifference, go home. But he could not. He shrank from the idea with a strength that surprised him; he sat on the edge of his bed in his austere little subterranean chamber, and looked around with an almost passionate fondness. He was being absurd, he told himself, as well as most unjust to Rose, who was as much a victim of circumstance as he was himself, whose appeals for help he had not always answered, whose miseries he had not tried sufficiently to understand because he did not wish to be cluttered up with them. At the recollection of those miseries, an almost physical antipathy rose in him at the thought of going home, an antipathy so energetic it propelled him off his bed and out of the villa across the road to the palace, where thick blue shadows, still warm from the day almost gone, lay across the dusty oblong of King Minos' Central Court.

They had had a *glendi* there but two days before, a Cretan festival, organized by Duncan Mackenzie with his instinctive Highland ability to know how to get the best out of the workmen. There had been a tug of war, a hundred men at either end of the rope, romantic and piratical in their great pleated breeches of dark blue cloth pushed into knee boots, their striped and embroidered waistcoats, their coloured headcloths. They had eaten and drunk afterwards, and then they had broken up into rhythmic circles, arms across each other's shoulders, in a strange, stamping, swinging dance. Where they had danced, Charlie now paced in the warm twilight air heavy with the summer scents of sage and tired grasses. What was intolerable about life at Buscombe, he realized, was that he was no longer his own master, no longer in charge of his life, had not been so since broken health and the closure of the offices in Swan Walk had taken away his goal and his independence. He was forty-four. There was still a daunting amount of his life left, too much to squander. Crete had made him confess that he could not bear any longer simply to let time pass, he wanted to *live*, fully and properly. But how on earth, given circumstances as they were, people as they had become, was such a desire to be gratified.

He wandered back to the villa as the sudden summer darkness fell thick and soft on the palace. He resolved as he walked, with relief but no self-admiration, upon a compromise. He would indeed go home, but not yet. He would make sure that he was home for Christmas but before that he would go west with Dr Mesara to Chania, and explore the remains of the Venetian Empire there, and the great White Mountains and the secret southern coast that lay beyond them. He would walk the fantastic gorge of Samaria, climb to the citadel of Rethymnon, swim in the deep and astounding waters of Soudha Bay, ride a mule up the Rodhopou Peninsula to the monastery of Ghonia, built like a fort, restored by the Venetians after desecration by the Turks. Fortified by all that, sated and steeped in the island and in seven months of sun, he would go home to face what had to be faced . . .

Dr Mesara had built himself a house in the classical style on a small promontory jutting into the sea to the east of

Chania, which gave him a view westwards of the bastion wall of the Venetian harbour, still proudly emblazoned with the lion of St Mark. He had been one of the first old families of Chania to move there when the arrival of Prince George of Greece in 1898 made the area suddenly fashionable. The house, washed dull terracotta, stood elegant and apart in a garden dense with umbrella pines, between the gently lapping shore and the coast road that ran from Chania eastwards to the Akrotiri with its caves and monasteries where the early Christian hermits had dwelt in their precipices above the sea. It was a quiet house, the silence broken only by the barely moving wavelets and the mule carts creaking companionably by, and from it Dr Mesara went forth each morning to his surgery in the central square, and each afternoon to his wards and clinics in the hospital in Dragoumi Street. Only a stone's throw from the house, also facing the indomitable lion across the bay, stood the British Consulate, a neoclassical building with a pretty balconied entrance framed in wrought iron, and here Charlie was given rooms looking out towards the sea, the harbour walls and the setting sun.

'I trust,' Dr Mesara said, 'that you will dine with us whenever possible, and make use of both my library and my knowledge. You must begin of course by exploring our city. I am bound to boast that it will astound you. There are streets where you can stand with Minoan remains upon the one hand, Venetian fragments upon the other and rising before you both a Turkish minaret and the façade of a Byzantine church. It is one – and I say this with great pride – one of the oldest continuously inhabited cities of the world. And I must warn you that it is my daughter Eleni's firm intention to take you to

335

the market. I believe she feels such a visit would be both instructive and beneficial after a summer spent among the stones—'

'We are to have a new market building,' Eleni said, leading him among the ropes and nets along the harbour. 'It is to be modelled on the market of Marseilles. Do you know Marseilles?'

Charlie stopped by a blue and a white fishing boat, lanterns in the prow, which was filled with grotesque pinkish fish, their heads crowned with a swirling fan shaped fin.

'Not the market building. What does that monster taste of?'

'It is quite good. Less oily than those—'

She pointed to two swordfish lying side by side in the bottom of the next boat, martial and elegant.

'I must give you our Chania oranges. Very excellent. Dark and very sweet. Come this way and I will show you the fruit and vegetable sellers. If I could paint, I would wish to paint them.'

In the narrow streets that ran up from the harbour, bordered by houses whose roofs were edged with a terracotta relief of shells or spearheads or acanthus leaves, the countrywomen squatted beside their baskets of produce, their huge and densely petticoated skirts swirling round them in the dust. Yellow and green globes of melons, pyramids of new oranges, peaches laid in leaf-lined baskets, grapes buzzing with flies, bunches of pink and white radishes as massive as carrots, brilliant green chillies like little Chinese lanterns – all lay spread out against the house walls among the skirts and the hens hobbled in pairs and the scavenging rail-thin cats with ears like wings.

'You could paint this?'

Charlie leaned against a warm and faded peach plastered wall.

'Yes. I could paint this. Those geraniums—'

'And the eggs. So beautiful, eggs. And to touch.'

He looked at her.

'Are you sure you cannot paint?'

'Quite sure. I have tried many times and I have decided that I only make myself cross. I do not care to be cross and so I now only perform – do you say? – the things I can perform because that makes me happy.'

She began to move forward along the street, and Charlie took her elbow so that they could still hear each other above the chatter and the squawking.

'Tell me what makes you happy. What do you like to do?'

She stooped to pick up a melon, pressed it gently, sniffed it, shook her head and put it back.

'I like to run a house. I like to look after people. It is such a misfortune for my father who is so progressive, that I do not wish to be the first woman doctor or lawyer in Crete. I am interested in healing, I am interested in law but I do not want to do that all the time, like a man. I have, you see, a very bad curiosity. I want to know everything about all the people I live with, and help them with their lives and feed them and see that they have clean linen and flowers on their tables. When they are in trouble, I want them to say, "Where is Eleni, I want to speak to Eleni." And now,' she said turning to Charlie, 'you will ask me why I am twenty-four and not a wife.'

'Very well,' Charlie said, laughing, 'why are you not a wife?'

Eleni stopped in front of a great wicker tray of perfect

337

oranges, most of them still winged with dark and shiny leaves.

'These we will buy. This woman has her own trees outside Perivolia and she is a widow and most proud of her independent life. If I buy twelve, will you carry them home for me?'

'Of course—'

'Thank you. Then tell me, please,' she began to pick out individual fruit and lay them in her basket, 'how you came to be married yourself?'

'I loved a young woman,' Charlie said, enjoying himself hugely, 'and so I asked her if she would marry me.'

'And what did she say?'

'She agreed.'

'No, do not take that one. Look, it is not perfectly ripe. Why did the young woman agree?'

'Because she loved me, I think.'

'Well, now you know why I am not a wife. And because my father is progressive and my mother is obedient to his will, I am not required to be the wife of someone I do not love.'

'Has such a person asked you?'

'Frequently,' Eleni said calmly. 'See what a useful wife I should make!' She looked at him and laughed. 'I am the good choice for a practical man!'

Charlie began to rattle for coins in his pocket.

'But you are not altogether practical. You are a romantic too. You wish to marry for love.'

'Please do not pay for the fruit. I wish to present them to you. I think it not at all practical to marry without love. It is not practical to be unhappy. You can do nothing if you are not happy.'

Charlie thought of Rose, and said nothing.

'I speak with a clumsy tongue,' Eleni said.

'An honest one—'

'It is not always kind to be honest. Now, come. We will find my old herb-seller. He has been selling herbs since I was a child, herbs for medicines.'

'Miss Mesara—'

'Please, Eleni.'

'Eleni.' He seized the basket of oranges and said, staring at them not at her, 'My wife is not happy.'

'No,' she said. 'I know that.' She waited a moment and then she said, 'If she were not unhappy and if you had not once loved her very much, why else should you be here?'

There was not a day when he did not go to the Mesara house. He went to sit in the blue shadowed garden, he went to pay brief court to the invalid mother in her darkened room, he went to borrow books and look at treasures and to be spoiled with *loukhoumadhes* and fresh figs and spoonfuls of clear pale honey from Sfakia. Above all, he went to talk to Eleni, drawn every day further and further into the deep enchantment of her competence and her calm. She was, he discovered, a woman of true compassion who did not judge however much human frailty she might perceive. Because of this, he could speak to her of Buscombe and of Rose, of Kate and Anna and the tiny boy he scarcely knew, and the seeming impasse they had all got themselves to. She never counselled him, only listened, and this lack of officiousness struck him so much that one day, as they stood by the garden wall above the sea and watched the sun slide down into the Venetian harbour, he asked her *why* she never offered him any advice.

'Because,' she said, 'my advice would not be – wait,

I do not know the English word—' and she went away to the house and returned a few minutes later to say, 'If I gave you advice, my advice would not be impartial. That was the word I did not know. I had to look for it in my father's dictionary.'

'Eleni—'

'We shall not have a conversation about this.'

'But, Eleni, I want, I long to tell you—'

'No,' she said firmly, turning upon him a look of pure love, 'we must not talk of it or everything will become bigger. It is very foolish of me to have given you even the very small idea. Come now. I must see about dinner and you must see about a clean shirt to eat it in.'

What an obtuse ass I am, he thought later, exultantly, tying his evening tie before the dim little glass in his room, how could I possibly not have seen before? Of *course*, that was why all these last weeks she had never suggested to me that I should go home – although I plainly should – why she let me go droning egotistically on about myself day after day. It is exactly the same reason that carries me across to that house every day in this idiotic and besotted manner, a reason no doubt perfectly obvious to her clear-eyed father who condemns, if I am right, as little about human affairs as Eleni does herself. Can it be, can it miraculously be that there really do exist human beings who are prepared to give so much and who apparently ask for so little in return? I do not believe – and this thought was at once perfectly natural and perfectly extraordinary – I do not even believe that dinner tonight is going to be in any way awkward . . .

It was not. There were other guests, a couple named Tiepolo claiming descent from the first- and thirteenth-century Venetian governor of Crete, a fellow doctor and his wife, and an expert on Byzantine books and documents from Athens who was spending some months working on the collection in the historical museum. Eleni wore a dress of cream lace that Charlie had seen several times before and gave him looks of great fondness in which there was not a trace of complicity or self-consciousness. He was afraid to drink too much, and lose his head, yet the temptation to celebrate this amazing state of things was very strong. Everything in the room seemed, to his delighted happy gaze, to bloom and glow, even the candles were more luminous than was customary, the ancient lovely glass more gleaming, the silver more brilliant. He looked up the table at Dr Mesara, fixing him with a gaze of astounded intensity, and Dr Mesara looked back at him with all the usual comfortable amiability and spoke only of Phokas, the great Byzantine emperor who had founded the first monastery on Mount Athos, and everything was both as it always had been and yet entirely changed. When he said good night at last and went down the steps to the road in the soft late September night, there was no extra pressure of any hand, no significant glances, no innuendo or inference, but for all that, he went humming home by the gentle sea and lay awake for hours in the warm darkness, smiling at himself and thinking of her.

In the morning, there was a letter from Kate, forwarded from the Villa Ariadne. It was brought up to him on his breakfast tray, among the bread and honey, and lay looking at him, inert yet vibrant with reproach. He spread honey on bread and ate it, poured coffee and drank that, and then walked out to his balcony and looked at the sea, and the distant lion on the harbour wall and at the house where Eleni would already be up and busy. Then he went back into his room and after a few practice tries at a handwriting less educated than his own, wrote 'Gone Away' on Kate's letter, underlined the Buscombe address she had put on the back of the envelope, and put the letter in his jacket pocket to post. He was not whole yet, he told himself, not mended through and through, not quite yet, but when he was, when he was entirely healed, and healthy in every fibre, *then* he would go home . . .

CHAPTER EIGHTEEN

1909

'I do not think,' Anna said in despair, 'that there is any disaster left to happen.'

They were sitting together in the blue late summer dusk, and spotted moths with pale and furry heads were tossing themselves recklessly at the hot globe of the lamp. On the floor below them they had left Ellen kneeling by a disconsolate Rose who had had one of her ceaselessly weeping days, and in another room Aunt Charlotte was shouting intemperately at an exhausted Elizabeth to go at once and fetch herself. On the table between them lay a letter from their grandmother du Cros, to tell them that their grandfather was still far from well after the stroke that had felled him a month earlier, leaving him without feeling all down one side, his poor mouth working soundlessly beneath pleading eyes.

'Except for you and me and little Rob,' Anna went on, 'everybody is simply falling to pieces. Aren't they?'

Kate said slowly, 'It's so strange, one almost gets used to it—'

'I don't.'

Kate looked up.

'I hate it,' Anna said. 'I hate the confusion and the

343

unhappiness and the servants not working properly because no-one tells them what to do. I hate those dusty old stones in the hall and the morning room looking so silly because Mother will not finish it, and everything being so shabby and sad-looking and no flowers anywhere and nobody caring. And what I hate most is people like Aunt Catherine and Father simply running away from it all and leaving us to face it and live here without help. It – it – oh!' she cried on a note of sudden piteousness. 'It isn't fair! We are not much more than children—'

'You are sixteen—'

'Kate. Kate, don't you see what I mean? Don't you hate it too?'

'Of course. But not so much as you—'

'I suppose you want to make an excuse for Father.' Kate sighed.

'There *is* some excuse. Not all, but some.'

'Thank heavens school begins again next week. But even that can't go on for ever. It's my last year and then what shall I do? We never meet anyone and we cannot have anyone here. Suppose I turn into a mad old maid like – like' – she got up suddenly and the moths flew up in a cloud at her movement – 'like the aunts or Aunt Charlotte. Suppose that is what happens if you stay in this horrible house too long?'

'It is not a horrible house.'

'It is, it is! Look what becomes of everyone who comes here! Happy people like Mother and Father, get – oh – sort of *blighted* – and can't be happy any more and turn into different people, strangers—'

'That wasn't the house!' Kate cried fiercely, springing up too. 'That was the people they found here! And Father's illness!'

344

'He did not have that before he came—'

'He was born with it!'

'Well, the people they found in the house who made life difficult were difficult because of the house—'

'No! No! They were difficult because times had changed and they could not change with them and they were so full of disappointments!'

Anna burst into tears.

'Oh look, oh look, now it is making us quarrel—'

'That is worry,' Kate said wearily, 'that is not Buscombe.'

'I *hate* worry!'

'Yes,' Kate said, 'it is pretty hateful—'

'Why should *we* have to bear it? Why does nobody think how it feels for *us*?'

'I don't know!' Kate shouted, suddenly furious. 'Why ask me? Why should I know?'

Anna stopped crying and said calmly, 'You see, you hate it as much as I do.'

Kate took a deep breath and went to the window, the high window from which they had watched Charlie and Rose come severally home from London and Arnold du Cros drive over from Marsham Court. It was too dark to see very much but the trees were whispering gently together and there were the comfortable mutterings of various feathered things going to their beds. Kate put her forehead against the glass.

'I don't hate it, Anna. I love this house and I am terribly sorry for it – somehow nobody manages to be happy in it. I could be, if only Father would come home and he and Mother could understand one another again. Sometimes, when I am playing with Rob—'

She broke off. Those times in the high sunny nursery, where she and Anna had slept when they first came to

345

Buscombe, with Rob on her knee, she felt an absolute, almost thrilling, contentment, however awful everyone else in the house was being that day. Certain corners, sudden unexpected moments, light on windowsills or pictures, little special atmospheres conferred here and there at particular times of day – all could give her the same feeling, the feeling of being at once satisfied and almost excited. She knew the house's many moods so well that she could plot where to be to capture what she was in search of at any one time.

'Rob!' Anna said. 'Wouldn't you think Father would want to come home to see *Rob*, even?'

Kate said, 'Come down to the tower room, I want to show you something.'

'I hate the tower room.'

'*Anna*. Nothing will ever be any good for you if you push things away all the time. Don't make any mistake about what I think about Mother. I am terribly sorry for her because she is the sort of person who so desperately needs someone to lean on, and her two props are gone just now, Father in Crete, Grandfather so ill. But Father isn't being callous for no reason. Please come down with me—'

'What do you want me to see?'

'Some drawings and writings—'

'I've seen *hundreds* of his drawings!'

'All right,' Kate said, 'I shall go alone,' and picked up the lamp to light herself down the stairs, not caring if she left Anna in the dark. Behind her Anna came trailing, complaining in a desultory way.

'I don't see the point—'

'Shh,' Kate said, stopping outside the nursery door. 'Listen. He's *snoring*. Oh, the dear—'

They giggled. The top flights of stairs were still

covered in oilcloth, horrible in winter, difficult to be silent on at any time. The first floor landings and staircase down to the hall were carpeted in grass green, chosen by Rose when she was in that brief happy period of being inclined to make an effort, and fastened down by brass rods that ended in little pineapples. The backstairs, up and down which Brixton and the maids laboured so constantly with hot water and scuttles of coal, were plain, scrubbed wood, and the walls were hung with grim little holy pictures at which the maids understandably never looked.

They stopped on the landing above the hall. No sound from Rose's room and only Pug's intermittent yaps from Aunt Charlotte's – Pug now grown as stout and immobile as a hassock from being denied exercise and fed incessantly upon petticoat tail shortbread. The lamp cast wavering shadows across the broad steps of the staircase, the pillars and glass cases of the hall, and threw the lumps of ancient masonry into craggy relief against the walls. It was all extremely quiet, and in the library there was a kind of dusty neglected atmosphere that intensified the silence. Anna shivered.

'Look at those curtains. They are simply in shreds—'

'Aunt Catherine said her father put them up when he was married, so they are rather venerable.'

'Why does nobody—'

'Anna!' Kate said warningly.

In the tower room, the blue evening shone darkly through the long windows.

'I always think there will be bats in here—'

'They can't get in. Look, come over here, where Father used to work.'

Kate moved across the room to the drawing boards and trestles Charlie had set up in the north light, and put the lamp down on his tall draughtsman's stool. His portfolios lay shut and silent, pens and brushes dry and neglected in their brass trays and pots, ink and paint bottles dusty in their neat rows.

'Look at this.'

Kate pulled towards the light a portfolio bearing a label lettered 'Buscombe' in Charlie's beautiful script. She opened it and pointed to a page of neat technical drawings under the heading 'Heating'. Below the drawings Charlie had written, 'Air to be sucked into basement, filtered through a screen sprayed with water for the right humidity, blown across hot pipes to warm it (? belt-driven machine – investigate) and into horizontal duct, connecting with ducts in all principal rooms with shutters to release warmed air when needed'.

Kate turned the page.

'And this.'

There were drawings of the ground- and first-floor plans of Buscombe, with a series of neat red lines running in the wall cavities and little red arrows pointing outward in the exterior walls, marked 'Ventilation'.

'What is it?'

Kate pointed. Anna bent forward and read out, 'Electricity, to be introduced in a series of ducts to carry the conduits, to be inserted in the floor space between the ground and cellar floors and the first and ground floors. Ventilation to be provided by a series of louvres in exterior walls.' Underneath Charlie had written, 'N.B. Ventilation and dry rot. Louvres to be installed too at semi-basement level to encourage the circulation of air.'

Anna stood up.

'Electric light? All over the house?'

'Yes,' Kate said, 'that's what he was planning all those lonely months. Read this bit—'

'We are in a period of building construction,' Anna read out, 'which has probably never been equalled for quality. In addition we are in an age of great architectural inventiveness; the lift, the radiator for hot water central heating systems, the installation of electricity for light and warmth all usher in what is undoubtedly a new age. For architects designing new buildings there is the most exciting of prospects. They can design with a freedom never experienced before, they can use space in a quite different manner because construction is so sophisticated and, by their use of space, guide, even change, the way humans occupy buildings. Architecture is the most public of arts, so much so that it is sometimes the least looked at, being so prevalent. We have now the chance to make it looked at anew, and to make buildings as remarkable to live in as they are to look at. We have an extraordinary power, because of tremendous technical advances, to influence and change the shape of people's everyday lives, both to make those lives easier and more exciting. Excitement, in one of its many forms, is, after all, the appetite for life which is fundamentally the only reason for living.'

Anna stopped reading.

'What does he mean?'

'Go on a bit,' Kate said.

'As a young man,' Anna read, 'I was powerfully influenced by the Arts and Crafts movement, and the necessity for humanity to infuse all corners of design. Looking back I think too many of the people in the Arts and Crafts movement simply fantasized about a clean, happy, full life and neither did nor could live it, but I still believe that design, and above all architecture, must be humane. Buildings must come to life because of the *people* in them; people must be as much part of design as the shape of windows, the proportion of rooms, yet building must always be the discipline, be in command, or it becomes pointless, without function. I have in Buscombe a building so shaped by people that its essential self is almost lost beneath the imposed layers of conflicting ways of life, and it is my aim and my duty to restore to it its essential purpose and dignity, while at the same time making it a place where useful and happy and convenient lives may be properly lived. It is in my hands to find the balance.'

There was a small silence, then Anna said, 'But if he was going to do all this, why did he go away?'

'Because he couldn't do it. Mother didn't really care and Aunt Charlotte said no to everything. And I don't think he could talk to anyone because none of us would really understand.'

'I'm not sure,' Anna said, 'that I do now—'

'I only do a bit,' said Kate, blushing in the kind darkness, 'because of Frank. He said nobody really understood how much Father had given up, how talented he was and how much he was admired and listened to. It was Frank who said I should look at this book one day when I got in a temper and said some unfair thing about Father being in Crete. And then I sort of saw how much he had to bear inside his head and how desperate he must have felt with nobody understanding or seeming to care, and his career all gone—'

'How did Frank know about these plans?'

'Father showed him. Very quietly. Frank said he was almost shy. Frank said, "It was a great lesson to me. I never knew what kind of man your father was."'

'I do wish,' Anna said wearily, 'that all our relations weren't so sad.'

'They *needn't* be.'

'Don't be so fierce.'

'I feel fierce. Come on, we had better go and see if Mother is all right.'

Anna closed the Buscombe portfolio.

'Has Mother seen this book?'

'I don't think so—'

'I wonder—' Anna said, but her voice trailed away. 'There wouldn't be any point, would there?'

'Not now—'

They carried the lamp into the dark library and closed the tower room door.

'You know,' Anna said, 'if Father had been able to, he might have made this a lovely house.'

In October, Harry retired from the army. He was a lieutenant colonel, he had done thirty-six years' service and the battalion was about to leave India and come home. Harry was not at all sure about being a peacetime soldier at home. India had been another matter. Even if his duties had been more a matter of policing than soldiering, it had been policing in Lucknow and Lahore and Bombay, and Harry had grown to love India. It was relatively new, this love, born of his spell of duty in Ceylon after the Boer War, guarding prisoners in the leafy camp at Rajaman, but it had grown very strong. He was ironically aware that Englishman and Indian were both so riddled with the caste system as to understand each other very well, but his love went beyond that. It went into the villages and the scruffy temples, into the absurd and wonderful palaces, into the endless offices filled with endless clerks, into the insatiable appetites for splendour and mystery and bureaucracy all together, into the dignity and the incompetence, the lovely girls and giggling old men, the dirt and the crowds and the soft exquisite twilights. Harry was not at all sure that his love for the regiment, powerful though it was, would manage to survive being taken from this more alluring love of India and being dumped in the Cambridge Barracks, Portsmouth.

'I am, I hope, a realist,' he wrote to his cousin Victoria, 'and the reality of the thing is that I am homing in fast on being sixty, and I do not want, at such an age, a change for the duller. So I shall resign and come home. Not to Somerset, never fear – I would not disturb my mother's reign there and I doubt we could live together and take much pleasure in it. Is there room for me, at least temporarily, in Swan Walk?'

Swan Walk now belonged entirely to Victoria. She had bought it, bit by bit from Charlie, and the ground floor rooms which had been his offices now housed the press which produced, each month, Victoria's magazine. It was called *The Alternative Grisette* and it was increasingly successful, appearing in the more liberal country houses on the hall table alongside copies of *Blackwood's Magazine* and *Country Life* and the *Pall Mall Gazette*. It was aimed, as it said uncompromisingly on its title page, at the thoughtful woman. This thoughtful woman, in Victoria's eyes, was also a universally competent and interested one, so that the articles ranged from the political through the artistic to pieces on garden design by Gertrude Jekyll and travel by Margaret Fountaine. Victoria's next ambition was a second press to print books, to be set up in the back room where Charlie had once stood with his drawing board and designed country houses for those newly successful men in love with the rural dream.

The first floor at Swan Walk was occupied by the offices and the army of slightly breathless girls, not always with quite enough of a sense of humour, who performed editorial and clerical duties with an almost slavish dedication. On the second floor Victoria lived alone and in great order, having collected, on Arnold du Cros's advice, some pieces by Charles Rennie Mackintosh whose combination of the practical and the aesthetic suited her perfectly. Her rooms were light and simple and uncluttered, the only colour in them provided by her books and a few severe flowers in season, disciplined flowers like tulips and gladioli. Her mother, gallivanting over from the jolly disorder of County Kildare with its doggy sofas and eighteenth-century portraits obscured by dirt, declared Victoria's flat had all the charm of a hospital ward. Victoria took no notice. Her rooms spelled calm and order and achievement to her, and she loved them.

Above her, on the third floor, were the rooms that had first been Charlie's, then hers and Maud's and now were let out at random to literary women in need. There seemed to be a surprising number of them, poets and novelists and political pamphleteers, eluding outraged fathers and tyrannical husbands and penury. Victoria's benevolence towards them extended to low rents and an unbiased look at their work. If it was good she either published them or helped them to find a publisher; if it was not – which was more often the case – she would make very plain the ultimate destructiveness of cherishing false hopes and gently move her lodgers out. At the moment she had rather a promising trio upstairs, one writing a novel about a country rector's daughter which looked as if it would prove particularly, accurately, poignant, one an ardent but level-headed suffragist and the third a quirky and talented painter of cats, who unselfishly kept them all by a quiet and steady stream of sales.

'So you see, I cannot offer you a roof just now,' Victoria wrote back to Harry, 'much as I would like to. But I do have a proposition to make to you which might solve your accommodation problem as well as many others at the same time. I so look forward to your return. If you go to your club, will you let me know the moment you are there, and come round to see me?'

He is looking extraordinarily young, she thought, admiring his brown face and still thick sunbleached hair against her white sitting room. How very odd, that he should be fifty-seven and I should be almost forty and yet I feel that we are as we have always been and that I am only a child to him which of course I am not any longer. We are both still alone which is perhaps what we are meant to be, except that I have the magazine and he no longer has the army which I do so hope is a loss he is conscious of so that he is receptive to my plans.

She gave him tea and a slice of the damp dark ginger-bread that the cat painter boiled up in a saucepan between pictures, and distributed throughout the building. It was, as she said, dreadfully sustaining. Harry ate it with enthusiasm and asked about the press and talked about India. Then he said, 'Now come on. What proposition?'

'It's Buscombe again—'

'Ah.'

'As you might have guessed.'

'Yes. Fire away.'

'First,' Victoria said, 'I think you had better read this.' She went to the mantelpiece and from behind a tall vase of white clouded glass which held a single cream carnation took a letter.

'It is from Kate. Poor child—'

Buscombe Priory
1 October, 1909

Dear Aunt Victoria,

I am very sorry to bother you when I know you are so busy with the magazine and giving talks, but Anna and I have got to a point where we do not know what to do next. We are sorry for everybody which just seems to make the muddle worse. I have tried writing to Father, but he does not seem to want to answer just now, which is why I am writing to you.

The thing is, I do not think anybody knows quite how bad things have got here. I thought Mrs Creighton knew, but she had gone to Madeira for the winter because Mr Creighton is ill, and I cannot really ask Frank Martineau because he is worried about his old father and anyway he is so busy. So I can't think of anyone else who might help us but you. I am sorry to keep saying this, but I really would not bother you if I could think of anyone else.

Mother is really in a sort of despair. She is so unhappy and doesn't seem to want to do anything, even go to London any more, so the servants just do as they like which isn't very much. It isn't any good asking Aunt Elizabeth because she is absolutely Aunt Charlotte's slave and Aunt Charlotte doesn't know what day it is any more or who any of us are or where she is. Luckily there is Ellen and we have a kind nurse for Rob who is adorable – but Ellen has to look after Mother most of the time as well as organize meals and try to keep the house in some sort of order. But she can't really, and the servants don't take much notice of her – except for Brixton whose arthritis is so awful that some days she is simply crying it hurts so much.

We have stopped coming home in the week because there wasn't anyone to take us any more, so we stay with the Masons who are the parents of Anna's friend Marian, and they are very kind to us though I think they think we are very peculiar. I am worried we ought to be paying them for being there so much, but I don't know what to do about it. They have a huge house in Lansdowne and I think they are quite rich, but it seems awkward all the same. We take them flowers from the conservatory when there are any nice ones, but the conservatory is in an awful state and some of the things are dying. We don't know what to do about them.

Aunt Catherine is in Syria and Turkey and says she won't be back for months because she wants to go to the Lebanon next and discover about Arab politics. I don't know when Father is coming back. I wrote to him at the Villa Ariadne but the letter has come back with 'Gone Away' on it. I thought of writing to Grandmother Mary, but Ireland is so far away and I know she doesn't really like leaving it, and Grandmother du Cros is too worried to think about anything but Grandpapa just now. Anna doesn't know what will happen to her at the end of this school year and that makes her unhappy. I am so sorry this is such a gloomy letter. I am writing it in bed very late at night which is probably a mistake. I expect I will feel better in the morning.

Love from Kate.

'You see?'

Harry said gruffly through incipient tears, 'Terrible. Simply terrible.'

'I must defend Charlie a little. He had dreadful disappointments and then he and Rose simply could not talk to each other any more. And then he was so ill.'

'So he fled?'

'There was provocation—'

'And left this gallant child to battle on in a madhouse. Provocation! And what the hell does Catherine think she is doing?'

'She doesn't know. She hasn't been home for several years. She didn't leave because she could not face things – she left because there was no place for her there, nothing for her to do.'

'There is now.'

'Do you think she *could* ?' Victoria said. 'Elizabeth has never listened to her, she sympathizes with Charlie, and she cannot run a house to save her life.'

'But those girls—'

'Yes. Those girls.'

'And Rose.'

'Yes.'

'What is the matter with Rose?'

'She has got nobody to look after her, for the first time in her life. No man, I mean. She is a darling, we all love her, but she simply cannot manage by herself and she knows she can't which makes it worse.'

'But the child, the boy—'

'Oh,' Victoria said, looking down, 'she did not mean to have him, she suffered very badly. She gets so frightened, you see.'

Harry got up and walked about the room, tapping the palm of his hand with Kate's letter.

'So I presume your proposition is that I go down to Buscombe and take charge?'

'Yes,' Victoria said.

'Rum do. Take over a house that isn't mine and all those women. How many? Five, six? And a baby. I have never run a house either—'

Victoria stood up.

'It isn't the housekeeping that matters. It is those

girls, and establishing a kind of order and security for them. Just the same kind of thing as organizing all your men, I shouldn't wonder, except that Kate and Anna are more intelligent. Just for the moment, Harry, just until Charlie comes home—'

'I love Buscombe—' Harry admitted.

Victoria waited and then she said, more as a statement than a question, 'Just until Christmas.'

'What happens at Christmas?'

'Perhaps I can get Charlie to come home. I don't think he has gone missing. I think he just could not bear the pressure and is lying very low. But if I write carefully in a few weeks, perhaps via the British School in Athens, then I think I might manage to make him see where his responsibilities lie.'

'It isn't like him—'

'No.'

Harry said doubtfully, 'Some sort of breakdown.'

'I think so. Of everything, all the important things. One can be angry with him, but not too angry.'

'And in the meantime, Uncle Harry to the rescue?'

'Yes. Please.'

'You are a very forceful woman.'

She smiled.

'May I write and tell Rose?'

He made a rueful face.

'You may. All I am thankful for is that the 28th can't see me now—'

Dressing to meet Harry's train at Bath took Rose hours. She was trembling with relief and gratitude and although she knew she was being exaggerated about his arrival, her behaviour was no exaggeration of her feelings. She was over-excited with thankfulness. With a man at the helm, her inadequacies could turn back into the charming and endearing dependency which was her natural state; there was no hypocrisy in her need for support for it was only in a supported state that she could flower and be her best. She felt that with Harry at Buscombe she could become herself again and abandon the hopeless lifeless self she became when ultimate responsibility was hers.

She looked worriedly in the glass. She was not quite forty-two and looked much younger, because of her ethereal colouring and her air of frail anxiety. Was this hat too much? A gigantic affair of pleated chiffon cascading roses, so absolutely flattering and meant to be flattering to Harry too, that she should dress up so for his coming. But Bath station? Bother Bath station. Her dress was lovely, Ellen so clever with a needle and these fluid lines suited her so well, smooth bands of grey wool around her waist and down the front of her skirt, soft bodice and gathered skirt panels of grey and pink crêpe, full at the back, gracefully sweeping as she moved. Her eyes filled with sudden hot tears of gratitude, for Harry, for Victoria, for darling Kate so stalwart and sensible. Had she become a hopeless mother? It was not what she had meant to be, not at all how it seemed when they were little, in London, in easy, happy London. Oh *Charlie*, she thought, with a sudden pang of longing for that lost life. Oh *Charlie* . . .

'Mother,' Anna said from the doorway, 'we are going to be late.'

CHAPTER NINETEEN

Christmas 1909

'I thought fondly I was a realist,' Harry wrote to Victoria in mid-November, 'but I am afraid I was deluding myself. I find that I am a hopeless romantic. If I were not, I could not be living here and what is more – breathe not a word to the regiment – enjoying it.'

Victoria wrote on a postcard, 'Thanks and praise to your Maker for your sense of humour.'

He did not think it was humour that carried him through, but rather his powerful fatherliness, the relish for protection and human order that had made him so popular a commanding officer. The sheer pathos of Buscombe, house and inmates, appealed to him strongly, even the sloppiness of the servants aroused in him reforming zeal rather than anger.

'I shall have to run it like a battalion, you know,' he said, smiling, to Rose, 'because that is the only thing I know how to run.'

'Oh!' she said, laughing, 'but that will be perfect. May we have a notice board for orders and reveille and a last post and if we are very obedient, may we dine with you in the mess?'

'Commanding officers are never teased. It is the first rule in the army's little red book.'

'Even in unorthodox battalions?'

'Particularly in unorthodox battalions.'

Rose began to sing again. She sang in the conservatory while she cut away papery dead trails of jasmine and made bouquets of fragrant calyanthus and deep blue tree violet to put around the house. She summoned a decorator from Bath and hummed while she considered paints and papers for the morning room, and she went about the house lightly, with little snatches of tune here and there, opening windows to the strangely mild November air, wanting pictures changed about, rugs cleaned, new cushions. Harry went into Bath with Kate and Anna, and made a discreet weekly arrangement with the Masons – they had, he discovered, been nursing a genteel but distinct grievance at what had seemed to them an upper class highhandedness – and then to the horse sales to buy a new pony for the trap and a better pair of bays for the carriage. He toured the buildings and the farm, visited Frank Martineau to discover that there was indeed no shortage of funds, and began upon a calm scheme of general refurbishment that aroused in Fred Bradstock's loyal heart almost as passionate a gratitude as there was in Rose's.

He even managed to make Elizabeth come down to dinner.

'But I cannot. I cannot possibly leave Mamma.'

'For one hour?'

'I never leave her except to sleep, when I am within call.'

'Then it is time you did.'

'I could not do it. She is so entirely dependent.'

'My dear Elizabeth, pitiable though it may be, most of the time my aunt is unable to distinguish between you or me or the door post. It is a needless martyrdom on your part.'

'It is my duty.'

'It is a duty you will perform much better for a little rest. Rose and I will expect you for dinner tonight.'

'Not tonight—'

'I am afraid, my dear Elizabeth, that we will be unable to eat unless you come. I shall personally come up to escort you downstairs.'

'Very well.'

She came. She did not say a great deal, being so absorbed by the habit of her preoccupation, but she ate, and she drank a glass of wine and she was very angry with Harry when he pointed out that she had exceeded her hour by three minutes. She came the next night and the next, and after a week she remarked upon the flowers on the table and asked after the girls. She stayed downstairs for two hours that evening and only went away because she confused and horrified herself by bursting into sudden and inexplicable tears. Rose was very kind to her as she always was – she had been the only person with a gentle word when she lost Freddie – but she could not allow herself to be comforted in front of Harry. Rose took her upstairs to the little room where Charlotte had briefly slept, next to her sitting room. It was not even pretty, a dull cheerless little room, for Elizabeth who had so loved pretty things.

'I do not know what came over me,' Elizabeth said.

Rose made her sit on the narrow bed.

'Relief, I think. We all feel it.'

'I am over-tired. I am not used to dining each night.'

'It does you good. It does us all good. Can you not feel how the house is changed?'

Elizabeth sniffed.

'I must go to Mamma.'

'May I not help you to bed?'

Elizabeth looked shocked.

'Not before I have seen to Mamma.'

Rose went down to the drawing room and waited for Harry. He was not long. He said solitary glasses of port wine were singularly pointless, so he would wait only long enough to satisfy the newly chastised servants, and then he would bring his glass into the drawing room. Rose pretended to sew but in truth she was just waiting to talk, or to listen. Harry told her about India, about Egypt and Malta and a great deal about Tommy. It was some weeks before he asked her about Charlie.

Rose said, 'Everything went wrong. It was so frightening. They were all things we could not help. It was like trying to stop huge runaway horses and knowing from the beginning that you had no chance. It all began with inheriting Buscombe which we had not expected and did not want.'

'I love it,' Harry said.

'Oh!' she cried, 'I know! The house is so different with you here! Kate loves it too.'

'Kate—'

She was on the point of confessing her feelings of inadequacy as a mother to Anna and Kate, but at the last second swerved aside and said instead, 'Kate thinks her father was beginning to love the house. But I don't think she is right. Not liking the house was one of the reasons he went away. One of them—'

'You do not have to say any more,' Harry said gently.

He was so sympathetic that she longed to, but she

363

knew it would be a mistake, so she just sat and stitched and let him look at her. On Fridays when the girls came home, they sat on the hearthrug in front of the fire between Rose and Harry and sometimes Kate illicitly went up to the nursery and collected the sleepy baby to join them. Harry adored him.

'Can't bear babies,' he said peering at Rob, 'can't see the point of them. Is Nurse looking? Splendid. Give him to me—'

These days, Rose herself went up to the nursery to visit Rob in the mornings when he had his bath in a kind of roofless tent in front of the fire made of clothes horses draped with towels. He was going to be as dark as his Irish grandmother, but his eyes were Taverner blue. She even took him to Marsham Court but her father was too ill to see them.

'It is too tragic,' Mrs du Cros said, surprisingly strong. 'He is simply a prisoner inside himself. I cannot bear to think of what he is suffering. How well you look, Rose. Better than you have for such a long time. And this,' she said, stooping over to kiss Rob in Nurse's arms, 'is a very handsome boy.'

Ellen went to Marsham Court to help nurse. She volunteered. She liked Harry – who could help liking Harry? – but she was uneasy, rootless because Rose was now turning to Harry after several years of clinging to her. Everything at Buscombe was so much better, the dead despair had gone, and yet there was something troubling around, something new and troubling. It made Ellen want to go away for a little, not on holiday where she would have too much time to think, but somewhere busy. Marsham Court was the obvious place.

She was invaluable, as she always was. Her intelligence was balm to Arnold, inarticulate as he had become yet sometimes frantic to be understood. He could still hear and she read to him, tirelessly. He began to hate it when she was not with him, and when she was with him and was not reading, she would talk of Buscombe to him and he would watch her devouringly as she talked. She could talk very freely, she found, and that was a relief to her, to be able to pour out the flood of her observations and reactions to those brilliant dark absorbing eyes. She spoke of Charlotte and Elizabeth, of the house, of the farm, of Anna and Kate and the baby, of Charlie and Rose, and Charlie's and Catherine's goings, and Harry's coming. She was talking this way, easily, one December afternoon when Arnold began suddenly to fight for breath, some great unseen struggle going on inside his poor, heavy body. She rang the bell and a parlourmaid came running to say that Mrs du Cros had gone to Bath, should she fetch Mrs Tilling?

'Yes,' Ellen said desperately, 'yes. And send for the doctor—'

So Meggy came, stout, grey-haired, taciturn, competent Meggy, housekeeper as she had desired to be, and between them, she and Ellen tried to lift Arnold to help him breathe more easily. But there was nothing to be done. There were only minutes more of battling to breathe and then Arnold wasn't breathing at all any more.

'''Tisn't right,' Meggy said, '''tisn't right for 'im to go with only you and me.'

'I don't know—'

Meggy grunted and Ellen, turning away, found that huge tears were rising and spilling, tears for Arnold and tears, even more, for Rose.

*   *   *

It was only natural that, when Ellen returned that night to Buscombe to break the news to Rose, Rose should at once go to Harry to be comforted. It was equally natural that Harry should escort her back to Marsham Court to condole with her mother, and that Ellen should go too in order, as Harry so sensibly suggested, that she might stay for a while as companion for Mrs du Cros. Harry and Ellen and Mrs du Cros behaved with perfect self-control, but Rose was dreadfully distressed, as shocked in her grief as if her father had not lain paralysed for almost four months and had been instead felled while in perfect health.

When they returned to Buscombe, Harry worried that there was no Ellen to help Rose to bed. He asked Elizabeth. Elizabeth was delighted. Between them, they consoled and fussed Rose into her fine lawn nightgown covered in exquisite tiny pin-tucks and got her into bed, and then Harry sat and talked gently to her until she cried herself to sleep. In the morning, it was Harry who went into Laurelbank, and Anna was summoned from her drawing class and Kate from French, while he broke the news of Grandpapa's death. They both cried but did not come to lean on his shoulders, and he took them to the Royal York Hotel for luncheon and made them talk about Grandpapa and then he asked them if they thought they could manage as he felt he should get back to Rose.

Kate nodded.

'Of course. May we see Grandmother?'

'On the way home on Friday. I will tell Fred.'

'Thank you for coming,' Anna said politely.

'Give our love to Mother,' Kate said and they both turned to go into the school and Harry drove away feeling that he had, in the most delicate manner, been chastised.

'I should not have gone,' he said to Rose, 'or rather, I should have taken you with me.'

'But I could not!'

'My dear Rose, you can do anything you want to. Particularly with me.'

When Arnold's will was read out, Rose needed Harry yet again. Arnold du Cros had left five thousand pounds to each of his grandchildren, the bulk of his fortune had been left to the newly formed National Art Collection Fund and his widow was to have a substantial investment in Taverner Warehouses and live comfortably upon the income. To Rose, he left nothing. The violence of this last-minute decision on his part – made only just before he was taken ill – struck her like a blow in the face. Harry's sympathy with her bewilderment and hurt and fury was both sweet to her and healing, and when she stormed over to Marsham Court to confront her mother, she took Harry as her bodyguard.

Mrs du Cros stood her ground with calm.

'He was full of remorse, my dear Rose, for the excessive spoiling he had lavished upon you all your life. He became convinced that your character had become warped by your comfortable circumstances and then, on top of those, by your legacy from Italy. He attributed, in the end, the disarray of your private life to money, and he was determined to contribute no further to the unhappiness of his grandchildren's lives. It is as simple as that.'

'But I thought he loved me!' Rose wailed.

'He did. Too much—'

'But to leave me *nothing*—'

'He did not leave you nothing. He only refused to

leave you money. He has left you furniture and pictures and books, and several little treasured possessions that have been his since childhood.'

'Oh!' Rose cried in a tone of scornful rage.

'Of course if you do not want such things, they can remain here until your children want them.' She rose. 'And now you must excuse me, my dear, I have an appointment with Mr Payne.'

'Mr Payne?'

'He is the new managing director of Taverner Warehouses. He has worked under your father for five years.' She paused and then said quietly, 'That sort of information, Rose, has always been here for the asking.'

By Christmas, Rose's spirits had risen again to a kind of fierce and gay defiance. She would *not* be hurt, she would *not* care, she would sing, loudly, and laugh, and organize the household into compulsory and hectic festivity. She sent Kate out with Fred Bradstock and the old pony wearing panniers, to fill with ivy and holly, and set Anna to gild fir cones which she set to dry on the old schoolroom windowsills like a little gold regiment. Ellen found a doll and dressed her in scraps and bits left over from dressing Rose, for the angel on top of the tree.

'A rather *secular* angel,' Kate said.

'Why should not angels be pretty?'

'Oh pretty, certainly, even beautiful, but not *modish*.'

'Perhaps that is her rather silly face.'

'Nobody will be able to see how silly her face is. Have you seen the size of the tree?'

Buscombe had never had so tall a tree. It rose incongruously out of the Minoan and Mycenaean ruins on the hall floor almost to the balustrades of the landing above, festooned with gold and scarlet ribbons and with a hundred precarious little candles wavering on its

368

branches. The angel was not to be put upon the topmost spike of the tree until Christmas Eve at midnight when Harry and Rose would go through an elaborate ritual of producing mysteriously filled stockings, even a tiny sock for Rob. An embarrassment that brought her close to tears kept Kate rigid in her bed, eyes screwed shut, while the fumbling laughing tiptoeing went on in the dark of her bedroom, and when the door closed she gave a savage kick and sent her stocking flying onto the floor.

'I can reach the tree from the landing,' Rose said. 'Look—'

'My dear, you must not, you will fall—'

'No. I won't. You hold me. Look, I don't have to lean very far. Just hold me while I tie her sash round the branch.'

She stretched over the banister rail with Harry's arms round her waist and tied the angel to the tree with gold gauze ribbons, and then she straightened and turned round and Harry did not take his arms away.

'Rose—'

She said nothing, because she was waiting.

'Beautiful, beloved, adorable Rose,' Harry said and kissed her, hard and lengthily. She did not pull away, rather he felt her pressing against him, her arms around his neck. When he lifted his head, she flung hers back and gave him a look of pride and triumph.

'At last,' Rose said.

'I completely lost my head,' Harry was to say, still astonished at himself, to Catherine years later. 'It was as if nothing else had any significance. In a way, I could see nothing else. It was an absolute and literal intoxication—'

For Ellen, the nameless trouble in the air suddenly had a name. Rose was alight with happiness, Harry almost walking into walls, the house resounding with an energy of joyful excitement that could, to the unobservant like Elizabeth, or the unsuspecting like the grandmothers, masquerade as the gaiety of Christmas. At dinner on Christmas night, at a table which had not seen such festivity since Rosamund was a new and excited bride, Ellen looked around at the ring of faces glowing in the candlelight and saw Kate's, and saw that she was close to tears. She fixed her with a gaze willing her to look up. At last she did, and across the table she and Ellen exchanged a look of sombre understanding, amid the crackers and the laughter and the tinsel stars.

Later that night, Kate was not in her bed and Ellen found her huddled in a blanket on the floor by Rob's cot. In whispers she was persuaded out and into the schoolroom where Ellen knelt, still in her evening frock, to blow a little life back into the dying fire.

'Kate—'

'I can't talk about it.'

'Are you angry?' Ellen asked, tucking cushions in around her for extra warmth.

'Oh, I'm everything. I am angry and sad and afraid.'

'I will try to speak to her.'

Kate said babyishly on a sudden sob, 'I want my father!'

'Oh, my dear.'

'It is *Christmas*!'

'I know.'

'It is my fault. I wrote to Aunt Victoria to ask for help. That is why Uncle Harry came.'

'It is not your fault. He was such a boon—' She stopped and then said, 'He is a kind man.'

Kate nodded wearily.

'Yes.'

'I think you should go to bed. Where is Anna?'

'Asleep,' Kate said briefly, and stood up, scattering cushions, holding the blanket tightly round her. Ellen looked at her blanched face, suddenly no more than the face of a lost child, that look Rose had so often – used to have so often . . .

'Your mother was so lonely,' she said gently, 'and she does so need to be loved, to have someone to love, it is part of the true womanliness of her—'

Kate said furiously, 'Ellen, this isn't the land of legend, you know, we are not living an Arthurian romance. This is 1909 and we are real, solid, ordinary people. At least I am. It's all right, I am going to bed. I really don't want to talk any more. Thank you for trying, but there isn't, given how you feel and how I feel, anything to say. I know you are sorry for us, I know you would like to help but you cannot because your own loyalties prevent you.'

'Will you not talk to someone else?' Ellen pleaded. 'To your grandmother?'

'No,' Kate said. 'No. Not anybody. If I talk it makes it real, so if I do not talk, it will simply go away.' She twitched the blanket higher round her shoulders and then looked at Ellen without smiling. 'Good night,' she said, and went out.

'I am taking you away,' Harry said. 'It is the only answer. It will solve everything.'

'Tell me—'

'We cannot stay here. We cannot be apart. I cannot conceive of a day without you.'

'But the girls—'

'They will come with us.'

Rose was illuminated with delight and anguish.

'But where will we *go*?'

'I shall find us a house.'

'But we cannot, it is impossible—'

'We *can.*'

'Harry—'

He took her shoulders.

'Listen to me. Do you want to stay here, in this house, and wait for Charlie to return home when it suits him, *if* it suits him – and to struggle on with him, unable to talk to him, neither of you understanding the other, with Charlotte and Elizabeth and the isolation? Is that what you *want*?'

'No,' Rose cried. 'No! You know it is not. But I am so afraid of what we must do to get away.'

Harry put his arms around her and said, 'Dearest, you must simply resign all those problems to me—' and then Elizabeth, who never came downstairs before luncheon, walked into the morning room in quest of a particular green Berlin wool for her embroidery that she knew Rose had, and found them.

Harry dropped his arms, but held tightly to one of Rose's hands.

'So!' said Elizabeth. Her face was working, her mouth and eyes and chin twitched. She said, 'Traitors! Hypocrites!'

Harry waited. He could feel Rose's trembling vibrating right up his own arm.

'Vipers in our bosom!' said Elizabeth. 'Deceivers! Snakes in the grass!' She clenched her hands and beat impotently at her sombre skirts. 'How could you?' she said to Rose.

Rose dropped her head.

'I think,' Harry said in the most level tones, 'that you do not understand what you see nor what you have seen in the last five years. Would you allow me to explain?'

Elizabeth took a huge breath.

'Never!'

'In that case,' said Harry, releasing Rose's hand and moving to hold the door open, 'there is no point in prolonging this regrettable encounter.'

'This will not be the end of the matter, you know!'

'I fear you are right,' Harry said politely.

'I believed you!' Elizabeth said to Rose. 'I believed you when you tried to comfort me!'

'Why should you not?' Rose whispered, bewildered. 'Why has that anything to do with this?'

'Judas,' said Elizabeth.

Gently, Harry took Elizabeth's arm and steered her towards the door. She shook him off.

'Do not *touch* me. You have polluted this house. You have made this house an unfit place for Christian people, for people of virtue.'

Harry regarded her gravely.

'Is that so.'

'You have caused our ruin,' said Elizabeth, and went out.

Elizabeth was filled with energy, the bright burning fuel of indignation. She wrote to an old friend, now a widow too, a friend of those far off days in Mount Street when they were young married women together, who was living in Cheltenham. Through her agency, Elizabeth took a house, a pretty Regency villa in Montpelier Terrace, with a canopied balcony over the street and a walled garden behind with a wisteria and a sundial. To this house, Elizabeth took Charlotte, carefully, with her familiar objects and her tartan rugs and her chair and lamp and Pug. Charlotte had not slept away from Buscombe for half a century, had not left her room for

373

half a decade; she had not tasted the air of another atmosphere for too long. She was bundled into a carriage for Bath, and then into a train to Swindon and a second train to Cheltenham, and she babbled and wept and turned her gaze piteously about in terror. Only once did she speak clearly and that was to ask for Brixton. Brixton, Elizabeth told her, was too old and arthritic to look after her any longer and had been dispatched to live with her sister in Essex. She did not say how reluctantly Brixton had left nor how she had pleaded to be allowed to remain for little more than her keep rather than be separated from Charlotte now. Elizabeth was beginning on a new life and only wanted the amenable, desirable parts of the old one to come along with her.

She had found a nurse to help her, a Miss Gaze, a parson's daughter from Middlesex who had trained at St Thomas's Hospital and then nursed her parents while they died, very slowly, one after the other. Elizabeth offered Miss Gaze two hundred pounds a year and Miss Gaze, who felt that Elizabeth was going to require as much care as Charlotte, albeit of a different sort, had no qualms about accepting it. She liked Charlotte's being titled, and she liked the prospect of Cheltenham and a good address, she liked the room she had been shown looking onto the garden. She wrote to several nursing friends inviting them to visit her, and when she had written, she asked Elizabeth, with elaborate deference, if she might ask a dear friend, very occasionally, to come? Elizabeth graciously assented.

The house was very charming. Elizabeth took all her own furniture from Buscombe, and drove out with her friend Grace to the furniture dealers of Cheltenham, to buy what she lacked. Grace found a kitchenmaid from a farm at Winchcombe, a parlourmaid who was sister to her own, and a gardener and handyman who came in daily from Shurdington on a bicycle. There was a butler Grace knew of who could be hired for small parties, and an excellent livery stable when one needed a carriage, and a doctor and a vicar who were not only patently gentlemen, but gave every evidence of being men of most delicate understanding.

To crown all this, there was precisely the kind of intense and hierarchical social life, composed of numerous small events vibrant with potential complication, that Elizabeth liked best. She discovered, like some hitherto unregarded talent, her health, a fascinating hobby which was to occupy her for the rest of her life. A circle of new friends crowded into her pretty sitting room to be impressed by the aura of Buscombe with which she had so assiduously filled it – pictures (many her own watercolours), mementoes, photographs taken superbly by Charlie and now standing in the forest of silver frames with which Elizabeth covered her un-played upon pianoforte. She was, within two months, so tremendously satisfied and fulfilled by her own life in Cheltenham that she quite failed to notice that Charlotte had fallen completely silent and sat upstairs, shrunken and white in her old chair, plucking at the rug on her knees and mouthing soundlessly at the frightening and unfamiliar view.

Harry too, found a house.
'Oh!' Rose cried. 'Where?'
Gently Harry said, 'Wales.'

'*Wales?*'

'Dearest Rose, we must be unobtrusive for a while. We will go abroad if you prefer, as is traditional, but I thought Wales would be easier for Anna and for Kate. It is a good house, just beyond Cardiff. A very pretty situation, I gather – in a village called Llanblethian.'

Rose began to laugh but tried to look doleful too.

'Oh Harry. Welsh Wales! What shall I do in Llan—'

'Llanblethian. You will make a wonderful life for us, assisted by a troupe of Welsh girls in red flannel petticoats. We will find a school for Kate in Cardiff and Anna shall become the belle of Glamorgan. And little Rob will grow up bilingual and sail coracles in his bath. What do you say to such a prospect?'

'That I love it.'

'Then perhaps we should propose it to Anna and to Kate.'

Rose hesitated.

'To Anna, perhaps—'

Rose had become afraid of Kate. She was not yet sixteen, yet she exuded such a strong sense already of being very much herself, that she made Rose hesitate. Rose suspected that Kate was grieving both for Charlotte and for Charlie, but could not quite bring herself to ask directly, and had to turn as usual to Ellen. Yes, Ellen said, Kate was distressed about both. To Rose, Ellen could not bring herself to say that Kate was shocked and angry too, any more than she could express her own astonishment at the turn events had taken.

'Could Anna speak to Kate? For me—'

'I think not,' Ellen said. 'They are not together a great deal just now.'

'It is quite absurd,' Rose said impatiently. 'It is

impossible to make plans if all the participants have taken a vow of silence.'

Ellen let a little pause elapse, and then she said, 'It may be very difficult to make Kate come with us at all. I know Anna wishes to complete the term at Laurelbank, staying with the Masons, but I think she will then come to Wales. But Kate is another matter.'

'She cannot stay here alone.'

'Perhaps – I might stay with her, Lady Rose?'

Rose said lightly, cutting Ellen, 'As you wish.'

Ellen found Kate reading *Ivanhoe* in the conservatory, eerie in the dull winter light and full of steamy warmth curling out of the ornate gratings in the floor. She did not look up when Ellen came to stand beside her so Ellen waited a little, and then she said,

'Kate, I want to make you an offer.'

Kate raised her head. She had been crying.

'Oh, Ellen—'

Ellen sat down in a second wrought-iron chair patterned with huge and hideously uncomfortable ferns.

'If you want to stay here, Kate, I will stay with you. Until – until there is – someone else, to look after you.'

'You are so kind, Ellen. Really you are. But I think I shall be all right.'

Ellen said, echoing Rose, 'You cannot stay here alone.'

'I know. I knew that all along. So I have made some plans. It was horrid being so secretive, but I was afraid I should be stopped.'

'Can you tell me?'

Kate looked at her doubtfully.

'As long as the plans remain a secret until they are complete.'

'They will.'

Kate had been to see Frank Martineau. She had walked to Combe Place one Sunday afternoon alone, in chill February drizzle, and found Frank with tweezers and a magnifying glass sorting his stamps. He had a magnificent collection which Kate had always envied. He had just managed to acquire a British Guiana two cent stamp of 1851 in mint condition and so he and Kate spent some time admiring it and checking its rarity in the Stanley Gibbons catalogue before Frank asked, 'Is anything the matter?'

Kate told him and was surprised to see, that although he looked most sorrowfully at her, he did not seem astonished or in any way taken unawares. He took her over to the wing chair where he usually sat himself, and poked the fire to a blaze and then, most unexpectedly, poured her a glass of Marsala. She looked at it doubtfully.

'You might like it. And I think it would help a bit.'

'Will you have some too?'

'Most certainly.'

He was so like her father, she thought, the same leanness, the same thin face and brown hair. He stood with his glass in his hand staring down into the flames, and then he said, 'It is so wrong that any of this should affect you.'

'Well it does.'

Frank turned his gaze from the fire to Kate.

'And you say that nobody has communicated with your father?'

'He hasn't been very good at letters. Three of mine have come back. You see,' her face twitched, 'I don't know where he has gone. He doesn't seem to be where he was, at the Villa Ariadne, any more.'

'I had no idea. One assumes, when nothing is said, that these rather unconventional arrangements exist by mutual consent. I shall telegraph. I shall start with Athens and work onwards from there. If necessary, I shall go myself to find him.'

'Oh. Oh, thank you, thank you – but you see, he can't get home in time to stop them, and even if he did come home, I don't *know* if Mother could be stopped – oh, Frank, even *should* be stopped – and he mustn't come home to an empty house, there mustn't be nobody there, *I* must stay, I must, I must—'

'Wait,' Frank said.

He left the fire and walked about a bit and Kate found that she was shaking so badly she could not hold her glass, and had to put it down by grasping one wrist with the other hand. Frank said, from the far window,

'If I could find somebody who would stay with you, you could remain, I think. Even your mother might countenance that. Would Miss Napier stay?'

'I think she would, but I cannot ask her, because she must be with Mother. That is how she is.'

'Even for a month?'

'I would rather not—'

'I have it!' Frank said, and came back to the fire. 'I shall telegraph Mrs Creighton, Lilian Creighton. She is so fond of you all. If her husband is well enough to leave, I am sure she would come, just long enough for this—'

Kate began abruptly to cry. Frank put his glass down and knelt beside her.

'My dear Kate, my dear. Why did you not come before, before everything became so unbearable?'

'Because – because – I hoped it wasn't happening – that Father would come, that it was all some silly dream – because you don't want to believe something

379

like this *is* happening. Oh dear, I am so sorry—'

He gave her a handkerchief.

'Not as sorry as I am.'

I am twenty years older than she is, he thought, and in all those extra twenty years I have not been faced with any human situation as bitter as she is facing, or felt as unsafe or lost. Can I ever forgive Rose, whom I once thought so wonderful, or Harry, whom I have admired all my life? Can I ever understand the kind of insanity that grips them or even the depth of this poor child's unhappiness? Am I really fit to help anybody since I have clearly lived so little myself?

'When you are telegraphing,' Kate said, 'perhaps you could try to find Aunt Catherine too. She was going to the Lebanon. She – understands Father, you see—'

'And your Aunt Victoria?'

Kate muttered.

'Kate?'

'I – don't know. I asked her for help before—'

'I shouldn't ask you things,' Frank said. 'You are worn out. Let me do things instead. Let me get the carriage to take you home at least.'

'May I,' Kate said hesitantly, blushing, 'may I stay here a little? In this chair, just not move, while you do your stamps. Would that annoy you?'

Frank shook his head.

'Can I ring for something for you, some tea, toast—'

'No thank you,' Kate said, 'I don't want anything except just not to move.'

'Then don't,' Frank said, smiling down at her.

He went back to his desk, and sat down, and began to sort his other, lesser British Guiana stamps around his new treasure, and when he looked up to make sure that Kate was not soundlessly in tears, he saw that she had fallen asleep.

In the first week of March, with a new year's sun beginning to encourage the astounding carpets of wild flowers to spread across the cliffs and hillsides of Crete, Maria the housekeeper opened the shutters of the Villa Ariadne to welcome a new digging season. The house had to be cleaned, the rugs beaten, beds aired and made up, china and glass washed and polished, food to be brought in and the first batch of the season's mail to be collected from the post office in Herakleion and arranged neatly and in date order on Sir Arthur's desk. All but four of the letters in the first mailbag were for Sir Arthur. Two of those were for Mr Mackenzie, one for the Norwegian photographer who had come for a month the previous summer, and the fourth was a telegram marked 'URGENT' several times, for Sir Charles Taverner. Maria considered this last envelope, and then put it on the hall table beneath the great bas-relief of the head of a charging bull that hung there, to make a decision about later. Duncan Mackenzie, arriving two days afterwards after a fiendish crossing from the mainland, as the first comer of the season, found the telegram, considered it also, and opened it. Then, leaving his bags scattered on the hall floor and Maria shouting hoarsely after him, he raced down the Villa garden to the road and managed to catch, just as he was turning, the driver who had brought him down from Herakleion. It was, it seemed, a matter of urgency. Holding a crumpled telegram, instructions for the telegraph offices in both Herakleion and Chania, and a helpful number of piastres, the driver whipped up his

381

horse and rattled northwards over the stony road. When he had seen him out of sight, Mackenzie walked back up the garden to the house, only pausing to lay an appreciative hand on Dionysius's unemotional, mythical, safely extra-human stone head.

CHAPTER TWENTY

1910

Kate was alone when Charlie came home to Buscombe. She had asked that it should be so and Victoria, who remembered most honestly the keenness of her own independence at Kate's age, took herself to Bath to visit a promising new friend Sarah Weston, at present moving an invalid mother into a sharply angled house on Gay Street. Victoria had been at Buscombe every Friday to Monday of the spring school holidays, and in the days in between, Lilian Creighton had provided Kate with sympathetic and remarkably sensible company. She had returned from Madeira upon the instant of receiving Frank's telegram, had never supposed that Kate should leave Buscombe to stay with her, and had kept Kate steadily but unobtrusively occupied. Kate admired her rather, not just her grace and prettiness, still remarkable at sixty, but her wry humour and her firm and courteous manner with the servants and her bouts of laughing self-deprecation.

'You are lucky to have been born when you were,' she said to Kate. 'Girls born when I was, and your aunts were, were made such fools of, ordered about and decided for until we were fit for almost nothing. The sheer foolishness of the lives we were expected to lead amazes me, looking back. And I was so compliant! No wonder I still agonize for ten minutes every morning over which colour handkerchief to take.'

For a lot of the time, she talked to Kate about Buscombe as it used to be, how she had first seen it over thirty years before, when it still felt, because of Charlotte's determined old-fashioned hand, an eighteenth-century house. Then Rosamund had come and wrenched it abruptly a hundred years forward.

'And now it is nothing really, is it,' Kate said. 'Mother did this and that, Father did this and that, but mostly everybody has just left it. And complained—'

Lilian, whose social circuit had included most of the massively fashionable country houses of southern England, and whose gentle irony had never quite been able to admire wholeheartedly their elaborate grandeur, said loyally that Buscombe was all the better for being a little faded, a little irregular.

'A little—!' Kate said.

Talk of Buscombe kept them away from unbearable talk. Whether Kate would or could not speak of her family fled to Wales was not plain, but the fact remained that they were not spoken of. Kate was very thin, a thinness emphasized by the hard leather belt she wore around the waists of her serge skirts, but she seemed to sleep and eat and only once did she say to Victoria in a most matter of fact voice, that she terribly missed her baby brother.

'He was one last week,' she said, 'he had a birthday,' and then she said, 'Do you think I should do German as well as French for School Certificate?' and Rob was not mentioned again.

What Charlie was expecting as he drove those

familiar uphill miles from Bath to Buscombe, he could not really tell himself, but it certainly was not the house's empty yellow face and standing before the front door, on the terrace, her solitude oddly theatrical for all its poignancy, his daughter Kate.

She had been there for a quarter of an hour, waiting for him. He got out of the carriage and said,

'Do you know, I think we should get a motor. We will be the last family in Somerset with a carriage before long.'

Kate said stiffly, 'We already are.'

She did not move. Charlie did not move. Fred drove the carriage away to the stableyard and left them in a great silence together. At last Kate said,

'I think – perhaps you should come in?'

'I should like to—'

'There is only me here.'

'Yes.'

'Mrs Creighton comes and Aunt Victoria is staying but today it is only me.'

Charlie climbed the steps until he was level with Kate on the terrace and looking down at her. He said gently, 'You don't look well.'

She nodded.

'Does that mean you think you do look well or that you know you do not?'

She muttered, 'A bit tired—'

'May we go in?'

She walked in front of him into the house, into the hall where his collection lay humped depressingly under dust sheets.

'It was Aunt Victoria's idea,' Kate said to his enquiring glance.

'Thoughtful of her.'

385

'Yes.'

He moved towards the stairs.

'Where have you put me to sleep?'

'In your dressing room.'

In the dressing room, Tom's old dressing room, where he had given Charlie the tin train and the architectural bricks on his wedding day, the floor still covered in the faded Turkey carpet on which Charlie had laid the bricks out in reverent lines . . .

'Ask Fred to bring my bags up there, would you?'

'Yes.'

'And then shall we have a cup of tea in the conservatory?'

'It's lovely in there,' Kate said with the first gleam of warmth she had shown. 'Mrs Creighton is so clever about flowers.'

'I will be ten minutes,' Charlie said.

Kate had already arranged for tea in the conservatory, and had put some narcissi in a vase – maddening how unhelpful flowers seemed to be in her hands – and ordered anchovy toast for her father. He was very pleased about that, and about the conservatory where the climbing pelargonium was already in bloom, and walked about with a piece of toast in his hand and commented delightedly on things. Then he came back to the table where Kate sat looking at her empty plate and said,

'Now look, my dearest and most faithful daughter, there is something we must get clear before we plunge into our new life. You have my undying gratitude for being here to welcome me and for your fidelity and courage and love, and I owe you, and offer you, my most earnest apology for allowing matters to run on until you found yourself in this miserable and frightening state. I shall not forget either what you have suffered, nor what you have done. But there my apology ends. It is my belief that you will in time come to understand why I went away and even why I stayed away, and such is my faith in your steady good sense that I will not muddy the waters by explanation. In my view an explanation is, in any case, neither called for, nor seemly. If you have any particular resentments, you should tell me directly because they only poison the air. If you do not, we must set about this house, and Anna's future and the business of retrieving your brother.'

'Getting Rob back!'

'Naturally,' Charlie said.

'Who will look after him?'

'You and me and a nurse and perhaps Anna.'

'But—'

'Kate, however good a man your cousin Harry is – and I believe him to be so – he is not Rob's father and cannot be permitted to bring him up. I am much less good but I am his father.'

Kate shut her eyes.

'Will there be a horrid fight?'

'I hope not. Would you like to go away for a while, abroad perhaps, until it is all over?'

'I should hate it.'

Charlie helped himself to more toast.

'Would you like me to tell you about Crete?'

'No,' Kate said stonily.

In the doorway, Palmer coughed. She had never recovered from proving an unsatisfactory lady's maid to Rose, whom she had nervously adored, and had relapsed into a permanent manner of mixed agitation and gloom. Lilian and Victoria had both encouraged her to enter rooms confidently after knocking, but she continued to sidle in unannounced except by a series of uncertain and unnatural coughs.

'Mr Martineau, Miss Kate, sir, Miss – Mr Martineau—'

'Thank you, Palmer.'

Frank stood warily under the jasmine fronds and looked at a point somewhere between Charlie and Kate.

'Frank, I have so much to thank you for.'

Frank shifted his gaze sideways to Kate.

'It is not me you should thank, Sir Charles.'

Kate went scarlet, said, 'Oh, will you excuse me—' and almost ran past Frank into the drawing room, across the hall, up the stairs, along the landing to the nursery stairs and up those to her room at the top of the house. Once there, the tremendous agitation that had propelled her upstairs vanished and she sat on the edge of her bed and felt extremely silly and therefore quite unable to go downstairs again as she wished to. She picked up a book and put it down again, and looked at herself unhappily in the mirror for a bit and unlaced and relaced her boots and then went to the window and saw that Charlie and Frank were walking slowly down to the lake, Charlie gesturing, Frank with his hands behind his back. Kate watched them until they reached the water and turned away out of sight towards the obelisk, and then she went into Anna's room next door and looked at its neat, bleak emptiness and felt suddenly and desperately solitary. So she sat down on the floor by Anna's bed, and burst into tears as she had so longed – but failed – to do on her father's arrival, tears of tiredness and of a quite vast relief.

'It is perfectly clear cut,' Frank said, 'legally, that is. Under the Matrimonial Causes Act you may obtain a dissolution of your marriage on the grounds of your wife's adultery. Those are the sole grounds open to a husband, and we may infer from the circumstances of both association and opportunity that Lady Taverner and Colonel Taverner provide proof of adultery.'

They had paused by the obelisk and were seated on the stone bench at its foot, Frank upright with folded arms in his lawyer's black, Charlie leaning his elbows on his knees and looking out across the pale and shining water.

'And my son?'

'You might include in your petition a prayer for custody of your son outlining your plans for his welfare, upbringing and education.'

Gazing steadily ahead, Charlie said, 'And if I do not choose to point a finger at my wife?'

'A wife,' Frank said woodenly, 'may apply for the dissolution of a marriage for reasons of bigamy, bestiality, sodomy, cruelty, adultery or desertion without cause for two years.'

'I have been absent less than one year.'

'Quite so.'

Charlie remained quite still, simply looking ahead with his eyes slightly screwed up against the reflection from the lake and then he said quietly,

'I have been adulterous too.'

Frank said nothing. After a while Charlie turned his head slowly, so that he could see Frank and said gently, 'I am sorry, old man. You know us all too well to be our lawyer with a quiet mind.'

'I – I am anxious not to be priggish—'

'Moral regret, even disapproval, is not necessarily priggish.'

'I must endeavour to give the best and most impartial advice in my power.'

Charlie turned back to look at the water.

'And what would that be?'

Frank said with some diffidence, 'I may be most presumptious, but since you and Lady Rose are, shall we say, in the same boat, might a reconciliation not be possible? Forgive me, but your situation is not at all uncommon in good society, in fact I believe it is commonplace. But *divorce*—'

'Is vulgar,' Charlie said, 'whereas adultery is perfectly acceptable socially as long as nobody says anything. Admirable.'

'I do not condone society's attitude, Sir Charles. I simply wondered if you and Lady Rose might be persuaded to talk the matter over—'

'*No!*' Charlie said.

'For your daughters. For Kate in particular—'

Charlie got up. He had acquired, Frank could not but notice, a distinct authority in his bearing and manner, as well as a new moustache and a brown complexion. He moved away from Frank down to the lake's edge, and stood there for a while, rattling things gently in his trouser pockets. Then he came back and said,

'The simple truth is, my dear Frank, that we do not want each other any more. We are not as we were. I do not wish to live with the woman circumstances, if you like, have made of Rose, and she evidently does not wish to live with the man circumstances have made of me.'

'Your son—'

'I do want my son. And I want my daughters though I would honour their own feelings in the matter. Naturally I will allow myself to be the guilty party in the dissolution of the marriage but I shall do everything in my power to retain the custody of my son. With your help.'

Frank stood up.

'I should imagine a court would be quite well disposed towards you on the matter of custody. For Robert to live here would satisfy society's requirements for orthodoxy and convention. Life with his mother under the present circumstances would certainly be awkward for him. Your case might perhaps be strengthened by applying to his maternal grandmother for her help.'

'Would she give it?'

'Mrs du Cros came to see me last week. Her one desire is to see her grandson restored to Buscombe.'

Beyond the dense dark mass of the shrubs behind them, the sound of carriage wheels and hooves could be heard on the gravelled drive. Charlie looked up.

'My sister perhaps—'

They turned and began to retrace their steps towards the house over the silent turf.

'What is the next step, Frank?'

'That I communicate with the firm of solicitors in Cardiff chosen by Lady Rose, both in the matter of divorce as well as the boy—'

'Particularly the boy.'

'I shall endeavour to obtain what you wish without recourse to the courts. Over your son, that is.'

'Spare Rose as much as you can.'

'That goes without saying, Sir Charles.'

Charlie stopped a moment.

'Have you ever wanted to marry, Frank?'

'Only intermittently – and in the abstract.'

'Sagacious fellow—'

On the terrace, Victoria was pulling off her gloves. She paused when she saw them coming, and waited, the empty fingers of her left hand glove hanging limply and unregarded. Frank stopped walking and turned to gaze intently and tactfully into an azalea and Charlie went on without him, across the drive and up the steps to the terrace, where he put his arms about his sister without a word, and much surprised Palmer, come belatedly and hesitantly to open the front door.

'Don't scold,' Charlie said, his cheek against the felt crown of her hat.

'My dear boy,' Victoria said, 'there is far too much to be done to waste time in that!'

The house in Llanblethian was charmingly set at the top of a sloping garden running south to a meadow and a stream and gentle hilly fields beyond. All the principal rooms faced the view with generous windows and glass doors, and there were pretty garden walks and an arbour under a latticed wooden arch left behind by a previous occupant with eighteenth-century rustic tastes. To the village, the family was simply Taverner, their desire for seclusion made natural by the assumption, left undispelled, that they had *all* been in India and had come home in search of lost peace and health. Servants, drawn from the village and from nearby Cowbridge, reported a very quiet and irreproachable family, a pretty mother and daughter attended by a devoted governess, a courteous father, a delightful baby. There were no callers to speak of, Mrs Taverner did not seem strong, only the Colonel appeared in church. They kept one riding horse – definitely not a lady's mount – and a pair for the carriage, which was seldom used. The wine merchant and the grocer spoke of moderate orders and prompt payment, and when the daughter and her governess went out for walks, they chose unfrequented paths and lonely times of day. Their reputation grew to be one of slow convalescence, rather than mystery.

Anna was afraid. However circumspect, she knew that someone would soon discover that Harry was not her father, nor Rob's. She had been sure that she would not dare to face life in Buscombe or Bath without her parents; now she knew it was worse to face it without Kate, and with a threat. She longed for her last school term to begin. She would say she had been staying with relations in Wales in the holidays which was, after all, the truth. Kate did not write to her. Kate did not answer her mother's letters. Kate was angry. Anna felt Kate was right and admirable to be angry and envied her strength of mind. She was not simply afraid in Llanblethian; she was bored and lonely and felt cut off as never before, worse even than at Buscombe. She spent hours in her bedroom frightening herself with imaginary incidents in which the unorthodoxy of the household was suddenly publicly revealed and she was stigmatized beyond all repair. Perhaps nobody would ever marry her; perhaps hiding in Llanblethian, unable even to show her face in church, was all that would ever happen to her. She clung fiercely to the prospect of her last term at Laurelbank and prayed that the Masons might be moved to wish to adopt her. She felt she could forgive them their good-hearted dullness, their bourgeois aspirations, their utter want of real taste – *anything*, for their security.

The week before term was to begin, Rose became very agitated. She spent hours closeted with Harry – an extra grave Harry – and wept a good deal and woke them all at night pacing about and opening and shutting doors loudly. When Anna went to see her and to ask about arrangements for her return to Laurelbank, Rose said that there was no need for any arrangement as Anna was to remain in Llanblethian.

'Not go back to school?' Anna was gripped with terror.

'No, my darling. I need you here. It is best that you remain here.'

'But, why? Why, why, why? I *must* go back! I want to!'

Rose was sitting at her bureau, half-turned towards Anna, her left hand on the chair back, her right on the pile of papers she had covered with an innocuous sheet as Anna came in. The pile was small, made up of four solicitor's letters and one of Charlie's. They were all polite and all firm, and they all in various ways informed her that she might sue Charlie for divorce upon the grounds of his admitted adultery with an unnamed woman, in Greece during the course of the previous year, and that she must return her son to Buscombe. Without making it explicit, the two courses of action were somehow put forward as the two halves of a bargain, with the added implication that the least fuss about any of this would benefit all those concerned, not least herself.

Harry, genuinely anguished at the thought of parting with the baby as well as at the spectacle of Rose's suffering, had said she must agree. A court would send Rob home in any case so it was better to agree without the hideous publicity and stress of a court case and the humiliation of a loss for all to see. He and Rose had quarrelled terribly. At the height of her despair, Rose had lost all control and had screamed at Harry that she had made a terrible mistake, and that she was going back to Charlie with the baby and with Anna, back to Buscombe. With commendable gentleness, Harry had made her reread Charlie's letter and forced her to realize that Charlie very plainly, indeed unmistakably, did not want her back again. He was, in a most gentlemanly but entirely decided manner, insisting upon a divorce. She did not have the choice of whether to go or to stay. She did not have a choice at all. Stay she must, and release the child she must.

'Then I must keep Anna!'

'Rose, Rose,' Harry said, exhausted, wrung with pity, 'you cannot. It would be too unkind. Think of her! She longs to be back where she feels herself irreproachable once more. Would you keep her here, make her a pariah, for your own ends?'

Rose said a great many foolish and sentimental things about being a mother, then she tried to send Harry away and tried not to speak to him as a punishment for being right, but she needed his reassuring presence too much for either. Even in her turmoil, she was astounded at his forgiveness. She said, trying to make amends,

'I should keep Anna here for a while, to try to protect her from any consequence of the – the divorce—'

'She is safest at school,' Harry said.

'They will ostracize her!'

'They need not know. Nobody need know yet. They will only suspect if you do something obvious and clumsy like keeping her from school on a pretext, when Kate returns—'

'She can go to school in Cardiff!'

'It is unfamiliar, she would be afraid of not being accepted. At Laurelbank she knows she is admired, for her looks and her voice and her graces.'

'I am her mother!' Rose said on a high note. 'I know what is best for her!'

'The one,' Harry said levelly, crushing down his rare but rising temper, 'does not in the least necessarily follow the other.'

'You may return to Laurelbank in the autumn per-haps,' Rose said now to Anna.

'But I am almost eighteen!'

'Do not scream at me—'

Anna said breathlessly, 'Excuse me – I must go – excuse me—' and fled through the house in search of Ellen. She was in the linen room sitting among airy piles of Rose's petticoats and bodices and nightgowns and reading a newspaper account of the coronation of George V, an event as remote as the moon to their present way of life. She turned as Anna burst wildly in and said, 'I thought you might come—'

'Everyone is *mad, mad, mad* – what is happening – why may I not return to school – what do Mother and Harry talk about all the time—?'

Ellen took a handkerchief of Harry's from a neat pile and held it out.

'Take this.'

'Tell me, *tell* me!' Anna screamed.

Ellen still held out the handkerchief.

'I know you do not like me!' Anna wailed, beside herself. 'You only like Mother and Kate! You have never liked me, nobody does, and now I am not even to be allowed to return to school, to the few friends I *do* have, I am quite alone, I want to *die*—'

'Sit down,' Ellen said sharply pushing Anna towards a wicker linen basket.

'I don't want to!'

'Then I can tell you nothing.'

Sobbing and shaking, Anna sat. Ellen put the hand-kerchief in her hand.

'Dry your eyes. Blow your nose.'

'I am so unhappy,' Anna said, obeying, awed by her own tragedy.

'I know,' said Ellen. 'My heart is wrung for you. I have seldom been so sorry for anybody.'

Anna looked up at her.

'What is happening?' she whispered.

'Your parents are to be divorced,' Ellen said, 'and little Rob is to go back to Buscombe.'

Anna stared.

'Di – divorced?'

'They are not to be married any more. There will be legal arrangements to separate them.'

'But they are my parents!'

'I know. They are people too.'

'Rob?'

'He must go home. To your father and to Kate. Mr Martineau and a nurse are to come to fetch him.'

She knelt by Anna and put her arms around her.

'Soon?'

'I believe so.'

Anna put trembling hands over her face.

'Ellen? What will happen to me?'

'You are seventeen, my dear,' Ellen said, 'a young woman. I think you must screw up all the courage in your being and decide that for yourself.'

It was a strange trio that boarded the Cardiff train at Bath station: Frank Martineau, tense with the delicacy of his mission, Aggie Tilling who had suckled Rob, beaming at the prospect of both an adventure and retrieving him, and Lilian Creighton, who had offered herself.

'I have after all,' she said to Charlie cheerfully, 'no moral standing in Taverner eyes, so that my presence might actually comfort Harry and Rose by making them feel themselves in the presence of a fellow traveller. And being a woman, I may soften the harshness of the blow at seeing the child delivered over to a lawyer. In any case, little Rob knows me.'

They sat in three of a carriage's four corners. Frank read, Lilian pretended to and Aggie looked alternately at each of them and out of the window. She wore a regrettable hat with large velvet violets in it and a tired feather. Lilian wore a high-waisted frock of finely embroidered green wool with a fringed overskirt. Frank wore black and a frown. Apart from the briefest courtesies they hardly spoke, Frank being quite given up to the wretchedness of the task ahead of him, and Lilian to an astonished contemplation of the ironies of life, one of which had now landed her in the same railway compartment as the daughter of the woman who had betrayed her thirty years before. Aggie found that the combination of an adventure and the eternally sliding landscape was very wearing and sensibly went to sleep, her chin on her chest and her velvet violets nodding in time with the rhythm of the train.

It was Lilian who carried them through. Even Frank, traditionally antagonistic to her as the bidder who had almost deprived his family of Combe Place, felt nothing but gratitude. To stand in the airy drawing room at Llanblethian with Rose whom he had so passionately admired, and Harry to whom his father owed the loan that had saved his land for him, was a situation of such emotional and social complexity that his wits felt entirely suspended. He literally could not speak. He heard Lilian's murmur, saw her brief kiss on Rose's cheek, her hand out to Harry, felt that same hand upon his own arm and was aware of her low voice speaking to him of papers. Harry looked as if made of granite, Rose was weeping bent over Rob who sat with unnatural stillness on her knee and turned a large dark blue enquiring gaze upon everyone in the room.

The formalities were awful, all hands shaking almost too much to sign, Frank aware amidst all his other miseries that he was displaying about as much professional dignity as a drunken duck. Still Lilian went on gently, soothingly, talking, guiding hands to sign, telling Rose that the separation was not for ever, and while this trance-like scene was going on, the door opened and Anna came in dressed in a green loden coat for travelling, and a sailor hat too young for her, and behind her came Ellen, carrying a bag.

'Anna,' Lilian said warmly.

'I am coming with you,' Anna said in a rush, 'I am coming back to Buscombe with you.'

Rose began to scream, and after her, bewildered, the baby. Ellen gave Anna a little push towards her mother. Above the hubbub Anna cried,

'I must to back to school, you see! I must go back to Laurelbank—'

'Yes,' Ellen said with emphasis to Rose, 'yes.'

Rose closed her mouth abruptly. The silence was dramatic. She turned to Harry.

'Is this a plot?'

'No.'

'*No*,' said Anna fiercely, possessive of those hours in which she had wrestled to be brave enough to act, 'it is my decision.'

'Take the baby,' Rose said suddenly. 'Go on, take him, *take* him—'

Anna stooped to pick him up. Immediately Lilian and Frank came nearer, drawn by an instinct both protective and achieving, and Rose, gasping, sprang to her feet and fled from the room. Lilian looked at Frank.

'We should go—'

He nodded. She moved over to Harry, rigid by the long windows looking down the pretty, sunny garden, and put her hand upon his arm.

'Look after her,' Lilian said, but he gazed down at her without seeing or hearing her because his mind had suddenly become possessed by a mingled image of both India and Catherine, an image so powerfully seductive that he was almost faint with longing for them both.

CHAPTER TWENTY-ONE

1912

The day after the SS *Titanic* had sunk, crushed by an
iceberg and plunging one thousand, five hundred and
thirteen passengers to the ocean floor, Catherine
Taverner arrived home to a shocked England. She was
sixty-four and she had not been home for over three
years. In her considerable luggage she had among other
things a camel saddle, a Berber headdress, and a curved
Arab sword, blade inlaid with brass, bargained for in the
souk in Muscat. She had been to Petra and Baalbek and
Leptis Magna; she had talked to Arab, Syrian, Turkish
and Lebanese politicians, she had talked to academics
at the universities of Ankara and Cairo and to priests
everywhere. She had become much interested in the
position of Muslim women. She had come home, she
told herself, merely to change her exhausted wardrobe
for a new one before returning to the fray. The fray was
represented by an interesting new friend, a woman in
her early forties named Gertrude Bell who was the first
woman to achieve a first class history degree at Oxford.
Gertrude Bell was an archaeologist and traveller, a
Persian scholar and an Alpinist. She had made marvellous journeys in Asia Minor and planned another

into Central Arabia proper where hardly a European woman had trodden. Catherine had encountered her in Baghdad over the autographing of her book *Amurath to Amurath* and they had become immediate friends. It was Catherine's intention to go too, on the expedition into Central Arabia.

She arrived at Swan Walk straight from the boat train, dressed in shabby but conventional black and over it a great sweeping travelling coat made of red and cream Moroccan cotton that reached to her feet. Her boxes and bags were labelled and corded fantastically, each piece hung about with objects like birdcages and drums and camping stools that had proved intractable to pack. Her handbag, in contrast to the tiny fringed pouches on silk cords being carried along fashionable London streets, was a large squashy affair apparently made of old Turkish carpet, which she wore slung over her shoulder on a leather strap. She had no jewellery, no gloves, and on her head she wore a red felt fez with a long black tassel.

The assiduous young women in inky overalls who operated Victoria's new printing presses on the ground floor of Swan Walk surged excitedly to the windows. So did the magazine staff on the floor above, and, on the top floor, the newest batch of aspiring and impoverished literary feminists. Catherine looked back at them with pleasure. Arriving in England to the stunned national horror of realizing that an unsinkable ship had sunk, to a coal strike, a dock strike and an impending transport strike had been decidedly discouraging, filling her with a fear that in her absence the country had trailed backwards rather than marched forwards. These windows full of eager faces were an indication that at least some parts of life were progressing.

'Oh,' Catherine said some minutes later standing in Victoria's pale and immaculate sitting room, 'what an old freak I must look! My dear, I shall shed sand everywhere—'

'Please do,' Victoria said, laughing and drawing off the travelling coat. 'I cannot tell you how pleased I am to see you. So will Anna be—'

'Anna?'

'She is staying with me. To take singing lessons. She is almost twenty.'

Catherine put her hands to her head.

'Twenty—'

'You are so brown!'

'I am an old lizard. It is so comfortable when it does not matter any more.' She looked about her. 'I should like you to choose yourself a present out of my traveller's store but really I cannot think of anything very appropriate. Perhaps a marble egg I bought in Marrakesh – May I stay a night or two? I must then go on to Cheltenham. Cheltenham!'

A girl in an apron with a knot of the green and purple ribbons of the Women's Suffrage Movement pinned to the bodice, came in with a tray of tea. She put it down on a low table beside Victoria and said, 'The page proofs are ready. Do you want them now or later? I've done my editing on them.'

Victoria said, 'Later,' and then she turned to Catherine and said, 'I print books now, you see. This is Florence West, my copy editor.'

Florence West looked all of sixteen. She smiled gravely at Catherine and left the room, and when she had gone Catherine said suddenly, 'Kate? What about Kate?'

'Oh,' Victoria said, remembering her irritation with

Charlie, 'her father wants her to go to Oxford and she wants to nurse.'

'So?'

'They are transforming Buscombe in the meantime and working out some kind of compromise. Milk or lemon?'

'Milk. And a great deal of sugar, please, a truly Middle Eastern amount. What do you mean, transforming Buscombe?'

Victoria smiled.

'You would hardly recognize it. There is electric light throughout, bathrooms at every turn, central heating, a telephone and in the garage, which has been made out of two of the old loose boxes, sits a Hispano Souza motorcar that everyone pretends not to be afraid of.'

'So Charlie—'

'Charlie is a man reborn.'

'And – Rose?'

Victoria said quietly, 'I do not see Rose.'

'Does anybody see Rose?'

'No.'

'It is ridiculous,' Catherine said. 'It is just like the absurd silence over Rosamund all those years ago. You cannot pretend someone is dead merely because they behave in a way you do not like. I shall see Rose.'

'She is with Harry—'

There was a tiny silence.

'Of course,' Catherine said flatly, 'I quite forgot.' She drank her tea. 'Did they marry?'

'I believe so.'

Catherine drank more tea and held out her cup.

'What news from Cheltenham?'

'Much as before. Aunt Charlotte knowing very little, Elizabeth—'

'Knowing far too much.'

'She is very contented.'

'And you?' Catherine said, shooting Victoria a sharp glance. 'Are you contented?'

'I am not *dis*contented.'

'Should you like to be married?'

'No,' Victoria said with emphasis.

Catherine finished her second cup of tea and put the cup down on the table.

'My generation were brought up to regard marriage as the only future. It was not simply a practical choice of what to do but a moral one. Spinsters definitely lacked the spiritual grace of wives and mothers. Never have I ceased to bless having a little money of my own. It has given me freedom and dignity. And you have done even better, you have *made* money of your own.'

'I have help. I have a partner in the book business, a friend called Sarah Weston. Frank Martineau is bowled over by her. She is a master printer in her own right and has an even better collection of stamps than he does.'

'It sounds,' Catherine said a little enviously, 'another world to Cheltenham.'

'Oh!' Victoria cried. 'Oh, I should hope indeed that it was!'

Miss Gaze made it very plain that she did not like having Catherine in Montpelier Terrace. Before Catherine came, she had manoeuvred the household with steely subtlety until it ran as best suited her, with her own sitting room almost as comfortably furnished as Elizabeth's and her own coterie of friends. When Catherine came, she had to give up her sitting room to provide an extra bedroom – it was terrible to her to see her room invaded with outlandish objects smelling of pepper and hides – and her friends stayed away lest their precarious gentility should in some way be contaminated by Catherine's unconventionality. There was a difficulty, too, over Charlotte. For three years Charlotte had been washed and brushed and fed and ignored like an old rag doll, but Catherine wished to speak and read to her.

'She cannot *hear* you,' Elizabeth said irritably.

'Just because she does not speak, it does not mean she cannot hear. Why does she weep sometimes?'

'I do not know,' Elizabeth said, 'the doctor cannot tell. It is one of the symptoms that show her mind is gone.'

Charlotte was tiny. Her back was bent, her trembling hands curved. Catherine tried to remember her dominating, domineering, but it was like trying to remember someone already dead. Elizabeth said Charlotte had no idea who Catherine was, but Charlotte watched Catherine without fear and sometimes made little mewing sounds and her mouth twitched as if she would smile if she could only remember how to. Catherine read her travel diaries out loud to her mother and Miss Gaze listened outside the door in order to be outraged if at all possible. Sometimes she was richly rewarded.

'I was rather apprehensive, riding into Sheveh,' Catherine read from her account of riding through Iraq on a mule, attended by an Armenian Turk called Hassan, 'after the narrow escape we had had among the fanatics at Samarah, especially as we could hear wild cries and music as we approached. The moon was full, white on the mountains, and the flames of a fire lit among the huts of the village threw eerie jumping shadows. As we came nearer the fire, we could see that the villagers were dancing, a kind of wild stamping, crying dance to an insistently beating drum and suddenly I could not bear to stay on my mule another minute, and I sprang off and cried to the men to let me join them. It was quite extraordinary. They turned and broke their circle to drag me in and I began to hop and turn and stamp and scream with them, a glorious free savage with them under the great white moon.'

'So coarse,' Miss Gaze reported to her friends, 'perfectly shocking. And to an innocent and sick old woman. Naturally I shall have to inform Miss Elizabeth.'

But Elizabeth did not seem interested. Elizabeth, though disconcerted at Catherine's eccentric new self-confidence, was pleased to see what an exotic cachet her travelled sister gave to her drawing room. Catherine was invited to give talks on her travels in the Pump Room, even in the Town Hall, and then in Gloucester and Tewkesbury and Hereford. People came constantly to the house to ask for her and a representative from the publishing house of Chapman & Hall arrived to discuss the editing of her diaries for a travel book. It was to be called *By Desert Ways: A Solitary Traveller in the Middle East*. Catherine was given an advance of one hundred and fifty pounds. In the midst of these excitements she knew that Charlotte was at last dying, very quietly, like a boat that has somehow slipped its moorings and is simply, silently, drifting out to the horizon across a calm, still sea. Upon an impulse Catherine wrote to Kate.

'I do not quite know why it is to you that I write, nor why I feel it is you that should come. She will not know you, of course, but I know you must see her yourself just once more. Of your generation, you are the only one with a sense of tradition, a sense of the house, of the family. It would, in any case, give me such pleasure to see you.'

A bedroom had to be made for Kate out of the sunny little upstairs room Elizabeth had taken as her boudoir. It was very small, being really only part of the landing at the half turn of the stairs, but it had a lovely window occupying almost all one wall, and a view of the garden. The walls were covered with family memorabilia, miniatures of Elizabeth and Catherine and Tom as children, portraits of Charlotte and her husband at the time of their marriage, photographs of Buscombe, inside and out, of Charlie and Victoria as children, Charlie as a page at Tom's wedding, Tommy in uniform, Tommy at two in a pony pannier wearing a sunbonnet like a cauliflower, Freddie Forrester dressed for shooting, Elizabeth herself, painting decorously under the tulip tree at Buscombe with her skirts spread around her in an enormous bell.

'Can you bear them all?' Catherine asked.

Kate nodded.

'I like them.'

'You are very thin—'

'I always seem to be thin. It doesn't matter. I've got heaps of energy. Oh Aunt Catherine, you should see the house!'

'Is it wonderful?'

'Very nearly. I can't seem to give it quite the right feeling, you know that warm capable feeling that houses run by women who are really good at it can have. But it's *so* much more alive than it has been for years and it has lost that sad neglected look.'

'So have you.'

'That is triumph,' Kate said.

'Triumph?'

'I am to go to St Bartholomew's Hospital as a student nurse in the autumn.'

Catherine held out her arms.

'My dear child!'

'I love Buscombe,' Kate said, 'but I can't stay at home any more and I know perfectly well I am not academic. The last year at school nearly killed me. You can't imagine the restrictions – even last summer, which was the hottest for a century or something, we had to play tennis and cricket in flannel blouses buttoned to our chins and our wrists—'

'*Cricket?*'

'Indeed yes. I am no mean spin bowler either. But I feel so *ignorant*. Of real life, I mean. Anna likes it, being sheltered and safe, but I really chafe at it. At least with nursing I shall get to know how bodies work. Do you realize,' her voice rose in indignation, 'that all I know about the arrival of babies and how they get there in the first place is from reading Ellen's copy of *Household Medicine*? It must be the most decorous book in England.'

'You girls,' Catherine said musingly, smiling, 'always seem so free compared with my own girlhood—'

'Well, not free *enough*. Yet. Father pretends to be very sceptical that I can manage in London on my own, but really I think he does not want to be left alone at Buscombe. I tell him he won't be alone because there is Rob, and all the paraphernalia of a little boy's life, human and otherwise. He *is* solitary anyway as if – as if he was missing someone. Perhaps—' She stopped and then said quickly, 'I think he should work again, but he says he has now missed the boat and that all his best ideas of eight or nine years ago have been overtaken by events.'

The days of Kate's visit were spent walking on Cleeve Hill, meeting Elizabeth's circle of indistinguishable friends, preparing with justified gratification for a talk Catherine had been invited to give to the Royal Geographical Society – 'Perhaps,' Kate said, 'they will even elect you a *member*! Women can be, now, can't they?' – sitting with Charlotte, and talking. Kate had never talked to anyone as she found she could talk to Catherine and describe her sad confused feelings about Rose, whom she had not seen for two years, and her concern that Rob – an anxious but loving child – should be growing up without a proper mother. She felt so able to confide that she even got to the point where she almost confessed her profound misery that Frank Martineau was plainly in love with Victoria's capable friend, Sarah Weston. That she finally said nothing was in obedience to an instinct to protect the extreme privacy of what had been, ever since she came to Buscombe as a child and Frank had been so unvaryingly kind to her, such a central emotion. She knew other people thought Frank dull, too clerkly, without real spark, but to Kate none of those things mattered besides his absolute and serious trustworthiness, his gentleness, his honour.

She spent a week in Cheltenham. The day after she left, Charlotte, alone in her room while Miss Gaze did errands in the town and Catherine and Elizabeth were writing letters at their several desks, gave a little sigh, more of relief than regret, and died. She might have lain there an hour or more, composedly dead, if Pug had not by his whinings and scurryings from bed to door and back again, brought Elizabeth and Catherine to Charlotte's room. They stood side by side and looked down at their mother and then Elizabeth, seized by a sudden sense of isolation and insecurity, took Catherine's hand and held it hard.

'Now,' Catherine said gently, 'now, my dear Elizabeth, you are quite free,' but Elizabeth, bursting into a sudden storm of tears, declared that that was the very last thing she had ever wanted to be.

'It is,' Charlie said to Frank Martineau, 'a perfectly outrageous suggestion. And there is no question of it.'

He brandished the letter in his hand and then tossed it down onto the library desk so that it spun across the surface like a flat stone on water. Frank fielded it neatly.

'Do I understand, Sir Charles, that your two cousins in Cheltenham now propose to return to Buscombe in order to assist in the bringing up of Robert?'

Charlie tramped to the window.

'It's preposterous.'

'Is it?'

'Of course it is. Don't tell me you are going to defend the idea?'

Frank said carefully, 'Kate is leaving for London in two months. That will leave the child with Aggie Tilling and a nurse, but no superior female guidance. In the circumstances, do you not think—'

'No!' Charlie shouted.

There was a knock at the door and Kate came in with a tray bearing the whisky decanter and two tumblers and a jug of water.

'Why are you shouting?'

'Frank seems unable to appreciate what a monstrous notion it is to have your old cousins back here.'

Kate avoided looking at Frank.

'Catherine is an influence for the good—'

Charlie came back to the desk and slammed the top with the flat of his hand.

'I see. We allow the house to become filled with prayer rugs and hubble-bubbles and dotty old experts on the churches of the Levant, only to have Catherine depart into the Arabian interior once more leaving us with all her clutter and undiluted Elizabeth?'

'Elizabeth—'

'Elizabeth is without exception the most restrictive human being on this earth. I can conceive of no more deadening influence on any child than Elizabeth's. Anyway, think of me.'

'We are,' Kate said, finally putting her tray down. 'You might be so lonely here.'

'I am lonely anyway.'

Kate flinched very slightly.

'I prefer loneliness,' Charlie said, 'to Elizabeth.'

'I suppose,' Frank suggested diffidently, 'Miss Napier could not be induced to return?'

Charlie picked up the decanter and poured whisky into the tumblers.

'Not your most tactful suggestion, Frank.'

Frank accepted his whisky in silence and then said, 'What about this business between Montenegro and Turkey? Do you think it is serious?'

'It might become so, if the Great Powers are asked to intervene. I'm not sure a Balkan squabble is worth getting our noses bloodied for, though. There *is* an uneasiness in the air, a sort of world uneasiness. Socialism brewing in Russia, strikes here, strikes in America—'

'Ever thought of following your cousin into politics, Sir Charles?'

Charlie grinned.

'Growing older is the damnedest thing. If you had asked me that ten years ago I should have looked at you as if you were mad. Now, three years short of fifty, the idea isn't so insane. Mind you, being divorced would probably be held against me. Look what victims our remarkably hypocritical society has made of both Dilke and Parnell.'

'I don't think,' Frank said slowly, turning his whisky in his hands, 'that this world of ours is going to last.'

Kate looked round at the library, at its almost unbearable familiarity.

'Not last?'

'It has been too rich, too successful, too pleased with itself for too long. There has been such a different air around since Edward VII died, almost as if an age died with him – well, a *decade* but a very distinct one. I don't know what is going to happen, but I don't think our children will know the same world that we know.'

'Does that prophecy,' Charlie said, 'include the protection of my son from his elderly relations?'

Frank smiled and stood up.

'Of course, if you wish it. Good night, Sir Charles.'

'Good night, Frank. Can you spare me an hour later in the week? I want to set up a trust for these independent young women of mine—'

Kate walked with Frank across the hall. He paused by the door to pick up his hat and said, turning it in his hands,

'Talking of changes and the future, Kate, there *is* a change that I should like you to know of before anyone else.'

Kate waited.

'I am to be married,' Frank said gently, looking straight at her. 'I think you have known for a long time

413

how much I admire Sarah Weston. She agreed last week to marry me.'

Kate nodded. Frank put out his hand and took one of hers.

'We have always been such friends, you and I. I can remember your coming here so clearly, and that first summer, meeting you barefoot all over the estate with your pinafore pocket full of pebbles and apple cores. It would make me so happy if you and Sarah came to be friends too. She so much admires your decision to nurse. So do I. You are the mainstay of this family but that is sometimes a crushing responsibility and it is time you had a rest from it.' He raised the hand he held and kissed it and then he went out of the door and across the terrace and down the steps to the drive where he had parked his car.

When he had gone, Kate went very quickly across the hall and out of the garden door and then ran, in the fading light, across the lawn, through the shrubbery and the door in the wall to the old granary on its stout stone legs. She pulled the door open and went up the stairs to the loft, and across the hay strewn floor to the long-forgotten apple store. It was like something out of *Sleeping Beauty*, the pagoda birdcage clotted with dead moths, gauzy curtains of cobweb between the chair legs and the rails of the ivory abacus, a general dusty furring and blurring across the globe and the musical box and the little looking glass, all the objects they had carried down from the attics that summer eight years ago when Charlie first was ill and everything began to go wrong. She put out a finger and wrote 'Kate' in the dust on the surface of the little sewing table. There was no point in crying or regretting anything, from Tommy's death to Frank's marriage, and all the upheavals in between. Gazing at the apple store was like looking at the essence of her childhood, a childhood that had slipped away when she wasn't looking. Perhaps even Frank was part of it?

She picked up the abacus and the globe and blew at their dustiness. Then she picked up the birdcage and descended the steps to the ground floor. It was almost dark and the evening star shone theatrically in the soft sky. Was Frank right, were changes coming? She thought of the *Titanic* and shivered. That had frightened everyone so, that human calculations could prove to be so utterly, tragically wrong. There were lights in the house, new and wonderful electric lights, one high up in Rob's nursery, one in her father's dressing room, a soft long gleam from the dining room where Palmer would be anxiously laying the table for dinner. She would go in and have a bath, in the marvellous new bathroom on the top floor where Charlie had installed a huge showerhead under a kind of china canopy at one end of the tub, a showerhead which released water with the violence of a tropical thunderstorm. Even the maids had a bathroom now, and the scullery pump had gone, and the lamp room, made redundant by the arrival of electricity, harnessed to a throbbing generator in the old coach house, was to become a dark-room in case Charlie's enthusiasm for photography grew.

As she came in through the garden door, Palmer was agitating in the hall. She sprang forward at the sight of Kate.

'A person – a lady in the morning room for you – to see Sir Charles – Miss Kate—'

Kate stopped.

'What sort of person, Palmer?'

'A lady. A dark lady with a child – a little boy – very pleasant—'

'Where is my father?'

Palmer jerked her head upwards in an endeavour to indicate that Charlie was bathing and changing without the indelicacy of actually having to say so.

'Such an odd time of day to call – has she been here long?'

'Oh, no – not above ten minutes – I was in the dining room, Miss Kate, when Fred came in – he went to the door when she rang—'

'I'll go in to her,' Kate said.

In the morning room, standing with her back to the fireplace and looking about her with interest, stood a dark woman in her twenties in a travelling coat and skirt of fawn gaberdine trimmed with black braid. Against her leaned a small boy, a very small boy, in a minute knickerbocker suit. Both of them exuded an air of extra-ordinary composure, so much so that Kate opened her mouth to say, 'May I help you?' and closed it again as the remark seemed entirely pointless. Instead she said, 'Good evening?' on a slightly questioning note and both the woman and the child turned a lively yet collected gaze upon her and smiled.

'I wonder if you could be Kate?'

She had a faint un-English intonation. Kate blushed. 'Yes—'

'I am so pleased to meet you. Your father always spoke so proudly of you. My name is Eleni Mesara. Your father and I became friends in Crete.'

'Crete!'

'And this is my son Carlo. He was christened Charles, but in Athens where we have been living, he had a Spanish nurse and Carlo was a compromise of sorts.'

The child detached himself from his mother and came across to Kate, standing close to her and holding up a round cheek.

'He expects to be kissed,' Eleni said. 'I am afraid he was much indulged in Athens and kissed all the time. The Greeks are very sentimental about children.'

Kate knelt and kissed Carlo's cheek. He put his nose against hers and pressed, peering brightly into her eyes.

'How old is he?'

'Two.'

'I have a little brother of three.'

There was a tiny pause and then Eleni said a little less relaxedly, 'Yes. That I know.'

Kate took her nose from Carlo's and looked up.

'You do? How do you know?'

Gently, Eleni said, 'Because your father told me so.'

'I think I should fetch my father.'

'Yes, my dear. So do I. But before you go—'

'Yes?'

Eleni paused and then she said, 'No. No explanations yet. Just tell your father I should be so glad to see him.'

Charlie's dressing room door was ajar. Inside he was standing in front of the glass shirtsleeves and braces, tying an evening tie. Kate stood behind him and said to his reflected face,

'There is a woman in the morning room asking to see you. She says her name is Eleni Mesara and she has brought her son with her, a little boy called Carlo.'

Charlie's eyes met Kate's in the glass. He became absolutely still.

'She says she has come from Athens. It's very odd. She seems quite at home—'

Charlie said, very softly, 'That is how she is,' and then he said, 'Eleni Mesara. Eleni. Good God—'

Kate stepped back.

'Who is she?'

Charlie was still facing the mirror. He said in a perfectly ordinary voice, 'She is the daughter of a doctor and archaeological scholar in Crete. I met her on my first visit and fell in love with her on my second.'

'I see,' Kate said.

Charlie turned round with extraordinary slowness. He looked suddenly extremely young.

'When I came home the second time from Crete, and found you here alone, the only one with sufficient love and courage to greet me, I think I remember saying to you that in time you would know why I had stayed away as well as why I went away. Why I went I think you knew long ago. A large measure of why I went for so long now waits downstairs. To my utter astonishment, I might say, since I have, to my great regret, heard nothing from Eleni for over a year. Judge if you must. All I ask is that you wait a while before you do.'

He picked up his coat and a brush and began with no apparent agitation, to brush the shoulders.

'Did you say there was a child with her?'

'Yes.'

'What age?'

'Two.'

'Called Carlo?'

'Christened Charles.'

Charlie put on his jacket and turned back to the glass to straighten it.

'*Say* something!' Kate shouted. 'Tell me what is going on! Don't you feel *anything*?'

'Certainly I do.'

He came towards Kate and bent his face until their eyes were only inches apart.

'The feeling I have, Kate, the sensation I have is that my heart is simply bursting in my chest,' and then before she could turn her face away from him he had kissed her cheek hard and she could hear his rapid footsteps going along the landing towards the stairs.

Catherine was, for all her lifelong policy of non-interference in the lives of loved ones, perfectly sure that Charlie was wrong. Rob should not grow up in a household of servants, however devoted, once Kate had gone to London. What if Charlie took it into his head to go off to Crete again, or Turkey, or mainland Greece? There were fascinating new excavations happening in all of them. If he did, Rob would become entirely isolated from his own kind. It had been bad enough for poor Tommy at Buscombe, without anyone else of his own age for company, but at least his grandmother and aunts had been there to supply him with the appropriate guidelines for his upbringing. It would be worse for Rob, brought up like a little emperor amid a sea of slaves, he would become like those ruined children allowed to behave tyrannically in the nurseries of India, the *baba-log* of three shouting imperious orders at a trembling ayah. There was more to it than that, of course, and she knew it. Having care of little Rob might in some measure fill the gap that Tommy had never ceased to leave.

Elizabeth agreed. Partly she agreed because she thought Catherine right about the servants, but mostly because she, as senior female relation, might now be mistress of Buscombe. Catherine would not endure to stay in England long – already she was planning her Arabian trip for the winter of next year – and she would be in sole charge of the house. To be sure, Charlie ran the estate most oddly, if what Kate had told them was to be believed. He had no interest in field sports himself, beyond a little trout fishing in early summer, and the acres upon which his great-uncle had grown wheat and oats and barley and his cousin Tom had latterly given up to grazing for sheep and the dairyherd or leased for shooting to Arnold du Cros and his cronies, were now used for beef cattle.

'Beef cattle?'

'For fattening,' Kate had said. 'They are sent down from Scotland as calves and we fatten them. Father says it means less capital outlay and fewer men but still makes a profit. You see, the thing is, farming isn't really of consequence any more.'

To Elizabeth, this seemed a wrong-headed, almost heretical attitude. She remembered Buscombe in her childhood, the harvest homes, the grain samples being taken to Bath market in linen bags, by Howitt in his brown bowler and gaiters, the October barns piled high. There was something so crude at the thought of all that meat on the hoof, something of the taint of trade almost as if Charlie were proposing to start a tannery. She was sure she could speak to him. She was sure he would welcome her domestic competence so that he would be free to travel as he wished. She was sixty-five, but her health – a source of intense interest to her but also a passionate pride – was excellent. If she was careful. She saw herself in Charlotte's bedroom, in Charlotte's chair in the drawing room, using the writing paper her father had commissioned specially for her birth and which Charlotte had unaccountably never used. She began to speak to her Cheltenham circle of family duty.

'Perhaps you would leave it to me to go down to Buscombe and explain?' Catherine said.

'Why so?'

'Because I shall not mind Charlie's rudeness and you will mind it very much. And he is certain to be rude.'

Elizabeth considered.

'Should we not go together? Would that not be altogether more suitable and – impressive?'

'I think it would look like bullying. And then we should never get what we want. I shall only be gone a night or two. And Elizabeth—'

'Yes?'

'If we succeed, if we return to Buscombe, we shall *not* go accompanied by Miss Gaze.'

'But Catherine—'

'But nothing.'

'She is so very respectable—'

'Respectable?' said Catherine. 'Ah, so *that* is what you call it.'

She wired to Charlie. He wired back.

'Delighted to see you. Position over Robert immovable.'

In the train going south she rehearsed her arguments. Charlie was surely too intelligent to wish anything but the best for his son, too realistic to dismiss her case before he had heard it? She was hopeful, at the least. The early autumn sun was shining comfortably on Buscombe's broad yellow face as she drove up, the drive was free of weeds and on the terrace there were urns of white geraniums and trailing dark blue lobelia instead of the stiff little bay trees Charlotte had always been so wedded to. And surely all the window frames looked particularly white and newly painted?

Palmer and Kate opened the door ineptly between them, and Kate came running down the steps in welcome. She looked extremely happy, had pinned her hair up rather badly and was wearing a pink and white striped shirt with a high white collar and a knot of dark blue ribbon at the neck. When they had kissed and Catherine had exclaimed over the house, she looked up and saw a neat dark woman in blue in the doorway with a small dark boy in either hand. A perfectly strange dark woman . . .

'Come on,' Kate said in a voice full of warmth, 'I have someone I want you to meet. And of course Rob, and Carlo—'

'Carlo?' Catherine said faintly. 'Who is—'

The dark woman came forward. Mediterranean, Catherine decided automatically, perhaps Italian, or Greek . . .

'Miss Taverner. It is such a pleasure to meet you. My name is Eleni Mesara and this is little Robert and this is my son, Carlo.'

Rob remained holding Eleni's hand but Carlo came forward beaming and held up a confident cheek.

'He expects you to kiss him,' Kate said.

Catherine did so.

'What an engaging child. Will little Rob speak to me?'

Rob turned and pressed his face into Eleni's skirts.

'In a moment perhaps. Will you come in?'

The morning room was full of flowers. In Cheltenham, Elizabeth only permitted what was proper, a carnation or two in a silver vase, a severely symmetrical fern in a Chinese pot. Here there were huge vases of cream chrysanthemums, bowls of yellow and white dahlias and in the window where she had sat so much of her young womanhood, stood a large and airy bright green bush starred, apparently, with little marguerites.

'Charming!' Catherine said.

Eleni and Kate exchanged glances.

'Palmer is horrified,' Kate said. 'She thinks us quite *démodé*, too cottagey for words. You should see what Eleni has done for your conservatory—'

'Mrs Mesara,' Catherine said, hoping she did not sound like Elizabeth, 'I imagine you are a guest at Buscombe.'

'For the moment,' Eleni said. 'Please won't you sit down?'

'I will fetch Father,' Kate said. 'He wanted to be told the moment you got here.'

Eleni looked across at Catherine with a smile.

'You must think us so extraordinary. And I hope you are not upset at finding me here. The moment Sir Charles comes, we will explain everything. Will you excuse me one moment while I take the children to the nursery?'

Alone in the morning room, Catherine struggled with herself for some degree of collectedness. The mixture of the extreme familiarity of the house – why, the morning room walls were still the faded duck egg blue of her childhood, now very shabby indeed – and the great unfamiliarity of the humans and human behaviour, made her feel confused and unsure. Who was this absolutely strange and disconcertingly pleasant woman with a child who, to look at, was almost a carbon copy of little Robert? Why was Kate so seemingly at ease? What on earth could the explanation be? Was she dreaming it all? She looked about her. There was the yellow velvet sofa, there were the unfortunate green linen Arts and Crafts curtains poor Rose had hung up, there were her mother's pretty Regency chairs and the dear old Turkey carpet sunbleached now in the places not under bits of furniture to straw and rose and grey. But the chairs were not in the same places and there was a strange workbasket by the fireplace and above all, all those extraordinary flowers . . .

'Catherine!' Charlie said from the doorway. He looked better than she had seen him look in years. 'This is an enormous pleasure! You can't have been here for ages. Of course, you will sleep in your old room—'

He kissed her vigorously. She said faintly, drawing away, 'Of course I am more than pleased to be here, I have not slept here for over three years. But Charlie, I do not understand—'

'Of course you don't. That is why I wished to see you as soon as you arrived, so that you should have an explanation at once.'

Catherine sat down on the yellow sofa.

'Well?'

Charlie came to sit next to her.

'Eleni Mesara is an old friend. I met her in Crete on my first visit and we became lovers on my second. She is the daughter of a doctor and a scholar and a member of one of the island's oldest families. The child is mine – though in fact I left Crete not knowing Eleni was pregnant. Crete is a small society and it was best for her family that she leave Chania for the mainland to live in Athens as her brother's housekeeper. We kept in touch, though she made no mention of the child and I imagined – she encouraged me to imagine – that she had simply become stifled by the restrictions of an island society. She knew of my difficulties with Rose, but waited a full two years before she came to find me. We are to be married and Rob will gain both a mother and a brother. That is all. It only remains for you to discover her worth for yourself.'

Catherine put a hand over her eyes.

'Oh, my dear—'

Charlie waited.

'Do you know,' Catherine said at last, her eyes still covered, 'that family life can make being pursued by a crowd of howling Muslim fanatics seem like a Temperance Society picnic?'

CHAPTER TWENTY-TWO

1913

It was not the isolation so much that Harry found hard
to bear, as the inactivity. Taught by long regimental
years, he made himself a timetable for each day which
was supposed to provide him with a full and productive
life, but in reality only gave him the illusion of one. He
rose early, leaving the first floor with elaborate quiet,
and rode for a couple of hours over Glamorgan's green
slopes, then returned to a solitary breakfast over which
he read *The Times*. The second Balkan war interested
him greatly – Bulgaria attacking Serbia and Greece,
Russia declaring war on Bulgaria, Serbia invading
Albania – and he tried to talk to Rose about it in order,
in some instinctive way, to ease the sharp pain of his
own nostalgia for military life. But Rose had lost even
the small interest she had once had in politics when her
father was alive, and it was to Ellen that Harry turned
for discussions on the alarming growth of Germany's
navy and the challenge that represented to the
supremacy of the island-Empire. Ellen at least had
advanced reading tastes, some of them quite difficult to
swallow; she had lent Harry a copy of a new book by
Thomas Mann called *Death in Venice* which had dis-

turbed him profoundly. It was not the homosexuality which troubled him so much – after all, he had had thirty-five years of soldiers buggering each other, whatever Army Rules tried to do to prevent it – as to see it portrayed as the self-destructive obsession of a highly civilized man. It was the obsessiveness that got to Harry, touched him on a raw nerve. Ellen wanted to lend him something else, called *Sons and Lovers*, but he didn't think, from the title, that he could take it quite yet.

He spent the morning at his desk and ambling about the garden – happy days were those when some specific and delicate job such as thinning out young grape bunches on the vine were to be done. Rose and he first met at luncheon. Afterwards, she paid or received calls – oh, how painful and delicate was this tiptoeing back into social acceptability! – and he, after a vigorous walk along one of two or three unvarying routes, returned for two hallowed hours upon what Rose called his memoirs. They were not memoirs in the strict sense, but more autobiographical reflections. Their theme was England's imperial role, both as trader and as influence for justice and for peace, and unflinchingly recorded the episodes, such as the Boer War, in which Harry felt both motive and action to have been questionable. Occasionally, he read pieces to Ellen. She admired his writing but, being one of that rare and extraordinary breed, a pacifist, could seldom admire his sentiments. Harry believed strongly in the military role; he was contemptuous of the vainglory of too many of his Army contemporaries and alarmed by the brutal simplicity of such soldiers as Kitchener, but the sword as an instrument to promote harmony, order and freedom, he saw as second to none. Ellen listened to him with great attention but was in no way moved. She thought the world had outgrown being able to settle differences by bashing at each other.

He and Rose met again for dinner and discussed their day. After dinner, they were joined by Ellen, and sat in the drawing room, reading or playing cards or fiddling about with bits of embroidery. At ten, four servants trooped in for prayers – the groom-chauffeur remained in his cottage behind the stableyard with his wife and children. At ten-twenty, Rose drifted up to her room, Ellen in attendance. Harry then lit a cigar, gave himself a glass of port and did some small soothing things with his hands, like tying fishing flies, rubbing beeswax into the bindings of favourite books or mending broken china, a skill at which he was particularly adept. Between eleven and eleven-thirty, he checked all the locks and the lamps, and took himself to bed, to dream often of India and sometimes of Malta and of Buscombe. The thing to avoid as he lay down to sleep, he had discovered, was any kind of introspection.

He was not exactly lonely. He had Rose, he had, in an odd but pleasant sort of way, Ellen, and he was on a number of local benevolent committees. He hunted twice a week in winter and they dined out perhaps a dozen times a year. But he was very conscious that he was rather passing the time than living life; nothing seemed to lead anywhere much. The hollow space this left inside him was not, she made it extremely clear, sympathetic to Rose. She indicated that she possessed a similar void, and that, obscurely, she was inclined to blame him for creating it. After a few unsuccessful attempts to discuss their private doubts and fears, Harry withdrew. It was better, plainly, to stick to everyday events.

Their old lives had not forgotten them. Harry still received letters from regimental colleagues and both Rose and he heard from Victoria and from Lilian Creighton. Their letters were read by him and Rose severally and without comment. When Lilian's letter came announcing Charlie's remarriage in a civil ceremony in Bath, Harry tried his best to comfort Rose, certain that she must need it. But she rebuffed him. He could only hope that if she needed to confide in anyone, she could turn to Ellen.

The marriage was not the only development. Rob had, it seemed, acquired overnight a half-Cretan half-brother, the child of Charlie's mistress, now wife, and the two boys were to be brought up together. Arthur Creighton had died, worn out by the final disappointments of his life, and his widow at once sold the house she had always detested and returned to London, to a graceful Mayfair house on Chesterfield Hill. To this house, at Lilian's invitation, Anna moved from Swan Walk, secretly thankful to be out of Victoria's household which, however vigorous and interesting and achieving, she could not but regard as unwomanly. Lilian planned to bring Anna out; she was sure Rose would be only too happy at such a plan? It was the ideal project for her, rich and without occupation and with an address book full of grandmothers with granddaughters of Anna's age.

Kate, it seemed, also went to Chesterfield Hill, on those days and half days too brief for her to return to Somerset. She was working indescribably hard, scrubbing floors, washing out dressings and bed pans in the sluice, dusting bedsprings and carrying around the wards huge wooden trays full of mugs of tea. She told Lilian that her back and her feet ached almost all the time, but the reward was a growing knowledge of human anatomy and functioning. After the bleakness of the nurses' hostel, where it was so difficult to find either hot bathwater or privacy, Kate delighted to bring friends to the welcoming comfort of Chesterfield Hill. Lilian reported all this faithfully to Rose.

'Is she malicious?' Rose said tearfully to Ellen. 'Is all this deliberate?'

Ellen shook her head.

'I think she is useful for the first time in her life and necessary, and of course that makes her very happy. If one is happy, one wants to tell other people about it.'

'Oh really?' Rose said. 'I really can't remember—' She gave a small, hard laugh. 'Happiness!' she said scornfully.

She rose and swished to the window.

'Happiness,' she said in the same hard, tight voice, 'is an illusion. It is only shown to you so that you may suffer the more when it is snatched away.'

And Ellen, whose great love for Rose was frequently stretched almost to breaking point these days, snapped, 'You cannot hope for happiness when you are eaten up with self-pity,' and fled from the room.

It was a mile and a half from the nurses' hostel to the hospital itself. The hostel was in a huge solid grey house overhung with sooty elms, there were no curtains at the windows and a general air of uncompromising gloom pervaded the place. Kate had a cubicle in a tall bare room that she shared with four others. They were divided from each other by cretonne curtains hung on rails six foot from the floor. There was no heating beyond that given off by a stout hot water pipe running along the skirting board of one wall, and the only light was a single low wattage bulb that hung nakedly from a long flex in the centre of the ceiling.

None of this discouraged Kate in the least – in itself. Even the single cold bathroom with its dangerously antique geyser designed to serve all thirty young nurses in the hostel was not so far removed in discomfort from the nursery bathroom at Buscombe, which Charlotte had considered suitable for the young. Linoleum floors, blank windows shaded only by crackling brown blinds, the cold, the functional furniture, empty cream gloss walls where the odd creeping crack assumed, in the absence of any decoration, the interest of a picture – all was as Kate had expected and, to an extent, relished as being outward and visible signs of inward and professional dedication. Her room-mates varied from likeable to tolerable and she was bent upon liking them anyhow. What was not so easy, were the hours – and the regulations.

Day duty was from seven-thirty until eight p.m. with three hours off; night duty from eight to eight for two months at a time. The nurses were supposed to catch trams into the City, but at six in the morning these were so crammed with workers that Kate often had to walk, carrying a case with clean aprons and changes of shoes and stockings. The nurses' changing room was up four flights of stone stairs, the refectory for breakfast in the basement.

'Nurses,' Matron said to all the new recruits, 'must be scrupulously punctual on duty. Nurses must be unvaryingly clean, tidy, and cheerful. Sitting down in the wards is forbidden. There is a month's probation, after which the unsuitable cases will return to non-medical life.'

When day duty was done, Kate ate supper in the refectory. Just before nine each evening, she would emerge into Smithfield Square, find that most of the hostel-bound trams were crammed full once more and frequently be forced to walk the weary mile and a half back again. After a day of dealing with rubber sheets and sputum cups and bed pans, visions of Charlie's great scalding showerbath at Buscombe swam like a mirage before her eyes; the reality was thirty people scrambling to use one bathroom, a geyser which no-one but the housekeeper was permitted to use and which could never manage more than half a tub of warm water in any case, and a house rule that every last light must be extinguished by ten at the latest. If it had not been for Chesterfield Hill on those blessed half days, she doubted that she would have made the suitable grade after that gruelling first month.

Going to Chesterfield Hill always made her laugh. She would gather up such hostel friends as had coincidental half days and trail with them by tram across London to Mayfair. They would always look awful, there was no way to avoid red hands and chapped faces and lank hair. Lilian's parlourmaid would open the door, and then press herself back against the wall as if she feared contamination from this dishevelled crew, and they would troop upstairs to Lilian's drawing room and find sometimes her, sometimes Anna, frequently with friends, and a rosy atmosphere of warmth and lace and soft padded surfaces. The welcome was always very warm. Then they would be let loose into the house's two splendid bathrooms and they became like puppies on a beach, emerging in the highest spirits to be fed the kind of teatime food that tasted like manna after the great, grey, flavourless meals of St Bartholomew's Hospital.

Lilian was in her element. Anna, in soft dresses of cream and pink that showed her pretty ankles, was such an asset, so compliant and grateful, such a charming voice. Kate, stamping in with her friends, all appallingly dressed, all resiliently cheerful and as hungry and appreciative as small boys, was in a different way, equally rewarding. She wrote jubilantly to Wales and to Buscombe. When Charlie was in London he came to see her and so did this most remarkable little new wife of his, who seemed to be transforming Buscombe in every respect. Sometimes Lilian thought of Tom and wondered what he would have said to a Greek chatelaine in his beloved house, and sometimes, with a stab of conscience and pity that she did not care to heed too much in her present contentment, she thought of Rose.

Anna, too, thought of Rose and she also managed to exclude from her thinking any imaginative sympathy. In Anna's mind, Rose had nearly ruined Anna's life – it was Lilian who had made it secure again and thus it was to Lilian she gave her best affection. Lilian spoiled her, and encouraged her to spoil herself. Lilian took her shopping and gave tea parties for her, and luncheon parties and encouraged her to go to the theatre and to enjoy herself. When young men showed an interest in Anna, and they often did, Lilian behaved with a charming diplomacy that was the envy of all Anna's girlfriends with tiresome mothers. Anna wrote to Rose every two or three weeks and told her about Bond Street and the Ritz and the newest plays and hats and gossip. They were heartless letters.

In the spring of 1914, Lilian proposed to take Anna on a European tour, to include the great opera houses for Anna's further education. Charlie, perturbed by the warmongering growls issuing from Germany against the Balkan Allies, objected to the inclusion of Vienna, Munich and Berlin on the projected tour. Lilian almost lost her head, forgetting she had no rights over Anna, and defied Charlie. He came up to London and was most alarming. If the trip were not confined to Italy, Spain and Portugal, Anna must return to Buscombe and the good sense of her stepmother.

'All tears and pleadings,' he said in disgust to Eleni later, 'perfectly idiotic. I pointed out to them that Germany is raising a capital levy of a thousand million marks for military purposes, not to mention conscripting over sixty thousand more men, and they opened their eyes wide and said what had that to do with opera—'

'But you won?'

'Oh yes. I won. Italy, Spain and Portugal it is, and as many fat tenors as their hearts desire.'

They were to be away three months.

'But my baths!' Kate said in horror to Lilian.

'They will continue. Young Mrs Martineau is to use the house during the week while she and Victoria launch their new list of books for this year. I shall instruct her that you are allowed unlimited hot water and walnut cake.'

Kate looked down.

'I have never met her—'

'Then it is time that you did. She is your aunt's partner and the wife of the family lawyer, after all, quite apart from being exceptionally nice. There now – I shall give you this key to the house and the freedom of it. You have shown great grit this winter and the least you deserve is a half day of comfort each week.'

It was almost a month before Kate arrived at Chesterfield Hill at a time when Sarah Martineau was also there. She let herself in, and found a sturdy open-faced young woman in the drawing room, sitting in a sea of books and papers with her reddish brown hair in engaging disorder and metal rimmed spectacles on her nose. When she observed Kate, she took off her spectacles and jumped up, scattering the papers on her lap, and marched across the books on the floor with her hand out in welcome.

'I am so glad to see you. I had so hoped we should coincide one day. I have a thousand things to ask you but I must let you have a bath first. Frank sends his best love and so, of course, does Victoria. My dear, you look all in.'

'Oh –' Kate said vaguely, 'you know—'

'I shall get Morris to run your bath.'

'No – no, please – I always do it myself—'

'Not today. And I think you should have sandwiches afterwards, beef if you like them. What the authorities think they are doing, working you girls as they do, I cannot imagine. It is undoubtedly the greatest curse of bureaucracy that every man and every department supposes another man and another department to be dealing with every difficulty.' She rang a bell and then turned to Kate with a sudden and brilliant smile. 'I cannot tell you what a pleasure it is to me to have you here.'

Half an hour later, Kate returned to the drawing room to a plate of hearty sandwiches and a pot of tea of a most decided strength. Both items sat in the soft, sweet room like vegetable marrows in a rosebed. She was terribly hungry.

'Well, you admirable creature, are you a little restored?'

Kate blushed.

'Very much.'

Sarah stooped to pick up a sheaf of manuscript.

'Your coming is so opportune. I am producing a series

of pamphlets on the abuse of women as labour in various fields. Sweatshops, seamstresses, spring at once to mind – women are such *humble* employees, no wonder they are so exploited – but nurses are just as much at risk. Does it not seem to you extraordinary that so much should be demanded of you for twenty pounds a year?'

Kate finished an enormous bite of sandwich.

'It isn't so much the money. It is our inefficiency – because we are so tired and because keeping clean is so difficult. If we were better housed and worked shorter hours and had enough hot water, we shouldn't be prey to all these headaches and infections and chills. In the whole hostel, I am the only one to be certain of even a weekly bath.'

Sarah was scribbling furiously.

'Can you give me any instance of this compulsory incompetence?'

Kate held up a bandaged finger.

'I have a septic finger which refuses to heal. But my first duty every morning is to set out the dressing trays for all the industrial accident cases, awful wounds some of them. Think of the risk of sepsis to them—'

Sarah took off her spectacles and looked at Kate.

Kate said quickly, 'It's inhumanity.'

'*Inhumanity?*'

Kate leaned forward, gesturing with a half eaten sandwich.

'Looking at the sisters on my ward, so efficient, so calm, makes me feel that they have made themselves immune to pity. That to be highly skilled necessarily means stamping out your human response to pain and suffering. I never want to lose that. If I do, I shall have lost my personality.'

436

'Have you worked on the obstetric ward at all?'

'No,' Kate said.

'I only asked,' Sarah said, turning her head aside as if searching for some further papers, 'because I am going to have a child.'

'Why do you tell me?'

'I felt I had a responsibility to tell you. You are the first person I have told.'

'You have no thought for my pride,' Kate said angrily and burst into tears.

Sarah said calmly, 'On the contrary. It is consideration for your pride that prompts me to tell you this news in person, rather than wait for the family tom-toms to beat out the message.'

Kate blew her nose.

'I'm sorry.'

'So am I. But I am also realistic which is a quality I believe we share.' She paused. It occurred to her to confide to Kate that this news of a coming child did not seem to be deflecting Frank from a new and alarming resolve of his to join one of the Gloucestershire Regiment's new territorial battalions. Briefly Sarah considered, decided it would not be fair at this precise moment and so said instead, with great directness, 'We both love Frank, so surely it is best for us both to use what we have in common to found a friendship upon? You have stopped eating.'

'I can't eat and cry—'

'Then don't cry.'

Kate began to smile and said, 'Oh, oh – bother—'

'Now,' Sarah said, settling herself with pad and pencil, 'I shall ask you questions about the hospital and you will reply between mouthfuls, if you would—'

After that, they met most weeks. There was a practicality in Sarah as sturdy as her frame which Kate found immediately attractive.

'Of course we should have the vote,' Sarah would say, 'but it is not the vote that will make women a force to be reckoned with, though it will help. It is economic independence that really counts, economic self-sufficiency. Look at Victoria, look at you, look at me—'

And look at Anna, Kate thought, trapped by her own choice in a way of life more Victorian than seemed credible in 1914. Sarah was kind about Anna, but she spoke of her with the indulgence of tone used when referring to children or to the handicapped. Somebody as apparently useless as Anna was genuinely puzzling to Sarah, for whom there was no aspect of life that could not, in some manner or measure, be made use of. It was Sarah who said to Kate one April afternoon as they sat companionably together,

'Of course, you must go and see your mother.'

Kate stared.

'But—'

'You will only be the loser if you don't. Who are you to condemn? And surely you have seen enough of life at the hospital now to know that humans are often as much victims of themselves as of circumstance.' She smiled broadly at Kate. 'Frank said he was infatuated with her once, she seemed to him the absolute epitome of everything essentially, adorably feminine. Wouldn't you think that, now, isolated and separated from all her children, she is terribly unhappy? Don't you think, if you are just, that she has suffered enough?'

Kate had had no leave in almost seven months, by her own choice. Now, armed with the fact that she had twice refused a week's break, she applied to the Matron

438

for leave to go down to Wales. It was granted with little difficulty. The difficulty was writing to Rose to invite herself and she knew the letter she dispatched was stiff and unnatural. The reply came back at once.

'Oh yes,' Rose wrote, 'yes, yes. Stay as long as you can. I cannot wait—'

At the beginning of May 1914, wearing a new dress and jacket of fine lilac wool sashed in purple petersham in honour of Rose, Kate climbed aboard the Cardiff-bound train from Paddington, carrying her bag, the voluminous mackintosh in which she had trudged through the winter rains between the hostel and St Bartholomew's, and a copy of *The Speaker* which she had bought, upon impulse, from the station bookstall.

It was a journey which, like that first summer at Buscombe eleven years before, was to remain a land-mark in later recollections of her youth. At the time it was simply a happening, a passage of hours, but even only a few months later, she saw it as yet another veil of innocence torn down to let experience in. The essence of the change lay in what she read as the train thundered west along Brunel's magnificent line, through country now dearly familiar to her, passing even within twenty miles of Buscombe. It was balm to think of Buscombe now, in Eleni's hands, a harmonious family house for the first time in almost fifty years, and Charlie so extra-ordinarily happy – the two little boys in the nursery, another on the way, projects and schemes for improve-ment all around.

It was when Somerset's green hills had rolled past, that Kate turned to *The Speaker*. She would not, instinc-tively, have bought a political paper, not, that is, before her new friendship with Sarah Martineau. But Sarah had made her ashamed of her ignorance, and eager to rectify it and the purchase of this paper was a first naive step that she was glad to make with no-one to see. The central article was on Germany. Kate was not interested, much, in Germany. Germany had had no relevance to her life beyond lessons at Laurelbank, and conjured up few images beyond steamer trips down the Rhine portrayed on pastel-tinted postcards and dismal hours spent peering at the dense Gothic script of German text books. She would have turned the page, eager to find some more attractively social political article, had not the first line of the text caught her eye.

'Are we blind or mad?' Kate read. 'War is inevitable, European war. Can we not see it, or do we refuse to see it?'

War? Kate looked up. There was the flat country of the Severn estuary outside the train. There was the usual complement of ordinary travellers inside it – a tired looking woman with a sleeping boy beside her, a weedy young man, doubtless a clerk, in a grubby collar and a stout old one with a bowler hat scribbling in a note book. *War?* She read on.

'The insularity of British politicians quite literally takes our breath away. So obsessed are they with Ireland – obsessed enough, we note with horror, to suggest refusing to pass the Army Annual Act, thus depriving the government of any disciplined force at such a tinder box time – that they quite fail to notice what is happening in Germany.

'Germany is preparing for war. Germany has almost written the date for war to commence, in her engagement diary for 1914. We have it on excellent authority that in approximately six weeks from now – the month of June – Germany and Austria will be free from all other preoccupations (we refer to the little matter of Germany's campaign against France) and able to join together, with large forces, against Russia. Germany has recovered all debts due to her from abroad; the gold reserve in the Reichsbank is at an unparalleled height. Germany is braced for war, fuelled and burnished and eager for war. All she lacks is a casus belli. Mark our words: she will supply that lack ere long.'

Kate stopped reading. Snatches and eddies of conversations about the Balkan wars had blown like dead leaves about her for several years, so had talk about strengthening our naval bases – she could remember the name Scapa Flow because she had liked the sound of it but she had no idea where it was or what it represented. She read on.

'When war breaks out – we say not if – where will England stand? Our view as Liberals is that she should remain neutral, but our view as realists is that she will not. It is unthinkable to the Conservatives by whom we are overruled that England can remain a spectator to a wrangle which will change the balance among the Central Powers, a balance so dear and so necessary to this nation, whose trading and financing interest – the greatest in the world – depends upon peace. Thus neutrality is unthinkable. So whose part shall she take? – That of France and Russia, or that of Germany and Austria? Nobody knows; nobody will decide. The cabinet is paralysed by disagreement. The neutrality of Belgium is the stumbling block to all. But decide they must. We are the voice of the prophet crying in the wilderness and what we cry is this: it is too late to stop the war, but it is not too late to decide what England will do when the storm breaks.'

When Cardiff came, Kate folded up the paper to take

with her, and then, obeying a sudden impulse of fear and repugnance, put it down on the seat behind her. The weedy young man cleared his throat.

'Excuse me, miss, but 'ave you finished your paper?'

'Yes,' Kate said.

'May I take it, then?'

'You won't like it,' Kate said, 'it is very alarmist. It says we will be at war in a few months.'

The young man laughed. He had stained teeth and a weak chin.

'Nah,' he said, 'don't you believe it. We 'aven't 'ad a war to really trouble us in a 'undred years,' and he tucked the paper under his arm and touched his hat to Kate and went off down the platform whistling.

Oh my God, Harry thought, looking at Kate across the dinner table, she is Catherine again, young Catherine. The same austere look, the same vulnerability underneath, the same fervour. Remember Catherine's bedroom and all those exhortations to feminine endeavour . . .

'I cannot believe you are here,' Rose said. 'I cannot believe that you are actually a nurse. Oh my dear! I simply *cannot* believe that you are twenty!'

'All those things,' Kate said gravely.

Rose's face had changed. A kind of softening had blurred it and her mouth was pinched.

'So I must be forty-six!' she cried with false gaiety.

Harry said gallantly, 'You do not look it.'

Rose was at once petulant.

'Oh, how can you tell! You see no-one to compare me with!'

'I can remember,' Harry said patiently.

Rose made a *moue*.

'To have a child of twenty—'

442

Kate opened her mouth to point out that Anna was twenty-one and closed it again. Instead she said, looking at the neat pinkish cutlets on her plate,

'This is delicious. Usually I eat awful food. Lots of it, but awful.'

'But *why*?'

'It is what we are given in the hospital. Good solid fare, all the same colour—'

'It does not seem to be making *you* very solid,' Harry said, yearning with affection for her and all she reminded him of. She smiled at him. He looked terribly sad, she thought, beaten somehow.

'I work so hard I burn it all up.'

'Tell us,' Harry said, 'tell us about the hospital. Tell us what you do.'

'Perhaps—' Kate looked doubtfully at her mother. Rose was in pearly taffeta with a collar of pink beads fastened round her neck with a tulle bow. Kate had gone to her bedroom while Ellen helped her to dress and she still, to Kate's amazement, wore the pink satin hip and rib pads to accentuate a tiny waist that Kate remembered being so intrigued by as a child. And she still billowed her pale hair out, over further pads and she still – Kate watched her at dinner – put up anxious hands to make sure that the pads were not showing, little fluttering gestures, pat-pat, pat-pat.

'I'd love to tell you about the hospital,' Kate said, 'it's so interesting. I've learned so much. But later—'

'I had a postcard from Anna!' Rose said triumphantly. 'Imagine! From Milan. She says the Italian women have the most marvellous jewels you ever saw and the spring clothes are so lovely, low, low waists over draped skirts and mad hats. Oh – I do long—' She stopped and then she said, 'She has been constantly to

443

the opera. I don't suppose you have the energy to go.'

'Or the time—' Harry said gently.

'I have become,' Kate said hesitantly, going pink, 'rather interested in politics. I have made a friend of Frank Martineau's wife – you know, she is Victoria's partner.'

Rose put her chin up.

'Of course, I never hear from Victoria.'

Harry said to Kate, 'Politics? What kind of politics? Knowing Victoria, the Women's Movement I am sure—'

'I bought a paper for the train,' Kate said, '*The Speaker*. Sarah recommended it to me because she said it was liberal. The chief article said that Germany is bent upon going to war with Russia, and that we can neither stop it nor help joining in. Is – is that really going to happen?'

'I think it likely—' Harry began, but Rose said sharply, 'Nonsense. Politics. What good did they ever do anybody? Kate, I have ordered a Charlotte Russe. Do you remember how you loved it when you were little?'

In the drawing room after dinner, Kate told them about the hospital. She did not know if Rose, sitting by the fire and gazing absently at it, was really listening or not. Ellen was listening all right and so was Harry. Ellen had grown so much older and also had a defeated air. She sat and listened to Kate and was consumed at once with envy and with self-disgust. Oh dear, oh dear, she cried to herself while Kate talked, where oh where, Ellen Napier, did you just silently, unconsciously, give up?

As the evening wore on, the awkwardness managed to grow worse. Rose's first ecstasy at seeing Kate was gone, the neutral subjects were explored and found inadequate and in the air the name of Buscombe hung in silent letters of flame. Nobody could mention it; nobody could think, increasingly, of anything else. At ten, the servants came in for prayers, at ten-twenty Rose kissed Kate with a kind of angry incipient tearfulness and rustled upstairs with Ellen. It was clearly Harry's time to be alone.

'Good night,' Kate said politely.

He turned to her.

'Must you go? Of course, if you are tired, after travelling—'

'Not at all.'

'I don't want to be selfish.'

'I'm not tired,' Kate said, 'at least not that kind of tired. Strained, perhaps.'

'Oh my dear. I am so sorry—'

He put a hand up to his eyes. Kate said, her heart suddenly wrung, 'Oh I would *like* to talk, really I would. I just thought this might be your private time.'

He said simply, 'I am so glad,' and went away to fetch the port. He returned and held the decanter up to her. 'Do you like it?'

'Yes. Yes, I do. It isn't supposed to be a very feminine drink, is it—'

'Women *should* drink it. Very nourishing. Particularly working women.'

How attractive he is, Kate thought, the same kind of lean Taverner as Father is, as I am. Poor man . . .

'Poor man, you are thinking,' Harry said.

Kate spilled her port.

'How *could* you—'

'It was written all over your face. Here, have this to mop up with. Port stains like blood. Blue blood. I am not a poor man even if I am in some ways a disap-

445

pointed one. Tell me—' He stopped, said, 'Do you mind?' brandishing a cigar, and when she shook her head, lit it slowly and carefully. 'Tell me, am I still regarded as a villain?'

'You never were.'

'No?'

'As – as someone behaving in a mad way, but not a villain. Not you. The odd thing is—' She paused and then said, looking directly at him with Catherine's forthright blue gaze, 'The odd thing is that in some ways everything is better than it's ever been. I mean, Buscombe—'

'Come on,' Harry said, 'come on, come on, *tell* me.'

She spread her hands.

'It's wonderful. It's a real family. The whole house is full of life. I don't think Father even remembers his asthma any more. Eleni is extraordinary. Never out of temper, very tolerant yet decided, too.' She looked at Harry. 'Catherine went to Buscombe, you know. Last autumn before she went back to Arabia. She and Eleni took to each other at once.'

There was a silence and then Harry said, 'Poor little Rose.'

'Yes.'

'That is my disappointment. I cannot seem to make her happy. Next winter I think I should take her abroad and spoil her a bit. The winters here are so long.'

'What if there is a war?'

Harry shrugged.

'What of little Rob?'

'Adorable as ever. Much more outgoing but still a serious little boy – you remember, enormous bright eyes taking everything in. He has company now, too—'

'She ought to see him. It's all wrong.'

'Eleni agrees with you.'

'Really? *Eleni?*'

'Certainly.'

'Then why has it not happened? If Charlie objects, surely Eleni can persuade him to anything?'

Kate said truthfully, 'I agreed with Father. Up until now. I was so angry with Mother, you see.'

'And now?'

Kate stood up.

'I am still a bit cross, but for other reasons. When I look at you and at Ellen it makes me cross. But mostly I am just sorry for her, now.' She looked around the softly lit room, at the rugs and cushions and the heavy gleaming fall of the curtains and remembered with a sharp stab, the drawing room in Campden Hill, severe and fresh, its decided flavour stamped for ever on her childhood memory. Where had that eager, friendly, pliant Rose gone? Was she still there, under the taffeta pillows, or had she been smothered to death?

'How long can you stay?'

'I must go back on Thursday.'

'Only three nights!'

'Oh!' Kate cried, 'I am so sorry! But really – really, I must get back to London. Do – do you see?'

'Yes,' he said, smiling, 'I see. In your place, so should I wish to get back.'

He came across the room and kissed her lightly, enveloping her in a breath of Hungary water and cigar smoke.

'Good night, dear Kate,' he said.

CHAPTER TWENTY-THREE

1916

On 16 July, the 4th Battalion of the Gloucesters and the 7th Worcesters were ordered to attack the German positions in front of Ovillers, on the Somme. The attack began at four in the afternoon and fighting continued without a pause until lunch time the following day. Crouched against the wall of one of the enemy trenches they had so triumphantly taken, Frank Martineau scribbled a pencilled note to his wife:

Dearest Sarah – Not a scratch! More to come I think, but don't worry – the 6th Battalion is on its way to relieve us. My love to you and a kiss to little Bay.
                                        Frank

There was no time to write more. The Germans were counter-attacking furiously but were steadily driven off. In the late afternoon of 18 July, the 4th Battalion was again ordered over the top to take the northern part of the village of Ovillers. It took them three hours, Frank led two charges with conspicuous gallantry, was shot through the hand in the course of the second and continued to stand upright after the wound, covering his men's advance by tearing the safety pins out of bombs with his teeth and hurling them into the enemy. When a second German shot passed harmlessly through the shoulder of his jacket, it threw him off balance, and he jerked helplessly forward, blowing himself up with the bomb he held, at that moment, only inches from his face.

For Kate, the Battle of the Somme had made its awful presence felt long before the news of Frank's death. The terrible and enormous convoys of stretchers bearing humped brown blankets had begun in the first week of July, a month she would always remember for the heat and the stink of damaged flesh. Hundreds of men, or bits of men, were borne in every day, their hideous gashes reeking and brilliant with gangrene – sometimes the wards, in their helpless confusion of cries and clattering, seemed a sort of hell, a place where humanity was to be punished for its sins by being left, quite literally, to rot.

Kate and her fellow nurses were moved into a hostel nearer the hospital which had been, in peacetime, used for medical students. It was a gaunt barrack of a place, but there was a bathroom on every floor supplied by a thundering gas boiler in the basement. Kate shared a tiny room with a fellow nurse called Sylvia Wallace, a girl who had intended to teach the piano until her fiancé had been killed in the Dardenelles. She was tall and gentle in appearance and manner, and quite relentless on duty.

'You see,' she said to Kate, 'one has to work off one's fierceness *somehow*.'

She came from the North, and sometimes at night, when for all their desperate fatigue they could not sleep for feeling, or imagining they felt, the vibrations from

449

the bombardment on the Western Front, she would tell Kate about the high and empty countryside of her home, where the grey walls ran snaking over the hills and the long winters had bred a granite strength into the people. Her fiancé had been her companion since childhood, her brother's greatest friend and she explained to Kate, in her soft and reasonable voice, that until the rage and despair in her was burnt out, she could not think what use she was to make of the great pointless lump of life left to her.

'Each man I nurse is him, you see. I hate the war, I hate the senseless waste and cruelty of it, yet I dread the war being over because then I will have to decide again, my mission will be over. What is more, is that I feel I will lose contact with him when I am not nursing the wounded any longer, I feel I will be breaking faith. And yet I can't bear the war to go on one more day.'

Kate had nothing to say to her except words of the most complete sympathy. Sylvia's attitude to her dead fiancé seemed not only understandable, but morally right, noble even. She felt that if Frank were killed she would have, in a way, some of the same sense of mission and the same fierce fuel would propel her tirelessly, like Sylvia, up and down the wards. So when Sarah Martineau toiled all across London on a baking afternoon and obtained permission from the Matron to tell Kate in person that Frank had been blown up and was to be awarded a posthumous Military Cross, Kate met the news with a kind of frenzied acceptance that Sarah first took to be the unbalanced result of extreme fatigue.

They sat in Kate's hostel room while the hot red afternoon burned on, and talked and cried together, and

Kate could hear herself making the kind of high-minded speeches that were not characteristic of herself at all, yet she could not stop. She told Sarah about Sylvia, and Sylvia's fiancé and her subsequent attitude to her work and to the war, and Sarah, suddenly understanding, said gently, 'But, my dear Kate, we must in a sense break faith with the dead if we are to be the slightest use to the living.'

Kate flung back her head. Her face was tear-stained.

'But what of the dead, and what they meant to us and what they died for?'

'None of that will suffer,' Sarah said more steadily than she felt inclined. 'Our love and our regret are inviolable. But if we feed the anger and the regret, we have no emotion left to give to the living. We penalize the living, if you like, by the energy of our homage to the dead. What kind of mother would I be to Bay, for example, if I gave her nothing to look forward to because I was so absorbed in the past and the futility of longing for what I could not have again?'

Kate drooped.

'You are so sensible—'

'It is my curse,' Sarah said. 'If it comforts you at all, I never loved Frank as he loved me, not with the same force. I am not even sure I have it in me to love with passion – except my child. That is really why I married Frank – to have children. I wanted a good, kind, stable man to be the father of my children.' She looked at Kate. 'Am I appalling you?'

'Yes,' Kate said.

'That I could marry for fondness and liking and no more?'

'Yes.'

451

'I am thirty, you know—'

'What difference does that make?'

'A difference of reflectiveness, I suppose, of self-knowledge perhaps. I don't want to patronize—'

'I don't want to be reflective about love,' Kate said fiercely, 'or about grief. Or the war, or nursing, or anything. Just now I want to exhaust myself, wear myself out—' She looked at Sarah. 'Sylvia thinks they will be sending us to France soon. I hope they do.'

Sarah stood up.

'Well – if they do, remember to nurse each man for his own sake, not for the sake of Frank. How would you like to be nursed by a girl who was pretending you were somebody else? By the way, Bay and I are going to move into the top floor of Swan Walk for a while. You see, Combe Place becomes mine but I can't disturb old Mrs Martineau there, and anyway, I cannot think what to do with it just yet. So if you want me, Swan Walk is where I will be.'

When she had gone, Kate lay dry eyed on her bed and was, for a while, very angry indeed. It should have been a sweet triumph, she realized, after Sarah's revelation, to know that she now had Frank's particular memory entirely to herself, but it was, unsatisfactorily, not so, somehow . . . In her mind she called Sarah disloyal, heartless, even scheming, but when the first fury had burned itself out and the vast dreary waste of reality crawled in to take its place, she found she could not sustain her condemnation. Sarah was an honest woman; she would have been honest with Frank and he, with his gentle level cast of character, would have accommodated himself very well to her candour. Perhaps he even quite liked it – after all, he had been rather given to worshipping, look at him with Rose. And of course

Sarah was right about her duty to Bay, that merry little bright eyed child whose given name of Barbara – after Miss Bodichon, a heroine of Sarah's – nobody ever used. What use to a child was a mother quite taken up with luxurious grief?

When Sylvia came in off duty, at once fagged and elated as she usually was, Kate tried to explain to her, sombrely, about, as Sarah had put it, the need to break faith with the dead. But Sylvia could not listen. There were two drafts of nurses being sent to France, and both she and Kate had applied to be included. That afternoon, Matron had sent for her, and told her that in ten days' time she and Nurse Taverner were to leave England for the 20th General Hospital at Etaples. In the interim, they were both given a week's leave.

Kate went at once to Buscombe. War or no war, it was the happiest week she had known for ages, a hot August idyll spent largely in the garden which Eleni was transforming bit by bit. She had become an admirer of Gertrude Jekyll – a natural admiration for someone brought up on an island where the spring flowers are so miraculous – and the enthusiasm for formal bedding out with which both Rosamund and Rose had disciplined the garden at Buscombe, was relaxing into the bold and natural groupings of colours and shapes that Miss Jekyll propounded and Charlotte would have considered cottagey. The long formal beds either side of the drive, parallel with the lily pond, in which regiments of salvias and begonias had so relentlessly marched all Kate's childhood, were dissolving into curving groups of flowering shrubs, red-leaved, grey-leaved, green-leaved, and there was a climbing rose showering petals out of the astonished tulip tree, and the great dark masses of the rhododendrons between the house and the lake were giving way in places before silvery waves of bamboo and birch.

The house too had relaxed, and gave the impression that after years of having its eyes shut, it had opened them wide to the sun. The less oppressive of the Greek and Minoan remains had been trundled into the library, the remainder to the stables, and the hall was painted yellow, with newly whitened pillars, at whose feet sat massive blue and white Chinese jardinières spilling ferns and speckled ivies. By the garden door there was a low sofa and chairs, and a table with magazines, and all that week the door stood open, and the boys ran in and out and Eleni left her garden boots on the step when she came hurrying inside. The morning room had been new washed its same familiar dim blue and the birdcage was back in the window with a conversational mynah bird inside and there were curtains of cream linen tied back with huge soft cords. The drawing room was unchanged except that all the furniture had been moved about to more encouraging positions, the library was deep green with velvet curtains crumpling onto the floor, and Eleni had refused to let Charlie pull down the tower.

'I like it.'

'It is a monstrosity. The Victorians had no tact about old houses. It is an insult to the house.'

'It is part of the family. It is a joke, if you like.'

'An extremely poor one.'

'Perhaps. But a traditional one. We will talk about it in one year?'

Eleni was pregnant. She took no notice whatsoever of being pregnant. She was up first and to bed last, and her fresh, strong personality blew through the house like a sea wind. She treated Rob and Carlo, as far as Kate could see, with absolutely the same measure of affection, discipline and humour. Ellen had come in July to fetch Rob to see his mother for a week, and he had disgraced himself and wept and clung to Eleni and then run away and tried to hide so successfully as not to be found. Carlo found him.

'You must go,' Carlo said, 'you are *seven*.'

He went, white and silent. He came back full of Harry. He hardly seemed to have noticed his mother and could only remember riding with Harry, playing cricket with Harry, going to the sea and rock climbing with Harry, having the top off Harry's egg every morning as well as his own whole egg, and going to Harry's room in the dawn to hear about India and the mongoose Harry had kept to kill the snakes in his bathroom. He jostled Carlo to be close to Eleni when he got back and he wanted his night light again, having given it up on his last birthday.

'It was right that he went,' Eleni said, 'and it will be right that he should go again. You cannot keep up barriers in natural relationships.'

Elizabeth, baulked of returning to Buscombe, had tried to put up just such a barrier. She wrote to Charlie expressing outrage at his treatment of herself and Catherine and a great many imperious opinions about the upbringing of Rob and the management of the estate. Charlie had flown into a fury, so Eleni took the letter and wrote a short reply, thanking Elizabeth for all her help and asking her to visit them. Winded, Elizabeth had floundered. She was angry with Charlie because he had, after her boasting, caused her to lose face in Cheltenham, and to admit she could not even go to Buscombe any more would mean further loss. So she compromised. She left the invitation lying about for friends to see the warmth of her welcome and the respect paid to her advice, and wrote a gracious refusal to Eleni. Next year, perhaps, when Catherine was returned and might accompany her. Catherine's expedition into Arabia had not been a success, and so, disheartened by that and reluctant to return to a war-torn Europe, she was immersing herself in Muslim women and planning a journey through southern Persia, from the blue domes of Isfahan, she wrote, to the rose gardens of Shiraz.

'She must please herself,' said Eleni of Elizabeth, and put the letter in a drawer. 'And so must you,' she said to Kate. 'Sleep when you want, do what you want, rest all you can.'

Despite the war, Charlie had a new commission, his first for twelve years. A Bristol businessman who had bought and renovated a fifteenth-century castle some twenty miles north of the city, and was impressed by Charlie's modernization of Buscombe, asked him to build a guest wing in sympathy with the house. Charlie dug Sir Thomas Taverner's Pugins out of the library and went joyfully to work on the sloping desks he had set up in the tower room a decade before. He was pleased to see Kate, proud of her, interested in her, but the central hall of his mind was occupied. The new commission made him love everyone and everything.

'To think,' he said to Kate, slapping down his hand upon the sketches of half-timbering he was playing with, 'to think I have even come to love this house. And do you know what? Eleni says she is going to turn it into a convalescent home for men wounded on the Somme. A convalescent home, I ask you! Still – we must do our bit—'

Two days before she was due to sail for France, Kate

456

returned to London and dined at Chesterfield Hill. After the almost salty strength of life at Buscombe, Chesterfield Hill was like stepping into a box padded in satin, and closing the lid. Lilian was doing a little elegant war work, and rolling bandages weekly in a friend's drawing room, and Anna was in love. Lilian said he was extremely suitable.

'His father is of very old family, and his mother comes from Scottish shipbuilding, so you see, there is plenty of money. He was wounded at Hedauville last year, lost a leg, poor boy, and has been learning to walk again with such gallantry. Anna met him at a little concert she and some friends gave for wounded officers. She is enchanting with him, such a grave little nurse—'

He was called Edward Harcourt, Anna said. She was very pleased with herself, and sorry for Kate without really taking in what Kate was going to do. She wore, Kate noticed, with irritation, a ring on a narrow blue satin ribbon round her neck and she twisted herself now and then to make sure Kate could see.

'You must meet him,' Anna said. 'I often talk about you to him, you know.'

She took Kate to a tea party at the house of a friend called Nell Fanshawe. There were about a dozen young women in soft afternoon dresses the colours of sweet peas, and seven young men in uniform, four visibly wounded. Nobody took any notice of Kate at all which was at once a relief and a humiliation. There was an extravagant tea and glasses of champagne and a phonograph to dance to. Three of the young officers physically could not dance, and one of them was Edward Harcourt. He was fair and good looking in an unremarkable way, and he gazed at Anna fixedly, grinning from his chair.

'I'm sorry about your leg,' Kate said awkwardly.

'A whizz bang,' he said, looking at Anna.

'We are so pleased about you and Anna—'

Anna was dancing with another girl and they were holding glasses of champagne and giggling and giving little shrieks.

'Topping. She's simply topping,' said Edward Harcourt. He called, 'Over here, over here!' and she came dancing over to him and gave him champagne from her glass and kissed him and went skipping off again. 'She's such ripping fun,' Edward Harcourt said, 'sings like an absolute angel.'

On the way home, in Lilian's new motor, Anna said triumphantly to Kate, 'There you are! Isn't he adorable and didn't it do you good to see some fun?'

The following day, Kate went to Swan Walk. The presses were clattering, the sales of *The Alternative Grisette* had doubled since the war began, and Victoria had started a cheerful weekly gazette to be circulated among the wounded in London's hospitals.

'It's jolly, schoolboyish sort of stuff really,' she told Kate. 'You know, jokes and anecdotes the men tell my journalists on their hospital rounds, such news of comrades as I can get hold of but, quite honestly, this summer it's been impossible, such thousands and thousands—'

It was called *The Lucifer*. On the top floor in her comfortable cluttered room, Sarah edited it, in between looking after Bay – 'Always so inky! Resembles a little dalmatian' – editing and proof-reading books, and going down to Somerset to see her old mother in Bath, and her mother-in-law, querulous and despondent, at Combe Place. The production of children for Edward had been the one aim of Alicia Martineau's life, and now that the sole achievement of that aim was dead, she was quite rudderless. Sarah looked exhausted.

'I am, of course. But then so is Victoria, and so are you when you have not rested at Buscombe. We all are. It is better that way, better to be too tired to think—'

Kate picked up Bay and sat her on her knee. Bay continued to post a penholder in and out of the central hole of a cotton reel, and looking over her russety curly head, Kate said,

'Do you know, Frank once said that something like this would happen. He didn't say a war, but he said he thought a great change was coming, and that our children would not know the world we knew. And of course they won't. They don't now. You would never have been able to bring Bay up like this, on your own, even when I was little—'

'Stuck—' Bay said, holding out the cotton reel.

'And yet,' Kate went on, pulling out the penholder and handing it and the cotton reel back to the child, 'and yet, the old order does go on still, somehow. Look at Buscombe. Blooming, flourishing, alive, with the Somme dragging on across the channel and convoy after convoy coming in every day. Eleni wants to take in convalescents.'

Sarah looked up.

'That will change it. I don't believe, when this war is over, that anybody or any aspect of life will be untouched. We'll never be so certain again, so secure. Take care of yourself, Kate. I mean that.'

Kate sat Bay on the floor, and stood up. She smiled down at her.

'You too,' she said to them both.

*　　*　　*

Between Etaples itself – scruffy and begrimed by army occupation – and the sea lay the hump-backed sand-hills, tufted with sharp grass like porcupines. Those sandhills were to become emblematic to Kate of her extraordinary twelve months in France, seeming both to be a literal physical barrier beyond which there was no longer any other world, and a symbol of the strange unreality of life, however exhausting, among those endless long wooden huts of the British camp. When-ever she closed her eyes in later years and saw the sandhills, domed and dun, against her lids, she could taste and see and hear her life in France again with a vividness that was almost painful. Above all she could remember, sharply, the intense longing and love for life that fired everyone there, soldier and civilian alike in a country where death's greed had apparently no limits.

The hut she shared with Sylvia was a small frail affair made of canvas and wood and known as an Alwyn hut. It contained two camp beds, a wooden chair and a couple of dozen nails hammered into a cross beam for hanging clothes. Its only advantage was that it opened directly onto a square of weary grass known as the Sisters' compound, and someone had planted nastur-tiums up all the surrounding hut walls, a riot of orange and yellow, which gave off their queer mustardy smell in the evening. There was also a clump of jolly dahlias and a tall butterfly speckled stand of double michaelmas daisies that made everyone poignantly homesick. The first night, among defiant jam jars of bright flowers and curtains and cushions of terrible cretonne patterned in emerald and scarlet, was fiercely lively.

'It's the German ward for you, Nurse,' Kate was told. 'You can call them what you like! They can't under-stand a word.'

The Germans lay in a great, damp marquee in a thick and stinking atmosphere while the temperature outside climbed into the nineties. Kate had never seen such wounds, or such desire for life, or felt, after the first shock of finding herself required to touch *German* flesh, such a common humanity. Often alone with two German orderlies only, she would toil for eight or nine hours at a time in the stench and heat, changing the great wads of stained gauze with which the wounds were packed, draining the rubber tubes that plunged so deeply into so many, desperately attempting to stop haemorrhages. Almost half the men were dying, which she knew as well as they did themselves. In a curtained alcove at one side, two officers lay apart, one delirious and muttering, the other appallingly wounded in the stomach and unbearably stoical. On Kate's third day, the delirious officer was given an injection which inadvertently threw him into convulsions of a violence Kate had never imagined possible. He was dead within two hours. She turned to the medical officer attached to the ward with a question all formed in her mouth but before she could utter it, he said brusquely, 'Syphilis. Not the last case you will see, by a long chalk.'

Between these long days in the crowded tent, where the new arrivals lay dumped on the floor in disgusting blankets and yelled for attention, and the old patients, not to be outdone, shouted above the racket, were periods off-duty of astonishing calm. With Sylvia, Kate would wander in the golden autumn light among the sandhills, picking up shells, talking idly, lying in the warm and yielding sand, and feeling, every so often, the vibration of distant gunfire under their tired shoulder blades. Once, in the cool dusk, they came upon a couple making love among the dunes, a medical officer and a small shy VAD who had seemed, since her arrival, too alarmed to speak to anybody. They were too absorbed to notice, and Kate and Sylvia slithered away in the silent sand.

'Perhaps,' Kate said, disturbed despite her daily intimacy with every other human function but sex, 'that is the only way she *can* communicate.'

'Or she is lonely—'

'Or she was simply *asked*—'

'What would you do,' Sylvia said, pausing and staring at Kate, 'if *you* were asked?'

'I should say no.'

'Would you?'

'If you are caught, you are dismissed, as a woman. Segregation may be silly and create tension but it's a rule.'

'Yes, Nurse.'

'*Sylvia*—'

'Do you think being made love to is any good at all if you are not *in* love?'

Kate gave her a push.

'How should I know?'

'I don't think,' Sylvia said, suddenly sober, 'that by temperament either of us is in a hurry to find out.'

With the winter, the nasturtiums collapsed into black strands, and a sharp wet wind blew in from the sea. A chill miasma rose in the German ward, and letters from England, which Kate read in snatched moments, described how grim and depressing everything was, food less plentiful, servants difficult to find or keep, men dispatched still, in relentless thousands, to feed the terrible trenches of the stalemate of the winter of 1916. Lilian and Anna, who was engaged to be married now,

tried moving into an hotel to avoid the servant difficulties at Chesterfield Hill, but disliked it, and moved
back, complaining faintly. Kate read their letters in her
rocking hut while the wind and rain turned the camp
into a swaying flapping old vessel floundering in a sea
of thin and pervasive mud, and felt impatience rise hotly
in her bosom. At least at Buscombe they were *trying* to
do something – Eleni reported that she had twenty men
now and she was afraid it was making the boys terribly
militaristic.

'Little Thomas is a good baby, fortunately, and
understood early the difference between day and night.
So necessary, for there is not a minute to spare. I have
two nurses living in, but otherwise only old Palmer is
actually resident in the house and I am relying on girls
from the village, and Fred's half-wit daughter. We think
of you so much—'

Christmas was chiefly remarkable for a sudden rush
of breathless blinded victims of mustard gas, their
bodies a burned mass of huge, weeping, sticky yellow
blisters. Kate was moved from the German ward to help
nurse them, and began a month of days which started
at 3.30 in the black raw dawns. Christmas Day was only
different from any other because she had a parcel from
Buscombe – books from Charlie, sheepskin slippers
from Eleni, and a cake of unbelievable rose geranium
scented soap – and because a young officer from the
next ward, who had been wounded in his left shoulder,
appeared holding an egg cup of cherry brandy for her.
He was called, he told her, Digby Payne, and his uncle
was running Taverner Warehouses, which was why,
having heard her name, he sought Kate out.

'Here's to 1917,' he said, raising his own egg cup,

463

'though I don't hold out much hope for it. I'm off on leave tomorrow, then I suppose back to the Front. Happy days!'

He drained his brandy, grinned at Kate, and was gone. She went back to the ward and found two convalescents among the mustard gas victims, dressed in jackboots and nurses' uniforms, giving an impromptu cabaret. She sat down by a patient and watched for a little and then, soothed by the cherry brandy and the warmth, and the tiny, impersonal contact with home, went soundly to sleep on an upright chair, her chin on her chest and her arms folded round her body as if to keep herself safe.

'The Czar of Russia has abdicated,' Charlie wrote to his daughter in March of 1917, 'and the revolution we have all been wondering about has happened. Extraordinary, if you think about it, in the midst of a world war. Or perhaps that is the ideal moment. What a winter – thirty degrees of frost last night, and coal at forty shillings a ton, if you can get it. We are worried that you are worn out – nine months is too long without leave. But the Americans are joining in, they say, so perhaps their new blood will break the deadlock that has bedevilled us so. We are all well and busy – the war doesn't seem to stop people building new houses any more than it deters Bolsheviks from having revolutions, and I have a queue, albeit a short one, of clients. Eleni is now running a full-scale hospital as far as I can tell – it is only a matter of days until my dressing room is commandeered for an operating theatre. Your sister is to be married in June – I hesitate to ask you to apply for leave for the wedding since I share your priorities, but think about it. Between you and me, I am getting more and more ashamed of my civilian togs, and cannot think how to behave in a future where I shall have to confess that I did not fight. I really can hardly face all Eleni's brave chaps as it is. You and what you are doing is my one solace. God bless.'

The long wet cold winter was dragging itself into a raw spring. On days off, Kate and Sylvia walked through the pine woods above Etaples and ate omelettes in cottage kitchens and worried that they were nursing less effectively than they had done the previous September.

'Well,' Sylvia said again and again, 'I *wanted* to burn the fierceness out, and I have. I feel old and sad and empty.'

'Me too.'

'We should apply for leave—'

'I'm afraid of stopping,' Kate said tiredly. 'I really don't want to go back to England just now – all the food shortages and servant difficulties make it sound much worse than this. They have even rationed bread now. Perhaps—' She glanced across at Sylvia. 'Perhaps we should apply to be posted somewhere else, or is that running away?'

'I don't know, I don't know—'

'That's the worst of war – weariness,' Kate said. 'In the end you can't make moral decisions any more.'

They applied, in a fit of boldness, for a transfer, two days before the Battle of Arras. The almost immediate deluge of convoys drove all other preoccupations out of their heads, and Kate was assigned to one of the acute surgical wards and a timetable that allowed her only six hours a night to stumble to her bed. She was assistant to the operating medical officer in his gruesome little canvas cubicle, assistant in every respect from lighting and cleaning of the oil lamps by which he worked to the fielding of grisly human bits and pieces, a job which left her, at the end of every spell of duty, indescribably filthy. Her first half day she spent entirely in a bath, and returned to the ward next morning to find it choked with new arrivals, awaiting their turn on the operating table with a mixture of resignation and rage. Moving among the filthy brown bundles on the ground, she heard a light and cultivated voice call out,

'Nurse! Nurse Taverner!'

She turned. A narrow faced, brown haired man was gesturing at her from a chair against the wall.

'Remember me? Digby Payne. Would you believe it, but Jerry got me again, six inches lower than last time—'

He looked quickly at the men either side of him and indicated his white swathed shoulder. Kate threaded her way towards him. Digby Payne watched her progress smiling, and remarked loudly that it was a good thing he was not left handed.

'Bit of luck, you still being here,' he said to Kate when she reached him.

'I ought to be on leave—'

'But this spot of bother at Arras got in your way? Rotten luck.'

He had a wide, boyish, friendly smile and his ears stuck out like pointed wings. She did not quite like either his face or his manner, but could think of no good reason for the dislike so said instead that she must go.

'So soon? See me again, though, won't you? I'm to go over to the officers' ward later but your chap here took the bullet out of me last night. Want to see it?'

'I've seen plenty, thank you,' Kate said and turned to step carefully back onto the narrow path left down the centre of the ward.

'If you can find the egg cups,' Digby Payne called after her, 'I'll find the cherry brandy.'

Scarlet among the sniggers, Kate hurried towards the operating room. At least, she thought crossly, she had had no contact with officers since she arrived in Etaples, and she did not, she told herself, mean to start now.

But Digby Payne would not leave her alone. Unharmed apart from the wound in his upper arm – miraculously two inches above the elbow – he was maddeningly able-bodied. On account of this, Kate prayed that he would, as was usual, be sent back to England to convalesce, but he puzzlingly stayed and stayed, appearing constantly in the ward on the pretext that seven men of his own company lay wounded there. Nobody but Kate seemed to object to him – indeed he was rather remarked upon for his solicitousness towards his men – but then nobody but Kate appeared to see insolence in his light eyes or a dangerous unreliability in his talk. She told herself she was tired and cross, and unreasonable as a result. Her manner to him varied from firm, but courteous, to extremely rude, and back he came for more of anything, sliding his eyes towards her with one of his frank young smiles and saying,

'How is the brightest star in the War Effort feeling today, then?'

One night he caught her almost alone on duty, dozing over a half written letter home among the muttered groans and cries of the darkened ward.

'May I speak to you?'

'On what subject?' Kate said without interest.

'I want to tell you about a dream I've got.'

She looked up. His voice was quite different, deeper, more serious. In the dull ochre light of her lamp, his eyes seemed to flicker less, to be steadier.

467

'You should not be here, Captain Payne.'

'Tosh. I've said good evening to your orderlies and told the MO that I'll be ten minutes checking the chaps. I'll check them with you. I say – do listen to me a minute. It's important.'

'Now?'

'Now might be the only chance I have.'

He squatted on a camp stool beside her.

'Look. I've wanted to tell you about this ever since I saw you again. You look so tired – you *are* so tired. I never saw anybody work as hard as you girls do. But look. This rotten war won't go on for ever, it can't. The Americans will finish it for us. Then what? Back to Blighty and post-war gloom and an office job? Can you imagine it? One would be better dead. But I've got the answer, I've got an alternative. The moment they blow the whistle on this show, I know what I am going to do and where I am going to do it.'

'Oh?' Kate said. 'Where?'

'Guess.'

She shook her head.

'Can't.'

He took a half breath and said, 'British East Africa. BEA.'

She sat up.

'Africa?'

'Listen,' he said, leaning forward, dropping his voice even lower, 'listen and I'll tell you about it. I've got an uncle farming coffee about ten miles from Nairobi, wonderful hill country, on the edge of a native reserve. The game is out of this world. You'd make a wonderful shot, you know. It's an absolutely outdoor life as well as being a chance to make a fortune. My uncle wants to sell up and move across into Uganda where they are very short of dairy farmers, so his place is going cheap. I'm going to try and scrape enough together to buy his farm. I'm going to live up there in those hills and ride and hunt and live like a king.' He looked at Kate and then he added, 'Have you any money?'

His insolence was so calmly expressed that it was quite easy to reply without heat,

'That is none of your business.'

'Ah,' he said, pleased, as if he had received precisely the answer he wanted, 'I thought you must have. Old du Cros was your grandfather after all, and my uncle said he made money out of anything he touched.'

'Oh,' Kate said, suddenly enraged, 'oh, do go *away*!'

Digby Payne stood up.

'You ought to know,' Kate said simultaneously conscious that she was being indiscreet and undignified, and that she was too furious to care, 'that my grandfather left almost all his fortune to prevent the art treasures of England being sold abroad. *That* is where the money went—'

'Oh I know,' Digby said maddeningly, 'but there was an awful lot of it – the money, I mean. I say, I ought to leave you to your ministrations—'

'Yes.'

'Look, I'll see you back in England. I'm going home to convalesce in three days. I'll look you up.'

'Don't bother—'

'It isn't,' Digby Payne said, 'any *bother* at all.'

The following week, Sylvia received news of a transfer to Malta. At the same time, Kate was given home leave, and was then to be recalled to Etaples. The distinction made between them was not to be explained, it seemed, and so although Sylvia was pleased at the prospect of sunshine, her pleasure was quite overshadowed by the inferred slight upon her war work; Kate, it appeared, was considered indispensable at the heart of things. It made for a coolness between them, and then a quarrel and then a disagreeable silence that neither of them seemed able to break and which continued, futile and painful, until Kate returned one day to their hut, and found Sylvia's half tidy and empty, both Sylvia and her possessions having set off for Malta. It was for Kate a moment of despair, a peak of miserable fury against a war which eventually destroyed everything, even a friendship which had been the one sustaining element in a breaking world. Discouraged to her depths, Kate packed her bags wearily for leave, and climbed aboard the train for Boulogne. The crossing was terrible, her arrival in England dejected and without spirit, and the newsboys hawking papers along the platform at Victoria were shouting hoarsely that the Battle of Passchendaele had begun.

CHAPTER TWENTY-FOUR

1919

Charlotte's old bedroom at Buscombe held six iron bedsteads, arranged in a double row. The pink and green curtains which had been drawn nightly by Brixton for over forty years had been bundled up and stowed away in the attics, and the windows were now shaded with white blinds and severely practical curtains of deep green linen union. The walls were painted cream, the floor covered in washable rubber. However, as the six officers who occupied it were aware, no hygienic measures could detract from the lovely cornice plasterwork nor the ceiling rose from which a single bright bulb hung, nor from the views to the lake to the south and across the croquet lawn to the Long Coppice to the west.

The same decorative treatment had been meted out to Catherine's room, Elizabeth's room and the dining room. The drawing room had become a mess for the officers, the library an administrative centre for the house, with the tower room, emptied of its Gothic furniture and incongruously filled with armchairs, a sitting room for the nursing staff. They slept, the five nurses, in the children's bedrooms on the top floor, except for Rob's old nursery which he now shared with Carlo. Charlie had put a north window into the old apple store at the end of the granary, and turned the whole building into a studio. He and Eleni and little Thomas occupied the lesser bedrooms looking east over the stable yard, and used the morning room as the one inviolable family room in the house. Buscombe smelled of linoleum and disinfectant and tobacco, and the hall was crisscrossed all day by the quick steps of the staff and the slow ones of men learning, with infinite trouble, how to walk again.

In Charlie's dressing room, a crib stood, containing Melina, born on Armistice Day. Melina had taken no notice of either of her parents and was born as corn blonde as her old cousin Elizabeth had once been – she was now dropsically stout and being pushed around Cheltenham in a bath chair by Miss Gaze. Melina was a determined baby, adored by her half-brother Rob, and a person to be reckoned with even at six months.

'She is all you,' Charlie said to Eleni.

'On the contrary,' Eleni replied, 'I never saw a child so like its father in temperament.'

Charlie had started a model farm; his aim was to make Buscombe as self-sufficient as possible. The old yard where his cousin had dreamed such dreams of agricultural progressiveness was being reorganized, the battered old barn corners where generations of hay-wains had turned too sharply, refaced with new quoins, an electrically driven grain drier installed and a new milking parlour. Half the week, Charlie stood at his drawing board, or paced West Country hillsides with prosperous clients from the business district of Bristol; the other half he considered disease-free strains of wheat and milk yields.

'This does not seem,' Kate said looking round at the charts and lists, 'to be very in character.'

She felt scratchy and out of place. It was her first visit home since the end of the war, and she had been put to sleep in a box room hastily made into a bedroom, a box room she remembered for wet afternoons with Anna, tunnelling among the old rugs and curtains cast aside by Rosamund.

'In character?'

'Yes,' Kate said. 'It is all so *practical*!' she said crossly. 'Where has all the vision gone, your vision? What are you doing weighing up the relative merits of a herd of cows and a herd of goats?'

'I am,' Charlie said carefully, 'trying to do my bit now we have peacetime to do it in.'

He was entirely grey now, but his thin face had colour.

'It depresses me,' Kate said. 'It's so sad to see you so – so *humdrum*. It's as if the fire had gone out of your belly.'

'Perhaps it has. I am fifty-four and a world war in which I was unfit to participate ended six months ago. Those of us who remember the atmosphere before the war very clearly – as you ought to do – are dismayed to find it cannot be recaptured. You can never turn the clock back. You cannot recapture artificially, deliberately, the creative passion of your youth, you know. You must allow for change.'

'It is as if,' Kate said unkindly, 'now you are personally happy, you are professionally empty. You did your best work when you were married to Mother and coping with the difficulties of that. Oh my God, what a depressing conclusion—'

*   *   *

'I wish you would talk to her,' Charlie said to Eleni, during the sacred half hour together in the morning room before they went to bed. 'She isn't like herself at all. She is unhappy and angry, and so she lashed out at me this afternoon for having become a pedestrian old bore. I am sure she needs some help, but I cannot think what except work, and she works far too hard as it is.'

'I will try,' Eleni said, but she said it doubtfully. 'She is angry with me, too, because I have made her home into a hospital, even though she would be the first to agree it was a good idea.' She sighed. 'But all the same, I will try. Poor girl. There must be millions like her, all the young—'

'No!' Kate almost shouted, two days later in the conservatory. 'No, there are almost none like me! Do you want to know what the people my age in London are doing? They are *dancing*! All night, literally. They are dancing in the Grafton Galleries under pictures of dying soldiers, that's what they are doing. Anna's among them. She has had her hair bobbed and Edward has taught her to smoke and drink cocktails. I can't *bear* it. I hate it all.' She had been dancing with them and their crowd and the silly frivolous innocence of the tea party where she had first met Edward, seemed to have hardened into something more disagreeable, almost depraved. Friends of Anna's had tried to make her dance with them, and she had accused them of being drunk, when they hardly were, and had then burst into public tears. Her brother-in-law had been disconcertingly kind.

'If you could join in with them, you would feel better, you know. We aren't dancing on the faces of the dead, we're just doing a bit of living now we can.'

Kate told him angrily he was wrong. She said it again,

now, to Eleni, and she said that Anna no longer seemed to be her sister, her behaviour was so trivial.

Eleni was perched on the corner of the wrought-iron table, watching Kate's angry pacing.

'But my dear, that is so natural. They are trying to get back the youth the war would not let them have. It makes them a little crazy, but it will not last. They have suffered so much. You must try to be a little tolerant.'

'It is so *cheap*,' Kate said. 'It belittles what all those men died for, it is so silly and tawdry.'

'But, what *you* do is not silly or tawdry. Nursing—'

Kate whirled round, almost knocking over a huge pot in which an amaryllis was slowly opening its gigantic coral-coloured trumpets.

'*Nursing!* Oh, Eleni, if you knew how unendurable it is to nurse back in England after France! All these stupid people imagining themselves ill, all the repetitive little complaints! Nobody is going to *die* of flat feet!'

Eleni found that she did not much want Kate to talk to her patients. Kate could not help dwelling upon the war, asking them about their own experiences in it and Eleni did not intend them to recall life before 11 November, it hindered their recoveries. Kate's grim unhappiness lay heavy on the house, even the children felt it. The strain of melancholy in Rob, his propensity for serious preoccupation, drove him to follow Kate about, irresistibly drawn by her despair. He would stand and watch her absorbedly, and she was furious with herself at finding his interest a balm, almost a luxury. I am taking myself so *seriously*, she cried inwardly, silently, and I cannot stop myself; I despise other people so for their lightness yet I hate the lack of it in me. I could hardly stand the war towards the end and now I can hardly stand its being over, and I *hate* the world it

475

has left us with, this unfamiliar, foolish, unprincipled world . . .

When she went back to London, Charlie and Eleni watched her leave with sorrow and relief.

'I hardly like to mention it,' Carlo said to them confidentially, as the Fred-chauffeured car pulled away, 'but she really is the most awful wet blanket. Don't you think?'

In her soft Welsh bedroom, Rose lay and wondered if the pain was worse or better than five minutes ago. Dr Rhys Evans had said it was colitis. Rose liked Dr Rhys Evans; he had practised in Paris in the nineties where, he said, colitis was all the rage, and no woman of fashion would have dared not to suffer from it. It was a nervous disorder, of course. He implied that only the most chic and sensitive of dispositions were eligible for colitis and that was some small comfort except when the pain was sharp and Rose was sick, when nothing much was comforting.

It was also the first ailment or physical trouble Rose had had, without Ellen, for sixteen years. Ellen's defection was in fact a worse pain than the colitis. She had hardly waited for the Armistice to be signed before she came to Rose and, in a torment of love and rage, had said that she could *not* sit in Llanblethian and just watch the poor old world trying to put itself back together again after the war. She was going to London. She was going to housekeep for Victoria and learn the rudiments of the printing trade and somehow – here she became very vehement and not at all clear – make herself useful to people who were pushing forward social frontiers. She talked a great deal about votes for women and the new heavens of psychology and philosophy, and rained down upon Rose a torrent of names, Freud and Jung and Bertrand Russell and Havelock Ellis and Rudolf Steiner. Harry found her in the middle of a confused tirade on behaviourism, and Rose in helpless tears, and took her away.

'Of course you must go,' he said to Ellen. 'It is ridiculous for a woman of your enterprise to stay here. But really, you must not bully her. Your going is quite enough for her to bear without being hectored as well.'

'I felt I must *explain*—'

Harry looked at her pityingly.

'Do you honestly think that Mr Russell's views on mysticism and logic will make a ha'porth of difference to her?'

'They do to me—'

'*Ellen*,' Harry said, and left her to go and comfort Rose. When he joined her – she was sitting at the drawing-room window staring blankly at the garden – she said, flatly and without looking at him,

'Well, it only needs you to abandon me now. So why do you not do it. Everyone else has, after all.'

He sat down and took her hand. She let it lie quite limp in his.

'I shall never abandon you.'

She turned a faintly accusing stare upon him.

'I am sure you would like to.'

'No.'

'Oh! Your voice is so *patient*. Of course you would like to! I am always so dismal.'

'I would *not* like to. I should, of course, like to make you happier, but I am at a loss as to how to achieve that. I think about it almost all the time—'

'How *could* she?' Rose said on a sudden high scream. 'How could Ellen leave me? Victoria is a witch, Victoria

477

and Ellen have plotted. That family will never forgive me, never. They are so patient, so terrifyingly patient. They will wait years and years and years for the right moment to punish me again. Next, it will be you. They'll find a way to take you. You'll see.'

'Nonsense,' Harry said tiredly.

'You don't *mean* nonsense!'

'What I mean,' Harry said, 'is what I said. You imagine persecutions where none exist, you imagine disloyalties with just the same force that you refuse to see love where that does exist. I will stay with you for ever and that is a fact. Ellen is not going because she does not love you, but because she is almost dead with frustration down here. She could just bear it before the war but now, with life so changed, she can bear it no longer—'

'It is so *selfish*,' Rose shrieked.

Harry got up.

'We will not, I think,' he said levelly, 'have a conversation about selfishness.'

And then he went away to his business room and left her crying again and, this time, there was no-one to go in and comfort her.

Ellen left in the New Year of 1919 and Rose began to have pains. She wrote to Ellen about the pains and Ellen wrote back to say how sorry she was, but that she was not to worry as colitis – she had looked it up – was very much affected by the patient's frame of mind which, in Rose's case, Ellen was sure would improve with the coming of spring. She sounded, Rose thought, impersonal, heartless, and unforgivably happy. It was appallingly difficult without her. Neither Harry nor Rose had had the smallest conception of how much domestic work Ellen had come to do during the war as the local girls went into the munitions factories, instead of opening the front door on Rose's at home afternoons. None of the village women wanted to live in any more. Two of them came to clean and the old gardener re-appeared brandishing an artificial arm after Italy, but that did not get the laundry or cooking done, or Rose's little correspondence sorted out, or clean vases of water set ready in the flower room for her arrangements, or her clothes and bedroom cared for so that she never had to trouble herself to consider them.

The pains in her stomach grew worse. Harry found that a travelling laundry van would pick up the household linen and wash it in Cowbridge, and he found a cottage woman who would look after Rose's clothes, but she was heavy handed after Ellen and tore and scorched things. A cook came from Cardiff, a cook with decided, and too frequently disgusting, ideas but nobody wanted to be parlourmaid any more, except on an impossibly casual basis. Rose retired to bed and Harry, forced to open his own front door for the first time in his life as often as not, in despair hired a nurse from London, a pleasant enough woman who was very happy to look after Rose and very unhappy to be asked to do anything else whatsoever.

In May, exhausted by domestic juggling and the impossible task of pleasing or appeasing Rose, Harry wrote to Kate. He wrote very carefully, anxious not to put any unfair pressure upon her, yet unable to resist appealing strongly to her to come.

'Your mother is not very well, I am afraid – discouraged like all of us by this depressing new world we find ourselves in. It would cheer her so much to see you. I know how committed you are, but could you not spare just one Friday to Monday? It would mean so much to us both.'

There was silence for two weeks and then she wrote that she would come. Rose thought the pain was better at hearing that Kate was coming, and on the morning of her arrival, she actually got up and fiddled about with some white tulips in a vase, but then the pain bit her and she had to sit down and Miss Hodges put her back to bed. She could not rest in bed, but twisted and turned and endlessly considered the pain and whether it was the same or better or worse. When Kate at last came in and stood at the end of her bed, so thin and unsmiling and dressed in a horrible brown coat and skirt that made her hair look dead, Rose knew the pain was definitely worse and was furious with Kate for making it so. Kate stooped to kiss her and then Miss Hodges, bristling in the presence of a real nursing sister, said, 'Now that's enough excitement until after luncheon,' and bustled about drawing curtains and shooing Kate out.

Over luncheon – halibut and unadorned potatoes and carrots with wooden cores – Harry said,

'I am reproaching myself for asking you. You don't look well yourself.'

'Oh, I'm *well*. I just can't shake myself out of this depression. I don't want to join in with all my age group in London and yet I resent not wanting to. The really awful thing is not knowing *what* I want any more. It's never happened to me before—'

'I don't think,' he said carefully, 'that experiences like war are shaken off in a matter of months. You have to wait and you have to *do*.'

Kate gave a sigh of impatience. She looked round the room and said petulantly, 'But I *am* doing!'

'I mean other interests than one's central core of doing. You probably think my life here trivial in the extreme, but I have two new and consuming interests – my luxuries if you like. Once a week I write to little Robert, to your brother – and all the rest of the week I am storing up things to tell him – and I have become passionately fond of jazz.'

'Jazz?'

'Certainly. I have a phonograph and all the recordings the Original Dixieland Jazz Band have made so far.'

'That,' Kate said cruelly, 'must be a great comfort.'

He paused and then with a great effort said simply, 'It is.'

She put down her knife and fork.

'Oh, that is all I needed to hear! Mother supposing herself ill to punish poor Ellen and you listening to black men playing saxophones in your business room! What on *earth* did you ask me here *for*? To tell me about that?'

Harry's hands were shaking. He put them in his lap and held them hard together. He waited for a few moments and then said in a voice so controlled it was almost expressionless,

'I asked you here to put a proposal to you. Already, within two hours of your being here, I see I was very much mistaken. The war has quite changed you and I cannot ask the Kate you now are what I might have asked the Kate you once were.'

'Which is?' she said, unrelenting.

'To give up your nursing for a while to come here and look after your mother. I have to admit that we are not managing well, and she is lonely and unhappy and feels herself quite cut off from her family.'

'Harry,' Kate said, 'colitis is a spasmodic inflammation of the colon particular to nervous individuals.

Treatment is to deal with the underlying nervous condition, not by pandering to it and getting expensive nurses and allowing the patient to believe herself seriously ill, but by distracting and encouraging her. If you ask me, Mother has an acute attack of self-pity and a minor one of colitis as a result.'

'No.'

'*No?*'

'I would be grateful if you would not keep echoing me in incredulous disbelief. Your mother *is* unhappy, certainly, but I also believe her to be more seriously ill than Dr Rhys Evans does.'

'The arrogance of laymen—'

Harry stood up.

'If you will excuse me, Kate, I shall leave you to finish your luncheon alone. I think it best that you do not even remain the night and I will arrange for you to be driven to the evening train. All I ask is that you do not speak to your mother this afternoon in anything but the kindest and most sympathetic of tones.'

In the train back to London, Kate was overwhelmed with a confusion of rage and remorse, and found herself trembling violently and quite unable to stop. Somewhat shaken by Harry's anger, she had attempted to be the daughter Rose wanted and had spent the afternoon sitting at her bedside, battling with a threatening ungraciousness. Rose had tried to rally and be gay, and had shown Kate the picture of a dress she meant to have for summer, a ridiculous, delightful dress that showed her ankles, with a skirt made entirely of floating panels pointed like handkerchiefs. Kate, deliberately plain in her brown gaberdine, struggled to feel anything but irritation.

'So you won't stay,' Rose said quietly, putting the picture down.

Kate, startled, stammered, 'N-no – no, I can't – the hospital—'

'Of course,' Rose said. 'I wish you could have a change though. It can't be good for you, going on and on and on like this, no fun. You are only twenty-five, poor Kate, and you have had no fun at all.'

'I don't want *fun*.'

'Don't you? I think that is because you have never had any and so you don't know what it is like. You shouldn't despise it, you know.'

She did not complain once, all the afternoon, and when Kate was leaving she managed to ask, tentatively, after Ellen.

'She's wonderfully well,' Kate said brutally. 'She is going to do an accountancy course so that she can do Victoria's books. She looks years younger.'

Rose looked away.

'She is thirty-nine. She will be forty on the first of June. Give her my love, won't you?' Her voice shook. 'I miss her—'

Kate said nothing. After a while, Rose turned her head back and said,

'You must not miss your train.'

'No.'

'Will you come again?'

'It's a bit difficult—'

'Of course,' Rose said, closing her eyes and turning her head away again. 'Of course. Goodbye, Kate.'

Kate stooped and kissed her averted cheek.

'Goodbye, Mother. Do try to pull yourself together a little.'

'I'll try—'

Harry did not come to see her off. She was driven away from Llanblethian without a single wave and in

483

revenge she did not look back at the graceful house above its sloping garden. She climbed onto the train in Cardiff, and almost at once was overcome by simultaneous fury at Rose's exploitation of Harry and genuine regret at her own grudging rudeness to them both. She was conscious, too, that she was for some quite unknown reason, afraid as well, with a cold and nauseating fear that was quite inexplicable and quite separate from the by now familiar fear of her own wretchedness. The train was terribly cold and unbearably slow and a raw grey twilight, more appropriate to March than May, deadened the landscape. Shivering and sick, unable either to sleep or to cry, Kate watched the fading light with sore eyes as the train crept on towards London.

When Digby Payne was shown into Victoria's sitting room, she was much surprised. A man in the house, in the first place, was something of a surprise, but a perfectly strange and curiously confident man was an added astonishment. He looked rather handsome, she thought, in a foxy way, standing easily in front of her in a double breasted suit of fawn flannel and a tie of corn yellow silk spotted in dark brown that he had just bought in the Burlington Arcade, as a small but jaunty snook to cock at a noted feminist.

'I am awfully impertinent,' he said, not meaning it. 'I mean, just bouncing in like this.'

She inclined her head. Her trim neat prettiness reminded him of the nurses at Etaples. She said, looking at his card,

'Captain Digby Payne.'

'Oxford and Bucks Light Infantry.'

'I see. Well, you had better tell me what you are doing here.'

She sounded exactly like Kate, he thought exultantly, *just* as crisp and unhelpful. Wonderful . . .

'I'm in search of another Miss Taverner and I hoped you might be able to help me. My sister reads your magazine which is how I came to hear your name, you see. I met a Kate Taverner nursing in France and I'd love to see her again. Is she any relation?'

'She is my niece.'

'I say!' Digby Payne cried. 'What luck!'

Victoria stood up and crossed to the window.

'Have you seen Kate since France?'

'No—'

'You will find her much changed.'

She was terribly changed, so changed that Victoria and Sarah found she had become their chief preoccupation. They spent whole nights worrying about Kate. They had tried to talk to her, but she had repelled all interest. She was just depressed, she insisted, like thousands of young people in 1919, there was nothing else the matter. Would they please leave her alone?

'Do you smoke?' Digby said.

'Thank you, no.'

'Do you mind—'

'Not at all.'

'What has happened to Kate?'

'I think,' Victoria said, bringing an ashtray like a china shell to Digby, 'that she is suffering very badly from the war being over. She hated it, naturally, but it has left her in an unbearable void.' She sat down and motioned him to a chair opposite to her. 'She has not the temperament for dancing the night away, you see.'

Digby leaned forward and said, 'I warned her that this might happen. I warned her in France. I told her England would be pretty grim after the war.' He leaned back again and drew on his cigarette. 'I'm not staying, you see.'

'No?'

'I'm going off to British East Africa, to Kenya. I'm only in London to raise a bit of money to buy out my uncle's coffee farm. I told Kate about that, in France. I made my mind up to it the first time I got hit.' He touched his left upper arm. 'Jerry got me twice but he did no real harm, I'm only a bit stiff, it won't stop me using a shotgun.'

'And does this Kenya plan have something to do with your wishing to see Kate once more?'

Digby raised his light eyes and looked directly at Victoria.

'Yes. It does. I think she is wonderful.'

Victoria looked down at her hands. If she did not tell this curiously unnerving young man where Kate was, he would surely find out from somebody else, and in any case, she had no idea of how far their friendship at Etaples had progressed and whether, indeed, Digby's opinion of Kate was warmly reciprocated and accounted in part for her present misery. Perhaps too, this African project, if not the answer, was at least the necessary distraction? All she could do, she thought rapidly, was to make perfectly certain that Captain Payne knew in how fragile a state Kate was just now. She looked up and found his gaze relaxedly upon her, as if he were waiting.

'Captain Payne—'

She stopped.

'If you are worried I might upset her,' he said easily, 'you needn't be. We've both been through the war, you see. I think we both want the same things out of life. Anyway, I've told you what I think of her, so that the last thing on my mind is upsetting her, isn't it? Obviously.'

'Obviously,' Victoria echoed faintly, and then she gathered breath and said, 'The trouble is, Captain Payne, that I believe she is on the edge of some nervous collapse. We are all extremely worried as she will not stop working, yet appears to detest what she does. It was in fact my intention to speak to the Matron of St Bartholomew's Hospital shortly, and I have only been checked by Kate's own fierce independence and insistence that nothing serious is wrong.'

'Ah,' Digby said, 'St Bartholomew's. Thank you, Miss Taverner.'

'I do beg you to be careful.'

He stood up.

'Of course I will be. But I may be just the cure she needs.'

He held out his hand, smiling his friendly and disconcerting smile, and then he said,

'I've never met anyone like her. I'm not going to risk damaging anything as rare as that, now am I?'

When he had gone, Victoria was very restless. She thought she would go and find Ellen – oh invaluable, committed and diligent Ellen! – but Ellen was out at the business college in Marylebone where she was learning accountancy and bookkeeping. Victoria went back to her sitting room and tried to analyse her unease. The man was plainly a gentleman and he and Kate had come to some very close understanding in France, so close perhaps as to explain why Kate had never mentioned him? That would be her way of course; all those years of her love for Frank Martineau of which she never spoke a syllable, or her apparent acceptance of her parents' parting with never a word of confidence, as far as Victoria knew, uttered to a soul – that was Kate's way

487

with the most private things. And why should Kenya not be the answer, offering freedom and sunshine and open air and superb physical chances? Was it the man himself, his sheer ease, almost insolent ease?

She sighed, and upon an impulse, ran up the narrow staircase to the top floor. Sarah was, as usual, working at her desk, and Bay was lying on her stomach on the hearthrug drawing with coloured chalks on a sheet of brown paper.

'Sarah—'

'My dear! What is it? You look quite shocked—'

'I'm so sorry to interrupt you,' Victoria said agitatedly, 'but I might have done the most awful thing. I think I have just arranged for Kate to be carried off to Africa by an almost unknown young man with no money!'

CHAPTER TWENTY-FIVE

1920

Kate became Mrs Digby Payne at the Westminster Register Office in April. She wore a low-waisted draped dress of grey blue wool challis and a broad brimmed felt hat with a single plumed grey feather. Her husband wore a double breasted flannel suit and an expression of carefree satisfaction. It was, however, apart from the vase of scarlet carnations on the Registrar's desk, not a particularly buoyant occasion and the two witnesses – Sarah Martineau and a friend of Digby's called Ned Hamilton – found that they did not wish to catch each other's eyes for fear of reading their own poorly disguised apprehension there.

It was at Kate's specific desire that none of her family was present. Whether this was directly as a result of Rose's recent death, even Kate herself could not be sure, any more than she was sure of any single thing above an urgent wish to be in this marvellous free country Digby told her of, breathing an exhilarating air that had never heard gunfire and treading raw red earth that had only known man and beast with an almost biblical simplicity of hunter and hunted. Digby had bought her a rifle and a shotgun; they were packed along with the boots and divided skirts that somehow became her overriding preoccupation as she made her promises before the Registrar. For her part, she had bought a farm. It astounded her. Without seeing an inch of it, she had put the whole of Arnold's five thousand pounds into a thousand acres on the southernmost slopes of the Aberdare Range, and those thousand acres, bearing coffee trees and flax fields and Kikuyu squatters, now waited for her, in the clean and singing upland air.

The farm had become hers the very day that Rose had died. Harry had summoned a specialist to see Rose in the winter of 1919, and he had diagnosed cancer of the stomach. He had indicated that she had perhaps six months to live, but she had only managed four. In the New Year of 1920, Ellen and Anna abandoned their London lives to go down to Llanblethian and they had nursed Rose – a strange, sweet, stoical Rose – until the last day of February when she died in the early winter twilight. Kate tried to go too. She wrestled and wept and raged with herself and could not do it.

'She is ill,' Eleni said to Charlie. 'She needs a doctor.'

'I know. But you cannot force her to go and she will not acknowledge that she should go. A doctor can do no good until she lets him.'

'You must talk to her. She needs you.'

He went sadly up to London and took Kate out to dinner at the Savoy. They had a table looking out at the river and Kate, smoking and only picking at her turbot, talked deliberately of Kenya, only Kenya.

'We must talk about you,' Charlie said clumsily, at last, when coffee came. 'We are all worried to death about you.'

'About me? What about me? I'm fine—'

'Everything about you. Your future, this marriage,

your attitude to your mother, the change in you—'

'You imagine it,' Kate said.

'Do I? And does Eleni and your mother and Anna and Harry and Victoria and Catherine? We all imagine it?'

'Yes,' Kate said.

'This marriage—'

'Is what I want. We have fun together. We like the same things. He is going to teach me to ride and shoot. His uncle's farm, the one I am buying—'

'I don't want to hear another word about the farm.'

'Oh?' Kate said. 'So now who is being unreasonable.'

Charlie went back to Buscombe in deeper gloom.

'It was hopeless.'

Eleni put her hand in his.

'Then we must hope and pray that deep down she really does know what she is doing.'

'Or we must simply stand by to pick up the pieces—'

All Eleni's officers had gone, limping off into the remnants of their lives. She was redecorating, turning the house back into a house with exactly the vigour she had turned it into a hospital. It was an invaluable occupation, diverting her weary mind from Kate and from Rob, wretched at his preparatory school and writing pleadingly to be allowed home, in secret letters he had to smuggle out since the boys' weekly official ones were always censored.

'I don't see why I must stay here. I could learn exactly the same things at home. I would work so hard, I promise I would. I am so sad all the time. I hate playing games. Carlo says they are fun, but they are not fun for me.'

Only eleven, Eleni thought, and he must bear this absurd English system. If he does not, he becomes a freak among other boys, a sissy they will despise, he will never fit in. She wrote to him as comfortingly as she could without disloyalty to Charlie, and Rob carried her letters about with him in a kind of passion of love for them, as if the pieces of paper were the last frail physical link between himself and home. She wrote to Kate too.

'My dear, please do not hurry, do not be in an impulsive rush. Perhaps a great change *is* what you need, even a change of country. But please be careful of the personal commitment, please think and think and think *without anger* before you take the final step.'

Kate tore the letter up. It was easy to be with Digby; he made all the running. He loved the chase of her, you could tell, he had an eager, impatient air like a dog longing for a stick to be thrown. He took her dancing and made her like it, he drove her out to Richmond Park and gave her crazy driving lessons over the rough grass among the startled deer, he took her on shopping expeditions for Africa and bought her breeches and a double Terai hat. And yet, although he was always with her, dancing around her like some high-spirited insect with his pointed ears and pale, bright gaze, he also left her in peace. He did not talk about love to her, he hardly tried even to kiss her, he did not badger her privacy. With him, she could thankfully, blessedly, close the door on the chamber where the nightmares dwelt, and from whose dark depths Rose called to her.

She did not go to the funeral. Instead, she went to the offices of Union Castle with Digby and booked their passages to Mombasa. Rose was buried on a green Welsh hillside, and Ellen and Harry and Victoria were there, and Charlie and Eleni came and brought the boys. Long afterwards, Rob remembered it as the most perplexing morning of his life, looking at Eleni while praying for his dead mother, seeing both Charlie and Harry regarding him with a most fatherly compassion; his reaction was to feel absolutely, terrifyingly solitary, belonging nowhere.

'I think it is better that she is dead,' Carlo said to him, misunderstanding his misery, 'I mean, for her. She was in awful pain.'

Carlo had never seen Rose, but he had seen her picture, which he worshipped. Nobody so unutterably pretty should be allowed to be in pain. He put an arm round Rob.

'She's safe now, you see.'

Rob turned upon him dark blue eyes haunted with despair.

'But I am not—'

Nobody spoke of Kate. Even Anna, begun upon some small self-righteous remark, checked herself. There was no victory to be gained from her absence, nothing but fear and the sadness that had now attended all thoughts of her for three years.

Harry looked terrible, defeated, crushed. Eleni found him in his business room after the funeral, turning papers over blindly, over and over, irrelevant papers about charity committees he sat on.

'Harry, what are you going to do about this house?'

He looked about him vaguely.

'Oh – oh, let it go, I think—'

'But where will you go? You have sold your mother's house, after all. You sold that when she died at the beginning of the war.'

'I never thought I should need it. It seemed imposs-ible I should ever leave Wales—'

'I know. But, Harry, you must live *somewhere*.'

He rubbed a hand over his eyes.

'I will find a place. Anywhere will do. Old soldiers aren't fussy, you know.'

She put a hand on his.

'Come home.'

He looked at her.

'Come to Buscombe. Live with us. We should all love it and you could be near Rob. Please—' She stopped because she had noticed that his eyes were suddenly full of tears. She gave his hand a little pat and stood up.

'Think about it,' she said, 'there is no hurry to decide. But we hope you decide – yes.'

After the wedding, Digby took Kate and Sarah and Ned to luncheon at the Mirabelle, on the strength of flax – and they had three hundred acres of it waiting for them at Kilima – being worth £500 a ton. It was not a success. Sarah's social principles could not adjust themselves to the Mirabelle, Digby and Ned drank too much and were uproarious, and Kate, unable to reconcile herself to the task of bridging the gap between them all, said very little. Sarah left quite soon after coffee was brought, stooping to say softly to Kate,

'You know your father is sending you a crate of things from Buscombe he thinks you might like to have? I think they are going straight to Mombasa. It was meant to be a surprise, but I was worried that you would not look for a crate you did not know you were supposed to look for. God bless you, Kate.'

This made Kate abruptly tearful, which embarrassed Digby and Ned and they jollied her out into Curzon Street and put her into Digby's motor, and drove her, whooping and zigzagging, around Hyde Park Corner until she stopped. Then the afternoon went quiet and dead upon them and Ned, who was also coming out to

Africa, to join a bachelor brother in Nairobi, went off
with murmured excuses of things needing attending to.
They left the motor in Lowndes Square, and walked
down by unspoken agreement to look at the African
elephants in the Natural History Museum, and standing
in front of the great family group, Kate felt suddenly
comfortable again and knew that this adventure in
Kenya was to be their bond. She put her arm through
Digby's.

'What now?'

'A surprise for you, old thing. A night at the Ritz.'

'The *Ritz*?'

He grinned.

'We are going to be rich, Mrs Payne. Very, very rich.
So let us start as we shall soon be able to go on.'

Their bedroom at the Ritz made Kate giggle. It was
entirely peach-coloured, carpet, curtains, satin bedspread, mirror glass, even bathroom towels, so that
one's colour sense was quite distorted, and Green Park
outside the windows looked by contrast exaggeratedly,
ridiculously green. Standing in the bathroom, looking
at her soft apricot reflection all around, Kate thought
abruptly, we share this. And then she thought in a cat-
aract, you are a nurse, you are absurd, there isn't an inch
of a male body you don't know about, has Digby ever,
before—? Damn, damn, *damn*, do I even want him to,
what am I doing, what have I done, of course it will be
all right, but where do I have left to go to now, where
he won't come too?

'Champagne,' Digby said behind her.

'Oh . . .'

'Come on, old thing. Do you know what I ordered
for Mombasa yesterday? A crate of gin and a crate of
French vermouth.'

495

'Oh!' Kate cried, relieved, laughing. 'But I told you to order *hens*, speckled Sussex. Six hens and a cock. I can't breed bottles of gin . . .'

'More's the pity.'

Dinner was fine, easy. Digby told her about Iain Hamilton, Ned's brother, who had fought with the East Africa Mounted Rifles in the war, and was a queer sort of fish, absolutely gone on Africa, an anthropologist with a bee in his bonnet about the Kikuyu, who ran weird safaris just to *look* at the animals, that crazy old professors and spinster aunts seemed to like. Kate told Digby about Catherine.

'She would adore that, living rough and stalking elephants, even if she is over seventy.'

'That's where you get it, then.'

'Get what?'

'Your spark,' Digby said, 'your go. What I like about you.'

They had brandy and then they danced and then they had more brandy and went up in the gilded lift to their peachy chamber, and then there was a kind of terrible urgent flurry and tussle, and Digby appeared wildly, savagely excited and tore at Kate's clothes and kissed her so that their teeth and jawbones ground against each other. She said at intervals, 'Wait, stop – oh, Digby, just a minute,' but he seemed unable to hear her, and groaned and writhed and raced his hands over her as if he were looking for something he could not find, and then suddenly he gave a great yell and leaped to his feet, pulling off the few garments that he had not already discarded.

'Look!' he shouted at her, naked and pointing at himself. 'Look! Look!'

Struggling amid the humiliating disorder of her

496

underclothes, Kate sat up and looked. He was as limp as a child. She put out a hand and he said fiercely,

'Do something, can't you? For God's sake, you're a bloody *nurse*, aren't you?'

She stared.

'Oh look, *look*, if you want to. I should have thought you'd seen enough cocks in your day to last a lifetime. But be my guest, old thing. You won't see another like this in a long while. This one won't do a bloody thing. Do you hear me? Drunk or sober, not a bloody *thing*!'

He stooped and pushed his face almost into hers.

'There,' he said, 'now what do you think of *that*, Sister Taverner?' and he leaped over the bed past her and went into the bathroom and slammed the door.

She remained quite still for a few moments, and then she got up and peeled off her collapsed stockings and rolled herself in a satin quilt from the bed. In the bathroom Digby turned on the shower full blast and began to sing harshly through it, 'Poor Butterfly' and other silly nightclub songs, his voice flat and loud and defiant through the waterfall of water. Kate made a nest of the pillows on the bed, and collected an ashtray, and then settled herself with a cigarette to wait. Digby was not long. He came out of the bathroom in his dark blue silk dressing gown over the scarlet silk pyjamas they had bought with much giggling in Jermyn Street, and sat on the edge of the bed and lit himself a cigarette from the case he had given Kate. After a while, she said,

'Is it just with women, or men too?'

'Nobody. Nothing.' He looked at her and his light, insolent stare had come back. 'I think I want to. I'm excited, I think I am going to. But nothing ever happens.'

Kate let a little silence fall.

'And so,' she said, 'you thought that you might try a nurse, who had seen every physical problem and would know what to do.'

'When I got really worked up, I thought you would know what to do. But mostly, I just knew you would not be shocked.'

'And it never struck you that I might be a human being as well as a nurse?'

'No more nor less than it never struck you to ask me anything about myself.'

Kate stubbed out her cigarette.

'We are married.'

He looked at his watch.

'Twelve hours . . .'

'Is – is it physical?' She gestured vaguely towards his groin.

'No.'

'Are you afraid?'

'I'm not afraid of anything *else* . . .'

She pulled the quilt tighter.

'Should you see a doctor?'

'Not for my sake,' Digby said, 'I'm pretty used to it. And I don't think for yours. Do you?'

She stared.

'I mean, old thing, that you don't want me to make love to you, do you? Even if I could. Let's face it. We don't want to touch each other. Perhaps you are like me, I don't know if women can be.'

Misery was settling on Kate like a raw fog.

'Oh!' she cried. 'What did we marry for?'

'We were lonely. We want to go to Africa. We don't fit in here . . .'

'I'm *normal*!' she shouted at him.

He paused and looked at her.

'Are you?' he said.

'Yes, yes I *am*! You're a brute. You're a cruel brute. What did you go through all that stupid performance for just now, if you don't really want to be like other men?'

He shrugged.

'Worth a try. Might have worked. Calm down, old thing. Face facts.'

'Facts!'

'Yes,' he said, getting up and looking down at her, 'facts. I had sex left out of me, and the war knocked it out of you. You don't like post-war England, I didn't even like it pre-war. We can give each other freedom, old thing. We get on fine, don't we?' He looked round the room. 'I'll sleep on the sofa, if you like.'

'Yes, please.'

He went across the room to the brass room service bell.

'What are you doing?'

'Ordering champagne.'

She flung herself out of the quilt.

'What have *we* got to celebrate?' she shouted.

He looked at her calmly.

'We've got everything sorted out now. And we are going to Africa in two days' time. Go and wash your face and come back showing a few of the guts I like in you.'

In the peach-coloured glass of the bathroom she looked at herself solemnly, from head to foot. There was no means of telling just by looking at her narrow body if she was normal or not, if that smooth tawny skin covered ordinary womanly appetites or none of them. She thought abruptly of walking through the sand dunes at Etaples with Sylvia, and the strange excitement of coming upon the couple illicitly making love, and at the memory, the same excitement flickered for a moment. But that of course, was no proof. Even Digby thought he was excited, now and then, and look at him. She peered at her face in the mirror and her newly cut smooth dark hair fell over one eye. Nice, she thought. She looked hard at herself. This, my girl, she told herself, is where you have got to, at the end of a long and tortuous path, this is where you have got *yourself*. Undersexed, oversexed, either, neither, none of that really matters just now. You are married, you are going to Africa and you are going out of this bathroom with your head *up*.

'Bubbly,' Digby shouted.

Kate turned the taps on full.

'Coming!'

From Port Said onwards, Kate could feel herself turning to the sun. It was a queer, instinctive thing, like a flower, a sensation at once healing and intoxicating, a raising of her face towards all that hot gold and blue. The smells at Port Sudan, smells of dung and oils and spices and sweat, stinks of dried fish and filth, filled her imagination with an exhilaration stronger than anything she had ever known, and she moved among the wrapped Arabs on the quay like someone in a heightened trance. Whole continents lay either side of her, deserts and plains, mountains and lakes, fantastic distances across which the camel trains swayed and rocked. She felt absurdly that she was standing on the threshold of a whole new world, that the chance for progress and expansion that the war had robbed her generation of, was waiting out there in that vast land mass, where farms a quarter the size of Wales were not uncommon, where ostriches ran in flocks on the plains, and in the cool uplands a fantastic heather grew as tall as a man.

Mombasa, when they reached it, across a shining blue sea barred with the long white rollers of the Indian Ocean, was all she could have asked of it. Built of coral, buff and dull yellow and pink, it offered its maze of narrow streets below the huge old fortress to Kate like an enchanted puzzle. The sun blazed upon the coral rock, scarlet acacias blazed from gardens and over walls and in squares flopped the heavy pointed leaves of the mango trees. There were dhows in the port and piratical sailors prowling the alleys and the coffee-sellers and coppersmiths shouted and hammered from open fronted booths along the harbour front. Digby took one look at it all and put an intoxicated Kate into a trolley car pushed by a massive African, for the Club.

Over a pink gin, Kate gazed at him in rapture.

'It's absolutely wonderful!'

'It's bloody *foreign* . . .'

Ned Hamilton's brother had left a letter of introduction for them at the Club. They were to be lent a bungalow for the night where they would find the Swahili servant he had hired for them.

'He is called Juma,' Iain Hamilton wrote. 'Do not forget that he is a Muslim. I have booked you first-class seats on the Nairobi train for Tuesday but you must provide yourselves with bedding. Juma knows the drill.'

Juma was tall and dignified and wore a long white kanzu, that reached to his feet. He showed them gravely about the wooden hut with its palm frond thatch that was to shelter them for three days, including pointing out, as serious objects of interest, a hornets' nest in the corner of the bedroom and a scurrying carpet of millipedes trekking across the verandah. Kate changed into a beaded dress of fawn silk, Digby into a white tropical dinner jacket, and back they went to the Club and a dinner of oxtail soup, chops and a crème caramel in its lake of dark syrup.

'All brown,' Digby said gloomily.

It was indeed disappointing. The chops, Kate felt, might at least have been cut from a Thompson's gazelle rather than an elderly and sinewy sheep. But the creak of the fan, the soft hot currents of air it blew about, the other diners with their hardened air of knowing Africa, the sheer exciting strangeness of it all was more than compensation for the institutional food of late Empire. When they got back to the bungalow, Juma had shrouded their beds in clouds of mosquito netting, and in the hot black night, Kate lay and listened to the insects' high singing whine as they cruised about the nets in search of entry. Out in the so-called garden where a weird old grey baobab tree stood in a whispering tangle of dry weeds, some tropical bird knocked and whistled, and every so often, through the soft air, came the sound of different human voices saying something so incomprehensibly strange that it sounded like an incantation. Kate lay and listened and smiled to herself and longed for the new day.

The locomotive, fired by eucalyptus logs that burned in an explosion of snapping sparks, lay like a dragon in Mombasa station. The platform was crowded with a few Asians, fewer Europeans and jolly hordes of Africans packing their friends and relations into third-class carriages with bulging baskets of yams and lumps of maize porridge parcelled up in banana leaves. The native women had babies tied to their backs with yards of bright cloth and balanced bundles of sugar cane on their heads, and trays of mangoes and eggs piled in ingenious pyramids. From her first-class seat, Kate watched them in rapture, a map of the protectorate on her knee. They were going northwest through Samburu to Voi – where, Juma informed them, they would alight for European dinner in the dak bungalow while he unrolled their bedding on the seats – and then on, sleeping, through Masongoleni and Makindu to the dawn on the plains south of Nairobi, where she would see her first elephant perhaps, her first giraffe, her first rhino standing as he did in picture books, ruminating beneath a thorn tree. She must look to the left of the train, Juma told her, because there all the animals were protected and could not be shot.

'They cross railway,' Juma said, turning her bed down with a precision she could not have bettered. 'They cross from that side to this. Not stupid.'

She slept to the jogging rhythm of the train and woke to the honey yellow plains in the early light, and a galloping herd of zebra and her hands and face and hair thinly veiled with the red dust of Africa. It seemed to her a baptism. In Nairobi, they slept in one of the square, bare bedrooms behind the bar of the Norfolk Hotel, hired a Kikuyu houseboy called Jogona, bought a car, saw all their crates of possessions loaded onto a train of ox carts, and were presented with a kind of wicker crate, which proved to contain two deerhound puppies as a present from Iain Hamilton, and a letter. He was presently away, he said, in Abyssinia on an expedition, but would be back in two months.

'I am afraid you may be dismayed by the state of Kilima. It has suffered from the war and your uncle's absence, but I think will not present an insuperable task to put to rights. The squatters have run riot a little. I

503

hope the puppies please you – I think you will see that the nobility and courtesy of the deerhound makes him the king of all breeds, and of course he is physically perfect for the African Highlands – aesthetically as well as athletically.'

'Man's mad,' Digby said. 'What does he mean about the farm?'

'He means, I think, that we have a lot of work to do . . .'

'But my uncle left it thriving!'

'It was thriving in 1914 . . .'

They drove up out of hot and dusty Nairobi north, into the cooler, bluer foothills of the Aberdare mountains. Juma, who was a man from the low baking coastline, sat in the back of the Ford and turned his eyes with slow disbelief, from one side to the other, as the hills grew higher and the deep cedar forests marched their straight trunked ranks alongside. The land rose and sank with the ridges of the hills, giving sudden sweeps of view down into the native reserve or the rift valley, sweeps of burned plain, freckled with wandering groups of wildebeest and elephant. The car jumped and bounced among the ruts and holes, the puppies whimpered in their wicker prison, Digby cursed softly, gripping the wheel, while the sun fell clear and yellow through the blue green cedars and Kate wanted to sing. She began, instead, to hum.

'I don't think,' Digby said, 'that there is going to be much to sing about, old thing.'

'Kilima', said a cracked and peeling painted board nailed askew to a juniper. Beyond the tree, a curving track led through land that had evidently once been cleared towards a huddle of reddish roofs visible on a slope about two miles away. The land had been planted too, once. Small bushes in regular rows struggled in a blanket of creepers and weeds and the track itself was edged with a ragged fringe of the coarse blades of couch grass. Trees had been planted to give the track dignity, at intervals of twenty yards, but some of these had been cut down, quite arbitrarily it seemed, and thrust their poor raw stumps upward among the exuberant under-growth.

From the back of the Ford, Juma, bolt upright still, began to make a low hissing moan of regret.

'Shut up,' Digby said.

Juma took no notice. His disapproval of the havoc outside the car windows filled the vehicle like gas. Kate turned to look at him.

'I am sure it is only *surface* neglect.'

Juma surveyed her, his long face set, his long hands folded in his white lap.

'No good, Memsahib.'

'You just wait,' Kate said.

The track wound down a slope, across a stretch of land that might once have been a flax field – Kate had been carrying about with her a mental picture of fields as blue as the sky that hung over them – and then climbed steadily for a mile in a gentle zigzag to emerge on a small sloping plateau, edged with trees where the wreck of a garden contained a low and shabby house with a collapsing verandah, facing the view. As the car pulled up, a number of African children began to ma-terialize out of the trees, standing at a discreet distance on the perimeter of the ruined lawn; there was a goat tethered to one of the verandah posts, and out of the centre of what had plainly started life as a flower bed, rose an enormous single pink hollyhock in sublime

505

disregard of the jungle creeping upon it from every side.

Kate glanced briefly at Digby. He had, she knew, envisaged pink gins on an emerald lawn brought by an immaculately starched Juma, a house panelled in native woods, coffee and flax machinery – the most advanced available – purring profitably away in whitewashed buildings, and a view as agriculturally ordered as the Kentish Weald, where his own coffee and his own flax grew in green and blue decorative discipline. Surveying the rampant decay and disorder he found instead must be causing him utter despair, she thought, but all he said was,

'Been let go a bit—' and then, after a long gaze at the dilapidated house, 'Not much like Buscombe—'

Kate said, 'I don't mind.'

'I say, old thing . . .'

'I don't. I don't mind at all. Let's look inside.'

If neglect had taken over outside, white ants had been busy within. It was a pleasant house, its main rooms opening onto the verandah and the view, but the door frames and doors were half devoured, a rank grey mildew lay in velvety blots along the skirting boards, and such pieces of furniture as had been left lurched and tottered and leaned against one another like elderly drunks. They went round the whole house, opening shutters and windows to the sun, while Juma moved behind them sighing, and fingering the knife he wore beneath his kanzu, as if to reassure himself in this frightful barbaric place. When they came out again, there was a ring of blanketed old men squatting on the grass, and waiting.

'What on earth do they want?'

'Perhaps they are our squatters—'

'But we can't speak to them!'

'We'll learn.'

'Oh God,' Digby said, turning his head away from that circle of little black watching eyes, 'what the hell have we done, Kate? What *have* we done—'

For Charlie, Kate's letters were a source of wonder and pride. Some magic had been at work, some African potion or charm and Kate was coming back to life. They had, she wrote, to buy entirely new machinery and two tractors, not to mention ploughs and hoes and spades. Because they had no money, she had secured an overdraft of two thousand pounds on the farm, at eight per cent, from the Bank of India in Nairobi. She had ordered thirty thousand coffee seedlings and two polo ponies for Digby and had taken on another Kikuyu houseboy whom Juma, with massive disapproval, was teaching to cook. They were both working a twelve-hour day themselves on the farm. There were turquoise blue and coral butterflies and green parakeets in the trees, and at night the fireflies dancing among the cedar trunks looked like an advancing troupe of lantern-bearing goblins. She wrote that the coffee seedlings must be planted in the rain with the tap root quite straight, that the best plough oxen were those trained by the Dutchmen and that to live at six thousand feet above sea level was the most exhilarating thing in the world. She did not write that Digby hated almost every single thing except the prospect of his polo ponies and the fact that Nairobi was only fourteen miles away.

Charlie felt stirrings of envy, reading Kate's letters. Ever since Rose's death, a dull melancholy had settled upon him, and a nagging regret for things he would not name that made him oddly pleased to have Harry in the house. He seemed to have a weary distaste for life since

507

the war had ended, and was dismayed to feel some stir-rings of that old, imprisoned restlessness that had driven him to Crete fourteen years before. Kate's letters made him itch, made him nostalgic, and this nostalgia for an adventure, for an escapade, conflicted uncomfortably with the other nostalgia, for Rose, the Rose he had loved and married. He found that he did not want to spend much time at home, so he was away from Buscombe on a commission whenever he could be, and in his absence Eleni and Harry companionably ran things together.

If Eleni felt herself excluded from Charlie's con-fidence, she gave no sign of it. She had missed her convalescent officers when they left, and so she turned her cossetting energies upon the family and its connec-tions and became a refuge and holiday home for Victoria, for Anna and her husband, for little Bay Martineau when her mother suddenly had a pang of conscience about London air. Buscombe's atmosphere had softened. There were a great many dogs, there were tennis racquets in the hall, a breath of Harry's pipe in the air and in the tower room stood a billiard table upon which Carlo and Rob played obsessively in the school holidays. Carlo won, almost always, with a great deal of generous grace outwardly, and considerable regret within.

'I can't lose *specially*,' he said to Harry, 'it would be so awfully patronizing. And anyway, he would spot I wasn't trying. But he gets so furious with himself that I sometimes think we oughtn't to play any more.'

They played tennis too, on the court Charlie had made from the old croquet lawn, whose mowing and marking had become the jealously guarded prerogative of Fred Bradstock. Fred was forty-eight. He had spent the war as a sergeant with the Glosters, pleased at the chance to be away from the neurotic jumpiness of his cottage where his wife's unhappy moodiness made daily life like tiptoeing through a minefield, but conscious throughout the three years he spent in the trenches that his heart was not really in any war, after Ladysmith and Tommy's death. The South African war had been Fred's war; he kept still uneaten the flat blue tin of chocolate that the Old Queen had sent to all her troops for Christmas of 1899. He showed it proudly to Carlo and to Rob who were, without any question, the two stars in his loyal firmament. Even at ten and eleven, they should have as immaculate a tennis lawn as it was in his power to provide them with.

He was not only their servant, but their encyclopaedia on Buscombe. As he had taught Anna and Kate, so he taught the boys to ride and to fish, and took them out with a shotgun after rabbits. Rob always needed a bit of urging about fishing and shooting, not so much lacking aptitude as seeming to be crippled by some incomprehensible anxiety about the possibility of cruelty to trout or rabbits. Everything worried Rob. Fred had never met a lad who took things so seriously, nor, since Tommy's father, a Taverner who loved the old place so much. It broke his heart three times a year to leave it to go back to school, you could tell it did, he'd have been weeping like a waterfall if he'd been a girl. That was the one aspect of Rob that comforted Fred – Buscombe had an heir who loved it above all things, at last, and in Fred's lifetime he would see it pass into loving hands.

He couldn't disguise it from himself, but Fred was frankly disappointed in Sir Charles. True enough, he'd modernized the place but piped water doesn't put the heart in a house. Her Ladyship did her best, and the Colonel was a very decent fellow, but the house didn't belong to them, and in Fred's view, houses turn to their *owners* for leadership, like dogs do. All his life, Sir Charles had been looking for something and Fred was sure he still hadn't found it, whatever it was, even when her Ladyship turned up out of the blue like that and rocked them all back on their heels. She was a good sort, her Ladyship, but she was a foreigner of course and she didn't have the sheer style of Lady Rose, God bless her, poor foolish creature. Fred missed her. He missed her sheer female glamour. Watching Sir Charles poking irritably about the place, Fred would have betted a pound to a penny that he was missing her too.

There were too many of them to miss. If it hadn't been for the school holidays of those two scamps, Fred would have found the missing very hard to bear. There was Miss Catherine, the only one to love Master Tommy as he had, gallivanting about the globe in breeches and now stuck in Cheltenham with Miss Elizabeth who had become, one gathered, a proper old handful. There was Kate of course, too. Next to Tommy, Fred cherished Kate. The only one of the family in the war, and a woman at that. Fred marvelled at Kate. And now there she was on some African hillside supervising darkies in her coffee plantation and dosing their nippers for worms. Sir Charles had told him she was learning the lingo. Fred rejoiced. He didn't care what it took – as long as she was emerging from the grim little misery she'd been two years ago and turning back into the Kate he remembered, wading in the farm pond looking for frog spawn with her dress tucked up into her knickers, he'd give it his backing.

Just as he would always give it to the house. It didn't matter to Fred what he was asked to do, as long as nothing took him from Buscombe again, so he was handyman and chauffeur, keeper and occasional butler, cleaned guns and boots, held ladders in the conservatory for her Ladyship while she pruned the dead trails of winter jasmine to encourage new growth and new flowers. Nothing that was going on missed Fred; he made it his business to know. So that, when a telegram came from Cheltenham to say that Elizabeth had suffered a massive heart attack in the night and was dead before dawn, Fred happened to be filling the hall log basket when her Ladyship rushed by on her way to find the Colonel. Fred was sorry about the old girl, but at least she was out of her misery and it set Miss Catherine free. He went off to the kitchen, where Cook and Palmer were having a cup of tea and discussing Cook's perennial grievance – her Ladyship's funny foreign notions about food – and stood by the table until they should observe he was heavy with portent. Cook put down her cup.

'Well, then?'

Fred cleared his throat.

'Miss Elizabeth's dead.'

Cook and Palmer clucked and muttered.

'Ah, poor soul—'

'Mercy, really—'

'Let me see now, she'd be seventy-three—'

'Seventy-four, come September—'

'Heart,' Fred said impressively.

'She'd got so big—'

'Oh, a *very* big person—'

'Poor Miss Catherine—'

Fred sat down and folded his arms on the table so that his face was on a level with theirs.

'Know what I think?'

'Not by looking,' Cook said, who believed in keeping Fred in his place. 'Not with a skull that thick—'

'Oo—' Palmer said admiringly.

Fred ignored them.

'What I think is – that Miss Catherine will come back here.'

'What of it? It's her home, isn't it?'

Fred looked knowing. He leaned forward.

'The Colonel.'

'What of the Colonel?'

'When I was a little kid, Miss Catherine and the Colonel were sweet on each other but her old Ladyship wouldn't have any of it. That's why he went soldiering. Now's his chance.'

Cook and Palmer went into squeals of mirth, and Palmer knocked over her teacup.

'Clumsy,' said Cook.

Fred stood up.

'You can laugh if you like, but you mark my words.'

'I like a nice wedding,' Palmer said.

Cook gave her a push.

'Well, you'll never see your own, *that's* for sure—'

Fred moved off to the outside door into the yard.

'I'd like to see that,' he said musing. 'The old place'd like it too. I'd like Miss Catherine to come home.'

CHAPTER TWENTY-SIX

Kenya, 1923

The view and the air together made up her elixir. She had the close pressing trees around the house at Kilima cut down so that she could, once a day, walk around her little plateau, and look south towards the stupendous plains, east to the bare dun desert land where giraffe and rhino moved among the thorn trees and then north and west to the green ridges and sweeps of foothills and forests swinging away to Mount Kenya. This was her favourite view. It looked over the Kikuyu Reserve and she liked the little smoke plumed clusters of their villages, and their shambas where the maize grew and which looked, from so high and far, as neat as green and yellow chessboards. Banana groves were no more than green shaving brushes, cattle on the grasslands mere specks. When she had looked all round, like the turning reflector in a lighthouse, she flung her head back and watched the high piled white clouds running before the wind from the northeast and felt, as she felt daily with an extraordinary delight that did not seem to diminish, that she was living, quite literally, up in the air.

It took her two years to concede what she had been told constantly by hearties at the bar of the Muthaiga

Club that Kilima was too high for coffee – successful coffee – because of frost and the wind from the plains and the chance of drought. Even now, with her little trees still two years away from bearing and four hundred acres patchily and disgustingly affected with the scabby seed pods of blackjack, she felt that given time she would make something of her plantation, because she so passionately wished and intended to. Also, she could not hide from herself the fact that she needed to.

The flax boom was over. Digby had, against all advice, planted a hundred acres, but not only had it not flourished but the Kikuyu seemed unable to grasp the techniques necessary to prepare the shiny, sticky flax fibre for sale. In any case, before the second crop was harvested, the market had plummeted. Flax was suddenly, terrifyingly, worth under a hundred pounds a ton, far less than it cost to produce. Digby had drunk a bottle of whisky neat and furiously set about his new and now useless machinery with a sledgehammer, watched by a whispering audience of Kikuyu.

'Grow tea,' Kate said.

'*Tea?*'

'Yes. I've been reading about it. We're at the right altitude, it's perfect land, and the natives would be able to pick it easily—'

'Shut up!' Digby yelled, 'shut up, shut up, at least until your bloody coffee is any less of a disaster!'

He slammed into Nairobi and into the Muthaiga Club, and then went missing. He was found two days later in the cheerful, filthy Swahili town which lay between the Club and Nairobi, and brought back to Kilima by Lars Nordstrom, a Swedish neighbour who worked like the devil for all of two months at a time, save three days, which he devoted to becoming insensibly drunk. He was sobering up as he brought Digby back to the farm, and in grave silence, he and Kate put Digby to bed and dealt with the gash on the side of his head.

'You must never let the land break you,' Lars said solemnly. 'It will if it can. You must make it work for you.'

'I thought perhaps tea—'

'I think pyrethrum. To make insecticides. My farm is lower than yours. I get more rain.'

Kate looked down at Digby. He was yellow white and stank like a distillery.

'Where did you find him?'

'In a hut. One of the boys at the club knew where.'

'It isn't the first time, you know—'

'It won't be the last,' Lars said. 'He does not like work. That is why the land will have the strong hand.'

When he had driven away across the northern ridges to his farm looking down on Lake Naivasha, Kate went into her sitting room and poured herself a drink. It was very quiet, midday, all the birds silent, no wind. The sitting room windows and doors were flung open to the verandah and the southern sun, and from the lawn beyond the verandah came the only faint sound to be heard, the soft mutterings of a group of Kilima's squatters who had been sitting there since dawn, waiting for Kate to arbitrate in the matter of a cow, traded by one to another, who had proved to be barren. Kate sat down just inside the threshold, so that they might not see her, and began her calming exercise, the steady quiet surveying of what lay around her.

The sitting room contained everything she loved most. The crate Charlie had sent from England contained, besides books and pictures – including a watercolour Elizabeth had painted of Buscombe in the hopeful months before her marriage – the two blue damask chairs with which she and Anna had once played houses in the apple store, the pagoda birdcage, and astoundingly the marble font and grieving swan Kate had so mockingly admired as a child. It stood now on the terrace outside the verandah, full of tumbling pelargoniums, the swan an object of admiring veneration to the Kikuyu. For all her profound delight in Kilima, Kate could not pass the swan without a stab of poignant longing for Buscombe; sometimes she went out of her way to pass it deliberately.

The sitting room had been panelled the year after they had arrived; Kate had borrowed more money against the farm. The watercolour of Buscombe hung above the fireplace where they burned great cedar logs in the chill upland evenings, and which was flanked by bookcases – how infinitely precious those books were in Kenya! The floor was covered with rugs from Buscombe, there were two bronze cherub lamps from Buscombe still wearing their pleated silk shades that Rosamund had once chosen, so incongruous in Africa, and zig-zagged against one wall stood the Chinese screen which had battled with the winter draughts at Buscombe that whistled from the tower room into the library.

'Do you mind,' Kate had said to Digby, 'that this room is so entirely Buscombe?'

He turned his light uncaring gaze upon her and said, 'Why should I mind?'

His only contribution to the room had been the head of a kudu he shot on their first safari. It hung above the sideboard and contrasted interestingly with the pink shaded cherub who pirouetted beneath it, a juxtaposition which gave certain visitors a lot of pleasure, but one that Kate had ceased to see or find funny. She looked at the kudu now, and he looked back with his yellow glass stare.

If only we could always be on safari, or playing polo, Digby would be quite happy, she thought. Safari is wonderful, magical even at times, but it's a pleasure we have to earn, labouring up here, like polo is, or all this gin, or a trip home sometime . . .

She closed her eyes. Living with Digby was not exactly unpleasant, but it was most peculiar. If they were riding or shooting, they had a friendly companionableness, the same cheerful, simple ease that characterized that first drink of the evening in front of the blazing cedar logs. But if they began to talk about the farm, or themselves, or politics, or the future, Digby would simply elude her and slide away, sometimes not replying, sometimes actually melting from the room. He was seldom angry, seldom rude, but bent, with a smiling determination, upon living the life he had come to Africa expressly to find. This life meant a great deal of sporting physical activity, a great deal of drink, and a great deal of mindless high spirits. Kate sometimes wondered if he even saw the natives on the farm; he certainly scarcely spoke to any but the houseboys and Juma, who came to Kate once a week to announce his intention of returning to Mombasa. At first she had pleaded, which meant a long and elusive wrangle, but now she simply said, 'Go, then,' and he would pad silently back to the kitchen. Digby shouted at him, as he shouted at the dogs. Neither Juma nor the deerhounds took the slightest flicker of notice. Sometimes Digby would get into the car, and just go. Kate did not always know where he had gone, and after the first year, did not mind very much. He went to the Muthaiga Club, she knew, and revelled in the rows and

517

heady little melodramas, and he went across the hill country to Jock Nelson's farm, or Gustav Behr, who both lived alone and had wild, ferocious tastes and habits. If he could persuade anyone to take him on safari, he went. Kate didn't mind. She liked her long upland days and she liked going down to Nairobi alone, and shopping, and having a haircut and lunch in the Norfolk Hotel. She had her own friends, and sometimes she brought one or two back to Kilima and rode with them among the blue gums, the deerhounds in attendance, looking for partridge.

Two of these friends were the Hamilton brothers. Ned had arrived in Africa only six months after the Paynes and Digby had been looking forward enormously to his coming. But when he came, and was established in his brother's house in Nairobi, he did not seem to be the same roistering companion he once had been. He was put to work. His brother first tried to make a research assistant of him, and after a crash course in the language, sent him out into the Reserve to attend Kikuyu Kiamas, the councils of elders which endlessly met to settle the endless disputes. After a few days with his notebook, bored to distraction by the circular and interminable haggling over sheep and goats, Ned picked up his rifle and joined a conveniently passing safari, as an unpaid white hunter to a party of Dutchmen. He returned to Nairobi with a lion skin, an empty notebook, and to a glacial reception. He was next sent on one of Iain Hamilton's camera and sketchbook safaris and almost allowed the Muslim porters to die of starvation because he had not provided the right food. He compounded this disaster by running out of camera film and by shooting two zebra in full view of his party. What his brother said to him on his return, no-one knew

– though the Muthaiga Bar, at once utterly perplexed and fascinated by Iain Hamilton's lack of orthodoxy and undoubted physical courage, was richly speculative – but Ned was suddenly very changed, almost subdued. Kate, meeting him one day in Government Road, was abruptly overcome with pity at his loss of swagger, and asked him up to Kilima.

He came, and he brought his brother. Iain Hamilton was enormously tall with the disconcerting gaze of a man who is most comfortable looking at objects more than two miles away. Kate thanked him profusely for the deerhounds, which he seemed almost to have forgotten giving her, being instantly absorbed by the painting of Buscombe and the books.

Iain was intensely interested in Kilima and what she had achieved, and was of great help to her in making her mare rideable, a half-made polo pony Digby had bought cheap and then lost interest in. In the process of schooling the mare, he made Kate an infinitely better horsewoman, so that when he and Ned and Kate played a limecutting – dashing past a lime stuck on a pole at full tilt and halving it with a single sword stroke – she could hold her own. He also taught her where her responsibilities lay with her squatters, what each owed to the other. Her role, she came to see, was judicial and protective, she must preside over disputes, dose sick totos, shield her people as much as she could from harassment, be it human or animal.

There was an old lame lion that was intermittently a nuisance – the kitchen toto would tuck up one arm and then scurry around the lawn on two feet and one hand to imitate it – stealing calves and goats when it failed to kill in the wild. It had grown very solitary and cunning and Kate had spent months trying to shoot it, even waiting up all night beside a fresh kill to which any ordinary lion would have been bound to return. She took a rifle everywhere she rode, but she only glimpsed it once, in months, fleeing crookedly among the thorn trees far beyond her rifle's range. It became a kind of Moby Dick to her and she felt that until the lion was dead, Kilima could not flourish.

'Then we must shoot it,' Iain said.

'Oh', she said, impatiently, 'I have been hunting it for *months*.'

'Then stop hunting it. Forget it. Then you will find it.'

They met it riding together a month later. Ned, nursing a hangover, had been left on the verandah with the solitaire board and a glass of Juma's cure-all, two raw eggs whisked into a measure of cognac. Kate was on her mare, and Iain on the cob she had bought for Digby to ride round the farm – wishful thinking, that had been – and they were dropping gently down into the reserve, hardly talking, very Sunday afternoon contented, when the mare stiffened and flung up her head. She stopped dead. Iain's hand shot out, warning Kate to silence.

'Shhh—' He slid from the cob and took his rifle from behind the saddle. She whispered, 'What?' He passed her the reins.

'Hold him. Hold them both. Reined right in. Sit tight.'

He moved from the rough path into the dry bushes beside it, and as he did so, the lame lion came out about fifty yards ahead, his huge old body swinging like a hammock from his spine, and turned and looked at Kate and at the horses. It was a long and hostile moment and then the mare bunched herself under Kate and put her head down and began to squeal, and the rifle sang out beside her and the lion fell with infinite heavy grace across the path. Then the mare flung up her head, wrenched herself and Kate away and sideways and began to tear in desperation across the scrubby land between the thorn trees. Kate lay flat, and prayed, pressing her face against the mare's neck to avoid the scratching grab of the thorn trees. The mare's mouth felt like iron. The humiliation of this happening, of being run away with like a child at its first meet, in front of Iain Hamilton, was absolutely appalling, worse than anything. She tried to reach along the mare's neck and hook her fingers in its nostrils but the shuddering jolting speed of their passage made it impossible. Then she heard the cob behind her and Iain's voice. The mare stopped dead, quite suddenly, and Kate fell off.

She sat where she had fallen and drooped her shamed and scarlet face. The mare stood close to her and blew like bellows. Iain came thundering to a halt, and swung himself off and came to crouch beside her.

'Well done!'

'Well done?'

'You didn't fall and she stopped.'

'I feel an utter ass.'

'Why?'

'I couldn't stop her.'

'Of course you couldn't. It was probably her first lion.' He put a hand under her arm and lifted her to her feet. 'You take the cob. I'll ride her back and show her the lion.'

'I'll come with you.'

The lion lay like a broken old tawny sofa across the path, his mouth open in a final roar of indignation, his crooked limb thrust stiffly away from his body like a defiant fist shaken at his foe. Iain knelt beside him and took Kate's hand and put it on the great body. He was warm still, the pelt curiously soft and thick. Iain took out his knife.

'No,' Kate said.

He eyed the lion critically.

'You are probably right. It isn't much of a skin, poor old boy—'

'Even if it was, you mustn't.'

He looked at her.

'He will be torn to pieces by the jackals, anyway,' he said gently. Kate was close to tears.

'I know. I know. But he would understand that. That is the savage way of nature that he always knew. But if we skin him, we humans, we demean him. We take away his dignity. He fought till the end, didn't he, man wounded him and still didn't break his spirit, did he? We must leave him to himself now, as he would want. Don't you see?'

Slowly Iain put the knife back in its sheath, and stood up. He looked down at the lion.

'Of course I see,' he said.

Kate was crying. She turned her head away so that he should not see her wet face.

'I felt he had to be killed,' she said, 'I thought it was Kilima or him. And now – and now, I'm – I'm desolate.'

Iain put his hands under her arms for the second time and lifted her up. He began to guide her back to the horses.

'He was old, Kate. He might have died slowly, of starvation, as his lameness got worse. Or taken more cattle. Or a toto.'

'Yes,' she said. 'Yes.'

'As it was,' Iain said, turning her face to him, 'he died

free. He died while he still had independence, some magnificence—'

He helped her onto the cob, then he led the mare down to where the lion lay and although she trembled she did not pull away but allowed herself to be shown the lion and, at the end, lowered her nose to within inches of his flanks. Then Iain mounted her, and together he and Kate rode back up the stony slopes to Kilima in silent sympathy.

Ned was still on the veranda. He said,

'I heard a shot.'

'Yes,' Iain said. He leaned over the solitaire board and hopped two marbles over one another. 'We shot the lion.'

'Good for you. Where's the skin?'

Kate was standing close behind Iain. His free hand stole back and touched hers in a tiny gesture of complicity.

'Wasn't worth skinning. Too old.'

'Oh? Pity.' Ned looked up at Kate and grinned. 'Well, that's that, then, isn't it? End of an episode.'

The episode of the lion, and Digby's being found on a mat in a hut in a Swahili town had both happened a year before, two years after their coming to Kenya. Because of the lion adventure and what had grown from it, Kate could now deal with Digby with dispassionate kindness when he needed her, and virtually forget him, as he wished her to, when he did not. Whenever he was in Nairobi, which was not so very often, Iain Hamilton came up to Kilima and brought wine and Turkish cigarettes and any books he could get hold of, and because of a strange certainty in his character, Kate knew he only came up to the farm because he wanted to come; if he had wanted to be anywhere else, he would have been there instead. He was a solitary. He was never seen at the wild parties in the White Highlands or on high society's romping safaris; there was a self-sufficiency in him that had about it an air of disdain for people who needed people.

He talked to her and taught her things, but mostly he listened. He would listen with immense quiet attention to anything she wanted to say to him, so she told him about her childhood and Buscombe, about her family and about the war, and sometimes she would stop herself and say, 'Oh, sorry, *sorry*, I've *told* you all that,' and he always replied, 'Yes, but not quite in the same way, there is always something new.' He had a streak of melancholy in him, and he loved Africa through and through. He went into the Reserve for weeks or months, living in a Kikuyu hut, emerging with notebooks and sketchbooks and his clothes impregnated with the strange rank smoke smell that clung about the native villages. He said lightly, once, that he should like Kate to go with him, because he wanted to study female circumcision and of course that was almost impossible for him, being a man. But he did not say it a second time, and soon after he said it, he vanished again to the district around Njoro which the Kikuyu were colonizing, and Kate went back to never knowing when his car would come jolting up the track, but always knowing that one day it would. Iain always seemed to know where Digby was, so Kate was always alone when the farm totos, who adored him, came tumbling into the house to tell her in a great excited chatter, that Bwana Lion was on his way.

It was inevitable that Kate should eventually arrive at the point when she told Iain about Digby's impotence.

He was sitting cross-legged in front of the fire between the deerhounds he had given her, and watching her with his usual attentiveness, and when at last she had finished he left a little pause and then said,

'Now then. Have you ever been to bed with anybody?'

'No. But, you see, perhaps I am not—'

'How old are you?'

'Twenty-nine.'

He didn't change his position in any way, or even gesture, but simply said,

'Then I think you should begin.'

'I am not sure if I – I mean, Digby seemed to feel – perhaps there is something missing—'

He regarded her gravely.

'Is that so.'

'I am afraid that it might be—'

'So that what was between us a year ago or more after I shot the lion had nothing sexual in it? So that we find no particular or intense pleasure in even sitting tamely in front of the same fire? So that if I reach out like this and close my hand around your bare wrist, you feel absolutely nothing at all and my hand might as well be your own other hand?'

Kate wrenched her hand away violently and said, 'No!'

'Then what did you feel when I touched you?'

'That I might be going to blow up. I *think*.'

He got easily to his feet.

'I think I had better show you what happens next.'

Her face was full of fear.

'Suppose I—'

He stopped to pull her to her feet.

'Suppose nothing. There is nothing odd about you except that you are a virgin at thirty and even that is not odd so much as a pity, given you. I have wanted to take you to bed for a year, and a year is a very long time to wait, particularly for me. Perhaps my patience is evidence of how much I want to do it.'

'Oh, Lord,' Kate said, suddenly scarlet and laughing, 'I feel such an *ass*—'

'In that case,' he said, 'there isn't a moment to lose,' and he swung her up into his arms and as he carried her out of the room, the deerhounds by the fire began to thump their tails approvingly on the floor.

Whether Digby knew that she had become Iain's mistress, she could not say. Nor would she have been able to declare definitely that he would care much, if he did. He wasn't at Kilima more than four months of the year now, having made for himself a job as a safari guide to parties of Germans, which he seemed curiously to relish, pulling up the left sleeve of his bush jacket to show them, with his mocking smile, the two lumpy purplish scars left by German bullets. He seemed to enjoy disconcerting them, yet they always came back for more; he was much in demand. Kate was pleased. It kept him occupied and paid for his drink and his polo, and when he came back to Kilima, he was usually in a good humour and would sometimes even gaily show visitors the scarred sledgehammer with which he had wrecked the flax machinery. She knew better, during those visits, than to confide in him that the coffee was an anxiety to her, and that she had borrowed almost up to the value of the farm in three years. There was more point in telling Iain, which she did, as she told him everything, and in any case, there were so many joys about just now that money could safely be put in its proper place.

She could, because of him, now speak to her squatters and begin to understand their circular and compensatory system of justice. She knew about animals now, and earth and plants and weather. She knew about her body, to her enormous delight, and she was learning – seeing her personality reflected in the mirror his interest held up to it – to like herself.

He made her ride and walk whenever she could.

'You must, if you are to see, really see. And if you don't see, you don't understand, and nothing works.'

'Don't you want to fly?'

He looked at her.

'I can,' he said easily, 'but I don't. You lose the essence, up there—'

The Kikuyu themselves always knew when Iain was at Kilima, and would come up to the farm for grave little ceremonials of welcome and farewell. On one occasion, an old chieftain in the Reserve lay sick and could not come, so Iain took Kate down to the stifling hut where she was presented with gifts of a chicken and a plaited leaf basket of eggs and then stood in the stinking smoking gloom while Iain and the old man talked long to one another. When they came out, the light was fading and they rode up to Kilima together in the indigo shadows, close and companiable, to find Digby on the verandah with a tumbler of whisky.

He was perfectly easy, greeted them both, explained he had another safari beginning in the next few days which was why he was home unexpectedly since he had left a huge supply of ammunition locked up in the store. Kate got drinks for herself and Iain, and they all three sat on the verandah and talked about game in a comfortable sort of way, and then Jogona came in to say that dinner was ready and Digby said, suddenly and furiously,

'I cannot stand that little bugger.'

'Jogona?'

'Cheeky little sod. Always does what I say but with such an air of impudence. Can't we get rid of him?'

'No,' Kate said calmly, 'we can't. He is invaluable. And he is never cheeky to me. Perhaps if you didn't shout at him—'

Digby grunted. Iain said quietly, 'If you'd be good enough to lend me a horse, I should be getting back to Nairobi.'

'How did you get up here, then?' Digby said.

'I came up from the Reserve—'

Digby gave a yelp of laughter. 'Mud-hutting again?'

Iain said coolly, 'Among other things.'

'Going back to Nairobi for a bath, then?'

Iain stood up, easily.

'And to shout at my brother.'

'No dinner?'

'Thank you, no.'

'But you were going to stay. Before you saw I was here.'

'Yes.'

'Then why not stay still? I don't mind.'

Iain waited. Kate could not look at either of them.

'Listen,' Digby said, 'I know perfectly well what's going on. All Nairobi does. It doesn't matter to me, one way or the other. Fact is, old thing,' he said, turning to Kate, 'if you want a divorce, it's fine by me. I can manage on my own now. It might be the best idea. Stay to dinner, Hamilton, and we'll talk about it.'

'No,' Kate said suddenly.

'Why not?'

'Not now. Not out of the blue like this—'

'Good idea, out of the blue. I didn't come home to

528

catch you two in flagrante, I came home to get my ammo. So I'm as off the cuff as you are. Come on, Hamilton, stay and thrash it out.'

Iain said, 'I cannot do that until I have talked to Kate alone—'

Digby looked at him with a knowing look.

'I see. I get it. Well, old thing, Hamilton, or no Hamilton, the offer's still open.'

'Can you not lend Iain the car,' Kate said desperately, 'to get him back to Nairobi?'

'Sorry, old chap, no can do. Need it myself first thing. But you can have a horse by all means. Take that little sod with you and he can bring it back.'

'Thank you,' Iain said quietly.

'I'll go and tell Jogona,' Kate said, 'I won't be a moment. There's a full moon at least—'

Mounted on Kate's now obliging mare, with Jogona trotting happily at her heels, Iain Hamilton set off to ride the fourteen miles by moonlight. Before he left, Digby told Jogona at the top of his voice that when he brought the horse back the next day, he was on no account to ride her, but was to lead her every step of the way. He repeated this command several times and the last time added that if Jogona disobeyed him he would answer for it. Kate pointed out that the mare was hers and Jogona often rode her, but all Digby did was to shout his order once more. As Iain was mounting, he paused and said deliberately to Kate, 'I will be back as soon as I can,' and then he swung himself into the saddle and went off down the track towards Nairobi with Jogona chanting behind him as he ran.

Kate and Digby then proceeded to have dinner. Digby ate moderately and drank enormously, and told

Kate about the last safari and how he thought he had landed a contract for safaris with Newland and Tarlton, and every so often he said things like, 'Good notion, a divorce, don't you think, now we've got things going?' and, 'Seeing as how we've got ourselves sorted out, no point staying married really, is there?' Kate listened mostly, and said No and Yes and Did you really, at intervals while her heart absolutely sang. She said at one point,

'Would we sell the farm? I mean, it is mine, I'd like to keep it—'

And he looked at her squinting through his wineglass and said, 'Well, if you could raise a couple of thousand for me, you do what you like with the rest, old thing.'

He seemed very cheerful, and at midnight she left him and his whisky by the fire and went off to bed, promising to wake him at dawn. She could not wake him at dawn. He had a hangover through which he seemed unable to see or hear her, and there was nothing to be done, but to leave him. He remained in bed and apparently unconscious all day, while Kate went about the farm in a state bordering upon the ecstatic. Every leaf and twig and lump of earth, every squatter woman hoeing in her shamba, every toto hopping and skirmishing in the dust, assumed a new and glorious attractiveness now that it might become hers alone. And every so often, she went across to the edge of the little plateau and looked down into the Reserve, and thought about Iain and the Kikuyu and how much they meant to one another and to her.

In the late afternoon, Digby staggered from his bed and went out onto the verandah in his pyjamas. He was exactly in time to see Jogona, somewhat naturally supposing the bwana to have left the farm as planned some ten or eleven hours before, riding Kate's mare up the track towards the house. Digby's fury was instantaneous and total. He sent Juma for two of the labourers from the coffee mill, and commanded them to drag Jogona off the mare, and to hold him down on the verandah while Digby flogged him with a sjambok, the rhino hide whip the Dutchmen used, which Gustav Behr had given him. When he had flogged Jogona for ten minutes or so, he tied him up with the rein from the mare's bridle and, ordering the two labourers to carry him, locked him in the store. It had a cement floor and contained nothing but boxes of ammunition. It was very cold at night.

When Kate came in from the farm at the fall of darkness, she asked if Jogona were back. Digby, who looked terrible, said a message had come up from Hamilton to say the mare needed a new left fore shoe – she had cast one on the journey down – and that he would send her up with Jogona in the morning. Juma looked terrible too, a kind of grey yellow beneath the blackness of his skin, but he often reacted badly to Digby and Digby was in a horrible humour. They ate dinner almost in silence, Kate preoccupied happily and profoundly with her own thoughts, and then she went to bed early to read and dream and to think about the day when Iain would come back. After dinner Digby went out to the store and found Jogona unconscious on the floor with his reins slackened, so he ordered the night watchman to help tighten them. The night watchman did not want to do this; he said he had heard Jogona wailing that he wanted to die. Digby said that was superstitious nonsense, and propped Jogona up against one of the posts that held up the store roof and lashed him tightly to it. He then summoned the kitchen-toto, a large headed child of ten who carried water and scrubbed vegetables, and told him to watch Jogona until dawn. He then went out and locked the store and went to bed. He could not sleep. At five he got up again and went back to the store, where the toto told him in great consternation that Jogona was dead. Digby sent the toto back to the kitchen, untied Jogona and laid him flat on the floor to feel his chest. There was neither beat nor breath. Digby took the reins off Jogona, and coiled them up and hung them on the wall, then he lifted down two boxes of ammunition, and carried them to the car. He came back to the store, hauled Jogona out of the building and left him slumped against the outside wall. He locked the store, put the key in his pocket, climbed into the car and set off for Nairobi. The kitchen-toto waited until the red tail lights had vanished in the distance and then ran like the wind for Kate's bedroom.

'Msabu, Msabu, Msabu, are you waking, Jogona is dead. Msabu, Jogona is dead, are you waking, Msabu—'

And he was dead, utterly, like a small black sack against the rough wall of the store, and there was not a mark upon him. The store was locked; Jogona was in the clothes in which he had left Kilima and the mare, with four shoes of identical wear, was contentedly in the stable with her mouth full. The syce said she had come back before nightfall and the stable toto had brought her from the house.

'Was there a message from Bwana Lion?'

'No message.'

Jogona was brought to the house and laid on the verandah in the shade. He looked quite impassive. Kate went into the sitting room to think and, on impulse, through to Digby's bedroom to wake him and found the

532

bed tumbled and empty and all his safari clothes gone. She ran back again, calling for Juma.

'Where is Bwana?'

'Gone,' Juma said, his eyes downcast.

'Where, gone where?'

'Nairobi, Memsahib. In the car.'

'When did he go?'

'Just before,' Juma said, 'kitchen-toto came for you.'

The lawn beyond the verandah was filling with the farm people, coming up in the early light, and squatting on the grass, waiting for her. Out of the crowd the night watchman came, and he stood at the foot of the steps and looked up at Kate and said,

'Msabu, Jogona is saying, I am dying, I am dying, and to the kitchen-toto he is saying, I am dead, and he is dead.'

'Why, why, was he ill—'

'No. No. Dying only.'

'But why did he die if he was not ill? Was he hurt? Did he fall from the mare?'

'Not fall, not hurting, only dying—'

Juma sent a runner down to Nairobi to find Iain, and when he came up in the afternoon, driving like the devil, Kate was beside herself with incomprehension and despair. What Juma could not tell Kate he could tell Bwana Lion and then, he knew, Bwana Lion could tell Memsahib about the Kikuyu, in certain circumstances, willing themselves to die. For his own part, he did not think Jogona had made up his mind to die at once, because the loosened reins indicated that he had tried to escape at the beginning, but as the night wore on, he had made up his mind finally and nothing could have moved him from that decision because it was what he wanted with every fibre of his being. So died he had.

533

In Juma's opinion, the flogging was not much, but being made a prisoner was a great deal. To be tied up in that way would weigh heavily on a man's mind.

When Kate saw Iain coming, his arrival was so appallingly different from the one she had planned that sheer disappointment released the tears she had been battling with all day. Iain was very gentle with her and made her sit down and gave her brandy, and then left her with the dogs while he went to talk to Juma and the night watchman and the totos from the stable and the kitchen. He was away a long time and Kate fell asleep, although she never meant to, and he had to wake her, to tell her what he had discovered.

'What will happen?'

'To Digby?'

'Yes.'

'We must report it. Or I must.'

'And then?'

'He will be charged, imprisoned and tried in the High Court in Nairobi.'

She gave a little shudder.

'What can I do for Jogona's family?'

'You could give them some cattle, a cow and a calf perhaps. They will understand the compensation for Jogona.'

'Oh Iain—'

'I know,' he said. He stooped and picked her out of her chair, and sat in it himself, cradling her on his knees.

'Do you know something?' he said. 'There is something so extraordinary, so marvellous about this strange will to die. If you have it, it means you can always elude your captors, you are master of an ultimate freedom, nobody can ever pin your wings. Jogona was in the end as fugitive as the wildest creature. It was as if he dwindled inside the cage Digby put round him until he was able to slip silently out through the bars. We can't do that. We are too civilized.'

Kate was silent for a bit. Then she said,

'I love that in them.'

'Yes.'

'You almost have it.'

'Oh my dear—'

'I know you do,' Kate said. 'I know about being free, for you. There's some part of me that understands that very well. So even if I am divorced—'

He waited.

'Even if I am divorced, and whatever happens to Digby, I shall go on farming here. At least I shall try to.'

'Kate—'

'Mm?'

'Kate, I would if I could—'

'But then you would be somebody different.'

'Yes.'

She got off his knee and stood up.

'I must order dinner. We should start for Nairobi early.'

'Are you coming?'

'Of course,' she said.

Digby was arrested just beyond Kitui and brought back to Nairobi. Kate went down to visit him twice a week for six weeks and took him soap and books and half bottles of whisky, but she avoided the hotels and the Club, and she did not see Iain who, on account of an agreement between them both, had gone up with Ned to the Northern Frontier Province to see, ostensibly, if it would make good safari country for serious-minded, anthropologically inclined travellers.

There was drought that year, and a hundred newly planted acres at Kilima were all dying as the coffee bushes came into flower because they had been planted badly with the tap root bent. Kate took full blame for that. She had ordered it done on the day Iain had taken her for a day-long and wonderful walk down the feathery wattle waved slopes towards the Reserve, among streams and little valleys and pastures fat with white clover, when she should have been supervising the planting. She spent hours on the plateau scanning the sky for clouds and sniffing the air for rain, but when the clouds did come, they went billowing over her shedding never a drop, and dissolved, dry and useless, over the blistering brown wastes of the Rift Valley.

The visits to Digby were difficult because there was so little to say. He seemed quite cheerful, and was certain no more than a reprimand would come his way, since nobody could die after thirty lashes from a man almost too hungover to stand up. In truth he preferred visits from cronies at the Club who could tell him the latest gossip and how much he figured in it. It seemed to Kate, driving up into the hills after seeing him, that he had already withdrawn into not being her husband any more, just as Jogona had withdrawn into death.

Four days before the trial, Iain came unexpectedly, racing the car up the slopes to the house to find her. He had bought a piece of land in the heart of Kikuyuland, at Nyeri – beautiful land in a great rift cleft by a river running down from the Aberdares, magical, untamed country. There was a house, a ramshackle charming old house put up years before by a man who had thought he might build a hotel there, with a special viewing platform above a waterhole where guests could watch the game come down to drink. He was going to take Kate there when the trial was over, and they would camp in the house and spend days exploring. He was alight with excitement. He was going down to Nairobi in the morning to make final the deed of purchase. He had brought champagne and they toasted the new land with tumblers of it. He held her against him and said that when the land was his he would go back to it, back to Nyeri, but that he would return to Nairobi on the day of the trial and he would come to find her, whatever the verdict.

They rose at first light and she went out to the car with him and saw him into it. He was laughing as he set off, roaring over the ruts, and she was too, thinking of the leafy valley at Nyeri with its tree house to spy upon the elephants. When she could not see the car any longer, she went back into the house and looked at their tumbled pillows and the marble swan and the empty champagne bottle, and then she pulled on breeches and boots and went out again, humming into the clear bright morning.

At midday, Iain met Hugh Brett-Williams, who owned the land at Nyeri, in the bar of the Norfolk Hotel and they spread out the deeds to the land on the bar, and held the corners flat with glasses of pink gin and signed, in the witnessing presence of the bartender, the land from one man to the other. Then they took a map into luncheon and weighted it with plates of lamb curry and Iain made marks on it with a pencil, as Hugh talked. They had coffee, and Hugh had brandy, and then Iain folded up all the papers, and put them in the pocket of his bush jacket, and they shook hands and walked amicably together into the street. Hugh mentioned the forthcoming trial – talk in the Norfolk bar was of little else – and because he knew what all Nairobi knew, asked how Digby's wife was bearing up.

'As you would expect,' Iain said. He tapped his pocket. 'I shall take her up there after Friday.'

'Perfect spot,' Brett-Williams said. Near them, someone began to scream. Then someone else shouted something warningly, and there was an uproar of screaming and shouting and through it, a growing bellowing, thundering noise like a runaway train. People began to scatter and dash about, still screaming, and into view came a driverless bullock cart, four demented oxen inspanned abreast, swerving and careering across the street and back again in a wild and terrible swathe of destruction.

Brett-Williams said later that Hamilton shouted to him to get back inside the bar, and then he was across the street like an arrow and onto the nearest oxen's back with the grace of a bullfighter, and the crowd began to cheer rather than scream and then he fell, down between two animals under those thundering sixteen hooves, and when the cart had bolted on, and they ran to take him up, he was quite dead, with his skull kicked in. The only mercy was that he had been killed instantly, with a single blow. This was the one crumb of comfort that Hugh Brett-Williams could pass on to Kate Payne at Kilima who was, in his view, the first and most relevant person to be informed.

When Digby Payne was sentenced to two years' Rigorous Imprisonment on a verdict of guilty of grievous harm, his wife could not be found. She was not in court and when Lars Nordstrom drove up to Kilima, she was not there either, and her houseboys said she had left very suddenly for Mombasa. They were in charge, they told him, until Msabu returned, though they did not know when that would be. Lars leaped into his car to go back to Nairobi, and even while he was jolting down from the hills, Kate was boarding a rusting German steamer that would take her as far as Hamburg. It was by no means the ideal ship, but at least it moved in the right direction, however slowly, and would take her most of the way back to Buscombe.

CHAPTER TWENTY-SEVEN

1925

Catherine and Harry were sitting beneath the tulip tree at Buscombe with a tea-tray between them set on a white painted wicker table. It was very hot. Harry wore a Panama hat with a black grosgrain band, and Catherine a huge shallow straw cone beneath which, in profile, only her chin was visible. On a rug at their feet Rob lay on his front, listening to their talk, while Carlo sat patient and cross-legged, holding a tennis racquet, and waiting for the game he had been longing for since lunch. Rob had seemed to want to play then, but now he had got all absorbed in this talk about Germany and Carlo knew that nagging would be useless since when Rob was really concentrating he simply couldn't *hear* you.

Rob was tall for sixteen and too thin. His heavy brown hair fell constantly into his eyes and when Eleni said to him, 'Oh my dear boy, your *clothes*—', he would look down at himself in genuine surprise, as if astonished to find he had dressed himself at all that morning, never mind achieving a finished result resembling an unmade bed. He was fierce and loving and frequently unhappy with the intensity he was all other things, so that even

540

playing tennis with him could easily mean twenty-five or thirty punishing games, and a walk to Rob wasn't a walk unless it involved more than ten miles and fifty per cent steep slopes in its course. He loved Buscombe and he loved Harry, he loved Carlo and Eleni, although he was fiercely jealous that Carlo was Eleni's son. He hated school, hated the prospect of orthodoxy in his future life, and regarded his father warily as a creature alarmingly without visible passion. Passion ruled Rob like a tempest, lifting him up to exultation and casting him down to despair.

Carlo rode these storms out with him with an extraordinarily good-tempered understanding. Nothing really shook Carlo beyond instances of injustice, when he became inflamed with rage and his already considerable physical strength doubled in power. They had had to pull him – literally – off an enormous member of the school's first fifteen whom he suspected of bullying an unfortunate new boy who wore spectacles and had made the mistake of explaining that he would rather read than play rugby. With his strong physique, open, handsome face and enormous friendliness, Carlo was deservedly popular. He possessed, too, an imaginative sympathy, the capacity to visualize how other people were feeling which was, his half-sister Kate considered, not only his most attractive quality, but the mark of the best sort of man.

It was this understanding that kept him unresentfully quiet while Harry explained why he thought this chap Adolf Hitler a potentially bad thing and Catherine disagreed with him and Rob listened. Harry and Catherine talked all day; you would find them in the conservatory or the morning room, even playing billiards in the tower room – Catherine was quite good and highly competitive – and they were always talking. Catherine said they had years to catch up on and Harry said that they had always had an aptitude for it. It was, for the boys, like having a pair of eccentric liberal, fresh-minded and unpossessive grandparents around, always available and pleasantly objective. When they argued, it puzzled Rob that they did not become inflamed in the defence of their own views, but Carlo saw that the arguing was only a kind of happy, energetic companionableness.

'Of course, Germany will want her revenge,' Harry said.

'What *do* you mean, of course?'

'She instigated the last war, she was all ready for it, to try to shift the balance of power in Europe in her own favour. She started it and then she lost it. She will be back for her revenge.'

'Nonsense,' said Catherine. The coolie hat shook with her vehemence. 'After the last war, there could not be another. It was so much more terrible than anyone could have supposed, that another is unthinkable. Revenge is childish.'

'National pride is childish.'

'Anyway,' said Catherine, 'what has all that got to do with Mr Hitler giving back some self-esteem to the Germans?'

'You take my point exactly. He gives them back their self-esteem through the Nazi Party and they begin to believe themselves invincible once more, and to wish to dominate Europe again.'

Catherine prodded Rob with her toe.

'Are you boys listening? What do you think?'

'I think it is wicked,' Rob said, at once, 'that anyone should dominate anyone else. It's feudal, it's *barbaric*—'

542

'It is human nature,' Harry said.

Rob sat up.

'But it's so *unjust*!'

'Life is unjust.'

'But you *can't* think that! You can't just sit there and say life is unjust and leave it at that. Don't you want to do something about it, don't you want to make the world *better*? Where are your *ideals*?'

'They have worn a little thin in seventy-three years.'

'Mine never will,' Rob said fiercely.

Catherine looked across at Carlo.

'What about yours, dear boy?'

'Awfully dull,' Carlo said cheerfully, 'I want to join the army for a bit and then I want to farm.'

Rob groaned.

'He doesn't even know the difference between ideals and ambitions—'

'Perhaps I think they're the same.'

'Blockhead—'

'When he gets abusive,' Carlo said imperturbably, 'you can always relax because it means he has temporarily lost interest in you.'

Harry was looking across the rose garden where the white dome of Eleni's rose-covered arch shone dramatically against the dark hedge behind it.

'Here's little Bay.'

Bay Martineau was eleven. Her reddish bobbed hair bounced against her cheeks as she ran towards them, and she was dressed, as usual while at Buscombe, in the boys' cast-off clothes. Out of her thin dark father and her small square mother, she had devised for herself a face which Catherine thought would in time be very beautiful indeed, with its straight nose, clear skin and remarkable eyes, shining with life. She spent most

543

school holidays at Buscombe and was, Eleni considered, the most self-sufficient of guests. When she reached the group under the tulip tree, she looked first at Rob rather ardently, and then at Carlo and the tennis racquet and said,

'Oh dear, are you longing?'

'With my usual fortitude. Are those my shorts?'

'They *were*.'

She flopped down on the rug and Harry held out a plate.

'My dear, have a sandwich.'

She took two, beaming.

'You looked as if you were arguing.'

'In a way. We were talking about Germany and about war and then about ideals.'

'Oh,' Bay said with some force, 'politics. Mother and Victoria and Ellen talk politics all day long. They don't want another war because it might stop one of them getting into Parliament, which is their Number One Topic.' She rolled her eyes. '*Imagine—*'

They were all laughing, even Rob.

'Lady Members of Parliament!'

'Lady Astor is,' Bay said reasonably.

'Should you like your mother to be a Member of Parliament?'

'Oh I shouldn't mind. I don't mind what she *does*, it's the talk, talk, talk that gets a bit much. You can't imagine,' she said confidingly, 'what that house is like with *all* women. Even my poor cat is a lady. When we did Other Religions in RK this term, we did the Greek Orthodox Church, and Mount Athos, where the monasteries are and no female creature is allowed. Swan Walk is like Mount Athos in reverse.'

544

'You are a precocious little puss,' Catherine said affectionately.

'I suppose,' Bay said, turning to Carlo, 'that I couldn't lure you to teach me how to hit a backhand while you wait for Rob?'

'I can't resist you. I suppose it's my shorts that do it.'

'They aren't a very good *fit*. But they are tremendously comfortable.' She got to her feet. 'I find that with backhands I tend to shut my eyes at the last minute, and then of course I usually miss.'

'Yes,' Carlo said, getting up too, 'you would.'

'Am I being a pest?'

'No more than usual.'

'That's all right then—'

They went off towards the tennis lawn, amiably bickering, and Catherine and Harry turned their heads to watch them.

'They make me feel most affectionate—'

'I know.'

'Look,' Rob said from the rug at their feet, 'look. About Hitler—'

When Kate had fled home in anguish eighteen months before, Eleni and Charlie had given her an unquestioning welcome, but it was to Eleni that she owed the subsequent privacy inside which she could heal at her own pace. Eleni had never asked her a single outright question, and had managed to muffle Charlie too.

'She will tell us when she wants to. If she wants to.'

'But she didn't before. She turned absolutely in on herself and did barmy things like marrying that Payne fellow.'

'That was not the same.'

545

'Of course it wasn't the same!'

'I mean *she* is not the same. Something very good happened to her in Africa as well as something bad, whatever it was, that put her husband in prison. But she is much stronger herself and she has an appetite for life.'

'Do you suppose,' Charlie said, 'that it could have been a man?'

'Of course it was a man. It always is.'

'Oh, my dearest Eleni—'

She looked at him.

'Am I impossible?'

She smiled.

'Not quite.'

'I feel – I feel so full of *disappointments* sometimes—'

'I know.'

He came up to her and gripped her arms.

'Do I make you unhappy?'

'Sometimes I feel that you are a very long way away but I do not think that is unhappiness. You have given me all this and a family and there is nowhere I would prefer to be and no-one I would prefer to be with.'

He gave her a quick, fierce kiss.

'You have as lovely a nature as our eldest son and that is saying something.'

'May I ask you something?'

'Anything you like.'

'That you are a little more patient with Rob.'

'*Patient?*'

'Yes. Try to see that because his views are not always yours, they are not always wrong.'

'He is an anarchist,' Charlie said.

'No. He is a growing boy. Please. He is experimenting with his mind. Please be patient. Were you not like him as a boy?'

'Never.'

'I don't believe you.'

'All right. I'll try. Now what was the second thing?'

'Could you,' Eleni said, 'however much you long to know, just stop yourself from asking Kate questions?'

Kate said nothing very revealing to anyone for months. She went to London and stayed with Victoria and Sarah, and then with her sister Anna who was struggling a little with motherhood.

'It's so exhausting, they never stop, and Edward hasn't had to change *his* life at all—'

She went to Chesterfield Hill and saw Lilian who had taken up a sedentary and querulous old age in her padded drawing room, complaining that she never saw anyone and nobody needed her, and then asking herself why that should surprise her as nobody ever had. After Lilian, Kate went to St Bartholomew's and found Sylvia still there, tipped for Under Matron, and as single-minded as ever. To them all she spoke of Africa and the farm and going on safari and learning to speak the language, but when it came to the topic of the future, she was evasive, and when Digby's name was mentioned, she was silent. When she had finished her round of visits she went back to Buscombe and, with quiet competence, almost took over the running of the farm.

'Are you *happy* to be here?' Charlie could not help asking her. 'Don't you want your independence again?'

'It is lovely here, just now, with Catherine and Harry and all the children—'

'But—'

'I like it,' Kate said.

'But your *own* farm—'

'It is in good hands,' she said. 'It's quite safe.'

Lars Nordstrom and Ned Hamilton had between

them found her a manager, a young Canadian who would farm the coffee in return for paying no rent. He was so young that Juma, who had refused to leave Kilima, bullied him like an old nanny and, Ned reported, would not let him move a single object in the house from the place Kate had elected for it. Ned had been quite astonishing. He had inherited everything of Iain's in Africa, and he had at once sold off the newly bought land at Nyeri and taken the proceeds to the National Bank of India and paid off Kate's mortgage at a single stroke.

'I am not writing to tell you of this so that you will thank me, but so that you will not worry. It is the least Iain would have wished.'

When it became evident, as it rapidly did, that Kilima could not support itself and young Donald Kean on coffee, it was Ned who paid for the replanting of the farm with tea and pyrethrum. He told Kate it was in the nature of a loan to Kean, but in reality it was, and Kate knew it, a gift to Kilima and therefore to herself. In some way, it seemed to her, Ned Hamilton was trying to compensate her for the marriage he had been witness to, which had failed, and then for Iain's dying, and his generosity was almost too touching to be borne.

'I can't express a hundredth of what I feel,' she wrote to him. 'I go round and round wondering and marvelling at why you should be so amazingly generous, and I always come to the same conclusion – that the why isn't really important, it's the fact that is so wonderful. I am literally bursting with gratitude. I don't know when I shall come back – or indeed if I ever shall – but you have provided me with an alternative that without you I should not have had.'

As it had been once before, on a long ago visit to

548

Cheltenham, it was to Catherine that Kate at last spoke freely. It was difficult to find Catherine alone these days on account of Harry's desire not to miss a moment of her now that he had found her again, and thus Kate had to wait until a day when Eleni drove him into Bath to order new spectacles. When she found Catherine in the rose garden, dead-heading in one of her huge old blue aprons and her coolie hat, and said, 'Oh – oh – may I talk to you?' Catherine replied, without looking up, 'I have been waiting for you to do that for a very long time.' She pulled a second pair of secateurs from her pocket.

'You dead-head too. We can talk as we work. Cut down to the first outgrowing spray with five leaves and a bud at the joint. It will encourage autumn flowering.'

'I wanted to grow English things at Kilima, it's so high, you see. Lavender and sage and thyme, that sort of thing. I expect it's cold enough for bulbs too. But I never got round to it.'

'What did you get round to?'

Kate stopped snipping. She gestured vaguely with her secateurs.

'Oh – I don't know – lots of things—'

'Like?' said Catherine, fixing her with a stern gaze from beneath her coolie hat.

Kate sat down on the grass path between the rose beds and said, 'I should not have married Digby, you see, because Digby should not really have married anybody,' and Catherine said, 'Do you mean that he is what Fred Bradstock would call a nancy boy?' and Kate said no, not that, but he was impotent – and after that it was all extremely easy. They moved to the stone seat Eleni had put in her white bower, and sat beneath the fragrant, airy canopy and Kate went steadily through

549

the whole story from their wedding night at the Ritz to the day, just under two years before, when the news of Iain's death had come up to her at Kilima, and she had panicked and bolted, like a rabbit going down its burrow.

'I could never have married him. He was the least marriable kind of man I ever met, but just knowing he was around was enough and gave me a kind of special energy and appetite. He did love me, I think, in his way, as much as he could love anything that wasn't Africa, but never as I loved him. And yet I know that kind of impulsive, exciting, erratic sort of love affair gets awfully neurotic if you do it for too long. I have tried convincing myself that if he had lived, Kilima would have been my marriage and Iain still, imperishably, my lover, but I don't really believe it. I miss him desperately but I wouldn't not have known him for one second.' She turned to Catherine, who had taken off her coolie hat exposing her neatly coiled still dim blond hair. 'When were you last in love?'

'When I was much younger than you are now.'

'Never since?'

'No. An old maid, my dear Kate, which you, I am thankful to say, will not now ever be.'

'Do you think that I will fall in love again?'

Catherine gave her a long look.

'Given your temperament, I should think it unlikely that you will feel anything quite so strong again. But then of course, if one is worth anything at all, one ceases to want to because one knows the value of its uniqueness. What about that husband of yours?'

'He comes out of prison,' Kate said in quite a different voice, 'in two months' time.'

'And shall you go back to Kenya?'

'I don't know—'

'You must *think*.'

'It's all very well for you,' Kate said, 'comfortably here with no more decisions ahead of you—'

'Rubbish. I am not comfortable here, not in my inmost self. Would you, in my place, like to feel that you had reached the end of a road, however pleasant? I have been back at Buscombe for five years and I am beginning to think that that is far too long. One thing I learned at about your age is that if one postpones decisions because they are difficult, the only person who suffers, ultimately, is oneself.'

'So?'

Catherine gave her a broad smile.

'So I am thinking very hard.'

'Isn't it odd,' Kate said, 'that the people who love this house the most seem to be the ones who have to get away from it? You, me, and I think dear Rob—'

Catherine's face clouded.

'Rob. Nothing will ever be easy for Rob.'

'No.'

'You know that he wants to be a doctor? He wants to go straight to medical school, not to Cambridge as Charlie wishes.'

'And is Father objecting?'

Catherine stood up.

'Sometimes your father resembles your grandfather Robert so closely that I almost despair of the progress of the human race.'

Rob had decided that if he did not tackle his father that summer, it would be too late. He had thought of approaching Eleni first, but had rejected that plan as cowardly, and so, with his usual tactless impetuosity, he bearded Charlie one morning in the library, upon

551

impulse, and declared that the notion of going to university was morally abhorrent to him, when he might be getting on with something socially useful. Charlie blew up and knocked over an inkstand, whose contents flowed in an oily stream across the carpet. They both fell to their knees to mop up the mess with handkerchiefs and continued to shout at each other, crawling about on their hands and knees while the ink crept under their fingernails and around the edge of Rob's shirt cuff. Drawn by the bellowing from the morning room across the hall, Eleni came in to find them thus. She said,

'What is going on?'

Charlie sat back on his heels.

'Rob is refusing the idea of Cambridge outright. He insists he wishes to be a doctor. He ignores – Let me finish!' he roared at Rob's attempted interruption. 'He ignores the fact that he has little or no scientific aptitude and that the social conscience he has suddenly discovered is no more than the woolly sentimentality that affects all adolescents at some stage. He is woefully young for his age and in my view needs three years at Cambridge to even *begin* to be some kind of adult. Do I make myself clear?'

Rob was trembling with rage. His voice rose to an uncertain shout.

'But don't you see, that if I can start training as a doctor next year, I shall have a much better chance of growing up than three years' more fooling about like school—'

'Would it not,' Eleni suggested gently, 'be quite good for you to fool about?'

'No, *no*, that's exactly what I detest about school.'

Charlie rose to his feet and dropped his sodden blue handkerchief into the wastepaper basket.

'You do not seem to realize,' he said to Rob, measuring out each word clearly and heavily, 'that you have a position to maintain, a duty. You will in due course inherit a baronetcy which is three hundred years old. For that, you must have the type and breadth of education necessary to fill that position and carry out that duty. You may not, do you hear me, think only of pleasing yourself.'

'But,' Rob cried in wild despair, 'that is exactly what I am *not* doing! I feel it is my duty to do something else, it isn't a pleasure, it's a torment. For God's sake,' he shouted, losing control entirely, 'talk to Carlo about duty and position, he's as stuck in the mud as you are, but leave me out of it,' and he fled from the room, slamming the door behind him with such vehemence that the portraits hanging either side of it clattered gently against the walls.

'Can you not—' Eleni began.

'My patience is exhausted. I won't have this kind of mindless rebelliousness. He must be made to see. For Heaven's sake,' he swung on her, 'don't you want him to go to Cambridge?'

'Of course I do—'

'What has got into him?'

'I think it was always there. He quite genuinely finds so much of what we have, what our kind of family has, unbearable.'

'Oh he does, does he? So unbearable he is unable to eat and drink and ride and fish here? So unbearable he refuses clothes and money and – and – cricket coaching—'

'He didn't want the cricket coaching—'

'Can't you see that he is no more than an immature fool?'

'I wish I thought it was only that,' Eleni said sadly, 'I wish I thought he would grow out of it.'

He looked at her.

'And you don't?'

She looked back at him.

'No,' she said, 'I don't.'

Kate found Rob in a storm of tears in Charlie's studio, once the old granary. Some instinct had led her there in the first place, and then the sound of wild sobbing guided her up to the first floor where he had cast himself down on the Kashmir rug Charlie stood on before his drawing board. When Rob heard Kate coming he leaped to his feet in horror, presenting her with a wild wet face and hair like a floor mop.

'It's so unfair,' he cried at her without preliminary, waving his arms at the drawing board, at the plans and sketches pinned around the walls, '*he* did what he wanted to! Why won't he let *me*?'

Kate said in a businesslike voice that she thought Charlie felt Rob did not know his own mind.

'He doesn't know *any* mind that isn't an exact copy of his own.'

Kate walked to the huge north window and looked out to the corn fields rippling golden away from her. It was going to be a good harvest.

'Look,' she said, 'I'll make some kind of bargain with you.'

He said nothing.

'Don't sulk,' she said without turning round.

'I'm not sulking.'

'Very well, then. I'm not going to support you against Father in this Cambridge business. He is right you should go, even if he is right for the wrong reasons. You

554

do need time to reflect before you decide finally because however old you may feel, I am afraid sixteen is not much more than a child—'

'But, *Kate*—'

'Let me finish. When you have been to Cambridge, I will give you my wholehearted backing in whatever you want to do next. I'll take Father on single-handed for you, if necessary, as long as what you want to do isn't actually *criminal*. So will Aunt Catherine. We have talked it over.'

'But she is old—'

'She is an extremely healthy and youthful seventy-five with opinions Father respects.'

Rob gave a shuddering sigh.

'I'll think about it.'

'There mustn't be any more rows.'

'But—'

'It isn't fair on anyone else. Think of Eleni.'

'She sides with Father—'

'Only because she thinks it best for you.'

'All right,' he said, 'all right, all right,' and he rushed past her and clattered down the wooden staircase into the sunshine.

Even at nine, Thomas Taverner was the most practical of his family. To him the mechanics of things were of absorbing interest – and efficiency came as a comfortable second nature, so that he was the only one entrusted regularly with messages. During the school holidays, when the post came after breakfast and after luncheon, he would take all the letters to his father, who sorted them out, kept his own, and sent Thomas off round the house delivering everyone else's. This not only pleased Thomas as a job, it allowed him to know, as all efficient people wish to know, what was going on. Discreet though he was with the information he gained, his curiosity was sometimes aroused to a point where he could not keep his mouth shut, and so when, on 1 September, an airmail letter came for Kate with uncommonly interesting stamps of zebras on it, he said to her,

'Unless you want those very much yourself, I would extremely like them. Are you going back to Africa?'

Kate was in her bedroom, the room that had once been Elizabeth's and which looked, as both the great bedrooms did, south over the drive towards the lake. She was sitting by the window doing farm accounts, and she took the thin letter from Thomas with a clutch of apprehension.

'Of course you may have the stamps.'

'If you went back to Africa, you could send me more. At birthdays and things like that.'

He watched her put her thumb under the flap of the envelope.

'It's better if you use a knife. Shall I show you?'

'Bossy boots,' Kate said.

Thomas took no notice. He slit the envelope neatly with the ruler lying among Kate's papers and handed it back.

'There.'

'Now, I suppose as your reward you wish to know what is in it.'

Thomas settled himself cross-legged on the floor.

'Yes please.'

Kate opened the letter. It was in Digby's handwriting and it was not long. She read it through twice, then she put it down on top of the milk yield lists and said,

'Digby says he does not want to stay in Kenya any more. He has met a man who has found a farm in

556

Rhodesia, which is further south in Africa than Kenya, and he wants Digby to go in as his partner. It is a ranch farm with huge herds of cattle. Digby needs seven thousand pounds to put into this farm, so he wants me to sell the farm in Kenya.'

Thomas thought for a bit.

'Is the farm your farm or his farm or both your farm?'

'It is mine.'

'Then don't sell it.'

'No,' said Kate, 'I don't think I will.'

'If it was me,' Thomas said, 'I would like a farm in Africa.'

'I do like it.'

'Then why are you here?'

'Because I ran away from some other things I didn't like.'

Thomas got up.

'I did that at school. The first time I was wicket keeper, I got hit by the ball, really socked, so I just walked away. They made me walk back again.'

'The problem is,' Kate said, 'where to find seven thousand pounds—'

'If you went back to Africa, I could come and visit you which would be very, very nice for me.'

'Thomas,' Kate said, 'go away.'

He was not in the least affronted.

'All right. I've got Uncle Harry's letters here, and Aunt Catherine's—'

Kate got up.

'Give me Aunt Catherine's, Thomas, there's a dear, I'll take them to her—'

'Of course you must go back,' Catherine said, 'at once. In the first place, it is time you did and in the second,

557

you cannot refuse to sell and release some money if you don't even want the farm yourself. That would be very wrong.'

They were standing by the north window in Catherine's bedroom where she liked to breakfast and look out at the rose garden. Kate had rushed straight to her with the letter.

'Suddenly,' Kate said, 'I am wild to be back there.'

'All that surprises me is that you have not felt wild *before*.'

Kate sat down in one of the low chairs that had lived in this room since Catherine's girlhood.

'All the time Digby was in prison, I felt, oh, sort of suspended, as if life had stopped for a while. But now he is out and being busy in Nairobi again, I suddenly want to be back there to stop him, at the very least, from selling anything that isn't his to sell. But seven thousand pounds . . .'

Catherine sat down opposite Kate. She wore what had now almost been her uniform for twenty years, a longish belted buttoned dress of buff drill vaguely military in appearance, full skirted and bristling with pockets. Catherine had designed the original herself and had had the first one made by an Indian tailor in Damascus. As a concession to life at Buscombe, she adorned these uncompromising garments with strings of lumpy quartz or amber beads, or enormous Arab and Turkish brooches of yellowish silver studded with cornelians and turquoises. Today she had wound a black knotted camel tether around her waist and pinned at her throat a huge blue pottery scarab set on a silver disc. She said,

'I have a proposal to make.'

'No,' Kate said quickly, 'you must not offer—'

'Listen to me. It is a bargain. I will lend you the money to give Digby if you will let me come to Kenya with you.'

Kate said, 'But, *Aunt Catherine*—'

'I am seventy-five, I know. But I am fiendishly well. I could probably give you five or ten years at least of usefulness, and if I become an old nuisance, there will be no nonsense, you must simply ship me home.' She paused and then she said in quite a different tone, 'Please.'

Kate slipped from her chair to kneel on the floor by Catherine.

'I should love it, you know I should, but *why*—'

Catherine flushed a little, hesitated and then said crossly,

'Because Harry has made a perfect fool of himself and asked me to marry him. I have said no, of course, and now I fear he will be extremely sad and we shall not be able to live here together companionably any more. It was so *stupid* of him. Men are so silly about romance, they never *think*. In any case, I was beginning to fidget here and I like the sound of Kenya.' She looked at Kate. 'I like natives, you know.'

Kate's eyes were shining.

'Uncle Harry proposed to you!'

'Yes. Last night in the conservatory. He wants us to buy a house near here and live happily ever after like two old apricots on a sunny wall, he said. He must be mad. Those moments are long past. I told him so—'

'You *told* him—'

'I told him,' Catherine said, her voice rising at her remembered indignation, 'that he was the only man I had ever loved or wanted to marry, but that I was now quite beyond wanting to marry even him. I vastly enjoy his company and feel a great affection but that is nothing like sufficient reason for marrying. I don't *need* to marry, you see.'

'Poor Harry.'

'He will get over it. You know what men are. It was probably an impulse—'

Kate was laughing.

'Of *course* you may come to Kilima with me. I should love it.'

Catherine stood up.

'Then waste no time. Telegraph Digby. And that nice sounding Hamilton man. Oh my dear, how wonderful, off again—'

On the bench below the obelisk by the lake, Bay Martineau found Harry gazing mournfully at nothing in particular. She was a habitually cheerful child, and so she sat down by him and showed him a broken pheasant's egg she had in her pocket and explained about the weed cutting going on in the stream to give the water greater flowing space before the winter rains. Harry, who could normally be relied upon to be very interested in this type of news item, remained looking abstracted and sad, so much so that he induced an abrupt pang of unhappiness in Bay and reminded her of something she had been trying not to think about.

'I have to go back to London on Friday. I hate London. I only like it here.'

'So do I,' said Harry, 'but not everybody seems to. It is incomprehensible to me.'

'I feel all shut up in London. I mean we play games and things, horrible lacrosse, but that isn't the same at all as being able to wander about where one likes all over the fields and things. And I really do like this house. It has a nice smell. Our house in London smells of ink and everyone is always so terrifically busy, rushing about and banging doors. If I bang a door here, Uncle Charlie growls at me like a tiger.'

'My dear little girl,' Harry said, 'would you leave me? Would you be a kind child and let me be alone?'

Crestfallen, Bay slipped from the bench and stood, hesitating, wondering whether to kiss, as was her instinct, that sad and handsome old face. Reluctantly, she decided against it, and went away on tiptoe out of a kind of intuitive respect for whatever was the matter with him. When she reached the corner where the path left the lakeside and ran up through the shrubbery to the house, she turned and looked back. He was sitting quite still, bolt upright with his soldierly old back like a ruler, but for all that he was so hung about with a miasma of misery that Bay could imagine she saw it, grey and clinging, like a veil wreathing his Panama hat.

CHAPTER TWENTY-EIGHT

1929

In the spring of 1928, at the age of eighteen, Rob gained a place at King's College, Cambridge, to read History and Economics. He was to go up the following October, just after his nineteenth birthday, a year or two older than most undergraduates, in the regulation uniform of tweed jacket and flannel bags, with the regulation library of volumes of poetry. At the same time, Carlo, at not quite eighteen and well over six foot, was to enter Sandhurst as an officer cadet, Thomas was to embark upon his first term at Winchester and Melina was to have a change of governess, having lost her battle to go to boarding school, on the grounds that, at ten, she was too young. She had contended that it was better to be too young at school than too bored at home.

'Is she bored?' Charlie asked Eleni.

'Of course not. But with all the boys going off, she thinks she is missing an adventure.'

For Rob, the adventure never began. In the middle of September he began to suffer an inexplicable chilliness which was followed by a burning fever and agonizing pains in his knees and shoulders. To Charlie's horror, haunted as he was by the memory of his own destructive illness in the very room to which Rob was now taken, the high temperature and the pain were only the beginning of a savage attack of rheumatic fever. In the dressing room, which looked north over the shrubbery where Meggy Bradstock had once hidden to wish her lover a furtive happy birthday, Rob lay restlessly in a condition of the extremest misery, his joints huge and hot and wincingly tender, unable sometimes to bear even the weight of the blankets. With a passionate sorrow, Charlie spent hours and hours by his bedside, reading *Middlemarch* to him, and Shakespearian sonnets, and describing, with an imaginative tenderness Rob had never seen in him before, the early autumn world beyond the window.

Occasionally, in moments when the fever and the pain subsided just a little, Rob wondered, dully and confusedly, why Charlie should sit there, day after day, suddenly so gentle and intuitive. His flexible draughtsman's hands were, of all the hands in the household, the most sure and delicate upon Rob's screaming scarlet flesh, his patience quite extraordinary in a man who usually relied upon his wife to induce in him even the smallest degree of endurance.

'My poor old boy,' Charlie would say over and over, his voice full of pity, 'it is too unjust. My poor old boy.'

The bitter echoes of Charlie's own illness grew worse. Rob's fever would not subside, there was an anxiety that the heart muscle was inflamed and a rash of scarlet blisters spread down his legs. As once with Charlie, the household drew into itself to concentrate upon the invalid, relays of nursing watches, trays of milk and glucose and fruit juice, anxious vigils by windows waiting for the doctor's now daily visits. Even Melina forgot to glare with suspicion at her new governess as she had intended, and found herself not only liking her quite by mistake, but relying upon her for comfort and sympathy, when misery broke helplessly through French irregular verbs and the great rivers of the Orient.

It was five weeks before Rob began to mend. He was as poor a convalescent as his father had been, as indignant to have been ill and as fretful and resentful at the failure of perfect health to return at once. His future tutor at King's sent him a parcel of books, which he read with a kind of ferocious hunger, but his supply of energy was pitiful. Moving about a room was only achieved at a snail's pace, and the stairs were a challenge only to be attempted twice a day, with a great deal of help and frequent stops. His state of mind was worse than his state of body. He could hardly bear to read the cheerful letters from Carlo and purposeful ones from Thomas that arrived at Buscombe while plainly, through incipient tears, burning to know how they did.

In the spring of 1929, after a gruelling winter for them all, Charlie took Rob to Spain and early sunshine. It was a peculiarly successful holiday. Charlie, Rob discovered, was extraordinarily knowledgeable on architectural history which made visits to the great Moorish cities memorable – Rob was never to forget the particular magic of a bright April afternoon at the Alhambra, standing gazing down through a fretted marble screen into a little secret court, while his father's voice beside him brought it all to life. Spain had another interesting aspect just then, being in political turmoil on the edge of becoming a republic. This fired Rob enormously, and led to the kind of rich political discussion he so relished. To his surprise, his father seldom lost his temper, contenting himself with telling Rob that his own raw socialist notions were at best, impractical. Rob

retorted that he at least believed in the essential goodness of humankind, at which Charlie would sigh and
his face become so full of a peculiarly poignant sadness
that even Rob, commonly so clumsy in the grip of his
passionate opinions, turned the conversation back to
the Cathedral at Valladolid or the chapel in the Escorial.

They were away three months. Charlie brought
Rob home in triumph, brown, heavier, hungrier and
energetic. Cambridge was patient and would allow
Rob to take up his place a year late. He read intensely
all summer, played tennis with Thomas, taught Bay
and Melina chess and backgammon, seemed more at
peace with the world than since his childhood. In
September, the temperature dropped suddenly; there
were early frosts and wild winds and the tender things
in the garden, taken by surprise, drooped darkly in the
borders. Rob, packing his possessions into his old
school trunk ready for the carrier to take it to Bath
Station en route for Cambridge, became aware of a
sinister sweating coldness around his head and neck
and a creeping ache across his shoulders. It was true
his room was cold, the little top floor room that had
been his since he was a baby, but his inner coldness
was more than could be accounted for by that. By
nightfall, he knew he had a temperature and before the
week was out, he was back in the dressing room with a
second bout of rheumatic fever.

Carlo, who had been going up to the Highlands for a
week's early stalking before Sandhurst began again,
cancelled Scotland and came home. Things, as they
were wont to do, steadied themselves on his arrival and
the emotional temperature of the household dropped by
visible degrees. Even so, Carlo could not avoid noticing
a frailty in the air for the first time, as if those rock solid

people of his childhood had developed fissures and cracks. Eleni, stalwart, indefatigable, optimistic Eleni, looked tired, moved a little less lightly, and her face in repose fell into lines Carlo had not noticed before. Charlie was wound up, no other phrase for it, by Rob's second illness, by the aimlessness of his own life that Rob's illness reminded him of so unavoidably, by the threat of income tax being put up to at least four and sixpence in the pound, by his declining interest in the model farm. Melina was a monkey and dear old Thomas no trouble at all, thank God. He had decided that a modern chap ought to be able to cook, so he took himself off to the kitchen every morning and Cook, who had at first tried to shoo him out, said he was a natural and would have her out of a job in no time. He made cakes mostly, because they were what he preferred to eat.

'When Rob is better,' Carlo said to his mother, having found her distractedly addressing envelopes for a charity committee and forced her to stop and sit peaceably for a while, 'you and Father should have a holiday.'

'But Melina—'

'Melina is eleven. She has Miss Thingummy—'

'Goddard—'

'Goddard, and you can have Bay to keep her company.'

'So dull for Bay. Bay is fifteen.'

'Nonsense.'

'Carlo darling, it is so difficult to leave.'

'Only because you have been here far too long.'

Eleni pulled a face.

'The army has made you very commanding.'

They were in the conservatory, where the September sun fell yellow upon the geraniums Fred fed so lovingly upon horse manure, and which responded by growing flowerheads the size of cauliflowers. Carlo got up from his chair, and walked about a bit, and then came back to his mother and said without preliminary,

'Do you feel you belong here?'

'Yes,' said Eleni.

'Why?'

'Because of your father and because this was my refuge, where I fled.'

'I'm half-Greek,' Carlo said, 'I look it but I don't feel it. Should I go to Greece?'

'Of course. One day, any day that you want to.'

'I don't even speak it—'

'You can learn. I'll teach you.'

Carlo looked at her.

'We are sort of refugees here, aren't we, you and I.'

Instantly, Eleni's brow puckered.

'Oh my dear, do you feel that?'

'I can't help feeling, in this house, all the Taverners who have lived in it, all the history and life and tradition, all the things Rob hates so much. I love it, but I am not really part of it. Perhaps my son will be—' He stopped, shook himself briskly and said, 'Talking of Rob, I've an idea.'

'Oh tell me—'

'He should go to Kenya. He ought to have a year or two in that sunshine. He could stay with Kate and preach socialism to her tea-pickers.'

'Yes, yes, but Cambridge. Father so wants him to go to Cambridge and now that he has been good and agreed—'

'Perhaps,' Carlo said, 'Cambridge will wait.'

Just before Christmas, a party of Taverners took Rob down to Southampton to see him off for Africa. Kate had been enthusiastic at his coming as long as he refrained from encouraging insurrection at Kilima, and King's had agreed to delay his place until he was properly strong once more. Carlo, newly commissioned a second lieutenant, arrived in his new Glosters uniform, escorting Bay who had played truant from the St Paul's School for Girls' Carol Service. She wore a narrow grey flannel coat with a small fur collar – 'Dyed bunny, I fear. Does it look very dyed? Or very bunny, for that matter—' and on her dark red curls framing her remarkable face, a close fitting grey felt hat with a silver arrow pinned to the side – 'Woolworths, would you believe? Wasn't it a find—'

Carlo had expected her to be very subdued on the train down from Waterloo, because she had, after all, been trailing about after Rob like a loving puppy since she was very small. It was only to be expected that the prospect of a separation of probably two years would prove very casting down. But she was so entranced at the thought of the Senior Choir singing *In Dulce Jubilo-o-o* without her, so pleased to be part of the little adventure of going to Kenya and so gratifyingly impressed by Carlo's appearance, that there seemed to be not a cloud on her mind.

'Mother is starting a new movement. It's called the Quarter Club. The aim is to get a quarter of the members of Parliament to be women. She's got a hundred and ninety members in ten days and they keep coming round and oh dear, not a grin among them. Is this a boat train?'

'Yes—'

'Do you wish you were going?'

'In a way—'

'What do you mean?'

'I mean,' said Carlo in a sudden rush of confidence, 'that I wish I was going abroad too. But in my case, to Greece.'

'Then why don't you? I'll come with you. We could start a revolution. Is there a king to overthrow?'

'You listen to Rob too much.'

Bay's face changed.

'I know,' she said reverently.

'I don't want to go to Greece to overthrow the King. I just wonder if I'll feel Greek when I get there.'

Bay looked at him.

'You look Greek.'

'And you look like a dyed rabbit.'

She collapsed in giggles.

'Carlo. Show me how to salute. Like this?'

'No. Hand at the wrong angle, heavens, Miss Martineau, civilians will think you are a *sailor*, dammit. No, like this.'

'I hope you are commander of the whole English army one day and then you can say to the stuffed shirts, sucks to you, I'm Greek.'

'What an extremely vulgar expression,' Carlo said in Eleni's voice.

'I know,' she said pleasedly.

'I could also tell them that I was born before my parents were married.'

Her eyes grew huge.

'*Were* you?'

'Yes.'

'Do you mind?'

'On and off.'

'On or off today?'

'Off.'

She looked at him, her head on one side.

'Most people in my form have a crush on you.'

He blushed.

'They've never seen me.'

'Yes, they have. I've shown them photographs. Is this Southampton?'

'Yes.'

'What do we do now?'

'We look for a tall skinny chap in a solar topee and crumpled shorts holding a spear and a flywhisk and that will be Rob.'

Rob, Kate realized within days of his arrival, was going to need an occupation. He was not in the least practical so, while being deeply and genuinely interested in the farm and its workers, and all the little gardening experiments with which Catherine surrounded herself, he was not in fact any use at any of them. Even teaching him to drive was going to present a problem since, if he was distracted by a particularly urgent train of thought, he was inclined to release all pedals and take both hands off the wheel, simultaneously, in order to gesticulate. The natives loved him at once because, from the beginning, and long before he learned to speak their own language, he was perfectly happy to spend hours squatting with them, apparently profoundly interested in the interminable seesaw of their bargainings over cows and compensation.

Kate took him down to Nairobi and bought him the brightly coloured corduroys and silk shirts that were currently *de rigueur* for the colony's young bloods. He wore them with the marvellous indifference he displayed towards all clothes, and after a few days of life with him around the farm, they assumed the same jumble sale air of the rest of his wardrobe. It was when he had used a scarlet silk shirt to bind up the hand of one of the tea pickers who had burned her hand badly on the drying drum, that what Rob might do struck Kate. She made arrangements for him to assist as unpaid orderly in the casualty room at the Native Hospital in Nairobi, and after a month of gashes, worms, emergency births and poisonings had passed beneath his fascinated gaze, he was given the old ammunition store as a surgery and allowed to dose and bind up the labourers and squatters of the farm, and their families as long, Kate made it plain, as their ailments or wounds were only of the simplest kind. Midwifery, she said, was on no account to be attempted, despite his eagerness, without her assistance.

'I am certain he does no harm,' she wrote staunchly back to Charlie, 'but I am not sure that he does great good except that the Kikuyu, loving him as they do, bring him problems that would just otherwise fester in their huts. He takes it terribly seriously. I have bought miles of bandage in one month and Catherine's newest idea is to make salves and ointments from her herb garden. You should *see* the garden under her care. We are the horticultural talk of Nairobi and two Americans came up yesterday just to photograph the freesias.'

Catherine was in her element. Beneath the blue gums to the north of the house was a kind of spring paradise now – primroses as well as the freesias, creamy clusters of narcissi, violets and scillas and hyacinths. She had lured two labourers away from Kate's new and highly successful pyrethrum acres, and put them on to digging her a pond, fed by a stream from the surrounding forests, which was now fringed with bright red canna lilies and blue and white irises, and the surface covered with the huge creamy pink cups of water lilies. She had planted magnolias and jasmines, and whole hedges of hydrangea along the drive, and the verandah was frothing with flowers in tubs and urns and winding themselves up the supporting posts. In addition, she had become passionately interested in Minorcan hens, was a great friend of all the old ladies of the shambas, and in due season, she made quantities of jam from the raspberries and blackberries she had planted, which she sold to the Norfolk Hotel in Nairobi. Her uniform of buff drill frocks had given way to bush shirts, breeches and gaiters and a huge Terai hat with a leopard skin band twisted around it; when she went down to Nairobi she was inclined to add a tie for formality and a string of beads for femininity to this costume, quite impervious to Kate's laughing suggestion that she looked dangerously like Radclyffe Hall.

They made up an extremely happy household, those three refugees from Buscombe, on their African ridge. Disinclined for high and raffish society – though Catherine, Kate observed, was an avid collector of gossip – they lived for and at Kilima, where ends never more than just met and Kate's only regret was that she saw little hope of paying Catherine back her seven thousand pounds. Catherine was quite unconcerned; having met Digby briefly in the Muthaiga Bar, she told Kate that she thought his payoff was cheap at the price.

'Just make sure he can't come back for more, that's all. He has a dangerously Micawberish look to him. I can't think why you don't get a divorce and marry the nice Hamilton man.'

To marry Kate was plainly what Ned Hamilton longed for. Rob, who thought him dull and worthy, said that he looked at Kate like a dog hoping for chocolate. He had sold off his brother's trading interests, but had kept the safari company, which he ran with tremendous attention to detail, and little imagination, so that it was enormously popular with German professors and Scandinavian spinsters and he was very successful indeed. He came up to Kilima every weekend that he was not away, bringing wine and imported soap and books for Kate, and what she called 'garden loot' for Catherine, boxes of any plant he thought might interest her. One time it was stapelias, which fascinated Rob, and he spent hours coaxing them to try morsels of liver pâté left over from dinner. Every time Ned came, kind and friendly and good humoured, Kate would look at him with gratitude and affection and notice regretfully for the thousandth time, how almost everything about him was but a leaden echo of his brother's golden flair.

Rob became, and remained, remarkably well. He made a friend in Nairobi, a young Indian lawyer called Hari Dayal, who had strong left-wing ideas and felt that the Indians in Kenya were very poorly treated. Together, he and Rob started a tiny newspaper, no more than a smudgy pamphlet, which they printed on an ancient press produced by one of Hari's numerous relations, in a shed behind a duka owned by another relation, in the Nairobi bazaar. The paper was called *Brotherhood*, and the first copy was sent to Ramsay MacDonald, as a tribute to his being elected Prime Minister of England. Both Rob and Hari were genuinely disappointed when MacDonald failed to acknowledge this journalistic bombshell. It was about this time that Rob stopped talking about wishing to be a doctor and started on other themes, such as newspapers or the Foreign Office. Kate and Catherine heard him out with tolerance. Often, Rob brought Hari up to Kilima, a neat, bespectacled, scrupulously polite young man, who only ate vegetables and pulses and was much shocked to see Kate drinking gin. He liked helping Catherine in the garden, and was very deft with her little seedlings, delivering long political diatribes the while in his soft and mannerly voice. It was while they were thus occupied, over a tray of delphiniums Catherine was planning to plant out in a specially dug trench full of manure from the farm oxen, that Catherine abruptly put her hand to her breast and said,

'Oh dear – how tiresome – stupid really – but I can't seem to breathe—'

'Perhaps you must sit down—'

'Perhaps,' she said, looking at once puzzled and irritated, and allowed him to lower her to the lawn, where she sat with her back against the marble font, and her head in the shadow cast by the swan. She could not seem to see very well, there was a curious buzzing in her ears and her palms prickled as if she had held handfuls of bees. She said muzzily, faintly, 'Kate, Kate—' but Hari had already sprinted to find her, calling and calling, running through the house like the wind. She was in the stables, worrying about a pony with horse sickness, and she gave one look at Hari's face and came with him.

'Where, where?' she cried.

'In the garden, by the white bird – we must go quickly—'

In the few minutes he had been away, a silent instinctive circle of farm people had gathered on the lawn around Catherine. She sat propped as Hari had left her, except that her head had fallen forward and she seemed to be sagging against the font, too weak to hold herself upright. Even before they stretched her out and opened her bush shirt, Kate knew that she was dead, and as she laid her ear to Catherine's ribs, Rob came running silently and knelt on her other side and when Kate lifted her head, he took her hands across Catherine's body and held them tightly, without speaking. A gentle murmur rose from the watchers, and they softly came in closer, like a living rampart of sympathy, so that Kate and Rob and Catherine were entirely circled by them, and as they moved, there was a flash of wings and a sapphire blue, scarlet throated East African starling alighted upon the marble swan's back and looked gravely down upon them.

They buried her in her spring garden.

'Now, mind there is no weeping and wailing,' – Catherine had written in a letter left for Kate and dated a year after her arrival at Kilima. 'Just you remember that I have had here with you the happiest time of my life, which I shall look forward to resuming when you join me in heaven. Tell old Harry he was the only man I ever loved, if he seems to need to know. I shall leave everything I have to you and to Victoria, because between you, you did as young women all I should have done and will have rich lives on account of it. If I die here, bury me in the spring garden, and when you next go home, plant something at Buscombe for me. Magnolia grandiflora, I think. Put it in sight of my bedroom windows. I'm sorry you will have the clearing up of me and my affairs to do, but there's no way round that. With much love to you, Katharine, from Catherine.'

Her affairs were very simple. The shares from her mother's family coalmines, which had provided her income, were divided between Kate and Victoria, her furniture and books were to remain at Buscombe where they had always been, and what she referred to as the unmemorabilia of her travels, the drums and camel saddles and animal skins and bizarre jewellery, were to be divided up, turn and turn about, among the children.

It was a loss that lay leaden on Kate for weeks and weeks. She missed her in the minutiae of daily life with an unvarying pain that simply would not diminish, and was constantly catching herself running to Catherine's room, or into the garden to tell her things. To add to the grief, Rob was becoming a nuisance. Besides his newspaper he was beginning to hold small public meetings in which he and Hari denounced the colonial administration of Kenya. There was a scuffle at one and an unpleasant episode between an Indian storekeeper and a policeman which ended with Rob, in a kind of hysteria, abusing the policeman and Kate being summoned to the police headquarters in Nairobi. She paid bail for Rob, and went to visit the storekeeper in his cell; he had gone to Rob's meeting believing it to be about the founding of some junior chamber of commerce which would help small shopkeepers such as himself, and had found himself helplessly caught up in an angry political scrimmage. Kate paid bail for him too, and took Rob home to Kilima in angry silence. She thrust him into a chair in the sitting room, poured herself a drink and then said, as a preliminary trumpet blast,

'Now.'

He said sulkily, 'Now what?'

'You have gone too far. You do not understand the complexity of society here, nor what people such as poor little Ram Singh really need. I won't have you behaving like a political agitator, first because you don't know what you are talking about, and second because you are dangerous and about to make life much worse for the people you profess to help.'

Rob began to shout. He said she was as bad as the police, that she was too right wing to care about the *people*, that the white administration of Kenya was exploiting the Africans and Indians, and that the days of overbearing imperial behaviour were over. It was difficult, Kate found, not to shout back.

'All this demonstrates,' she said in a voice tight with control, 'is that you are politically and in most other ways shockingly immature. It is time you went home and went to Cambridge.'

Rob sagged.

'It is too late. I am too old. I shall be twenty-three soon and most undergraduates are only eighteen—'

'You behave as if you were eighteen.'

Rob covered his face with his hands. He stayed like that for a long time and then he took them away and said in a voice that was little more than a whisper,

'But Kate, I *do* care. I care about people like Ram Singh, I honestly do. That is what our meetings are for. I can't bear to see people like him oppressed by more powerful people. I'm really sorry he went to jail, that he got beaten up—'

Kate said, on a long sigh, 'We'll go home together.'

'What – what about here?'

'I'll only be away a few months. They can manage without me for that time. It isn't the picking season after all. And I'd like to plant Catherine's tree. Rob – Rob, you *must* go to Cambridge, old or not, if they will still have you. For your own good as well as everyone else's, you have to grow up.'

'I know, I know,' Rob said bitterly, 'I've got to grow up to be a good little baronet.'

*   *   *

They went home, dashingly, by plane, on the newly opened Cape Town to London run, which Imperial Airways had just started, and which took ten days. The African part of the journey was extremely exciting, with the navigator sitting with a map on his knee. The plane, a Hanno, broke down at Alexandria, which gave them a chance to drive out to the barracks where both Harry and Tommy had swatted at the Egyptian flies, and when they finally landed at Croydon, there was Carlo to greet them, twice the size he had been three years before it seemed, and in uniform.

'Oh, my dear,' Kate said, hugging him and glancing at his shoulder. 'Oh Carlo, a *lieutenant*—'

'A month ago. They had to, because my size made all the other ensigns look silly, and they complained. I say, Rob—'

They looked at each other for a long moment.

'Hello—'

'You look – pretty fit—'

'Oh yes—'

'Kenya suited you—'

'Oh yes—'

'Better than Gravesend, where I've been stuck—'

'Not difficult—'

They grinned.

'What do we do now?' Kate asked.

'We climb into my new Ford with which I am hopelessly besotted and I drive you to Buscombe.'

'Buscombe—'

'Any news? Any news from Buscombe?'

'More of the same, really. Father isn't too good, wheezing a lot, Mother is running every committee in the county, Thomas has decided to be an engineer and

Melina is in a rage because she said no-one ever told her that boarding school would mean she had to play hockey. I say, let me carry that.'

'And London?' Kate said, hurrying beside him. 'What news from London?'

Carlo stopped walking abruptly.

'Oh, I knew there was something I had to tell you. Lilian Creighton died and left everything to Anna. Apparently Anna is now frightfully rich and Father is in a ferment about it. Can't think why. I say, I am so pleased that you are home.' He swung on them both his wide and affectionate smile. 'Aren't you pleased? To be home, I mean, to be going back to Buscombe?'

CHAPTER TWENTY-NINE

1933

In the year that Adolf Hitler was appointed Chancellor of Germany, Rob Taverner at last took up his place at King's College, Cambridge. Instead of the volumes of poetry that he might have had on his bookshelves had he gone up as intended at eighteen, he now had a copy of Leon Trotsky's *History of the Russian Revolution*, Jung's *Modern Man in Search of a Soul* and Cardinal von Faulhaber's anti-Nazi treatise. His rooms were large, and dark with old panelling, the sitting room shared with a tall, slight, fair young man called Douglas Barr Taylor, a mathematician who had just been to the University of Göttingen in Germany, on sabbatical leave from Cambridge. As most undergraduates were public-school men, Douglas Barr Taylor had heard of Rob from a cousin of his who had been a Wykhamist too, and knew about Buscombe and the baronetcy. This caused Rob obscure irritation until he noticed, in the pile of books Barr Taylor had tossed onto the ancient sofa, another copy of Trotsky's *History of the Russian Revolution*. At the time, Rob said nothing of this, but when after a week of getting used to living with one another, he found a pamphlet edition of Marx and

Engels' *Manifesto of the Communist Party* lying on their communal table, and evidently much read, he asked Barr Taylor outright what his politics were. Douglas eyed him coolly.

'I'll tell you,' he said, 'when I know you better.'

They had been put together because they were both older than the average. The drinking and horseplay sessions among the younger undergraduates reminded Rob of nothing so much as the results of a heavy night's carousing in the Muthaiga Bar, and he wanted none of it. Drink, he had discovered in Kenya, made him feel, after a brief interlude of elation, appallingly ill and he had had enough of illness to last him for a very long time. He was not by nature part of the philistine and aristocratic set and because of a certain aloofness in his character, was not likely to be elected to the Apostles, who regarded themselves not only as intellectual stars, but as great cultivators of superior personal friendships. Girls, who except for brotherly affection for Bay Martineau, had not loomed large in Rob's consciousness as yet, were imprisoned in their colleges and were not allowed even to have tea in a man's room without a chaperone. Rob's stimulant, and he wished for no other, was talk.

At the beginning, the political talk discouraged him, being as it was so profoundly Tory. He had been deeply depressed on coming back to England from Kenya, to find that the peace with Germany appeared to be breaking down, that unemployment was on a massive scale, so that even his contemporaries, old schoolfellows, were caught up in the scarcity of jobs, and that nothing much appeared to be being done about either problem. He was sure that somewhere in Cambridge, particularly among the experimental physicists who seemed so universally admired, would be men who shared his despair over traditional economic and social policies, and his enthusiasm for left-wing solutions. Barr Taylor was clearly a sympathizer, but Rob sensed that he was somehow on trial, that Barr Taylor was watching and waiting, before he spoke with any intimacy. It was a month – a long month to Rob out of an eight-week term – before Douglas held out his hand to Rob, displaying a button lying in the palm, and said,

'Mean anything to you?'

Rob peered. The button bore a hammer and sickle.

'Yes.' He looked up. 'You know it does.'

'My brother went down last year. He is unemployed. So are five out of seven of his closest friends. What about your brother?'

Rob looked away.

'He is in the army.'

'Are you in close touch?'

'No.'

'I've got something to tell you,' Douglas said. 'I might have done it earlier, but I was waiting to see which way you would jump. I saw your article in the *Cambridge Left*, and I knew you were sound, not just flirting with ideas. You see, I am a Marxist.'

'Yes,' Rob said, bursting with a sudden excitement.

Douglas cast himself down along the length of the sofa and lit a cigarette.

'It happened in Göttingen. I hadn't been faintly interested in politics before, only in mathematics. That's why I went there, to study under Hilbert. I can't tell you what Göttingen is like. It is completely Nazi dominated, the streets are full of armed police and they have drunken all-night meetings and behave in a way that is more repulsive in its brutality and domination than anything I ever imagined, let alone saw. Do you realize,' he swung his legs onto the floor and jabbed at the air with his cigarette, 'do you realize that they have taken the works of Heine out of the library and *burned* them? I'd never come across anti-Semitism before, and it's the ugliest thing I have seen in my life. The Nazi treatment of Jews in Göttingen is no less than deliberate and outrageous persecution. There was a demonstration, a demonstration against the police. I joined it. I was arrested and jailed. In Braunschweig prison. I was there for a month. I'd probably be there still if some Marxists I'd made friends with hadn't somehow manoeuvred my release. I came home and joined the British Communist Party.' He looked at Rob. 'I'm starting a cell in Cambridge.'

Rob let out a long, unsteady breath.

'I've been through your books with a toothcomb,' Douglas said. He smiled. 'I should say that you were in the same state of moral shock as I am. Do you realize that if we don't do something to stop it, we shall be fighting a war – we are just the right age – that we don't want and we don't believe in?'

'I know!' Rob said. 'I know, I know!' His voice rose to a shout. 'I have such a disgust for our politicians you cannot imagine! They want to re-arm Germany and send her eastwards, it's outrageous. And do you realize, do you *realize*, that its *our* class in England who are so smug and – and so hypocritically selfish and so—'

'Yes,' Douglas said, 'of course I do. That's what we have in common, you and I. The disgust is under our own skins.'

Rob got up from the armchair on whose edge he had been crouching and began to walk rapidly about the room. He was at once extremely excited and possessed

583

with a curious and calming sense of homecoming, as if he had found the Holy Grail and yet only upon the moment of its discovery, realized that it was indeed what he had been looking for. He wheeled on Barr Taylor.

'We have the cure!'

'If we go about it the right way.'

'So. So what happens next?'

Douglas stood up.

'They are showing *Our Fighting Navy* at the Tivoli next week. It's the most appalling bit of jingoism you ever saw. We are leading a demonstration to stop the film even being run, if we can manage it. I'd like your help.'

'Of course,' Rob said. His whole face was glowing. 'Anything you want. Anything you ask me to do, at all. *Anything.*'

It was a wet and windy November night, with leaves thick and slippery on the pavements. The demonstration, indistinguishable in dress from the queue of cinema-goers waiting to go in, marched up to the doors bearing placards in favour of pacifism. Rob was one of three at the head of the demonstration, holding up a huge plywood banner on which he had painted, 'War! The true oppressor of all mankind', and thus, because of the prominence of his position, he was one of the first to be fallen upon by the surge of university Tories who erupted suddenly from the darkness, howling like banshees. The man who seized Rob had him on the pavement in a single skilful movement, had broken the placard across his knee, and had yelled furiously, inches from Rob's face, 'You are nothing but a cad and a coward!' Rob attempted to get up, shouting too, and was punched with great accuracy on the left side of his jaw. When he came groggily to, he was being held up in a sitting position on the kerb, his head between his knees, and Douglas Barr Taylor was saying triumphantly,

'Well, that will do us nothing but good.'

'What,' Rob said dimly, fighting a humming in his ears, 'what?'

'Those thugs have played us straight into the hands of the pacifist socialists. You'll see. We'll make something of the Poppy Day Rag, now. It's perfect.'

Rob shook his head as if to shake a better comprehension into it.

'Poppy Day? What rag?'

Douglas crouched in front of him. His breath, lit faintly by the gas lamp overhead, came out of his mouth in steamy little puffs as he spoke.

'It's an awful thing. It's supposed to be nothing to do with politics – just a sort of drunken binge with everyone dressing up and careering through Cambridge collecting money. The money is for ex-servicemen's funds. After this, though, we can exploit it very usefully. We can turn it into an anti-war demonstration, because the town will favour pacifists after that display by the Tory thugs. Come on, Rob. Get up. Get up. You'll have to learn to slug them back.'

'But if I'm a pacifist—'

Douglas stooped and put a hand under Rob's arm to haul him to his feet.

'Even the best principles, Comrade Taverner, need defending on occasion.'

The plans they laid for Poppy Day were meticulous. The demonstration, it was decided at a number of fervently attended meetings, should not confine itself to being simply against the Great War and all its destructive horrors but against what were to be described as 'similar crimes of Imperialism'. The phrase was painted on banners, printed in pamphlets, and inscribed across the ribbon which garlanded the poppy wreath they were to carry. The day before the demonstration, Rob returned to his rooms after a long round of pushing pamphlets through letterboxes and found, sitting at his table and going shamelessly through his books and papers, not Douglas as he might have expected, but Bay Martineau. She appeared perfectly composed, both at having played truant from a lecture on Schiller at the University of London, and at having managed to sneak illicitly into a men's Cambridge college. When Rob came in, she stood up and pulled off her hat and beamed at him. He was aghast.

'What *are* you doing here?'

'I've come to see you.'

'But you can't – why didn't you write? What on earth have you come for?'

'I told you. To see you. I could have written, I suppose, but I suddenly had an impulse that it would be more fun just to come.' She looked round her. 'I've never been to Cambridge.'

'Well, you aren't going to be here long—'

Bay took no notice of him. She put her hand on the top-most book near to her.

'Are you a Communist?'

'Oh my *God*—' Rob said desperately.

'Well, are you? I don't suppose you have all this lying about as a smokescreen for being really a Fascist.'

'It's none of your business what I am. You have no right to sneak in here and go through my stuff like some amateur sleuth. It's dishonourable. I'm taking you back to the station—'

'Suppose I agree with you.'

'*Agree* with me?'

'Yes. Suppose I don't like the look of society either and I think Marxist solutions may be the right ones. Suppose I sympathize?'

Rob groaned.

'You don't know what you think. You are just a silly little schoolgirl having an adventure.'

'And you are a mature and considered man whose views have more value on account of your sex and age—'

The door opened.

'Good Lord,' Douglas Barr Taylor said, 'who are you?'

Rob said, 'She is called Bay Martineau. She has grown up with us all. She is just on her way back to London.'

'No, I'm not,' Bay said.

Douglas stayed in the doorway.

'If I'm interrupting something—'

'Only a quarrel. Rob declines to believe I could share his political sympathies because I am only a girl and only nineteen.'

Douglas came into the room and shut the door behind him.

'What *is* going on?'

Bay explained. Rob said, suddenly furious, 'Can't you see I don't *want* you here, sympathy or no sympathy? I don't want *any* of you here. I want to be left *alone*—'

Douglas, struck by both Bay's face and her self-possession, came over to her so that he could look at her closely.

'Are you running away from something?'

'Only a couple of lectures on Schiller. I can make the work up easily. I just thought I'd come and see Rob and find out what he was up to. Whatever it was, I knew it wouldn't be orthodox.'

'Do you want to make yourself useful?'

Bay looked straight back at him.

'In what way?'

'Carry a banner tomorrow, in our demonstration. You would be the only woman. Perhaps, on second thoughts, you should carry the wreath. It would be most effective.'

Bay sat down on the sofa amid the tangle of gowns and scarves that littered it.

'Explain.'

Rob said, 'Don't involve her. For God's sake. It will be all round the family in no time.'

'Does that matter?'

'Of course it matters. It makes everything I do twice as difficult, for the cause. There'll be such a stink. Can't you see?'

Douglas was still gazing at Bay.

'All I can see is that she'd be the most wonderful publicity.'

'On your own head then—'

'I'll find you a boarding house for tonight,' Douglas said to Bay. 'Have you any money? There's a final meeting tonight and you can come along to that.'

'I'd love it—'

Rob said fiercely, 'All right, all right, but not a *word* at home, do you hear me, not a *word*—'

'Why should I?'

'Because you always—'

'Shut up,' Douglas said. 'This is no moment for

588

family scraps. Come on,' he said to Bay, 'let's find you somewhere for the night.'

She stood up. Excitement glittered round her in a sort of electric crackle.

'I'm pretty bona fide, you know. My mother is a socialist journalist.'

'Lucky you.'

She turned to Rob.

'You'll be pleased I came, tomorrow. You wait and see.'

Thirty-six hours later Bay climbed on the London train with a folded newspaper under her arm and a promise to Douglas Barr Taylor that she would keep in touch. He saw her off; Rob, with the excuse of an economics tutorial, did not. When the train had pulled out of the station, and Bay was sure that no-one else in the compartment could overlook her, she opened the paper. A photograph of the Peace March almost filled the top half of the front page, and the most prominent figure in the picture was herself, carrying the wreath of poppies, bareheaded and with a borrowed scarf wound round the collar of her coat. Either side of her, in polo necked jerseys and tweed jackets, strode Rob and Douglas, each holding the pole of a vast banner, which proclaimed above her head, 'Workers by hand and brain unite against war'. Behind them marched the ranks of under-graduates and dons, Communists, Christians, pacifists and socialists, who made up the demonstration, and beside the column, on each side, were a few indulgent looking policemen. It was a most dramatic photograph.

When she arrived back in Swan Walk, both Victoria and her mother were out. She had left a message on the kitchen table two days before to say she was staying with a friend and that they were not to worry. She now left a second to say that she was back and had gone in to college, slipped the newspaper down her bed, and departed, in the highest spirits, for north London. Ellen, finding the note an hour later, went up to Bay's room and put her hand down the bed to see if it could do with a hot water bottle to air it before evening, and found the newspaper.

She took it down to the kitchen, to think about it over a cup of tea. Bay, she considered, had always been given extraordinary freedoms and she had hinted to Sarah that they might one day prove dangerous. Sarah had always defended Bay's essential good sense, and as mother and daughter were very open with one another, she perhaps already knew where Bay had been and what she had been doing. Bay was at least extremely truthful; Ellen could ask her directly what she had been up to and whether her mother knew, and be certain of a straight answer.

Rob, however, was quite another matter. Ellen's feelings about Rob were so bound up with and distorted by the catastrophe he had innocently brought into Rose's life, that she could not see him as a person, only as some kind of agent. If Rob had become a pacifist, even a socialist, Ellen could only sympathize, but she was unnerved by his behaving so publicly, so prominently, and she was alarmed that he should seem to have inveigled Bay into a demonstration which might well – Sarah had told her a great deal about this – be a cover for some kind of extreme political ends. Suppose that the Fascists were really behind it, and Rob had embroiled Bay in something really sinister which she, in her idealistic innocence, would not have spotted?

Ellen made a sudden resolve. She got up and fetched

the scissors Victoria kept in the kitchen to chop parsley and remove the rind from bacon, and carefully cut out the photograph. She then wrote a short note to Charlie who, she told herself, she had a duty to inform which must override her personal feelings of animosity towards him as yet another instrument of Rose's unhappiness. She put both letter and cutting into an envelope, and went out into the twilight on the Embankment to catch the tea-time post. Then she returned to the house, and went into the little office where she kept the magazine and publishing accounts, to work until she heard Bay's returning step upon the stairs, and might have a private word with her.

Rob's agitation when Charlie came to Cambridge was intensified by observing how awful his father looked. Always lean, he was now painfully thin, and the flesh of his face hung limply from his cheekbones, forming dark pouches under his eyes. He was sixty-eight and looked at least ten years older, his dark hair quite grey now, his movements hesitant. Eleni had been terribly anxious about his going alone, but he had been absolutely determined.

'In the first place, don't treat me like an old dotard, and in the second, I don't want to turn up in Cambridge in a damn *deputation*.'

When he reached Rob's sitting room he was extremely short of breath, and lay back in an armchair recovering while Rob shouted for his bedder to make tea and hovered about with a kind of clumsy solicitude. Tea came, with a bag of doughty buns which Rob had bought upon an impulse of awkward hospitality, and Charlie struggled to sit up, and said,

'Made yourself quite snug, I see.'

He looked round, at the clutter of garments, the piles of books and sliding stacks of paper, the pipes and tobacco tins and walking sticks.

'Who's this Barr Taylor?'

'His cousin was at Winchester at the same time as me. A college man. This one is clever too, a mathematician.'

Charlie grunted.

'Do I get to meet him?'

'No.'

'And why not?'

'Because I don't want your visit turning into some sort of inquisition.'

Charlie gulped a mouthful of tea.

'I see.'

'I don't really know why you have come,' Rob said rashly.

'Oh?'

'Do you think most fathers race across England at the sight of their son's photograph in a provincial newspaper?'

'Don't provoke me,' Charlie said. 'And you know damn well that the photograph was in *The Times* the following day and no doubt Stalin has a copy on his desk by this morning.'

Rob said nothing.

'Look,' Charlie said, 'I haven't come to laugh off your communist sympathies as a kind of minor adolescent affliction that I am patronizingly certain you will grow out of. If I thought you would grow out of it in time, I would have stayed at home. I am here because I think your convictions are serious, and because your future life and career will frankly be a ruinous mess, unless you can be persuaded to change them.'

Rob put down his bun.

'Oh?' he said. His voice was not quite steady. 'How so?'

'Because within five or ten years, you will be a baronet, and Buscombe, and all it means in terms of tradition and responsibility to its past and future and the people who work for it at present, will be yours. Because I know to my cost what it is not to have a career as well as a possession like Buscombe in an age like ours when the landed gentry is in every way an anachronism. I am afraid it is not possible to be a Marxist as well as a baronet, and that any career in public life, or indeed any distinction in any other career worth having, would become barred to you if you were known to be a public Communist.'

Rob got up. Six weeks ago he would have blown instantly and stormed at his father, but under Douglas's careful tuition he was learning self-control of a kind. He went over to the table and picked up his copy of the *Communist Manifesto*, and brought it back to his chair opposite his father's, holding it as a sort of talisman. He said with great deliberateness,

'You have actually hit the nail on the head. You say the landed gentry is an anachronism and you are perfectly right. Take that fact and draw it out to its logical conclusion and you will see that the whole of capitalist society will disappear for the same reasons – society has progressed, grown beyond the hidebound rules of history. What we are living in now, this decaying mess, this confusion and hypocrisy, is simply the death convulsions of a system which the world has outgrown. We cannot cling on, even if it were morally right to do so, which it absolutely is not.'

'My dear boy,' Charlie said tiredly, 'please do not start on morality. You will be preaching to me next on

593

the essential goodness and loving kindness of humanity, particularly working class humanity.'

'I believe it.'

'It is a most unintelligent belief.'

'Why so?'

'Because it refuses to recognize the inescapable facts about humanity, the facts proven again and again by history, the regrettable facts of human aggression and avarice, of—'

'But don't you *see*,' Rob said, leaning forward in his eagerness, 'that Communism will *change* all that?'

Charlie closed his eyes.

'Please do not show yourself as credulous as well as stupid.'

Rob's knuckles were white as he gripped the *Manifesto*.

'Our society is a criminal mess.'

'Maybe so,' Charlie said, 'but Communism is not the answer.' He sat up abruptly and said in a much less weary voice, 'But I haven't come half across England to argue politics with you. I have come to tell you that if you are not, at the very least, less overt about your current views, you have little or no future. What does Buscombe mean to you? Nothing? Is it just a house?'

Rob looked away.

'Of course not.'

'Tell me. Tell me what you feel.'

'I love it,' Rob said, 'you know I do. It conflicts with everything I believe and I still know I love it, which must be proof to you of my sincerity.'

'Listen,' Charlie said, 'Buscombe is a burden you can't put down. You *can't*. You will be baronet after me, like it or not. Buscombe will be yours, like it or not. Your hands are tied. You are not free to embrace a doctrine like Marxism. It is not for you.'

Rob put his head in his hands. They were both silent for a long while, sitting there together in the companionable masculine muddle, while the afternoon grew dark, and undergraduates back from the games fields thundered up the wooden staircases past Rob's door to their rooms. Charlie said at last,

'I seem to be rather tired. I think I shall go to the hotel. You will dine with me, of course?'

Rob's voice was muffled by his hands.

'Of course.'

Charlie began to struggle to his feet.

'Don't think I don't sympathize with your position, even if I can't sympathize with your politics. Heaven knows,' he gave a short laugh, 'heaven knows your life has echoed mine well enough to make me more painfully aware of what you feel than anyone else possibly could. I sometimes think that if it were in my power to free you, and I felt that freedom would make you happy, free you I would. But you are so young yet. Buscombe will grow upon you, you'll see. What you cannot conceive of wanting at twenty-four becomes a dearly loved possession at sixty-four.' He looked down at Rob, still drooped over his hands. 'Will you come home for Christmas, dear boy?'

Rob looked up. There were tears on his cheeks.

'Oh yes,' he said.

Christmas that year was oddly successful – oddly because of anxiety over Charlie's health and Rob's politics, and disappointment at Carlo's enforced absence. He was stationed at Catterick and could not get leave.

'Dull, dull, dull,' he wrote from Yorkshire. 'The

whole battalion obsessed with rugby and boxing, at both of which we seem determined to beat the rest of the army. Mustn't whinge, though – I'm to be made a captain and the hunting is wonderful.'

He made no reference to Rob, except to wish him an affectionate happy Christmas, and merely sent a teasing message to Bay, telling her she was too pretty to be a revolutionary and no-one would take her cause seriously. He had written privately to her a month before, and she had burned the letter unanswered.

'I know you think I am a blockhead, a philistine military heavy – perhaps I am, compared with Rob. But don't dismiss reason and sense as qualities too pedestrian to be countenanced. I have to tell you – you know why – that I think Communism dangerous because at the heart of it lies an hypocrisy as bad, worse, than that of capitalism. Communism, it seems to me, under a mask of preaching equality, fundamentally despises the great masses it claims to want to elevate. Communism is not about human happiness and self-achievement, nor is it about freedom. It will throw up a hierarchy as oppressive as any dictatorship, in time – it's only human nature and you can't change that. I expect you will burn this. I only hope that you will have *really* read it first.'

Bay was given Catherine's old room to sleep in, over Christmas. Through the wall, in the little room adjoining Charlotte's where Elizabeth had slept in her last years at Buscombe, Melina played 'Stormy Weather' and 'Smoke Gets in Your Eyes' endlessly on her gramophone. This conflicted interestingly, if doors were left open, with the saxophones and trombones of Harry's beloved jazz. Sarah had Kate's room, and Victoria the room looking east where Charlie and Rose had slept when they came to Buscombe thirty years before, the room where Rob had been both conceived and born. Eleni had excelled herself. A huge tree rose toweringly in the hall, the landing balustrades were garlanded with ivy and spruce and every picture was crowned with a scratchy bunch of holly. On Christmas Eve, the servants and the outdoor staff – including Fred and poor anxious Mrs Fred, and three children and five grandchildren, the youngest but a baby – came in to stand around and consume mince pies and a dangerous hot punch Rob and Thomas had brewed with reckless disregard for its effect – 'I say, it's horribly sweet. Must be all that cider. Gin will sharpen it up a bit, lots of it . . .' – and then trail off into the night clutching parcels Eleni had organized, leaving behind them an atmosphere of satisfaction, relief and self-consciousness.

Controversy was studiously avoided. No comment was made when Rob, announcing that he was now naturally an atheist, declined to come to church, and Bay, after a deep breath and an elaborate avoidance of her mother's eye, elected to join him. Rob gave his father a copy of George Orwell's *Down and Out in Paris and London*, Melina said that the only thing she wanted in the whole world beside a London haircut was to be taken to see Mae West in *She Done Him Wrong*, and Thomas spent most of Christmas lunch informing his family that he had decided to read engineering at Cambridge since his ambition was to rescue Taverner Warehouses from the clutches of the Payne family, and make it into the most modern dockside plant in England. Like most of his explanations, this took some time and involved a great deal of rearrangement of spoons and forks to illustrate his plans, and piles of walnuts and tangerines to represent capital and borrowings. He was still unfinished when Palmer came

597

in with the Christmas Day post, and there, as if by telepathy, was a letter from Mrs Payne of Kilima, who wrote to say first that she had won first prize at Nairobi flower show for roses – 'So appropriate – from the bed I planted for Catherine' – second, that there seemed to be a great enthusiasm for British Fascism in Kenya – 'Super-loyalty to the Crown, they *say*' – and thirdly that she was to be married.

'To that nice Mr Hamilton, as Catherine called him, of course. There is no point in not, any more. I have been saying no, no, no, for four years and then the other day he said to me, "Am I simply too *dull*?" which was not only endearing, but made me realize that it was far from true, either. I think we will go on much as before. He'll keep the house in Nairobi and I'll keep this, and he'll go on running safaris which he is so good at and which are so lucrative, and we will juggle about together as much as possible. Juma is very pleased – you wouldn't think a Somali could be so full of European bourgeois convention. Perhaps I have taught it to him. Anyway, I hope this gets to you before Christmas Day, so you can drink our health. I am very happy and tremendously relieved somehow. Will you send Thomas out to us between school and university?'

'You bet,' Thomas said.

Only Eleni remembered to go round the table to comfort Harry, who suffered anguish at any mention of Kenya, where his Catherine had died and was now buried. Her death had been a terrible blow to him; he had always cherished a little flame of hope that she would find, once in Kenya, that she missed him, and come home to him. But she had flourished in Kenya, and then she had died there and Harry's appetite for life had died with her. Even his beloved jazz was not the comfort it once was, being travestied these days by some gin palace stuff called 'swing'. When Eleni put her hand on his shoulder, he turned his face to her in pain and gratitude, but could not speak.

On Boxing Day, Anna and her husband Edward and two slender pale children in matching coats with velvet collars arrived by car. Anna wore furs and careful makeup and had an amber cigarette holder. She was very animated.

'Oh, but of course, we are moving into Chesterfield Hill. My dear, it's taken nearly three years to badger Edward, hasn't it, darling—'

'I was rather fond of my garden,' he said mildly.

'– But, of course, I *knew* he'd see it was best, and then we can buy a deevy country house and everybody can have everything they want, and it will be poor little me rushing madly between the two. No, Eleni darling, thank you, not a morsel of cake. I've swelled like a balloon over the dread Chrimbo – look' – patting weasel hips – 'Oh, but it's a treat to be here again!'

'I am your Uncle Thomas,' Thomas said impressively to the two pale children. 'I am going to be an engineer. What about you?'

John said he was going to play cricket and Susan said she didn't know. Thomas took John into the long corridor that led to the kitchens and gave him a tennis racquet as a cricket bat, and then bowled at him with a tennis ball. John was immediately enslaved. Susan stayed in the drawing room and held her father's hand and gazed apprehensively about her and when he stooped down to say something encouraging she whispered, 'Are these all my aunts?'

Eleni took Susan to sit by her at tea, but the kindness of this was rather undermined by a huge, dark scowling uncle on her other side, who gave her an enormous slab of cake she did not want – and she had tried to say, in a strangled voice, that she did not – and then ignored her. After tea, her mother sang 'Night and Day' and 'I'm Getting Sentimental Over You' while her fascinating looking young aunt Melina played the piano, and it should have been lovely – everyone else seemed to think so and clapped and asked for more – but was instead only, and as usual, squirm-making. A tremendously pretty girl, who might for all Susan knew, be yet another relation, came up to her and said kindly,

'Can you sing too?'

Susan shook her head.

'Nor can I,' Bay said, 'I can't do anything feminine except cry like mad. Are you a crier?'

Susan nodded vehemently, tears rising at the very thought.

'Have you ever been here before?'

'No—'

'Shall I show you round?'

'No, thank you,' Susan said.

'Not even the room your mother had as a little girl?'

'Go on, dear,' her father said. 'Wouldn't you like to see that?'

Reluctantly, Susan put her hand in Bay's. They went up and up and up onto the top floor where it was terribly cold and there was only hard shiny stuff on the floor. Bay talked all the time but Susan couldn't really listen because she was so longing for the little expedition to be over. She thought her mother's childhood room awful, so cold and bare with horrid slopey ceilings and no carpet. She almost pulled Bay downstairs in her eagerness to get back to the drawing room.

'Well, duckie,' her father said, 'tell me what it was like—'

Susan put her face on his shoulder so that she could whisper.

'I want to go home.'

The next day, Bay and Sarah and Victoria went back to London by train. Bay tried to have a moment alone with Rob, but he was in a most peculiar mood tramping round and round the house and garden wearing a devouring expression, as if making a mental inventory of every leaf, every stick of furniture, and refused to be cornered. Instead she found that she was cornered herself, by Sarah and Victoria, in the train compartment, who told her, without heat, that she was making a great fool of herself.

'Are you in love with Rob?' Victoria asked her. 'Is that the reason for all this overexcited enthusiasm?'

Bay blushed.

'I really don't know. Sometimes I think yes, hugely, and other times I think I just love the enthusiasm and excitement he generates.'

'So,' Sarah said, 'if we were to generate a similar excitement for Roman Catholicism or Fascism or Buddhism, you would follow him as slavishly?'

'I'm not slavish.'

'I am afraid,' Victoria said, 'that you do not give the impression of a young woman who has really thought out her opinions for herself.'

'Just because they do not coincide with yours—'

Victoria said sharply, 'Don't be silly.'

'Sorry—'

Sarah put her hand on her daughter's.

'Listen. Look at us. You want careers like ours, don't you? You might even get into serious politics instead of hovering on the edge like us. But political extremism, revolutionary behaviour, will *bar* you. Do you understand that?'

'But if Rob is willing to risk—'

'My dear little goose, Rob really believes what he believes, just now. I am not at all convinced that you do. Don't throw away your chances – there you are, top of your year, the German *and* the French prize now – for something you don't wholeheartedly believe in.'

'Are you going to *do* anything about it?' Bay asked.

Sarah stared at her.

'Of course not. Apart from talk to you. Why should a liberal upbringing suddenly became a dictatorial one? I trust you.'

'Oh good,' Bay said. 'Sorry I asked. I just wanted to know.'

'Do you think,' Sarah said to Victoria later, 'that we made any impression on her?'

'Oh yes,' Victoria said comfortingly, 'I am sure we did. She is so sensible. Girls don't get carried away by romantic ideals, like young men do.'

In January, Rob returned to Cambridge. His frame of mind was not entirely straightforward, being confused by a month at Buscombe in which his lifelong love for the place had done angry battles with his much newer belief that houses like Buscombe, and all they stood for, were doomed. Because of this raggedness of emotion, compounded by a rather indifferent greeting from Douglas Barr Taylor, the two of them fell into a quarrel within an hour of seeing one another again. It was their first quarrel, and as is usual with quarrels, the first stage of hurling petty personal insults at each other soon gave way to deeper grievances and fears. Douglas accused

Rob of harbouring lingering treacherous loyalties to bourgeois principles and when Rob, stung, pointed out that Douglas came from a remarkably similar background to his own, the reason for Douglas's anxiety, the true reason, emerged.

He had not been home for Christmas to the Barr Taylor stronghold in Suffolk, but to Moscow instead. A Russian, an interpreter, whom he had met in Cambridge had arranged this. He was visibly shaken as a result. The Russian Revolution and its aftermath were not, it seemed, without a savagery and fear that seemed to Douglas incompatible with even the most basic altruistic concern for the common weal, and, more disturbingly, the idealistic words of Marx and Engels. He talked for a long time about this and then he said,

'You see, I don't think the Russian way is the British way. Don't get me wrong, I believe Communism is the only answer for our society and for most of Western Europe, but I don't think purges are the way to go about it. When I was in Moscow, I kept remembering Göttingen, somehow—'

'I understand,' Rob said.

They looked at each other.

'I'm in an awful dilemma, too,' Rob said. 'I am violently opposed to a society which allows a house like Buscombe to continue, and yet I am hampered by having been born there and knowing every stone of it. Just as you are hampered in the direct pursuit of your beliefs by your liberal and humanitarian upbringing.'

Douglas lit his pipe.

'Can one *compromise* with Communism?'

'We may have to. We are English after all.'

'And Marxists.'

'To the death—'

Douglas grinned at him.

'Sorry, old man.'

'Me too.'

For a few weeks, term-time life took over, the round of lectures and tutorials and frenzied essays, meetings of the peace movements, Marxist gatherings in the rooms of like-minded dons and undergraduates, long nights of talk, clouded with pipe smoke. Bay tried to come to Cambridge but Rob was adamant she should not – to him she represented, in one person, his incompatible longings for both Buscombe and Marxism. Bay was angry and wrote to say so.

'I shall not sneak behind your back and write to Douglas, because I know he would encourage me to come. But it would do you good to see me. I have friends who are starting a Marxist newspaper, and I am going to Vienna in the summer to look at practical Communism, in order to make up my mind. I don't expect you want to know what I think, but I'll tell you all the same. You are just *playing* at politics in Cambridge. It's all a sort of isolated idealism, quite safe really, within your medieval walls. You won't have a hope of making your mind up until you see a bit of *reality*.'

Had she but known it, reality was but a week away. It was on a bleak day in February, with the wind whining along the Cam and the grey stone seeming to suck in the damp grey sky, that the first hunger marchers that the city had seen came through on their ragged way from Tyneside to London. There had been of course warning that they would come, and schools had been offered to shelter them, and soup kitchens set up to feed them, and a large proportion of the university as well as the townspeople were lining the streets in sympathy and curiosity.

Rob and Douglas had taken up their positions soon after dawn, on the corner of Sidney Street and Green Street. They were elated, keyed up, at the prospect of seeing this first great demonstration of a huge crack splitting up capitalist society, the first visible *proof* to them, that their Marxist convictions were as visible as they both believed and wished them to be. When the column at last trudged through, at midday, the shock was no less than sickening. The pinched and pallid faces, despite the determinedly cheerful smiles spread across them, the broken old boots, the torn and filthy mackintoshes, the stale, sour, unwashed smell of under-nourished poverty bore no relation to Rob's vision of robust and overalled Marxist workers. As the column moved on, one man dropped out to retie the length of grubby twine that bound the remains of his boot to his foot – a naked, white-grey foot – and as he straightened up again, his eye caught Rob's, staring at him. For a second or two, they regarded one another, and as the man's expression changed from slightly defiant jaunti-ness to one of wonder, Rob knew that the horror and fear spreading through his whole being like a violent nausea, was writ large upon his face.

He was rooted to the spot. Marcher after marcher went by, while Rob's appalled and frightened gaze took in each pathetic and shocking detail, and when the last man had gone, shuffling and hobbling behind his mates, Rob turned like some wild thing and fought his way through the crowd behind him, ignoring Douglas's cries, and ran and ran and ran.

It took him over a week to compose the letter to his father, partly because the ferment and agitation into which he had been thrown made him unable to be even faintly coherent. He wrote it at last under Douglas's moderating eye – 'Don't use such savage adjectives, you can make your point perfectly well without them. Better' – and even when it was at last done and sealed up he tore open the envelope and altered words and phrases. When it was finally and irrevocably posted, he felt a singing relief, the sensation of cleanliness and directness of purpose he had experienced when Douglas had confided to him, the autumn before, that he too was a Marxist.

> *King's College*
> *Cambridge*
> *25 February, 1934*

Dear Father,

I am writing to tell you that I have at last made up my mind about my future, and my decision is final. I wish to work in the practical world of socialist politics ['Don't put Communist,' Douglas said. 'He knows what you mean, and why wave a red rag at a bull?'] which necessitates my severing as many connections with Buscombe and my upbringing as it is in my power to do.

If it were possible for me to disclaim the baronetcy, and give it to Carlo, I would do so tomorrow. As it is out of the question, I will simply, when the time comes, never use it. But it is in my power to decline the house, the estate and a way of life repugnant to me and irrelevant to our future world. And that I do. I would be grateful if a document might be drawn up to that effect so that there can be no shadow of doubt as to the future ownership of Buscombe.

All I shall keep is the income that became mine on my twenty-first birthday, which I will devote to the cause. There is nothing to be gained from remaining at Cambridge in academic isolation, when there is so much to be done in the

field. At the end of this term, in just over two weeks' time, I
shall go to London, and begin my political work.

   I am quite open with you, because I trust you not to inter-
vene. I heard you out, but my mind cannot be moved from
what has become a true and profound belief and purpose.
                                                    Rob.

Charlie was never to read the letter, on account of the
bitter irony of his dying the day it was written. He had
been no frailer than before, not particularly overtired or
stressed, but simply said to Eleni that he would go up
to bed before her as she was still poring over her plans
for summer bedding plants. He went upstairs before her
quite often, so she simply looked up and smiled absently
and said she would only be half an hour, and went
back to her antirrhinums and wallflowers. When she did
go up, some three quarters of an hour later, after the
nightly ritual of shutting up dogs and locking doors, of
turning off lights and checking that Harry was soundly
asleep, she found Charlie was not yet in bed, so went
along to his dressing room and discovered him fully
dressed on the floor, except for one shoe he had
managed to take off. He was quite dead. After she
had made sure of that, Eleni sat down on the floor
beside him, and took his hand on her lap and began to
stroke his hair and his face, and to talk to him gently.
She stayed like that for an hour, and then the clock from
the hall below struck midnight, and she stooped to kiss
his forehead and said to him in Greek, 'Goodbye, my
darling,' and then she went downstairs to telephone the
doctor.

CHAPTER THIRTY

1935

'If,' Sarah said often these days, 'I could be as philosophical as Eleni, I should really have nothing left to
wish for.'

The problem, of course, was Bay. Bay had been a
problem, a matter for concern, for two years now,
two years in which she had gained a first-class degree
in languages, which was splendid, and demonstrated
frequently and publicly against the Fascists and then
disappeared to Vienna for anxious months, which was
not. Sarah admired her principles and deplored her
reckless way of living by them. The Vienna episode had
shaken Sarah badly. Bay had simply gone off, just *gone*,
leaving no more information than one of her telegram-
matic kitchen table notes, and the next thing Sarah
knew was a postcard from Vienna, from some street in
the ninth district, where Bay said she was living with a
Jewish family and having a 'proper look at things'.

For the first time in her life, Sarah panicked. She went
down to Buscombe and begged Eleni to persuade Carlo
to go to Austria and bring Bay home.

'You must understand how I feel, having Rob so
disruptive and troublesome.'

'I do,' Eleni said. Her hair had at last begun to go grey, almost as a token of mourning Charlie, the odd silver strand in the dramatic glossy darkness. 'I do, but I don't think rushing off to Vienna and forcing her to come home is the answer. She is a young adult. One may deplore what these naughty children do, but they are well beyond the age of nursery discipline.' She smiled at Sarah. 'We have brought them up to be independent, my dear Sarah, and these are the fruits of it.'

'Then you will not approach Carlo?'

'No,' Eleni said.

'Then I must go myself!'

Carlo was much startled to see Sarah appear in Yorkshire. A letter was brought to him in camp asking him to meet her at the little hotel in Richmond. He was sure some terrible catastrophe must have happened to Eleni, and drove like a maniac through Swaledale to the hotel, to find Sarah in her customary wrappings of indeterminate woolly garments, fidgeting in the lounge.

'It's Bay,' Sarah cried to him without preliminary.

He blanched.

'What about Bay—'

'She has run away to Vienna!'

Carlo took a deep breath. He steered Sarah to a chair, ordered tea, sat down opposite her and said levelly,

'I know she has gone to Vienna.'

'But you don't seem to understand! I asked your mother, and she did not understand either! I mean, about how fearfully dangerous Austria is now, not just the city life itself with everyone so hungry and Europe refusing to help in case it brings the Hapsburgs back, but because it is an absolute *hotbed* of political intrigue and she is living with Jews and she will be sucked into

609

the political underground in a flash, she is so im-
pressionable, and she hasn't a ghost of an idea how to
cope with espionage and secret causes – oh!' Sarah
cried, pulling a handkerchief out of a subterranean
pocket, 'I am simply distraught! You *must* go out and
find her!'

Tea and a plate of muffins was put down on the table
between them. Carlo poured out, gave Sarah a cup, put
two muffins on her plate, pushed the jampot towards
her and said,

'Do you *know* all this? Or is it just speculation?'

'Look,' Sarah said, 'look.' She put down her muffin,
picked up her handbag, and from its packed interior –
all paper, Carlo could not help interestedly noticing, not
a powder compact in sight – produced an airmail letter.
'Read that.'

It was a single sheet of thin blue paper.

Latschkagasse
Vienna
20 February, 1935

Dear Mother,

    *There isn't much time to write but I've left such a long gap
– I'll try and do better soon. Please don't worry – I really am
one of life's survivors, and I wouldn't be anywhere but here
in the world just now, even if the coffee is made of acorns –
simply horrible – and the bread is always black. I can't write
very freely for obvious reasons, but I know now that socialism
isn't enough to deal with Fascism, you need something
stronger. The police here charge with sabres – enough said?
It's driving everyone worthwhile underground. As a little
English fräulein of usefully impeccable background, I don't
have restraints, so I can be of some use. What a blessing
women are so practical. I'm saving up for a single schlagober*

at the Café Heinrichshof this week – how's that for decadence?

                    Much love, Bay

'You see,' Sarah said, clutching her teacup in both hands, 'I think she is helping smuggle Communists out of Vienna. That's what I read between the lines. That's why I'm having sleepless nights and why I want you to go and persuade her to come back.'

Carlo said, 'I'm afraid I'm the last person—'

'You? The last person? Nonsense!'

'Yes,' he said patiently, 'because I have been on at her about Communism for over a year already and because my motives, although certainly political, are not primarily so, and are not fraternal either.'

'But you are so fond of her!'

'Exactly,' Carlo said.

Sarah put down her teacup.

'Oh my dear—'

'For goodness' sake,' Carlo said, 'don't be sorry for me. But you see why I can't go. She knows I am in love with her so she wouldn't give me two seconds of listening time. Anyway, I don't think dragging her back will make any difference. If she is in earnest, she will simply start on the whole process in another place.'

'But she is in such danger!'

'Revolutionary politics always are.'

There was a pause, during which Carlo refilled their cups, and then Sarah said,

'Are you afraid of alienating Bay still further?'

'I'm not *afraid*. I'd go tomorrow if I thought there was any chance of success. But the only thing that will change Bay's mind is *her* mind and I can't influence that. In every way, I'm the last person, not just because

I love her but because I now sort of own Buscombe –
Rob seems to want me to, but the lawyers don't like it
and are waiting for him to change from red to blue
overnight and go home – and therefore stand for everything she and Rob despise.'

Sarah drank her tea.

'How sad. How sad that you should all have grown
up together and been such friends and now this great
gulf.'

Carlo's face clouded.

'It will get worse. There's bound to be another war,
the question is when not if, and here I am, a regular
soldier, and there they are, writing politically contro-
versial novels and smuggling dissidents out of Central
Europe. You think of that and you think of Buscombe
and you can't believe the two exist in the same world.'

Sarah began to gather up scarf and bag and papers.

'Can you think of anything else I can do?'

'Oh yes,' Carlo said, 'I can. Go and ask Rob. Bay
listens to him—'

Between them, Rob and Douglas Barr Taylor had taken
a house in Rotherhithe Street. One side almost had its
feet in the river, the other looked at a vast and depressing block of Victorian workers' flats built of dirty
red brick with evil stone staircases lined with chipped
tiles. There was a warehouse on one side and the beginnings of a discouraged looking terrace on the other,
built about thirty years before with a great many rusti-
cated quoins and stained glass fanlights, mostly now
broken and the spaces crammed with rags and old
newspapers.

The house was a kind of commune. On the drawing
room floor – a handsome room running from front to

back – was the haphazard muddle of bookshelves and tables and filing cabinets that they liked to call the office. Above, was a warren of bedrooms, through which wandered a random procession of men and women, the only sacred room being the tiny one looking over the river where Rob wrote the novels that were turning him into a minor cause célèbre. He had written the first one, *Jarrow Lad*, in a white heat of passion after coming down from Cambridge, some of the energy contributed, had he but acknowledged it, by a violent and anguished grief for his father. It sold two thousand copies, was reprinted, and sold another three. The second novel, about pacifism rather than social ills, and entitled *The Undeclared Warrior*, had an initial print run of three thousand and had sold out in weeks. He was now on his third. It was anti-Fascist and called *Witch Craze*. He worked on it for seven or eight hours a day, in between organizing or attending meetings, long hours spent wrangling on inner-party matters, and going off with Douglas to Lyons' Corner Houses for sustaining mountains of fish and chips. He was not pleased to see Sarah, and not sympathetic to her anxieties either.

'If Bay is really doing what you think, I'm proud of her and I certainly wouldn't think of stopping her. She is working by the sound of it, with what I often feel are the real Communists, the serious ones who will be the ones who move mountains. What on earth made you come and ask me, of all people?'

'Because Carlo suggested you. Because Bay would listen to what you say.'

'Carlo!'

Carlo had been for one night to Rotherhithe Street. Somewhat inevitably, it was not a success. He was dismayed by the number of bottles around, by the casual promiscuity, by the general air of upper class intellectual dropping out.

'This is all so *affected*,' he said unhappily to Rob, waving an arm at the squalid disorder in the kitchen. 'It's just what I always imagined it would be. You're just playing at it, aren't you?'

After he had gone, Rob sent an angry letter after him, pointing out that the sales of his books were neither affected nor playing at anything.

'Rant if you want to,' Carlo wrote back. 'I still think you have kid gloves on in your mind, however many dirty dishes there are on the kitchen floor. You would be helping the people you profess to support far more by joining the local Labour Party, or even employing a woman from the flats opposite to clean up that pigsty you live in.'

There had been silence between them since. And now, inexplicably, Carlo had sent Sarah Martineau to Rotherhithe Street.

'Carlo says Bay would listen to you.'

'Bay doesn't listen to anybody.'

'But she *would*, to you, if you were in earnest.'

'I should not be in earnest.'

Sarah gathered herself up to go.

'What a heartless business Communism is.'

'You don't change the world,' Rob said, 'by selfishly giving in to fear or pity.'

Sarah looked at him. She was abruptly extremely angry.

'It seems,' she said, 'that your politics have made you both stupid and pompous,' and then she fled from the house and wept bitterly on the omnibus which took an hour to get her back to Chelsea. That night Ellen offered to go to Vienna herself, and this shocked Sarah out of her distraction.

'Oh my dear, I wouldn't think of it. I had sooner go myself. No, no. I must get the whole thing back in proportion and just work like mad until Bay comes home of her own accord.'

When Bay did return, in the summer, it was to Rotherhithe Street she went, and not to Swan Walk. Her aim, coming back bursting with the explosive reality of European politics, was to help organize from England a kind of network for escaping political refugees. She brought with her a list of European contacts and her intention was to use Rob and Douglas to furnish an equivalent English one and between the two, a sort of railway of sympathy could be built up between Central Europe and England, along which might travel those endangered by the bludgeoning advance of Nazism. She had, with her excellent French and better German, no trouble at all in securing well paid freelance work translating contracts for businessmen and industrialists, and often acting as interpreter as well, at meetings. She took over a bedroom at Rotherhithe Street, refused to share it with anyone – except occasionally with Douglas who, although an inept lover, she felt, obscurely, she had to extend comradeship to in every way possible – and endeavoured to create some kind of order out of the leisurely chaos of the household.

Rob disliked having her there. She brought into the house a salty energy that made him feel hounded. On account of her looks and her Viennese experience, she was a great draw, and there appeared to be a party almost every night, materializing out of nowhere and going on until the small hours, with not enough to eat and too much to drink and people throwing bottles, and sometimes each other, out of the windows into the river. Bay joined the Bermondsey Labour Party and went to meetings and to visit local dockers' families and organized fund-raising to help send aid to Hitler's Jewish victims. Hurrying to one of these meetings on a wet October evening, she slipped and broke her thigh. She was taken to Guy's Hospital, put in plaster and told she must remain there for ten days. After three, she tried to discharge herself, was chased by two nurses in an attempt to retrieve her, fell once more and broke her leg again, three inches lower. Rob, tired of Bay's theatricals, summoned Sarah. Sarah was in a very different mood to the one of intense maternal anxiety that had made her so vulnerable six months before.

'We are *all* sick and tired of you,' she said.

Bay was in considerable pain and had a temperature. She regarded her mother with a certain apprehension from her pillow and could not, for the first occasion in a very long time, think of anything to say.

'What depresses me most,' Sarah went on relentlessly, 'is that someone as manifestly intelligent as you are should behave with a stupidity and exhibitionism one would be sorry to see in an unbalanced fourteen year old. You are not going back to Rotherhithe Street.'

'But—'

'There is no question of it. Tell me something. Are you a card-carrying Communist?'

Bay turned her head away.

'*Are* you?'

She whispered, 'No.'

'That's one thing to be thankful for. Another is that you have one wonderful friend left in the world who is

616

prepared to nurse you for the next few months. Eleni says you may go to Buscombe.'

'But I can't—'

'You can't do anything else.'

Tears began to slide down Bay's cheeks.

'I don't think you understand how much what I was trying to do *matters*.'

Sarah put a hand on hers.

'Yes, I do,' she said, much more gently, 'but you are going about it in such a headlong, clumsy way that you will end up hindering the people you want to help. I don't agree with Rob about much, but I do agree on the terrible danger reckless courage brings about. You'll have time at Buscombe to think about everything, not least of all what you really want, what you really are going to do.'

Fred Bradstock drove Eleni up to London, and between them they tucked Bay up onto the back seat of the Ford, making no conversation beyond murmurs about her comfort, and then drove her back to Buscombe. She was ashamed and startled to feel the surge of relief and happiness that rose in her as the car rounded the bend in the drive off the Bath road, and there was Buscombe's yellow face in the yellow afternoon sun and the harsh calling of the ducks from the lake and Harry waving in welcome from the terrace among the bounding dogs. They had made a bedroom for her out of the tower room, setting a screen around the bedhead, filling the room with flowers and books, circling it with electric fires.

'I am so worried you will be cold,' Eleni said. 'This terrible room! But best for you to be on the ground floor and you can see all round from here. Palmer is dying to

617

look after you, but quite honestly she is as wobbly as you are, so we shall have to let her think she is helping and in reality give the work to Aggie Tilling, who is as strong as an ox.'

Bay was, she discovered, terribly tired. It was a tiredness that took disconcerting forms like hopeless tearfulness and feeling herself completely isolated from everyone else in the house, as if she were watching them all from down the wrong end of a telescope. Neither Eleni nor Harry spoke of Vienna or of Rotherhithe Street unless she brought up either place as a subject herself and she found she did not want to do that very much. It was easy to be with them, they were so companionable and comfortable.

'I am unbelievably fortunate,' Harry said to Bay. 'Ever since I retired, I have been handed from one magnificent woman to another.' He was smiling, but his eyes were regretful. 'And of course I have come back to this house—'

It shook Bay to realize how much it meant to be back in the house. She lay awake at night and looked up into the arching Gothic peaks of the tower room ceiling, and remembered playing billiards there as a child and finding that if she rubbed the gilded flowers on the paintwork with a licky finger, they sprang briefly to brilliant golden life until the lick dried and they subsided once again. She was glad of her screen; Eleni had hung long falls of crimson cloth at the windows but still the draughts sidled in and ruffled papers she had left scattered about. She liked lying there, thinking of the tulip tree blowing in the wind to her left, and the lake shimmering away to her right, and sending her imagination out to walk through the silent night-time library – only Harry used it now, to read *The Times* in, after breakfast

– and across the hall with its rugs and tubs of ferns and flowers, into the morning room, where Eleni might have left her mending on the sofa, and then back across the hall to the drawing room, its cushions patted plumply as a late night ritual, and to the dining room where, almost two Christmases ago, she had observed Charlie and Rob watching each other whenever the other wasn't looking. Then she would go down the passage where the gun and rod racks were, and the croquet box lay in winter, to the kitchen, where Cook had now learned – mutter, mutter, mutter – to add cumin seed and coriander to dishes of lamb as Eleni liked, and then on past the larder (half an apple pie left on the slab) and the pantry (rows and rows of jams and chutney and bottled fruit) to the game larder and the old dairy where they now washed the vegetables Fred brought in from the garden which his middle son, the one with the cleft palate, tended with such ferocious devotion. After that she turned back up the passage to the hall and began to climb the staircase to the galleried landing. She had never managed to reach it before falling asleep.

By the Christmas holidays, she had graduated from crutches to sticks and was talking of going back to London. Thomas came down from Cambridge and showed none of his mother's delicacy or reticence.

'Frankly, I think you are pretty lucky to have got away with a broken leg. If you ask me—'

'I didn't.'

'– If you ask me, you were playing with fire. Nothing is going to stop the next war, because nothing will stop German aggression except a war. It's the lesson they have to learn and quite honestly, it's up to us to teach it to them.'

'It's the *wrong* way, war—'

'It's the only way. You are absolutely out of touch if you think otherwise.'

'Do you have to be so dogmatic?'

Thomas looked surprised.

'I always talk like this.'

Melina came home from school and spun about the house singing 'Begin the Beguine'. She spent a lot of time on the telephone, and then disappeared to London, to stay with Anna and go to parties.

'Wouldn't you like to come?' she said to Bay.

'Not in the least, thank you.'

'Well, I'm packing in as much fun as I can before Thomas's war begins. I call it Thomas's because, from the way he talks, you'd think it was not only his idea but he was going to run it singlehanded.'

On Christmas Eve, unannounced, Carlo arrived from Yorkshire.

'Good and bad news,' he said. 'Good is that here I am. Bad is – though not really for me, I have exhausted the possibilities of Catterick – that we are off to Egypt in January. A little tap on the nose to Mussolini.' He looked at Bay on her sticks and said, 'Mending, then?'

She nodded and tossed her head.

'Thomas thinks it is a very small punishment for a very great folly.'

Carlo hugged his mother.

'Look at the arrogance university breeds. Now if you had sent Thomas straight into the army, he would have learned humility and obedience.'

Eleni laughed.

'*Thomas?*'

It was as it usually was when Carlo returned; the house seemed to relax into itself like a dog that has at last found a comfortable arrangement of itself in a basket. There were long hours spent with Eleni on farm business – she was managing the land with the steady competence she brought to everything else, there were scrambles over the roofs with Fred – 'Now you take care, my lad' – inspecting valleys and gutters, and rides out around the land to look at the state of the hedges and fences. Thomas often accompanied Carlo on these rides, and lectured him on agricultural subsidies.

'If you ask me, they are absolutely absurd. Five and a half million on sugar beet! Now listen. In my view, world trade, and our own for that matter, would benefit far more if we spent all these subsidies on buying food from the impoverished countries. Are you listening?'

'No.'

Thomas was very patient; he had to be.

'Well, what do you think?'

Carlo surveyed the graceful slope below Long Coppice where the winter wheat had been planted.

'I think, my dear old gasbag, that we shall shortly have the strategic need of being self-sufficient in wartime, for food. So I shall continue to grow crops on every inch I have.'

'I say,' Thomas said, in serious admiration, 'that's a very sound theory. Very sound indeed, if you ask me.'

Only to Eleni did Carlo confide his anxiety about Buscombe. It was now almost two years since Charlie's death, two years since Rob had declared that he wished Carlo to have his inheritance of Buscombe and the land, and nothing legal had happened at all.

'I wish,' Eleni said, 'I wish we had not transferred to Arthur Creighton's old firm when Frank was killed. It was an emotional reaction, I think; your father couldn't bear the thought of anyone in that firm but a Martineau. But Creightons are so terribly fuddy-duddy, and so

621

outraged at the thought that a baronet might not wish to *be* a baronet, that they are quite paralysed.'

Carlo was standing by the sitting-room window looking over the drive, his shoulders blocking out a good deal of the light Eleni needed for darning a sock of Harry's.

'I just feel a bit insecure, you see. There's nothing in life I want more than this house and to work the land – after I come out of the army – but I daren't believe it's mine until there is a document to say so.' He turned round. 'It sounds as if I don't trust Rob.'

'Creightons say we must wait three years after your father's death.'

'Then I suppose I must just bide my time. It's only a year to go and I shall be away, anyway. I say—'

'Yes?'

'Are you all right, Mother, I mean—'

Eleni looked up at him with a twinkling glance.

'That is not a question I ever ask myself.'

Until Christmas itself was over, Bay and Carlo avoided being left alone together. Bay felt unaccountably shy, and Carlo, for a whole number of reasons he did not care to dwell on, extremely nettled. On a grey day in the queer no-man's-land of time between Christmas and the New Year, Bay managed the stairs triumphantly, and limped along to Catherine's old room for a poke about. After Catherine had died, Kate sent most of her possessions home.

'I am keeping a few tiny things, strings of beads, etc., for my own remembrance, but everything else will get eaten by white ants in a trice if they stay here. The camel saddle she always used as a footstool, and the drum was her bedside table. Can they all go back into her old room?'

Her old room was a microcosm of her life, from the

622

pretty, girlish half tester bed to the rich and battered clutter acquired on her travels. The walls were thickly hung with photographs, the bookcases crammed with books and pamphlets, including two copies of her *By Desert Ways* – 'I shall never write another,' she had said to Kate. 'Dreadfully boring. Killed the pleasure of recollection stone dead' – and on every surface lay fossils and bells and carvings, lumps of interesting rock, branches of coral, objects of ivory and brass, pieces of jewellery, shells and peacock blue Arabian pottery, bright and fragile. Carlo, passing the open door on his way to collect another jersey before going out, saw Bay on the floor, her damaged leg stuck out stiffly in front of her, clicking the black glass beads of an abacus Catherine had bought in Beirut, determined that the mastery of it would solve all her accounting problems.

'Bay?'

She looked up.

'You don't look awfully comfortable.'

'Oh, I am—'

Carlo came in and crouched on the floor beside her. Bay touched her sticks. Her voice was light and brittle.

'I simply *sprang* upstairs. First time! You should have seen. I'll be fit to go back to London any minute.'

'And what will you do?' Carlo said.

'Oh,' she said, 'it wouldn't interest you.'

He settled himself more comfortably, propping one arm across the camel saddle.

'You think I am not interested in what interests you?'

Bay blushed. Carlo picked up a string of dull silver beads that rang like little bells, and ran them through his fingers.

'Tell me,' he said casually, 'about Vienna.'

'Oh, oh that's all over—'

623

'But it was terribly important.'

Bay said, a little choked, 'Terribly—'

'Tell me.'

'I joined something called the Revolutionary Socialists.'

'Were they Communist?'

'Some of them—'

'Go on,' Carlo said.

'You see, the government and the Heimwehr – that was a kind of private army – were bent on stamping out all the Socialists. They even shelled the two biggest blocks of workers' flats in Vienna – the Karl Marx Hof and the Goethe Hof – and I was there just after they did it, and we dug all night trying to find anyone left alive. I helped two men to hide, in my bedroom. That's how it all began, you see. I managed to get them onto a train going up into Italy and then I couldn't stop, could I? I could *help*. I got them clothes and food and hid them till we could forge papers and buy rail tickets. I suppose I hid about twenty altogether.'

Carlo's face betrayed nothing. He laid the beads out in a figure of eight on the carpet.

'And why did you come home?'

Bay said nothing.

'Why?'

She said angrily, 'I was frightened.'

'Were you threatened?'

'I thought I was. I thought I was being watched.'

'So the waters were deeper than you thought?'

She nodded.

'And so,' Carlo said, not looking at her, 'you thought you would ease your conscience at leaving by coming home and endeavouring to set up a welcome committee for Communists in Rotherhithe Street?'

Bay gazed at him in silence.

'With Europe in such turmoil,' Carlo went on, 'you thought you would introduce a few experienced political dissidents into England, just to spice the mixture we already have of the depression and unemployment and a threatening war?'

Bay said, 'But we believe in freedom of thought and speech here—'

'So it is fair to allow our tolerance to be exploited by revolutionaries?'

'You sound so *angry*,' she whispered.

'I am angry.'

'But *why*?' She turned a pleading face on him. 'Can't you see how much I had to help these oppressed people? *Noble* Communists—'

'Name me,' Carlo said, 'a noble Communist.'

'Trotsky, Marx—'

'Neither Trotsky nor Marx ever *practised* Communism.'

He got up and began to walk with difficulty about the room, impeded by objects at every second step.

'Bay.'

'Yes.' She sounded very subdued.

'If we had Communism here, there would not be houses like this any more.'

'I know.'

'Do you want that?'

'No.' Almost a whisper.

'And when all this bother comes to a head and war breaks out, and the Nazis threaten us and find us unable to present a united front because we are weakened by political dissension, do you think that a good idea, either morally or practically?'

'Oh,' Bay said, putting her head on her crooked knee. 'Do stop—'

'Why?'

'Because,' she shouted, bursting into sudden tears, 'you have never spoken to me like this before and anyway, everyone is allowed to make mistakes. I am only twenty-one.' She raised a wet face to Carlo. 'You used to be such *fun*!'

'So,' he said, smiling at her, 'did you. Left wing politics don't seem to be compatible with fun—'

'Can I have a handkerchief?'

Carlo produced a vast yellow square.

'I found these in a box in the dressing room. The box was marked, "Campaigning Handkerchiefs – 1888". I suppose that was old cousin Tom on his Whig kick. Look, Bay—'

She was blowing ferociously but she nodded to show she could hear all the same.

'I can't disguise that I am furious to think you even contemplated introducing some kind of fifth column into England just now, even just a handful of people. I do understand your altruism, though, in fact I—' He stopped and then said hurriedly, 'Promise you won't go back to Rotherhithe Street.'

'But—'

'Promise.'

'Look, I won't try to continue—'

'Promise!'

Bay stuck her chin out.

'Why?'

He came and crouched beside her long enough to say, 'Because I can't *stand* thinking of you there.'

There was silence and then Bay said a little unsteadily that she supposed she could go back to Swan Walk.

'Yes.'

'I'll have to get a job—'

'Of course. You are very employable.'

She picked up her sticks.

'Will you help me up?'

He lifted her competently to her feet, and together they went out onto the landing. It was almost dark, and looking over the banisters they could see two long shafts of light falling like fingers across the hall, one from the sitting room where Melina and Harry could be heard playing bezique – 'Oh I shall scream if I lose again!' – and one from the dining room where shuffles and irregular clattering indicated that Palmer was attempting to lay the table. Harry's spaniel came out of the sitting room and pattered along the shafts of light to the dining room and looked in. Palmer, who was afraid of dogs however loving, said, 'Shoo!' and sneezed. Unaffronted, the spaniel pattered back again. Carlo said,

'I'll think of all this while I am tilting at pyramids this year. They say the Italian officers fight in silk shirts.' He looked at Bay's faint profile in the gloom. 'Are you all right?'

'Yes,' she said. 'Are you?'

'More or less. More, I think—'

'I once asked you if you minded being born before your parents were married and you said on and off.'

'Did I? How extraordinary. I haven't thought about it for ages. I say, there's Melina. Shh—'

Melina came out of the sitting room and fumbled on the wall beside her for a light switch. Carlo leaned over the banister and said, 'Boo,' loudly. Melina leapt and shrieked.

'Most satisfactory,' Carlo said.

'Beast, hateful beast!'

Carlo blew her a kiss.

'Simply hateful,' he agreed contentedly and went off

627

along the landing in the delayed pursuit of his jersey.

In the first week of January, Carlo sailed for Egypt, and Bay went back to Swan Walk. The following week she applied for a job with the BBC World Service, was completely open about her recent left wing sympathies and was refused. She tried various civil service departments and was rebuffed by them all.

'May I say,' she said more cheerfully to her mother than she felt, 'serve me right, before you do?'

'My dear, it never occurred—'

'Well, it occurred to *me*.'

She took her courage in both hands and sought out Victoria.

'Do you think I am politically suspect?'

'If you mean, do I think you still wish to be a Communist, no.'

'Then will you give me a job?'

'I have no job to give you, Bay.'

'You could make one. I could translate French and German women's literature for you, and vice versa.'

Victoria eyed her.

'Has the idea just popped into your head?'

'Yes,' Bay said truthfully.

'Well, go away and think about it more carefully, and I will think about it too. Of course, there are plenty of other publishing houses.' She put a trade paper down on her desk and pointed to an advertisement. 'Look. Victor Gollancz has started a Left Book Club. What about him?'

Bay wandered out onto the Embankment, the better to think. She limped still, and was stiff, but it only hurt if she got cold. People looked at her more than ever on the streets now that a limp was incongruously allied to her startling face. She caught a bus up to Sloane Square, and dawdled along among the crowds on the pavements and saw, in a bookshop, a great pile of yellow wrapped books, a shouting pyramid with placard leaning against it saying '*Witch Craze* by Robert Taverner'. She put one shoulder against the window and leaned there for a long time, staring and thinking. She thought about Rob and Cambridge and Rotherhithe Street; she thought about her mother and Victoria and Ellen; she thought about Carlo steaming east towards hot Egyptian days and of Buscombe and Eleni and Harry and the children.

'Penny for 'em,' a man said at her elbow.

She turned her wide smile on him.

'Heavens,' she said, 'they're not worth half that,' and then she took her shoulder from the window and limped away from him, unhurried and somehow extremely dismissive, towards the King's Road.

CHAPTER THIRTY-ONE

1936

Harry woke with the anxious feeling that something was the matter. He lay and considered this for some time, and could not define what it was. He felt ill, he felt awful, but he could not say that anything hurt or that there was a specific part of him that did not feel itself, he just felt terrible, all over. He put out a thin old arm in a blue shadow striped pyjama sleeve and turned on his bedside light. Ill or not, the instant miracle of electricity never failed to delight him. He looked at his watch. It was half past three. Beside his watch was the little brass bell Eleni had put there with strict instructions that he was to ring it the moment he needed her. He picked it up, then put it down again. She had looked tired tonight, and in any case, the ill feeling might well disperse as mysteriously as it had come.

He arranged himself cautiously in a different position to see if that made him feel better. Briefly, he thought that it did. He must now think cheerful thoughts, which meant not thinking about Catherine or Rose or Rob – Rob, almost worst of all, that boy he had cherished and written to so faithfully, every week for almost ten years, who was now lost to some awful rebellious folly. No, no, mustn't think about that. Must think about Eleni and the lovely September weather and the dogs and – rather cautiously – about God. God had lost Harry – or to be scrupulously fair, probably the other way about – somewhere in India. But Eleni was very decided about Him, and although brought up as a Catholic, had adopted Buscombe's little church, and had taken Harry along so that he and God could, as it were, get to know each other again. God, it seemed, was not going to hold it against you if you had virtually ignored Him, beyond a little aesthetic marvelling at His works when in particularly beautiful places, for thirty-five years. He was also, Harry found, an extraordinary comfort; it was much easier to be philosophical about things, take a long, sage view of things, even at eighty-four with a lot of dead hopes cluttering up your mind, if you knew God was there. Harry had come to realize, because of God, that his parting from Catherine was only a very temporary thing, and that when they were reunited, he, Harry, would be very careful not to make his earthly mistakes of either neglecting or stifling her. He had visions of her heavenly journeys in the Moroccan travelling coat and when he asked himself, 'Am I being perfectly absurd?' he would seem to hear God assuring him that decidedly he was not.

The ill feeling was, if anything, getting worse. He tried to turn away from the light, but could not seem to move, and the light was behaving in a peculiar and horrible way, swelling and blurring, swaying at him like a monster flower on a stalk. He thought that he must, after all, call Eleni, so he tried to stretch out an arm to ring his bell, but it would not do more than flap about wildly and he knocked the bell to the floor and then his arm would not come back into bed with him. When

Eleni came, alert for even the faintest sound from his room, he said to her, 'I don't seem to be quite the thing, my dear,' but although he could hear the words quite clearly in his head, they did not seem to come out in the air. He tried again. Still silence. To his shame he could feel tears of frustration brimming. Eleni said,

'It's all right, Harry. I understand. Don't try to talk.'

She picked up the errant arm and put it back into bed with him and tucked the covers round him, then she stooped and said,

'I am going to telephone the doctor, I won't be long. I will come straight back to you.'

He wished the light would keep still, it was probably these damned tears that made it look so unnatural. He tried to shut his eyes, but they wouldn't obey him either, and he was forced to go on looking at the light. Eleni seemed to be an age. The light stopped dancing and looming at him and began to dance away instead, which was at first rather a relief and then rather alarming as it dwindled and dwindled into a smaller and smaller yellow blob down a long black tunnel, and he could not seem to help going down the tunnel too. He thought he must keep the light in sight, so he tried to hurry to catch up with it and then it simply went out, quite silently, and when Eleni came back, after only five minutes away, Harry was lying just as she had left him, just like someone tucked up to sleep snugly, except that he was dead.

Buscombe Church was packed for Harry's funeral, so packed that John Cornwell, who had replaced the egregious Mr Aubrey, and was a clergyman of a very different cut, ordered the west door left open to the September sun, so that the people for whom there was literally no room might stand outside and look in. Harry's coffin was carried by six men of the Glosters and his cap and cane lay on top of it. Behind it walked the men from the estate, as they had done for Charlie's funeral, bareheaded with Fred Bradstock leading them.

Rob had come down from London. Somewhat to Eleni's surprise, he had not just come in time for the funeral, but had arrived two days before, and had attempted to be helpful.

'I know it isn't like having Carlo here, but I'll do anything I can—'

She was touched but there was not very much to be done which she, with the regretful practice of burying Charlie less than two years before, could not do better and more easily herself. Harry's affairs were very simple; in an austere soldierly way he had amassed very few possessions, and his money he left divided among Charlie's children – four thousand pounds each – and the rest to his old regiment to assist old or disabled soldiers. His papers were neatly ordered and labelled, the only personal things being a packet of photographs which contained pictures of Catherine and Rose and Rob, and a great many military ones, including one of the SS *India* leaving Calcutta on 25 September 1899, with all the officers lined up at the rail, moustachioed, eyes screwed up against the sun, helmets in hand – Harry was in the centre of the photograph, Tommy, chin as high as he could get it, was second from the right – and the manuscript of Harry's memoirs and reflections. Eleni considered, very briefly, as to whether she should give those to Rob, but decided rapidly against it, and took the papers and the photographs down to the library, labelled them as Harry's and put them in a drawer of the huge old eighteenth-century desk, which held the ephemeral and random relics of at least four generations of Taverners. Harry's jazz records were, for some reason, too poignant to touch just yet, so Eleni left them where they were in his room, beside the silent gramophone with its huge handle like a crank.

Rob was unaffronted by being assigned no role in the ceremonial of Harry's burial. He had been fond of Harry, at one time violently so, to the point where his love for Harry made him wish Harry were his father instead of Charlie, but those last years of Charlie's life had made such a bitter, passionate, splendid difference. He and Carlo had been two of the coffin bearers for Charlie, but he was quite content that the Glosters should carry Harry – it was, after all, what Harry had wished. But what did dismay him was the huge turn out for Harry, even people like the Masons from Bath and the Walgraves and old Mrs du Cros, people they hardly saw, at least half again as many people as had come to bury his father.

He did not like to ask Eleni why this should be and could not think who else to ask, until he found Fred, after the service, about to join the soldiers whom Cook and Palmer and Aggie Tilling were plying with fruit cake in the kitchen. Fred, as head man about the place, was waiting until they were all assembled before he made his entrance, and had paused, for a moment's sombre reflection, in the kitchen passage when Rob called to him.

'I want to ask you something,' Rob said. 'It's a bit odd really, and perhaps you won't know the reason either, but why are there so many more people today than came to my father's funeral?'

Fred hesitated. It was always tricky addressing Sir Robert, because he refused to let you call him Sir Robert, and Fred was darned if he knew what to call him instead. It was also important to put the answer to his question delicately.

'It's like this,' Fred said, checking himself at the last second from saying 'sir', 'it's the Colonel being, as it were, the old guard, sir – sorry, sir – it's the Colonel being the last of the old family, if you see what I mean, the last of your uncle's generation.'

Fred felt he was not doing very well. Rob looked as if he might be about to resent an implied slight upon his father.

'You see, sir,' Fred went on hastily, 'what with the world being so uncertain and it looking as if there's another war coming, people tend to cling to the old things a bit. Makes them feel safer, I suppose. And they remember the Colonel as a young man, some of them, before there were any wars, before even the South African war, and he's always been there, if you see what I mean, sir, and his passing affects them.' Fred looked at Rob with pity; he had always felt sorry for him, always felt he had never known where he was with his father. 'It's no slur upon Sir Charles, sir,' Fred said gently. 'Folk hadn't had a chance to get to know him like they had the Colonel. They had twenty years more of the Colonel, you see. I think, sir, her Ladyship will be wanting you in the drawing room.'

'Don't call me sir,' Rob said, but he said it absently and gave Fred's square shoulder a brief touch, before he turned and went up the passage to the hall. Fred watched him go, and then he went impressively into the kitchen, and to his enormous pleasure, all the young soldiers round the table sprang to their feet and stopped chewing. Fred made a deprecating gesture.

'That's all right, lads,' he said, 'you sit down and enjoy yourselves.'

Palmer brought tea and a slice of cake to his particular wooden chair at one end of the dresser. Her eyes were pink with crying. Fred patted her arm.

'Come on now, Violet, he'd a good innings, the old fellow—'

'It's not 'im I'm crying for,' Palmer said, pulling up her apron skirt to mop at her eyes, 'it's all of us. With 'im gone, it's the end of the old way of things. It'll never be the same again 'ere, never. That's what I'm crying for, Fred Bradstock.'

Bay had come down to Buscombe with her mother and with Victoria. She still had a slight limp, which she took no notice of, and wore the black coat Sarah had bought her for Charlie's funeral, and under it a black georgette frock onto which she had sewn, as a private signal to Harry, little scarlet buttons shaped like hearts. She was amazed to discover the size of the gap he had left, the alarming way that the absence of his gentle, interested, affectionate presence had suddenly removed the human backcloth from Buscombe, and left the remaining figures looking dwarfed and insecure. He had been to her the grandfather she had never had, she supposed, as he had been to Rob and Carlo, to Thomas and Melina. Carlo was stuck in North Africa, some place called Mersa Matruh, and couldn't get back, but all the others were there, poor Melina crying and crying and Thomas patiently handing her one large masculine handkerchief after another.

'It's so awful,' Melina said angrily between sobs, 'that you don't realize how much you love someone until they aren't there to tell any more.'

She looked about twelve, crying as hard as that. It was difficult to believe she was almost eighteen, that school was behind her, and that she was going to Montreux in the New Year to learn French and how to ski. She thought she was going sailing on spring evenings with gallant young men on Lake Geneva, but Bay told her she would be cooped up by grim Swiss schoolmistresses who feared only for her virtue and refused to employ music masters younger than sixty-five. In an obscure way, Bay rather envied her, in the essence of her getting away, at least. Bay had found a job at last, with a rather obscure little avant-garde publisher, who was trying to make a name for himself with a list of modern European novels. Bay was called an editor, but mostly she was just a translator, and too many of the books were entirely word-bound in their earnest desire to explain man to himself. Her old tutor had suggested that she return to do a PhD but she was uncertain that she wanted to go back to being academic, at least not just yet. I am only twenty-two, she told herself, I have plenty of time, heaps of people don't know what they want to do for ages and ages, and I've done a lot already, more than most . . .

Rob was not exactly avoiding her, but they did not seem to come across each other naturally. She had bought *Witch Craze*, and admired it very much, and managed briefly to tell him so. He said,

'Oh. Thanks. Yes, it's doing quite well. We are going to start a newspaper.'

'You and Douglas?'

'Yes. It'll help finance some of Douglas's welfare work.'

Bay thought of Douglas's impersonal, almost chilly way of dealing with his fellow humans.

'*Welfare?*'

'Oh yes. People in the Party who've gone sick or who

haven't any money. Anyone who needs it really. We've taken in quite a few in Rotherhithe Street, but of course, we haven't much space. I took Carlo's advice and got a woman from the Buildings to clean up a bit. She doesn't seem to mind at all. Amazing.'

Bay was afraid that the subject of her own politics might come up so she just said, 'Not really, if she needs the money,' and went away to find Eleni. Eleni was looking terribly tired. Whenever she could corner her, Victoria tried to explain that now she had some time on her hands, she could become involved in philanthropic and cultural activities on a *county* level.

'You are perfect OBE material,' Victoria said.

Eleni laughed.

'I am also a Greek—'

She turned from the flowers she was doing as Bay came in and said,

'Oh, chrysanthemums, chrysanthemums. Are they the flowers of funerals because so many people die in the autumn?'

'Are you going to be all right?' Bay said.

Eleni turned her candid gaze upon her.

'I honestly do not know. For the first time I seem to have nobody to look after. I am sure someone will need it, sooner or later, but just now everyone seems very young and healthy and independent.'

Bay picked up a heavy white flowerhead and began to spin it in her fingers.

'Why,' she said, 'don't you give yourself a little holiday in Crete?'

There was a pause. Eleni went on arranging and Bay went on twirling her flowerhead.

'I think,' Eleni said, 'that I am a little afraid to.' She gave a little laugh. 'Perhaps I am absurd, but just now

I feel that Crete will have forgotten me, that I could never belong there again—'

Bay flung her arms round Eleni.

'You belong *here*!'

Eleni kissed her and disengaged herself, smiling.

'Darling child, you do not need to comfort me. Though – though I do thank you. I have a role here certainly, a job, a place, but I do not belong in my – my *essence*. That remains Greek. Yet living here has shaped me in such a different way than the Greek way, that I could not live there again as a pure Greek. Do you see?'

'I wasn't suggesting *living* there,' Bay said. 'We wouldn't let you anyway, we are all far too selfish for that. I just thought you might like to have a look at Crete again. You know, to refresh the essence – and – to help you get over Charlie and Harry. You have been here for nearly a quarter of a century looking after Taverners and me.'

Eleni put in the last flower and stepped back to look at the whole effect.

'Such *solid* flowers—'

'Eleni?'

She turned.

'My very dear Bay, I think your suggestion intriguing – and attractive. But I should not like to go alone, without a purpose. If you were to come with me and I could show you the places of my growing up, then I should have both a companion and a purpose. Would you do that?'

Bay was pink with pleasure.

'Oh I should adore it – but my job – and oh, Eleni, it should be Carlo going with you—'

'Perhaps you could get a month's leave? Would you ask? As for Carlo, yes, yes, it probably should be him since he was born in Athens. But it can't be, can it? And if it cannot be him, then the person, my dear child, that I should like to come with me, is you—'

Bay and Eleni sailed in the first week of November, seen off by a sturdy group of well-wishers all intent upon telling them that this was the worst possible time to be going to the eastern Mediterranean, and that the weather and the winds would be appalling, and demanding to know why they did not wait until the spring? Eleni smiled and said that she needed a holiday now, and that the weather in Crete, though chilly, often held until after Christmas.

'In any case,' Bay said firmly to her mother, 'we are not going for the *weather*—'

Much as she liked Eleni, Sarah was opposed to the trip. Almost everything Bay had done since returning from Vienna had made Sarah uneasy, with the exception of her job. The publisher, though unorthodox, definitely had cachet in intellectual circles, and the nature of the work kept up Bay's French and German. It troubled Sarah to see Bay take six weeks' unpaid leave; it seemed to her almost inevitable that the job would have gone to someone else when Bay returned. Bay, as usual, was quite unconcerned by this, and maddeningly, appeared to regard her journey to Crete with Eleni as some kind of pilgrimage.

'You are so melodramatic,' Sarah said accusingly.

Bay was quite unmoved.

'Nonsense. I just happen to know when something unconventional is really important, and this is.'

Even Rob had come to Southampton to see them off. He seemed uncharacteristically interested, even down to such details as to when they should return.

'Before Christmas,' Eleni said, kissing him, 'and in the meantime, our luxury will be to hear as little of you all as possible.' She stood back a little and looked at him. 'You are so like your father. Look at you! Racked with frightening illnesses whenever you are required to do something you do not wish to do, and fit as a fiddle when you lead your chosen life. Impossible men!' She held Bay's hand and laughed. 'Oh my dear – this is such an adventure!'

Buscombe, to his intense satisfaction, was in the care of Fred Bradstock. Even the new farm manager Mr Carlo had found – a nice enough young fellow called Price – was required to have a meeting with Fred once a week, and of course the garden was in the hands of Fred's George, and therefore, to all intents and purposes, in Fred's own hands, George being a biddable lad. In her Ladyship's absence, the house was to be seen to in detail, every windowframe and slate checked for rot and leaks, the paintwork washed down with sugar soap, the huge chandelier in the drawing room to be cleaned by a specialist firm in Bath, a father and son who came with ladders and buckets and chamois leathers and worked, Fred was pleased to note, in suitable silence. Her Ladyship had left Fred a list as long as his arm, and it was his intention that she should return to find the whole place in the best order for years. He knew there was a good deal of sniggering directed at him from the kitchen, but he was adept at ignoring silly women; he'd had plenty of practice after all, thirty-three years of wedlock to one of the most foolish. Funny that, how like his own mother she was. What was it in Bradstock men – and he knew himself to be very like his father – that made them pick women as daft as brushes?

Robin Price, the new farm manager, knew exactly how to handle Bradstock. In his reliability, loyalty, efficiency and self-importance he closely resembled old Evans who all but ran his father's estate in Glamorgan. Robin was to inherit that estate, to which end he had been to agricultural college at Cirencester, had worked on a ducal estate in Rutland for a spell, and was now completing his experience at Buscombe. He knew of the Taverners from the enigmatic, reclusive couple who had lived ten miles from his childhood home in Wales – she had a reputation as a kind of local Lady of Shalott, beautiful, imprisoned and doomed – and then his younger brother had gone into the army and met another Taverner at some regimental binge who seemed to be looking for someone to keep an eye on two thousand acres. It was all a bit odd, since no-one seemed to know who the place belonged to just now. There were intriguing stories of the current baronet wanting to disclaim the title and being a Communist. But there was nothing wrong with the chap Robin met, Carlo Taverner, in fact he was a terrific fellow, very straight. And there was nothing wrong with the cottage he was offered or the local hunting, or the autonomy of the job. He had a weekly meeting each Thursday morning with Bradstock, at which he reported what was happening on the farm and what plans he had, with a judicious mixture of deference and confidence, and apart from that he was left marvellously alone with his crew of seventeen workmen and an interestingly mixed estate to apply them to.

It was therefore a surprise, on his return to his cottage one late afternoon beneath a spectacular coral streaked winter sky, to find Bradstock on the doorstep. He had been there, he said, but five minutes.

'I'm sorry to trouble you, sir,' Fred said, in a voice much less rich than usual with its fruity notes of competence, 'but I've a slight difficulty and I'd be much obliged for your advice.'

Robin led him inside. The cottage was the prettily set one below the Long Coppice where Fred had spent his childhood, and Lilian had visited on that fatal afternoon over half a century before, and it always gave Fred a shock not to find it as it always had been, a tumbling racketing pile of children with his poor old mother twitching helplessly in their midst. Sir Charles had done it up a bit and put wooden floors down on the old red tiles – Fred's grandfather had trodden beaten earth – and Mr Price had put in some very gentlemanly bits of furniture that to Fred's mind looked most out of place and made him ill at ease and unable to sit down, even when invited to.

'I'll stand if it's all the same to you, sir.'

Robin put a match to the fire, and then began to fill his pipe.

'How can I help you?'

'It's very difficult, sir—'

Robin glanced up from his pipe. The poor fellow looked really distressed, shrunken somehow.

'It's Sir Robert,' Bradstock said.

'*Sir* Robert? But I thought—'

'Oh, it's just my way, sir. I can't get my tongue out of calling Sir Robert what's proper. The thing is, sir, he's come home, and he's brought with him a whole crew that to be honest with you, sir, I don't like the look of at all. I'm afraid that they are lefties, sir, most of them not well and all of them with a down and out look. I don't think her Ladyship would like them in the house at all. I've locked her bedroom' – he did not add that he had had to defy Rob openly to do so – 'but they are everywhere else. I'm in a proper fix, sir, with her Ladyship away and Mr Carlo overseas and the property so unsettled—'

Robin said, 'But I thought it was Mr Carlo's?'

'That's the tricky bit, sir. Sir Robert wrote his father a letter two years ago saying that it was to go to Mr Carlo, but Sir Charles died before the lawyers could make it shipshape and Sir Robert hasn't mentioned it again, and the lawyers are dilly-dallying until he does. It's all been on trust, sir, understood, nothing official. So Sir Robert says to me that it's his house to do what he likes with, and legally it is. But it isn't right to do this, and behind her Ladyship's back. And I don't like the look of them, sir.'

'Have you spoken to Sir Robert?'

Fred looked unhappier than ever.

'I tried, sir.'

'Then perhaps I had better come up to the house with you, now.'

'I'd be more than grateful, sir.'

Robin had only been inside the house once. His interview with Carlo had been a friendly affair over lunch in the Army and Navy Club a year before, and then he had had a pleasant half hour with Carlo's mother and a nice old boy in a pretty sitting room about which he couldn't remember much except sunlight pouring in, because of being so taken with the old colonel's spaniel being such a mirror image of his own. He almost thought that the resemblance had been the final element to decide him that Buscombe was the job for him. Certainly, going in to Buscombe now, he couldn't have found his way back to the same room. Fred led him in through the door of the stableyard and up a long passage to a big square hall with a galleried landing, and long before they reached it, he could hear the sound of voices, a lot of voices, and hear feet moving about and strange thuds as if furniture was being shifted around.

Rob, in a battered old Army greatcoat with the pips torn off the epaulettes and the collar turned up, was standing in the centre of the hall shouting up at someone on the landing. There were a lot of boxes lying about and a sack or two and several exhausted looking suitcases bound up with rope and straps.

'There's half a dozen more rooms on the top floor,' Rob was shouting. 'Absolutely no need to cram in all together, plenty of beds. I'll get someone to find sheets and things. Just keeping opening doors until you find what you want—'

'Sir Robert,' Fred said.

Rob turned, frowning.

'Don't—' He saw Robin. 'Who is this?'

'I'm Robin Price. I manage the farm. We met briefly at Colonel Taverner's funeral.'

'I don't remember,' Rob said.

'The management of the house,' Robin said ignoring him, 'is of course no business of mine, but Bradstock here—'

'It is no business of his, either.'

'In Lady Taverner's absence—'

'It is my house,' Rob said.

Robin wondered if he was drunk. He was pale and fervent looking, but seemed in perfect control, except of his manners.

'Are these friends of yours, Sir Robert?'

He glanced up at the gallery. A few interested people

645

had gathered to watch and were leaning comfortably on the landing balustrade. Beside him, Robin could feel Fred pulsing with outrage.

'Certainly,' Rob said. 'They are all comrades in need of a rest. Some are quite ill. I happen to be the owner of a large house in the country, at present empty, in which they can recover before returning to the fray. It is appalling that such a house should not be used for the people when it is required and luckily it is in my power to order its use. You are quite right, Mr Price, it is no concern of yours.'

'I understood that the house and estate were, by your wish, to be the property of your brother?'

Rob regarded him.

'Eventually. When I decide, Mr Price. When, if the time ever comes, I do not need it. In the meantime, as I believe you are my employee, I would ask you please to get out.'

Robin did not move.

'I am not your employee. I am the employee of Lady Taverner and Captain Carlo Taverner—'

A tall fair man came out of the library and said, 'What the hell is going on? I can't hear myself telephone.'

'Take no notice. This is my farm manager making a fuss—'

Douglas came over to Robin and held out a hand.

'Barr Taylor. Is something the matter?'

Robin, whose temper had been rising rapidly alongside a barely controllable desire to shout 'Cheat!' at Rob, took a deep breath and said,

'It seems that something is indeed the matter that Lady Taverner's absence should be taken advantage of in this way.'

'But, Mr – er – Price? – Buscombe Priory belongs to Robert.'

'Then why did he not come down when Lady Taverner was here and ask her permission openly?'

Douglas did not even glance at Rob.

'We are only using the house in her absence. I am sure everyone will be sufficiently recovered to return to London before Christmas. It would indeed have inconvenienced Lady Taverner if we had attempted to use the house while she was here. I can assure you, Mr Price, that we have some extremely sick men here.'

'I wonder,' Robin said, 'if I might see over the house?'

'No,' Rob said.

Douglas moved a single step to take Rob's arm and whisper briefly. He then turned to Robin and said,

'Would you follow me?'

Fred attempted to attach himself to Robin, but Rob said, 'There is no need for you to go, Bradstock,' in a tone that filled Fred with such sudden and simultaneous anger and misery that he felt quite giddy. He stood where he was, gazing down at the black and blond squares on the floor and wondered what extraordinary discipline it was within him that prevented him from taking this unruly boy whom he had taught to ride and fish and shoot across his knee, and tanning his insolent hide for him. If he couldn't hit him with his hand, he could, he reflected, strike with his tongue. He lifted his head and looked up at Rob, standing quite still beside him and watching Douglas and Robin retreating up the stairs.

'What you are doing, my lad,' Fred Bradstock said quietly but distinctly, 'is underhand. And for all your high words, you know it. You weren't man enough to face her Ladyship so you sneaked in when her back was turned. You know what I'm saying is true, or you wouldn't come so high and mighty with me all of a sudden. Your father must be turning in his grave with shame at what a son of his could do, and to a lady that's treated him like an angel. You are right not to call yourself Sir Robert. You're not fit to bear the title.'

Rob did not move.

'Get out.'

'Certainly, sir,' Bradstock said, 'I've said all I've to say. I'll wait in the kitchen for Mr Price.'

The atmosphere in the kitchen was thick with indignation. During Eleni's absence, Cook had gone to stay with her sister in Broadstairs who ran a genteel boarding house and could always do with an extra pair of hands, leaving Palmer and Aggie in happy companionship cleaning the house and spending long hours over the new Aga in the kitchen with cups of tea and copies of *Home Chat*. Palmer had cherished a faint and fantastic hope that Eleni might be moved to take her too, as lady's maid, like people in her position, Palmer was convinced, should do. But the notion had not even seemed to occur to her Ladyship, and although Palmer would have liked the somewhat anxious distinction of going – she saw herself laying out evening frocks in a ship's stateroom, answering the door of hotel suites to bellboys delivering significant messages – she was in truth pleased enough to be left alone with Aggie who was the only person in Palmer's entire life to have obeyed her, always and without question. That obedience was going to come in very handy right now.

'I don't care,' Palmer said, when Fred came into the kitchen, 'if he's the crowned king of England, I'm not waiting on that lot of ragamuffins. And nor is Aggie. Are you, Aggie?'

Aggie shook her head. Fred crossed to his chair at the dresser end and sat down.

'Put the kettle on, Violet, would you? I don't know if there'll be any waiting to do. Lefties don't hold with that kind of thing.'

Palmer snorted.

'This lot are cottoning on pretty quick. I've had a message in from Sir Robert to say that he'd like Aggie and me to make up every bed in the house. I haven't budged and I shan't. The linen room key is in my pocket and it's staying there. He said dinner for twenty-five. There's nothing in the house but the dry stores and a mutton chop for Aggie's and my supper, and they're not having *that*.' She filled the kettle noisily and banged it on the Aga. 'I knew it would all come to this. I knew it would, when the Colonel died, I said so, didn't I? And now the King is having these goings on with some American woman who's already married to someone else. If the King himself can do that, what's to stop Sir Robert filling this house with a crowd of dirty old down-and-outs? All I say is, he can fill it, but I won't lift a finger to help them and mind you don't either, Fred Bradstock. Nobody can manage the boiler but you, so mind you just don't manage it.'

'Then,' Aggie said, 'they'll just be dirtier than ever, them men.'

Palmer threw up her chin.

'Say what you like, but I'm not making them so much as a cup of tea, and that's final.'

There was a knock at the door and Robin Price put his head round it. Fred got at once to his feet.

'Well, sir?'

'There's nothing harmed, though they've moved some of the beds and chairs about a bit.' He came into the room and said to Palmer, 'I think I should put away Lady Taverner's ornaments and things. They don't look destructive to me, but they might be careless.'

'I don't like it, sir,' Fred said.

'No,' Robin said, 'nor do I.'

He had not liked his tour through the house. The comrades had looked on the whole an inoffensive lot, mostly too run down and grey with fatigue and under-nourishment to be any bother, but they had, according to their creed, simply appropriated Buscombe in a few hours with a casualness that bordered upon insolence. They had moved furniture to make comfortable separate corners of rooms, strewn their grey and disagreeable belongings across chairs and carpets, hauled bed-spreads and blankets off beds in which to roll themselves as they sat by fires, and filled the air of the house, the air that was usually faintly scented with beeswax polish and sometimes flowers, with a thick raw stench of cheap tobacco. A lot of them, Robin observed, conscious of his profoundly capitalist appearance by contrast with theirs, had extremely intelligent faces and he had no doubt but that if Rob had asked them to respect his stepmother's possessions rather than ap-propriating it all to himself and ordering them to behave with a free hand, they would not have their boots on chairs or be tossing cigarette butts inaccurately towards the drawing-room fireplace. Some of them had stirred uneasily at Robin's entering and had attempted clumsily to straighten a rucked bedspread or replace a chair in its accustomed place. As they came out of Catherine's room, where two men were lying humped on her bed, one of them coughing disagreeably, Robin said,

'This is a bit of brazen stupidity, you know.'

Douglas looked unabashed.

'I don't think so. It may be inconvenient for the rest of the family, but the house is Rob's after all.'

'I believe he has a house in London.'

'Too small,' Douglas said briefly. He looked sideways at Robin. 'I think Rob had forgotten you were here. We only expected to find old Bradstock, not you.'

'Then,' Robin said, 'you have been singularly unfortunate, haven't you?'

As he and Fred left the kitchen and went out into the stableyard, Fred said anxiously,

'But what are we to do, sir?'

'First, I think you and the other servants must keep your tempers as best you can, and do what you are asked within reason. Second, I shall go to the family lawyers in the morning – you know the name? – and I shall telegraph Lady Taverner and Captain Taverner. And at the smallest sign of bother, I shall go to the police.'

Fred let his breath out in a long sigh. He had been extremely scornful that the farm was to be run by some college student – what had book learning to do with farming, he'd like to know? – but now he felt for Robin Price's natural assumption of command a happy and familiar gratitude and understanding. In the darkness, Fred touched the peak of his cap to him.

'Very good, sir,' he said.

Early on the morning of 10 December, Eleni and Bay arrived at Victoria to an alarming line of newspaper placards announcing that the King was abdicating.

'Poor man,' Eleni said, 'I should think he is thankful. What an intolerable burden if you know yourself to be the wrong person.'

Nobody watching them, Eleni in a narrow dark coat with a fur collar and a little fur hat, Bay in a blue checked jacket over a short blue skirt with her red curls wild in the wind, would have imagined that they were anything other than two women composedly finishing a holiday together. Indeed, from Eleni's astounding self-command ever since she received the telegram, Bay would hardly have imagined anything other herself. The telegram had reached them in Chania, where they were staying in the hotel that had been made of the old British Consulate, where Charlie had slept almost twenty years before. Eleni opened it, read it, read it once more and handed it to Bay saying,

'It was stupid of me not to think that something like this would happen.'

Bay was horrified.

'But this is the most terrible thing to do! They might wreck the place, there's no knowing – oh, Eleni, Eleni, how could he, how *could* he?'

'Because I am afraid he is taking a long time to grow up.'

'It is spite, it is personal, oh it is simply *horrible*—'

Eleni took the telegram back.

'It is not spite, my dear, it is folly. He has never been quite sure that anyone really loved him and that is why he has embraced Communism with such fervour. His little childhood was so confusing—' She took a deep breath. 'Now. I shall wire to this most sensible Mr Price of ours and tell him on no account to worry Carlo. And we shall go back to Herakleion today and take the night boat to the mainland. Then we shall take a train. If you would pack—'

There had been a dreadful exhilaration to that train journey back and, fearful though she was of what they might find at the end of it, Bay could not help feeling, as they flew through Yugoslavia and Italy, through Switzerland and France, that she was on some gallant mission. And then it struck her, with a kind of horror, that this heady mixture of fear and elation was exactly the cocktail that had fuelled her so recklessly in Vienna, and that this time she must use the energy she thus created with the utmost care, no outbursts, no loss of temper, no wild misplaced damaging acts of unthought-out generosity.

Fred Bradstock was waiting at Bath station with the Morris. He tucked Eleni up into the back seat with particular fervour, and settled himself behind the wheel, prepared to answer a barrage of questions. But Eleni, experienced by twenty years of exactly the same amiable busybodying in Thomas, merely remarked that she was pleased to be home and asked about the abdication.

'We have hardly had a moment to spare from our own troubles, your Ladyship—'

'Come, Fred. The whole nation must be talking of nothing else!'

'To be honest, your Ladyship, with so much on my mind—'

'Nobody's mind,' Eleni said, 'can have too much on it not to notice when there is a rather unusual change of King.'

'I'm sure I wish him well, your Ladyship, but what with the problems at the house—'

'Oh, he'll be well, now, Fred, poor man. You could see from his face how he hated being King.'

Bay began to giggle. Inadvertently she caught Fred's eye in the driving mirror.

'Go on, Fred,' she said, 'you'll have to give in—'

Buscombe looked exactly the same as they drove up,

except for two bicycles leaning against the terrace wall, and a large red flag bearing a hammer and sickle hanging out of what had once been Elizabeth's bedroom window. Eleni gave Bay's hand a light squeeze as the car stopped, allowed Fred to hand her out and went up the steps conscious that this was the second time in her life that she had entered this house with a thorny task before her. The first time, however, she was looking for something, and this time she had come to protect what she had found.

The house was very quiet. The air did not exactly smell unpleasant, just over-used, and the old table tennis table had been put up on the hall flagstones and was littered with tin lids and saucers used as ashtrays. One saucer, she noticed, belonged to the Minton tea service. She had not advanced more than ten paces when Palmer sprang from the kitchen passage, almost sobbing with relief.

'Oh, your Ladyship, it's too good to be true to see you back, oh you've no idea—'

'Good afternoon, Palmer,' Eleni said. 'Where are all our guests?'

'In the drawing room, it's the King – I mean, it's not the King no more, he's going to marry that Mrs Simpson—'

With Bay close behind her, Eleni opened the drawing room door. The air was grey blue with smoke. In the centre of the room stood the sofa table shrouded in a blanket (Palmer's idea) and bearing a great many cups and mugs, and in the centre, Eleni's own wireless set. All around the table men were grouped on chairs and stools and sofas, facing the wireless, and as Eleni opened the door, Edward VIII was saying,

'This was a thing I had to judge for myself. The other

654

person most nearly concerned has tried, up to the last, to persuade me to take a different course. I have made this, the most serious decision of my life, only upon a single thought of what would in the end be best for all—'

Eleni closed the door quietly with one hand, and with the other hand drew Bay behind her into the room silently. They sat down on two chairs at the edge of the group. From the far side of the room Rob's face was a mask of incredulity; he leaped up, mouthing, but Eleni simply said quietly, 'Shh, I'm listening,' and all eyes swung amazedly upon her while Edward VIII said,

'I now quit altogether public affairs, and I lay down my burden. It may be some time before I return to my native land, but I shall always follow the fortunes of the British race and Empire with profound interest—'

Someone snorted.

'Don't look round,' Eleni whispered.

'And now we all have a new King. I wish him and you, his people, happiness and prosperity with all my heart. God bless you all. God save the King.'

The moment he had finished, Rob sprang to his feet.

'Look here—'

Eleni took no notice of him. She stood up, smiled and said, 'I wonder if you would all be good enough to put the furniture back where you found it and leave me with my son for a few moments?'

'What is this,' Rob said savagely. 'Some kind of conspiracy?'

Bay was furious.

'You should know about *those*—'

'Be quiet,' Eleni said, 'the pair of you. No – that sofa goes at right angles to the fire and the table at its back. No, not that table, that belongs by the window. Would you empty all the ashtrays? Thank you so much. Rob,

655

do not even open your mouth until the room is empty. Bay, will you help those gentlemen with the console table? It goes under Charlotte's portrait. I wonder if someone would kindly open the window and let some of the smoke out—'

To Bay's admiring astonishment, it seemed to occur to nobody to do other than what they were asked to do. A kind of dumb obedience seemed to be propelling men about the room carrying chairs and occasional tables while Rob stood facing the wall with his hands thrown up against it in an exaggerated attitude of despair. When the last piece was back to Eleni's satisfaction, and the last man had departed bemusedly into the hall, he swung round and said hoarsely,

'Now look here, this is *my* house, mine by law—'

Eleni sat down and looked into the fireplace, empty of everything but cigarette butts. The room was cold and cheerless.

'We will not begin, Rob, at a point of high emotion.'

'I *feel* highly emotional. I bring down a group of sick workers to my own house, and by some unpleasant conniving on the part of Price and Fred, you make a wholly unnecessary grand entrance and treat these men like servants, and me like a small boy, humiliating me before them—'

'You are behaving like a small boy. *Don't* interrupt me.'

Rob banged on the sofa table with his fist. 'Look—'

'No,' she said, turning her gaze from the fireplace to him, 'no. It is you who must listen first. I am afraid, Rob, that it is not possible for you to have your cake and eat it. By all means use the title and come down to live here and run the estate, or leave me to do it for you. Or, alternatively, by all means decline to use the title and

656

remain in London writing your novels and looking after your political friends. But you may not do both. This house is yours to use, not to abuse. It is my home and the home of your brothers and your sister. I have always respected your political honesty, even if I could not share your views, but I cannot respect this exploitation and cowardice. I must ask you to request your friends to prepare to leave in the morning, and to spend this evening replacing furniture in all the rooms I imagine they have disarranged as they did this.' She stood up. 'Perhaps breaking your word no longer means much to you, but I must remind you that I have your written plea that this house and land should become Carlo's since you wished no part of such an outmoded capitalist possession.'

Rob had been pacing about feverishly as she spoke, and when she finished he came to a halt in front of her, and said angrily,

'Carlo. That's it, really. *Carlo.*'

'What do you mean?'

'You only resent my being here because you want it for Carlo. It's Carlo's house you are defending, throwing my friends out. I should have known, I should have guessed. It's always been Carlo first, hasn't it, whatever you—'

Bay stepped swiftly across from the conservatory door where she had been standing, and hit him. She hit him with a force that amazed her, so hard that he staggered and fell sideways against the sofa. Then he lay where he had fallen, quite quiet.

'You should not have done that,' Eleni said, but she did not sound admonishing.

'It might be,' Bay said indignantly, 'the only language he understands.'

She stooped and put a hand on Rob's shoulder. He shook her off.

'You are twenty-seven,' Bay said. 'Isn't this all pretty silly?'

Rob said nothing.

'Oh well,' she said, 'I'm going to play with your Communists if you won't speak to me.'

She stood up and gave Eleni a look of enquiry. Eleni smiled, a tiny, sorrowful smile. Bay nodded and went off towards the door, and as she closed it behind her, she thought she heard the sound of someone beginning, in a painful, strangled, awful way, to sob.

Eleni's first telegram had been too late to prevent Robin Price sending for Carlo. Carlo's battalion was coming back in the following January anyway, so it was no difficulty for him to get leave to precede it by three weeks, on an amazing journey of flying boats and planes and trains that brought him to Buscombe only hours after the comrades had left, and in a towering rage. Bay had forgotten how enormous he was, and now that he was beside himself with fury – she had never seen him angry, *ever*, before – he was like some superhuman embodiment of tempest and temper. He would listen to nobody, not even to his mother. He propelled Rob into the tower room – Bay could visualize every detail after those hours she had lain there nursing her leg – and from it their raised and angry voices could be heard going on and on, minutes dragging into hours. After a while Bay could not bear it, and took herself off to Catherine's room and the queerly comforting chaos of Catherine's possessions. She had tried to comfort Eleni, but Eleni for once, brave, calm, forgiving Eleni, was inconsolable at hearing, for the first time in their lives, Rob and Carlo tearing at each other like lions.

After it had been dark for some time, Carlo came up to Catherine's room. Bay had been hoping that he would, but when he came, it was not at all as she had imagined it might be. He said a great many things about the immature folly of her politics, and the way that these had encouraged someone much weaker than herself, namely Rob, to behave in a delinquent manner. He told her she was a hypocrite, sympathizing with Rob yet perfectly prepared to be spoiled by Eleni and welcomed at Buscombe. He accused her of troublemaking and lack of loyalty and he refused to hear one syllable from her in reply. He concluded by informing her that Fred Bradstock had the Morris at the door, and was ready to take her to Bath station the moment her things were packed. Then he went out and shut the door, and left her where he had found her, clutching in her arms Catherine's cream and scarlet travelling coat, a single Turkish slipper, and a little Buddhist temple bell of beaten brass.

CHAPTER THIRTY-TWO

1938

In September, during the week in which primitive air raid trenches were being hastily dug in the London parks, and the few anti-aircraft guns that the nation possessed were being dusted off, Thomas Taverner bought himself a house in Bristol. He paid a thousand pounds for it. It was a tall and graceful terrace house, with a balcony on the first floor, and a dramatic view down to the Clifton suspension bridge. Thomas did not intend to live in it for the moment because, like his brother Carlo, he had no faith in Chamberlain's peace negotiations, and was certain there was going to be a war. When that was over, however, Thomas meant to return to Bristol and begin his grand design upon Taverner Warehouses in which he had already bought five hundred shares. He had also been to see Reginald Payne, the managing director, announced that he had a degree in engineering and was interested in the modernization of dockside handling. When he had gone, Reginald Payne was left with the impression that about a hundred very capable people all talking very loudly had marched purposefully through his office and left all the doors and windows wide open.

With Payne dealt with, Thomas turned to his next projects. The first was to make his house as weather-proof and as sound as possible – he meant to rewire it personally – and the next, to enlist in the navy. Thomas had always admired the navy. It was, he knew, far superior to the combined navies of Germany and Italy. In Thomas's opinion, when the war came, the navy ought to go over to a two ocean standard and establish a separate fleet in the Far East to counter any threat from Japan, and would need, in the circumstances, more men. Doubtless if Thomas had happened to meet an admiral anywhere, he would have instructed him in this opinion. Thomas was heading for the Royal Naval Scientific service, being particularly interested in the stresses ships have to withstand from torpedoes and mines, with as clear an idea of what he wished to be involved with there as he was in every other area of his life.

He was twenty-two. To look at, he was pure Thomas Taverner, big and fair and open faced, despite his dark parents and siblings. His sister Melina said he was pompous, but he knew he was not; there was a world of difference between pomposity and taking things seriously.

'Do I,' he said to his mother, 'have no sense of humour?'

'Oh my darling Thomas—'

'I thought not,' he said good humouredly. 'Isn't it odd? It's just missing, like only having one leg.'

And to Bay, with whom he had become great friends in the last two years, he said,

'Am I tremendously boring or only a bit?'

She was always truthful and particularly with Thomas.

'Only a bit.'

He beamed.

'That's all right then.'

While Thomas hammered away that autumn at Meridan Crescent, Bay came down every Friday from London, catching the 5.30 from Paddington to Bristol Temple Meads. Thomas met her punctually and took her up to the Crescent in his little Ford and gave her a beaker of tinned tomato soup, bread and butter, and a banana. The ritual and menu never varied. Sometimes, friends of Thomas's were staying, sometimes Melina came, and often Eleni would arrive from Buscombe with a ham and a basket of apples and one of the huge game pies which, being about the only thing Cook really liked making, for some reason, was thus about the only really excellent thing she made.

Meridan Crescent was sketchily furnished with things from Buscombe. It was very neat. Bay's job at weekends was to shop and cook for whoever was there, and to stand at the foot of stepladders holding pliers and screwdrivers and the spirit level, saying, 'Just to the right a fraction', and, 'Simply perfect' at intervals. If Melina came, she was supposed to do likewise, but usually she lay on the floor and made jokes and read bits out of whatever novel she was reading – she was passionate about *Rebecca* and longed loudly for a Maxim de Winter – or played repeatedly on the gramophone a song called 'Flat Foot Floogie with the Floy Floy' because it annoyed Thomas so satisfactorily. She was extremely pretty in the same doll-like way as her half-sister Anna, in whose house on Chesterfield Hill she had a room, from which she sallied forth each morning to a gallery in Bond Street and spent the day dusting the pictures and getting orders wrong on the telephone.

'There is no need for you to be so silly,' Eleni would scold, 'you have a perfectly good intelligence.'

Melina was unabashed.

'The thing *is*, that nothing has come along yet that I want to use my intelligence for—'

She liked coming to Bristol for the weekends because the house was, being usually full of people, great fun. Robin Price, in the final year of his contract to Carlo, came whenever he thought there might be a chance of a kind word from Bay, or even, when those seemed dismally hopeless to wish for, to be in the same room with her. Quite a lot of Thomas's Cambridge friends had not found a job, so they drifted through the Crescent and Thomas made them sand down window frames and crawl through the house painting the seemingly endless miles of skirting board. They ate a great deal of corned beef and bread, and when Bay came at weekends, huge stews and the saucepan gingerbread that had been a staple of Swan Walk since her childhood, and in the evenings, they would roll back the rugs in what would one day be a most handsome first floor drawing room and dance to 'I've Got My Love to Keep Me Warm'. Sometimes they would pile into Thomas's Ford and drive down to the Mendips to walk. If Bay hadn't come to stay Thomas went to Buscombe, but Bay wouldn't go, even though Eleni pleaded.

'No. No, I really honourably can't until Carlo relents and says that I may. It is his house now after all, properly his house, and as he threw me out I really must wait until he throws me back—'

'It was a burst of temper,' Eleni said, 'that's all. I'm sure he regretted it at once.'

'He hasn't said so, and I must wait until he does.'

'Shall I ask him?'

'No!' Bay said, horrified, 'I'd die of shame if you asked him. Please wait. *Please.*'

Carlo was stationed at Plymouth, helping to mechanize his men into a machine gun battalion. Everything that had happened after his return from North Africa had demonstrated a different Carlo, a Carlo who had inherited far more of his father's cutting edge than he had shown during his childhood and adolescence. He had taken Rob with him down to Creighton's in Bath, and they had sat in the senior partner's room where Arthur Creighton had once dreamed of great alliances for his daughters, and social and professional acceptance for himself, and hammered out, in an astonishingly short space of time, a document that finally gave Buscombe to Carlo. Rob had been queerly acquiescent. He looked exhausted and ill and Carlo was afraid that he might be about to go down with yet another bout of rheumatic fever. When they left Creighton's finally and came out into the sharp January air of Queen's Square, Rob said, with a curious diffidence,

'Actually, it's the best thing. I – I'm going to Spain—'

Carlo took his arm.

'How odd. When the Civil War began and everyone started rushing off there to clout Franco, I wondered why you didn't go. It seemed just your kind of thing.'

'Yes. It will be doing, rather than writing or thinking. *Doing.* That's what I was trying to achieve, I suppose—'

'Enough said.'

'Yes.'

Rob and Douglas Barr Taylor took a train down to Marseilles, fell in with a huge disorganized band of volunteers from all over Europe, sailed with them to Valencia and were herded off to the training camp for the International Brigade at Albacete. None of them had had any training before, and they were not given much now. Within weeks, both men were at the front near Madrid in all the confusion and muddy bloodiness of a poorly organized foot soldier's life. Rob wrote one letter in six months. He was keeping a war diary he said, and he was completely happy. No-one was to worry.

'With Rob,' Eleni said, 'worry is always at your shoulder.'

Perhaps it was because she felt she honourably must stay away from Buscombe that Bay allowed herself to be drawn so much to Thomas; if she could not have the cake, she would make as much as she could of the crumbs. Thomas was a very substantial crumb in his own right. He had come down from Cambridge in the summer of 1937, had found himself a job as a handler at the East India Docks, and become the first man to sleep at Swan Walk since Charlie had left it over thirty years before.

'I simply do not know what came over me,' Victoria said to an astonished Sarah. 'I found that I had said that most certainly he might use my spare bedroom without the actual thought even seeming to be in my mind.'

If Thomas noticed he was living in a house filled exclusively with women, he gave no sign of it. He was undeniably useful, and was wholly unsqueamish about emptying mouse traps. The magazine had distinctly had its heyday, the women for whom it was originally conceived now being the mothers of daughters for whom the vote and a career came as second nature. Gently, Victoria allowed it to become more literary, but she knew in her heart that it was fading, and that her better alternative was now the printing presses which still religiously turned out their slender and distinguished volumes of verse and prose. Victoria was sixty-seven.

'I sometimes wonder,' she would say to Sarah, 'if we haven't become two old curiosities, you and I? I feel we simply stopped moving at some point, without noticing, and are fossilized for all time as two excellent examples of early professional female endeavour.'

When Thomas, after a year in the docks, announced that he had seen enough to satisfy himself, Victoria felt uncharacteristic regret at seeing him go. They had all grown not just used to him, but dependent upon him, and Bay, who had kept a sharp eye upon things, observed that earnest little Florence, who had been Victoria's copy editor for over a decade, was going to suffer a badly broken heart at his departure. He went off to Bristol to buy his house and a chilly blankness descended upon Swan Walk. In that hotbed of feminist fervour, no-one quite liked to articulate – though most were thinking it – that Thomas's sheer maleness, let alone his amiability and competence, had given the household a roundness and a richness that on their own they could not seem to supply.

'This is no moment, with a war coming,' Sarah said firmly, 'to let ourselves droop and decline.'

There was a pause. Victoria took off her spectacles and put her palms into her eye sockets.

'I think I am just very, very tired. I have never wanted to rest before, but suddenly I am almost *fantasizing* about resting. I was wondering, even, whether I might not go home to Buscombe.'

'Buscombe?' Sarah said. 'Go home to Buscombe? My dear, if you were to do that, you would only be doing what all Taverners seem to do, in the end—'

*   *   *

In Plymouth, Carlo dreamed of Buscombe and, when he could not prevent himself, of Bay. He sometimes felt quite exhausted between the two undeniable sides of his personality, the puritanical, industrious side inherited from Charlie which almost drove him to deny himself the things he loved most on moral principle, and the imaginative and passionate Mesara side that so relished humanity and beauty and had such a profound sense of history. Sometimes, on exercise on Dartmoor, he would think to himself incredulously, what *am* I doing, being a soldier, what possessed me, when all I want to do and should be doing, lies waiting for me at Buscombe? At other times, exhausted, wet through, driving his men only a little less hard than he drove himself, he would feel quite exalted by the sheer rigorousness of his life, and know that when war came, and he had to fight in it, he would know, with Buscombe now his, what he was fighting *for*.

Two things, in the last half dozen years, had honed Carlo's personality, that benign and tolerant personality to which nobody had paid a great deal of heed in the past simply because it gave them no trouble. The first was his dawning consciousness of how much he wanted Buscombe, at first suppressed because it simply could not be his, but stealing irresistibly back as Rob's political sympathies swung further and further left. All his childhood, Rob's attachment to Buscombe had been so intense, so remarked upon by everyone that it seemed, at the least, only decent for Carlo to love it temperately, conventionally, as a home like any other boy's home, but no more. To realize in his late teens that he could not really conceive of living anywhere else, and that his satisfaction at being there was almost exalted sometimes, was rather alarming. It was a bit like finding yourself violently in love with someone else's wife who in return was not remotely interested in you. The only solution seemed to Carlo to be to get away. He had always said he wanted to be a soldier, so a soldier he became, in the family regiment where there were men who remembered Harry and Tommy, and to whom he could practise speaking of Buscombe with nonchalance.

When Charlie died, and Carlo found that somehow he was not allowed to mourn his father as passionately as he wished, that monopoly now being Rob's, an unbelievable consolation suddenly bloomed before him like flowers in a desert. Rob, it seemed, did not want Buscombe. Buscombe might, incredibly, miraculously, become his. He held his breath. Nothing happened; lawyers dithered, Rob did no more, Carlo was sent overseas. He fought tremendous battles with himself, between the half that longed to have it out with Rob, and, if need be, to wrest the treasure from him, and the half that said you must be patient, you must be discreet and decent. He listened mostly to the second voice because in Egypt he had no option to act in any other way, but then the telegram came from Robin Price at Buscombe and the first voice began to shout so loudly that he was entirely deaf to any other. He had obtained leave to precede the regiment home, and found a plane leaving Alexandria for the first leg of the journey, within two hours of reading the telegram. The white heat of temper with which he had dashed aboard had not abated one whit when he roared into Buscombe, lambasted Rob for two hours and threw Bay out. It was hardly cooler when he dragged Rob into Bath and banged the table at Creighton's. When it finally abated, it was replaced by such a violent excitement at finding

Buscombe to be finally his, that Eleni felt she could hardly tell the difference.

'My dear, my dear, do try to calm down—'

'In my own good time!' Carlo shouted, 'when I have felt absolutely everything I want to feel!'

He went back to Plymouth singing. He put photographs of Buscombe up all over his quarter like pin-ups and before he went to sleep, he took mental walks through Long Coppice in autumn while pheasants rose clattering from the bracken and a sharp frosty moon rose behind the silhouetted trees. For a few weeks, he did not think of Bay at all; she was just Unfinished Business. Then she started to become Unsatisfactory Unfinished Business and he thought of her far too much and to no conclusion.

The moment when you fall from liking someone you have known all your life into loving them as someone you see for the first time with all beguiling clarity, is usually without drama. The drama lies in the change. Carlo could not recall when the remarkable looking child in his cast-off shorts with her persistent questions and desire to be played with, turned into Bay. Perhaps it was not until, with growing misery, he began to perceive that her own childhood affection for Rob was turning into something more adult. When she became politically sympathetic to Rob, and when she went to Vienna and came home in that feverish state of excitement, savagely independent and very clearly a virgin no longer, Carlo was in real pain. It was made worse because they simply could not seem to capture the camaraderie of childhood any more; they had grown up – and apart.

When Bay had broken her leg and, as it were, her wings, Carlo had been full of hope. But it was short lived. She was touchy and unapproachable and still, it seemed, involved with Rotherhithe Street. Carlo had absolutely no doubt that she had supported Rob's crazy notion to turn Buscombe into some Bolshevik rest home – in fact, it might even have been her idea. Eleni swore to the contrary, that she adored the place and was only anxiously waiting to be asked back. Carlo believed his mother simply wished to make the peace, and was not going to parade his jealousy of Rob yet again beneath Bay's indifferent nose. All the same, she would not remain out of his thoughts, and his only consolation at her nagging presence was to feel that at least no-one knew, except for Sarah Martineau, how he felt.

When the telegram came announcing that Rob had been killed on the Valencia road during some of the heaviest days of artillery bombardment of the war – and only three months before the British were to recognize Franco as the rightful ruler of Spain – Eleni at once tried to telephone Carlo. She was told he was out on a three-day exercise. She then rang Thomas. Thomas was alone in the Crescent except for a friend with whom he was sanding the floors, using a marvellous and deafening machine that filled their ears and noses with a fine choking yellow dust. Thomas was very silent for a minute and then he said,

'Are you all right?'

'Yes.'

'Are you all right enough for me to go to Plymouth and just find him somehow, rather than to come home?'

'Yes.'

'Look,' said Thomas, 'just don't tell anyone else until I telephone. All right?'

'But why—'

'I've got to find something out,' said Thomas, 'first, that is.'

'But I must tell Victoria.'

'Oh. Oh, yes. Never mind. I'll think of another plan.'

'So you will tell Carlo?'

'Yes. I'll drive down now. Mother—'

'Yes?'

'Poor old fellow—'

'I know,' Eleni said and her voice was thick with tears, 'poor Rob, poor Rob—'

Thomas left his friend sanding, with a variety of shouted instructions, and climbed into the Ford. First things being first, he did not trouble to dust himself off, and simply drove away with his blondness queerly emphasized by a kind of dry yellow bloom. After he had passed Axbridge, he realized that his blurred vision was accounted for by his dusty eyelashes, so he stopped the Ford, wiped his eye sockets with a dubious handkerchief and drove on, perfectly unconscious of his comic mask. At Taunton, he was suddenly overcome by grief for Rob and had to stop the Ford in a side street, and give way for a few minutes. Then he got out of the Ford and went into a corner shop to buy a pasty and an apple from the startled proprietress – his face was now streaked with tears in addition to the dust – and resumed his journey.

Eleni had telephoned at ten in the morning. Rather under twelve hours later, Thomas and the Ford chugged wearily up to the Glosters' camp at Plymouth. The guard on duty was at first entirely uninclined to permit this extraordinary looking creature, however authoritative, into the camp, but Thomas finally persuaded him to allow him to speak to the commanding officer by telephone. The Ford and Thomas were then escorted to the officers' mess, where Carlo's commanding officer was sitting over a typewriter with a labrador at his feet and a tumbler of whisky at his elbow. He took one look at Thomas and handed him a large khaki handkerchief.

'You'll find a mirror over there. I'd like to see what you look like underneath.'

'I was sanding a floor, you see—'

'Urgent dash, this?'

Thomas turned round from the mirror.

'Our eldest brother has been killed in Spain. My mother couldn't get through. She was told Carlo was out on exercise.' He remembered something. 'Sir.'

Two soldiers were instantly despatched to Dartmoor, and Thomas was shown pointedly to a bathroom and then to Carlo's bed. He did not mean to sleep, he meant to stay awake until Carlo's return, but then, suddenly, there Carlo was, shaking his shoulder and saying,

'Thomas, old man, Thomas—'

He sat up. Carlo was in combat dress, with a streak of mud on his cheek. Out of the tiny window, the first silvery stripe of dawn was slipping over the sky. Carlo sat down on the edge of the bed.

'What is it, Thomas? Mother—'

'No,' Thomas said, 'not Mother. She's fine. The fact is—' He stopped and then said in a rush, 'Fact is, Rob's been killed in Spain. On the Valencia road. Five days ago. Instantaneous death—'

Carlo's look gripped him. His whole face was frozen with concentration. After a moment he put out a hand to clutch Thomas's arm, and then he said hoarsely, 'Sorry, old man, a bit of Greek perhaps,' and fell across Thomas's knees, heaving with sobs. Thomas gave him a pat or two. He longed to join in but felt that to do so would not somehow be helpful. Instead he said,

'The thing is, he didn't really have a future. Did he?' which was the remark he had tried to comfort himself with all the drive down to Plymouth, but he didn't like the sound of it, said out loud.

There was a knock at the door. Carlo sprang upright.

'Come in.'

It was a soldier with a tray of tea.

'Thank you, Baynes.'

'I'd like to offer my condolences, sir—'

'Thank you, Baynes.'

When the door had shut, Carlo blew his nose tremendously and handed Thomas a mug.

'You're a brick to come and tell me.'

'Mother tried—'

'How is she?'

'Oh, you know,' Thomas said, 'how she manages things.'

Carlo flung an arm up across his eyes.

'How could I—'

'You couldn't know.'

He took a gulp of tea.

'I suppose,' he said, 'that you are Sir Charles now.'

Carlo gazed at him.

'God, God, oh my *God*—' and then he suddenly seized Thomas so that a brown wave of tea leaped from the mug across the white sheet. 'What about Bay, who has told Bay?'

'Mother was telephoning Victoria.'

There was a brief silence and then Thomas said,

'You ought to go to London.'

'She wouldn't want me.'

'She would,' Thomas said.

'But it was Rob—'

'I lived in Swan Walk for a year,' Thomas said firmly, 'and Bay is in Bristol almost every weekend. People think I only understand engines, because that's all I talk about if I get the chance. People are wrong.'

'But Mother—'

'I'm going home straight away. You telephone her. Then you go to London.'

'Thomas?'

'Yes.'

'You are being splendid.'

'It's easier for me than for you, just now. Rob was my half-brother too, but I wasn't as bound up in him as you were. If *you* were dead, *I'd* be feeling as you are now.'

Carlo stood up.

'I almost feel *guilty*—'

'Guilty?'

'Because of Buscombe. Because I wanted it so much.'

Thomas began to climb out of bed.

'Rob didn't really want it. He didn't know what he wanted, poor old chap. He was full of desire for something but he never quite knew what for. Very confusing. Enough to send you off your head, really.'

Briefly, Carlo put an arm around his brother's shoulders.

'Old man, I think you are wasted on engines.'

Bay, too, had been stricken with guilt as well as grief at hearing of Rob's death. Victoria, perceiving this at once, had taken her into her sitting room and said decidedly,

'It would be arrogance, my dear, to assume you were in any way to blame for this. Even if Rob were secretly pleased, even flattered, by your espousal of his cause, he would never have been influenced by it.'

'But Carlo said—' Bay cried, wincing at the memory.

Victoria looked at her sharply.

'I don't know much about love, it not being a subject that has ever interested me a great deal, but I have observed it in others. And it can make a noble character behave most ignobly sometimes.'

'What has love to do with any of this?'

'A great deal, my dear, as you at twenty-four should well know.'

Bay looked aghast.

'I am twenty-four! Oh Victoria, look what a little nothing—'

'There's plenty of time. People do their growing up at very different ages. Poor Rob hadn't even begun at almost thirty.'

'I have simply got,' Bay said looking hunted, 'to go and have a tremendous cry about Rob.'

'I don't mind that. Cry for Rob as much as you need to. Just make sure that you aren't shedding a single tear for yourself.'

Bay telephoned her publisher and said that she thought she had flu. He was terrified of germs and begged her to stay away until she was fully recovered. She went up to her bedroom at the top of the house and lay down and was extremely unhappy for a long while, and then she remembered Carlo saying, in the course of his tirade to her the last time they had met at Buscombe, that she seemed to have lost her fun and her gaiety. She rolled over onto her back and thought about this. Sarah had often spoken to her of Kate, and how the Great War had knocked the appetite for life out of her very badly for a while, and she had only found it again in Kenya. Bay had no war to blame and you couldn't blame just the prospect of one. If Bay had lost her zest, she had lost it wastefully into the wrong things, and to end up working drearily for a firm she neither much liked or admired was the destiny of a creature fatally in love with her own impulses. Sitting in that dreary little room high in Russell Square reading French and German novels of exhausting intensity and integrity was a fit punishment for what had gone before. Perhaps Rob's death marked the *coup de grâce* of a period of really serious, even damaging, folly, and the fact that he had never been happier than during his eighteen months of bashing away at Fascists in Spanish mud, was proof that his driving forces had been as immature as her own. Fighting, however glorious the cause, should not in itself make a grown man *happy*.

Bay sat up. Someone was coming up the stairs. She could tell from the footsteps that it was Ellen; she was not far off sixty, but her movements were as brisk and purposeful as when she had buttoned Anna and Kate into pinafores over thirty years before. She opened Bay's door and said,

'Up you get, dear. You've got a visitor.'

Ellen came into the room, picked up Bay's hairbrush and held it out to her.

'Carlo. He's driven all the way from Plymouth and he looks as if he should sleep for a week.'

'Oh,' Bay said, panicking, ignoring the hairbrush, 'oh, I don't think I could—'

'Nonsense.'

Ellen had more hopes centred in Bay than she cared to acknowledge. She was entirely opposed to her job as being a dead-end, and unworthy of her, and saw before her eyes, every time she thought of Bay, the spectre of her own life and its deserts and plateaux. When Cyril Connolly's *Enemies of Promise* had appeared earlier that year, she had bought a copy for Bay and handed it to her saying that if Bay couldn't see what the enemies to her own promise were, she, Ellen, most certainly could. Bay had read some of it and put it down with a sinking heart. It lay beside her bed now, and she *knew* Ellen would have noticed the postcard she was using as a bookmark had not recently advanced a single millimetre.

'Ellen—' Bay said pleadingly.

Ellen began to brush Bay's red curls with practised briskness, in silence.

'Why has he come?' Bay said.

'He will tell you that for himself.'

'I don't want another lecture—'

Ellen had a sudden vision of Anna sitting on the laundry basket in the linen room at Llanblethian, pleading for help.

'Courage is one thing you don't lack,' Ellen said, stopping brushing, 'so use it to get yourself downstairs. I'm going to make him some tea and a sandwich.'

Victoria's sitting room was unchanged, except for, every ten years, a fresh coat of paint. The same Mackintosh chairs – Sarah thought them awful and referred to them as Victoria's snakes-and-ladders furniture – stood against the walls, the same sofa and chairs in their severe overcoats of cream linen stood around the low table which bore a clouded glass vase containing three white chrysanthemums. The room also had, intact, the same atmosphere of austere calm which Sarah said was the emanation of a single-minded woman. It was certainly, despite having not a bow or a frill, an extremely feminine room, so that a man standing in it, as Carlo now was, looked exaggeratedly, almost crudely, male.

He was looking out, as all guests invariably did, over the river. When the door opened and Bay came in, he

didn't turn but simply said, 'Hello,' and went on looking, so that she had to say, 'It's nice of you to come,'
nervously, to his back.

'Ellen said she is bringing you some tea—'

'That's kind. I drove without stopping—' He turned
then, and added, 'I don't know why I didn't stop. Melodramatic, really.'

He was still in combat dress, and his eyes were huge
and smudged darkly with fatigue.

'You look so *tired*—'

'I was out on exercise when Thomas came to find me,
night exercise. And then I just got into the car and came
here.'

Bay said startled, 'But – but haven't you been to
Buscombe?'

'No. I'll go on to Buscombe—'

Ellen opened the door and came in with a tray.

'There, my dear. Sardine. Don't go until your aunt
gets back, she'll want to see you. I'll be in my office if
you need me. How is your mother?'

'Wonderful,' Carlo said.

'She is,' Ellen said simply. 'I couldn't see it at first,
but she is. Just what the Taverners need, you know, a
drop or two of vigorous outside blood. If you're still
hungry after that, there's the usual gingerbread.'

'Thank you,' Carlo said. 'This will be fine, it's very
kind—'

When Ellen had gone, Bay said,

'You'd better eat.'

'It's most peculiar, but I'm not really hungry—'

He picked up a sandwich reluctantly.

'I say,' Bay said, 'you hate sardines. Don't you?'

'Not as much as I did.'

678

'Shall I make you another? Ellen will never know. The cat will love these—'

'No. No, don't bother.'

He put the sandwich down again.

'Carlo. Carlo, are you all right?'

He looked at her, properly, for the first time.

'I really came – to see if you are.'

'*Me?*' She was filled with sudden shame.

'Yes. Because you were in love with Rob.'

A queer resounding silence seemed to take possession of her skull, as if a gong were being struck but somehow she could only hear the echo of its boom. She said, with difficulty out of this resonant cavern inside her head,

'Oh no.'

He was waiting, staring at her. She moved awkwardly to pour the tea and splashed it onto the smooth surface of Victoria's table and discovered that she was shaking far too much to have any hope of connecting tea and teacup, so she put the pot down with an unintentional bang and said,

'Oh no, I wasn't. I was very caught up, you know, with – with everything, while he was at Cambridge, but it wasn't him.' Her face was burning. She said, half laughing, 'I kept doing that, falling – falling in – for causes, confusing people and ideas—' and then some most disconcerting tears, hot and huge, began to spill childishly down her cheeks. 'I – I suppose – if you have a lot of fervour – it's – it's easy to believe that you have found somewhere to put it, you know, just because you so want to—'

'Bay.'

She nodded vigorously. Tears were now falling into the pool of tea.

'Look at me.'

'Can't, can't, can't—'

'Please.'

She said fiercely to the table top, 'But I'm so full of shame. I made a divide between you and Rob. You are really my family and then I helped to divide you up—'

'I love you,' Carlo said.

There was silence.

'I expect I always have. I've certainly known about it for three years, but I think it has been there for longer, much longer. But I thought you were in love with Rob because you shared the same ideals. Here – you need a handkerchief.'

He left his chair and came and knelt by hers and wiped her eyes. She did not move to stop him.

'I'm sorry it's one more thing to contend with, knowing that I'm in love with you,' Carlo said, 'and I'm sorry that believing you were in love with Rob led me to behave in such a classic jealous lover's way last time at Buscombe. It's an extraordinary feeling, instinct takes over from the head, a sort of fevered blind rage. But I don't blame you for anything. You didn't come between Rob and me. We just grew up, and apart. The divide was there, in our two personalities.' He bent to peer into Bay's face. 'Could you say something?'

She shook her head. He got off his knees and sat down on the sofa beside her, and stretched out past her to pour out the tea.

'I don't seem to be very steady, either. Here, drink this.'

She gulped obediently.

'Bay. Look, could you manage some kind of reply? It's a bit difficult to proceed with this conversation if I can't see any reaction except hair. I mean, could you tell me what you feel? Honestly, that is.'

She put her teacup down and turned to him. Her face was white except for her nose and eyes which were pink with crying, but she looked strangely composed.

'I feel, I think, that I've come home.'

'Oh my God,' Carlo said.

Bay was sitting quite upright, her hands in her lap.

'Is this love, this feeling that I simply can't bear you to go out of this room and drive off to Buscombe tonight?'

'Don't ask *me*!' he said, nearly shouting. 'Of course I'll say yes!'

'Then say yes.'

'Yes. Yes, you love me.'

'I think I do. Don't touch me a minute—'

She leaned forward and put her mouth on his. After a few seconds he wrenched his head back and said furiously,

'What do you mean, don't *touch* you—'

'Touch me now.'

He flung her back on Victoria's cream linen sofa and kissed and kissed her.

'Come with me to Buscombe. Come tonight. I can't leave you here.'

'I can't be left—'

He stooped to pick her up, and stood up, cradling her against him like a child.

'Marry me,' he said, his face inches from hers.

'Yes.'

'Just yes!'

'Well, yes please then—'

'No, ass, idiot, darling idiot, I mean, oh how wonderful, yes, and how heavenly, let's do it at once, yes—'

'All that then. Why – Carlo – your eyes are full of tears—'

He began to whirl round the room with her still in his arms.

'Of course they are, of course they are, of course, of course! Wouldn't yours be, with all this, all you, and Buscombe too?'

CHAPTER THIRTY-THREE

1939

'Not even Hitler,' Kate wrote exultantly to Carlo, 'will stop me coming to your wedding. Or perhaps I should say, *particularly* not Hitler. I have agreed to take in some Jewish refugees from Germany, but can postpone them until the end of April I think. My pyrethrum is going to be my own personal war effort. Someone told me that we spent eight million pounds delousing the troops in the last war, but that was before dear old pyrethrum had caught on. I've got a lovely journey planned as I haven't left Kenya for ten years, and probably can't again for a while on account of Herr H. I shall climb on an assortment of trains and boats to make my way up through the Sudan and Egypt, then by sea to Venice and the Simplon-Orient express to Paris, and finally a plane to Croydon. I land on 6 April. Can you meet me?'

She was, it seemed, coming alone. Ned Hamilton, at forty-four and not apparently content with the long agony of the Somme in his early twenties, was determined to enlist with the Kenya Regiment. Call-up had not yet begun, but it was rumoured that it would be soon – the smaller telephone exchanges had been instructed to remain open a further three hours each evening to facilitate this – and he did not want to miss it. He had temporarily closed the safari business, and had retreated to Kilima with Kate where he was filling in time by, with great foresight, erecting a small canning factory in anticipation of supplying an army at war. The great tea plantation, only a moderate success, was ploughed up and sown with root vegetables, destined for the cans. It was a year of terrible drought, so besides building his factory, Ned was harnessing water from two blessed natural springs in the forest behind the house. His relationship with Kate was one of profoundly contented and hardworking co-existence – based on a mutual recognition that neither was going to look the providential gift horse of the other in the mouth. When Kate announced she wished to go home for a Buscombe wedding, Ned's only stricture was that if war broke out while she was away, she would not attempt to cross Europe, but would sail to the Cape and take another boat up to Mombasa, however lengthy the journey. On the morning of her departure, they kissed each other companionably, exchanged instructions about the drying of pyrethrum flowers and the obtaining of particular carrot seeds from a specialist firm in Ipswich, and then Kate climbed into the car beside Juma – now an admirable driver – who was to take her down to the station in Nairobi. She looked back at the beloved and battered little house in its horseshoe of blue gums and cedars to wave once, then turned briskly in her seat to give Juma final injunctions about the hens and the hives and all her other cherished little personal projects. On the day she reached Alexandria over a week later, news had come through that Hitler had invaded Czechoslovakia.

★   ★   ★

It was not Carlo who was waiting for Kate at Croydon airport, but Sarah Martineau, a small round figure in woolly tweeds waving like a windmill.

'Carlo did so want to come, but he is only being allowed a week's leave to be married and honeymooned in, so I said I was sure you would understand if he saved that week for Bay—'

'Of course. And I am thrilled to see you.' She looked about her. 'I just wondered if perhaps Anna—'

Sarah took Kate's arm and began to steer her out of the building.

'Anna, my dear Kate, has evacuated herself already. Quite extraordinary. She has sent Susan and John to America, to stay with some connections of Edward's and she, if you please, has gone to Wales with some women friends—'

'*Wales?*'

'She contacted the nice doctor who bought Llanblethian from Harry, found that he has a rather nervous wife whom he was anxious about leaving since he expects to be called up, so Anna's war work looks as if it will be spent cosily nursing a hypochondriac. Victoria even went down to have a look, and there was Anna and a bevy of just the kind of woman I can't bear, drinking gin, and shrieking with laughter in Rose's drawing room. We simply can't get over it. The war hasn't even *begun*.'

Kate said, bewildered,

'But she hated that house. She virtually ran away from it—'

'The devil you know?'

'She has spent all her life running away from *some-thing*. Why didn't she go to Buscombe?'

'Buscombe is for Bay and Carlo.'

685

'But Eleni will be there.'

'Oh no,' Sarah said, 'Eleni won't.'

If she could help it, Eleni never came to London. In her entire life she had only lived once in a city, in Athens for the first two years of Carlo's life, and that had been more than enough for her. As she grew older, the strong rural island roots of her childhood bedded her more and more firmly in her garden and the open air, so it was a great surprise to Sarah and Victoria to see Eleni arrive at Swan Walk in the New Year. It could not be to celebrate the engagement again, since that had been done resoundingly at Christmas, despite Rob's pathetic little funeral where the tiny congregation had been literally choked by regrets they could not voice. Eleni did not leave them in suspense long; she was, after all, anxious to get back to Paddington and the certain security of the Great Western Railway. She sat down in the comfortable clutter of Sarah's upstairs sitting room – it was the room Charlie had first occupied as a student in the nineties – accepted a cup of tea, and said directly,

'I wondered if you might let me look after Combe Place?'

'My dear!'

'Would you think about it? I know the present tenant is leaving and I know you don't much want it for yourself. And there are all these evacuation plans beginning. I could take in a great many city children there and I should make sure the house came to no harm. And I should be close to Buscombe. I did think of going back to Crete, after Bay and I had been there, but that would be a mistake. I think I should be very lonely. Islands like that,' she gave a quick laugh, 'don't forget little irregularities in one's life.'

Sarah was immediately excited. She scurried downstairs to find Victoria who was showing a new employee how to proof-read without actually reading the text.

'Eleni has such a notion! She has offered to live in Combe Place! Is that not an answer to prayer? And if we have to leave here, we can move the presses down there—'

Victoria straightened up. She looked extremely and profoundly tired.

'Well, I had thought of returning to Buscombe before all these wedding plans popped up. I suppose that Combe Place is the next best thing. Dear me, is this a defeat? Are we all giving in?'

'No!' Sarah cried. 'No! It is a victory and a beginning.'

'And so,' she said now to Kate, shutting her into the Morris, 'we are in the midst of moving. I do hope you aren't frightened by my driving, I am really quite competent for someone who did not even attempt it until they were forty. Doesn't it change one's life? I am taking you to Combe Place now. I do hope you don't mind.'

Kate was uncertain whether she minded or not. She had looked forward with an almost childish eagerness to being in Buscombe again, to waking to familiar views, to the sound of the whirring long case clock in the hall, to opening Catherine's bedroom door upon the idiosyncratic mementoes of her life. On the other hand, she had looked forward just as much to seeing Buscombe like a new white page for Carlo and Bay to write upon, because they seemed to Kate, Hitler or no Hitler, to have a more absolutely fresh start in the house than any Taverner had had for generations. It would of course be interesting to stay at Combe Place, where Frank had grown up, the house built, in part, by Harry's money, on land that had been part of her father's cousin's inheritance. When she walked in, and was ushered into the drawing room where she had once slept the exhausted sleep of despair while Frank comfortingly sorted his stamps, she felt a sudden rush of past Kates come pressing round her, pricking her insistently with small forgotten memories.

Eleni had been at the room with her usual decided flair. Flowers cascaded from urns and pedestals, cushions were heaped welcomingly in chairs, books and sewing gave the room the air of one that is lived in, not withdrawn to. There was a tray of drinks and a dish of cheese straws and the curtains were still open to a raw pale spring twilight. They stood around the fire – Kate sniffed, apple wood – and raised their glasses to one another and Victoria said,

'Oh dear, oh dear, how we do endure, we Taverner women. We just seem to go on and on. Thank heaven for Carlo and for Thomas, and may Bay be blessed with a dozen sons!'

It rained early on the wedding morning, and then the sun came out and made the wet pebbles on the drive and the leaves on the shrubs glitter with little bright points of light. The jasmine in the conservatory, fortunately delayed by a hard winter, was in tremendous flower and scent, filling the house with as sensational and lush a smell as the lilies had on Tom and Rosamund's wedding day over sixty years before. In the tower room, the wedding presents had been spread out like a window display at Asprey's – 'Oh, oh, oh,' Bay had cried, 'three pairs of grape scissors and four ice buckets and no less than a dozen beastly bridge packs with our initials! How can I be even untruthfully grateful for any of them when all I want is you, and perhaps a puppy?' – and on the dining-room table stood Cook's tour de force, a towering white cake surmounted by a silver vase of freesias. Bay, unable to wear the family tiara since that had gone long ago to Italy with Rosamund, wore instead the little circlet of pearls Arnold du Cros had given his daughter on her wedding day. Melina was her only attendant; Thomas was best man.

As at Harry's funeral, the church was packed. Young Lady Walgrave, whose mother-in-law had attended Tom's coming of age, looked about her in the church, and could see no memorial tablets that weren't to Taverners (large) or to Bradstocks (small). She had married Lord Walgrave as his second wife, and although in his eyes she seemed able to do no wrong, she was quite mesmerized by the two Taverner men at the altar steps, one dark, one fair, both young and both so wonderfully *huge*. She was pleased to think of Bay at Buscombe. It would be nice to have a young neighbour and now that old Mrs du Cros was dead, there was a good chance that a youngish couple might buy Marsham Court, if they weren't put off by all that awful art deco.

Bay was astoundingly pretty. Lady Walgrave tried to visualize her own neat little smart face and felt at once eclipsed. She glanced at her husband and he immediately stopped looking at Bay in her heavy cream panelled satin, and looked lovingly down at her instead. It was annoying that his adoration was not as satisfying as it should have been. She whispered, 'She's very lovely,' and he whispered back on cue, 'But not a patch on you!' They sang 'Love Divine' and 'The Lord's my Shepherd' to the tune of Crimond, and Bay and Carlo came buoyantly down the aisle, man and wife, and Lady Walgrave glimpsed Kate and Anna watching them, Kate smiling, Anna's discontented scarlet mouth struggling to do likewise. Both the Taverner men were in uniform and the organ was pouring out Purcell and there in the sunlight, beyond the guard of honour of the Glosters, the estate children had formed a second arch with trembling branches of hazel catkins. Heedless of her mascara, Lady Walgrave began to cry.

Fred Bradstock was close to tears, too. He had had, in the last few years, to make so many massive re-adjustments to his beliefs and hopes that he was no longer certain that he was even the same man. That Rob, who had given every appearance of loving the house and estate as they should be loved, had, to Fred's mind, just gone clean off his head was a terrible blow. His death was another. Her Ladyship taking off to Combe Place – Fred shook his head as if to clear it of swarming, buzzing, stinging thoughts. But there was something good in all this, and there it was, climbing into the Daimler that old Mrs du Cros had left Mr Car— Sir Charles. Fred's recognition that Carlo was the right heir for Buscombe, fought daily battles with his profound feeling that the oldest son should inherit. But Sir Charles was the man for the job and he had married the right girl, no doubt about that. Fred stepped up to the Daimler, and through the open window gravely offered Bay a posy of primroses gathered that morning from Long Coppice. She said,

'Oh Fred—'

He did not trust himself to speak.

'Thank you, oh, thank you—'

Fred's George, who was driving, put the car into gear. Fred stepped back amid the crowd of children jigging and hopping to get a better look, and, to relieve his feelings, rounded upon them.

'Where are your manners, then? Pushing and shoving – Get back, will you, get back and show a little respect—'

Inside the car, Bay was crying happily into her primroses.

'Oh don't,' Carlo begged, 'darling, don't, don't—'

She looked up at him with shining eyes.

'Don't worry. I like it. It's just that everything is suddenly so *perfect*!'

They had elected to spend the remaining six days of Carlo's leave at Buscombe, practising, as Bay put it, the kind of life they would lead there once the war was over. The days were soft and damp, the evenings chilly, so that Fred still had the excuse of coming in to clear fire grates each morning and bringing in huge wicker baskets of logs. Cook threw away all the remaining cumin seeds and provided them with the kind of only slightly superior school food which was not only what she liked cooking, but also what she considered morally right. They were out in the open air all day so they were ready to eat anything by evening, bathed and changed and brought cocktails by Palmer in the conservatory.

'This is playing houses,' Bay said.

'We don't have the option to do anything else but play at it, just now.'

Bay took a deep breath.

'When you go—'

'Yes—'

'When you go, I think I shall stay here and farm like crazy. I should like a job, translating telegrams or something, but I fear I've burned my boats as far as that's concerned. I'm not sufficiently politically clean. If I get called up—'

'No,' said Carlo.

'It might become intolerable to stay here.'

'It will be intolerable for me if you don't. You would be far more useful growing food than doing anything else. I've thought that for ages. Ask Thomas—'

'But if you go – I mean, when you go—'

He took her hand. She said,

'It's going to be so awful to be left behind.'

'Would going anywhere else, if we can't be together, which we can't, make it any better?'

'No,' she said, 'I don't suppose it would.'

'If it's any comfort to you, it will help me so much, more than you know—'

'Yes,' she said, 'yes.'

Their last day was wet, with that fine insidious rain of an English spring that blurs the landscape with a soft watercolour wash. They rode in the morning, out to all the tenants' cottages to say goodbye, and came back damp and hungry at lunchtime, to find a perfectly strange little Austin in the drive, and Fred in a state of great agitation.

'There's a gentleman to see you, Sir Charles. Will not give his name. I've shown him into the hall and I'm not letting him go no farther. Says he's here on official business—'

In the hall, clutching a clipboard to his chest and reflectively tapping a pencil against his teeth, stood a small, moustachioed, bespectacled man in a blue suit. He was surveying the galleried landing and when he heard their feet on the floor, he turned and said with a wide and empty smile,

'Sir Charles Taverner?'

'Yes—'

The small man transferred the pencil to his left hand, held out his right and said,

'Rigby, Leonard Rigby. I am requisitioning officer for the area.'

'Requisitioning officer?'

'Government programme for the evacuation, principally of children, from the cities before hostilities begin. I am sure you are aware that we expect an initial heavy bombardment of urban areas, so those must be cleared well in advance.'

'Mr Rigby, I am not at all clear—'

'Why I am here? To enlist your help, if I might.'

Bay, who was unbuckling her mackintosh belt, had a sudden leap of horrified insight.

'Have you come to requisition *this house*?'

Mr Rigby smiled.

'I have indeed, Lady Taverner.'

Carlo seized her hand. There was a small silence and then he said,

'Would you come into the library, so that we may talk?'

'Only too pleased—'

Carlo gave Mr Rigby a chair facing the light and sat Bay and himself at either side. Mr Rigby sat neatly with his feet together and his clipboard balanced on his knees, and turned his face from one to another as he spoke, his spectacle lenses gleaming like little headlights.

'I am sure you are aware that an Emergency Powers Act is on the way. We expect it to become law in under a month, about the third week of May. It will give the government almost unlimited authority over British citizens and their property.'

Carlo offered Bay a cigarette. She shook her head. He lit one for himself with, she observed admiringly, almost completely steady hands.

'You are, I believe, Sir Charles, a regular soldier?'

'Correct.'

'And your regiment will form part of a British expeditionary force should that become necessary?'

'Correct.'

'And that you and Lady Taverner are newly married and have no children and are the sole occupants of this house?'

They did not catch each other's eyes.

'Yes,' Carlo said.

Mr Rigby made little ticks against remarks written on his clipboard.

'This area is one of the least vulnerable to air attack being almost entirely rural. We have therefore been designated a reception area for the inhabitants of such closely populated areas as the East End of London.'

'You mean,' Bay said, horror struck, 'that I've got to look after dozens of evacuees?'

'Oh no, Lady Taverner,' Mr Rigby said, flashing his spectacles and his smile at her, 'not that at all unless, of course, you choose to stay. Buscombe Priory being such a sizeable property makes it an admirable proposition as the home, for the duration of hostilities, for an entire school. That is what I propose. From a preliminary glance, I think that we could accommodate here St Michael's Church School from Wapping Stairs.' He stood up and gave a little bow. 'Would you oblige me by showing me the remaining accommodation of the property?'

Carlo said, struggling to his feet, 'Forgive us, but we are a little – winded by this information—'

'Naturally,' Mr Rigby said. He smiled. 'I doubt that there's a country house in England that won't feel the change. But we all have to do our bit.'

Bay whispered frantically to Carlo, 'I can't stay now, I can't—'

He put his arm round her.

'We'll think again. Don't panic.'

'Sorry,' she said, fighting tears, '*sorry*—'

'We are all sorry, madam,' Mr Rigby said. 'We are very loath to cause inconvenience. Will you lead the way?'

In the doorway he paused and smiled at them.

'I can give you one crumb of comfort. We do not expect the evacuation programme to begin until June at the earliest. There will be plenty of time to make the house ready.'

When Carlo had gone, and Bay was left to the empty house, her first instinct – one she was subsequently much ashamed of – was to ask Eleni for help. Eleni had, after all, emptied the house once for her convalescent officers and in any case, Eleni always knew what to do. Bay's hand, with all the dogs watching her in their anxiously interested way, was actually on the telephone receiver to ring Combe Place when Palmer came in with the post, adopting the exaggeratedly cautious walk she always used while in the vicinity of even a silent telephone. Bay took her hand off the receiver. There would be a letter from Carlo; there always was, every day.

Palmer said, 'Oo madam, I never meant—'

'It doesn't matter. I'd rather read letters than telephone.'

She took them into the conservatory, where George Bradstock's huge white climbing geranium, lovingly fed on nothing but well rotted manure, was already in bloom, filling the air with its curious sweet pepper scent. Bay sat down in one of the astoundingly uncomfortable iron chairs and opened Carlo's letter:

My darling, we are very much as we were yesterday – except that I trod on my wristwatch this morning – and spend all our time going over and over the same manoeuvres.

Some things I said to you are very much on my conscience. I have absolutely no right to insist you stay at Buscombe among a crowd of unhousetrained little East Enders, and bite your nails worrying about me, just because I prefer to think of you at Buscombe. Of course you must spend this coming war as is most bearable for you.

I miss you like steady toothache. Now that I'm not with you, I realize how much, in such a short time, I have become dependent on the sheer radiance of your personality,
Carlo

PS I had a very Thomas-ish letter from Thomas. He says the Navy are starting a women's branch, recruiting now. Might that . . . ?

Bay put down the letter and whistled to the dogs and went out of the garden doors of the conservatory onto the wet grass. The dear old mulberries had tiny rosy green buds of folded leaves, and there were even a few little cyclamens pushing up under them. She walked up towards the rose garden, to Eleni's bower in the centre, and then turned so that she could look back at the house. It looked back at her with the comforting and dispassionate calm with which it had surveyed her as a little child, familiar yet dignified, a little remote, full of the self-possession of simply having stood there so long, weathered so much. A school couldn't harm it!

Buscombe was a match for any inhabitants. Perhaps indeed, in an indulgent experienced way, it might quite *like* fifty or sixty children rampaging about it, using every corner, sliding down the banisters. And however they behaved, even, as Mr Rigby had tried delicately to warn her, if they were, on account of tenement dwelling, uncertain what lavatories were for, they could not behave worse in that respect than some of the roistering Stuart and Georgian Taverners, staggering from the dinner table to relieve themselves in chamber pots kept in the sideboard.

As for the farm, Fred and George could manage that. George, whose speech was almost unintelligible on account of his acutely cleft palate and hare lip – Fred held darkly superstitious views about both – was unlikely to be passed fit for the forces. Aggie could lend a hand outside, being as sturdy and tireless as her mother had been, and showing no desire to marry, indeed no desire to do anything beyond remaining working at Buscombe with all the unimaginative re-liability of a little traction engine.

Strangely comforted, Bay went slowly back to the house, and instead of telephoning to Combe Place, asked the operator to find her the London number of the Admiralty Board.

By the end of May, Buscombe was ready for its share in the war. Curtains, the good furniture and rugs, the pictures and the ornaments, had all been taken down, rolled up and packed away, and were stacked, with mili-tary precision on a system devised by Fred, in the huge dry haylofts that ran above the stables. Along the aisles left between the blocks of objects lay a trail of mouse-traps, and every block was shrouded in a rick cloth. It had been a mammoth operation and it had taken a month of ceaseless and filthy labour. When she felt that the end was in sight and her absence would be honourable, Bay drove herself to Bath station and climbed on a train to London.

The lieutenant who interviewed her in a small square room at the back of the Admiralty building in Whitehall said his name was Swain, and that he was looking for recruits to embark on an officers' training course for women at the Royal Naval College at Greenwich.

'Our aim, Lady Taverner, is to train women to do a great many shore duties – communications for example – which will free more men for seagoing duties. We are founding, if you like, the Women's Royal Navy Service.'

Bay explained about her French and German. Lieutenant Swain looked pleased about this and wrote it down with emphasis. She watched him as he wrote and realized with a sinking heart that he was so *upright* looking, so immaculately neat and clean, with his scrubbed fingernails and entirely obedient hair, that she was going to have to make her customary confession.

'I must tell you—'

He looked up.

'Yes?'

'I must tell you that between the ages of eighteen and twenty-two – I am now twenty-five – I was extremely interested in Communism. Not so much for itself, you understand, as because it seemed the strongest weapon available to combat Fascism. I went to Vienna in 1935 and became very briefly involved with the political underground.'

Lieutenant Swain sat back and flicked an imaginary speck of dust off his gold ringed blue sleeve.

'Were you ever a member of a Communist Party?'

698

'No.'

'Are you a member of the Labour Party?'

'No.'

'I have a brother,' Lieutenant Swain said, 'who was up at Cambridge and took part in the Peace March of 1933. I remember him saying that I ought to read the *Communist Manifesto*.' He smiled at Bay. 'He is a clergyman now. Volunteered last week as a military chaplain. When I was eighteen, I thought the only thing I wanted to do was paint. I still do a bit, seascapes and so on. One does these things.'

Bay said, swallowing, 'Then do you mean that it doesn't – that it wouldn't matter?'

Lieutenant Swain folded his square pink hands – not painter's hands, Bay thought – round one another and leaning across the desk said,

'You are hardly likely to confess all this to me if you are still at it, now are you? In any case, you do not look to me a woman of guile.'

'Then—'

'Then I am going to send you down to Greenwich for them to have a look at you.' He wrote something and said, '*Lady* Taverner. That will look splendid when you become an admiral. Funny thing, on my last ship, one of my ratings was the Earl of Suffolk. I think the seamen just called him Mike.' He held out a piece of paper to Bay. 'Good luck.'

She stood up.

'Thank you very much – sir.'

He laughed.

'All we need is a war now, isn't it?'

On 1 September 1939, Lieutenant Colonel the Hon N. F. Somerset DSO MC was ordered to mobilize the 61st battalion of the Glosters, and to proceed with them to join the Third Division at Lyme Regis. Among his officers was Captain Sir Charles Taverner. On 3 September, war was declared between England and Germany, and the order was given for the Third Division to proceed to Europe through the French port of Cherbourg. There was a week before embarkation.

During that week, Carlo obtained permission for a day's absence. In the early light of a spectacular September day, he set off north from Lyme Regis and drove up through Chard and Crewkerne, through Yeovil and Shepton Mallet, through Radstock and Bath, to Buscombe. He turned off the familiar road into the drive, parked the car under the trees by the gate, and climbed out.

It could not have looked more perfect, a still, clear, golden day with every detail sharp. He walked around the curve of the drive until the house was in view, and then he simply stood and looked. It was very quiet. Somewhere in there, fifty-two little Londoners were learning to read and write, having slept beneath that roof and washed – hopefully – in the fantastic bathrooms installed by his father. When their lessons were over, they would come spilling out of the front door and the conservatory door and the garden door, just as he had done thousands of times in his childhood, and scatter across the garden and the farm. They had been there since 1 September, and the reports of them were on the whole good – Fred had only caught one of them unscrewing door knobs for sale as scrap, they had almost all had head lice and a handful bewilderingly persisted in peeing in the corners of rooms.

'I ain't done it on the *carpet*!' one of them had screamed uncomprehendingly at Palmer.

As he watched, Fred came round the corner of the house with a wheelbarrow. Carlo waved to attract his attention. Fred put the wheelbarrow down at once and came hurrying down the drive at a speed compatible with both pleasure and dignity.

'I never thought to see you again, sir,' Fred said, 'not before you went off to France that is.' They shook hands.

'I thought I should like one more look.'

'Well, don't you come no closer, Sir Charles. Not just now. Little varmints. Don't you worry, sir, there's been no harm done, and there won't be none done either. Keeping well, sir?'

'Pretty fit. And yourself?'

'Can't grumble,' Fred said. He adjusted his hat. 'Got a bumper crop of tomatoes, sir. Her Ladyship will be pleased.'

'I'll tell her.'

'You do that, sir.' Fred began to shift on the gravel. 'I ought to be getting on, Sir Charles—'

Carlo roused himself.

'So should I, Fred.'

Fred grinned.

'You've got a war to win, haven't you, sir?'

Carlo smiled at him.

'That's right.'

'When I went off more than forty years ago, I was a soldier of the Queen,' Fred said. He straightened at the memory.

'I think,' Carlo said, 'I'll fight for this place, rather than the King. If that doesn't seem disrespectful.'

They both turned to survey the house. After a while Fred said,

'You could do worse, sir,' and then they shook hands

again and Fred went back to his wheelbarrow and Carlo to his car. As he turned it to drive back south to Lyme, a duck and a drake came out of the bushes, and crossed the drive in front of him unhurriedly, on their way back to the lake. As he passed, the drake paused a moment, and gave Carlo a level, comical and slightly admonishing glance before following his wife. One of the evacuees, who had become addicted to natural history and was playing truant from lessons among the bushes by the drive, reported that he had seen the lord driving to war that morning and he seemed to be laughing his head off.

THE END

CITY OF GEMS
by Caroline Harvey

A romantic adventure set in the lush and enchanting world of Mandalay . . .

On the day that Maria Beresford celebrated her eighteenth birthday in Bombay, in faraway Burma the formidable and unpredictable Queen had ordered eighty members of the royal family to be clubbed to death.

On that day in 1879 Maria knew nothing of Mandalay, the fairytale City of Gems. The selfish, difficult but beautiful daughter of a failed tea-planter devoted herself only to pleasure and social advancement. But when her father was sent to Burma, and she had to accompany him, she became embroiled in an exotic world of political intrigue. Her friendship with the Queen – a dangerous and mercurial figure – and her growing closeness to Archie Tennant, a young man who had come east to seek his fortune after the ruin of his family business, brought her both power and menace, and the key to her destiny.

Caroline Harvey is the pseudonym of the award-winning writer Joanna Trollope.

0 552 14686 2

A SELECTED LIST OF FINE NOVELS
AVAILABLE FROM CORGI AND BLACK SWAN

THE PRICES SHOWN BELOW WERE CORRECT AT THE TIME OF GOING
TO PRESS. HOWEVER TRANSWORLD PUBLISHERS RESERVE THE RIGHT
TO SHOW NEW RETAIL PRICES ON COVERS WHICH MAY DIFFER FROM
THOSE PREVIOUSLY ADVERTISED IN THE TEXT OR ELSEWHERE.

☐	14537 8	APPLE BLOSSOM TIME	*Kathryn Haig*	£5.99
☐	14538 6	A TIME TO DANCE	*Kathryn Haig*	£5.99
☐	14567 X	THE CORNER HOUSE	*Ruth Hamilton*	£5.99
☐	13872 X	LEGACY OF LOVE	*Caroline Harvey*	£5.99
☐	13917 3	A SECOND LEGACY	*Caroline Harvey*	£5.99
☐	14299 9	PARSON HARDING'S DAUGHTER	*Caroline Harvey*	£5.99
☐	14407 X	THE STEPS OF THE SUN	*Caroline Harvey*	£5.99
☐	14429 7	LEAVES FROM THE VALLEY	*Caroline Harvey*	£5.99
☐	14553 X	THE BRASS DOLPHIN	*Caroline Harvey*	£5.99
☐	14686 2	CITY OF GEMS	*Caroline Harvey*	£5.99
☐	14692 7	THE PARADISE GARDEN	*Joan Hessayon*	£5.99
☐	14599 8	FOOTPRINTS ON THE SAND	*Judith Lennox*	£5.99
☐	14603 X	THE SHADOW CHILD	*Judith Lennox*	£5.99
☐	14492 4	THE CREW	*Margaret Mayhew*	£5.99
☐	14693 5	THE LITTLE SHIP	*Margaret Mayhew*	£5.99
☐	14659 5	WHAT BECAME OF US	*Imogen Parker*	£5.99
☐	14752 4	WITHOUT CHARITY	*Michelle Paver*	£5.99
☐	10375 6	CSARDAS	*Diane Pearson*	£5.99
☐	14715 X	MIDSUMMER MEETING	*Elvi Rhodes*	£5.99
☐	14671 4	THE KEYS TO THE GARDEN	*Susan Sallis*	£5.99
☐	99494 4	THE CHOIR	*Joanna Trollope*	£6.99
☐	99410 3	A VILLAGE AFFAIR	*Joanna Trollope*	£6.99
☐	99442 1	A PASSIONATE MAN	*Joanna Trollope*	£6.99
☐	99470 7	THE RECTOR'S WIFE	*Joanna Trollope*	£6.99
☐	99492 8	THE MEN AND THE GIRLS	*Joanna Trollope*	£6.99
☐	99549 5	A SPANISH LOVER	*Joanna Trollope*	£6.99
☐	99643 2	THE BEST OF FRIENDS	*Joanna Trollope*	£6.99
☐	99700 5	NEXT OF KIN	*Joanna Trollope*	£6.99
☐	99788 9	OTHER PEOPLE'S CHILDREN	*Joanna Trollope*	£6.99
☐	99872 9	MARRYING THE MISTRESS	*Joanna Trollope*	£6.99
☐	14740 0	EMILY	*Valerie Wood*	£5.99

All Transworld titles are available by post from:

Bookpost, P.O. Box 29, Douglas, Isle of Man IM99 1BQ

Credit cards accepted. Please telephone 01624 836000,
fax 01624 837033, Internet http://www.bookpost.co.uk or
e-mail: bookshop@enterprise.net for details.

Free postage and packing in the UK. Overseas customers allow
£1 per book (paperbacks) and £3 per book (hardbacks).